PENGUIN BOOKS

On Broadway

Damon Runyon was born in Kansas in 1884 and grew up in Pueblo, Colorado. As a teenager he wrote articles for the local newspapers and in 1898, at the age of fourteen, enlisted in the Spanish–American War. He returned to work on various newspapers and became a sportswriter for the New York *American* in 1911. During the First World War he was a war correspondent for the Hearst newspapers and after the war continued to work as a Hearst columnist. He died in 1946.

Runyon's stories are famous for their individual style and grew out of his knowledge of the amiable low-life of Broadway and the New York sporting scene. They were published over a number of years and first collected in *Guys and Dolls* (1932). His other collections of stories include *Blue Plate Special* (1934) and *Take It Easy* (1938). Together with Howard Lindsay he wrote a play, *A Slight Case of Murder* (1935). Many of his stories were made into successful film and stage productions, including the hit musical, *Guys and Dolls*.

On Broadway

containing all the stories from

More Than Somewhat
Furthermore
Take It Easy

DAMON RUNYON

PENGUIN BOOKS

PENGUIN BOOKS

Published by the Penguin Group
Penguin Books Ltd, 27 Wrights Lane, London W8 5TZ, England
Penguin Putnam Inc., 375 Hudson Street, New York, New York 10014, USA
Penguin Books Australia Ltd, Ringwood, Victoria, Australia
Penguin Books Canada Ltd, 10 Alcorn Avenue, Toronto, Ontario, Canada M4V 3B2
Penguin Books India (P) Ltd, 11, Community Centre, Panchsheel Park, New Delhi – 110 017, India
Penguin Books (NZ) Ltd, Private Bag 102902, NSMC, Auckland, New Zealand
Penguin Books (South Africa) (Pty) Ltd, 5 Watkins Street, Denver Ext 4, Johannesburg 2094, South Africa

Penguin Books Ltd, Registered Offices: Harmondsworth, Middlesex, England

This omnibus edition first published by Constable and Company 1950
Published in Penguin Books 1990
Reprinted in Penguin Classics 2000
1

Printed in England by Clays Ltd, St Ives plc

Contents

More Than Somewhat

Introduction by E. C. Bentley

Before Damon Runyon began writing his stories of the bandits of Broadway, he had made himself a national reputation in America as a newspaper-man; a descriptive reporter who could deal with any event in the day's doings, from a horserace at Miami to an electrocution at Ossining, in a manner that put him in a class by himself. In particular, he wrote of sporting matters with a style and a fund of expert knowledge that were enjoyed from ocean to ocean. But this was not, by its nature, the sort of work that endures. He broke into literature, quite suddenly, with a hilarious short story of the gangsters and crooks infesting a certain section of Broadway, the main artery of New York's life – the Hardened Artery, as Walter Winchell has called it. He followed it up with many others of the same sort; all of them, in fact, told by the same imaginary narrator, and told in a tone and a language that make up one of the richest contributions to comic literature in our time.

So, at least, I think; and I have not yet met any critical reader of Runyon's tales who does not think so too.

I have made this selection of Damon Runyon's stories with the idea of showing as many aspects as possible of his narrative genius, ranging as they do from the most uproarious farce to such sadness as goes to the depths of the heart. The note of pathos is not often touched, it is true: when it is, it gains force from the contrast with its setting of quaint, unemotional, unconscious cynicism. If, after reading *The Lily of St. Pierre* in this book you do not agree with that judgment, then – as Runyon's narrator would say – you must be such a guy as will never be moved by anything short of an earthquake.

In the little world inhabited by Runyon's people every male human being is a guy, every female a doll. There are in that world other names for dolls, it is true, such as broads, or pancakes, or tomatoes; but the narrator prefers not to use such terms, which he claims are not respectful. Do not ask me if there really is such a world. I only know that it is a world, and a very lively world, at that. But it is certainly founded on fact, if you like things founded on fact. We have been hearing of guys like Dave the Dude, and Benny South Street, and Germany Schwartz, and Franky Ferocious (whose square monicker is Ferroccio), and Milk Ear Willie, and Izzy Cheesecake, for many years past; ever since gangsters and racketeers began to be news: also of dolls like Rosa Midnight, and Miss Cleghorn, the Arabian Acrobatic dancer, and Miss Muriel O'Neill, who works in the Half Moon night club, and the doll named Silk, who associates so much more with guys than she does with other dolls that she finally gets so she thinks like a guy, and has a guy's slant on things in general. We have heard of them all before; but Damon Runyon puts life into them as no other writer has done yet, and I do not expect any other in the future to make crime, and violence, and dissipation, and predatory worthlessness, together with occasional off-hand decency where you would least expect it, as keenly interesting and as frantically funny as Damon Runyon does.

You cannot help liking his guys and dolls. I do not mean that they – the guys, anyway – would be nice to know, or even safe. In fact, if it is left to me, I will as soon go in bathing with a school of sharks, or maybe sooner. (I am sorry, but I find it impossible not to drift into Runyonese when writing of the creatures of his brain.) I do not mean that they are unselfish, good-hearted, high-minded guys and dolls. I do not mean that you will shed tears when Angie the Ox gets cooled off by Lance McGowan, or when Joey Perhaps gets what is coming to him from Ollie Ortega, which is a short knife in the throat, or when The Brain gets carved up quite some, and finally hauls off and dies. I merely mean that they have a reckless, courageous vitality that makes you like hearing about them; that is, if you are an ordinary human being, such as has always liked hearing about desperados. As a certain newspaper guy in one of the Runyon stories puts it, many legitimate guys are much interested in the doings of tough guys, and consider them very romantic. I do not see anything against this, so long as you also consider them very indefensible, and are strongly in favour of discouraging them in a severely practical manner.

But what you will probably like without reserve is the endless comedy that Damon Runyon extracts from their dangerous and disreputable way of life, and the wonderful style in which he gives it expression.

Just as I, an Englishman, cannot say how far the New York underworld he shows you corresponds to the real thing, so I do not know if the talk of these guys and dolls is the sort of conversation you will actually hear in the section between Times Square and Columbus Circle. But those who ought to know give both them and their speech a high character for trueness to life. Heywood Broun, for instance, who lives quite near at hand, declares that he recognizes Runyon's characters as actual people, and that their talk is put down almost literally.

That 'almost' is, no doubt, quite necessary. Damon Runyon, an artist in words, must have worked up his raw material with loving care; and in all likelihood he has made some contribution of his own. For Runyon, be it said, has long been among the recognized personal influences in the development of current American slang. In the days when he was known mainly as a sports-writer with a vast public, he was included in a short list of such influences by W. J. Funk, the New York publisher; and so high an authority as Henry Mencken, in his work on *The American Language*, has approved of that inclusion. It is doubtful if the ineffable felicity of so many passages in these stories could have been achieved by any merely phonographic method.

Nevertheless, the style of them is exclusively a conversational style. They are all talk; the talk of the guy who is telling them, or of other guys as reported by him. For English readers, I suppose, the most curious thing about that guy's talk will be his resolute avoidance of the past tense; the remarkable things he does with the historic present. The same thing is known in our own vulgar tongue, of course; but it is incidental, and apt to take a debased form – for example, 'So I says to him, "Did you hear what I said?"' In Runyonese this would be, 'So I say to him, "Do you hear what I say?"' Runyon's guy will say, 'About three weeks ago, Big Nig is down taking the waters in Hot Springs, and anything else there may be to take in Hot Springs.' He will not say, 'When I heard Bugs Lonigan say this, I wished I had never been born'; he will say, 'When I hear Bugs Lonigan say this, I wish I am never born.' There is a sort of ungrammatical purity about it, an almost religious exactitude, that to me, at least, has the strongest appeal. In all the Runyon stories, as published in America, I have found only one single instance of a verb in the past tense. It occurs in one of those included in this book; and you may try to find it, if – as Runyon's guy might say – you figure there is any percentage in doing so. And, as that same guy might go on to say, I will lay plenty of 6 to 5 that it is nothing but a misprint; but I do not think it is the proper caper for me to improve on Runyon's prose, so I leave it.

I do not know what the history of this dread of the past tense may be. Possibly it is quite a long history. From the literature of the cattle industry in the West – I mean the serious literature – it is to be seen that the cowboy of half a century ago, when West was West indeed, had a dialect all his own, in which the past tense did not figure. For instance, Alfred Henry Lewis's old cattleman, calling on his memories of long ago, says:

The most ornery party I ever knows is Curly Ben. This yere Ben is killed, final, by old Captain Moon, when Curly is playin' kyards. He's jest dealin', when Moon comes Injunin' up from the r'ar, an' drills Curly through the head with a ·45 Colt's. Which the queer part is this: Curly, as I states – an' he never knows what hits him, an' is as dead as Santa Anna in a moment – is dealin' the kyards. He's got the deck in his hands. An' yet, when the public picks Curly off the floor, he's pulled his two guns, an' has got one cocked.

A psychological curiosity which would have fitted very nicely into Runyon's account of the cooling off of various guys.

Very interesting, to my mind, is the personality of the guy who tells these stories. He does not give himself a name at any time, but it will do no harm to call him X. In some ways X is a strange guy to be mobbed up with such characters as he tells about. He is a nervous guy, for one thing; and even more remarkable, in the circumstances, than his nervousness, is his passion for respectability. He is 'greatly opposed to guys who violate the law,' as he insists again and again; and he can think of a million things he will rather do than be seen in the company of such guys. But as he is, on his own showing, practically never in any other kind of society, he must spend a harassing time. The truth is, X is very far from being one of the high shots, but is simply known to one and all as a guy who is just around. In fact, they figure him as harmless as a bag of marsh-mallows. Just the same, X is well known to every wrong gee on Broadway; and if one of them sees him and gives him a huge hello, what can X do? It would be very unsafe indeed if X tried playing the chill for such a guy. There are the professional assassins, like Ropes McGonnigle. There are the casual and temperamental killers, like Rusty Charley, the genial but uncertain-tempered guy in whose presence even such citizens as Nick the Greek or Joey Uptown become silent and nervous. There are the dangerous criminals, like Big Jule, who is wanted for robbery and burglary in a dozen different States, and who claims that he will catch cold if he goes out of doors without the holsters under his arms. There are various guys who are known to have cooled other guys off from time to time, and who are regarded consequently as rather suspicious characters. There are the git-em-up guys like Dancing Dan; and the guys who open safes for a living, like Big Butch; and the guys who are on the snatch (which it is very illiterate to call kidnapping), like Spanish John; and the guys who ride the tubs – that is to say, who live by cheating at cards on the Atlantic liners – like Little Manuel; and the guys who specialize in telling the tale, like the Lemon Drop Kid. There is also Pussy McGuire, who does very well at stealing valuable dogs and cats.

Besides these, there are of course the influential citizens who are interested in wet merchandise; for the Runyon stories reach back into the days of Prohibition, and if they 'date' at all, I suppose it will be because of that – though I am never sure that the importing dodge is so very dead, at that, considering what the taxation is on legal liquor. Naturally, guys who are interested in wet merchandise do not count seriously as illegal characters; but then many of them are also interested in artichokes, and extortion, and gambling joints, and other hot propositions. All such guys as these know X well, and seem to have a liking for his company; and X will often make himself useful to such guys by taking a message, for instance, to some citizen that it would be a good idea if he left town, and stayed away, instead of bringing beer into another guy's territory. In fact, if you come right down to it, the chances are that the nearest X ever comes to having a job of any kind is being more or less on the pay-roll of guys like Dave the Dude; which is not such a bum connection, at that, as Dave the Dude handles nothing but genuine champagne and Scotch, wishing no part in that trade in cut goods which brings in plenty of scratch to other importers who are not so particular.

The one and only guy in X's circle of acquaintance who is strictly legit is Judge Henry G. Blake. Of course, Judge Blake is not a judge, and never has been a judge, but he is called Judge because he looks like a judge, and talks slow, and puts in many long words. Judge Blake is very good at poker; and at pool he is just naturally a curly wolf; so he makes a living by building up suckers into playing against him for real money at these games.

Much as X is opposed to law-breaking, he is not bigoted about it. When he happens to hear of a promising job of burglary, with a little blackmail as a chaser, he remembers Harry the Horse, and throws it his way; for he knows that Harry the Horse is feeling the economic depression keenly, because if nobody is making any money, there is nobody for him to rob. Furthermore, Harry the Horse is never a bargain at any time, and is such a guy as you would much rather stand good with than have sored up at you for any reason.

Another curious feature of X's passion for legality is that it does not make him at all fond of policemen. In fact, the way X figures it, there are far too many coppers in this world. He believes, naturally, in being courteous to them at all times, but he does not care for them, even when they are fairly good guys, such as the copper who has the tears come into his eyes when he tells about the poor people who have all their lifetime savings in Israel Ib's busted jug.

Another way in which X seems to be a somewhat inconsistent guy is in his attitude towards liquor. To hear him tell it, he is by no means a rumpot, and indeed very seldom indulges in fermented beverages in any form. Yet from the derogatory things X says about the liquor in Good Time Charley's little speak, and in various other deadfalls, it is clear that he knows more than somewhat about the subject. Furthermore, at least two of X's adventures happen when he certainly has his pots on, rye whisky being the raw material in both cases; and he knows what it is like to have such a noggin the morning after that he does not feel much more than a hop ahead of the undertaker. So if X's putting himself away as an abstemious guy is not a lie, it will do until a lie comes along; and the chances are he is not the only guy in the same position, at that.

Whatever the truth may be about X as regards wine, his reactions to woman and song are fairly clear. X is a good, even an exacting, judge of dolls, and many of his remarks on the subject are well worth bearing in mind. He is by no means blind to the possibilities of romance as between young guys and dolls; he knows that the right conditions, such as the moon shining on the river, and what not, may be a dead cold set-up for love. But X is not such a guy as will get a high blood pressure over any doll; he has never been in love, and barring a bad break, never expects to be in love, to say nothing of being married. Most of the guys in his circle are bachelors, and the rest wish they were, but at the same time many of them take a great practical interest in dolls, including The Brain, who maintains four separate establishments, and guesses that love costs him about as much dough as any guy that ever lives. But The Brain can easily afford this, being the biggest guy in gambling operations in the East.

On the other hand, X is an enthusiast about song. If there is one thing he loves to do more than anything else, it is to sing in quartet, taking the baritone part. He likes to sing in quartet in Good Time Charley's little joint, because Good Time Charley sings a nice bass, and there are seldom any customers there until after the other places are closed; so that it is fairly quiet in there until about 5 a.m. Though you can never be quite sure, at that, because things may happen such as when Jack O'Hearts looks in unexpectedly, and outs with the old equalizer and shoots the right ear off Louie the Lug, who is singing a very fair tenor in the quartet, and then chases Louie out the back door and gets another crack at him which finishes him. Of course this breaks up the quartet, and nobody is happy, not even Jack O'Hearts, who complains that the light in Charley's dump is no good, as he ought to get Louie the first shot, and it is very sloppy work.

Another taste which X has strongly developed is horse-race betting; a taste which he shares with practically every guy mentioned in these stories. In fact, the only guys I can think of at the moment who do not back horses are two guys who happen to be book-makers. Some of X's friends, like Hot Horse Herbie, are such guys as never think of anything else in this world but betting on horses; but those who are mainly interested in crime, and so cannot be considered as serious horse-players, mostly devote a good deal of the proceeds to this form of amusement. Playing the horses is a necessary part of X's life. He despises football, and he cannot imagine why anybody takes an interest in such a thing as lawn tennis; baseball means nothing to him, and as for pugilism, X will not give you a bad two-bit piece to see a fight anywhere, because half the time the result is arranged beforehand, and X does not believe in encouraging dishonesty. His thoughts, and the thoughts of most of his acquaintance, are apt to express themselves in terms of betting; as for instance when the monkey steals the baby and carries it off to the roof of a house, and seems disposed to heave the baby into the street, and Big Nig, the crap shooter, is around among the hysterical crowd offering to lay 7 to 5 against the baby, which, X observes, is not a bad price, at that.

The most renowned short-story-teller of New York life in the past was O. Henry, whose work has long been the delight of a multitude of readers in this country. The question of a comparison between O. Henry and Damon Runyon is therefore bound to arise; and it can be easily answered. The two have hardly anything in common, apart from the faculty of invention. To begin with, O. Henry wrote of the New York life of thirty to forty years ago, which is a long time in the history of that metropolis. Also, while he knew its rich and its poor, its clerks and its shopgirls, its politicians and its sportsmen and its loafers, there is no sign – despite one or two romantic efforts of the Jimmy Valentine sort – that he had much acquaintance with the habitual criminal class. Again, if he had known it as it was in his day, he would have known a class very different from the one to which most of Runyon's characters belong, children as they are of a new age of crime, equipped with all the technical resources of the twentieth century; freed at the same time, by the advance of a brutish materialism, from the last rags of scruple and compassion; and to a great extent financed as crime never was financed before, first, by the enormous profits of a generally tolerated, not to say welcomed, smuggling trade, and then by the even easier money from organized extortion on a grand scale. O. Henry did not live to see national Prohibition, and never heard of racketeering.

His style and method, too, were wholly different from Damon Runyon's. All of the Runyon stories, as I have said, are told with the mouth and in the distinctive speech of one of the characters, who is a very real person indeed. O. Henry seldom resorted to this way of story-telling; and when he did – as in *The Gentle Grafter* – both the imaginary narrator and his talk were obviously not intended to be like life; they were meant merely for the producing of burlesque effect.

One English reader of these stories made the remark – so I am told – that a glossary would help you to understand them. I do not suppose he really meant this: if he did, I cannot imagine a more abject confession of dullness. Let us take it that he was paying an indirect compliment to the freshness and pungency of this variety of American speech. The truth is, X is particularly easy to understand. It is the greatest of the many merits of his style. Even if a term or a phrase is unfamiliar the context tells you instantly what it means. It may be news to you that to cool a guy off means to kill him; or that a doll taking a run-out powder on her husband means her deserting him; or that playing the duck for a guy means trying to avoid him: but if when you read these things in a Runyon story you do not understand what they mean, then you must be such a guy as will never understand much of anything in this world.

I can recall several cases of glossaries attached to English editions of American stories; and they always struck me as fussy and even, in a vague way, offensive, implying that the kind of slang in question was an unintelligible lingo of barbarians. One of the most famous of modern American novels was gravely introduced to English readers with a glossary, from which one could learn, with surprise, that a getaway meant an escape, or that junk meant rubbish. I have no idea of insulting readers by providing them with a glossary to help them to tear out the hidden significance of the statement, for example, that Israel Ib has a large snozzle and is as homely as a mud fence, but is well known to be a company guy in the banking dodge. The only terms I can think of that are not self-explanatory refer to sums of money: it is, from time to time, important to remember that a thousand dollars are a grand, or a G; a hundred dollars, a yard, or a C; ten dollars, a sawbuck; five dollars, a finnif, a fin, or a pound note; two dollars, a deuce; one dollar, a buck, or a bob.

Speaking generally, all this affectation about American speech being an alien thing is tiresome and many years out of date. Every office-boy uses the terms he has picked up from the Hollywood films; and our more sophisticated slang-users of both sexes have a much larger vocabulary drawn from American books. In fact, we produce little slang of our own to-day: what we have that is English is of old standing. Our borrowing in this way is, I suppose, one of the results of the enormous impression made on us (whether we like it or not) by the vigour, the vivacity, the originality, the self-sufficiency, the drama and melodrama of American life. And it is because we are under that impression that I believe English readers will welcome and enjoy these stories by Damon Runyon.

Breach of Promise

One day a certain party by the name of Judge Goldfobber, who is a lawyer by trade, sends word to me that he wishes me to call on him at his office in lower Broadway, and while ordinarily I do not care for any part of lawyers, it happens that Judge Goldfobber is a friend of mine, so I go to see him.

Of course Judge Goldfobber is not a judge, and never is a judge, and he is 100 to 1 in my line against ever being a judge, but he is called Judge because it pleases him, and everybody always wishes to please Judge Goldfobber, as he is one of the surest-footed lawyers in this town, and beats more tough beefs for different citizens than seems possible. He is a wonderful hand for keeping citizens from getting into the sneezer, and better than Houdini when it comes to getting them out of the sneezer after they are in.

Personally, I never have any use for the professional services of Judge Goldfobber, as I am a law-abiding citizen at all times, and am greatly opposed to guys who violate the law, but I know the Judge from around and about for many years. I know him from around and about the night clubs, and other deadfalls, for Judge Goldfobber is such a guy as loves to mingle with the public in these spots, as he picks up much law business there, and sometimes a nice doll.

Well, when I call on Judge Goldfobber, he takes me into his private office and wishes to know if I can think of a couple of deserving guys who are out of employment, and who will like a job of work, and if so, Judge Goldfobber says, he can offer them a first-class position.

'Of course,' Judge Goldfobber says, 'it is not steady employment, and in fact it is nothing but piece-work, but the parties must be extremely reliable parties, who can be depended on in a pinch. This is out-of-town work that requires tact, and,' he says, 'some nerve.'

Well, I am about to tell Judge Goldfobber that I am no employment agent, and go on about my business, because I can tell from the way he says the parties must be parties who can be depended on in a pinch, that a pinch is apt to come up on the job any minute, and I do not care to steer any friends of mine against a pinch.

But as I get up to go, I look out of Judge Goldfobber's window, and I can see Brooklyn in the distance beyond the river, and seeing

Brooklyn I get to thinking of certain parties over there that I figure must be suffering terribly from the unemployment situation. I get to thinking of Harry the Horse, and Spanish John and Little Isadore, and the reason I figure they must be suffering from the unemployment situation is because if nobody is working and making any money, there is nobody for them to rob, and if there is nobody for them to rob, Harry the Horse and Spanish John and Little Isadore are just naturally bound to be feeling the depression keenly.

Anyway, I finally mention the names of these parties to Judge Goldfobber, and furthermore I speak well of their reliability in a pinch, and of their nerve, although I cannot conscientiously recommend their tact, and Judge Goldfobber is greatly delighted, as he often hears of Harry the Horse, and Spanish John and Little Isadore.

He asks me for their addresses, but of course nobody knows exactly where Harry the Horse and Spanish John and Little Isadore live, because they do not live anywhere in particular. However, I tell him about a certain spot in Clinton Street where he may be able to get track of them, and then I leave Judge Goldfobber for fear he may wish me to take word to these parties, and if there is anybody in this whole world I will not care to take word to, or to have any truck with in any manner, shape, or form, it is Harry the Horse, and Spanish John and Little Isadore.

Well, I do not hear anything more of the matter for several weeks, but one evening when I am in Mindy's restaurant on Broadway enjoying a little cold borscht, which is a most refreshing matter in hot weather such as is going on at the time, who bobs up but Harry the Horse, and Spanish John and Little Isadore, and I am so surprised to see them that some of my cold borscht goes down the wrong way, and I almost choke to death.

However, they seem quite friendly, and in fact Harry the Horse pounds me on the back to keep me from choking, and while he pounds so hard that he almost caves in my spine, I consider it a most courteous action, and when I am able to talk again, I say to him as follows:

'Well, Harry,' I say, 'it is a privilege and a pleasure to see you again, and I hope and trust you will all join me in some cold borscht, which you will find very nice, indeed.'

'No,' Harry says, 'we do not care for any cold borscht. We are looking for Judge Goldfobber. Do you see Judge Goldfobber round and about lately?'

Well, the idea of Harry the Horse and Spanish John and Little Isadore looking for Judge Goldfobber sounds somewhat alarming to me, and I figure maybe the job Judge Goldfobber gives them turns out bad and they wish to take Judge Goldfobber apart, but the next minute Harry says to me like this:

'By the way,' he says, 'we wish to thank you for the job of work you throw our way. Maybe some day we will be able to do as much for you. It is a most interesting job,' Harry says, 'and while you are snuffing your cold borscht I will give you the details, so you will understand why we wish to see Judge Goldfobber.'

It turns out [Harry the Horse says] that the job is not for Judge Goldfobber personally, but for a client of his, and who is this client but Mr. Jabez Tuesday, the rich millionaire, who owns the Tuesday string of one-arm joints where many citizens go for food and wait on themselves. Judge Goldfobber comes to see us in Brooklyn in person, and sends me to see Mr. Jabez Tuesday with a letter of introduction, so Mr. Jabez Tuesday can explain what he wishes me to do, because Judge Goldfobber is too smart a guy to be explaining such matters to me himself.

In fact, for all I know maybe Judge Goldfobber is not aware of what Mr. Jabez Tuesday wishes me to do, although I am willing to lay a little 6 to 5 that Judge Goldfobber does not think Mr. Jabez Tuesday wishes to hire me as a cashier in any of his one-arm joints.

Anyway, I go to see Mr. Tuesday at a Fifth Avenue hotel where he makes his home, and where he has a very swell layout of rooms, and I am by no means impressed with Mr. Tuesday, as he hems and haws quite a bit before he tells me the nature of the employment he has in mind for me. He is a little guy, somewhat dried out, with a bald head, and a small mouser on his upper lip, and he wears specs, and seems somewhat nervous.

Well, it takes him some time to get down to cases, and tell me what is eating him, and what he wishes to do, and then it all sounds very simple, indeed, and in fact it sounds so simple that I think Mr. Jabez Tuesday is a little daffy when he tells me he will give me ten G's for the job.

What Mr. Tuesday wishes me to do is to get some letters that he personally writes to a doll by the name of Miss Amelia Bodkin, who lives in a house just outside Tarrytown, because it seems that Mr. Tuesday makes certain cracks in these letters that he is now sorry for, such as speaking of love and marriage and one thing and another to Miss Amelia Bodkin, and he is afraid she is going to sue him for breach of promise.

'Such an idea will be very embarrassing to me,' Mr. Jabez Tuesday says, 'as I am about to marry a party who is a member of one of the most high-toned families in this country. It is true,' Mr. Tuesday says, 'that the Scarwater family does not have as much money now as formerly, but there is no doubt about its being very, very high-toned, and my fiancée, Miss Valerie Scarwater, is one of the high-tonedest of them all. In fact,' he says, 'she is so high-toned that the chances are she will be very huffy about anybody suing me for breach of promise, and cancel everything.'

Well, I ask Mr. Tuesday what a breach of promise is, and he explains to me that it is when somebody promises to do something and fails to do this something, although of course we have a different name for a proposition of this nature in Brooklyn, and deal with it accordingly.

'This is a very easy job for a person of your standing,' Mr. Tuesday says. 'Miss Amelia Bodkin lives all alone in her house the other side of Tarrytown, except for a couple of servants, and they are old and harmless. Now the idea is,' he says, 'you are not to go to her house as if you are looking for the letters, but as if you are after something else, such as her silverware, which is quite antique and very valuable.

'She keeps the letters in a big inlaid box in her room,' Mr. Tuesday says, 'and if you just pick up this box and carry it away along with the silverware, no one will ever suspect that you are after the letters, but that you take the box thinking it contains valuables. You bring the letters to me and get your ten G's,' Mr. Tuesday says, 'and,' he says, 'you can keep the silverware, too. Be sure you get a Paul Revere teapot with the silverware,' he says. 'It is worth plenty.'

'Well,' I say to Mr. Tuesday, 'every guy knows his own business best, and I do not wish to knock myself out of a nice soft job, but,' I say, 'it seems to me the simplest way of carrying on this transaction is to buy the letters off this doll, and be done with it. Personally,' I say, 'I do not believe there is a doll in the world who is not willing to sell a whole post-office full of letters for ten G's, especially in these times, and throw in a set of Shakespeare with them.'

'No, no,' Mr. Tuesday says. 'Such a course will not do with Miss Amelia Bodkin at all. You see,' he says, 'Miss Bodkin and I are very, very friendly for a matter of maybe fifteen or sixteen years. In fact, we are very friendly, indeed. She does not have any idea at this time that I wish to break off this friendship with her. Now,' he says, 'if I try to buy the letters from her, she may become suspicious. The idea,' Mr. Tuesday says, 'is for me to get the letters first, and then explain to her about breaking off the friendship, and make suitable arrangements with her afterwards.

'Do not get Miss Amelia Bodkin wrong,' Mr. Tuesday says. 'She is an excellent person, but,' he says, 'you know the saying, "Hell hath no fury like a woman scorned." And maybe Miss Amelia Bodkin may figure I am scorning her if she finds out I am going to marry Miss Valerie Scarwater, and furthermore,' he says, 'if she still has the letters she may fall into the hands of unscrupulous lawyers, and demand a very large sum, indeed. But,' Mr. Tuesday says, 'this does not worry me half as much as the idea that Miss Valerie Scarwater may learn about the letters and get a wrong impression of my friendship with Miss Amelia Bodkin.'

Well, I round up Spanish John and Little Isadore the next afternoon, and I find Little Isadore playing klob with a guy by the name of Educated Edmund, who is called Educated Edmund because he once goes to Erasmus High school and is considered a very fine scholar, indeed, so I invite Educated Edmund to go along with us. The idea is, I know Educated Edmund makes a fair living playing klob with Little Isadore, and I figure as long as I am depriving Educated Edmund of a living for awhile, it is only courteous to toss something else his way. Furthermore, I figure as long as letters are involved in this proposition it may be a good thing to have Educated Edmund handy in case any reading becomes necessary, because Spanish John and Little Isadore do not read at all, and I read only large print.

We borrow a car off a friend of mine in Clinton Street, and with me driving we start for Tarrytown, which is a spot up the Hudson River, and it is a very enjoyable ride for one and all on account of the scenery. It is the first time Educated Edmund and Spanish John and Little Isadore ever see the scenery along the Hudson although they all reside on the banks of this beautiful river for several years at Ossining. Personally, I am never in Ossining, although once I make Auburn, and once Comstock, but the scenery in these localities is nothing to speak of.

We hit Tarrytown about dark, and follow the main drag through this burg, as Mr. Tuesday tells me, until finally we come to the spot I am looking for, which is a little white cottage on a slope of ground above the river, not far off the highway. This little white cottage has quite a piece of ground around it, and a low stone wall, with a driveway from the highway to the house, and when I spot the gate to the driveway I make a quick turn, and what happens but I run the car slapdab into a stone gatepost, and the car folds up like an accordion.

You see, the idea is we are figuring to make this a fast stick-up job without any foolishness about it, maybe leaving any parties we come across tied up good and tight while we make a getaway, as I am greatly opposed to housebreaking, or sneak jobs, as I do not consider them dignified. Furthermore, they take too much time, so I am going to run the car right up to the front door when this stone post gets in my way.

The next thing I know, I open my eyes to find myself in a strange bed, and also in a strange bedroom, and while I wake up in many a strange bed in my time, I never wake up in such a strange bedroom as this. It is all very soft and dainty, and the only jarring note in my surroundings is Spanish John sitting beside the bed looking at me.

Naturally I wish to know what is what, and Spanish John says I am knocked snoring in the collision with the gatepost, although none of the others are hurt, and that while I am stretched in the driveway with the blood running out of a bad gash in my noggin, who pops out of the house but a doll and an old guy who seems to be a butler, or some such, and the doll insists on them lugging me into the house, and placing me in this bedroom.

Then she washes the blood off of me, Spanish John says, and wraps my head up and personally goes to Tarrytown to get a croaker to see if my wounds are fatal, or what, while Educated Edmund and Little Isadore are trying to patch up the car. So, Spanish John says, he is sitting there to watch me until she comes back, although of course I know what he is really sitting there for is to get first search at me in case I do not recover.

Well, while I am thinking all this over, and wondering what is to be done, in pops a doll of maybe forty odd, who is built from the ground up, but who has a nice, kind-looking pan, with a large smile, and behind her is a guy I can see at once is a croaker, especially as he is packing a little black bag, and has a grey goatee. I never see a nicer-looking doll if you care for middling-old dolls, although personally I like them young, and when she sees me with my eyes open, she speaks as follows:

'Oh,' she says, 'I am glad you are not dead, you poor chap. But,' she says, 'here is Doctor Diffingwell, and he will see how badly you are injured. My name is Miss Amelia Bodkin, and this is my house, and this is my own bedroom, and I am very, very sorry you are hurt.'

Well, naturally I consider this a most embarrassing situation, because here I am out to clip Miss Amelia Bodkin of her letters and her silverware, including her Paul Revere teapot, and there she is taking care of me in first-class style, and saying she is sorry for me.

But there seems to be nothing for me to say at this time, so I hold still while the croaker looks me over, and after he peeks at my noggin, and gives me a good feel up and down, he states as follows:

'This is a very bad cut,' he says. 'I will have to stitch it up, and then he must be very quiet for a few days, otherwise,' he says, 'complications may set in. It is best to move him to a hospital at once.'

But Miss Amelia Bodkin will not listen to such an idea as moving me to a hospital. Miss Amelia Bodkin says I must rest right where I am, and she will take care of me, because she says I am injured on her premises by her gatepost, and it is only fair that she does something for me. In fact, from the way Miss Amelia Bodkin takes on about me being moved, I figure it is the old sex appeal, although afterwards I find out it is only because she is lonesome, and nursing me will give her something to do.

Well, naturally I am not opposing her idea, because the way I look at it, I will be able to handle the situation about the letters, and also the silverware, very nicely as an inside job, so I try to act even worse off than I am, although of course anybody who knows about the time I carry eight slugs in my body from Broadway and Fiftieth Street to Brooklyn will laugh very heartily at the idea of a cut on the noggin keeping me in bed.

After the croaker gets through sewing me up, and goes away, I tell Spanish John to take Educated Edmund and Little Isadore and go back to New York, but to keep in touch with me by telephone, so I can tell them when to come back, and then I go to sleep, because I seem to be very tired. When I wake up later in the night, I seem to have a fever, and am really somewhat sick, and Miss Amelia Bodkin is sitting beside my bed swabbing my noggin with a cool cloth, which feels very pleasant, indeed.

I am better in the morning, and am able to knock over a little breakfast which she brings to me on a tray, and I am commencing to see where being an invalid is not so bad, at that, especially when there are no coppers at your bedside every time you open your eyes asking who does it to you.

I can see Miss Amelia Bodkin gets quite a bang out of having somebody to take care of, although of course if she knows who she is taking care of at this time, the chances are she will be running up the road calling for the gendarmes. It is not until after breakfast that I can get her to go and grab herself a little sleep, and while she is away sleeping the old guy who seems to be the butler is in and out of my room every now and then to see how I am getting along.

He is a gabby old guy, and pretty soon he is telling me all about Miss Amelia Bodkin, and what he tells me is that she is the old-time sweetheart of a guy in New York who is at the head of a big business, and very rich, and of course I know this guy is Mr. Jabez Tuesday, although the old guy who seems to be the butler never mentions his name.

'They are together many years,' he says to me. 'He is very poor when they meet, and she has a little money, and establishes him in business, and by her management of this business, and of him, she makes it a very large business, indeed. I know, because I am with them almost from the start,' the old guy says. 'She is very smart in business, and also very kind, and nice, if anybody asks you.

'Now,' the old guy says, 'I am never able to figure out why they do not get married, because there is no doubt she loves him, and he loves her, but Miss Amelia Bodkin once tells me that it is because they are too poor at the start, and too busy later on to think of such things as getting married, and so they drift along the way they are, until all of a sudden he is rich. Then,' the old guy says, 'I can see he is getting away from her, although she never sees it herself, and I am not surprised when a few years ago he convinced her it is best for her to retire from active work, and move out to this spot.

'He comes out here fairly often at first,' the old guy says, 'but gradually he stretches the time between his visits, and now we do not see him once in a coon's age. Well,' the old guy says, 'it is just such a case as often comes up in life. In fact, I personally know of some others. But Miss Amelia Bodkin still thinks he loves her, and that only business keeps him away so much, so you can see she either is not as smart as she looks or is kidding herself. Well,' the old guy says, 'I will now bring you a little orange-juice, although I do not mind saying you do not look to me like a guy who drinks orange-juice as a steady proposition.'

Now I am taking many a gander around the bedroom to see if I can case the box of letters that Mr. Jabez Tuesday speaks of, but there is no box such as he describes in sight. Then in the evening, when Miss Amelia Bodkin is in the room, and I seem to be dozing, she pulls out a drawer in the bureau, and hauls out a big inlaid box, and sits down at a table under a reading-lamp, and opens this box and begins reading some old letters. And as she sits there reading those letters, with me watching her through my eyelashes, sometimes she smiles, but once I see little tears rolling down her cheeks.

All of a sudden she looks at me, and catches me with my eyes wide open, and I can see her face turn red, and then she laughs, and speaks to me, as follows:

'Old love-letters,' she says, tapping the box. 'From my old sweetheart,' she says. 'I read some of them every night of my life. Am I not foolish and sentimental to do such a thing?'

Well, I tell Miss Amelia Bodkin she is sentimental all right, but I do not tell her just how foolish she is to be letting me in on where she plants these letters, although of course I am greatly pleased to have this information. I tell Miss Amelia Bodkin that personally I never write a love-letter, and never get a love-letter, and in fact, while I hear of these propositions, I never even see a love-letter before, and this is all as true as you are a foot high. Then Miss Amelia Bodkin laughs a little, and says to me as follows:

'Why,' she says, 'you are a very unusual chap, indeed, not to know what a love-letter is like. Why,' she says, 'I think I will read you a few of the most wonderful love-letters in this world. It will do no harm,' she says, 'because you do not know the writer, and you must lie there and think of me, not old and ugly, as you see me now, but as young, and maybe a little bit pretty.'

So Miss Amelia Bodkin opens a letter and reads it to me, and her voice is soft and low as she reads, but she scarcely ever looks at the letter as she is reading, so I can see she knows it pretty much by heart. Furthermore, I can see that she thinks this letter is quite a masterpiece, but while I am no judge of love-letters, because this is the first one I ever hear, I wish to say I consider it nothing but great nonsense.

'Sweetheart mine,' this love-letter says, 'I am still thinking of you as I see you yesterday standing in front of the house with the sunlight turning your dark brown hair to wonderful bronze. Darling,' it says, 'I love the colour of your hair. I am so glad you are not a blonde. I hate blondes, they are so empty-headed, and mean, and deceitful. Also they are bad-tempered,' the letter says. 'I will never trust a blonde any farther than I can throw a bull by the tail. I never see a blonde in my life who is not a plumb washout,' it says. 'Most of them are nothing but peroxide, anyway. Business is improving,' it says. 'Sausage is going up. I love you now and always, my baby doll.'

Well, there are others worse than this, and all of them speak of her as sweetheart, or baby, or darlingest one, and also as loveykins, and precious, and angel, and I do not know what all else, and several of them speak of how things will be after they marry, and as I judge these are Mr. Jabez Tuesday's letters, all right, I can see where they are full of dynamite for a guy who is figuring on taking a run-out powder on a doll. In fact, I say something to this general effect to Miss Amelia Bodkin, just for something to say.

'Why,' she says, 'what do you mean?'

'Well,' I say, 'documents such as these are known to bring large prices under certain conditions.'

Now Miss Amelia Bodkin looks at me a moment as if wondering what is in my mind, and then she shakes her head as if she gives it up, and laughs and speaks as follows:

'Well,' she says, 'one thing is certain, my letters will never bring a price, no matter how large, under any conditions, even if anybody ever wants them. Why,' she says, 'these are my greatest treasure. They are my memories of my happiest days. Why,' she says, 'I will not part with these letters for a million dollars.'

Naturally I can see from this remark that Mr. Jabez Tuesday makes a very economical deal with me at ten G's for the letters, but of course I do not mention this to Miss Amelia Bodkin as I watch her put her love-letters back in the inlaid box, and put the box back in the drawer of the bureau. I thank her for letting me hear the letters, and then I tell her good night, and I go to sleep, and the next day I telephone to a certain number in Clinton Street and leave word for Educated Edmund and Spanish John and Little Isadore to come and get me, as I am tired of being an invalid.

Now the next day is Saturday, and the day that comes after is bound to be Sunday, and they come to see me on Saturday, and promise to come back for me Sunday, as the car is now unravelled and running all right, although my friend in Clinton Street is beefing no little about the way his fenders are bent. But before they arrive Sunday morning, who is there ahead of them bright and early but Mr. Jabez Tuesday in a big town car.

Furthermore, as he walks into the house, all dressed up in a cutaway coat, and a high hat, he grabs Miss Amelia Bodkin in his arms, and kisses her ker-plump right on the smush, which information I afterwards receive from the old guy who seems to be the butler. From upstairs I can personally hear Miss Amelia Bodkin crying more than somewhat, and then I hear Mr Jabez Tuesday speak in a loud, hearty voice as follows:

'Now, now, now, 'Mely,' Mr. Tuesday says. 'Do not be crying, especially on my new white vest. Cheer up,' Mr. Tuesday says, 'and listen to the arrangements I make for our wedding to-morrow, and our honeymoon in Montreal. Yes, indeed, 'Mely,' Mr. Tuesday says, 'you are the only one for me, because you understand me from A to Izzard. Give me another big kiss, 'Mely, and let us sit down and talk things over.'

Well, I judge from the sound that he gets his kiss, and it is a very large kiss, indeed, with the cut-out open, and then I hear them chewing the rag at great length in the living-room downstairs. Finally I hear Mr. Jabez Tuesday speak as follows:

'You know, 'Mely,' he says, 'you and I are just plain ordinary folks without any lugs, and,' he says, 'this is why we fit each other so well. I am sick and tired of people who pretend to be high-toned and mighty, when they do not have a white quarter to their name. They have no manners whatever. Why, only last night,' Mr. Jabez Tuesday says, 'I am calling on a high-toned family in New York by the name of Scarwater, and out of a clear sky I am grossly insulted by the daughter of the house, and practically turned out in the street. I never receive such treatment in my life,' he says. ' 'Mely,' he says, 'give me another kiss, and see if you feel a bump here on my head.'

Of course, Mr. Jabez Tuesday is somewhat surprised to see me present later on, but he never lets on he knows me, and naturally I do not give Mr. Jabez any tumble whatever at the moment, and by and by Educated Edmund and Spanish John and Little Isadore come for me in the car, and I thank Miss Amelia Bodkin for her kindness to me, and leave her standing on the lawn with Mr. Jabez Tuesday waving us good-bye.

And Miss Amelia Bodkin looks so happy as she snuggles up close to Mr. Jabez Tuesday that I am glad I take the chance, which is always better than an even-money chance these days, that Miss Valeria Scarwater is a blonde, and send Educated Edmund to her to read her Mr. Tuesday's letter in which he speaks of blondes. But of course I am sorry that this and other letters that I tell Educated Edmund to read to her heats her up so far as to make her forget she is a lady and causes her to slug Mr. Jabez Tuesday on the bean with an 18-carat vanity case, as she tells him to get out of her life.

So [Harry the Horse says] there is nothing more to the story, except we are now looking for Judge Goldfobber to get him to take up a legal matter for us with Mr. Jabez Tuesday. It is true Mr. Tuesday pays us the ten G's, but he never lets us take the silverware he speaks of, not even the Paul Revere teapot, which he says is so valuable, and in fact when we drop around to Miss Amelia Bodkin's house to pick up these articles one night not long ago, the old guy who seems to be the butler lets off a double-barrelled shotgun at us, and acts very nasty in general.

So [Harry says] we are going to see if we can get Judge Goldfobber to sue Mr. Jabez Tuesday for breach of promise.

Romance in the Roaring Forties

Only a rank sucker will think of taking two peeks at Dave the Dude's doll, because while Dave may stand for the first peek, figuring it is a mistake, it is a sure thing he will get sored up at the second peek, and Dave the Dude is certainly not a man to have sored up at you.

But this Waldo Winchester is one hundred per cent. sucker, which is why he takes quite a number of peeks at Dave's doll. And what is more, she takes quite a number of peeks right back at him. And there you are. When a guy and a doll get to taking peeks back and forth at each other, why, there you are indeed.

This Waldo Winchester is a nice-looking young guy who writes pieces about Broadway for the *Morning Item*. He writes about the goings-on in night clubs, such as fights, and one thing and another, and also about who is running around with who, including guys and dolls.

Sometimes this is very embarrassing to people who may be married and are running around with people who are not married, but of course Waldo Winchester cannot be expected to ask one and all for their marriage certificates before he writes his pieces for the paper.

The chances are if Waldo Winchester knows Miss Billy Perry is Dave the Dude's doll, he will never take more than his first peek at her, but nobody tips him off until his second or third peek, and by this time Miss Billy Perry is taking her peeks back at him and Waldo Winchester is hooked.

In fact, he is plumb gone, and being a sucker, like I tell you, he does not care whose doll she is. Personally, I do not blame him much, for Miss Billy Perry is worth a few peeks, especially when she is out on the floor of Miss Missouri Martin's Sixteen Hundred Club doing her tap dance. Still, I do not think the best tap-dancer that ever lives can make me take two peeks at her if I know she is Dave the Dude's doll, for Dave somehow thinks more than somewhat of his dolls.

He especially thinks plenty of Miss Billy Perry, and sends her fur coats, and diamond rings, and one thing and another, which she sends back to him at once, because it seems she does not take presents from guys. This is considered most surprising all along Broadway, but people figure the chances are she has some other angle.

Anyway, this does not keep Dave the Dude from liking her just the same, and so she is considered his doll by one and all, and is respected accordingly until this Waldo Winchester comes along.

It happens that he comes along while Dave the Dude is off in the Modoc on a little run down to the Bahamas to get some goods for his business, such as Scotch and champagne, and by the time Dave gets back Miss Billy Perry and Waldo Winchester are at the stage where they sit in corners between her numbers and hold hands.

Of course nobody tells Dave the Dude about this, because they do not wish to get him excited. Not even Miss Missouri Martin tells him, which is most unusual because Miss Missouri Martin, who is sometimes called 'Mizzoo' for short, tells everything she knows as soon as she knows it, which is very often before it happens.

You see, the idea is when Dave the Dude is excited he may blow somebody's brains out, and the chances are it will be nobody's brains but Waldo Winchester's, although some claim that Waldo Winchester has no brains or he will not be hanging around Dave the Dude's doll.

I know Dave is very, very fond of Miss Billy Perry, because I hear him talk to her several times, and he is most polite to her and never gets out of line in her company by using cuss words, or anything like this. Furthermore, one night when One-eyed Solly Abrahams is a little stewed up he refers to Miss Billy Perry as a broad, meaning no harm whatever, for this is the way many of the boys speak of the dolls.

But right away Dave the Dude reaches across the table and bops One-eyed Solly right in the mouth, so everybody knows from then on that Dave thinks well of Miss Billy Perry. Of course Dave is always thinking fairly well of some doll as far as this goes, but it is seldom he gets to bopping guys in the mouth over them.

Well, one night what happens but Dave the Dude walks into the Sixteen Hundred Club, and there in the entrance, what does he see but this Waldo Winchester and Miss Billy Perry kissing each other back and forth friendly. Right away Dave reaches for the old equalizer to shoot Waldo Winchester, but it seems Dave does not happen to have the old equalizer with him, not expecting to have to shoot anybody this particular evening.

So Dave the Dude walks over and, as Waldo Winchester hears him coming and lets go his strangle-hold on Miss Billy Perry, Dave nails him with a big right hand on the chin. I will say for Dave the Dude that he is a fair puncher with his right hand, though his left is not so good, and he knocks Waldo Winchester bow-legged. In fact, Waldo folds right up on the floor.

Well, Miss Billy Perry lets out a screech you can hear clear to the Battery and runs over to where Waldo Winchester lights, and falls on top of him squalling very loud. All anybody can make out of what she says is that Dave the Dude is a big bum, although Dave is not so big, at that, and that she loves Waldo Winchester.

Dave walks over and starts to give Waldo Winchester the leather, which is considered customary in such cases, but he seems to change his mind, and instead of booting Waldo around, Dave turns and walks out of the joint looking very black and mad, and the next anybody hears of him he is over in the Chicken Club doing plenty of drinking.

This is regarded as a very bad sign indeed, because while everybody goes to the Chicken Club now and then to give Tony Bertazzola, the owner, a friendly play, very few people care to do any drinking there, because Tony's liquor is not meant for anybody to drink except the customers.

Well, Miss Billy Perry gets Waldo Winchester on his pegs again, and wipes his chin off with her handkerchief, and by and by he is all okay except for a big lump on his chin. And all the time she is telling Waldo Winchester what a big bum Dave the Dude is, although afterwards Miss Missouri Martin gets hold of Miss Billy Perry and puts the blast on her plenty for chasing a two-handed spender such as Dave the Dude out of the joint.

'You are nothing but a little sap,' Miss Missouri Martin tells Miss Billy Perry. 'You cannot get the right time off this newspaper guy, while everybody knows Dave the Dude is a very fast man with a dollar.'

'But I love Mr. Winchester,' says Miss Billy Perry. 'He is so romantic. He is not a bootlegger and a gunman like Dave the Dude. He puts lovely pieces in the paper about me, and he is a gentleman at all times.'

Now of course Miss Missouri Martin is not in a position to argue about gentlemen, because she meets very few in the Sixteen Hundred Club and anyway, she does not wish to make Waldo Winchester mad as he is apt to turn around and put pieces in his paper that will be a knock to the joint, so she lets the matter drop.

Miss Billy Perry and Waldo Winchester go on holding hands between her numbers, and maybe kissing each other now and then, as young people are liable to do, and Dave the Dude plays the chill for the Sixteen Hundred Club and everything seems to be all right. Naturally we are all very glad there is no more trouble over the proposition, because the best Dave can get is the worst of it in a jam with a newspaper guy.

Personally, I figure Dave will soon find himself another doll and forget all about Miss Billy Perry, because now that I take another peek at her, I can see where she is just about the same as any other tap-dancer, except that she is red-headed. Tap-dancers are generally blackheads, but I do not know why.

Moosh, the doorman at the Sixteen Hundred Club, tells me Miss Missouri Martin keeps plugging for Dave the Dude with Miss Billy Perry in a quiet way, because he says he hears Miss Missouri Martin make the following crack one night to her: 'Well, I do not see any Simple Simon on your lean and linger.'

This is Miss Missouri Martin's way of saying she sees no diamond on Miss Billy Perry's finger, for Miss Missouri Martin is an old experienced doll, who figures if a guy loves a doll he will prove it with diamonds. Miss Missouri Martin has many diamonds herself, though how any guy can ever get himself heated up enough about Miss Missouri Martin to give her diamonds is more than I can see.

I am not a guy who goes around much, so I do not see Dave the Dude for a couple of weeks, but late one Sunday afternoon little Johnny McGowan, who is one of Dave's men, comes and says to me like this: 'What do you think? Dave grabs the scribe a little while ago and is taking him out for an airing!'

Well, Johnny is so excited it is some time before I can get him cooled out enough to explain. It seems that Dave the Dude gets his biggest car out of the garage and sends his driver, Wop Joe, over to the *Item* office where Waldo Winchester works, with a message that Miss Billy Perry wishes to see Waldo right away at Miss Missouri Martin's apartment on Fifty-ninth Street.

Of course this message is nothing but the phonus bolonus, but Waldo drops in for it and gets in the car. Then Wop Joe drives him up to Miss Missouri Martin's apartment, and who gets in the car there but Dave the Dude. And away they go.

Now this is very bad news indeed, because when Dave the Dude takes a guy out for an airing the guy very often does not come back. What happens to him I never ask, because the best a guy can get by asking questions in this man's town is a bust in the nose.

But I am much worried over this proposition, because I like Dave the Dude, and I know that taking a newspaper guy like Waldo Winchester out for an airing is apt to cause talk, especially if he does not come back. The other guys that Dave the Dude takes out for airings do not mean much in particular, but here is a guy who may produce trouble, even if he is a sucker, on account of being connected with a newspaper.

I know enough about newspapers to know that by and by the editor or somebody will be around wishing to know where Waldo Winchester's pieces about Broadway are, and if there are no pieces from Waldo Winchester, the editor will wish to know why. Finally it will get around to where other people will wish to know, and after a while many people will be running around saying: 'Where is Waldo Winchester?'

And if enough people in this town get to running around saying where is So-and-so, it becomes a great mystery and the newspapers hop on the cops and the cops hop on everybody, and by and by there is so much heat in town that it is no place for a guy to be.

But what is to be done about this situation I do not know. Personally, it strikes me as very bad indeed, and while Johnny goes away to do a little telephoning, I am trying to think up some place to go where people will see me, and remember afterwards that I am there in case it is necessary for them to remember.

Finally Johnny comes back, very excited, and says: 'Hey, the Dude is up at the Woodcock Inn on the Pelham Parkway, and he is sending out the word for one and all to come at once. Good Time Charley Bernstein just gets the wire and tells me. Something is doing. The rest of the mob are on their way, so let us be moving.'

But here is an invitation which does not strike me as a good thing at all. The way I look at it, Dave the Dude is no company for a guy like me at this time. The chances are he either does something to Waldo Winchester already, or is getting ready to do something to him which I wish no part of.

Personally, I have nothing against newspaper guys, not even the ones who write pieces about Broadway. If Dave the Dude wishes to do something to Waldo Winchester, all right, but what is the sense of bringing outsiders into it? But the next thing I know, I am in Johnny McGowan's roadster, and he is zipping along very fast indeed, paying practically no attention to traffic lights or anything else.

As we go busting out the Concourse, I get to thinking the situation over, and I figure that Dave the Dude probably keeps thinking about Miss Billy Perry, and drinking liquor such as they sell in the Chicken Club, until finally he blows his topper. The way I look at it, only a guy who is off his nut will think of taking a newspaper guy out for an airing over a doll, when dolls are a dime a dozen in this man's town.

Still, I remember reading in the papers about a lot of different guys who are considered very sensible until they get tangled up with a doll, and maybe loving her, and the first thing anybody knows they hop out of windows, or shoot themselves, or somebody else, and I can see where even a guy like Dave the Dude may go daffy over a doll.

I can see that little Johnny McGowan is worried, too, but he does not say much, and we pull up in front of the Woodcock Inn in no time whatever, to find a lot of other cars there ahead of us, some of which I recognize as belonging to different parties.

The Woodcock Inn is what is called a road house, and is run by Big Nig Skolsky, a very nice man indeed, and a friend of everybody's. It stands back a piece off the Pelham Parkway and is a very pleasant place to go to, what with Nig having a good band and a floor show with a lot of fair-looking dolls, and everything else a man can wish for a good time. It gets a nice play from nice people, although Nig's liquor is nothing extra.

Personally, I never go there much, because I do not care for road houses, but it is a great spot for Dave the Dude when he is pitching parties, or even when he is only drinking single-handed. There is a lot of racket in the joint as we drive up, and who comes out to meet us but Dave the Dude himself with a big hello. His face is very red, and he seems heated up no little, but he does not look like a guy who is meaning any harm to anybody, especially a newspaper guy.

'Come in, guys!' Dave the Dude yells. 'Come right in!'

So we go in, and the place is full of people sitting at tables, or out on the floor dancing, and I see Miss Missouri Martin with all her diamonds hanging from her in different places, and Good Time Charley Bernstein, and Feet Samuels, and Tony Bertazzola, and Skeets Boliver, and Nick the Greek, and Rochester Red, and a lot of other guys and dolls from around and about.

In fact, it looks as if everybody from all the joints on Broadway are present, including Miss Billy Perry, who is all dressed up in white and is lugging a big bundle of orchids and so forth, and who is giggling and smiling and shaking hands and going on generally. And finally I see Waldo Winchester, the scribe, sitting at a ringside table all by himself, but there is nothing wrong with him as far as I can see. I mean, he seems to be all in one piece so far.

'Dave,' I say to Dave the Dude, very quiet, 'what is coming off here? You know a guy cannot be too careful what he does around this town, and I will hate to see you tangled up in anything right now.'

'Why,' Dave says, 'what are you talking about? Nothing is coming off here but a wedding, and it is going to be the best wedding anybody on Broadway ever sees. We are waiting for the preacher now.'

'You mean somebody is going to be married?' I ask, being now somewhat confused.

'Certainly,' Dave the Dude says. 'What do you think? What is the idea of a wedding, anyway?'

'Who is going to be married?' I ask.

'Nobody but Billy and the scribe,' Dave says. 'This is the greatest thing I ever do in my life. I run into Billy the other night and she is crying her eyes out because she loves this scribe and wishes to marry him, but it seems the scribe has nothing he can use for money. So I tell Billy to leave it to me, because you know I love her myself so much I wish to see her happy at all times, even if she has to marry to be that way.

'So I frame this wedding party, and after they are married I am going to stake them to a few G's so they can get a good running start,' Dave says. 'But I do not tell the scribe and I do not let Billy tell him as I wish it to be a big surprise to him. I kidnap him this afternoon and bring him out here and he is scared half to death thinking I am going to scrag him.

'In fact,' Dave says, 'I never see a guy so scared. He is still so scared nothing seems to cheer him up. Go over and tell him to shake himself together, because nothing but happiness for him is coming off here.'

Well, I wish to say I am greatly relieved to think that Dave intends doing nothing worse to Waldo Winchester than getting him married up, so I go over to where Waldo is sitting. He certainly looks somewhat alarmed. He is all in a huddle with himself, and he has what you call a vacant stare in his eyes. I can see that he is indeed frightened, so I give him a jolly slap on the back and I say: 'Congratulations, pal! Cheer up, the worst is yet to come!'

'You bet it is,' Waldo Winchester says, his voice so solemn I am greatly surprised.

'You are a fine-looking bridegroom,' I say. 'You look as if you are at a funeral instead of a wedding. Why do you not laugh ha-ha, and maybe take a dram or two and go to cutting up some?'

'Mister,' says Waldo Winchester, 'my wife is not going to care for me getting married to Miss Billy Perry.'

'Your wife?' I say, much astonished. 'What is this you are speaking of? How can you have any wife except Miss Billy Perry? This is great foolishness.'

'I know,' Waldo says, very sad. 'I know. But I got a wife just the same, and she is going to be very nervous when she hears about this. My wife is very strict with me. My wife does not allow me to go around marrying people. My wife is Lola Sapola, of the Rolling

Sapolas, the acrobats, and I am married to her for five years. She is the strong lady who juggles the other four people in the act. My wife just gets back from a year's tour of the Interstate time, and she is at the Marx Hotel right this minute. I am upset by this proposition.'

'Does Miss Billy Perry know about this wife?' I ask.

'No,' he says. 'No. She thinks I am single-o.'

'But why do you not tell Dave the Dude you are already married when he brings you out here to marry you off to Miss Billy Perry?' I ask. 'It seems to me a newspaper guy must know it is against the law for a guy to marry several different dolls unless he is a Turk, or some such.'

'Well,' Waldo says, 'if I tell Dave the Dude I am married after taking his doll away from him, I am quite sure Dave will be very much excited, and maybe do something harmful to my health.'

Now there is much in what the guy says, to be sure. I am inclined to think, myself, that Dave will be somewhat disturbed when he learns of this situation, especially when Miss Billy Perry starts in being unhappy about it. But what is to be done I do not know, except maybe to let the wedding go on, and then when Waldo is out of reach of Dave, to put in a claim that he is insane, and that the marriage does not count. It is a sure thing I do not wish to be around when Dave the Dude hears Waldo is already married.

I am thinking that maybe I better take it on the lam out of here, when there is a great row at the door and I hear Dave the Dude yelling that the preacher arrives. He is a very nice-looking preacher, at that, though he seems somewhat surprised by the goings-on, especially when Miss Missouri Martin steps up and takes charge of him. Miss Missouri Martin tells him she is fond of preachers, and is quite used to them, because she is twice married by preachers, and twice by justices of the peace, and once by a ship's captain at sea.

By this time one and all present, except maybe myself and Waldo Winchester, and the preacher and maybe Miss Billy Perry, are somewhat corned. Waldo is still sitting at his table looking very sad and saying 'Yes' and 'No' to Miss Billy Perry whenever she skips past him, for Miss Billy Perry is too much pleasured up with happiness to stay long in one spot.

Dave the Dude is more corned than anybody else, because he has two or three days' running start on everybody. And when Dave the Dude is corned I wish to say that he is a very unreliable guy as to temper, and he is apt to explode right in your face any minute. But he seems to be getting a great bang out of the doings.

Well, by and by Nig Skolsky has the dance floor cleared, and then he moves out on the floor a sort of arch of very beautiful flowers. The idea seems to be that Miss Billy Perry and Waldo Winchester are to be married under this arch. I can see that Dave the Dude must put in several days planning this whole proposition, and it must cost him plenty of the old do-re-mi, especially as I see him showing Miss Missouri Martin a diamond ring as big as a cough drop.

'It is for the bride,' Dave the Dude says. 'The poor loogan she is marrying will never have enough dough to buy her such a rock, and she always wishes a big one. I get it off a guy who brings it in from Los Angeles. I am going to give the bride away myself in person, so how do I act, Mizzoo? I want Billy to have everything according to the book.'

Well, while Miss Missouri Martin is trying to remember back to one of her weddings to tell him, I take another peek at Waldo Winchester to see how he is making out. I once see two guys go to the old warm squativoo up in Sing Sing, and I wish to say both are laughing heartily compared to Waldo Winchester at this moment.

Miss Billy Perry is sitting with him and the orchestra leader is calling his men dirty names because none of them can think of how 'Oh, Promise Me' goes, when Dave the Dude yells: 'Well, we are all set! Let the happy couple step forward!'

Miss Billy Perry bounces up and grabs Waldo Winchester by the arm and pulls him up out of his chair. After a peek at his face I am willing to lay 6 to 5 he does not make the arch. But he finally gets there with everybody laughing and clapping their hands, and the preacher comes forward, and Dave the Dude looks happier than I ever see him look before in his life as they all get together under the arch of flowers.

Well, all of a sudden there is a terrible racket at the front door of the Woodcock Inn, with some doll doing a lot of hollering in a deep voice that sounds like a man's, and naturally everybody turns and looks that way. The doorman, a guy by the name of Slugsy Sachs, who is a very hard man indeed, seems to be trying to keep somebody out, but pretty soon there is a heavy bump and Slugsy Sachs falls down, and in comes a doll about four feet high and five feet wide.

In fact, I never see such a wide doll. She looks all hammered down. Her face is almost as wide as her shoulders, and makes me think of a great big full moon. She comes in bounding-like, and I can see that she is all churned up about something. As she bounces in, I hear a gurgle, and I look around to see Waldo Winchester slumping down to the floor, almost dragging Miss Billy Perry with him.

Well, the wide doll walks right up to the bunch under the arch and says in a large bass voice: 'Which one is Dave the Dude?'

'I am Dave the Dude,' says Dave the Dude, stepping up. 'What do you mean by busting in here like a walrus and gumming up our wedding?'

'So you are the guy who kidnaps my ever-loving husband to marry him off to this little red-headed pancake here, are you?' the wide doll says, looking at Dave the Dude, but pointing at Miss Billy Perry.

Well now, calling Miss Billy Perry a pancake to Dave the Dude is a very serious proposition, and Dave the Dude gets very angry. He is usually rather polite to dolls, but you can see he does not care for the wide doll's manner whatever.

'Say, listen here,' Dave the Dude says, 'you better take a walk before somebody clips you. You must be drunk,' he says. 'Or daffy,' he says. 'What are you talking about, anyway?'

'You will see what I am talking about,' the wide doll yells. 'The guy on the floor there is my lawful husband. You probably frighten him to death, the poor dear. You kidnap him to marry this red-headed thing, and I am going to get you arrested as sure as my name is Lola Sapola, you simple-looking tramp!'

Naturally, everybody is greatly horrified at a doll using such language to Dave the Dude, because Dave is known to shoot guys for much less, but instead of doing something to the wide doll at once, Dave says: 'What is this talk I hear? Who is married to who? Get out of here!' Dave says, grabbing the wide doll's arm.

Well, she makes out as if she is going to slap Dave in the face with her left hand, and Dave naturally pulls his kisser out of the way. But instead of doing anything with her left, Lola Sapola suddenly drives her right fist smack-dab into Dave the Dude's stomach, which naturally comes forward as his face goes back.

I wish to say I see many a body punch delivered in my life, but I never see a prettier one than this. What is more, Lola Sapola steps in with the punch, so there is plenty on it.

Now a guy who eats and drinks like Dave the Dude does cannot take them so good in the stomach, so Dave goes 'oof,' and sits down very hard on the dance floor, and as he is sitting there he is fumbling in his pants pocket for the old equalizer, so everybody around tears for cover except Lola Sapola, and Miss Billy Perry, and Waldo Winchester.

But before he can get his pistol out, Lola Sapola reaches down and grabs Dave by the collar and hoists him to his feet. She lets go her hold on him, leaving Dave standing on his pins, but teetering around somewhat, and then she drives her right hand to Dave's stomach a second time.

The punch drops Dave again, and Lola steps up to him as if she is going to give him the foot. But she only gathers up Waldo Winchester from off the floor and slings him across her shoulder like he is a sack of oats, and starts for the door. Dave the Dude sits up on the floor again and by this time he has the old equalizer in his duke.

'Only for me being a gentleman I will fill you full of slugs,' he yells.

Lola Sapola never even looks back, because by this time she is petting Waldo Winchester's head and calling him loving names and saying what a shame it is for bad characters like Dave the Dude to be abusing her precious one. It all sounds to me as if Lola Sapola thinks well of Waldo Winchester.

Well, after she gets out of sight, Dave the Dude gets up off the floor and stands there looking at Miss Billy Perry, who is out to break all crying records. The rest of us come out from under cover, including the preacher, and we are wondering how mad Dave the Dude is going to be about the wedding being ruined. But Dave the Dude seems only disappointed and sad.

'Billy,' he says to Miss Billy Perry, 'I am mighty sorry you do not get your wedding. All I wish for is your happiness, but I do not believe you can ever be happy with this scribe if he also has to have his lion tamer around. As Cupid I am a total bust. This is the only nice thing I ever try to do in my whole life, and it is too bad it does not come off. Maybe if you wait until we can drown her, or something—'

'Dave,' says Miss Billy Perry, dropping so many tears that she seems to finally wash herself right into Dave the Dude's arms, 'I will never, never be happy with such a guy as Waldo Winchester. I can see now you are the only man for me.'

'Well, well, well,' Dave the Dude says, cheering right up. 'Where is the preacher? Bring on the preacher and let us have our wedding anyway.'

I see Mr. and Mrs. Dave the Dude the other day, and they seem very happy. But you never can tell about married people, so of course I am never going to let on to Dave the Dude that I am the one who telephones Lola Sapola at the Marx Hotel, because maybe I do not do Dave any too much of a favour, at that.

Dream Street Rose

Of an early evening when there is nothing much doing anywhere else, I go around to Good Time Charley's little speak in West Forty-seventh Street that he calls the Gingham Shoppe, and play a little klob with Charley, because business is quiet in the Gingham Shoppe at such an hour, and Charley gets very lonesome.

He once has a much livelier spot in Forty-eighth Street that he calls the Crystal Room, but one night a bunch of G-guys step into the joint and bust it wide open, besides confiscating all of Charley's stock of merchandise. It seems that these G-guys are members of a squad that comes on from Washington, and being strangers in the city they do not know that Good Time Charley's joint is not supposed to be busted up, so they go ahead and bust it, just the same as if it is any other joint.

Well, this action causes great indignation in many quarters, and a lot of citizens advise Charley to see somebody about it. But Charley says no. Charley says if this is the way the government is going to treat him after the way he walks himself bow-legged over in France with the Rainbow Division, making the Germans hard to catch, why, all right. But he is not going to holler copper about it, although Charley says he has his own opinion of Mr. Hoover, at that.

Personally, I greatly admire Charley for taking the disaster so calmly, especially as it catches him with very few potatoes. Charley is a great hand for playing the horses with any dough he makes out of the Crystal Room, and this particular season the guys who play the horses are being murdered by the bookies all over the country, and are in terrible distress.

So I know if Charley is not plumb broke that he has a terrible crack across his belly, and I am not surprised that I do not see him for a couple of weeks after the government guys knock off the Crystal Room. I hear rumours that he is at home reading the newspapers very carefully every day, especially the obituary notices, for it seems that Charley figures that some of the G-guys may be tempted to take a belt or two at the merchandise they confiscate, and Charley says if they do, he is even for life.

Finally I hear that Charley is seen buying a bolt of gingham in Bloomington's one day, so I know he will be in action again very soon, for all Charley needs to go into action is a bolt of gingham and a few bottles of Golden Wedding. In fact, I know Charley to go into action without the gingham, but as a rule he likes to drape a place of business with gingham to make it seem more homelike to his customers, and I wish to say that when it comes to draping gingham, Charley can make a sucker of Joseph Urban, or anybody else.

Well, when I arrive at the Gingham Shoppe this night I am talking about, which is around ten o'clock, I find Charley in a very indignant state of mind, because an old tomato by the name of Dream Street Rose comes in and tracks up his floor, just after Charley gets through mopping it up, for Charley does his mopping in person, not being able as yet to afford any help.

Rose is sitting at a table in a corner, paying no attention to Charley's remarks about wiping her feet on the Welcome mat at the door before she comes in, because Rose knows there is no Welcome mat at Charley's door, anyway, but I can see where Charley has a right to a few beefs, at that, as she leaves a trail of black hoofprints across the clean floor as if she is walking around in mud somewhere before she comes in, although I do not seem to remember that it is raining when I arrive.

Now this Dream Street Rose is an old doll of maybe fifty-odd, and is a very well-known character around and about, as she is wandering through the Forties for many a year, and especially through West Forty-seventh Street between Sixth and Seventh Avenues, and this block is called Dream Street. And the reason it is called Dream Street is because in this block are many characters of one kind and another who always seem to be dreaming of different matters.

In Dream Street there are many theatrical hotels, and rooming houses, and restaurants, and speaks, including Good Time Charley's Gingham Shoppe, and in the summer time the characters I mention sit on the stoops or lean against the railings along Dream Street, and the gab you hear sometimes sounds very dreamy indeed. In fact, it sometimes sounds very pipe-dreamy.

Many actors, male and female, and especially vaudeville actors, live in the hotels and rooming houses, and vaudeville actors, both male and female, are great hands for sitting around dreaming out loud about how they will practically assassinate the public in the Palace if ever they get a chance.

Furthermore, in Dream Street are always many hand-bookies and horse players, who sit on the church steps on the cool side of Dream Street in the summer and dream about big killings on the races, and there are also nearly always many fight managers, and sometimes fighters, hanging out in front of the restaurants, picking their teeth and dreaming about winning championships of the world, although up to this time no champion of the world has yet come out of Dream Street.

In this street you see burlesque dolls, and hoofers, and guys who write songs, and saxophone players, and newsboys, and newspaper scribes, and taxi drivers, and blind guys, and midgets, and blondes with Pomeranian pooches, or maybe French poodles, and guys with whiskers, and night-club entertainers, and I do not know what all else. And all of these characters are interesting to look at, and some of them are very interesting to talk to, although if you listen to several I know long enough, you may get the idea that they are somewhat daffy, especially the horse players.

But personally I consider all horse players more or less daffy anyway. In fact, the way I look at it, if a guy is not daffy he will not be playing the horses.

Now this Dream Street Rose is a short, thick-set, square-looking old doll, with a square pan, and square shoulders, and she has heavy iron-grey hair that she wears in a square bob, and she stands very square on her feet. In fact, Rose is the squarest-looking doll I ever see, and she is as strong and lively as Jim Londos, the wrestler. In fact, Jim Londos will never be any better than 6 to 5 in my line over Dream Street Rose, if she is in any kind of shape.

Nobody in this town wishes any truck with Rose if she has a few shots of grog in her, and especially Good Time Charley's grog, for she can fight like the dickens when she is grogged up. In fact, Rose holds many a decision in this town, especially over coppers, because if there is one thing she hates and despises more than somewhat it is a copper, as coppers are always heaving her into the old can when they find her jerking citizens around and cutting up other didoes.

For many years Rose works in the different hotels along Dream Street as a chambermaid. She never works in any one hotel very long, because the minute she gets a few bobs together she likes to go out and enjoy a little recreation, such as visiting around the speaks, although she is about as welcome in most speaks as a G-guy with a search warrant. You see, nobody can ever tell when Rose may feel like taking the speak apart, and also the customers.

She never has any trouble getting a job back in any hotel she ever works in, for Rose is a wonderful hand for making up beds, although several times, when she is in a hurry to get off, I hear she makes up beds with guests still in them, which causes a few mild beefs to the management, but does not bother Rose. I speak of this matter only to show you that she is a very quaint character indeed, and full of zest.

Well, I sit down to play klob with Good Time Charley, but about this time several customers come into the Gingham Shoppe, so Charley has to go and take care of them, leaving me alone. And while I am sitting there alone I hear Dream Street Rose mumbling to herself over in the corner, but I pay no attention to her, although I wish to say I am by no means unfriendly with Rose.

In fact, I say hello to her at all times, and am always very courteous to her, as I do not wish to have her bawling me out in public, and maybe circulating rumours about me, as she is apt to do, if she feels I am snubbing her.

Finally I notice her motioning to me to come over to her table, and I go over at once and sit down, because I can see that Rose is well grogged up at this time, and I do not care to have her attracting my attention by chucking a cuspidor at me. She offers me a drink when I sit down, but of course I never drink anything that is sold in Good Time Charley's, as a personal favour to Charley. He says he wishes to retain my friendship.

So I just sit there saying nothing much whatever, and Rose keeps on mumbling to herself, and I am not able to make much of her mumbling, until finally she looks at me and says to me like this:

'I am now going to tell you about my friend,' Rose says.

'Well, Rose,' I say, 'personally I do not care to hear about your friend, although,' I say, 'I have no doubt that what you wish to tell me about this friend is very interesting. But I am here to play a little klob with Good Time Charley, and I do not have time to hear about your friend.'

'Charley is busy selling his poison to the suckers,' Rose says. 'I am now going to tell you about my friend. It is quite a story,' she says. 'You will listen.'

So I listen.

It is a matter of thirty-five years ago [Dream Street Rose says] and the spot is a town in Colorado by the name of Pueblo, where there are smelters and one thing and another. My friend is at this time maybe sixteen or seventeen years old, and a first-class looker in every respect. Her papa is dead, and her mamma runs a boarding-house for the guys who work in the smelters, and who are very hearty eaters. My friend deals them off the arm for the guys in her mamma's boarding-house to save her mamma the expense of a waitress.

Now among the boarders in this boarding-house are many guys who are always doing a little pitching to my friend, and trying to make dates with her to take her places, but my friend never gives them much of a tumble, because after she gets through dealing them off the arm all day her feet generally pain her too much to go anywhere on them except to the hay.

Finally, however, along comes a tall, skinny young guy from the East by the name of Frank something, who has things to say to my friend that are much more interesting than anything that has been said to her by a guy before, including such things as love and marriage, which are always very interesting subjects to any young doll.

This Frank is maybe twenty-five years old, and he comes from the East with the idea of making his fortune in the West, and while it is true that fortunes are being made in the West at this time, there is little chance that Frank is going to make any part of a fortune, as he does not care to work very hard. In fact, he does not care to work at all, being much more partial to playing a little poker, or shooting a few craps, or maybe hustling a sucker around Mike's pool room on Santa Fe Avenue, for Frank is an excellent pool player, especially when he is playing a sucker.

Now my friend is at this time a very innocent young doll, and a good doll in every respect, and her idea of love includes a nice little home, and children running here and there and around and about, and she never has a wrong thought in her life, and believes that everybody else in the world is like herself. And the chances are if this Frank does not happen along, my friend will marry a young guy in Pueblo by the name of Higginbottom, who is very fond of her indeed, and who is a decent young guy and afterwards makes plenty of potatoes in the grocery dodge.

But my friend goes very daffy over Frank and cannot see anybody but him, and the upshot of it all is she runs away with him one day to Denver, being dumb enough to believe that he means it when he tells her that he loves her and is going to marry her. Why Frank ever bothers with such a doll as my friend in the first place is always a great mystery to one and all, and the only way anybody can explain it is that she is young and fresh, and he is a heel at heart.

'Well, Rose,' I say, 'I am now commencing to see the finish of this story about your friend, and,' I say, 'it is such a story as anybody can hear in a speak at any time in this town, except,' I say, 'maybe your story is longer than somewhat. So I will now thank you, and excuse myself, and play a little klob with Good Time Charley.'

'You will listen,' Dream Street Rose says, looking me slap-dab in the eye.

So I listen.

Moreover, I notice now that Good Time Charley is standing behind me, bending in an ear, as it seems that his customers take the wind after a couple of slams of Good Time Charley's merchandise, a couple of slams being about all that even a very hardy customer can stand at one session.

Of course [Rose goes on] the chances are Frank never intends marrying my friend at all, and she never knows until long afterward that the reason he leads her to the parson is that the young guy from Pueblo by the name of Higginbottom catches up with them at the old Windsor Hotel where they are stopping and privately pokes a six-pistol against Frank's ribs and promises faithfully to come back and blow a hole in Frank you can throw a watermelon through if Frank tries any phenagling around with my friend.

Well, in practically no time whatever, love's young dream is over as far as my friend is concerned. This Frank turns out to be a most repulsive character indeed, especially if you are figuring him as an ever-loving husband. In fact, he is no good. He mistreats my friend in every way any guy ever thought of mistreating a doll, and besides the old established ways of mistreating a doll, Frank thinks up quite a number of new ways, being really quite ingenious in this respect.

Yes, this Frank is one hundred per cent heel.

It is not so much that he gives her a thumping now and then, because, after all, a thumping wears off, and hurts heal up, even when they are such hurts as a broken nose and fractured ribs, and once an ankle cracked by a kick. It is what he does to her heart, and to her innocence. He is by no means a good husband, and does not know how to treat an ever-loving wife with any respect, especially as he winds up by taking my friend to San Francisco and hiring her out to a very loose character there by the name of Black Emanuel, who has a dance joint on the Barbary Coast, which, at the time I am talking about, is hotter than a stove. In this joint my friend has to dance with the customers, and get them to buy beer for her and one thing and another, and this occupation is most distasteful to my friend, as she never cares for beer.

It is there Frank leaves her for good after giving her an extra big thumping for a keepsake, and when my friend tries to leave Black Emanuel's to go looking for her ever-loving husband, she is somewhat surprised to hear Black Emanuel state that he pays Frank three C's for her to remain there and continue working. Furthermore, Black Emanuel resumes the thumpings where Frank leaves off, and by and by my friend is much bewildered and downhearted and does not care what happens to her.

Well, there is nothing much of interest in my friend's life for the next thirty-odd years, except that she finally gets so she does not mind the beer so much, and, in fact, takes quite a fondness for it, and also for light wines and Bourbon whisky, and that she comes to realize that Frank does not love her after all, in spite of what he says. Furthermore, in later years, after she drifts around the country quite some, in and out of different joints, she realizes that the chances are she will never have a nice little home, with children running here and there, and she often thinks of what a disagreeable influence Frank has on her life.

In fact, this Frank is always on her mind more than somewhat. In fact, she thinks of him night and day, and says many a prayer that he will do well. She manages to keep track of him, which is not hard to do, at that, as Frank is in New York, and is becoming quite a guy in business, and is often in the newspapers. Maybe his success is due to my friend's prayers, but the chances are it is more because he connects up with some guy who has an invention for doing something very interesting in steel, and by grabbing an interest in this invention Frank gets a shove toward plenty of potatoes. Furthermore, he is married, and is raising up a family.

About ten or twelve years ago my friend comes to New York, and by this time she is getting a little faded around the edges. She is not so old, at that, but the air of the Western and Southern joints is bad on the complexion, and beer is no good for the figure. In fact, my friend is now quite a haybag, and she does not get any better-looking in the years she spends in New York as she is practically all out of the old sex appeal, and has to do a little heavy lifting to keep eating. But she never forgets to keep praying that Frank will continue to do well, and Frank certainly does this, as he is finally spoken of everywhere very respectfully as a millionaire and a high-class guy.

In all the years she is in New York my friend never runs into Frank, as Frank is by no means accustomed to visiting the spots where my friend hangs out, but my friend goes to a lot of bother to get acquainted with a doll who is a maid for some time in Frank's town house in East Seventy-fourth Street, and through this doll my friend keeps a pretty fair line on the way Frank lives. In fact, one day when Frank and his family are absent, my friend goes to Frank's house with her friend, just to see what it looks like, and after an hour there my friend has the joint pretty well cased.

So now my friend knows through her friend that on very hot nights such as to-night Frank's family is bound to be at their country place at Port Washington, but that Frank himself is spending the night at his town house, because he wishes to work on a lot of papers of some kind. My friend knows through her friend that all of Frank's servants are at Port Washington, too, except my friend's friend, who is in charge of the town house, and Frank's valet, a guy by the name of Sloggins.

Furthermore, my friend knows through her friend that both her friend and Sloggins have a date to go to a movie at 8.30 o'clock, to be gone a couple of hours, as it seems Frank is very big-hearted about giving his servants time off for such a purpose when he is at home alone; although one night he squawks no little when my friend is out with her friend drinking a little beer, and my friend's friend loses her door key and has to ring the bell to the servants' entrance, and rousts Frank out of a sound sleep.

Naturally, my friend's friend will be greatly astonished if she ever learns that it is with this key that my friend steps into Frank's house along about nine o'clock to-night. An electric light hangs over the servants' entrance, and my friend locates the button that controls this light just inside the door and turns it off, as my friend figures that maybe Frank and his family will not care to have any of their high-class neighbours, or anyone else, see an old doll who has no better hat than she is wearing, entering or leaving their house at such an hour.

It is an old-fashioned sort of house, four or five stories high, with the library on the third floor in the rear, looking out through French windows over a nice little garden, and my friend finds Frank in the library where she expects to find him, because she is smart enough to figure that a guy who is working on papers is not apt to be doing his work in the cellar.

But Frank is not working on anything when my friend moves in on him. He is dozing in a chair by the window, and, looking at him, after all these years, she finds something of a change, indeed. He is much heavier than he is thirty-five years back, and his hair is white, but he looks pretty well to my friend, at that, as she stands there for maybe five minutes watching him. Then he seems to realize somebody is in the room, as sleeping guys will do, for his regular breathing stops with a snort, and he opens his eyes, and looks into my friend's eyes, but without hardly stirring. And finally my friend speaks to Frank as follows:

'Well, Frank,' she says, 'do you know me?'

'Yes,' he says, after a while, 'I know you. At first I think maybe you are a ghost, as I once hear something about your being dead. But,' he says, 'I see now the report is a canard. You are too fat to be a ghost.'

Well, of course, this is a most insulting crack, indeed, but my friend passes it off as she does not wish to get in any arguments with Frank at this time. She can see that he is upset more than somewhat and he keeps looking around the room as if he hopes he can see somebody else he can cut in on the conversation. In fact, he acts as if my friend is by no means a welcome visitor.

'Well, Frank,' my friend says, very pleasant, 'there you are, and here I am. I understand you are now a wealthy and prominent citizen of this town. I am glad to know this, Frank,' she says. 'You will be surprised to hear that for years and years I pray that you will do well for yourself and become a big guy in every respect, with a nice family, and everything else. I judge my prayers are answered,' she says. 'I see by the papers that you have two sons at Yale, and a daughter in Vassar, and that your ever-loving wife is getting to be very high mucky-mucky in society. Well, Frank,' she says, 'I am very glad. I pray something like all this will happen to you.'

Now, at such a speech, Frank naturally figures that my friend is all right, at that, and the chances are he also figures that she still has a mighty soft spot in her heart for him, just as she has in the days when she deals them off the arm to keep him in gambling and drinking money. In fact, Frank brightens up somewhat, and he says to my friend like this:

'You pray for my success?' he says. 'Why, this is very thoughtful of you, indeed. Well,' he says, 'I am sitting on top of the world. I have everything to live for.'

'Yes,' my friend says, 'and this is exactly where I pray I will find you. On top of the world,' she says, 'and with everything to live for. It is where I am when you take my life. It is where I am when you kill me as surely as if you strangle me with your hands. I always pray you will not become a bum,' my friend says, 'because a bum has nothing to live for, anyway. I want to find you liking to live, so you will hate so much to die.'

Naturally, this does not sound so good to Frank, and he begins all of a sudden to shake and shiver and to stutter somewhat.

'Why,' he says, 'what do you mean? Are you going to kill me?'

'Well,' my friend says, 'that remains to be seen. Personally,' she says, 'I will be much obliged if you will kill yourself, but it can be arranged one way or the other. However, I will explain the disadvantages of me killing you.

'The chances are,' my friend says, 'if I kill you I will be caught and a very great scandal will result, because,' she says, 'I have on my person the certificate of my marriage to you in Denver, and something tells me you never think to get a divorce. So,' she says, 'you are a bigamist.'

'I can pay,' Frank says. 'I can pay plenty.'

'Furthermore,' my friend says, paying no attention to his remark, 'I have a sworn statement from Black Emanuel about your transaction with him, for Black Emanuel gets religion before he dies from being shivved by Johnny Mizzoo, and he tries to round himself up by confessing all the sins he can think of, which are quite a lot. It is a very interesting statement,' my friend says.

'Now then,' she says, 'if you knock yourself off you will leave an unsullied, respected name. If I kill you, all the years and effort you have devoted to building up your reputation will go for nothing. You are past sixty,' my friend says, 'and any way you figure it, you do not have so very far to go. If I kill you,' she says, 'you will go in horrible disgrace, and everybody around you will feel the disgrace, no matter how much dough you leave them. Your children will hang their heads in shame. Your ever-loving wife will not like it,' my friend says.

'I wait on you a long time, Frank,' my friend says. 'A dozen times in the past twenty years I figure I may as well call on you and close up my case with you, but,' she says, 'then I always persuade myself to wait a little longer so you would rise higher and higher and life will be a bit sweeter to you. And there you are, Frank,' she says, 'and here I am.'

Well, Frank sits there as if he is knocked plumb out, and he does not answer a word; so finally my friend outs with a large John Roscoe which she is packing in the bosom of her dress, and tosses it in his lap, and speaks as follows:

'Frank,' she says, 'do not think it will do you any good to pot me in the back when I turn around, because,' she says, 'you will be worse off than ever. I leave plenty of letters scattered around in case anything happens to me. And remember,' she says, 'if you do not do this job yourself, I will be back. Sooner or later, I will be back.'

So [Dream Street Rose says] my friend goes out of the library and down the stairs, leaving Frank sprawled out in his chair, and when she reaches the first floor she hears what may be a shot in the upper part of the house, and then again maybe only a door slamming. My friend never knows for sure what it is, because a little later as she nears the servants' entrance she hears quite a commotion outside, and a guy cussing a blue streak, and a doll teeheeing, and pretty soon my friend's friend, the maid, and Sloggins, the valet, come walking in.

Well, my friend just has time to scroonch herself back in a dark corner, and they go upstairs, the guy still cussing and the doll still giggling, and my friend cannot make out what it is all about except that they come home earlier than she figures. So my friend goes tippy-toe out of the servants' entrance, to grab a taxi not far from the house and get away from this neighbourhood, and now you will soon hear of the suicide of a guy who is a millionaire, and it will be all even with my friend.

'Well, Rose,' I say, 'it is a nice long story, and full of romance and all this and that, and,' I say, 'of course I will never be ungentlemanly enough to call a lady a liar, but,' I say, 'if it is not a lie, it will do until a lie comes along.'

'All right,' Rose says. 'Anyway, I tell you about my friend. Now,' she says, 'I am going where the liquor is better, which can be any other place in town, because,' she says, 'there is no chance of liquor anywhere being any worse.'

So she goes out, making more tracks on Good Time Charley's floor, and Charley speaks most impolitely of her after she goes, and gets out his mop to clean the floor, for one thing about Charley, he is as neat as a pin, and maybe neater.

Well, along toward one o'clock I hear a newsboy in the street outside yelling something I cannot make out, because he is yelling as if he has a mouthful of mush, as newsboys are bound to do. But I am anxious to see what goes in the first race at Belmont, on account of having a first-class tip, so I poke my noggin outside Good Time Charley's and buy a paper, and across the front page, in large letters, it states that the wealthy Mr. Frank Billingsworth McQuiggan knocks himself off by putting a slug through his own noggin.

It says Mr. McQuiggan is found in a chair in his library as dead as a door-nail with the pistol in his lap with which he knocks himself off, and the paper states that nobody can figure what causes Mr. McQuiggan to do such a thing to himself as he is in good health and has plenty of potatoes and is at the peak of his career. Then there is a lot about his history.

When Mr. McQuiggan is a young fellow returning from a visit to the Pacific Coast with about two hundred dollars in his pocket after paying his railroad fare, he meets in the train Jonas Calloway, famous inventor of the Calloway steel process. Calloway, also then young, is desperately in need of funds and he offers Mr. McQuiggan a third interest in his invention for what now seems the paltry sum of one hundred dollars. Mr. McQuiggan accepts the offer and thus paves the way to his own fortune.

I am telling all this to Good Time Charley while he is mopping away at the floor, and finally I come on a paragraph down near the finish which goes like this: 'The body was discovered by Mr. McQuiggan's faithful valet, Thomas Sloggins, at eleven o'clock. Mr. McQuiggan was then apparently dead a couple of hours. Sloggins returned home shortly before ten o'clock with another servant after changing his mind about going to a movie. Instead of going to see his employer at once, as is his usual custom, Sloggins went to his own quarters and changed his clothes.

' "The light over the servants' entrance was out when I returned home," the valet said, "and in the darkness I stumbled over some scaffolding and other material left near this entrance by workmen who are to regravel the roof of the house to-morrow, upsetting all over the entranceway a large bucket of tar, much of which got on my apparel when I fell, making a change necessary before going to see Mr. McQuiggan." '

Well, Good Time Charley keeps on mopping harder than ever, though finally he stops a minute and speaks to me as follows:

'Listen,' Charley says, 'understand I do not say the guy does not deserve what he gets, and I am by no means hollering copper, but,' Charley says, 'if he knocks himself off, how does it come the rod is still in his lap where Dream Street Rose says her friend tosses it? Well, never mind,' Charley says, 'but can you think of something that will remove tar from a wood floor? It positively will not mop off.'

The Old Doll's House

Now it seems that one cold winter night, a party of residents of Brooklyn comes across the Manhattan Bridge in an automobile wishing to pay a call on a guy by the name of Lance McGowan, who is well known to one and all along Broadway as a coming guy in the business world.

In fact, it is generally conceded that, barring accident, Lance will someday be one of the biggest guys in this country as an importer, and especially as an importer of such merchandise as fine liquors, because he is very bright, and has many good connections throughout the United States and Canada.

Furthermore, Lance McGowan is a nice-looking young guy and he has plenty of ticker, although some citizens say he does not show very sound business judgment in trying to move in on Angie the Ox over in Brooklyn, as Angie the Ox is an importer himself,

besides enjoying a splendid trade in other lines, including artichokes and extortion.

Of course Lance McGowan is not interested in artichokes at all,
and very little in extortion, but he does not see any reason why he
shall not place his imports in a thriving territory such as Brooklyn,
especially as his line of merchandise is much superior to anything
handled by Angie the Ox.

Anyway, Angie is one of the residents of Brooklyn in the party
that wishes to call on Lance McGowan, and besides Angie the
party includes a guy by the name of Mockie Max, who is a very
prominent character in Brooklyn, and another guy by the name of
The Louse Kid, who is not so prominent, but who is considered a
very promising young guy in many respects, although personally I
think The Louse Kid has a very weak face.

He is supposed to be a wonderful hand with a burlap bag when
anybody wishes to put somebody in such a bag, which is considered
a great practical joke in Brooklyn, and in fact The Louse Kid has
a burlap bag with him on the night in question, and they are
figuring on putting Lance McGowan in the bag when they call on
him, just for the laugh. Personally, I consider this a very crude
form of humour, but then Angie the Ox and the other members of
his party are very crude characters, anyway.

Well, it seems they have Lance McGowan pretty well cased, and
they know that of an evening along toward ten o'clock he nearly
always strolls through West Fifty-fourth street on his way to a
certain spot on Park Avenue that is called the Humming Bird
Club, which has a very high-toned clientele, and the reason Lance
goes there is because he has a piece of the joint, and furthermore he
loves to show off his shape in a tuxedo to the swell dolls.

So these residents of Brooklyn drive in their automobile along
this route, and as they roll past Lance McGowan, Angie the Ox
and Mockie Max let fly at Lance with a couple of sawed-offs, while
The Louse Kid holds the burlap bag, figuring for all I know that
Lance will be startled by the sawed-offs and will hop into the bag
like a rabbit.

But Lance is by no means a sucker, and when the first blast of
slugs from the sawed-offs breezes past him without hitting him,
what does he do but hop over a brick wall alongside him and drop
into a yard on the other side. So Angie the Ox, and Mockie Max
and The Louse Kid get out of their automobile and run up close to
the wall themselves because they commence figuring that if Lance

McGowan starts popping at them from behind this wall, they will be taking plenty the worst of it, for of course they cannot figure Lance to be strolling about without being rodded up somewhat.

But Lance is by no means rodded up, because a rod is apt to create a bump in his shape when he has his tuxedo on, so the story really begins with Lance McGowan behind the brick wall, practically defenceless, and the reason I know this story is because Lance McGowan tells most of it to me, as Lance knows that I know his real name is Lancelot, and he feels under great obligation to me because I never mention the matter publicly.

Now, the brick wall Lance hops over is a wall around a pretty fair-sized yard, and the yard belongs to an old two-story stone house, and this house is well known to one and all in this man's town as a house of great mystery, and it is pointed out as such by the drivers of sightseeing buses.

This house belongs to an old doll by the name of Miss Abigail Ardsley, and anybody who ever reads the newspapers will tell you that Miss Abigail Ardsley has so many potatoes that it is really painful to think of, especially to people who have no potatoes whatever. In fact, Miss Abigail Ardsley has practically all the potatoes in the world, except maybe a few left over for general circulation.

These potatoes are left to her by her papa, old Waldo Ardsley, who accumulates same in the early days of this town by buying corner real estate very cheap before people realize this real estate will be quite valuable later on for fruit-juice stands and cigar stores.

It seems that Waldo is a most eccentric old bloke, and is very strict with his daughter, and will never let her marry, or even as much as look as if she wishes to marry, until finally she is so old she does not care a cuss about marrying, or anything else, and becomes very eccentric herself.

In fact, Miss Abigail Ardsley becomes so eccentric that she cuts herself off from everybody, and especially from a lot of relatives who are wishing to live off her, and any time anybody cuts themselves off from such characters they are considered very eccentric, indeed, especially by the relatives. She lives in the big house all alone, except for a couple of old servants, and it is very seldom that anybody sees her around and about, and many strange stories are told of her.

Well, no sooner is he in the yard than Lance McGowan begins

looking for a way to get out, and one way he does not wish to get out is over the wall again, because he figures Angie the Ox and his sawed-offs are bound to be waiting for him in Fifty-fourth Street. So Lance looks around to see if there is some way out of the yard in another direction, but it seems there is no such way, and pretty soon he sees the snozzle of a sawed-off come poking over the wall, with the ugly kisser of Angie the Ox behind it, looking for him, and there is Lance McGowan all cornered up in the yard, and not feeling so good, at that.

Then Lance happens to try a door on one side of the house, and the door opens at once and Lance McGowan hastens in to find himself in the living-room of the house. It is a very large living-room with very nice furniture standing around and about, and oil paintings on the walls, and a big old grandfather's clock as high as the ceiling, and statuary here and there. In fact, it is such a nice, comfortable-looking room that Lance McGowan is greatly surprised, as he is expecting to find a regular mystery-house room such as you see in the movies, with cobwebs here and there, and everything all rotted up, and maybe Boris Karloff wandering about making strange noises.

But the only person in this room seems to be a little old doll all dressed in soft white, who is sitting in a low rocking-chair by an open fireplace in which a bright fire is going, doing some tatting.

Well, naturally Lance McGowan is somewhat startled by this scene, and he is figuring that the best thing he can do is to guzzle the old doll before she can commence yelling for the gendarmes, when she looks up at him and gives him a soft smile, and speaks to him in a soft voice, as follows:

'Good evening,' the old doll says.

Well, Lance cannot think of any reply to make to this at once, as it is certainly not a good evening for him, and he stands there looking at the old doll, somewhat dazed, when she smiles again and tells him to sit down.

So the next thing Lance knows, he is sitting there in a chair in front of the fireplace chewing the fat with the old doll as pleasant as you please, and of course the old doll is nobody but Miss Abigail Ardsley. Furthermore, she does not seem at all alarmed, or even much surprised, at seeing Lance in her house, but then Lance is never such a looking guy as is apt to scare old dolls, or young dolls either, especially when he is all slicked up.

Of course Lance knows who Miss Abigail Ardsley is, because he often reads stories in the newspapers about her the same as everybody else, and he always figures such a character must be slightly daffy to cut herself off from everybody when she has all the potatoes in the world, and there is so much fun going on, but he is very courteous to her, because after all he is a guest in her home.

'You are young,' the old doll says to Lance McGowan, looking him in the kisser. 'It is many years since a young man comes through yonder door. Ah, yes,' she says, 'so many years.'

And with this she lets out a big sigh, and looks so very sad that Lance McGowan's heart is touched.

'Forty-five years now,' the old doll says in a low voice, as if she is talking to herself. 'So young, so handsome, and so good.'

And although Lance is in no mood to listen to reminiscences at this time, the next thing he knows he is hearing a very pathetic love story, because it seems that Miss Abigail Ardsley is once all hotted up over a young guy who is nothing but a clerk in her papa's office.

It seems from what Lance McGowan gathers that there is nothing wrong with the young guy that a million bobs will not cure, but Miss Abigail Ardsley's papa is a mean old waffle, and he will never listen to her having any truck with a poor guy, so they dast not let him know how much they love each other.

But it seems that Miss Abigail Ardsley's ever-loving young guy has plenty of moxie, and every night he comes to see her after her papa goes to the hay, and she lets him in through the same sidedoor Lance McGowan comes through, and they sit by the fire and hold hands, and talk in low tones, and plan what they will do when the young guy makes a scratch.

Then one night it seems Miss Abigail Ardsley's papa has the stomach ache, or some such, and cannot sleep a wink, so he comes wandering downstairs looking for the Jamaica ginger, and catches Miss Abigail Ardsley and her ever-loving guy in a clutch that will win the title for any wrestler that can ever learn it.

Well, this scene is so repulsive to Miss Abigail Ardsley's papa that he is practically speechless for a minute, and then he orders the young guy out of his life in every respect, and tells him never to darken his door again, especially the side-door.

But it seems that by this time a great storm is raging outside, and Miss Abigail Ardsley begs and pleads with her papa to let the young guy at least remain until the storm subsides, but between being all sored up at the clutching scene he witnesses, and his stomach ache, Mr. Ardsley is very hard-hearted, indeed, and he makes the young guy take the wind.

The next morning the poor young guy is found at the side-door frozen as stiff as a board, because it seems that the storm that is raging is the blizzard of 1888, which is a very famous event in the history of New York, although up to this time Lance McGowan never hears of it before, and does not believe it until he looks the matter up afterwards. It seems from what Miss Abigail Ardsley says that as near as anyone can make out, the young guy must return to the door seeking shelter after wandering about in the storm a while, but of course by this time her papa has the door all bolted up, and nobody hears the young guy.

'And,' Miss Abigail Ardsley says to Lance McGowan, after giving him all these details, 'I never speak to my papa again as long as he lives, and no other man ever comes in or out of yonder door, or any other door of this house, until your appearance to-night, although,' she says, 'this side-door is never locked in case such a young man comes seeking shelter.'

Then she looks at Lance McGowan in such a way that he wonders if Miss Abigail Ardsley hears the sawed-offs going when Angie the Ox and Mockie Max are tossing slugs at him, but he is too polite to ask.

Well, all these old-time memories seem to make Miss Abigail Ardsley feel very tough, and by and by she starts to weep, and if there is one thing Lance McGowan cannot stand it is a doll weeping, even if she is nothing but an old doll. So he starts in to cheer Miss Abigail Ardsley up, and he pats her on the arm, and says to her like this:

'Why,' Lance says, 'I am greatly surprised to hear your statement about the doors around here being so little used. Why, Sweetheart,' Lance says, 'if I know there is a doll as good-looking as you in the neighbourhood, and a door unlocked, I will be busting in myself every night. Come, come, come,' Lance says, 'let us talk things over and maybe have a few laughs, because I may have to stick around here a while. Listen, Sweetheart,' he says, 'do you happen to have a drink in the joint?'

Well, at this Miss Abigail Ardsley dries her eyes, and smiles again, and then she pulls a sort of rope near her, and in comes a guy who seems about ninety years old, and who seems greatly surprised to see Lance there. In fact, he is so surprised that he is practically tottering when he leaves the room after hearing Miss

Abigail Ardsley tell him to bring some wine and sandwiches.

And the wine he brings is such wine that Lance McGowan has half a mind to send some of the lads around afterwards to see if there is any more of it in the joint, especially when he thinks of the unlocked side-door, because he can sell this kind of wine by the carat.

Well, Lance sits there with Miss Abigail Ardsley sipping wine and eating sandwiches, and all the time he is telling her stories of one kind and another, some of which he cleans up a little when he figures they may be a little too snappy for her, and by and by he has her laughing quite heartily indeed.

Finally he figures there is no chance of Angie and his sawed-offs being outside waiting for him, so he says he guesses he will be going, and Miss Abigail Ardsley personally sees him to the door, and this time it is the front door, and as Lance is leaving he thinks of something he once sees a guy do on the stage, and he takes Miss Abigail Ardsley's hand and raises it to his lips and gives it a large kiss, all of which is very surprising to Miss Abigail Ardsley, but more so to Lance McGowan when he gets to thinking about it afterwards.

Just as he figures, there is no one in sight when he gets out in the street, so he goes on over to the Humming Bird Club, where he learns that many citizens are greatly disturbed by his absence, and are wondering if he is in The Louse Kid's burlap bag, for by this time it is pretty well known that Angie the Ox and his fellow citizens of Brooklyn are around and about.

In fact, somebody tells Lance that Angie is at the moment over in Good Time Charley's little speak in West Forty-ninth Street, buying drinks for one and all, and telling how he makes Lance McGowan hop a brick wall, which of course sounds most disparaging of Lance.

Well, while Angie is still buying these drinks, and still speaking of making Lance a brick-wall hopper, all of a sudden the door of Good Time Charley's speak opens and in comes a guy with a Betsy in his hand and this guy throws four slugs into Angie the Ox before anybody can say hello.

Furthermore, the guy throws one slug into Mockie Max, and one slug into The Louse Kid, who are still with Angie the Ox, so the next thing anybody knows there is Angie as dead as a door-nail, and there is Mockie Max even deader than Angie, and there is The Louse making a terrible fuss over a slug in his leg, and nobody can remember what the guy who plugs them looks like, except a couple of stool pigeons who state that the guy looks very much like Lance McGowan.

So what happens but early the next morning Johnny Brannigan, the plain-clothes copper, puts the arm on Lance McGowan for plugging Angie the Ox, and Mockie Max and The Louse Kid, and there is great rejoicing in copper circles generally because at this time the newspapers are weighing in the sacks on the coppers quite some, claiming there is too much lawlessness going on around and about and asking why somebody is not arrested for something.

So the collar of Lance McGowan is water on the wheel of one and all because Lance is so prominent, and anybody will tell you that it looks as if it is a sure thing that Lance will be very severely punished, and maybe sent to the electric chair, although he hires Judge Goldstein, who is one of the surest-footed lawyers in this town, to defend him. But even Judge Goldstein admits that Lance is in a tough spot, especially as the newspapers are demanding justice, and printing long stories about Lance, and pictures of him, and calling him some very uncouth names.

Finally Lance himself commences to worry about his predicament, although up to this time a little thing like being charged with murder in the first degree never bothers Lance very much. And in fact he will not be bothering very much about this particular charge if he does not find the D. A. very fussy about letting him out on bail. In fact, it is nearly two weeks before he lets Lance out on bail, and all this time Lance is in the sneezer, which is a most mortifying situation to a guy as sensitive as Lance.

Well, by the time Lance's trial comes up, you can get 3 to 1 anywhere that he will be convicted, and the price goes up to 5 when the prosecution gets through with its case, and proves by the stool pigeons that at exactly twelve o'clock on the night of January 5th, Lance McGowan steps into Good Time Charley's little speak and plugs Angie the Ox, Mockie Max and The Louse Kid.

Furthermore, several other witnesses who claim they know Lance McGowan by sight testify that they see Lance in the neighbourhood of Good Time Charley's around twelve o'clock, so by the time it comes Judge Goldstein's turn to put on the defence, many citizens are saying that if he can do no more than beat the chair for Lance he will be doing a wonderful job.

Well, it is late in the afternoon when Judge Goldstein gets up and looks all around the courtroom, and without making any opening statement to the jury for the defence, as these mouthpieces usually do, he says like this:

'Call Miss Abigail Ardsley,' he says.

At first nobody quite realizes just who Judge Goldstein is calling for, although the name sounds familiar to one and all present who read the newspapers, when in comes a little old doll in a black silk dress that almost reaches the floor, and a black bonnet that makes a sort of a frame for her white hair and face.

Afterwards I read in one of the newspapers that she looks like she steps down out of an old-fashioned ivory miniature and that she is practically beautiful, but of course Miss Abigail Ardsley has so many potatoes that no newspaper dast to say she looks like an old chromo.

Anyway, she comes into the courtroom surrounded by so many old guys you will think it must be recess at the Old Men's Home, except they are all dressed up in claw-hammer coat tails, and high collars, and afterwards it turns out that they are the biggest lawyers in this town, and they all represent Miss Abigail Ardsley one way or another, and they are present to see that her interests are protected, especially from each other.

Nobody ever sees so much bowing and scraping before in a courtroom. In fact, even the judge bows, and although I am only a spectator I find myself bowing too, because the way I look at it, anybody with as many potatoes as Miss Abigail Ardsley is entitled to a general bowing. When she takes the witness-stand, her lawyers grab chairs and move up as close to her as possible, and in the street outside there is practically a riot as word goes around that Miss Abigail Ardsley is in the court, and citizens come running from every which way, hoping to get a peek at the richest old doll in the world.

Well, when all hands finally get settled down a little, Judge Goldstein speaks to Miss Abigail Ardsley as follows:

'Miss Ardsley,' he says, 'I am going to ask you just two or three questions. Kindly look at this defendant,' Judge Goldstein says, pointing at Lance McGowan, and giving Lance the office to stand up. 'Do you recognize him?'

Well, the little old doll takes a gander at Lance, and nods her head yes, and Lance gives her a large smile, and Judge Goldstein says:

'Is he a caller in your home on the night of January fifth?' Judge Goldstein asks.

'He is,' Miss Abigail Ardsley says.

'Is there a clock in the living-room in which you receive this defendant?' Judge Goldstein says.

'There is,' Miss Abigail Ardsley says. 'A large clock,' she says. 'A grandfather's clock.'

'Do you happen to notice,' Judge Goldstein says, 'and do you now recall the hour indicated by this clock when the defendant leaves your home?'

'Yes,' Miss Abigail Ardsley says, 'I do happen to notice. It is just twelve o'clock by my clock,' she says. 'Exactly twelve o'clock,' she says.

Well, this statement creates a large sensation in the courtroom, because if it is twelve o'clock when Lance McGowan leaves Miss Abigail Ardsley's house in West Fifty-fourth Street, anybody can see that there is no way he can be in Good Time Charley's little speak over five blocks away at the same minute unless he is a magician, and the judge begins peeking over his specs at the coppers in the courtroom very severe, and the cops begin scowling at the stool pigeons, and I am willing to lay plenty of 6 to 5 that the stools will wish they are never born before they hear the last of this matter from the gendarmes.

Furthermore, the guys from the D. A.'s office who are handling the prosecution are looking much embarrassed, and the jurors are muttering to each other, and right away Judge Goldstein says he moves that the case against his client be dismissed, and the judge says he is in favour of the motion, and he also says he thinks it is high time the gendarmes in this town learn to be a little careful who they are arresting for murder, and the guys from the D. A.'s office do not seem to be able to think of anything whatever to say.

So there is Lance as free as anybody, and as he starts to leave the courtroom he stops by Miss Abigail Ardsley, who is still sitting in the witness-chair surrounded by her mouthpieces, and he shakes her hand and thanks her, and while I do not hear it myself, somebody tells me afterwards that Miss Abigail Ardsley says to Lance in a low voice, like this:

'I will be expecting you again some night, young man,' she says.

'Some night, Sweetheart,' Lance says, 'at twelve o'clock.'

And then he goes on about his business, and Miss Abigail Ardsley goes on about hers; and everybody says it is certainly a wonderful thing that a doll as rich as Miss Abigail Ardsley comes forward in the interests of justice to save a guy like Lance Mc-Gowan from a wrong rap.

But of course it is just as well for Lance that Miss Abigail Ardsley does not explain to the court that when she recovers from the shock of the finding of her ever-loving young guy frozen to death, she stops all the clocks in her house at the hour she sees him last, so for forty-five years it is always twelve o'clock in her house.

Blood Pressure

It is maybe eleven-thirty of a Wednesday night, and I am standing at the corner of Forty-eighth Street and Seventh Avenue, thinking about my blood pressure, which is a proposition I never before think much about.

In fact, I never hear of my blood pressure before this Wednesday afternoon when I go around to see Doc Brennan about my stomach, and he puts a gag on my arm and tells me that my blood pressure is higher than a cat's back, and the idea is for me to be careful about what I eat, and to avoid excitement, or I may pop off all of a sudden when I am least expecting it.

'A nervous man such as you with a blood pressure away up in the paint cards must live quietly,' Doc Brennan says. 'Ten bucks, please,' he says.

Well, I am standing there thinking it is not going to be so tough to avoid excitement the way things are around this town right now, and wishing I have my ten bucks back to bet it on Sun Beau in the fourth race at Pimlico the next day, when all of a sudden I look up, and who is in front of me but Rusty Charley.

Now if I have any idea Rusty Charley is coming my way, you can go and bet all the coffee in Java I will be somewhere else at once, for Rusty Charley is not a guy I wish to have any truck with whatever. In fact, I wish no part of him. Furthermore, nobody else in this town wishes to have any part of Rusty Charley, for he is a hard guy indeed. In fact, there is no harder guy anywhere in the world. He is a big wide guy with two large hard hands and a great deal of very bad disposition, and he thinks nothing of knocking people down and stepping on their kissers if he feels like it.

In fact, this Rusty Charley is what is called a gorill, because he is known to often carry a gun in his pants pocket, and sometimes to shoot people down as dead as door-nails with it if he does not like the way they wear their hats – and Rusty Charley is very critical of hats. The chances are Rusty Charley shoots many a guy in this man's town, and those he does not shoot he sticks with his shiv – which is a knife – and the only reason he is not in jail is because he just gets out of it, and the law does not have time to think up something to put him back in again for.

Anyway, the first thing I know about Rusty Charley being in my neighbourhood is when I hear him saying: 'Well, well, well, here we are!'

Then he grabs me by the collar, so it is no use of me thinking of taking it on the lam away from there, although I greatly wish to do so.

'Hello, Rusty,' I say, very pleasant. 'What is the score?'

'Everything is about even,' Rusty says. 'I am glad to see you, because I am looking for company. I am over in Philadelphia for three days on business.'

'I hope and trust that you do all right for yourself in Philly, Rusty,' I say; but his news makes me very nervous, because I am a great hand for reading the papers and I have a pretty good idea what Rusty's business in Philly is. It is only the day before that I see a little item from Philly in the papers about how Gloomy Gus Smallwood, who is a very large operator in the alcohol business there, is guzzled right at his front door.

Of course, I do not know that Rusty Charley is the party who guzzles Gloomy Gus Smallwood, but Rusty Charley is in Philly when Gus is guzzled, and I can put two and two together as well as anybody. It is the same thing as if there is a bank robbery in Cleveland, Ohio, and Rusty Charley is in Cleveland, Ohio, or near there. So I am very nervous, and I figure it is a sure thing my blood pressure is going up every second.

'How much dough do you have on you?' Rusty says. 'I am plumb broke.'

'I do not have more than a couple of bobs, Rusty,' I say. 'I pay a doctor ten bucks to-day to find out my blood pressure is very bad. But of course you are welcome to what I have.'

'Well, a couple of bobs is no good to high-class guys like you and me,' Rusty says. 'Let us go to Nathan Detroit's crap game and win some money.'

Now, of course, I do not wish to go to Nathan Detroit's crap game; and if I do wish to go there I do not wish to go with Rusty Charley, because a guy is sometimes judged by the company he keeps, especially around crap games, and Rusty Charley is apt to be considered bad company. Anyway, I do not have any dough to shoot craps with, and if I do have dough to shoot craps with, I will not shoot craps with it at all, but will bet it on Sun Beau, or maybe take it home and pay off some of the overhead around my joint, such as rent.

Furthermore, I remember what Doc Brennan tells me about avoiding excitement, and I know there is apt to be excitement around Nathan Detroit's crap game if Rusty Charley goes there, and maybe run my blood pressure up and cause me to pop off very unexpected. In fact, I already feel my blood jumping more than somewhat inside me, but naturally I am not going to give Rusty Charley any argument, so we go to Nathan Detroit's crap game.

This crap game is over a garage in Fifty-second Street this particular night, though sometimes it is over a restaurant in Forty-seventh Street, or in back of a cigar store in Forty-fourth Street. In fact, Nathan Detroit's crap game is apt to be anywhere, because it moves around every night, as there is no sense in a crap game staying in one spot until the coppers find out where it is.

So Nathan Detroit moves his crap game from spot to spot, and citizens wishing to do business with him have to ask where he is every night; and of course almost everybody on Broadway knows this, as Nathan Detroit has guys walking up and down, and around and about, telling the public his address, and giving out the password for the evening.

Well, Jack the Beefer is sitting in an automobile outside the garage in Fifty-second Street when Rusty Charley and I come along, and he says 'Kansas City,' very low, as we pass, this being the password for the evening; but we do not have to use any password whatever when we climb the stairs over the garage, because the minute Solid John, the doorman, peeks out through his peephole when we knock, and sees Rusty Charley with me, he opens up very quick indeed, and gives us a big castor-oil smile, for nobody in this town is keeping doors shut on Rusty Charley very long.

It is a very dirty room over the garage, and full of smoke, and the crap game is on an old pool table; and around the table, and packed in so close you cannot get a knitting-needle between any two guys with a mawl, are all the high shots in town, for there is plenty of money around at this time, and many citizens are very prosperous. Furthermore, I wish to say there are some very tough guys around the table, too, including guys who will shoot you in the head, or maybe the stomach, and think nothing whatever about the matter.

In fact, when I see such guys as Harry the Horse, from Brooklyn, and Sleepout Sam Levinsky, and Lone Louie, from Harlem, I know this is a bad place for my blood pressure, for these are very tough guys indeed, and are known as such to one and all in this town.

But there they are wedged up against the table with Nick the Greek, Big Nig, Grey John, Okay Okun, and many other high shots, and they all have big coarse G notes in their hands which they are tossing around back and forth as if these G notes are nothing but pieces of waste paper.

On the outside of the mob at the table are a lot of small operators who are trying to cram their fists in between the high shots now and then to get down a bet, and there are also guys present who are called Shylocks, because they will lend you dough when you go broke at the table, on watches or rings, or maybe cuff-links, at very good interest.

Well, as I say, there is no room at the table for as many as one more very thin guy when we walk into the joint, but Rusty Charley lets out a big hello as we enter, and the guys all look around, and the next minute there is space at the table big enough not only for Rusty Charley but for me, too. It really is quite magical the way there is suddenly room for us when there is no room whatever for anybody when we come in.

'Who is the gunner?' Rusty Charley asks, looking all around.

'Why, you are, Charley,' Big Nig, the stick man in the game, says very quick, handing Charley a pair of dice, although afterward I hear that his pal is right in the middle of a roll trying to make nine when we step up to the table. Everybody is very quiet, just looking at Charley. Nobody pays any attention to me, because I am known to one and all as a guy who is just around, and nobody figures me in on any part of Charley, although Harry the Horse looks at me once in a way that I know is no good for my blood pressure, or for anybody else's blood pressure as far as this goes.

Well, Charley takes the dice and turns to a little guy in a derby hat who is standing next to him, scrooching back so Charley will not notice him, and Charley lifts the derby hat off the little guy's head, and rattles the dice in his hand and chucks them into the hat and goes 'Hah!' like crap shooters always do when they are rolling the dice. Then Charley peeks into the hat and says 'Ten,' although he does not let anybody else look in the hat, not even me, so nobody knows if Charley throws a ten, or what.

But, of course, nobody around is going to up and doubt that Rusty Charley throws a ten, because Charley may figure it is the same thing as calling him a liar, and Charley is such a guy as is apt to hate being called a liar.

Now Nathan Detroit's crap game is what is called a head-and-head game, although some guys call it a fading game, because the guys bet against each other rather than against the bank, or house. It is just the same kind of game as when two guys get together and start shooting craps against each other, and Nathan Detroit does not have to bother with a regular crap table and layout such as they have in gambling houses. In fact, about all Nathan Detroit has to do with the game is to find a spot, furnish the dice and take his percentage, which is by no means bad.

In such a game as this there is no real action until a guy is out on a point, and then the guys around commence to bet he makes this point, or that he does not make this point, and the odds in any country in the world that a guy does not make a ten with a pair of dice before he rolls seven, is 2 to 1.

Well, when Charley says he rolls ten in the derby hat nobody opens their trap, and Charley looks all around the table, and all of a sudden he sees Jew Louie at one end, although Jew Louie seems to be trying to shrink himself up when Charley's eyes light on him.

'I will take the odds for five C's,' Charley says, 'and Louie, you get it' – meaning he is letting Louie bet him $1000 to $500 that he does not make his ten.

Now Jew Louie is a small operator at all times and more of a Shylock than he is a player, and the only reason he is up there against the table at all at this moment is because he moves up to lend Nick the Greek some dough; and ordinarily there is no more chance of Jew Louie betting a thousand to five hundred on any proposition whatever than there is of him giving his dough to the Salvation Army, which is no chance at all. It is a sure thing he will never think of betting a thousand to five hundred a guy will not make ten with the dice, and when Rusty Charley tells Louie he has such a bet, Louie starts trembling all over.

The others around the table do not say a word, and so Charley rattles the dice again in his duke, blows on them, and chucks them into the derby hat and says 'Hah!' But, of course, nobody can see in the derby hat except Charley, and he peeks in at the dice and says 'Five.' He rattles the dice once more and chucks them into the derby and says 'Hah!' and then after peeking into the hat at the dice he says 'Eight.' I am commencing to sweat for fear he may heave a seven in the hat and blow his bet, and I know Charley has no five C's to pay off with, although, of course, I also know Charley has no idea of paying off, no matter what he heaves.

On the next chuck, Charley yells 'Money!' – meaning he finally makes his ten, although nobody sees it but him; and he reaches out his hand to Jew Louie, and Jew Louie hands him a big fat G note, very, very slow. In all my life I never see a sadder-looking guy than Louie when he is parting with his dough. If Louie has any idea of asking Charley to let him see the dice in the hat to make sure about the ten, he does not speak about the matter, and as Charley does not seem to wish to show the ten around, nobody else says anything either, probably figuring Rusty Charley isn't a guy who is apt to let anybody question his word, especially over such a small matter as a ten.

'Well,' Charley says, putting Louie's G note in his pocket, 'I think this is enough for me to-night,' and he hands the derby hat back to the little guy who owns it and motions me to come on, which I am glad to do, as the silence in the joint is making my stomach go up and down inside me, and I know this is bad for my blood pressure. Nobody as much as opens his face from the time we go in until we start out, and you will be surprised how nervous it makes you to be in a big crowd with everybody dead still, especially when you figure it a spot that is liable to get hot any minute. It is only just as we get to the door that anybody speaks, and who is it but Jew Louie, who pipes up and says to Rusty Charley like this:

'Charley,' he says, 'do you make it the hard way?'

Well, everybody laughs, and we go on out, but I never hear myself whether Charley makes his ten with a six and a four, or with two fives – which is the hard way to make a ten with the dice – although I often wonder about the matter afterward.

I am hoping that I can now get away from Rusty Charley and go on home, because I can see he is the last guy in the world to have around a blood pressure, and, furthermore, that people may get the wrong idea of me if I stick around with him, but when I suggest going to Charley, he seems to be hurt.

'Why,' Charley says, 'you are a fine guy to be talking of quitting a pal just as we are starting out. You will certainly stay with me because I like company, and we will go down to Ikey the Pig's and play stuss. Ikey is an old friend of mine, and I owe him a complimentary play.'

Now, of course, I do not wish to go to Ikey the Pig's, because it is a place away downtown, and I do not wish to play stuss, because this is a game which I am never able to figure out myself, and, furthermore, I remember Doc Brennan says I ought to get a little sleep now and then; but I see no use in hurting Charley's feelings, especially as he is apt to do something drastic to me if I do not go.

So he calls a taxi, and we start downtown for Ikey the Pig's, and the jockey who is driving the short goes so fast that it makes my blood pressure go up a foot to a foot and a half from the way I feel inside, although Rusty Charley pays no attention to the speed. Finally I stick my head out of the window and ask the jockey to please take it a little easy, as I wish to get where I am going all in one piece, but the guy only keeps busting along.

We are at the corner of Nineteenth and Broadway when all of a sudden Rusty Charley yells at the jockey to pull up a minute, which the guy does. Then Charley steps out of the cab and says to the jockey like this:

'When a customer asks you to take it easy, why do you not be nice and take it easy? Now see what you get.'

And Rusty Charley hauls off and clips the jockey a punch on the chin that knocks the poor guy right off the seat into the street, and then Charley climbs into the seat himself and away we go with Charley driving, leaving the guy stretched out as stiff as a board. Now Rusty Charley once drives a short for a living himself, until the coppers get an idea that he is not always delivering his customers to the right address, especially such as may happen to be drunk when he gets them, and he is a pretty fair driver, but he only looks one way, which is straight ahead.

Personally, I never wish to ride with Charley in a taxicab under any circumstances, especially if he is driving, because he certainly drives very fast. He pulls up a block from Ikey the Pig's, and says we will leave the short there until somebody finds it and turns it in, but just as we are walking away from the short up steps a copper in uniform and claims we cannot park the short in this spot without a driver.

Well, Rusty Charley just naturally hates to have coppers give him any advice, so what does he do but peek up and down the street to see if anybody is looking, and then haul off and clout the copper on the chin, knocking him bow-legged. I wish to say I never see a more accurate puncher than Rusty Charley, because he always connects with that old button. As the copper tumbles, Rusty Charley grabs me by the arm and starts me running up a side street, and after we go about a block we dodge into Ikey the Pig's.

It is what is called a stuss house, and many prominent citizens of the neighbourhood are present playing stuss. Nobody seems any too glad to see Rusty Charley, although Ikey the Pig lets on he is tickled half to death. This Ikey the Pig is a short fat-necked guy who will look very natural at New Year's, undressed, and with an apple in his mouth, but it seems he and Rusty Charley are really old-time friends, and think fairly well of each other in spots.

But I can see that Ikey the Pig is not so tickled when he finds Charley is there to gamble, although Charley flashes his G note at once, and says he does not mind losing a little dough to Ikey just for old time's sake. But I judge Ikey the Pig knows he is never going to handle Charley's G note, because Charley puts it back in his pocket and it never comes out again even though Charley gets off loser playing stuss right away.

Well, at five o'clock in the morning, Charley is stuck one hundred and thirty G's, which is plenty of money even when a guy is playing on his muscle, and of course Ikey the Pig knows there is no chance of getting one hundred and thirty cents off of Rusty Charley, let alone that many thousands. Everybody else is gone by this time and Ikey wishes to close up. He is willing to take Charley's marker for a million if necessary to get Charley out, but the trouble is in stuss a guy is entitled to get back a percentage of what he loses, and Ikey figures Charley is sure to wish this percentage even if he gives a marker, and the percentage will wreck Ikey's joint.

Furthermore, Rusty Charley says he will not quit loser under such circumstances because Ikey is his friend, so what happens but Ikey finally sends out and hires a cheater by the name of Dopey Goldberg, who takes to dealing the game and in no time he has Rusty Charley even by cheating in Rusty Charley's favour.

Personally, I do not pay much attention to the play, but grab myself a few winks of sleep in a chair in a corner, and the rest seems to help my blood pressure no little. In fact, I am not noticing my blood pressure at all when Rusty Charley and I get out of Ikey the Pig's, because I figure Charley will let me go home and I can go to bed. But although it is six o'clock, and coming on broad daylight when we leave Ikey's, Charley is still full of zing, and nothing will do him but we must go to a joint that is called the Bohemian Club.

Well, this idea starts my blood pressure going again, beause the Bohemian Club is nothing but a deadfall where guys and dolls go when there is positively no other place in town open, and it is run by a guy by the name of Knife O'Halloran, who comes from down around Greenwich Village and is considered a very bad character. It is well known to one and all that a guy is apt to lose his life in Knife O'Halloran's any night, even if he does nothing more than drink Knife O'Halloran's liquor.

But Rusty Charley insists on going there, so naturally I go with him; and at first everything is very quiet and peaceful, except that a lot of guys and dolls in evening clothes, who wind up there after being in night clubs all night, are yelling in one corner of the joint. Rusty Charley and Knife O'Halloran are having a drink together out of a bottle which Knife carries in his pocket, so as not to get it mixed up with the liquor he sells his customers, and are cutting up old touches of the time when they run with the Hudson Dusters together, when all of a sudden in comes four coppers in plain clothes.

Now these coppers are off duty and are meaning no harm to anybody, and are only wishing to have a dram or two before going home, and the chances are they will pay no attention to Rusty Charley if he minds his own business, although of course they know who he is very well indeed and will take great pleasure in putting the old sleeve on him if they only have a few charges against him, which they do not. So they do not give him a tumble. But if there is one thing Rusty Charley hates it is a copper, and he starts eyeing them from the minute they sit down at a table, and by and by I hear him say to Knife O'Halloran like this:

'Knife,' Charley says, 'what is the most beautiful sight in the world?'

'I do not know, Charley,' Knife says. 'What is the most beautiful sight in the world?'

'Four dead coppers in a row,' Charley says.

Well, at this I personally ease myself over toward the door, because I never wish to have any trouble with coppers and especially with four coppers, so I do not see everything that comes off. All I see is Rusty Charley grabbing at the big foot which one of the coppers kicks at him, and then everybody seems to go into a huddle, and the guys and dolls in evening dress start squawking, and my blood pressure goes up to maybe a million.

I get outside the door, but I do not go away at once as anybody with any sense will do, but stand there listening to what is going on inside, which seems to be nothing more than a loud noise like ker-bump, ker-bump, ker-bump. I am not afraid there will be any shooting, because as far as Rusty Charley is concerned he is too smart to shoot any coppers, which is the worst thing a guy can do in this town, and the coppers are not likely to start any blasting because they will not wish it to come out that they are in a joint such as the Bohemian Club off duty. So I figure they will all just take it out in pulling and hauling.

Finally the noise inside dies down, and by and by the door opens and out comes Rusty Charley, dusting himself off here and there with his hands and looking very much pleased indeed, and through the door before it flies shut again I catch a glimpse of a lot of guys stretched out on the floor. Furthermore, I can still hear guys and dolls hollering.

'Well, well,' Rusty Charley says, 'I am commencing to think you take the wind on me, and am just about to get mad at you, but here you are. Let us go away from this joint, because they are making so much noise inside you cannot hear yourself think. Let us go to my joint and make my old woman cook us up some breakfast, and then we can catch some sleep. A little ham and eggs will not be bad to take right now.'

Well, naturally ham and eggs are appealing to me no little at this time, but I do not care to go to Rusty Charley's joint. As far as I am personally concerned, I have enough of Rusty Charley to do me a long, long time, and I do not care to enter into his home life to any extent whatever, although to tell the truth I am somewhat surprised to learn he has any such life. I believe I do once hear that Rusty Charley marries one of the neighbours' children, and that he lives somewhere over on Tenth Avenue in the Forties, but nobody really knows much about this, and everybody figures if it is true his wife must lead a terrible dog's life.

But while I do not wish to go to Charley's joint, I cannot very well refuse a civil invitation to eat ham and eggs, especially as Charley is looking at me in a very much surprised way because I do not seem so glad, and I can see that it is not everyone that he invites to his joint. So I thank him, and say there is nothing I will enjoy more than ham and eggs such as his old woman will cook for us, and by and by we are walking along Tenth Avenue up around Forty-fifth Street.

It is still fairly early in the morning, and business guys are open-ing up their joints for the day, and little children are skipping along the sidewalks going to school and laughing tee-hee, and old dolls are shaking bedclothes and one thing and another out of the windows of the tenement houses, but when they spot Rusty Charley and me everybody becomes very quiet indeed, and I can see that Charley is greatly respected in his own neighbourhood. The business guys hurry into their joints, and the little children stop skipping and tee-heeing and go tip-toeing along, and the old dolls yank in their noodles, and a great quiet comes to the street. In fact, about all you can hear is the heels of Rusty Charley and me hitting on the sidewalk.

There is an ice wagon with a couple of horses hitched to it standing in front of a store, and when he sees the horses Rusty Charley seems to get a big idea. He stops and looks the horses over very carefully, although as far as I can see they are nothing but horses, and big and fat, and sleepy-looking horses, at that. Finally Rusty Charley says to me like this :

'When I am a young guy,' he says, 'I am a very good puncher with my right hand, and often I hit a horse on the skull with my fist and knock it down. I wonder,' he says, 'if I lose my punch. The last copper I hit back there gets up twice on me.'

Then he steps up to one of the ice-wagon horses and hauls off and biffs it right between the eyes with a right-hand smack that does not travel more than four inches, and down goes old Mister Horse to his knees looking very much surprised indeed. I see many a hard puncher in my day including Dempsey when he really can punch, but I never see a harder punch than Rusty Charley gives this horse.

Well, the ice-wagon driver comes busting out of the store all heated up over what happens to his horse, but he cools out the minute he sees Rusty Charley, and goes on back into the store leaving the horse still taking a count, while Rusty Charley and I keep walking. Finally we come to the entrance of a tenement house that Rusty Charley says is where he lives, and in front of this house is a wop with a push-cart loaded with fruit and vegetables and one thing and another, which Rusty Charley tips over as we go into the house, leaving the wop yelling very loud, and maybe cussing us in wop for all I know. I am very glad, personally, we finally get somewhere, because I can feel that my blood pressure is getting worse every minute I am with Rusty Charley.

We climb two flights of stairs, and then Charley opens a door and we step into a room where there is a pretty little red-headed doll about knee high to a flivver, who looks as if she may just get out of the hay, because her red hair is flying around every which way on her head, and her eyes seem still gummed up with sleep. At first I think she is a very cute sight indeed, and then I see something in her eyes that tells me this doll, whoever she is, is feeling very hostile to one and all.

'Hello, tootsie,' Rusty Charley says. 'How about some ham and eggs for me and my pal here? We are all tired out going around and about.'

Well, the little red-headed doll just looks at him without saying a word. She is standing in the middle of the floor with one hand behind her, and all of a sudden she brings this hand around, and what does she have in it but a young baseball bat, such as kids play ball with, and which cost maybe two bits; and the next thing I know I hear something go ker-bap, and I can see she smacks Rusty Charley on the side of the noggin with the bat.

Naturally I am greatly horrified at this business, and figure Rusty Charley will kill her at once, and then I will be in a jam for witnessing the murder and will be held in jail several years like all witnesses to anything in this man's town; but Rusty Charley only falls into a big rocking-chair in a corner of the room and sits there with one hand to his head, saying, 'Now hold on, tootsie,' and 'Wait a minute there, honey.' I recollect hearing him say, 'We have company for breakfast,' and then the little red-headed doll turns on me and gives me a look such as I will always remember, although I smile at her very pleasant and mention it is a nice morning.

Finally she says to me like this:

'So you are the trambo who keeps my husband out all night, are you, you trambo?' she says, and with this she starts for me, and I start for the door; and by this time my blood pressure is all out of whack, because I can see Mrs. Rusty Charley is excited more than somewhat. I get my hand on the knob and just then something hits me alongside the noggin, which I afterward figure must be the baseball bat, although I remember having a sneaking idea the roof caves in on me.

How I get the door open I do not know, because I am very dizzy in the head and my legs are wobbling, but when I think back over the situation I remember going down a lot of steps very fast, and by and by the fresh air strikes me, and I figure I am in the clear. But all of a sudden I feel another strange sensation back of my head and something goes plop against my noggin, and I figure at first that maybe my blood pressure runs up so high that it squirts out the top of my bean. Then I peek around over my shoulder just once to see that Mrs. Rusty Charley is standing beside the wop peddler's cart snatching fruit and vegetables of one kind and another off the cart and chucking them at me.

But what she hits me with back of the head is not an apple, or a peach, or a rutabaga, or a cabbage, or even a casaba melon, but a brickbat that the wop has on his cart to weight down the paper sacks in which he sells his goods. It is this brickbat which makes a lump on the back of my head so big that Doc Brennan thinks it is a tumour when I go to him the next day about my stomach, and I never tell him any different.

'But,' Doc Brennan says, when he takes my blood pressure again, 'your pressure is down below normal now, and as far as it is concerned you are in no danger whatever. It only goes to show what just a little bit of quiet living will do for a guy,' Doc Brennan says. 'Ten bucks, please,' he says.

The Bloodhounds of Broadway

One morning along about four bells, I am standing in front of Mindy's restaurant on Broadway with a guy by the name of Regret, who has this name because it seems he wins a very large bet the year the Whitney filly, Regret, grabs the Kentucky Derby, and can never forget it, which is maybe because it is the only very large bet he ever wins in his life.

What this guy's real name is I never hear, and anyway names make no difference to me, especially on Broadway, because the chances are that no matter what name a guy has, it is not his square name. So, as far as I am concerned, Regret is as good a name as any other for this guy I am talking about, who is a fat guy, and very gabby, though generally he is talking about nothing but horses, and how he gets beat three dirty noses the day before at Belmont, or wherever the horses are running.

In all the years I know Regret he must get beat ten thousand noses, and always they are dirty noses, to hear him tell it. In fact, I never once hear him say he is beat a clean nose, but of course this is only the way horse-racing guys talk. What Regret does for a living besides betting on horses I do not know, but he seems to do pretty well at it, because he is always around and about, and generally well dressed, and with a lot of big cigars sticking up out of his vest pocket.

It is generally pretty quiet on Broadway along about four bells in the morning, because at such an hour the citizens are mostly in speakeasies, and night clubs, and on this morning I am talking about it is very quiet, indeed, except for a guy by the name of Marvin Clay hollering at a young doll because she will not get into a taxicab with him to go to his apartment. But of course Regret and I do not pay much attention to such a scene, except that Regret remarks that the young doll seems to have more sense than you will expect to see in a doll loose on Broadway at four bells in the morning, because it is well known to one and all that any doll who goes to Marvin Clay's apartment, either has no brains whatever, or wishes to go there.

This Marvin Clay is a very prominent society guy, who is a great hand for hanging out in night clubs, and he has plenty of scratch which comes down to him from his old man, who makes it out of railroads and one thing and another. But Marvin Clay is a most obnoxious character, being loud and ungentlemanly at all times, on account of having all this scratch, and being always very rough and abusive with young dolls such as work in night clubs, and who have to stand for such treatment from Marvin Clay because he is a very good customer.

He is generally in evening clothes, as he is seldom around and about except in the evening, and he is maybe fifty years old, and has a very ugly mugg, which is covered with blotches, and pimples, but of course a guy who has so much scratch as Marvin Clay does not have to be so very handsome, at that, and he is very welcome indeed wherever he goes on Broadway. Personally, I wish no part of such a guy as Marvin Clay, although I suppose in my time on Broadway I must see a thousand guys like him, and there will always be guys like Marvin Clay on Broadway as long as they have old men to make plenty of scratch out of railroads to keep them going.

Well, by and by Marvin Clay gets the doll in the taxicab, and away they go, and it is all quiet again on Broadway, and Regret and I stand there speaking of this and that, and one thing and another, when along comes a very strange-looking guy leading two very strange-looking dogs. The guy is so thin I figure he must be about two pounds lighter than a stack of wheats. He has a long nose, and a sad face, and he is wearing a floppy old black felt hat, and he has on a flannel shirt, and baggy corduroy pants, and a see-more coat, which is a coat that lets you see more hip pockets than coat.

Personally, I never see a stranger-looking guy on Broadway, and I wish to say I see some very strange-looking guys on Broadway in my day. But if the guy is strange-looking, the dogs are even stranger-looking because they have big heads, and jowls that hang down like an old-time faro bank dealer's, and long ears the size of bed sheets. Furthermore, they have wrinkled faces, and big, round eyes that seem so sad I half expect to see them bust out crying.

The dogs are a sort of black and yellow in colour, and have long tails, and they are so thin you can see their ribs sticking out of their hides. I can see at once that the dogs and the guy leading them can use a few hamburgers very nicely, but then so can a lot of other guys on Broadway at this time, leaving out the dogs.

Well, Regret is much interested in the dogs right away, because he is a guy who is very fond of animals of all kinds, and nothing will do but he must stop the guy and start asking questions about what sort of dogs they are, and in fact I am also anxious to hear myself, because while I see many a pooch in my time I never see anything like these.

'They is bloodhounds,' the sad-looking guy says in a very sad voice, and with one of these accents such as Southern guys always have. 'They is man-tracking bloodhounds from Georgia.'

Now of course both Regret and me know what bloodhounds are because we see such animals chasing Eliza across the ice in Uncle Tom's Cabin when we are young squirts, but this is the first time either of us meet up with any bloodhounds personally, especially on Broadway. So we get to talking quite a bit to the guy, and his story is as sad as his face, and makes us both feel very sorry for him.

In fact, the first thing we know we have him and the bloodhounds in Mindy's and are feeding one and all big steaks, although Mindy puts up an awful squawk about us bringing the dogs in, and asks us what we think he is running, anyway. When Regret starts to tell him, Mindy says never mind, but not to bring any more Shetland ponies into his joint again as long as we live.

Well, it seems that the sad-looking guy's name is John Wangle, and he comes from a town down in Georgia where his uncle is the high sheriff, and one of the bloodhounds' name is Nip, and the other Tuck, and they are both trained from infancy to track down guys such as lags who escape from the county pokey, and bad niggers, and one thing and another, and after John Wangle gets the kinks out of his belly on Mindy's steaks, and starts talking good, you must either figure him a high-class liar, or the hounds the greatest man-trackers the world ever sees.

Now, looking at the dogs after they swallow six big sirloins apiece, and a lot of matzoths, which Mindy has left over from the Jewish holidays, and a job lot of goulash from the dinner bill, and some other odds and ends, the best I can figure them is hearty eaters, because they are now lying down on the floor with their faces hidden behind their ears, and are snoring so loud you can scarcely hear yourself think.

How John Wangle comes to be in New York with these bloodhounds is quite a story, indeed. It seems that a New York guy drifts into John's old home town in Georgia when the bloodhounds are tracking down a bad nigger, and this guy figures it will be a wonderful idea to take John Wangle and the dogs to New York and hire them out to the movies to track down the villains in the pictures. But when they get to New York, it seems the movies have other arrangements for tracking down their villains, and the guy runs out of scratch and blows away, leaving John Wangle and the bloodhounds stranded.

So here John Wangle is with Nip and Tuck in New York, and they are all living together in one room in a tenement house over in West Forty-ninth Street, and things are pretty tough with them, because John does not know how to get back to Georgia unless he walks, and he hears the walking is no good south of Roanoke.

When I ask him why he does not write to his uncle, the high sheriff down there in Georgia, John Wangle says, there are two reasons, one being that he cannot write, and the other that his uncle cannot read.

Then I ask him why he does not sell the bloodhounds, and he says it is because the market for bloodhounds is very quiet in New York, and furthermore if he goes back to Georgia without the bloodhounds his uncle is apt to knock his ears down. Anyway, John Wangle says he personally loves Nip and Tuck very dearly, and in fact he says it is only his great love for them that keeps him from eating one or the other and maybe both, the past week, when his hunger is very great indeed.

Well, I never before see Regret so much interested in any situation as he is in John Wangle and the bloodhounds, but personally I am getting very tired of them, because the one that is called Nip finally wakes up and starts chewing on my leg, thinking it is maybe more steak, and when I kick him in the snoot, John Wangle scowls at me, and Regret says only very mean guys are unkind to dumb animals.

But to show you that John Wangle and his bloodhounds are not so dumb, they come moseying along past Mindy's every morning after this at about the same time, and Regret is always there ready to feed them, although he now has to take the grub out on the sidewalk, as Mindy will not allow the hounds in the joint again. Naturally Nip and Tuck become very fond of Regret, but they are by no means as fond of him as John Wangle, because John is commencing to fat up very nicely, and the bloodhounds are also taking on weight.

Now what happens but Regret does not show up in front of Mindy's for several mornings hand running, because it seems that Regret makes a very nice score for himself one day against the horses, and buys himself a brand-new tuxedo, and starts stepping out around the night clubs, and especially around Miss Missouri Martin's Three Hundred Club, where there are many beautiful young dolls who dance around with no more clothes on them than will make a pad for a crutch, and it is well known that Regret dearly loves such scenes.

Furthermore, I hear reports around and about of Regret becoming very fond of a doll by the name of Miss Lovey Lou, who works in Miss Missouri Martin's Three Hundred Club, and of him getting in some kind of a jam with Marvin Clay over this doll, and smacking Marvin Clay in the kisser, so I figure Regret is getting a little simple, as guys who hang around Broadway long enough are bound to do. Now, when John Wangle and Nip and Tuck come around looking for a hand-out, there is nothing much doing for them, as nobody else around Mindy's feels any great interest in bloodhounds, especially such interest as will cause them to buy steaks, and soon Nip and Tuck are commencing to look very sad again, and John Wangle is downcast more than somewhat.

It is early morning again, and warm, and a number of citizens are out in front of Mindy's as usual, breathing the fresh air, when along comes a police inspector by the name of McNamara, who is a friend of mine, with a bunch of plain-clothes coppers with him, and Inspector McNamara tells me he is on his way to investigate a situation in an apartment house over in West Fifty-fourth Street, about three blocks away, where it seems a guy is shot; and not having anything else to do, I go with them, although as a rule I do not care to associate with coppers, because it arouses criticism from other citizens.

Well, who is the guy who is shot but Marvin Clay, and he is stretched out on the floor of the living-room of his apartment in evening clothes, with his shirt front covered with blood, and after Inspector McNamara takes a close peek at him, he sees that Marvin Clay is plugged smack dab in the chest, and that he seems to be fairly dead. Furthermore, there seems to be no clue whatever to who does the shooting, and Inspector McNamara says it is un-doubtedly a very great mystery, and will be duck soup for the newspapers, especially as they do not have a good shooting mystery for several days.

Well, of course all this is none of my business, but all of a sudden I happen to think of John Wangle and his bloodhounds, and it seems to me it will be a great opportunity for them, so I say to the Inspector as follows:

'Listen, Mac,' I say, 'there is a guy here with a pair of man-tracking bloodhounds from Georgia who are very expert in track-ing down matters such as this, and,' I say, 'maybe they can track down the rascal who shoots Marvin Clay, because the trail must be hotter than mustard right now.'

Well, afterwards I hear there is much indignation over my sug-gestion, because many citizens feel that the party who shoots Marvin Clay is entitled to more consideration than being tracked with bloodhounds. In fact, some think the party is entitled to a medal, but this discussion does not come up until later.

Anyway, at first the Inspector does not think much of my idea, and the other coppers are very sceptical, and claim that the best way to do under the circumstances is to arrest everybody in sight and hold them as material witnesses for a month or so, but the trouble is there is nobody in sight to arrest at this time, except maybe me, and the Inspector is a broad-minded guy, and finally he says all right, bring on the bloodhounds.

So I hasten back to Mindy's, and sure enough John Wangle and Nip and Tuck are out on the sidewalk peering at every passing face in the hope that maybe one of these faces will belong to Regret. It is a very pathetic sight, indeed, but John Wangle cheers up when I explain about Marvin Clay to him, and hurries back to the apartment house with me so fast that he stretches Nip's neck a foot, and is pulling Tuck along on his stomach half the time.

Well, when we get back to the apartment, John Wangle leads Nip and Tuck up to Marvin Clay, and they snuffle him all over, because it seems bloodhounds are quite accustomed to dead guys. Then John Wangle unhooks their leashes, and yells something at them, and the hounds begin snuffling all around and about the joint, with Inspector McNamara and the other coppers watching with great interest. All of a sudden Nip and Tuck go busting out of the apartment and into the street, with John Wangle after them, and all the rest of us after John Wangle. They head across Fifty-fourth Street back to Broadway, and the next thing anybody knows they are doing plenty of snuffling around in front of Mindy's.

By and by they take off up Broadway with their snozzles to the sidewalk, and we follow them very excited, because even the coppers now admit that it seems to be a sure thing they are red hot on the trail of the party who shoots Marvin Clay. At first Nip and Tuck are walking, but pretty soon they break into a lope, and there we are loping after them, John Wangle, the Inspector, and me, and the coppers.

Naturally, such a sight as this attracts quite some attention as we go along from any citizens stirring at this hour, and by and by milkmen are climbing down off their wagons, and scavenger guys are leaving their trucks standing where they are, and newsboys are dropping everything, and one and all joining in the chase, so by the time we hit Broadway and Fifty-sixth there is quite a delegation following the hounds with John Wangle in front, just behind Nip and Tuck, and yelling at them now and then as follows:

'Hold to it, boys!'

At Fifty-sixth the hounds turn east off Broadway and stop at the door of what seems to be an old garage, this door being closed very tight, and Nip and Tuck seem to wish to get through this door, so the Inspector and the coppers kick the door open, and who is in the garage having a big crap game but many prominent citizens of Broadway. Naturally, these citizens are greatly astonished at seeing the bloodhounds, and the rest of us, especially the coppers, and they start running every which way trying to get out of the joint, because crap shooting is quite illegal in these parts.

But the Inspector only says Ah-ha, and starts jotting down names in a note-book as if it is something he will refer to later, and Nip and Tuck are out of the joint almost as soon as they get in and are snuffling on down Fifty-sixth. They stop at four more doors in Fifty-sixth Street along, and when the coppers kick open these doors they find they are nothing but speakeasies, although one is a hop joint, and the citizens in these places are greatly put out by the excitement, especially as Inspector McNamara keeps jotting down things in his note-book.

Finally the Inspector starts glaring very fiercely at the coppers with us, and anybody can see that he is much displeased to find so much illegality going on in this district, and the coppers are starting in to hate Nip and Tuck quite freely, and one copper says to me like this:

'Why,' he says, 'these mutts are nothing but stool pigeons.'

Well, naturally, the noise of John Wangle's yelling, and the gabble of the mob following the hounds makes quite a disturbance, and arouses many of the neighbours in the apartment houses and hotels in the side streets, especially as this is summer, and most everybody has their windows open.

In fact, we see many tousled heads poked out of windows, and hear guys and dolls inquiring as follows:

'What is going on?'

It seems that when word gets about that bloodhounds are tracking down a wrongdoer it causes great uneasiness all through the Fifties, and in fact I afterwards hear that three guys are taken to the Polyclinic suffering with broken ankles and several bruises from hopping out of windows in the hotels we pass in the chase, or from falling off of fire-escapes.

Well, all of a sudden Nip and Tuck swing back into Seventh Avenue, and pop into the entrance of a small apartment house, and go tearing up the stairs to the first floor, and when we get there these bloodhounds are scratching vigorously at the door of Apartment B-2, and going woofle-woofle, and we are all greatly excited, indeed, but the door opens, and who is standing there but a doll by the name of Maud Milligan, who is well known to one and all as the ever-loving doll of Big Nig, the crap shooter, who is down in Hot Springs at this time taking the waters, or whatever it is guys take in Hot Springs.

Now, Maud Milligan is not such a doll as I will care to have any part of, being red-headed, and very stern, and I am glad Nip and Tuck do not waste any more time in her apartment than it takes for them to run through her living-room and across her bed, because Maud is commencing to put the old eye on such of us present as she happens to know. But Nip and Tuck are in and out of the joint before you can say scat, because it is only a two-room apartment, at that, and we are on our way down the stairs and back into Seventh Avenue again while Inspector McNamara is still jotting down something in his note-book.

Finally, where do these hounds wind up, with about four hundred citizens behind them, and everybody perspiring quite freely indeed from the exercise, but at the door of Miss Missouri Martin's Three Hundred Club, and the doorman, who is a guy by the name of Soldier Sweeney, tries to shoo them away, but Nip runs between the Soldier's legs and upsets him, and Tuck steps in the Soldier's eye in treating over him, and most of the crowd behind the hounds tread on him in passing, so the old Soldier is pretty well flattened out at the finish.

Nip and Tuck are now more excited than somewhat, and are going zoople-zoople in loud voices as they bust into the Three Hundred Club with John Wangle and the law, and all these citizens behind them. There is a very large crowd present and Miss Missouri Martin is squatted on the back of a chair in the middle of the dance floor when we enter, and is about to start her show when she sees the mob surge in, and at first she is greatly pleased because she thinks new business arrives, and if there is anything Miss Missouri Martin dearly loves, it is new business.

But before she can say hello, sucker, or anything else whatever, Nip runs under her chair, thinking maybe he is a dachshund, and dumps Miss Missouri Martin on the dance floor, and she lays there squawking no little, while the next thing anybody knows, Nip and Tuck are over in one corner of the joint, and are eagerly crawling up and down a fat guy who is sitting there with a doll alongside of him, and who is the fat guy but Regret!

Well, as Nip and Tuck rush at Regret he naturally gets up to defend himself, but they both hit him at the same time, and over he goes on top of the doll who is with him, and who seems to be nobody but Miss Lovey Lou. She is getting quite a squashing with Regret's heft spread out over her, and she is screaming quite some, especially when Nip lets out a foot of tongue and washes her make-up off her face, reaching for Regret. In fact, Miss Lovey Lou seems to be more afraid of the bloodhounds than she does of being squashed to death, for when John Wangle and I hasten to her rescue and pull her out from under Regret she is moaning as follows:

'Oh, do not let them devour me – I will confess.'

Well, as nobody but me and John Wangle seem to hear this crack, because everybody else is busy trying to split out Regret and the bloodhounds, and as John Wangle does not seem to understand what Miss Lovey Lou is mumbling about, I shove her off into the crowd, and on back into the kitchen, which is now quite deserted, what with all the help being out watching the muss in the corner, and I say to her like this:

'What is it you confess?' I say. 'Is it about Marvin Clay?'

'Yes,' she says. 'It is about him. He is a pig,' she says. 'I shoot him, and I am glad of it. He is not satisfied with what he does to me two years ago, but he tries his deviltry on my baby sister. He has her in his apartment and when I find it out and go to get her, he says he will not let her go. So I shoot him. With my brother's pistol,' she says, 'and I take my baby sister home with me, and I hope he is dead, and gone where he belongs.'

'Well, now,' I say, 'I am not going to give you any argument as to where Marvin Clay belongs, but,' I say, 'you skip out of here and go on home, and wait until we can do something about this situation, while I go back and help Regret, who seems to be in a tough spot.'

'Oh, do not let these terrible dogs eat him up,' she says, and with this she takes the breeze and I return to the other room to find there is much confusion indeed, because it seems that Regret is now very indignant at Nip and Tuck, especially when he discovers that one of them plants his big old paw right on the front of Regret's shirt bosom, leaving a dirty mark. So when he struggles to his feet, Regret starts letting go with both hands, and he is by no means a bad puncher for a guy who does not do much punching as a rule.

In fact, he flattens Nip with a right-hand to the jaw, and knocks Tuck plumb across the room with a left hook.

Well, poor Tuck slides over the slick dance floor into Miss Missouri Martin just as she is getting to her feet again, and bowls her over once more, but Miss Missouri Martin is also indignant by this time, and she gets up and kicks Tuck in a most unladylike manner. Of course, Tuck does not know so much about Miss Martin, but he is pretty sure his old friend Regret is only playing with him, so back he goes to Regret with his tongue out, and his tail wagging, and there is no telling how long this may go on if John Wangle does not step in and grab both hounds, while Inspector McNamara puts the arm on Regret and tells him he is under arrest for shooting Marvin Clay.

Well, of course everybody can see at once that Regret must be the guilty party all right, especially when it is remembered that he once had trouble with Marvin Clay, and one and all present are looking at Regret in great disgust, and saying you can see by his face that he is nothing but a degenerate type.

Furthermore, Inspector McNamara makes a speech to Miss Missouri Martin's customers in which he congratulates John Wangle and Nip and Tuck on their wonderful work in tracking down this terrible criminal and at the same time putting in a few boosts for the police department, while Regret stands there paying very little attention to what the Inspector is saying, but trying to edge himself over close enough to Nip and Tuck to give them the old foot.

Well, the customers applaud what Inspector McNamara says, and Miss Missouri Martin gets up a collection of over two C's for John Wangle and his hounds, not counting what she holds out for herself. Also the chef comes forward and takes John Wangle and Nip and Tuck back into the kitchen and stuffs them full of food, although personally I will just as soon not have any of the food they serve in the Three Hundred Club.

They take Regret to the jail-house, and he does not seem to understand why he is under arrest, but he knows it has something to do with Nip and Tuck and he tries to bribe one of the coppers to put the bloodhounds in the same cell with him for awhile, though naturally the copper will not consider such a proposition. While Regret is being booked at the jail-house, word comes around that Marvin Clay is not only not dead, but the chances are he will get well, which he finally does, at that.

Moreover, he finally bails Regret out, and not only refuses to prosecute him but skips the country as soon as he is able to move, although Regret lays in the sneezer for several weeks, at that, never letting on after he learns the real situation that he is not the party who plugs Marvin Clay. Naturally, Miss Lovey Lou is very grateful to Regret for his wonderful sacrifice, and will no doubt become his ever-loving wife in a minute, if Regret thinks to ask her, but it seems Regret finds himself brooding so much over the idea of an ever-loving wife who is so handy with a Roscoe that he never really asks.

In the meantime, John Wangle and Nip and Tuck go back to Georgia on the dough collected by Miss Missouri Martin, and with a big reputation as man-trackers. So this is all there is to the story, except that one night I run into Regret with a suit-case in his hand, and he is perspiring very freely, although it is not so hot, at that, and when I ask him if he is going away, he says this is indeed his general idea. Moreover, he says he is going very far away. Naturally, I ask him why this is, and Regret says to me as follows:

'Well,' he says, 'ever since Big Nig, the crap shooter, comes back from Hot Springs, and hears how the bloodhounds track the shooter of Marvin Clay, he is walking up and down looking at me out of the corner of his eye. In fact,' Regret says, 'I can see that Big Nig is studying something over in his mind, and while Big Nig is a guy who is not such a fast thinker as others, I am afraid he may finally think himself to a bad conclusion.

'I am afraid,' Regret says, 'that Big Nig will think himself to the conclusion that Nip and Tuck are tracking me instead of the shooter, as many evil-minded guys are already whispering around and about, and that he may get the wrong idea about the trail leading to Maud Milligan's door.'

Tobias the Terrible

One night I am sitting in Mindy's restaurant on Broadway partaking heartily of some Hungarian goulash which comes very nice in Mindy's, what with the chef being personally somewhat Hungarian himself, when in pops a guy who is a stranger to me and sits down at my table.

I do not pay any attention to the guy at first as I am busy looking over the entries for the next day at Laurel, but I hear him tell the waiter to bring him some goulash, too. By and by I hear the guy making a strange noise and I look at him over my paper and see that he is crying. In fact, large tears are rolling down his face into his goulash and going plop-plop as they fall.

Now it is by no means usual to see guys crying in Mindy's restaurant, though thousands of guys come in there who often feel like crying, especially after a tough day at the track, so I commence weighing the guy up with great interest. I can see he is a very little guy, maybe a shade over five feet high and weighing maybe as much as a dime's worth of liver, and he has a moustache like a mosquito's whiskers across his upper lip, and pale blond hair and a very sad look in his eyes.

Furthermore, he is a young guy and he is wearing a suit of clothes the colour of French mustard, with slanting pockets, and I notice when he comes in that he has a brown hat sitting jack-deuce on his noggin. Anybody can see that this guy does not belong in these parts, with such a sad look and especially with such a hat.

Naturally, I figure his crying is some kind of a dodge. In fact, I figure that maybe the guy is trying to cry me out of the price of his Hungarian goulash, although if he takes the trouble to ask anybody before he comes in, he will learn that he may just as well try to cry Al Smith out of the Empire State Building.

But the guy does not say anything whatever to me but just goes on shedding tears into his goulash, and finally I get very curious about this proposition, and I speak to him as follows:

'Listen, pally,' I say, 'if you are crying about the goulash, you better dry your tears before the chef sees you, because,' I say, 'the chef is very sensitive about his goulash, and may take your tears as criticism.'

'The goulash seems all right,' the guy says in a voice that is just about his size. 'Anyway, I am not crying about the goulash. I am crying about my sad life. Friend,' the guy says, 'are you ever in love?'

Well, of course, at this crack I know what is eating the guy. If I have all the tears that are shed on Broadway by guys in love, I will have enough salt water to start an opposition ocean to the Atlantic and Pacific, with enough left over to run the Great Salt Lake out of business. But I wish to say I never shed any of these tears personally, because I am never in love, and furthermore, barring a bad break, I never expect to be in love, for the way I look at it love is strictly the old phedinkus, and I tell the little guy as much.

'Well,' he says, 'you will not speak so harshly of love if you are acquainted with Miss Deborah Weems.'

With this he starts crying more than somewhat, and his grief is such that it touches my heart and I have half a notion to start crying with him as I am now convinced that the guy is levelling with his tears.

Finally the guy slacks up a little in his crying, and begins eating his goulash, and by and by he seems more cheerful, but then it is well known to one and all that a fair dose of Mindy's goulash will cheer up anybody no matter how sad they feel. Pretty soon the guy starts talking to me, and I make out that his name is Tobias Tweeney, and that he comes from a spot over in Bucks County, Pennsylvania, by the name of Erasmus, or some such.

Furthermore, I judge that this Erasmus is not such a large city, but very pleasant, and that Tobias Tweeney is born and raised there and is never much of any place else in his life, although he is now rising twenty-five.

Well, it seems that Tobias Tweeney has a fine position in a shoe store selling shoes and is going along all right when he happens to fall in love with a doll by the name of Miss Deborah Weems, whose papa owns a gas station in Erasmus and is a very prominent citizen. I judge from what Tobias tells me that this Miss Deborah Weems tosses him around quite some, which proves to me that dolls in small towns are just the same as they are on Broadway.

'She is beautiful,' Tobias Tweeney says, speaking of Miss Deborah Weems. 'I do not think I can live without her. But,' he says, 'Miss Deborah Weems will have no part of me because she is daffy over desperate characters of the underworld such as she sees in the movies at the Model Theatre in Erasmus.

'She wishes to know,' Tobias Tweeney says, 'why I cannot be a big gunman and go around plugging people here and there and talking up to politicians and policemen, and maybe looking picturesque and romantic like Edward G. Robinson or James Cagney or even Georgie Raft. But, of course,' Tobias says, 'I am not the type for such a character. Anyway,' he says, 'Constable Wendell will never permit me to be such a character in Erasmus.

'So Miss Deborah Weems says I have no more nerve than a catfish,' Tobias says, 'and she goes around with a guy by the name of Joe Trivett, who runs the Smoke Shop, and bootlegs ginger extract to the boys in his back room and claims Al Capone once says "Hello" to him, although,' Tobias says, 'personally, I think Joe Trivett is nothing but a great big liar.'

At this, Tobias Tweeney starts crying again, and I feel very sorry for him indeed, because I can see he is a friendly, harmless little fellow, and by no means accustomed to being tossed around by a doll, and a guy who is not accustomed to being tossed around by a doll always finds it most painful the first time.

'Why,' I say, very indignant, 'this Miss Deborah Weems talks great foolishness, because big gunmen always wind up nowadays with the score nine to nought against them, even in the movies. In fact,' I say, 'if they do not wind up this way in the movies, the censors will not permit the movies to be displayed. Why do you not hit this guy Trivett a punch in the snoot,' I say, 'and tell him to go on about his business?'

'Well,' Tobias says, 'the reason I do not hit him a punch in the snoot is because he has the idea of punching snoots first, and whose snoot does he punch but mine. Furthermore,' Tobias says, 'he makes my snoot bleed with the punch, and he says he will do it again if I keep hanging around Miss Deborah Weems. And,' Tobias says, 'it is mainly because I do not return the punch, being too busy stopping my snoot from bleeding, that Miss Deborah Weems renounces me for ever.

'She says she can never stand for a guy who has no more nerve than me,' Tobias says, 'but,' he says, 'I ask you if I am to blame if my mother is frightened by a rabbit a few weeks before I am born, and marks me for life?

'So I leave town,' Tobias says. 'I take my savings of two hundred dollars out of the Erasmus bank, and I come here, figuring maybe I will meet up with some big gunmen and other desperate characters of the underworld, and get to know them, and then I can go back to Erasmus and make Joe Trivett look sick. By the way,' he says, 'do you know any desperate characters of the underworld?'

Well, of course I do not know any such characters, and if I do know them I am not going to speak about it, because the best a guy can get in this town if he goes around speaking of these matters is a nice kick in the pants. So I say no to Tobias Tweeney, and tell him I am more or less of a stranger myself, and then he wishes to know if I can show him a tough joint, such as he sees in the movies.

Naturally, I do not know of such a joint, but then I get to thinking about Good Time Charley's little Gingham Shoppe over in Forty-seventh Street, and how Charley is not going so good the last time I am in there, and here is maybe a chance for me to steer a little trade his way, because, after all, guys with two yards in their pocket are by no means common nowadays.

So I take Tobias Tweeney around to Good Time Charley's, but the moment we get in there I am sorry we go, because who is present but a dozen parties from different parts of the city, and none of these parties are any bargain at any time. Some of these parties, such as Harry the Horse and Angie the Ox, are from Brooklyn, and three are from Harlem, including Little Mitzi and Germany Schwartz, and several are from the Bronx, because I recognize Joey Uptown, and Joey never goes around without a few intimate friends from his own neighbourhood with him.

Afterwards I learn that these parties are to a meeting on business matters at a spot near Good Time Charley's, and when they get through with their business they drop in to give Charley a little complimentary play, for Charley stands very good with one and all in this town. Anyway, they are sitting around a table when Tobias Tweeney and I arrive, and I give them all a big hello, and they hello me back, and ask me and my friend to sit down as it seems they are in a most hospitable frame of mind.

Naturally I sit down because it is never good policy to decline an invitation from parties such as these, and I motion Tobias to sit down, too, and I introduce Tobias all around, and we all have a couple of drinks, and then I explain to those present just who Tobias is, and how his ever-loving doll tosses him around, and how Joe Trivett punches him in the snoot.

Well, Tobias begins crying again, because no inexperienced guy can take a couple of drinks of Good Time Charley's liquor and not bust out crying, even if it is Charley's company liquor, and one and all are at once very sympathetic with Tobias, especially Little Mitzi, who is just tossed around himself more than somewhat by a doll. In fact, Little Mitzi starts crying with him.

'Why,' Joey Uptown says, 'I never hear of a greater outrage in my life, although,' he says, 'I can see there is some puppy in you at that, when you do not return this Trivett's punch. But even so,' Joey says, 'if I have time I will go back to this town you speak of with you and make the guy hard to catch. Furthermore,' he says, 'I will give this Miss Deborah Weems a piece of my mind.'

Then I tell them how Tobias Tweeney comes to New York figuring he may meet up with some desperate characters of the underworld, and they hear this with great interest, and Angie the Ox speaks as follows:

'I wonder,' Angie says, 'if we can get in touch with anybody who knows such characters and arrange to have Mr. Tweeney meet them, although personally,' Angie says, 'I loathe and despise characters of this nature.'

Well, while Angie is wondering this there comes a large knock at the front door, and it is such a knock as only the gendarmes can knock, and everybody at the table jumps up. Good Time Charley goes to the door and takes a quiet gander through his peephole and we hear a loud, coarse voice speaking as follows:

'Open up, Charley,' the voice says. 'We wish to look over your guests. Furthermore,' the voice says, 'tell them not to try the back door, because we are there, too.'

'It is Lieutenant Harrigan and his squad,' Charley says as he comes back to the table where we are all standing. 'Someone must tip him off you are here. Well,' Charley says, 'those who have rods to shed will shed them now.'

At this, Joey Uptown steps up to Tobias Tweeney and hands him a large Betsy and says to Tobias like this:

'Put this away on you somewhere,' Joey says, 'and then sit down and be quiet. These coppers are not apt to bother with you,' Joey says, 'if you sit still and mind your own business, but,' Joey says, 'it will be very tough on any of us they find with a rod, especially any of us who owe the state any time, and,' Joey says, 'I seem to remember I owe some.'

Now of course what Joey says is very true, because he is only walking around and about on parole, and some of the others present are walking around the same way, and it is a very serious matter for a guy who is walking around on parole to be caught with a John Roscoe in his pocket. So it is a very ticklish situation, and somewhat embarrassing.

Well, Tobias Tweeney is somewhat dazed by his couple of drinks of Good Time Charley's liquor and the chances are he does not realize what is coming off, so he takes Joey's rod and puts it in his hip kick. Then all of a sudden Harry the Horse and Angie the Ox and Little Mitzi, and all the others step up to him and hand him their Roscoes and Tobias Tweeney somehow manages to stow the guns away on himself and sit down before Good Time Charley opens the door and in come the gendarmes.

By this time Joey Uptown and all the others are scattered at different tables around the room, with no more than three at any one table, leaving Tobias Tweeney and me alone at the table where we are first sitting. Furthermore, everybody is looking very innocent indeed, and all hands seem somewhat surprised at the intrusion of the gendarmes, who are all young guys belonging to Harrigan's Broadway squad, and very rude.

I know Harrigan by sight, and I know most of his men, and they know there is no more harm in me than there is in a two-year-old baby, so they pay no attention to me whatever, or to Tobias Tweeney, either, but go around making Joey Uptown, and Angie the Ox, and all the others stand up while the gendarmes fan them to see if they have any rods on them, because these gendarmes are always laying for parties such as these hoping to catch them rodded up.

Naturally the gendarmes do not find any rods on anybody, because the rods are all on Tobias Tweeney, and no gendarme is going to fan Tobias Tweeney looking for a rod after one gander at Tobias, especially at this particular moment, as Tobias is now half-asleep from Good Time Charley's liquor, and has no interest whatever in anything that is going on. In fact, Tobias is nodding in his chair.

Of course the gendarmes are greatly disgusted at not finding any rods, and Angie the Ox and Joey Uptown are telling them that they are going to see their aldermen and find out if law-abiding citizens can be stood up and fanned for rods, and put in a very undignified position like this, but the gendarmes do not seem disturbed by these threats, and Lieutenant Harrigan states as follows:

'Well,' he says, 'I guess maybe I get a bum steer, but,' he says, 'for two cents I will give all you wrong gees a good going-over just for luck.'

Of course this is no way to speak to parties such as these, as they are all very prominent in their different parts of the city, but Lieutenant Harrigan is a guy who seldom cares how he talks to anybody. In fact, Lieutenant Harrigan is a very tough copper.

But he is just about to take his gendarmes out of the joint when Tobias Tweeney nods a little too far forward in his chair, and then all of a sudden topples over on the floor, and five large rods pop out of his pockets and go sliding every which way around the floor, and the next thing anybody knows there is Tobias Tweeney under arrest with all the gendarmes holding on to some part of him.

Well, the next day the newspapers are plumb full of the capture of a guy they call Twelve-Gun Tweeney, and the papers say the police state that this is undoubtedly the toughest guy the world ever sees, because while they hear of two-gun guys, and even three-gun guys, they never before hear of a guy going around rodded up with twelve guns.

The gendarmes say they can tell by the way he acts that Twelve-Gun Tweeney is a mighty bloodthirsty guy, because he says nothing whatever but only glares at them with a steely glint in his eyes, although of course the reason Tobias stares at them is because he is still too dumbfounded to think of anything to say.

Naturally, I figure that when Tobias comes up for air he is a sure thing to spill the whole business, and all the parties who are in Good Time Charley's when he is arrested figure the same way, and go into retirement for a time. But it seems that when Tobias finally realizes what time it is, he is getting so much attention that it swells him all up and he decides to keep on being Twelve-Gun Tweeney as long as he can, which is a decision that is a very nice break for all parties concerned.

I sneak down to Judge Rascover's court the day Tobias is arraigned on a charge of violation of the Sullivan law, which is a law against carrying rods, and the courtroom is packed with citizens eager to see a character desperate enough to lug twelve rods, and among these citizens are many dolls, pulling and hauling for position, and some of these dolls are by no means crows. Many photographers are hanging around to take pictures of Twelve-Gun Tweeney as he is led in handcuffed to gendarmes on either side of him, and with other gendarmes in front and behind him.

But one and all are greatly surprised and somewhat disappointed when they see what a little squirt Tobias is, and Judge Rascover looks down at him once, and then puts on his specs and takes another gander as if he does not believe what he sees in the first place. After looking at Tobias awhile through his specs, and shaking his head as if he is greatly puzzled, Judge Rascover speaks to Lieutenant Harrigan as follows:

'Do you mean to tell this court,' Judge Rascover says, 'that this half-portion here is the desperate Twelve-Gun Tweeney?'

Well, Lieutenant Harrigan says there is no doubt whatever about it, and Judge Rascover wishes to know how Tobias carries all these rods, and whereabouts, so Lieutenant Harrigan collects twelve rods from the gendarmes around the courtroom, unloads these rods, and starts in putting the guns here and there on Tobias as near as he can remember where they are found on him in the first place, with Tobias giving him a little friendly assistance.

Lieutenant Harrigan puts two guns in each of the side pockets of Tobias's coat, one in each hip pocket, one in the waistband of Tobias's pants, one in each side pocket of the pants, one up each of Tobias's sleeves, and one in the inside pocket of Tobias's coat. Then Lieutenant Harrigan states to the court that he is all finished, and that Tobias is rodded up in every respect as when they put the arm on him in Good Time Charley's joint, and Judge Rascover speaks to Tobias as follows:

'Step closer to the bench,' Judge Rascover says. 'I wish to see for myself just what kind of a villain you are.'

Well, Tobias takes a step forward, and over he goes on his snoot, so I see right away what it is makes him keel over in Good Time Charley's joint, not figuring in Charley's liquor. The little guy is naturally top-heavy from the rods.

Now there is much confusion as he falls and a young doll who seems to be fatter than somewhat comes shoving through the crowd in the courtroom yelling and crying, and though the gendarmes try to stop her she gets to Tobias and kneels at his side, and speaks as follows:

'Toby, darling,' she says, 'it is nobody but Deborah who loves you dearly, and who always knows you will turn out to be the greatest gunman of them all. Look at me, Toby,' she says, 'and tell me you love me, too. We never realize what a hero you are until we get the New York papers in Erasmus last night, and I hurry to you as quickly as possible. Kiss me, Toby,' the fat young doll says, and Tobias raises up on one elbow and does same, and it makes a very pleasing scene, indeed, although the gendarmes try to pull them apart, having no patience whatever with such matters.

Now Judge Rascover is watching all this business through his specs, and Judge Rascover is no sucker, but a pretty slick old codger for a judge, and he can see that there is something wrong somewhere about Tobias Tweeney being a character as desperate as the gendarmes make him out, especially when he sees that Tobias cannot pack all these rods on a bet.

So when the gendarmes pick the fat young doll off of Tobias and take a few pounds of rods off of Tobias, too, so he is finally able to get back on his pins and stand there, Judge Rascover adjourns court, and takes Tobias into his private room and has a talk with him, and the chances are Tobias tells him the truth, for the next thing anybody knows Tobias is walking away as free as the little birdies in the trees, except that he has the fat young doll clinging to him like a porous plaster, so maybe Tobias is not so free, at that.

Well, this is about all there is to the story, except that there is afterwards plenty of heat between the parties who are present in Good Time Charley's joint when Tobias is collared, because it seems that the meeting they all attend before going to Charley's is supposed to be a peace meeting of some kind and nobody is supposed to carry any rods to this meeting just to prove their confidence in each other, so everybody is very indignant when it comes out that nobody has any confidence in anybody else at the meeting.

I never hear of Tobias Tweeney but once after all this, and it is some months afterwards when Joey Uptown and Little Mitzi are over in Pennsylvania inspecting a brewery proposition, and finding themselves near the town that is called Erasmus, they decide it will be a nice thing to drop in on Tobias Tweeney and see how he is getting along.

Well, it seems Tobias is all married up to Miss Deborah Weems, and is getting along first class, as it seems the town elects him constable, because it feels that a guy with such a desperate reputation as Tobias Tweeney's is bound to make wrongdoers keep away from Erasmus if he is an officer of the law, and Tobias's first official act is to chase Joe Trivett out of town.

But along Broadway Tobias Tweeney will always be considered nothing but an ingrate for heaving Joey Uptown and Little Mitzi into the town sneezer and getting them fined fifty bobs apiece for carrying concealed weapons.

The Snatching of Bookie Bob

Now it comes on the spring of 1931, after a long hard winter, and times are very tough indeed, what with the stock market going all to pieces, and banks busting right and left, and the law getting very nasty about this and that, and one thing and another, and many citizens of this town are compelled to do the best they can.

There is very little scratch anywhere and along Broadway many citizens are wearing their last year's clothes and have practically nothing to bet on the races or anything else, and it is a condition that will touch anybody's heart.

So I am not surprised to hear rumours that the snatching of certain parties is going on in spots, because while snatching is by no means a high-class business, and is even considered somewhat illegal, it is something to tide over the hard times.

Furthermore, I am not surprised to hear that this snatching is being done by a character by the name of Harry the Horse, who comes from Brooklyn, and who is a character who does not care much what sort of business he is in, and who is mobbed up with other characters from Brooklyn such as Spanish John and Little Isadore, who do not care what sort of business they are in, either.

In fact, Harry the Horse and Spanish John and Little Isadore are very hard characters in every respect, and there is considerable indignation expressed around and about when they move over from Brooklyn into Manhattan and start snatching, because the citizens of Manhattan feel that if there is any snatching done in their territory, they are entitled to do it themselves.

But Harry the Horse and Spanish John and Little Isadore pay no attention whatever to local sentiment and go on the snatch on a pretty fair scale, and by and by I am hearing rumours of some very nice scores. These scores are not extra large scores, to be sure, but they are enough to keep the wolf from the door, and in fact from three different doors, and before long Harry the Horse and Spanish John and Little Isadore are around the race-tracks betting on the horses, because if there is one thing they are all very fond of, it is betting on the horses.

Now many citizens have the wrong idea entirely of the snatching business. Many citizens think that all there is to snatching is to round up the party who is to be snatched and then just snatch him, putting him away somewhere until his family or friends dig up enough scratch to pay whatever price the snatchers are asking. Very few citizens understand that the snatching business must be well organized and very systematic.

In the first place, if you are going to do any snatching, you cannot snatch just anybody. You must know who you are snatching, because naturally it is no good snatching somebody who does not have any scratch to settle with. And you cannot tell by the way a party looks or how he lives in this town if he has any scratch, because many a party who is around in automobiles, and wearing good clothes, and chucking quite a swell is nothing but the phonus bolonus and does not have any real scratch whatever.

So of course such a party is no good for snatching, and of course guys who are on the snatch cannot go around inquiring into bank accounts, or asking how much this and that party has in a safe-deposit vault, because such questions are apt to make citizens wonder why, and it is very dangerous to get citizens to wondering why about anything. So the only way guys who are on the snatch can find out about parties worth snatching is to make a connection with some guy who can put the finger on the right party.

The finger guy must know the party he fingers has plenty of ready scratch to begin with, and he must also know that this party is such a party as is not apt to make too much disturbance about being snatched, such as telling the gendarmes. The party may be a legitimate party, such as a business guy, but he will have reasons why he does not wish it to get out that he is snatched, and the finger must know these reasons. Maybe the party is not leading the right sort of life, such as running around with blondes when he has an ever-loving wife and seven children in Mamaroneck, but does not care to have his habits known, as is apt to happen if he is snatched, especially if he is snatched when he is with a blonde.

And sometimes the party is such a party as does not care to have matches run up and down the bottom of his feet, which often happens to parties who are snatched and who do not seem to wish to settle their bill promptly, because many parties are very ticklish on the bottom of the feet, especially if the matches are lit. On the other hand maybe the party is not a legitimate guy, such as a party who is running a crap game or a swell speakeasy, or who has some other dodge he does not care to have come out, and who also does not care about having his feet tickled.

Such a party is very good indeed for the snatching business, because he is pretty apt to settle without any argument. And after a party settles one snatching, it will be considered very unethical for anybody else to snatch him again very soon, so he is not likely to make any fuss about the matter. The finger guy gets a commission of twenty-five per cent. of the settlement, and one and all are satisfied and much fresh scratch comes into circulation, which is very good for the merchants. And while the party who is snatched may know who snatches him, one thing he never knows is who puts the finger on him, this being considered a trade secret.

I am talking to Waldo Winchester, the newspaper scribe, one night and something about the snatching business comes up, and Waldo Winchester is trying to tell me that it is one of the oldest dodges in the world, only Waldo calls it kidnapping, which is a title that will be very repulsive to guys who are on the snatch nowadays. Waldo Winchester claims that hundreds of years ago guys are around snatching parties, male and female, and holding them for ransom, and furthermore Waldo Winchester says they even snatch very little children and Waldo states that it is all a very, very wicked proposition.

Well, I can see where Waldo is right about it being wicked to snatch dolls and little children, but of course no guys who are on the snatch nowadays will ever think of such a thing, because who is going to settle for a doll in these times when you can scarcely even give them away? As for little children, they are apt to be a great nuisance, because their mammas are sure to go running around hollering bloody murder about them, and furthermore little children are very dangerous, indeed, what with being apt to break out with measles and mumps and one thing and another any minute and give it to everybody in the neighbourhood.

Well, anyway, knowing that Harry the Horse and Spanish John and Little Isadore are now on the snatch, I am by no means pleased to see them come along one Tuesday evening when I am standing at the corner of Fiftieth and Broadway, although of course I give them a very jolly hello, and say I hope and trust they are feeling nicely.

They stand there talking to me a few minutes, and I am very glad indeed that Johnny Brannigan, the strong-arm cop, does not happen along and see us, because it will give Johnny a very bad impression of me to see me in such company, even though I am not responsible for the company. But naturally I cannot haul off and walk away from this company at once, because Harry the Horse and Spanish John and Little Isadore may get the idea that I am playing the chill for them, and will feel hurt.

'Well,' I say to Harry the Horse, 'how are things going, Harry?'

'They are going no good,' Harry says. 'We do not beat a race in four days. In fact,' he says, 'we go overboard to-day. We are washed out. We owe every bookmaker at the track that will trust us, and now we are out trying to raise some scratch to pay off. A guy must pay his bookmaker no matter what.'

Well, of course this is very true, indeed, because if a guy does not pay his bookmaker it will lower his business standing quite some, as the bookmaker is sure to go around putting the blast on him, so I am pleased to hear Harry the Horse mention such honourable principles.

'By the way,' Harry says, 'do you know a guy by the name of Bookie Bob?'

Now I do not know Bookie Bob personally, but of course I know who Bookie Bob is, and so does everybody else in this town that ever goes to a race-track, because Bookie Bob is the biggest book-maker around and about, and has plenty of scratch. Furthermore, it is the opinion of one and all that Bookie Bob will die with this scratch, because he is considered a very close guy with his scratch. In fact, Bookie Bob is considered closer than a dead heat.

He is a short fat guy with a bald head, and his head is always shaking a little from side to side, which some say is a touch of palsy, but which most citizens believe comes of Bookie Bob shaking his head 'No' to guys asking for credit in betting on the races. He has an ever-loving wife, who is a very quiet little old doll with grey hair and a very sad look in her eyes, but nobody can blame her for this when they figure that she lives with Bookie Bob for many years.

I often see Bookie Bob and his ever-loving wife eating in differ-ent joints along in the Forties, because they seem to have no home except an hotel, and many a time I hear Bookie Bob giving her a going-over about something or other, and generally it is about the price of something she orders to eat, so I judge Bookie Bob is as tough with his ever-loving wife about scratch as he is with every-body else. In fact, I hear him bawling her out one night because she has on a new hat which she says cost her six bucks, and Bookie Bob wishes to know if she is trying to ruin him with her extravagances.

But of course I am not criticizing Bookie Bob for squawking about the hat, because for all I know six bucks may be too much for a doll to pay for a hat, at that. And furthermore, maybe Bookie Bob has the right idea about keeping down his ever-loving wife's appetite, because I know many a guy in this town who is practi-cally ruined by dolls eating too much on him.

'Well,' I say to Harry the Horse, 'if Bookie Bob is one of the bookmakers you owe, I am greatly surprised to see that you seem to have both eyes in your head, because I never before hear of Bookie Bob letting anybody owe him without giving him at least one of their eyes for security. In fact,' I say, 'Bookie Bob is such a guy as will not give you the right time if he has two watches.'

'No,' Harry the Horse says, 'we do not owe Bookie Bob. But,' he says, 'he will be owing us before long. We are going to put the snatch on Bookie Bob.'

Well, this is most disquieting news to me, not because I care if they snatch Bookie Bob or not, but because somebody may see me talking to them who will remember about it when Bookie Bob is snatched. But of course it will not be good policy for me to show Harry the Horse and Spanish John and Little Isadore that I am nervous, so I only speak as follows:

'Harry,' I say, 'every man knows his own business best, and I judge you know what you are doing. But,' I say, 'you are snatching a hard guy when you snatch Bookie Bob. A very hard guy, indeed. In fact,' I say, 'I hear the softest thing about him is his front teeth, so it may be very difficult for you to get him to settle after you snatch him.'

'No,' Harry the Horse says, 'we will have no trouble about it. Our finger gives us Bookie Bob's hole card, and it is a most surprising thing, indeed. But,' Harry the Horse says, 'you come upon many surprising things in human nature when you are on the snatch. Bookie Bob's hole card is his ever-loving wife's opinion of him.

'You see,' Harry the Horse says, 'Bookie Bob has been putting himself away with his ever-loving wife for years as a very important guy in this town, with much power and influence, although of course Bookie Bob knows very well he stands about as good as a broken leg. In fact,' Harry the Horse says, 'Bookie Bob figures that his ever-loving wife is the only one in the world who looks on him as a big guy, and he will sacrifice even his scratch, or anyway some of it, rather than let her know that guys have such little respect for him as to put the snatch on him. It is what you call psychology,' Harry the Horse says.

Well, this does not make good sense to me, and I am thinking to myself that the psychology that Harry the Horse really figures to work out nice on Bookie Bob is tickling his feet with matches, but I am not anxious to stand there arguing about it, and pretty soon I bid them all good evening, very polite, and take the wind, and I do not see Harry the Horse or Spanish John or Little Isadore again for a month.

In the meantime, I hear gossip here and there that Bookie Bob is missing for several days, and when he finally shows up again he gives it out that he is very sick during his absence, but I can put two and two together as well as anybody in this town and I figure that Bookie Bob is snatched by Harry the Horse and Spanish John and Little Isadore, and the chances are it costs him plenty.

So I am looking for Harry the Horse and Spanish John and Little Isadore to be around the race-track with plenty of scratch and betting them higher than a cat's back, but they never show up, and what is more I hear they leave Manhattan, and are back in Brooklyn working every day handling beer. Naturally this is very surprising to me, because the way things are running beer is a tough dodge just now, and there is very little profit in same, and I figure that with the scratch they must make off Bookie Bob, Harry the Horse and Spanish John and Little Isadore have a right to be taking things easy.

Now one night I am in Good Time Charley Bernstein's little speak in Forty-eighth Street, talking of this and that with Charley, when in comes Harry the Horse, looking very weary and by no means prosperous. Naturally I give him a large hello, and by and by we get to gabbing together and I ask him whatever becomes of the Bookie Bob matter, and Harry the Horse tells me as follows:

Yes [Harry the Horse says], we snatch Bookie Bob all right. In fact, we snatch him the very next night after we are talking to you, or on a Wednesday night. Our finger tells us Bookie Bob is going to a wake over in his old neighbourhood on Tenth Avenue, near Thirty-eighth Street, and this is where we pick him up.

He is leaving the place in his car along about midnight, and of course Bookie Bob is alone as he seldom lets anybody ride with him because of the wear and tear on his car cushions, and Little Isadore swings our flivver in front of him and makes him stop. Naturally Bookie Bob is greatly surprised when I poke my head into his car and tell him I wish the pleasure of his company for a short time, and at first he is inclined to argue the matter, saying I must make a mistake, but I put the old convincer on him by letting him peek down the snozzle of my John Roscoe.

We lock his car and throw the keys away, and then we take Bookie Bob in our car and go to a certain spot on Eighth Avenue where we have a nice little apartment all ready. When we get there I tell Bookie Bob that he can call up anybody he wishes and state that the snatch is on him and that it will require twenty-five G's, cash money, to take it off, but of course I also tell Bookie Bob that he is not to mention where he is or something may happen to him.

Well, I will say one thing for Bookie Bob, although everybody is always weighing in the sacks on him and saying he is no good – he takes it like a gentleman, and very calm and businesslike.

Furthermore, he does not seem alarmed, as many citizens are when they find themselves in such a situation. He recognizes the justice of our claim at once, saying as follows:

'I will telephone my partner, Sam Salt,' he says. 'He is the only one I can think of who is apt to have such a sum as twenty-five G's cash money. But,' he says, 'if you gentlemen will pardon the question, because this is a new experience to me, how do I know everything will be okay for me after you get the scratch?'

'Why,' I say to Bookie Bob, somewhat indignant, 'it is well known to one and all in this town that my word is my bond. There are two things I am bound to do,' I say, 'and one is to keep my word in such a situation as this, and the other is to pay anything I owe a bookmaker, no matter what, for these are obligations of honour with me.'

'Well,' Bookie Bob says, 'of course I do not know you gentlemen, and, in fact, I do not remember ever seeing any of you, although your face is somewhat familiar, but if you pay your bookmaker you are an honest guy, and one in a million. In fact,' Bookie Bob says, 'if I have all the scratch that is owing to me around this town, I will not be telephoning anybody for such a sum as twenty-five G's. I will have such a sum in my pants pocket for change.'

Now Bookie Bob calls a certain number and talks to somebody there but he does not get Sam Salt, and he seems much disappointed when he hangs up the receiver again.

'This is a very tough break for me,' he says. 'Sam Salt goes to Atlantic City an hour ago on very important business and will not be back until to-morrow evening, and they do not know where he is to stay in Atlantic City. And,' Bookie Bob says, 'I cannot think of anybody else to call up to get this scratch, especially anybody I will care to have know I am in this situation.'

'Why not call your ever-loving wife?' I say. 'Maybe she can dig up this kind of scratch.'

'Say,' Bookie Bob says, 'you do not suppose I am chump enough to give my ever-loving wife twenty-five G's, or even let her know where she can get her dukes on twenty-five G's belonging to me, do you? I give my ever-loving wife ten bucks per week for spending money,' Bookie Bob says, 'and this is enough scratch for any doll, especially when you figure I pay for her meals.'

Well, there seems to be nothing we can do except wait until Sam Salt gets back, but we let Bookie Bob call his ever-loving wife, as Bookie Bob says he does not wish to have her worrying about his absence, and tells her a big lie about having to go to Jersey City to sit up with a sick Brother Elk.

Well, it is now nearly four o'clock in the morning, so we put Bookie Bob in a room with Little Isadore to sleep, although, personally, I consider making a guy sleep with Little Isadore very cruel treatment, and Spanish John and I take turns keeping awake and watching out that Bookie Bob does not take the air on us before paying us off. To tell the truth, Little Isadore and Spanish John are somewhat disappointed that Bookie Bob agreed to settle so promptly, because they are looking forward to tickling his feet with great relish.

Now Bookie Bob turns out to be very good company when he wakes up the next morning, because he knows a lot of race-track stories and plenty of scandal, and he keeps us much interested at breakfast. He talks along with us as if he knows us all his life, and he seems very nonchalant indeed, but the chances are he will not be so nonchalant if I tell him about Spanish John's thought.

Well, about noon Spanish John goes out of the apartment and comes back with a racing sheet, because he knows Little Isadore and I will be wishing to know what is running in different spots although we do not have anything to bet on these races, or any way of betting on them, because we are overboard with every bookmaker we know.

Now Bookie Bob is also much interested in the matter of what is running, especially at Belmont, and he is bending over the table with me and Spanish John and Little Isadore, looking at the sheet, when Spanish John speaks as follows:

'My goodness,' Spanish John says, 'a spot such as this fifth race with Questionnaire at four to five is like finding money in the street. I only wish I have a few bobs to bet on him at such a price,' Spanish John says.

'Why,' Bookie Bob says, very polite, 'if you gentlemen wish to bet on these races I will gladly book to you. It is a good way to pass away the time while we are waiting for Sam Salt, unless you will rather play pinochle?'

'But,' I say, 'we have no scratch to play the races, at least not much.'

'Well,' Bookie Bob says, 'I will take your markers, because I hear what you say about always paying your bookmaker, and you put yourself away with me as an honest guy, and these other gentlemen also impress me as honest guys.'

Now what happens but we begin betting Bookie Bob on the different races, not only at Belmont, but at all the other tracks in the country, for Little Isadore and Spanish John and I are guys who like plenty of action when we start betting on the horses. We write out markers for whatever we wish to bet and hand them to Bookie Bob, and Bookie Bob sticks these markers in an inside pocket, and along in the late afternoon it looks as if he has a tumour on his chest.

We get the race results by 'phone off a poolroom downtown as fast as they come off, and also the prices, and it is a lot of fun, and Little Isadore and Spanish John and Bookie Bob and I are all little pals together until all the races are over and Bookie Bob takes out the markers and starts counting himself up.

It comes out then that I owe Bookie Bob ten G's, and Spanish John owes him six G's, and Little Isadore owes him four G's, as Little Isadore beats him a couple of races out west.

Well, about this time, Bookie Bob manages to get Sam Salt on the 'phone, and explains to Sam that he is to go to a certain safe-deposit box and get out twenty-five G's, and then wait until midnight and hire himself a taxicab and start riding around the block between Fifty-first and Fifty-second, from Eighth to Ninth Avenues, and to keep riding until somebody flags the cab and takes the scratch off him.

Naturally Sam Salt understands right away that the snatch is on Bookie Bob, and he agrees to do as he is told, but he says he cannot do it until the following night because he knows there is not twenty-five G's in the box, and he will have to get the difference at the track the next day. So there we are with another day in the apartment and Spanish John and Little Isadore and I are just as well pleased because Bookie Bob has us hooked and we naturally wish to wiggle off.

But the next day is worse than ever. In all the years I am playing the horses I never have such a tough day, and Spanish John and Little Isadore are just as bad. In fact, we are all going so bad that Bookie Bob seems to feel sorry for us and often lays us a couple of points above the track prices, but it does no good. At the end of the day, I am in a total of twenty G's, while Spanish John owes fifteen, and Little Isadore fifteen, a total of fifty G's among the three of us.

But we are never any hands to hold post-mortems on bad days, so Little Isadore goes out to a delicatessen store and lugs in a lot of nice things to eat, and we have a fine dinner, and then we sit around with Bookie Bob telling stories, and even singing a few songs together until time to meet Sam Salt.

When it comes on midnight Spanish John goes out and lays for Sam, and gets a little valise off of Sam Salt. Then Spanish John comes back to the apartment and we open the valise and the twenty-five G's are there okay, and we cut this scratch three ways.

Then I tell Bookie Bob he is free to go on about his business, and good luck to him, at that, but Bookie Bob looks at me as if he is very much surprised, and hurt, and says to me like this:

'Well, gentlemen, thank you for your courtesy, but what about the scratch you owe me? What about these markers? Surely, gentlemen, you will pay your bookmaker?'

Well, of course we owe Bookie Bob these markers, all right, and of course a man must pay his bookmaker, no matter what, so I hand over my bit and Bookie Bob puts down something in a little note-book that he takes out of his kick.

Then Spanish John and Little Isadore hand over their dough, too, and Bookie Bob puts down something more in the little note-book.

'Now,' Bookie Bob says, 'I credit each of your accounts with these payments, but you gentlemen still owe me a matter of twenty-five G's over and above the twenty-five I credit you with, and I hope and trust you will make arrangements to settle this at once because,' he says, 'I do not care to extend such accommodations over any considerable period.'

'But,' I say, 'we do not have any more scratch after paying you the twenty-five G's on account.'

'Listen,' Bookie Bob says, dropping his voice down to a whisper, 'what about putting the snatch on my partner, Sam Salt, and I will wait over a couple of days with you and keep booking to you, and maybe you can pull yourselves out. But of course,' Bookie Bob whispers, 'I will be entitled to twenty-five per cent. of the snatch for putting the finger on Sam for you.'

But Spanish John and Little Isadore are sick and tired of Bookie Bob and will not listen to staying in the apartment any longer, because they say he is a jinx to them and they cannot beat him in any manner, shape or form. Furthermore, I am personally anxious to get away because something Bookie Bob says reminds me of something.

It reminds me that besides the scratch we owe him, we forget to take out six G's two-fifty for the party who puts the finger on Bookie Bob for us, and this is a very serious matter indeed, because anybody will tell you that failing to pay a finger is considered a very dirty trick. Furthermore, if it gets around that you fail to pay a finger, nobody else will ever finger for you.

So [Harry the Horse says] we quit the snatching business because there is no use continuing while this obligation is outstanding against us, and we go back to Brooklyn to earn enough scratch to pay our just debts.

We are paying off Bookie Bob's IOU a little at a time, because we do not wish to ever have anybody say we welsh on a bookmaker, and furthermore we are paying off the six G's two-fifty commission we owe our finger.

And while it is tough going, I am glad to say our honest effort is doing somebody a little good, because I see Bookie Bob's everloving wife the other night all dressed up in new clothes and looking very happy, indeed.

And while a guy is telling me she is looking so happy because she gets a large legacy from an uncle who dies in Switzerland, and is now independent of Bookie Bob, I only hope and trust [Harry the Horse says] that it never gets out that our finger in this case is nobody but Bookie Bob's ever-loving wife.

The Lily of St. Pierre

There are four of us sitting in Good Time Charley Bernstein's little joint in Forty-eighth Street one Tuesday morning about four o'clock, doing a bit of quartet singing, very low, so as not to disturb the copper on the beat outside, a very good guy by the name of Carrigan, who likes to get his rest at such an hour.

Good Time Charley's little joint is called the Crystal Room, although of course there is no crystal whatever in the room, but only twelve tables, and twelve hostesses, because Good Time Charley believes in his customers having plenty of social life.

So he has one hostess to a table, and if there are twelve different customers, which is very seldom, each customer has a hostess to talk with. And if there is only one customer, he has all twelve hostesses to gab with and buy drinks for, and no customer can ever go away claiming he is lonesome in Good Time Charley's.

Personally, I will not give you a nickel to talk with Good Time Charley's hostesses, one at a time or all together, because none of them are anything much to look at, and I figure they must all be pretty dumb or they will not be working as hostesses in Good Time Charley's little joint. I happen to speak of this to Good Time Charley, and he admits that I may be right, but he says it is very difficult to get any Peggy Joyces for twenty-five bobs per week.

Of course I never buy any drinks in Good Time Charley's for hostesses, or anybody else, and especially for myself, because I am a personal friend of Good Time Charley's, and he will not sell me any drinks even if I wish to buy any, which is unlikely, as Good Time Charley figures that anybody who buys drinks in his place is apt to drink these drinks, and Charley does not care to see any of his personal friends drinking drinks at his place. If one of his personal friends wishes to buy a drink, Charley always sends him to Jack Fogarty's little speak down the street, and in fact Charley will generally go with him.

So I only go to Good Time Charley's to talk with him, and to sing in quartet with him. There are very seldom any customers in Good Time Charley's until along about five o'clock in the morning after all the other places are closed, and then it is sometimes a very hot spot indeed, and it is no place to sing in quartet at such hours, because everybody around always wishes to join in, and it ruins the harmony. But just before five o'clock it is okay, as only the hostesses are there, and of course none of them dast to join in our singing, or Good Time Charley will run them plumb out of the joint.

If there is one thing I love to do more than anything else, it is to sing in quartet. I sing baritone, and I wish to say I sing a very fine baritone, at that. And what we are singing – this morning I am talking about – is a lot of songs such as 'Little White Lies,' and 'The Old Oaken Bucket,' and 'My Dad's Dinner Pail,' and 'Chloe,' and 'Melancholy Baby,' and I do not know what else, including 'Home, Sweet Home,' although we do not go so good on this because nobody remembers all the words, and half the time we are all just going ho-hum-hum-ho-hum-hum, like guys nearly always do when they are singing 'Home, Sweet Home.'

Also we sing 'I Can't Give You Anything but Love, Baby,'

which is a very fine song for quartet singing, especially when you have a guy singing a nice bass, such as Good Time Charley, who can come in on every line with a big bum-bum like this:

I can't give you anything but luh-huh-vuh,
  Bay-hay-bee!
    BUM-BUM!

I am the one who holds these last words, such as love, and baby, and you can hear my fine baritone very far indeed, especially when I give a little extra roll like bay-hay-ay-ay-BEE! Then when Good Time Charley comes in with his old bum-bum, it is worth going a long way to hear.

Well, naturally, we finally get around to torch songs, as guys who are singing in quartet are bound to do, especially at four o'clock in the morning, a torch song being a song which guys sing when they have the big burnt-up feeling inside themselves over a battle with their dolls.

When a guy has a battle with his doll, such as his sweetheart, or even his ever-loving wife, he certainly feels burnt up inside himself, and can scarcely think of anything much. In fact, I know guys who are carrying the torch to walk ten miles and never know they go an inch. It is surprising how much ground a guy can cover just walking around and about, wondering if his doll is out with some other guy, and everybody knows that at four o'clock in the morning the torch is hotter than at any other time of the day.

Good Time Charley, who is carrying a torch longer than anybody else on Broadway, which is nearly a year, or ever since his doll, Big Marge, gives him the wind for a rich Cuban, starts up a torch song by Tommy Lyman, which goes as follows, very, very slow, and sad:

Gee, but it's tough
When the gang's gone home.
Out on the corner
You stand alone.

Of course there is no spot in this song for Good Time Charley's bum-bum, but it gives me a great chance with my fine baritone, especially when I come to the line that says Gee, I wish I had my old gal back again.

I do not say I can make people bust out crying and give me money with this song like I see Tommy Lyman do in night clubs, but then Tommy is a professional singer, besides writing this song for himself, so naturally he figures to do a little better with it than me. But I wish to say it is nothing for me to make five or six of the hostesses in Good Time Charley's cry all over the joint when I hit this line about Gee, I wish I had my old gal back again, and making five or six hostesses out of twelve cry is a fair average anywhere, and especially Good Time Charley's hostesses.

Well, all of a sudden who comes popping into Good Time Charley's by way of the front door, looking here and there, and around and about, but Jack O'Hearts, and he no sooner pokes his snozzle into the joint than a guy by the name of Louie the Lug, who is singing a very fair tenor with us, jumps up and heads for the back door.

But just as he gets to the door, Jack O'Hearts outs with the old equalizer and goes whangity-whang-whang at Louie the Lug. As a general proposition, Jack O'Hearts is a fair kind of a shot, but all he does to Louie the Lug is to knock his right ear off. Then Louie gets the back door open and takes it on the lam through an area-way, but not before Jack O'Hearts gets one more crack at him, and it is this last crack which brings Louie down half an hour later on Broadway, where a copper finds him and sends him to the Polyclinic.

Personally, I do not see Louie's ear knocked off, because by the second shot I am out the front door, and on my way down Forty-eighth Street, but they tell me about it afterwards.

I never know Jack O'Hearts is even mad at Louie, and I am wondering why he takes these shots at him, but I do not ask any questions, because when a guy goes around asking questions in this town people may get the idea he is such a guy as wishes to find things out.

Then the next night I run into Jack O'Hearts in Bobby's chop-house, putting on the hot meat, and he asks me to sit down and eat with him, so I sit down and order a hamburger steak, with plenty of onions, and while I am sitting there waiting for my hamburger, Jack O'Hearts says to me like this:

'I suppose,' he says, 'I owe you guys an apology for busting up your quartet when I toss those slugs at Louie the Lug?'

'Well,' I say, 'some considers it a dirty trick at that, Jack, but I figure you have a good reason, although I am wondering what it is.'

'Louie the Lug is no good,' Jack says.

Well, of course I know this much already, and so does everybody else in town for that matter, but I cannot figure what it has to do with Jack shooting off ears in this town for such a reason, or by and by there will be very few people left with ears.

'Let me tell you about Louie the Lug,' Jack O'Hearts says. 'You will see at once that my only mistake is I do not get my shots an inch to the left. I do not know what is the matter with me lately.'

'Maybe you are letting go too quick,' I say, very sympathetic, because I know how it annoys him to blow easy shots.

'Maybe,' he says. 'Anyway, the light in Charley's dump is no good. It is only an accident I get Louie with the last shot, and it is very sloppy work all around. But now I tell you about Louie the Lug.'

It is back in 1924 [Jack O'Hearts says] that I go to St. Pierre for the first time to look after some business matters for John the Boss, rest his soul, who is at this time one of the largest operators in high-grade merchandise in the United States, especially when it comes to Scotch. Maybe you remember John the Boss, and the heat which develops around and about when he is scragged in Detroit? John the Boss is a very fine character, and it is a terrible blow to many citizens when he is scragged.

Now if you are never in St. Pierre, I wish to say you miss nothing much, because what is it but a little squirt of a burg sort of huddled up alongside some big rocks off Newfoundland, and very hard to get to, any way you go. Mostly you go there from Halifax by boat, though personally I go there in 1924 in John the Boss's schooner by the name of the *Maude*, in which we load a thousand cases of very nice merchandise for the Christmas trade.

The first time I see St. Pierre I will not give you eight cents for the whole layout, although of course it is very useful to parties in our line of business. It does not look like much, and it belongs to France, and nearly all the citizens speak French, because most of them are French, and it seems it is the custom of the French people to speak French no matter where they are, even away off up yonder among the fish.

Well, anyway, it is on this trip to St. Pierre in 1924 that I meet an old guy by the name of Doctor Armand Dorval, for what happens to me but I catch pneumonia, and it looks as if maybe I am a gone gosling, especially as there is no place in St. Pierre where a guy can have pneumonia with any comfort. But this Doctor Armand Dorval is a friend of John the Boss, and he takes me into his house and lets me be as sick there as I please, while he does his best to doctor me up.

Now this Doctor Armand Dorval is an old Frenchman with whiskers, and he has a little granddaughter by the name of Lily, who is maybe twelve years old at the time I am talking about, with her hair hanging down her back in two braids. It seems her papa, who is Doctor Armand's son, goes out one day looking for cod on the Grand Banks when Lily is nothing but a baby, and never comes back, and then her mamma dies, so old Doc raises up Lily and is very fond of her indeed.

They live alone in the house where I am sick with this pneumonia, and it is a nice, quiet little house and very old-fashioned, with a good view of the fishing boats, if you care for fishing boats. In fact, it is the quietest place I am ever in in my life, and the only place I ever know any real peace. A big fat old doll who does not talk English comes in every day to look after things for Doctor Armand and Lily, because it seems Lily is not old enough to keep house as yet, although she makes quite a nurse for me.

Lily talks English very good, and she is always bringing me things, and sitting by my bed and chewing the rag with me about this and that, and sometimes she reads to me out of a book which is called *Alice in Wonderland*, and which is nothing but a pack of lies, but very interesting in spots. Furthermore, Lily has a big, blonde, dumb-looking doll by the name of Yvonne, which she makes me hold while she is reading to me, and I am very glad indeed that the *Maude* goes on back to the United States and there is no danger of any of the guys walking in on me while I am holding this doll, or they will think I blow my topper.

Finally, when I am able to sit up around the house of an evening I play checkers with Lily, while old Doctor Armand Dorval sits back in a rocking-chair, smoking a pipe and watching us, and sometimes I sing for her. I wish to say I sing a first-class tenor, and when I am in the war business in France with the Seventy-seventh Division I am always in great demand for singing a quartet. So I sing such songs to Lily as 'There's a Long, Long Trail,' and 'Mademoiselle from Armentières,' although of course when it comes to certain spots in this song I just go dum-dum-dee-dum and do not say the words right out.

By and by Lily gets to singing with me, and we sound very good together, especially when we sing the 'Long, Long Trail,' which Lily likes very much, and even old Doctor Armand joins in now and then, although his voice is very terrible. Anyway, Lily and me and Doctor Armand become very good pals indeed, and what is more I meet up with other citizens of St. Pierre and become friends with them, and they are by no means bad people to know, and it is certainly nice to be able to walk up and down without being afraid every other guy you meet is going to chuck a slug at you, or a copper put the old sleeve on you and say that they wish to see you at headquarters.

Finally I get rid of this pneumonia and take the boat to Halifax, and I am greatly surprised to find that Doctor Armand and Lily are very sorry to see me go, because never before in my life do I leave a place where anybody is sorry to see me go.

But Doctor Armand seems very sad and shakes me by the hand over and over again, and what does Lily do but bust out crying, and the first thing I know I am feeling sad myself and wishing that I am not going. So I promise Doctor Armand I will come back some day to see him, and then Lily hauls off and gives me a big kiss right in the smush and this astonishes me so much that it is half an hour afterwards before I think to wipe it off.

Well, for the next few months I find myself pretty busy back in New York, what with one thing and another, and I do not have time to think much of Doctor Armand Dorval and Lily, and St. Pierre, but it comes along the summer of 1925, and I am all tired out from getting a slug in my chest in the run-in with Jerk Donovan's mob in Jersey, for I am now in beer and have no more truck with the boats.

But I get to thinking of St. Pierre and the quiet little house of Doctor Armand Dorval again, and how peaceful it is up there, and nothing will do but I must pop off to Halifax, and pretty soon I am in St. Pierre once more. I take a raft of things for Lily with me, such as dolls, and handkerchiefs, and perfume, and a phonograph, and also a set of razors for Doctor Armand, although afterwards I am sorry I take these razors because I remember the old Doc does not shave and may take them as a hint I do not care for his whiskers. But as it turns out the Doc finds them very useful in operations, so the razors are a nice gift after all.

Well, I spend two peaceful weeks there again, walking up and down in the daytime and playing checkers and singing with Lily in the evening, and it is tough tearing myself away, especially as Doctor Armand Dorval looks very sad again and Lily busts out crying, louder than before. So nearly every year after this I can hardly wait until I can get to St. Pierre for a vacation, and Doctor Armand Dorval's house is like my home, only more peaceful.

Now in the summer of 1928 I am in Halifax on my way to St. Pierre, when I run across Louie the Lug, and it seems Louie is a lammister out of Detroit on account of some job or other, and is broke, and does not know which way to turn. Personally, I always figure Louie a petty-larceny kind of guy, with no more moxie than a canary bird, but he always dresses well, and always has a fair line of guff, and some guys stand for him. Anyway, here he is in trouble, so what happens but I take him with me to St. Pierre, figuring he can lay dead there until things blow over.

Well, Lily and old Doctor Armand Dorval are certainly glad to see me, and I am just as glad to see them, especially Lily, for she is now maybe sixteen years old and as pretty a doll as ever steps in shoe leather, what with her long black hair, and her big black eyes, and a million dollars' worth of personality. Furthermore, by this time she swings a very mean skillet, indeed, and gets me up some very tasty fodder out of fish and one thing and another.

But somehow things are not like they used to be at St. Pierre with this guy Louie the Lug around, because he does not care for the place whatever, and goes roaming about very restless, and making cracks about the citizens, and especially the dolls, until one night I am compelled to tell him to keep his trap closed, although at that the dolls in St. Pierre, outside of Lily, are no such lookers as will get Ziegfeld heated up.

But even in the time when St. Pierre is headquarters for many citizens of the United States who are in the business of handling merchandise out of there, it is always sort of underhand that such citizens will never have any truck with the dolls at St. Pierre. This is partly because the dolls at St. Pierre never give the citizens of the United States a tumble, but more because we do not wish to get in any trouble around there, and if there is anything apt to cause trouble it is dolls.

Now I suppose if I have any brains I will see that Louie is playing the warm for Lily, but I never think of Lily as anything but a little doll with her hair in braids, and certainly not a doll such as a guy will start pitching to, especially a guy who calls himself one of the mob.

I notice Louie is always talking to Lily when he gets a chance, and sometimes he goes walking up and down with her, but I see nothing in this, because after all any guy is apt to get lonesome at St. Pierre and go walking up and down with anybody, even a little young doll. In fact, I never see Louie do anything that strikes me as out of line, except he tries to cut in on the singing between Lily and me, until I tell him one tenor at a time is enough in any singing combination. Personally, I consider Louie the Lug's tenor very flat, indeed.

Well, it comes time for me to go away, and I take Louie with me, because I do not wish him hanging around St. Pierre alone, especially as old Doctor Armand Dorval does not seem to care for him whatever, and while Lily seems as sad as ever to see me go I notice that for the first time she does not kiss me good-bye. But I figure this is fair enough, as she is now quite a young lady, and the chances are a little particular about who she kisses.

I leave Louie in Halifax and give him enough dough to go on to Denver, which is where he says he wishes to go, and I never see him again until the other night in Good Time Charley's. But almost a year later, when I happen to be in Montreal, I hear of him. I am standing in the lobby of the Mount Royal Hotel thinking of not much, when a guy by the name of Bob the Bookie, who is a hustler around the race-tracks, gets to talking to me and mentions Louie's name. It brings back to me a memory of my last trip to St. Pierre, and I get to thinking that this is the longest stretch I ever go in several years without a visit there and of the different things that keep me from going.

I am not paying much attention to what Bob says, because he is putting the blast on Louie for running away from an ever-loving wife and a couple of kids in Cleveland several years before, which is something I do not know about Louie, at that. Then I hear Bob saying like this:

'He is an awful rat any way you take him. Why, when he hops out of here two weeks ago, he leaves a little doll he brings with him from St. Pierre dying in a hospital without a nickel to her name. It is a sin and a shame.'

'Wait a minute, Bob,' I say, waking up all of a sudden. 'Do you say a doll from St. Pierre? What-for looking kind of a doll, Bob?' I say.

'Why,' Bob says, 'she is black-haired, and very young, and he calls her Lily, or some such. He is knocking around Canada with her for quite a spell. She strikes me as a t. b., but Louie's dolls always look this way after he has them a while. I judge,' Bob says, 'that Louie does not feed them any too good.'

Well, it is Lily Dorval, all right, but never do I see such a change in anybody as there is in the poor little doll I find lying on a bed in a charity ward in a Montreal hospital. She does not look to weigh more than fifty pounds, and her black eyes are sunk away back in her head, and she is in tough shape generally. But she knows me right off the bat and tries to smile at me.

I am in the money very good at this time, and I have Lily moved into a private room, and get her all the nurses the law allows, and the best croakers in Montreal, and flowers, and one thing and another, but one of the medicos tells me it is even money she will not last three weeks, and 7 to 5 she does not go a month. Finally Lily tells me what happens, which is the same thing that happens to a million dolls before and will happen to a million dolls again. Louie never leaves Halifax, but cons her into coming over there to him, and she goes because she loves him, for this is the way dolls are, and personally I will never have them any other way.

'But,' Lily whispers to me, 'the bad, bad thing I do is to tell poor old Grandfather I am going to meet you, Jack O'Hearts, and marry you, because I know he does not like Louie and will never allow me to go to him. But he loves you, Jack O'Hearts, and he is so pleased in thinking you are to be his son. It is wrong to tell Grandfather this story, and wrong to use your name, and to keep writing him all this time making him think I am your wife, and with you, but I love Louie, and I wish Grandfather to be happy because he is very, very old. Do you understand, Jack O'Hearts?'

Now of course all this is very surprising news to me, indeed, and in fact I am quite flabbergasted, and as for understanding it, all I understand is she gets a rotten deal from Louie the Lug and that old Doctor Armand Dorval is going to be all busted up if he hears what really happens. And thinking about this nice old man, and thinking of how the only place I ever know peace and quiet is now ruined, I am very angry with Louie the Lug.

But this is something to be taken up later, so I dismiss him from my mind, and go out and get me a marriage licence and a priest, and have this priest marry me to Lily Dorval just two days before she looks up at me for the last time, and smiles a little smile, and then closes her eyes for good and all. I wish to say, however, that up to this time I have no more idea of getting myself a wife than I have of jumping out the window, which is practically no idea at all.

I take her body back to St. Pierre myself in person, and we bury her in a little cemetery there, with a big fog around and about, and the siren moaning away very sad, and old Doctor Armand Dorval whispers to me like this:

'You will please to sing the song about the long trail, Jack O' Hearts.'

So I stand there in the fog, the chances are looking like a big sap, and I sing as follows:

'There's a long, long trail a-winding
 Into the land of my dreams,
Where the nightingale is singing,
 And the white moon beams.'

But I can get no farther than this, for something comes up in my throat, and I sit down by the grave of Mrs. Jack O'Hearts, who was Lily Dorval, and for the first time I remember I bust out crying.

So [he says] this is why I say Louie the Lug is no good.

Well, I am sitting there thinking that Jack O'Hearts is right about Louie, at that, when in comes Jack's chauffeur, a guy by the name of Fingers, and he steps up to Jack and says, very low:

'Louie dies half an hour ago at the Polyclinic.'

'What does he say before he goes?' Jack asks.

'Not a peep,' Fingers says.

'Well,' Jack O'Hearts says, 'it is sloppy work, at that. I ought to get him the first crack. But maybe he had a chance to think a little of Lily Dorval.'

Then he turns to me and says like this:

'You guys need not feel bad about losing your tenor, because,' he says, 'I will be glad to fill in for him at all times.'

Personally I do not think Jack's tenor is as good as Louie the Lug's especially when it comes to hitting the very high notes in such songs as Sweet Adeline, because he does not hold them long enough to let Good Time Charley in with his bum-bum.

But of course this does not go if Jack O'Hearts hears it, as I am never sure he does not clip Louie the Lug just to get a place in our quartet, at that.

Hold 'em, Yale!

What I am doing in New Haven on the day of a very large football game between the Harvards and the Yales is something which calls for quite a little explanation, because I am not such a guy as you will expect to find in New Haven at any time, and especially on the day of a large football game.

But there I am, and the reason I am there goes back to a Friday night when I am sitting in Mindy's restaurant on Broadway thinking of very little except how I can get hold of a few potatoes to take care of the old overhead. And while I am sitting there, who comes in but Sam the Gonoph, who is a ticket speculator by trade, and who seems to be looking all around and about.

Well, Sam the Gonoph gets to talking to me, and it turns out that he is looking for a guy by the name of Gigolo Georgie, who is called Gigolo Georgie because he is always hanging around night clubs wearing a little moustache and white spats, and dancing with old dolls. In fact, Gigolo Georgie is nothing but a gentleman bum, and I am surprised that Sam the Gonoph is looking for him.

But it seems that the reason Sam the Gonoph wishes to find Gigolo Georgie is to give him a good punch in the snoot, because it seems that Gigolo Georgie promotes Sam for several duckets to the large football game between the Harvards and the Yales to sell on commission, and never kicks back anything whatever to Sam. Naturally Sam considers Gigolo Georgie nothing but a rascal for doing such a thing to him, and Sam says he will find Gigolo Georgie and give him a going-over if it is the last act of his life.

Well, then, Sam explains to me that he has quite a few nice duckets for the large football game between the Harvards and the Yales and that he is taking a crew of guys with him to New Haven the next day to hustle these duckets, and what about me going along and helping to hustle these duckets and making a few bobs for myself, which is an invitation that sounds very pleasant to me, indeed.

Now of course it is very difficult for anybody to get nice duckets to a large football game between the Harvards and the Yales unless they are personally college guys, and Sam the Gonoph is by no means a college guy. In fact, the nearest Sam ever comes to a college is once when he is passing through the yard belonging to the Princetons, but Sam is on the fly at the time as a gendarme is after him, so he does not really see much of the college.

But every college guy is entitled to duckets to a large football game with which his college is connected, and it is really surprising how many college guys do not care to see large football games even after they get their duckets, especially if a ticket spec such as Sam the Gonoph comes along offering them a few bobs more than the duckets are worth. I suppose this is because a college guy figures he can see a large football game when he is old, while many things are taking place around and about that it is necessary for him to see while he is young enough to really enjoy them, such as the Follies.

Anyway, many college guys are always willing to listen to reason when Sam the Gonoph comes around offering to buy their duckets, and then Sam takes these duckets and sells them to customers for maybe ten times the price the duckets call for, and in this way Sam does very good for himself.

I know Sam the Gonoph for maybe twenty years, and always he is speculating in duckets of one kind and another. Sometimes it is duckets for the world's series, and sometimes for big fights, and sometimes it is duckets for nothing but lawn-tennis games, although why anybody wishes to see such a thing as lawn tennis is always a very great mystery to Sam the Gonoph and everybody else.

But in all those years I see Sam dodging around under the feet of the crowds at these large events, or running through the special trains offering to buy or sell duckets, I never hear of Sam personally attending any of these events except maybe a baseball game, or a fight, for Sam has practically no interest in anything but a little profit on his duckets.

He is a short, chunky, black-looking guy with a big beezer, and he is always sweating even on a cold day, and he comes from down around Essex Street, on the lower East Side. Moreover, Sam the Gonoph's crew generally comes from the lower East Side, too, for as Sam goes along he makes plenty of potatoes for himself and branches out quite some, and has a lot of assistants hustling duckets around these different events.

When Sam is younger the cops consider him hard to get along with, and in fact his monicker, the Gonoph, comes from his young days down on the lower East Side, and I hear it is Yiddish for thief, but of course as Sam gets older and starts gathering plenty of potatoes, he will not think of stealing anything. At least not much, and especially if it is anything that is nailed down.

Well, anyway, I meet Sam the Gonoph and his crew at the information desk in Grand Central the next morning, and this is how I come to be in New Haven on the day of the large football game between the Harvards and the Yales.

For such a game as this, Sam has all his best hustlers, including such as Jew Louie, Nubbsy Taylor, Benny South Street and old Liverlips, and to look at these parties you will never suspect that they are top-notch ducket hustlers. The best you will figure them is a lot of guys who are not to be met up with in a dark alley, but then ducket-hustling is a rough-and-tumble dodge and it will scarcely be good policy to hire female impersonators.

Now while we are hustling these duckets out around the main gates of the Yale Bowl I notice a very beautiful little doll of maybe sixteen or seventeen standing around watching the crowd, and I can see she is waiting for somebody, as many dolls often do at football games. But I can also see that this little doll is very much worried as the crowd keeps going in, and it is getting on toward game time. In fact, by and by I can see this little doll has tears in her eyes and if there is anything I hate to see it is tears in a doll's eyes.

So finally I go over to her, and I say as follows: 'What is eating you, little Miss?'

'Oh,' she says, 'I am waiting for Elliot. He is to come up from New York and meet me here to take me to the game, but he is not here yet, and I am afraid something happens to him. Furthermore,' she says, the tears in her eyes getting very large, indeed, 'I am afraid I will miss the game because he has my ticket.'

'Why,' I say, 'this is a very simple proposition. I will sell you a choice ducket for only a sawbuck, which is ten dollars in your language, and you are getting such a bargain only because the game is about to begin, and the market is going down.'

'But,' she says, 'I do not have ten dollars. In fact, I have only fifty cents left in my purse, and this is worrying me very much, for what will I do if Elliot does not meet me? You see,' she says, 'I come from Miss Peevy's school at Worcester, and I only have enough money to pay my railroad fare here, and of course I cannot ask Miss Peevy for any money as I do not wish her to know I am going away.'

Well, naturally all this is commencing to sound to me like a hard-luck story such as any doll is apt to tell, so I go on about my business because I figure she will next be trying to put the lug on me for a ducket, or maybe for her railroad fare back to Worcester, although generally dolls with hard-luck stories live in San Francisco.

She keeps on standing there, and I notice she is now crying more than somewhat, and I get to thinking to myself that she is about as cute a little doll as I ever see, although too young for anybody to be bothering much about. Furthermore, I get to thinking that maybe she is on the level, at that, with her story.

Well, by this time the crowd is nearly all in the Bowl, and only a few parties such as coppers and hustlers of one kind and another are left standing outside, and there is much cheering going on inside, when Sam the Gonoph comes up looking very much disgusted, and speaks as follows:

'What do you think?' Sam says. 'I am left with seven duckets on my hands, and these guys around here will not pay as much as face value for them, and they stand me better than three bucks over that. Well,' Sam says, 'I am certainly not going to let them go for less than they call for if I have to eat them. What do you guys say we use these duckets ourselves and go in and see the game? Personally,' Sam says, 'I often wish to see one of these large football games just to find out what makes suckers willing to pay so much for duckets.'

Well, this seems to strike one and all, including myself, as a great idea, because none of the rest of us ever see a large football game either, so we start for the gate, and as we pass the little doll who is still crying, I say to Sam the Gonoph like this:

'Listen, Sam,' I say, 'you have seven duckets, and we are only six, and here is a little doll who is stood up by her guy, and has no ducket, and no potatoes to buy one with, so what about taking her with us?'

Well, this is all right with Sam the Gonoph, and none of the others object, so I step up to the little doll and invite her to go with us, and right away she stops crying and begins smiling, and saying we are very kind indeed. She gives Sam the Gonoph an extra big smile, and right away Sam is saying she is very cute, indeed, and then she gives old Liverlips an even bigger smile, and what is more she takes old Liverlips by the arm and walks with him, and old Liverlips is not only very much astonished, but very much pleased. In fact, old Liverlips begins stepping out very spry, and Liverlips is not such a guy as cares to have any part of dolls, young or old.

But while walking with old Liverlips, the little doll talks very friendly to Jew Louie and to Nubbsy Taylor and Benny South Street, and even to me, and by and by you will think to see us that we are all her uncles, although of course if this little doll really knows who she is with, the chances are she will start chucking faints one after the other.

Anybody can see that she has very little experience in this wicked old world, and in fact is somewhat rattleheaded, because she gabs away very freely about her personal business. In fact, before we are in the Bowl she lets it out that she runs away from Miss Peevy's school to elope with this Elliot, and she says the idea is they are to be married in Hartford after the game. In fact, she says Elliot wishes to go to Hartford and be married before the game.

'But,' she says, 'my brother John is playing substitute with the Yales to-day, and I cannot think of getting married to anybody before I see him play, although I am much in love with Elliot. He is a wonderful dancer,' she says, 'and very romantic. I meet him in Atlantic City last summer. Now we are eloping,' she says, 'because my father does not care for Elliot whatever. In fact, my father hates Elliot, although he only sees him once, and it is because he hates Elliot so that my father sends me to Miss Peevy's school in Worcester. She is an old pill. Do you not think my father is unreasonable?' she says.

Well, of course none of us have any ideas on such propositions as this, although old Liverlips tells the little doll he is with her right or wrong, and pretty soon we are inside the Bowl and sitting in seats as good as any in the joint. It seems we are on the Harvards' side of the field, although of course I will never know this if the little doll does not mention it.

She seems to know everything about this football business, and as soon as we sit down she tries to point out her brother playing substitute for the Yales, saying he is the fifth guy from the end among a bunch of guys sitting on a bench on the other side of the field all wrapped in blankets. But we cannot make much of him from where we sit, and anyway it does not look to me as if he has much of a job.

It seems we are right in the middle of all the Harvards and they are making an awful racket, what with yelling, and singing, and one thing and another, because it seems the game is going on when we get in, and that the Harvards are shoving the Yales around more than somewhat. So our little doll lets everybody know she is in favour of the Yales by yelling, 'Hold 'em, Yale!'

Personally, I cannot tell which are the Harvards and which are the Yales at first, and Sam the Gonoph and the others are as dumb as I am, but she explains the Harvards are wearing the red shirts and the Yales the blue shirts, and by and by we are yelling for the Yales to hold 'em, too, although of course it is only on account of our little doll wishing the Yales to hold 'em, and not because any of us care one way or the other.

Well, it seems that the idea of a lot of guys and a little doll getting right among them and yelling for the Yales to hold 'em is very repulsive to the Harvards around us, although any of them must admit it is very good advice to the Yales, at that, and some of them start making cracks of one kind and another, especially at our little doll. The chances are they are very jealous because she is out-yelling them, because I will say one thing for our little doll, she can yell about as loud as anybody I ever hear, male or female.

A couple of Harvards sitting in front of old Liverlips are imitat-ing our little doll's voice, and making guys around them laugh very heartily, but all of a sudden these parties leave their seats and go away in great haste, their faces very pale, indeed, and I figure maybe they are both taken sick at the same moment, but afterwards I learn that Liverlips takes a big shiv out of his pocket and opens it and tells them very confidentially that he is going to carve their ears off.

Naturally, I do not blame the Harvards for going away in great haste, for Liverlips is such a looking guy as you will figure to take great delight in carving off ears. Furthermore, Nubbsy Taylor and Benny South Street and Jew Louie and even Sam the Gonoph commence exchanging such glances with other Harvards around us who are making cracks at our little doll that presently there is almost a dead silence in our neighbourhood, except for our little doll yelling, 'Hold 'em, Yale!' You see by this time we are all very fond of our little doll because she is so cute looking and has so much zing in her, and we do not wish anybody making cracks at her or at us either, and especially at us.

In fact, we are so fond of her that when she happens to mention that she is a little chilly, Jew Louie and Nubbsy Taylor slip around among the Harvards and come back with four steamer rugs, six mufflers, two pairs of gloves, and a thermos bottle full of hot coffee for her, and Jew Louie says if she wishes a mink coat to just say the word. But she already has a mink coat. Furthermore, Jew Louie brings her a big bunch of red flowers that he finds on a doll with one of the Harvards, and he is much disappointed when she says it is the wrong colour for her.

Well, finally the game is over, and I do not remember much about it, although afterwards I hear that our little doll's brother John plays substitute for the Yales very good. But it seems that the Harvards win, and our little doll is very sad indeed about this, and is sitting there looking out over the field, which is now covered with guys dancing around as if they all suddenly go daffy, and it seems they are all Harvards, because there is really no reason for the Yales to do any dancing.

All of a sudden our little doll looks toward one end of the field, and says as follows:

'Oh, they are going to take our goal posts!'

Sure enough, a lot of Harvards are gathering around the posts at this end of the field, and are pulling and hauling at the posts, which seem to be very stout posts, indeed. Personally, I will not give you eight cents for these posts, but afterwards one of the Yales tells me that when a football team wins a game it is considered the proper caper for this team's boosters to grab the other guys' goal posts. But he is not able to tell me what good the posts are after they get them, and this is one thing that will always be a mystery to me.

Anyway, while we are watching the goings-on around the goal posts, our little doll says come on and jumps up and runs down an aisle and out on to the field, and into the crowd around the goal posts, so naturally we follow her. Somehow she manages to wiggle through the crowd of Harvards around the posts, and the next thing anybody knows she shins up one of the posts faster than you can say scat, and pretty soon is roosting out on the cross-bar between the posts like a chipmunk.

Afterwards she explains that her idea is the Harvards will not be ungentlemanly enough to pull down the goal posts with a lady roosting on them, but it seems these Harvards are no gentlemen, and keep on pulling, and the posts commence to teeter, and our little doll is teetering with them, although of course she is in no danger if she falls because she is sure to fall on the Harvards' noggins, and the way I look at it, the noggin of anybody who will be found giving any time to pulling down goal posts is apt to be soft enough to break a very long fall.

Now Sam the Gonoph and old Liverlips and Nubbsy Taylor

and Benny South Street and Jew Louie and I reach the crowd around the goal posts at about the same time, and our little doll sees us from her roost and yells to us as follows:

'Do not let them take our posts!'

Well, about this time one of the Harvards who seems to be about nine feet high reaches over six other guys and hits me on the chin and knocks me so far that when I pick myself up I am pretty well out of the way of everybody and have a chance to see what is going on.

Afterwards somebody tells me that the guy probably thinks I am one of the Yales coming to the rescue of the goal posts, but I wish to say I will always have a very low opinion of college guys, because I remember two other guys punch me as I am going through the air, unable to defend myself.

Now Sam the Gonoph and Nubbsy Taylor and Jew Louie and Benny South Street and old Liverlips somehow manage to ease their way through the crowd until they are under the goal posts, and our little doll is much pleased to see them, because the Harvards are now making the posts teeter more than somewhat with their pulling, and it looks as if the posts will go any minute.

Of course Sam the Gonoph does not wish any trouble with these parties, and he tries to speak nicely to the guys who are pulling at the posts, saying as follows:

'Listen,' Sam says, 'the little doll up there does not wish you to take these posts.'

Well, maybe they do not hear Sam's words in the confusion, or if they do hear them they do not wish to pay any attention to them, for one of the Harvards mashes Sam's derby hat down over his eyes, and another smacks old Liverlips on the left ear, while Jew Louie and Nubbsy Taylor and Benny South Street are shoved around quite some.

'All right,' Sam the Gonoph says, as soon as he can pull his hat off his eyes, 'all right, gentlemen, if you wish to play this way. Now, boys, let them have it!'

So Sam the Gonoph and Nubbsy Taylor and Jew Louie and Benny South Street and old Liverlips begin letting them have it, and what they let them have it with is not only their dukes, but with the good old difference in their dukes, because these guys are by no means suckers when it comes to a battle, and they all carry something in their pockets to put in their dukes in case of a fight, such as a dollar's worth of nickels rolled up tight.

Furthermore, they are using the old leather, kicking guys in the stomach when they are not able to hit them on the chin, and Liverlips is also using his noodle to good advantage, grabbing guys by their coat lapels and yanking them into him so he can butt them between the eyes with his noggin, and I wish to say that old Liverlips' noggin is a very dangerous weapon at all times.

Well, the ground around them is soon covered with Harvards, and it seems that some Yales are also mixed up with them, being Yales who think Sam the Gonoph and his guys are other Yales defending the goal posts, and wishing to help out. But of course Sam the Gonoph and his guys cannot tell the Yales from the Harvards, and do not have time to ask which is which, so they are just letting everybody have it who comes along. And while all this is going on our little doll is sitting up on the crossbar and yelling plenty of encouragement to Sam and his guys.

Now it turns out that these Harvards are by no means soft touches in a scrabble such as this, and as fast as they are flattened they get up and keep belting away, and while the old experience is running for Sam the Gonoph and Jew Louie and Nubbsy Taylor and Benny South Street and old Liverlips early in the fight, the Harvards have youth in their favour.

Pretty soon the Harvards are knocking down Sam the Gonoph, then they start knocking down Nubbsy Taylor, and by and by they are knocking down Benny South Street and Jew Louie and Liverlips, and it is so much fun that the Harvards forget all about the goal posts. Of course as fast as Sam the Gonoph and his guys are knocked down they also get up, but the Harvards are too many for them, and they are getting an awful shellacking when the nine-foot guy who flattens me, and who is knocking down Sam the Gonoph so often he is becoming a great nuisance to Sam, sings out:

'Listen,' he says, 'these are game guys, even if they do go to Yale. Let us cease knocking them down,' he says, 'and give them a cheer.'

So the Harvards knock down Sam the Gonoph and Nubbsy Taylor and Jew Louie and Benny South Street and old Liverlips just once more and then all the Harvards put their heads together and say rah-rah-rah, very loud, and go away, leaving the goal posts still standing, with our little doll still roosting on the cross-bar, although afterwards I hear some Harvards who are not in the fight get the posts at the other end of the field and sneak away with them. But I always claim these posts do not count.

Well, sitting there on the ground because he is too tired to get up from the last knockdown, and holding one hand to his right eye, which is closed tight, Sam the Gonoph is by no means a well guy, and all around and about him is much suffering among his crew. But our little doll is hopping up and down chattering like a jaybird and running between old Liverlips, who is stretched out against one goal post, and Nubbsy Taylor, who is leaning up against the other, and she is trying to mop the blood off their kissers with a handkerchief the size of a postage stamp.

Benny South Street is laying across Jew Louie and both are still snoring from the last knockdown, and the Bowl is now pretty much deserted except for the newspaper scribes away up in the press box, who do not seem to realize that the Battle of the Century just comes off in front of them. It is coming on dark, when all of a sudden a guy pops up out of the dusk wearing white spats and an overcoat with a fur collar, and he rushes up to our little doll.

'Clarice,' he says, 'I am looking for you high and low. My train is stalled for hours behind a wreck the other side of Bridgeport, and I get here just after the game is over. But,' he says, 'I figure you will be waiting somewhere for me. Let us hurry on to Hartford, darling,' he says.

Well, when he hears this voice, Sam the Gonoph opens his good eye wide and takes a peek at the guy. Then all of a sudden Sam jumps up and wobbles over to the guy and hits him a smack between the eyes. Sam is wobbling because his legs are not so good from the shellacking he takes off the Harvards, and furthermore he is away off in his punching as the guy only goes to his knees and comes right up standing again as our little doll lets out a screech and speaks as follows:

'Oo-oo!' she says. 'Do not hit Elliot! He is not after our goal posts!'

'Elliot?' Sam the Gonoph says. 'This is no Elliot. This is nobody but Gigolo Georgie. I can tell him by his white spats,' Sam says, 'and I am now going to get even for the pasting I take from the Harvards.'

Then he nails the guy again and this time he seems to have a little more on his punch, for the guy goes down and Sam the Gonoph gives him the leather very good, although our little doll is still screeching, and begging Sam not to hurt Elliot. But of course the rest of us know it is not Elliot, no matter what he may tell her, but only Gigolo Georgie.

Well, he rest of us figure we may as well take a little something out of Georgie's hide, too, but as we start for him he gives a quick wiggle and hops to his feet and tears across the field, and the last we see of him is his white spats flying through one of the portals.

Now a couple of other guys come up out of the dusk, and one of them is a tall, fine-looking guy with a white moustache and anybody can see that he is somebody, and what happens but our little doll runs right into his arms and kisses him on the white moustache and calls him daddy and starts to cry more than somewhat, so I can see we lose our little doll then and there. And now the guy with the white moustache walks up to Sam the Gonoph and sticks out his duke and says as follows:

'Sir,' he says, 'permit me the honour of shaking the hand which does me the very signal service of chastising the scoundrel who just escapes from the field. And,' he says, 'permit me to introduce myself to you. I am J. Hildreth Van Cleve, president of the Van Cleve Trust. I am notified early to-day by Miss Peevy of my daughter's sudden departure from school, and we learn she purchases a ticket for New Haven. I at once suspect this fellow has something to do with it. Fortunately,' he says, 'I have these private detectives here keeping tab on him for some time, knowing my child's schoolgirl infatuation for him, so we easily trail him here. We are on the train with him, and arrive in time for your last little scene with him. Sir,' he says, 'again I thank you.'

'I know who you are, Mr. Van Cleve,' Sam the Gonoph says. 'You are the Van Cleve who is down to his last forty million. But,' he says, 'do not thank me for putting the slug on Gigolo Georgie. He is a bum in spades, and I am only sorry he fools your nice little kid even for a minute, although,' Sam says, 'I figure she must be dumber than she looks to be fooled by such a guy as Gigolo Georgie.'

'I hate him,' the little doll says. 'I hate him because he is a coward. He does not stand up and fight when he is hit like you and Liverlips and the others. I never wish to see him again.'

'Do not worry,' Sam the Gonoph says. 'I will be too close to Gigolo Georgie as soon as I recover from my wounds for him to stay in this part of the country.'

Well, I do not see Sam the Gonoph or Nubbsy Taylor or Benny South Street or Jew Louie or Liverlips for nearly a year after this, and then it comes on fall again and one day I get to thinking that here it is Friday and the next day the Harvards are playing the Yales a large football game in Boston.

I figure it is a great chance for me to join up with Sam the Gonoph again to hustle duckets for him for this game, and I know Sam will be leaving along about midnight with his crew. So I go over to the Grand Central station at such a time, and sure enough he comes along by and by, busting through the crowd in the station with Nubbsy Taylor and Benny South Street and Jew Louie and old Liverlips at his heels, and they seem very much excited.

'Well, Sam,' I say, as I hurry along with them, 'here I am ready to hustle duckets for you again, and I hope and trust we do a nice business.'

'Duckets!' Sam the Gonoph says. 'We are not hustling duckets for this game, although you can go with us, and welcome. We are going to Boston,' he says, 'to root for the Yales to kick hell out of the Harvards and we are going as the personal guests of Miss Clarice Van Cleve and her old man.'

'Hold 'em, Yale!' old Liverlips says, as he pushes me to one side and the whole bunch goes trotting through the gate to catch their train, and I then notice they are all wearing blue feathers in their hats with a little white Y on these feathers such as college guys always wear at football games, and that moreover Sam the Gonoph is carrying a Yale pennant.

Earthquake

Personally, I do not care for coppers, but I believe in being courteous to them at all times, so when Johnny Brannigan comes into Mindy's restaurant one Friday evening and sits down in the same booth with me, because there are no other vacant seats in the joint, I give him a huge hello.

Furthermore, I offer him a cigarette and say how pleased I am to see how well he is looking, although as a matter of fact Johnny Brannigan looks very terrible, what with big black circles under his eyes and his face thinner than somewhat.

In fact, Johnny Brannigan looks as if he is sick, and I am secretly hoping that it is something fatal, because the way I figure it there are a great many coppers in this world, and a few less may be a good thing for one and all concerned.

But naturally I do not mention this hope to Johnny Brannigan, as Johnny Brannigan belongs to what is called the gunman squad and is known to carry a black-jack in his pants pocket and furthermore he is known to boff guys on their noggins with this jack if they get too fresh with him, and for all I know Johnny Brannigan may consider such a hope about his health very fresh indeed.

Now the last time I see Johnny Brannigan before this is in Good Time Charley Bernstein's little joint in Forty-eighth Street with three other coppers, and what Johnny is there for is to put the arm on a guy by the name of Earthquake, who is called Earthquake because he is so fond of shaking things up.

In fact, at the time I am speaking of, Earthquake has this whole town shaken up, what with shooting and stabbing and robbing different citizens, and otherwise misconducting himself, and the law wishes to place Earthquake in the electric chair, as he is considered a great knock to the community.

Now the only reason Brannigan does not put the arm on Earthquake at this time is because Earthquake picks up one of Good Time Charley Bernstein's tables and kisses Johnny Brannigan with same, and furthermore, Earthquake outs with the old equalizer and starts blasting away at the coppers who are with Johnny Brannigan, and he keeps them so busy dodging slugs that they do not have any leisure to put the arm on him, and the next thing anybody knows, Earthquake takes it on the lam out of there.

Well, personally, I also take it on the lam myself, as I do not wish to be around when Johnny Brannigan comes to, as I figure Johnny may be somewhat bewildered and will start boffing people over the noggin with his jack thinking they are all Earthquake, no matter who they are, and I do not see Johnny again until this evening in Mindy's.

But in the meantime I hear rumours that Johnny Brannigan is out of town looking for Earthquake, because it seems that while misconducting himself Earthquake severely injures a copper by the name of Mulcahy. In fact, it seems that Earthquake injures him so severely that Mulcahy hauls off and dies, and if there is one thing that is against the law in this town it is injuring a copper in such a manner. In fact, it is apt to cause great indignation among other coppers.

It is considered very illegal to severely injure any citizen in this town in such a way as to make him haul off and die, but naturally it is not apt to cause any such indignation as injuring a copper, as this town has more citizens to spare than coppers.

Well, sitting there with Johnny Brannigan, I get to wondering if he ever meets up with Earthquake while he is looking for him, and if so how he comes out, for Earthquake is certainly not such a guy as I will care to meet up with, even if I am a copper.

Earthquake is a guy of maybe six foot three, and weighing a matter of two hundred and twenty pounds, and all these pounds are nothing but muscle. Anybody will tell you that Earthquake is one of the strongest guys in this town, because it seems he once works in a foundry and picks up much of his muscle there. In fact, Earthquake likes to show how strong he is at all times, and one of his ways of showing this is to grab a full-sized guy in either duke and hold them straight up in the air over his head.

Sometimes after he gets tired of holding these guys over his head, he will throw them plumb away, especially if they are coppers, or maybe knock their noggins together and leave them with their noggins very sore indeed. When he is in real good humour, Earthquake does not think anything of going into a night club and taking it apart and chucking the pieces out into the street, along with he owner and the waiters and maybe some of the customers, so you can see Earthquake is a very high-spirited guy, and full of fun.

Personally, I do not see why Earthquake does not get a job in a circus as a strong guy, because there is no percentage in wasting all this strength for nothing, but when I mention this idea to Earthquake one time, he says he cannot bear to think of keeping regular hours such as a circus might wish.

Well, Johnny Brannigan does not have anything to say to me at first as we sit there in Mindy's, but by and by he looks at me and speaks as follows:

'You remember Earthquake?' he says. 'You remember he is very strong?'

'Strong?' I say to Johnny Brannigan. 'Why, there is nobody stronger than Earthquake. Why,' I say, 'Earthquake is strong enough to hold up a building.'

'Yes,' Johnny Brannigan says, 'what you say is very true. He is strong enough to hold up a building. Yes,' he says, 'Earthquake is very strong indeed. Now I will tell you about Earthquake.'

It is maybe three months after Earthquake knocks off Mulcahy [Johnny Brannigan says] that we get a tip he is in a town by the name of New Orleans, and because I am personally acquainted with him, I am sent there to put the arm on him. But when I get to this New Orleans, I find Earthquake blows out of there and does not leave any forwarding address.

Well, I am unable to get any trace of him for some days, and it looks as if I am on a bust, when I happen to run into a guy by the name of Saul the Soldier, from Greenwich Village. Saul the Soldier winds up in New Orleans following the horse races, and he is very glad indeed to meet a friend from his old home town, and I am also glad to meet Saul, because I am getting very lonesome in New Orleans. Well, Saul knows New Orleans pretty well, and he takes me around and about, and finally I ask him if he can tell me where Earthquake is, and Saul speaks as follows:

'Why,' Saul says, 'Earthquake sails away on a ship for Central America not long ago with a lot of guys that are going to join a revolution there. I think,' Saul says, 'they are going to a place by the name of Nicaragua.'

Well, I wire my headquarters and they tell me to go after Earthquake no matter where he is, because it seems the bladders back home are asking what kind of a police force do we have, anyway, and why is somebody not arrested for something.

I sail on a fruit steamer, and finally I get to this Nicaragua, and to a town that is called Managua.

Well, for a week or so I knock around here and there looking for Earthquake, but I cannot find hide or hair of him, and I am commencing to think that Saul the Soldier gives me a bum steer.

It is pretty hot in this town of Managua, and of an afternoon when I get tired of looking for Earthquake I go to a little park in the centre of the town where there are many shade trees. It is a pretty park, although down there they call it a plaza, and across from this plaza there is a big old two-story stone building that seems to be a convent, because I see many nuns and small female kids popping in and out of a door on one side of the building, which seems to be the main entrance.

One afternoon I am sitting in the little plaza when a big guy in sloppy white clothes comes up and sits down on another bench near me, and I am greatly surprised to see that this guy is nobody but Earthquake.

He does not see me at first, and in fact he does not know I am present until I step over to him and out with my jack and knock him bow-legged; because, knowing Earthquake, I know there is no use starting out with him by shaking hands. I do not boff him so very hard, at that, but just hard enough to make him slightly insensible for a minute, while I put the handcuffs on him.

Well, when he opens his eyes, Earthquake looks up at the trees, as if he thinks maybe a coconut drops down and beans him, and it is several minutes before he sees me, and then he leaps up and roars, and acts as if he is greatly displeased. But then he discovers that he is handcuffed, and he sits down again and speaks as follows:

'Hello, copper,' Earthquake says. 'When do you get in?'

I tell him how long I am there, and how much inconvenience he causes me by not being more prominent, and Earthquake says the fact of the matter is he is out in the jungles with a lot of guys trying to rig up a revolution, but they are so slow getting started they finally exasperate him, and he comes into town.

Well, finally we get to chatting along very pleasant about this and that, and although he is away only a few months, Earthquake is much interested in what is going on in New York and asks me many questions, and I tell him that the liquor around town is getting better.

'Furthermore, Earthquake,' I say, 'they are holding a nice warm seat for you up at Ossining.'

'Well, copper,' Earthquake says, 'I am sorry I scrag Mulcahy, at that. In fact,' he says, 'it really is an accident. I do not mean to scrag him. I am aiming at another guy, copper,' he says. 'In fact,' he says, 'I am aiming at you.'

Now about this time the bench seems to move from under me, and I find myself sitting on the ground, and the ground also seems to be trying to get from under me, and I hear loud crashing noises here and there, and a great roaring, and at first I think maybe Earthquake takes to shaking things up, when I see him laid out on the ground about fifty feet from me.

I get to my pins, but the ground is still wobbling somewhat and I can scarcely walk over to Earthquake, who is now sitting up very indignant, and when he sees me he says to me like this:

'Personally,' he says, 'I consider it a very dirty trick for you to boff me again when I am not looking.'

Well, I explain to Earthquake that I do not boff him again, and that as near as I can figure out what happens is that we are overtaken by what he is named for, which is an earthquake, and looking around and about, anybody can see that this is very true, as great clouds of dust are rising from piles of stone and timber where fair-sized buildings stand a few minutes before, and guys and dolls are running every which way.

Now I happens to look across at the convent, and I can see that it is something of a wreck and is very likely to be more so any minute, as the walls are teetering this way and that, and mostly they are teetering inward. Furthermore, I can hear much screeching from inside the old building.

Then I notice the door in the side of the building that seems to be the main entrance to the convent is gone, leaving the doorway open, and now I must explain to you about this doorway, as it figures quite some in what later comes off. It is a fairly wide doorway in the beginning with a frame of heavy timber set in the side of the stone building, with a timber arch at the top, and the wall around this doorway seems to be caving in from the top and sides, so that the doorway is now shaped like the letter V upside down, with the timber framework bending, instead of breaking.

As near as I can make out, this doorway is the only entrance to the convent that is not closed up by falling stone and timber, and it is a sure thing that pretty soon this opening will be plugged up, too, so I speak to Earthquake as follows:

'Earthquake,' I say, 'there are a lot of nuns and kids in this joint over here, and I judge from the screeching going on inside that some of them are very much alive. But,' I say, 'they will not be alive in a few minutes, because the walls are going to tip over and make jelly of them.'

'Why, yes,' Earthquake says, taking a peek at the convent, 'what you say seems reasonable. Well, copper,' he says, 'what is to be done in this situation?'

'Well,' I say, 'I see a chance to snatch a few of them out of there if you will help me. Earthquake,' I say, 'I understand you are a very strong guy?'

'Strong?' Earthquake says. 'Why,' he says, 'you know I am maybe the strongest guy in the world.'

'Earthquake,' I say, 'you see the doorway yonder? Well, Earthquake, if you are strong enough to hold this doorway apart and keep it from caving in, I will slip in through it and pass out any nuns and kids that may be alive.'

'Why,' Earthquake says, 'this is as bright an idea as I ever hear from a copper. Why,' he says, 'I will hold this doorway apart until next Pancake Tuesday.'

Then Earthquake holds out his dukes and I unlock the cuffs. Then he runs over to the doorway of the convent, and I run after him.

This dorway is now closing in very fast indeed, from the weight of tons of stones pressing against the timber frame, and by the time we get there the letter V upside down is so very narrow from top to bottom that Earthquake has a tough time wedging himself into what little opening is left.

But old Earthquake gets in, facing inward, and once in, he begins pushing against the door-frame on either side of him, and I can see at once how he gets his reputation as a strong guy. The doorway commences to widen, and as it widens Earthquake keeps spraddling his legs apart, so that pretty soon there is quite a space between his legs. His head is bent forward so far his chin is resting on his wishbone, as there is plenty of weight on Earthquake's neck and shoulders, and in fact he reminds me of pictures I see of a guy by the name of Atlas holding up the world.

It is through the opening between his spraddled-out legs that I pop, looking for the nuns and the kids. Most of them are in a big room on the ground floor of the building, and they are all huddled up close together screeching in chorus.

I motion them to follow me, and I lead them back over the wreckage, and along the hall to the spot where Earthquake is holding the doorway apart, and I wish to state at this time he is doing a very nice job of same.

But the weight on Earthquake's shoulders must be getting very hefty indeed, because his shoulders are commencing to stoop under it, and his chin is now almost down to his stomach, and his face is purple.

Now through Earthquake's spraddled-out legs, and into the street outside the convent wall, I push five nuns and fifteen female kids. One old nun refuses to be pushed through Earthquake's legs, and I finally make out from the way she is waving her hands around and about that there are other kids in the convent, and she wishes me to get them, too.

Well, I can see that any more delay is going to be something of a strain on Earthquake, and maybe a little irritating to him, so I speak to him as follows:

'Earthquake,' I say, 'you are looking somewhat peaked to me, and plumb tired out. Now then,' I say, 'if you will step aside, I will hold the doorway apart awhile, and you can go with this old nun and find the rest of the kids.'

'Copper,' Earthquake says, speaking from off his chest because he cannot get his head up very high, 'I can hold this doorway apart with my little fingers if one of them is not sprained, so go ahead and round up the rest.'

So I let the old nun lead me back to another part of the building, where I judge she knows there are more kids, and in fact the old nun is right, but it only takes one look to show me there is no use taking these kids out of the place.

Then we go back to Earthquake, and he hears us coming across the rubbish and half-raises his head from off his chest and looks at me, and I can see the sweat is dribbling down his kisser and his eyes are bugging out, and anybody can see that he is quite upset. As I get close to him he speaks to me as follows:

'Get her out quick,' he says. 'Get the old doll out.'

So I push the old nun through Earthquake's spraddled-out legs into the open, and I notice there is not as much space between these legs as formerly, so I judge the old mumblety-pegs are giving out. Then I say to Earthquake like this:

'Well, Earthquake,' I say, 'it is now time for you and me to be going. I will go outside first,' I say, 'and then you can ease yourself out, and we will look around for a means of getting back to New York, as headquarters will be getting worried.'

'Listen, copper,' Earthquake says, 'I am never going to get out of this spot. If I move an inch forward or an inch backward, down comes this whole shebang. But, copper,' he says, 'I see before I get in here that it is a hundred to one against me getting out again, so do not think I am trapped without knowing it. The way I look at it,' Earthquake says, 'it is better than the chair, at that. I can last a few minutes longer,' he says, 'and you better get outside.'

Well, I pop out between Earthquake's spraddled-out legs, because I figure I am better off outside than in, no matter what, and when I am outside I stand there looking at Earthquake and wondering what I can do about him. But I can see that he is right when he tells me that if he moves one way or another the cave-in will come, so there seems to be nothing much I can do.

Then I hear Earthquake calling me, and I step up close enough to hear him speak as follows:

'Copper,' he says, 'tell Mulcahy's people I am sorry. And do not forget that you owe old Earthquake whatever you figure your life is worth. I do not know yet why I do not carry out my idea of letting go all holds the minute you push the old nun out of here, and taking you with me wherever I am going. Maybe,' he says, 'I am getting soft-hearted. Well, good-bye, copper,' he says.

'Good-bye, Earthquake,' I say, and I walk away.

So [Johnny Brannigan says], now you know about Earthquake.

'Well,' I say, 'this is indeed a harrowing story, Johnny. But,' I say, 'if you leave Earthquake holding up anything maybe he is still holding it up, because Earthquake is certainly a very strong guy.'

'Yes,' Johnny Brannigan says, 'he is very strong indeed. But,' he says, 'as I am walking away another shock hits, and when I get off the ground again and look at the convent, I can see that not even Earthquake is strong enough to stand off this one.'

'Gentlemen, the King!'

On Tuesday evening I always go to Bobby's Chop House to get myself a beef stew, the beef stews in Bobby's being very nourishing, indeed, and quite reasonable. In fact, the beef stews in Bobby's are considered a most fashionable dish by one and all on Broadway on Tuesday evenings.

So on this Tuesday evening I am talking about, I am in Bobby's wrapping myself around a beef stew and reading the race results in the *Journal*, when who comes into the joint but two old friends of mine from Philly, and a third guy I never see before in my life, but who seems to be an old sort of guy, and very fierce looking.

One of these old friends of mine from Philly is a guy by the name of Izzy Cheesecake, who is called Izzy Cheesecake because he is all the time eating cheesecake around delicatessen joints, although of course this is nothing against him, as cheesecake is very popular in some circles, and goes very good with java. Anyway, this Izzy Cheesecake has another name, which is Morris something, and he is slightly Jewish, and has a large beezer, and is considered a handy man in many respects.

The other old friend of mine from Philly is a guy by the name of Kitty Quick, who is maybe thirty-two or three years old, and who is a lively guy in every way. He is a great hand for wearing good clothes, and he is mobbed up with some very good people in Philly in his day, and at one time has plenty of dough, although I hear that lately things are not going so good for Kitty Quick, or for anybody else in Philly, as far as that is concerned.

Now of course I do not rap to these old friends of mine from Philly at once, and in fact I put the *Journal* up in front of my face, because it is never good policy to rap to visitors in this town, especially visitors from Philly, until you know why they are visiting. But it seems that Kitty Quick spies me before I can get the *Journal* up high enough, and he comes over to my table at once, bringing Izzy Cheesecake and the other guy with him, so naturally I give them a big hello, very cordial, and ask them to sit down and have a few beef stews with me, and as they pull up chairs, Kitty Quick says to me like this:

'Do you know Jo-jo from Chicago?' he says, pointing his thumb at the third guy.

Well, of course I know Jo-jo by his reputation, which is very alarming, but I never meet up with him before, and if it is left to me, I will never meet up with him at all, because Jo-jo is considered a very uncouth character, even in Chicago.

He is an Italian, and a short wide guy, very heavy set, and slow moving, and with jowls you can cut steaks off of, and sleepy eyes, and he somehow reminds me of an old lion I once see in a cage in Ringling's circus. He has a black moustache, and he is an old-timer out in Chicago, and is pointed out to visitors to the city as a very remarkable guy because he lives as long as he does, which is maybe forty years.

His right name is Antonio something, and why he is called Jo-jo I never hear, but I suppose it is because Jo-jo is handier than Antonio. He shakes hands with me, and says he is pleased to meet me, and then he sits down and begins taking on beef stew very rapidly while Kitty Quick says to me as follows:

'Listen,' he says, 'do you know anybody in Europe?'

Well, this is a most unexpected question, and naturally I am not going to reply to unexpected questions by guys from Philly without thinking them over very carefully, so to gain time while I think, I say to Kitty Quick:

'Which Europe do you mean?'

'Why,' Kitty says, greatly surprised, 'is there more than one Europe? I mean the big Europe on the Atlantic Ocean. This is the Europe where we are going, and if you know anybody there we will be glad to go around and say hello to them for you. We are going to Europe on the biggest proposition anybody ever hears of,' he says. 'In fact,' he says, 'it is a proposition which will make us all rich. We are sailing to-night.'

Well, offhand I cannot think of anybody I know in Europe, and if I do know anybody there I will certainly not wish such parties as Kitty Quick, and Izzy Cheesecake, and Jo-jo going around saying hello to them, but of course I do not mention such a thought out loud. I only say I hope and trust that they have a very good *bon voyage* and do not suffer too much from seasickness. Naturally I do not ask what their proposition is, because if I ask such a question they may think I wish to find out, and will consider me a very nosey guy, but I figure the chances are they are going to look after some commercial matter, such as Scotch, or maybe cordials.

Anyway, Kitty Quick and Izzy Cheesecake and Jo-jo eat up quite a few beef stews, and leave me to pay the check, and this is the last I see or hear of any of them for several months. Then one day I am in Philly to see a prizefight, and I run into Kitty Quick on Broad Street, looking pretty much the same as usual, and I ask him how he comes out in Europe.

'It is no good,' Kitty says. 'The trip is something of a bust, although we see many interesting sights, and have quite a few experiences. Maybe,' Kitty says, 'you will like to hear why we go to Europe? It is a very unusual story, indeed, and is by no means a lie, and I will be pleased to tell it to someone I think will believe it.'

So we go into Walter's restaurant, and sit down in a corner, and order up a little java, and Kitty Quick tells me the story as follows:

It all begins [Kitty says] with a certain big lawyer coming to me here in Philly, and wishing to know if I care to take up a proposition which will make me rich, and naturally I say I can think of nothing that will please me more, because at this time things are very bad indeed in Philly, what with investigations going on here and there, and plenty of heat around and about, and I do not have more than a few bobs in my pants pocket, and can think of no way to get any more.

So this lawyer takes me to the Ritz-Carlton hotel, and there he introduces me to a guy by the name of Count Saro, and the lawyer says he will okay anything Saro has to say to me 100 per cent., and then he immediately takes the wind as if he does not care to hear what Saro has to say. But I know this mouthpiece is not putting any proposition away as okay unless he knows it is pretty much okay, because he is a smart guy at his own dodge, and everything else, and has plenty of coconuts.

Now this Count Saro is a little guy with an eyebrow moustache, and he wears striped pants, and white spats, and a cutaway coat, and a monocle in one eye, and he seems to be a foreign nobleman, although he talks English first rate. I do not care much for Count Saro's looks, but I will say one thing for him he is very business-like, and gets down to cases at once.

He tells me that he is the representative of a political party in his home country in Europe which has a King, and this country wishes to get rid of the King, because Count Saro says Kings are out of style in Europe, and that no country can get anywhere with a King these days. His proposition is for me to take any assistants I figure I may need and go over and get rid of this King, and Count Saro says he will pay two hundred G's for the job in good old American scratch, and will lay twenty-five G's on the line at once, leaving the balance with the lawyer to be paid to me when everything is finished.

Well, this is a most astonishing proposition, indeed, because while I often hear of propositions to get rid of other guys, I never before hear of a proposition to get rid of a King. Furthermore, it does not sound reasonable to me, as getting rid of a King is apt to attract plenty of attention, and criticism, but Count Saro explains to me that his country is a small, out-of-the-way country, and that his political party will take control of the telegraph wires and everything else as soon as I get rid of the King, so nobody will give the news much of a tumble outside the country.

'Everything will be done very quietly, and in good order,' Count Saro says, 'and there will be no danger to you whatever.'

Well, naturally I wish to know from Count Saro why he does not get somebody in his own country to do such a job, especially if he can pay so well for it, and he says to me like this:

'Well,' he says, 'in the first place there is no one in our country with enough experience in such matters to be trusted, and in the second place we do not wish anyone in our country to seem to be tangled up with getting rid of the King. It will cause internal complications,' he says. 'An outsider is more logical,' he says, 'because it is quite well known that in the palace of the King there are many valuable jewels, and it will seem a natural play for outsiders, especially Americans, to break into the palace to get these jewels, and if they happen to get rid of the King while getting the jewels, no one will think it is anything more than an accident, such as often occurs in your country.'

Furthermore, Count Saro tells me that everything will be laid out for me in advance by his people, so I will have no great bother getting into the palace to get rid of the King, but he says of course I must not really take the valuable jewels, because his political party wishes to keep them for itself.

Well, I do not care much for the general idea at all, but Count Saro whips out a bundle of scratch, and weeds off twenty-five large coarse notes of a G apiece, and there it is in front of me, and looking at all this dough, and thinking how tough times are, what with banks busting here and there, I am very much tempted indeed, especially as I am commencing to think this Count Saro is some kind of a nut, and is only speaking through his hat about getting rid of a King.

'Listen,' I say to Count Saro, as he sits there watching me, 'how do you know I will not take this dough off of you and then never do anything whatever for it?'

'Why,' he says, much surprised, 'you are recommended to me as an honest man, and I accept your references. Anyway,' he says, 'if you do not carry out your agreement with me, you will only hurt yourself, because you will lose a hundred and seventy-five G's more and the lawyer will make you very hard to catch.'

Well, the upshot of it is I shake hands with Count Saro, and then go out to find Izzy Cheesecake, although I am still thinking Count Saro is a little daffy, and while I am looking for Izzy, who do I see but Jo-jo, and Jo-jo tells me that he is on vacation from Chicago for awhile, because it seems somebody out there claims he is a public enemy, which Jo-jo says is nothing but a big lie, as he is really very fond of the public at all times.

Naturally I am glad to come across a guy such as Jo-jo, because he is most trustworthy, and naturally Jo-jo is very glad to hear of a proposition that will turn him an honest dollar while he is on his vacation. So Jo-jo and Izzy and I have a meeting, and we agree that I am to have a hundred G's for finding the plant, while Izzy and Jo-jo are to get fifty G's apiece, and this is how we come to go to Europe.

Well, we land at a certain spot in Europe, and who is there to meet us but another guy with a monocle, who states that his name is Baron von Terp, or some such, and who says he is representing Count Saro, and I am commencing to wonder if Count Saro's country is filled with one-eyed guys. Anyway, this Baron von Terp takes us travelling by trains and automobiles for several days, until finally after an extra long hop in an automobile we come to the outskirts of a nice-looking little burg, which seems to be the place we are headed for.

Now Baron von Terp drops us in a little hotel on the outskirts of the town, and says he must leave us because he cannot afford to be seen with us, although he explains he does not mean this as a knock to us. In fact, Baron von Terp says he finds us very nice travelling companions, indeed, except for Jo-jo wishing to engage in target practice along the route with his automatic Roscoe, and using such animals as stray dogs and chickens for his targets. He says he does not even mind Izzy Cheesecake's singing, although personally I will always consider this one of the big drawbacks to the journey.

Before he goes, Baron von Terp draws me a rough diagram of the inside of the palace where we are to get rid of the King, giving me a layout of all the rooms and doors. He says usually there are guards in and about this palace, but that his people arrange it so these guards will not be present around nine o'clock this night, except one guy who may be on guard at the door of the King's bedroom, and Baron von Terp says if we guzzle this guy it will be all right with him, because he does not like the guy, anyway.

But the general idea, he says, is for us to work fast and quietly, so as to be in and out of there inside of an hour or so, leaving no trail behind us, and I say this will suit me and Izzy Cheesecake and Jo-jo very well, indeed, as we are getting tired of travelling, and wish to go somewhere and take a long rest.

Well, after explaining all this, Baron von Terp takes the wind, leaving us a big fast car with an ugly-looking guy driving it who does not talk much English, but is supposed to know all the routes, and it is in this car that we leave the little hotel just before nine o'clock as per instructions, and head for the palace, which turns out to be nothing but a large square old building in the middle of a sort of park, with the town around and about, but some distance off.

Ugly-face drives right into this park and up to what seems to be the front door of the building, and the three of us get out of the car, and Ugly-face pulls the car off into the shadow of some trees to wait for us.

Personally, I am looking for plenty of heat when we start to go into the palace, and I have the old equalizer where I can get at it without too much trouble, while Jo-jo and Izzy Cheesecake also have their rods handy. But just as Baron von Terp tells us, there are no guards around, and in fact there is not a soul in sight as we walk into the palace door, and find ourselves in a big hall with paintings, and armour, and old swords, and one thing and another hanging around and about, and I can see that this is a perfect plant, indeed.

I out with my diagram and see where the King's bedroom is located on the second floor, and when we get there, walking very easy, and ready to start blasting away if necessary, who is at the door but a big tall guy in a uniform, who is very much surprised at seeing us, and who starts to holler something or other, but what it is nobody will ever know, because just as he opens his mouth, Izzy Cheesecake taps him on the noggin with the butt of a forty-five, and knocks him cock-eyed.

Then Jo-jo grabs some cord off a heavy silk curtain which is hanging across the door, and ties the guy up good and tight, and wads a handkerchief into his kisser in case the guy comes to, and wishes to start hollering again, and when all this is done, I quietly turn the knob of the door to the King's bedroom, and we step into a room that looks more like a young convention hall than it does a bedroom, except that it is hung around and about with silk drapes, and there is much gilt furniture here and there.

Well, who is in this room but a nice-looking doll, and a little kid of maybe eight or nine years old, and the kid is in a big bed with a canopy over it like the entrance to a night club, only silk, and the doll is sitting alongside the bed reading to the kid out of a book. It is a very homelike scene; indeed, and causes us to stop and look around in great surprise, for we are certainly not expecting such a scene at all.

As we stand there in the middle of the room somewhat confused the doll turns and looks at us, and the little kid sits up in bed. He is a fat little guy with a chubby face, and a lot of curly hair, and eyes as big as pancakes, and maybe bigger. The doll turns very pale when she sees us, and shakes so the book she is reading falls to the floor, but the kid does not seem scared, and he says to us in very good English like this:

'Who are you?' he says.

Well, this is a fair question, at that, but naturally we do not wish to state who we are at this time, so I say:

'Never mind who we are, where is the King?'

'The King?' the kid says, sitting up straight in the bed, 'why, I am the King.'

Now of course this seems a very nonsensical crack to us, because we have brains enough to know that Kings do not come as small as this little squirt, and anyway we are in no mood to dicker with him, so I say to the doll as follows:

'Listen,' I say, 'we do not care for any kidding at this time, because we are in a great hurry. Where is the King?'

'Why,' she says, her voice trembling quite some, 'this is indeed the King, and I am his governess. Who are you, and what do you want? How do you get in here?' she says. 'Where are the guards?'

'Lady,' I say, and I am greatly surprised at myself for being so patient with her, 'this kid may be a King, but we want the big King. We want the head King himself,' I say.

'There is no other,' she says, and the little kid chips in like this:

'My father dies two years ago, and I am the King in his place,' he says. 'Are you English like Miss Peabody here?' he says. 'Who is the funny looking old man back there?'

Well, of course Jo-jo is funny looking, at that, but no one ever before is impolite enough to speak of it to his face, and Jo-jo begins growling quite some, while Izzy Cheesecake speaks as follows:

'Why,' Izzy says, 'this is a very great outrage. We are sent to get rid of a King, and here the King is nothing but a little punk. Personally,' Izzy says, 'I am not in favour of getting rid of punks, male or female.'

'Well,' Jo-jo says, 'I am against it myself as a rule, but this is a pretty fresh punk.'

'Now,' I say, 'there seems to be some mistake around here, at that. Let us sit down and talk things over quietly, and see if we cannot get this matter straightened out. It looks to me,' I say, 'as if this Count Saro is nothing but a swindler.'

'Count Saro,' the doll says, getting up and coming over to me, and looking very much alarmed. 'Count Saro, do you say? Oh, sir, Count Saro is a very bad man. He is the tool of the Grand Duke Gino of this country, who is this little boy's uncle. The Grand Duke will be King himself if it is not for this boy, and we suspect many plots against the little chap's safety. Oh, gentlemen,' she says, 'you surely do not mean any harm to this poor orphan child?'

Well, this is about the first time in their lives that Jo-jo and Izzy

Cheesecake are ever mentioned by anybody as gentlemen, and I can see that it softens them up quite some, especially as the little kid is grinning at them very cheerful, although of course he will not be so cheerful if he knows who he is grinning at.

'Why,' Jo-jo says, 'the Grand Duke is nothing but a rascal for wishing harm to such a little guy as this, although of course,' Jo-jo says, 'if he is a grown-up King it will be a different matter.'

'Who are you?' the little kid says again.

'We are Americans,' I say, very proud to mention my home country. 'We are from Philly and Chicago, two very good towns, at that.'

Well, the little kid's eyes get bigger than ever, and he climbs right out of bed and walks over to us looking very cute in his blue silk pyjamas, and his bare feet.

'Chicago?' he says. 'Do you know Mr. Capone?'

'Al?' says Jo-jo. 'Do I know Al? Why, Al and me are just like this,' he says, although personally I do not believe Al Capone will know Jo-jo if he meets him in broad daylight. 'Where do you know Al from?' he asks.

'Oh, I do not know him,' the kid says. 'But I read about him in the magazines, and about the machine guns, and the pineapples. Do you know about the pineapples?' he says.

'Do I know about the pineapples?' Jo-jo says, as if his feelings are hurt by the question. 'He asks me do I know about the pineapples. Why,' he says, 'look here.'

And what does Jo-jo do but out with a little round gadget which I recognize at once as a bomb such as these Guineas like to chuck at people they do not like, especially Guineas from Chicago. Of course I never know Jo-jo is packing this article around and about with him, and Jo-jo can see I am much astonished, and by no means pleased, because he says to me like this:

'I bring this along in case of a bear fight,' he says. 'They are very handy in a bear fight.'

Well, the next thing anybody knows we are all talking about this and that very pleasant, especially the little kid and Jo-jo, who is telling lies faster than a horse can trot, about Chicago and Mr. Capone, and I hope and trust that Al never hears some of the lies Jo-jo tells, or he may hold it against me for being with Jo-jo when these lies come off.

I am talking to the doll, whose name seems to be Miss Peabody, and who is not so hard to take, at that, and at the same time I am keeping an eye on Izzy Cheesecake, who is wandering around the room looking things over. The chances are Izzy is trying to find a few of the valuable jewels such as I mention to him when telling him about the proposition of getting rid of the King, and in fact I am taking a stray peek here and there myself, but I do not see anything worth while.

This Miss Peabody is explaining to me about the politics of the country, and it seems the reason the Grand Duke wishes to get rid of the little kid King and be King himself is because he has a business deal on with a big nation near by which wishes to control the kid King's country. I judge from what Miss Peabody tells me that this country is no bigger than Delaware county, Pa., and it seems to me a lot of bother about no more country than this, but Miss Peabody says it is a very nice little country, at that.

She says it will be very lovely indeed if it is not for the Grand Duke Gino, because the little kid King stands okay with the people, but it seems the old Grand Duke is pretty much boss of everything, and Miss Peabody says she is personally long afraid that he will finally try to do something very drastic indeed to get rid of the kid King on account of the kid seeming so healthy. Well, naturally I do not state to her that our middle name is drastic, because I do not wish Miss Peabody to have a bad opinion of us.

Now nothing will do but Jo-jo must show the kid his automatic, which is as long as your arm, and maybe longer, and the kid is greatly delighted, and takes the rod and starts pointing it here and there and saying boom-boom, as kids will do. But what happens but he pulls the trigger, and it seems that Jo-jo does not have the safety on, so the Roscoe really goes boom-boom twice before the kid can take his finger off the trigger.

Well, the first shot smashes a big jar over in one corner of the room, which Miss Peabody afterwards tells me is worth fifteen G's if it is worth a dime, and the second slug knocks off Izzy Cheesecake's derby hat, which serves Izzy right, at that, as he is keeping his hat on in the presence of a lady. Naturally these shots are very disturbing to me at the moment, but afterwards I learn they are a very good thing indeed, because it seems a lot of guys who are hanging around outside, including Baron von Terp, and several prominent politicians of the country, watching and listening to see what comes off, hurry right home to bed, figuring the King is got rid of as per contract, and wishing to be found in bed if anybody comes around asking questions.

Well, Jo-jo is finally out of lies about Chicago and Mr. Capone, when the little kid seems to get a new idea and goes rummaging around the room looking for something, and just as I am hoping he is about to donate the valuable jewels to us he comes up with a box, and what is in this box but a baseball bat, and a catcher's mitt, and a baseball, and it is very strange indeed to find such homelike articles so far away from home, especially as Babe Ruth's name is on the bat.

'Do you know about these things?' the little kid asks Jo-jo. 'They are from America, and they are sent to me by one of our people when he is visiting there, but nobody here seems to know what they are for.'

'Do I know about them?' Jo-jo says, fondling them very tenderly, indeed. 'He asks me do I know about them. Why,' he says, 'in my time I am the greatest hitter on the West Side Blues back in dear old Chi.'

Well, now nothing will do the kid but we must show him how these baseball articles work, so Izzy Cheesecake, who claims he is once a star back-stopper with the Vine Streets back in Philly, puts on a pad and mask, and Jo-jo takes the bat and lays a small sofa pillow down on the floor for a home plate, and insists that I pitch to him. Now it is years since I handle a baseball, although I wish to say that in my day I am as good an amateur pitcher as there is around Gray's Ferry in Philly, and the chances are I will be with the A's if I do not have other things to do.

So I take off my coat, and get down to the far end of the room, while Jo-jo squares away at the plate, with Izzy Cheesecake behind it. I can see by the way he stands that Jo-jo is bound to be a sucker for a curve, so I take a good windup, and cut loose with the old fadeaway, but of course my arm is not what it used to be, and the ball does not break as I expect, so what happens but Jo-jo belts the old apple right through a high window in what will be right field if the room is laid off like Shibe Park.

Well Jo-jo starts running as if he is going to first, but of course there is no place in particular for him to run, and he almost knocks his brains out against a wall, and the ball is lost, and the game winds up right there, but the little kid is tickled silly over this business, and even Miss Peabody laughs, and she does not look to me like a doll who gets many laughs out of life, at that.

It is now nearly ten o'clock, and Miss Peabody says if she can find anybody around she will get us something to eat, and this sounds very reasonable, indeed, so I step outside the door and bring in the guy we tie up there, who seems to be wide awake by now and very much surprised, and quite indignant, and Miss Peabody says something to him in a language which I do not understand. When I come to think it all over afterwards, I am greatly astonished at the way I trust Miss Peabody, because there is no reason why she shall not tell the guy to get the law, but I suppose I trust her because she seems to have an honest face.

Anyway, the guy in the uniform goes away rubbing his noggin, and pretty soon in comes another guy who seems to be a butler, or some such, and who is also greatly surprised at seeing us, and Miss Peabody rattles off something to him and he starts hustling in tables, and dishes, and sandwiches, and coffee, and one thing and another in no time at all.

Well, there we are, the five of us sitting around the table eating and drinking, because what does the butler do but bring in a couple of bottles of good old pre-war champagne, which is very pleasant to the taste, although Izzy Cheesecake embarrasses me no little by telling Miss Peabody that if she can dig up any considerable quantity of this stuff he will make her plenty of bobs by peddling it in our country, and will also cut the King in.

When the butler fills the wine-glasses the first time, Miss Peabody picks hers up, and looks at us, and naturally we have sense enough to pick ours up, too, and then she stands up on her feet and raises her glass high above her head, and says like this:

'Gentlemen, the King!'

Well, I stand up at this, and Jo-jo and Izzy Cheesecake stand up with me, and we say, all together:

'The King!'

And then we swig our champagne, and sit down again and the little kid laughs all over and claps his hands and seems to think it is plenty of fun, which it is, at that, although Miss Peabody does not let him have any wine, and is somewhat indignant when she catches Jo-jo trying to slip him a snort under the table.

Well, finally the kid does not wish us to leave him at all, especially Jo-jo, but Miss Peabody says he must get some sleep, so we tell him we will be back some day, and we take our hats and say good-bye, and leave him standing in the bedroom door with Miss Peabody at his side, and the little kid's arm is around her waist, and I find myself wishing it is my arm, at that.

Of course we never go back again, and in fact we get out of the country this very night, and take the first boat out of the first seaport we hit and return to the United States of America, and the gladdest guy in all the world to see us go is Ugly-face, because he has to drive us about a thousand miles with the muzzle of a rod digging into his ribs.

So [Kitty Quick says] now you know why we go to Europe.

Well, naturally, I am greatly interested in his story, and especially in what Kitty says about the pre-war champagne, because I can see that there may be great business opportunities in such a place if a guy can get in with the right people, but one thing Kitty will never tell me is where the country is located, except that it is located in Europe.

'You see,' Kitty says, 'we are all strong Republicans here in Philly, and I will not get the Republican administration of this country tangled up in any international squabble for the world. You see,' he says, 'when we land back home I find a little item of cable news in a paper which says the Grand Duke Gino dies as a result of injuries received in an accident in his home some weeks before.

'And,' Kitty says, 'I am never sure but what these injuries may be caused by Jo-jo insisting on Ugly-face driving us around to the Grand Duke's house the night we leave and popping his pineapple into the Grand Duke's bedroom window.'

A Nice Price

One hot morning in June, I am standing in front of the Mohican Hotel in the city of New London, Conn., and the reason I am in such a surprising spot is something that makes a long story quite a bit longer.

It goes back to a couple of nights before, when I am walking along Broadway and I run into Sam the Gonoph, the ticket speculator, who seems to have a very sour expression on his puss, although, even when Sam the Gonoph is looking good-natured his puss is nothing much to see.

Now Sam the Gonoph is an old friend of mine, and in fact I

sometimes join up with him and his crew to hustle duckets to one thing and another when he is short-handed, so I give him a big hello, and he stops and the following conversation ensues:

'How is it going with you, Sam?' I say to Sam the Gonoph, although of course I do not really care two pins how it is going with him. 'You look as if you are all sored up at somebody.'

'No,' Sam says, 'I am not sored up at anybody. I am never sored up at anybody in my life, except maybe Society Max, and of course everybody knows I have a perfect right to be sored up at Society Max, because look at what he does to me.'

Well, what Sam the Gonoph says is very true, because what Society Max does to Sam is to steal Sam's fiancée off of him a couple of years before this, and marry her before Sam has time to think. This fiancée is a doll by the name of Sonia, who resides up in the Bronx, and Sam the Gonoph is engaged to her since the year of the Dempsey–Firpo fight, and is contemplating marrying her almost any time, when Society Max bobs up.

Many citizens afterwards claim that Max does Sam the Gonoph a rare favour, because Sonia is commencing to fat up in spots, but it breaks Sam's heart just the same, especially when he learns that Sonia's papa gives the happy young couple twenty big G's in old-fashioned folding money that nobody ever knows the papa has, and Sam figures that Max must get an inside tip on this dough and that he takes an unfair advantage of the situation.

'But,' Sam the Gonoph says, 'I am not looking sored up at this time because of Society Max, although of course it is well known to one and all that I am under oath to knock his ears down the first time I catch up with him. As a matter of fact, I do not as much as think of Society Max for a year or more, although I hear he deserts poor Sonia out in Cincinnati after spending her dough and leading her a dog's life, including a few off-hand pastings – not that I am claiming Sonia may not need a pasting now and then.

'What I am looking sored up about,' Sam says, 'is because I must get up into Connecticut to-morrow to a spot that is called New London to dispose of a line of merchandise.'

'Why, Sam,' I say, 'what can be doing in such a place?'

'Oh,' Sam says, 'a large boat race is coming up between the Harvards and the Yales. It comes up at New London every year, and is quite an interesting event from what I read in the papers about it, but the reason I am sored up about going to-morrow is because I wish to spend the week-end on my farm in New Jersey to see how my onions are doing. Since I buy this farm in New Jersey, I can scarcely wait to get over there on weekends to watch my onions grow.

'But,' Sam the Gonoph says, 'this is an extra large boat race this year, and I am in possession of many choice duckets, and am sure to make plenty of black ink for myself, and business before pleasure is what I always say. By the way,' Sam says, 'do you ever see a boat race?'

Well, I say that the only boat races I ever see are those that come off around the race tracks, such a race being a race that is all fixed up in advance, and some of them are pretty raw, if you ask me, and I am by no means in favour of things of this kind unless I am in, but Sam the Gonoph says these races are by no manner of means the same thing as the boat races he is talking about.

'I never personally witness one myself,' Sam says, 'but the way I understand it is a number of the Harvards and the Yales, without any clothes on, get in row boats and row, and row, and row until their tongues hang out, and they are all half-dead. Why they tucker themselves out in this fashion I do not know and,' Sam says, 'I am too old to start trying to find out why these college guys do a lot of things to themselves.

'But,' Sam says, 'boat racing is a wonderful sport, and I always have a nice trade at New London, Conn., and if you wish to accompany me and Benny South Street and Liverlips and maybe collect a few bobs for yourself, you are as welcome as the flowers in May.'

So there I am in front of the Mohican Hotel in New London, Conn., with Sam the Gonoph and Benny South Street and old Liverlips, who are Sam the Gonoph's best hustlers, and all around and about is a very interesting sight, to be sure, as large numbers of the Harvards and the Yales are passing in and out of the hotel and walking up and down and back and forth, and making very merry, one way and another.

Well, after we are hustling our duckets for a couple of hours and it is coming on noon, Benny South Street goes into the hotel lobby to buy some cigarettes, and by and by he comes out looking somewhat excited, and states as follows:

'Say,' Benny says, 'there's a guy inside with his hands full of money offering to lay three to one that the Yales win the boat race. He says he has fifteen G's cash with him to wager at the price stated.'

'Are there any takers?' Sam the Gonoph asks.

'No, not many,' Benny says. 'From all I hear, the Yales figure. In fact, all the handicappers I speak with have them on top, so the Harvards do not care for any part of the guy's play. But,' Benny says, 'there he is, offering three to one.'

'Three to one?' Sam the Gonoph says, as if he is mentioning these terms to himself. 'Three to one, eh? It is a nice price.'

'It is a lovely price,' old Liverlips puts in.

Well, Sam the Gonoph stands there as if he is thinking, and Benny South Street seems to be thinking, too, and even old Liverlips seems to be thinking, and by and by I even find myself thinking, and finally Sam the Gonoph says like this:

'I do not know anything about boat races,' Sam says, 'and the Yales may figure as you say, but nothing between human beings is one to three. In fact,' Sam the Gonoph says, 'I long ago come to the conclusion that all life is six to five against. And anyway,' he says, 'how can anybody let such odds as these get away from them? I think I will take a small nibble at this proposition. What about you, Benny?'

'I will also nibble,' Benny South Street says. 'I will never forgive myself in this world if I let this inviting offer go and it turns out the Harvards win.'

Well, we all go into the hotel lobby, and there is a big, grey-haired guy in a white cap and white pants standing in the centre of a bunch of other guys, and he has money in both hands. I hear somebody say he is one of the real old-time Yales, and he is speaking in a loud voice as follows:

'Why,' he says, 'what is the matter, Harvards, are you cowards, or are you just broke? If you are broke, I will take your markers and let you pay me on the instalment plan. But,' he says, 'bet me. That is all, just bet me.'

Personally, I have a notion to let on I am one of the Harvards and slip the guy a nice marker, but I am afraid he may request some identification and I do not have anything on me to prove I am a college guy, so I stand back and watch Sam the Gonoph shove his way through the crowd with a couple of C notes in his hand, and Benny South Street is right behind him.

'I will take a small portion of the Harvards at the market,' Sam the Gonoph says, as he offers the grey-haired guy his dough.

'Thank you, my friend,' the guy says, 'but I do not think we are acquainted,' he says. 'Who do you wish to hold the stakes?'

'You hold them yourself, Mr. Campbell,' Sam the Gonoph says. 'I know you, although you do not know me, and I will gladly trust you with my dough. Furthermore, my friend here, who also wishes a portion of the Harvards, will trust you.'

So the grey-haired guy says that both Sam the Gonoph and Benny South Street are on at 3 to 1, and thanks again to them, at that, and when we get outside, Sam explains that he recognizes the guy as nobody but Mr. Hammond Campbell, who is a very important party in every respect and who has more dough than Uncle Sam has bad debts. In fact, Sam the Gonoph seems to feel that he is greatly honoured in getting to bet with Mr. Hammond Campbell, although from the way Mr. Campbell takes their dough, I figure he thinks that the pleasure is all his.

Well, we go on hustling our duckets but neither Sam the Gonoph nor Benny South Street seem to have much heart in their work, and every now and then I see one or the other slip into the hotel lobby, and it comes out that they are still nibbling at the 3 to 1, and finally I slip in myself and take a little teensy nibble for twenty bobs myself, because the way I look at it, anything that is good enough for Sam the Gonoph is good enough for me.

Now Sam the Gonoph always carries quite a little ready money on his body, and nobody will deny that Sam will send it along if he likes a proposition, and by and by he is down for a G on the Harvards, and Benny South Street has four C's going for him, and there is my double saw, and even old Liverlips weakens and goes for a pound note, and ordinarily Liverlips will not bet a pound that he is alive.

Furthermore, Mr. Hammond Campbell says we are about the only guys in town that do bet him and that we ought to get degrees off the Harvards for our loyalty to them, but of course what we are really loyal to is the 3 to 1. Finally, Mr. Cambell says he has to go to lunch, but that if we feel like betting him any more we can find him on board his yacht, the *Hibiscus*, out in the river, and maybe he will boost the price up to 3½ to 1.

So I go into the hotel and get a little lunch myself, and when I am coming out a nice-looking young doll who is walking along in front of me accidentally drops her poke from under her arm, and keeps right on walking. Naturally, I pick it up, but several parties who are standing around in the lobby see me do it, so I call to the young doll and when she turns around I hand her the poke, and she is very grateful to me, to be sure. In fact, she thanks me several times, though once will do, and then all of a sudden she says to me like this:

'Pardon me,' the young doll says, 'but are you not one of the gentlemen I see wagering with my papa that the Harvards will win the boat race?'

'Yes,' I say, 'and what is more, we may keep on wagering him. In fact,' I say, 'a friend of mine by the name of Sam the Gonoph is just now contemplating wiring home for another G to accept your papa's generous offer of three-and-a-half to one.'

'Oh,' the young doll says, 'do not do it. You are only throwing your money away. The Harvards have no chance whatever of winning the boat race. My papa is never wrong on boat races. I only wish he is to-day.'

And with this she sits down in a chair in the lobby and begins crying boo-hoo until her mascara is running down her cheeks, and naturally I am greatly embarrassed by this situation, as I am afraid somebody may come along and think maybe she is my step-child and that I am just after chastising her.

'You see,' the young doll says, 'a boy I like a very, very great deal belongs to the Harvards' crew and when I tell him a couple of weeks ago that my papa says the Yales are bound to win, he grows very angry and says what does my papa know about it, and who is my papa but an old money-bags, anyway, and to the dickens with my papa. Then when I tell him my papa always knows about these things, Quentin grows still angrier, and we quarrel and he says all right, if the Harvards lose he will never, never, never see me again as long as he lives. And Quentin is a very obstinate and unreasonable boy, and life is very sad for me.'

Well, who comes along about now but Sam the Gonoph and naturally he is somewhat surprised by the scene that is presented to his eyes, so I explain to him, and Sam is greatly touched and very sympathetic, for one thing about Sam is he is very tender-hearted when it comes to dolls who are in trouble.

'Well,' Sam says, 'I will certainly be greatly pleased to see the Harvards win the boat race myself, and in fact,' he says, 'I am just making a few cautious inquiries around here and there to see if there is any chance of stiffening a couple of the Yales, so we can have a little help in the race.

'But,' Sam says, 'one great trouble with these college propositions is they are always levelling, though I cannot see why it is necessary. Anyway,' he says, 'it looks as if we cannot hope to do any business with the Yales, but you dry your eyes, little miss, and maybe old Sam can think up something.'

At this the young doll stops her bawling and I am very glad of it, as there is nothing I loathe and despise so much as a doll bawling, and she looks up at Sam with a wet smile and says to him like this:

'Oh, do you really think you can help the Harvards win the boat race?'

Well, naturally Sam the Gonoph is not in a position to make any promises on this point, but he is such a guy as will tell a doll in distress anything whatever if he thinks it will give her a little pleasure for a minute, so he replies as follows:

'Why, who knows?' Sam says. 'Who knows, to be sure? But anyway do not bawl any more, and old Sam will give this matter further consideration.'

And with this Sam pats the young doll on the back so hard he pats all the breath out of her and she cannot bawl any more even if she wishes to, and she gets up and goes away looking very happy, but before she goes she says:

'Well, I hear somebody say that from the way you gentlemen are betting on the Harvards you must know something and,' she says, 'I am very glad I have the courage to talk to you. It will be a wonderful favour to Quentin and me if you help the Harvards win, even though it costs my papa money. Love is more than gold,' she says.

Personally, I consider it very wrong for Sam the Gonoph to be holding out hope to a young doll that he is unable to guarantee, but Sam says he does not really promise anything and that he always figures if he can bring a little joy into any life, no matter how, he is doing a wonderful deed, and that anyway we will never see the young doll again, and furthermore, what of it?

Well, I cannot think what of it just off-hand, and anyway I am glad to be rid of the young doll, so we go back to disposing of the duckets we have left.

Now the large boat race between the Harvards and the Yales takes place in the early evening, and when it comes on time for the race one and all seem to be headed in the direction of the river, including all the young guys with the stir haircuts, and many beautiful young dolls wearing blue and red flowers, and old guys in sports pants and flat straw hats, and old dolls who walk as if their feet hurt them, and the chances are they do, at that.

Well, nothing will do Sam the Gonoph but we must see the boat race, too, so we go down to the railroad station to take the very train for which we are hustling duckets all day, but by the time we get there the race train is pulling out, so Benny South Street says the next best thing for us to do is to go down to the dock and hire a boat to take us out on the river.

But when we get to the dock, it seems that all the boats around are hired and are already out on the river, but there is an old pappy guy with a chin whisker sitting in a rickety-looking little motor-boat at the dock, and this old guy says he will take us out where we can get a good peek at the race for a buck apiece.

Personally, I do not care for the looks of the boat, and neither does Benny South Street nor old Liverlips, but Sam the Gonoph is so anxious to see the race that finally we all get into the boat and the old guy heads her out into the river, which seems to be filled with all kinds of boats decorated with flags and one thing and another, and with guys and dolls walking back and forth on these boats.

Anybody must admit that it is quite a sight, and I am commencing to be glad I am present, especially when Benny South Street tells me that these guys and dolls on the boats are very fine people and worth plenty of money. Furthermore, Benny South Street points out many big white boats that he says are private yachts, and he tells me that what it costs to keep up these private yachts is a sin and a shame when you start to figure out the number of people in the world who are looking for breakfast money. But then Benny South Street is always talking of things of this kind, and sometimes I think maybe he is a dynamiter at heart.

We go putt-putting along under a big bridge and into a sort of lane of boats, and Benny South Street says we are now at the finish line of the large boat race and that the Harvards and the Yales row down this lane from away up the river, and that it is here that they have their tongues hanging out and are nearly all half-dead.

Well, it seems that we are in the way, because guys start yelling at us from different boats and shaking their fists at us, and it is a good thing for some of them that they are not close enough for us to get a pop at them, but the old pappy guy keeps the motor-boat putt-putting and sliding in and out among the boats until we come to a spot that he says is about a hundred yards above the finish and a great spot to see the best part of the race.

We are slipping alongside of a big white boat that Benny South Street says is a private yacht and that has a little set of stair steps running down one side almost into the water, when all of a sudden Sam the Gonoph notices his feet are wet, and he looks down and sees that the motor-boat is half-full of water and furthermore that the boat is commencing to sink.

Now this is quite a predicament, and naturally Sam the Gonoph lets out a slight beef and wishes to know what kind of accommodations we are paying for, anyway, and then the old pappy guy notices the water and the sinking, and he seems somewhat put out about the matter, especially as the water is getting up around his chin whiskers.

So he steers the boat up against the stair steps on the yacht and all of us, including the old pappy guy, climb out on to the stairs just as the motor-boat gives a last snort and sinks from sight. The last I see of the motor-boat is the hind end sticking up in the air a second before it disappears, and I remember the name that is painted on the hind end. The name is *Baby Mine*.

Well, Sam the Gonoph leads the way up the stairs to the deck of the yacht, and who meets us at the head of the stairs but Mr. Hammond Campbell in person, and who is right behind him but the young doll I am talking with in the hotel lobby, and at first Mr. Campbell thinks that we come out to his yacht to pick up a little of his $3\frac{1}{2}$ to 1, and he is greatly disappointed when he learns that such is by no means our purpose and that we are merely the victims of disaster.

As for the young doll, whose name turns out to be Clarice, she gazes at Sam the Gonoph and me with her eyes full of questions, but we do not get a chance to talk to her as things begin occurring at once.

There are quite a number of guys and dolls on the yacht, and it is a very gay scene to be sure, as they walk around laughing and chatting, when all of a sudden I see Sam the Gonoph staring at a guy and doll who are leaning over the rail talking very earnestly and paying no attention to what is going on around and about them.

The guy is a tall, dark-complected young guy with a little moustache, and he is wearing white flannel pants and a blue coat with brass buttons, and white shoes, and he is a very foreign-looking guy, to be sure. The doll is not such a young doll, being maybe around middle age, giving her a few points the best of it, but she is a fine-looking doll, at that, especially if you like dolls with grey hair, which personally I am not so much in favour of.

I am close enough to Sam the Gonoph to hear him breathing heavily as he stares at this guy and doll, and finally the dark-complected young guy looks up and sees Sam and at the same instant Sam starts for him, and as Sam starts the young guy turns and takes to running in the other direction from Sam along the deck, but before he takes to running I can see that it is nobody but Society Max.

Naturally, I am somewhat surprised at seeing Society Max at a boat-race between the Harvards and the Yales, because I never figure him such a guy as will be interested in matters of this kind, although I remember that Society Max is once a life guard at Coney Island, and in fact it is at Coney Island that Sonia gets her first peek at his shape and is lost for ever to Sam the Gonoph, so I get to thinking that maybe Society Max is fond of all aquatic events.

Now of course the spectacle of Sam the Gonoph pursuing Society Max along the deck is quite surprising to one and all, except Benny South Street and old Liverlips and myself, who are aware of the reason, and Mr. Hammond Campbell wishes to know what kind of game they are playing, especially after they round the deck twice, with Society Max showing much foot, but none of us feel called on to explain. Finally the other guys and dolls on the yacht enter into the spirit of the chase, even though they do not know what it is all about, and they shout encouragement to both Sam the Gonoph and Society Max, although Max is really the favourite.

There is no doubt but what Society Max is easily best in a sprint, especially as Sam the Gonoph's pants legs are wet from the sinking motor-boat and he is carrying extra weight, but Sam is a wonderful doer over a route, and on the third trip around the deck, anybody can see that he is cutting down Max's lead.

Well, every time they pass the grey-haired doll that Society Max is talking to when we come on the yacht she asks what is the matter, Max, and where are you going, Max, and other questions that seem trivial at such a time, but Max never has an opportunity to answer, as he has to save all his breath to keep ahead of Sam the Gonoph, and in fact Sam the Gonoph stops talking, too, and just keeps plugging along with a very determined expression on his puss.

Well, now all the whistles on the boats in the river around us start blowing, and it seems this is because the large boat race between the Harvards and the Yales is now approaching the finish, and one and all on our yacht rush to the side of the yacht to see it, forgetting about everything else, and the side they rush to is the same side the stair steps are on.

But I am too much interested in Sam the Gonoph's pursuit of Society Max to pay any attention to the boat race, and as they come around the deck the fifth or sixth time, I can see that Sam will have Max in the next few jumps, when all of a sudden Society Max runs right down the stairs and dives off into the river, and he does it so fast that nobody seems to notice him except Sam the Gonoph and me and the grey-haired doll, and I am the only one that notices her fall in a big faint on the deck as Max dives.

Naturally, this is not a time to be bothering with fainting dolls, so Sam the Gonoph and me run to the side of the yacht and watch the water to see where Society Max comes up, but he does not appear at once, and I remember hearing he is a wonderful diver when he is a life guard, so I figure he is going to keep under water until he is pretty sure he is too far away for Sam the Gonoph to hit him with anything, such as maybe a slug from a Betsy.

Of course Sam the Gonoph does not happen to have a Betsy on him, but Society Max can scarcely be expected to know this, because the chances are he remembers that Sam often has such an article in his pants pocket when he is around New York, so I suppose Society Max plays it as safe as possible.

Anyway, we do not see hide or hair of him and in the meantime the excitement over the large boat race between the Harvards and the Yales is now so terrific that I forget Society Max and try to get a peek at it.

But all I remember is seeing the young doll, Clarice, kissing Sam the Gonoph smack-dab on his homely puss, and jumping up and down in considerable glee, and stating that she knows all along that Sam will figure out some way for the Harvards to win, although she does not know yet how he does it, and hearing Mr. Hammond Campbell using language even worse than Sam the Gonoph employs when he is pursuing Society Max, and saying he never sees such a this-and-that boat race in all his born days.

Then I get to thinking about the grey-haired doll, and I go over and pick her up and she is still about two-thirds out and is saying to herself, as follows:

'Max, oh, my dear, dear Max.'

Well, by and by Mr. Hammond Campbell takes Sam the Gonoph into a room on the yacht and pays him what is coming to all of us on the race, and then he takes to asking about Society Max, and when Sam the Gonoph explains how Max is a terrible fink and what he does to Sonia and all, Mr. Hammond Campbell hands Sam five large G's extra, and states to him as follows:

'This,' he says, 'is for preventing my sister, Emma, from making a fool of herself. She picks this Max up somewhere in Europe and he puts himself away with her as a Russian nobleman, and she is going to marry him next week, although from what you tell me it will be bigamy on his part. By the way,' Mr. Hammond Campbell says, 'not that it makes any difference, but I wonder whatever becomes of the guy?'

I am wondering this somewhat myself, not that I really care what becomes of Society Max, but I do not find out until later in the evening when I am at the Western Union office in New London, Conn., sending a telegram for Sam the Gonoph to the guy who runs his farm in New Jersey telling the guy to be sure and watch the onions, and I hear a newspaper scribe talking about the large boat race.

'Yes,' the newspaper scribe says, 'the Yales are leading by a boat length up to the last hundred yards and going easy, and they seem to be an absolute cinch to win, when No. 6 man in their boat hits something in the water and breaks his oar, throwing the rest of the crew out of kilter long enough for the Harvards to slip past and win. It is the most terrible upset of the dope in history,' he says.

'Now,' the scribe says, 'of course a broken oar is not unheard of in a boat race, but what No. 6 says he hits is a guy's head which pops out of the water all of a sudden right alongside the Yales' boat, and which disappears again as the oar hits it.

'Personally,' the scribe says, 'I will say No. 6 is seeing things but for the fact that a Coast Guard boat which is laying away down the river below the finish just reports that it picks up a guy out of the river who seems to be alive and all right except he has a lump on his noggin a foot high.'

I do not see Sam the Gonoph again until it comes on fall, when I run into him in Mindy's restaurant on Broadway, and Sam says to me like this:

'Say,' he says, 'do you remember what a hit I make with the little doll because she thinks I have something to do with the Harvards winning a large boat-race? Well,' Sam the Gonoph says, 'I just get a note from her asking me if I can do anything about a football game that the Harvards have coming up with the Dartmouths next month.'

Broadway Financier

Of all the scores made by dolls on Broadway the past twenty-five years, there is no doubt but what the very largest score is made by a doll who is called Silk, when she knocks off a banker by the name of Israel Ib, for the size of Silk's score is three million one hundred bobs and a few odd cents.

It is admitted by one and all who know about these matters that the record up to this time is held by a doll by the name of Irma Teak, who knocks off a Russian duke back in 1911 when Russian dukes are considered very useful by dolls, although of course in these days Russian dukes are about as useful as dandruff. Anyway, Irma Teak's score off this Russian duke is up around a million, and she moves to London with her duke and chucks quite a swell around there for a time. But finally Irma Teak goes blind, which is a tough break for her as she can no longer see how jealous she is making other dolls with her diamonds and sables and one thing and another, so what good are they to her, after all?

I know Irma Teak when she is a show doll at the old Winter Garden, and I also know the doll by the name of Mazie Mitz, who is a Florodora revival, and who makes a score of maybe three hundred G's off a guy who has a string of ten-cent stores, and three hundred G's is by no means hay. But Mazie Mitz finally hauls off and runs away with a saxophone player she is in love with and so winds up back of the fifteen ball.

Furthermore, I know Clara Simmons, the model from Rickson's, who gets a five-story town house and a country place on Long Island off a guy in Wall Street for birthday presents, and while I never meet this guy personally, I always figure he must be very dumb because anybody who knows Clara Simmons knows she will be just as well satisfied with a bottle of perfume for a birthday

present. For all I know, Clara Simmons may still own the town
house and the country place, but she must be shoving on toward
forty now, so naturally nobody on Broadway cares what becomes
of her.

I know a hundred other dolls who run up different scores, and
some of them are very fair scores, indeed, but none of these scores
are anything much alongside Silk's score off Israel Ib, and this
score is all the more surprising because Silk starts out being greatly
prejudiced against bankers. I am no booster for bankers myself, as I
consider them very stony-hearted guys, but I am not prejudiced
against them. In fact, I consider bankers very necessary, because
if we do not have bankers many citizens will not be able to think
of anybody to give a cheque on.

It is quite a while before she meets Israel Ib that Silk explains to
me why she is prejudiced against bankers. It is when she is nothing
but a chorus doll in Johnny Oakley's joint on Fifty-third Street,
and comes into Mindy's after she gets through work, which is
generally along about four o'clock in the morning.

At such an hour many citizens are sitting around Mindy's resting from the crap games and one thing and another, and dolls from
the different joints around and about, including chorus dolls and
hostesses, drop in for something to eat before going home, and
generally these dolls are still in their make-up and very tired.

Naturally they come to know the citizens who are sitting around,
and say hello, and maybe accept the hospitality of these citizens,
such as java and Danish pastry, or maybe a few scrambled eggs,
and it is all very pleasant and harmless, because a citizen who is all
tuckered out from shooting craps is not going to get any high
blood pressure over a tired chorus doll or a hostess, and especially a
hostess.

Well, one morning Silk is sitting at my table guzzling a cup of
java and a piece of apple pie, when in comes The Greek looking
very weary, The Greek being a high shot who is well known far
and wide. He drops into a chair alongside me and orders a Bismarck herring with sliced onions to come along, which is a dish
that is considered most invigorating, and then The Greek mentions
that he is playing the bank for twenty-four hours hand running, so
right away Silk speaks up as follows:

'I hate banks,' she says. 'Furthermore,' she says, 'I hate bankers.
If it is not for a banker maybe I will not be slaving in Johnny
Oakley's dirty little drum for thirty bobs per week. Maybe my

mamma will still be alive, and I will be living at home with her instead of in a flea bag in Forty-seventh Street.

'My mamma once saves up three hundred bobs from scrubbing floors in an office building to send me to school,' Silk says, 'and a banker in one of the buildings where she does this scrubbing tells her to put her dough in his bank, and what happens but the bank busts and it is such a terrible blow to my mamma that she ups and dies. I am very small at the time,' Silk says, 'but I can remember standing in front of the busted bank with my mamma, and my mamma crying her eyes out.'

Well, personally, I consider Silk's crack about Johnny Oakley's joint uncalled for, as it is by no means little, but I explain to her that what The Greek is talking about is a faro bank, and not a bank you put your money in, as such a bank is called a jug, and not a bank at all, while faro bank is a gambling game, and the reason I explain this to Silk is because everybody always explains things to her.

The idea is everybody wishes Silk to be well smartened up, especially everybody who hangs out around Mindy's because she is an orphan and never has a chance to go to school, and we do not wish her to grow up dumb like the average doll, as one and all are very fond of Silk from the first minute she bobs up around Mindy's.

Now at this time Silk is maybe seventeen years old and weighs maybe ninety pounds, sopping wet, and she is straight up and down like a boy. She has soft brown hair and brown eyes that seem too big for her face, and she looks right at you when she talks to you and she talks to you like one guy to another guy. In fact, I always claim there is more guy in Silk than there is doll, as she finally gets so she thinks like a guy, which is maybe because she associates more with guys than she does with other dolls and gets a guy's slant on things in general.

She loves to sit around Mindy's in the early morning gabbing with different citizens, although she does more listening than gabbing herself, and she loves to listen to gab about horse-racing and baseball and fights and crap-shooting and to guys cutting up old touches and whatever else is worth gabbing about, and she seldom sticks in her oar, except maybe to ask a question. Naturally a doll who is willing to listen instead of wishing to gab herself is bound to be popular because if there is anything most citizens hate and despise it is a gabby doll.

So then many citizens take a real interest in Silk's education, including Regret, the horse-player, who explains to her how to build up a sucker to betting on a hot horse, although personally I do not consider such knowledge of any more value to a young doll just starting out in the world than the lesson Big Nig, the crap-shooter, gives her one night on how to switch in a pair of tops on a craps game.

Then there is Doc Daro, who is considered one of the highest-class operators that ever rides the tubs in his day, being a great hand for travelling back and forth across the ocean and outplaying other passengers at bridge and poker and one thing and another, but who finally gets rheumatism in his hands so bad he can no longer shuffle the cards. And of course if Doc Daro cannot shuffle the cards there is no sense whatever in him trying to play games of skill any more.

Doc Daro is always telling Silk what rascals guys are and explaining to her the different kinds of business they will try to give her, this being the same kind of business the Doc gives dolls himself in his time. The Doc has an idea that a young doll who is battling Broadway needs plenty of education along such lines, but Silk tells me privately that she is jerry to the stuff Doc is telling her when she is five years old.

The guy I figure does Silk the most good is an old pappy guy by the name of Professor D, who is always reading books when he is not busy doping the horses. In fact, Professor D is considered somewhat daffy on the subject of reading books, but it seems he gets the habit from being a teacher in a college out in Ohio before he becomes a horse-player. Anyway, Professor D takes to giving Silk books to read, and what is more she reads them and talks them over afterward with the professor, who is greatly pleased by this.

'She is a bright little doll,' Professor D says to me one day. 'Furthermore,' the professor says, 'she has soul.'

'Well,' I say, 'Big Nig claims she can palm a pair of dice as good as anybody he ever sees.'

But the professor only says heigh-ho, and goes along, and I can see he does not consider me a character worth having much truck with, even though I am as much interested in Silk's education as anybody else.

Well, what happens one night but the regular singer in Johnny Oakley's joint, a doll by the name of Myrtle Marigold, hauls off and catches the measles from her twelve-year-old son, and as

Johnny has enough trouble getting customers into his joint without giving them the measles after getting them there he gives Myrtle Marigold plenty of wind at once.

But there he is without anybody to sing 'Stacker Lee' to his customers, 'Stacker Lee' being a ditty with which Myrtle Marigold panics the customers, so Johnny looks his chorus over and finally asks Silk if she can sing. And Silk says she can sing all right, but that she will not sing 'Stacker Lee,' because she considers it a low-down lullaby, at best. She says she will sing something classical and, being desperate for singing, Johnny Oakley says go ahead. So what does Silk do but sing a very old song called 'Annie Laurie,' which she learns from her mamma, and she sings this song so loud that sobs are heard all over the joint.

Of course if anybody investigates they will learn that the sobbing is being done by Professor D and Big Nig and The Greek, who happen to be in the joint at the time, and what they are sobbing about is the idea of Silk singing at all, but Johnny Oakley considers her a big hit and keeps her singing 'Annie Laurie' right along, and one night Harry Fitz, the booking agent, drops in and hears her singing and tells Ziegfeld he discovers a doll with a brand-new style.

Naturally Ziggie signs her up at once for the Follies, because he has great faith in Harry Fitz's judgment but after Ziggie hears Silk sing he asks her if she can do anything else, and is greatly relieved when he learns she can dance.

So Silk becomes a Ziegfeld dancer, and she is quite a sensation with the dramatic critics on the night she opens because she dances with all her clothes on, which is considered a very great novelty indeed. The citizens around Mindy's chip in and send Silk a taxi-cab full of orchids, and a floral pillow, and Professor D contributes a book called *The Outline of History*, and Silk is the happiest doll in town.

A year goes by, and what a year in the Follies does for Silk is most astonishing. Personally, I never see a lot of change in her looks, except her figure fills out so it has bumps here and there where a doll is entitled to have bumps, and her face grows to fit her eyes more, but everybody else claims she becomes beautiful, and her picture is always in the papers and dozens of guys are always hanging around after her and sending her flowers and one thing and another.

One guy in particular starts sending her jewellery, which Silk always brings around to Mindy's for Jewellery Joe to look at, this Jewellery Joe being a guy who peddles jewellery along Broadway for years, and who can tell you in a second what a piece of jewellery is worth.

Jewellery Joe finds that the jewellery Silk brings around is nothing much but slum, and naturally he advises her to have no further truck with any party who cannot send in anything better than this, but one morning she shows up in Mindy's with an emerald ring the size of a cake of soap, and the minute Jewellery Joe sees the emerald he tells Silk that whoever donates this is worthy of very careful consideration.

Now it seems that the party who sends the emerald is nobody but Israel Ib, the banker who owns the jug down on the lower East Side that is called the Bank of the Bridges, and the way Silk comes to connect with him is most unusual. It is through a young guy by the name of Simeon Slotsky, who is a teller in Israel Ib's jug, and who sees Silk dancing one night in the Follies and goes right off his ka-zip about her.

It is this Simeon Slotsky who is sending the jewellery that Silk first brings around, and the way he is buying this jewellery is by copping a little dough out of the jug now and then which does not belong to him. Naturally this is a most dishonest action, and by and by they catch up with Simeon Slotsky in the jug, and Israel Ib is going to place him in the pokey.

Well, Simeon Slotsky does not wish to be placed in the pokey and not knowing what else to do, what does he do but go to Silk and tell her his story, explaining that he commits his dishonest business only because he is daffy about her, even though Silk never gives him a tumble, and in fact never says as much as two words to him before.

He tells her that he comes of respectable old parents down on the lower East Side, who will be very sad if he is placed in the pokey, especially his mamma, but Israel Ib is bound and determined to put him away, because Israel Ib is greatly opposed to anybody copping dough out of his jug. Simeon Slotsky says his mamma cries all over Israel Ib's vest trying to cry him out of the idea of placing her son in the pokey, but that Israel Ib is a very hard-hearted guy and will not give in no matter what, and furthermore he is very indignant because Simeon's mamma's tears spot up his vest. So Simeon says it looks as if he must go to the pokey unless Silk can think of something.

Now Silk is very young herself and very tender hearted and she is sorry for Simeon Slotsky, because she can see he is nothing but a hundred-per-cent chump, so she sits down and writes a letter to Israel Ib asking him to call on her backstage at the Follies on a matter of great importance. Of course Silk does not know that it is not the proper caper to be writing a banker such a letter, and ordinarily it is a thousand to one, according to the way The Greek figures the odds, that a banker will pay no attention to such a letter except maybe to notify his lawyer.

But it seems that the letter tickles Israel Ib, as he always secretly wishes to get a peek backstage at the Follies to see if the dolls back there wear as few clothes as he hears, so he shows up the very same night, and in five minutes Silk has him all rounded up as far as Simeon Slotsky is concerned. Israel Ib says he will straighten out everything and send Simeon to a job in a jug out West.

So the next day Simeon Slotsky comes around and thanks Silk for all she does for him, and bawls quite some, and gets a photograph off her with her name signed to it which he says he will give to his mamma so she can stick it up on her wall on the East Side to always remember the doll who saves her son, and then Simeon Slotsky goes on about his business, and for all I know becomes a very honest and useful citizen. And forty-eight hours later, Silk is wearing the emerald from Israel Ib.

Now this Israel Ib is by no means a Broadway character, and in fact few ever hear of him before he bobs up sending Silk an emerald ring. In fact, it seems that Israel Ib is a quiet, industrious guy, who has nothing on his mind but running his jug and making plenty of scratch until the night he goes to see Silk.

He is a little short fat guy of maybe forty-odd at this time with a little round stomach sticking out in front of him and he always wears a white vest on his stomach, with a pair of gold-rimmed cheaters hanging on a black ribbon across the vest. He has a large snozzle and is as homely as a mud fence, anyway you take him, but it is well known to one and all that he is a coming guy in the banking dodge.

Silk is always making jokes about Israel Ib, because naturally she cannot see much to such a looking guy, but every morning she comes into Mindy's with all kinds of swag, such as bracelets and rings and brooches, and Jewellery Joe finally speaks to her very severely and tells her that a guy who can send her such merchandise is no joking matter.

There is no doubt that Israel Ib is dizzy about her, and personally I consider it very sad that a guy as smart as he must be lets himself get tangled up in such a situation. But then I remember that guys ten thousand times smarter than Israel Ib let themselves get tangled up the same way, so it is all even.

The upshot of the whole business is that Silk begins to pay a little serious attention to Israel Ib, and the next thing anybody knows she quits the Follies and takes to living in a large apartment on Park Avenue and riding around in a big car with a guy in uniform driving her, and she has enough fur coats for a tribe of Eskimos, including a chinchilla flogger that moves Israel back thirty G's.

Furthermore, it comes out that the apartment house she is living in is in her own name, and some citizens are greatly surprised, as they do not figure a doll just off Broadway smart enough to get anything in her own name, except maybe a traffic summons. But Professor D says he is not surprised because he once makes Silk read a book entitled *The Importance of Property.*

We do not see much of Silk any more these days, but every now and then we hear rumours of her getting more apartment houses and business buildings in her own name, and the citizens around Mindy's are greatly pleased because they figure it proves that the trouble they take educating Silk is by no means wasted. Finally we hear Silk goes to Europe, and for nearly two years she is living in Paris and other spots, and some say the reason she sticks around Europe is because she finds out all of a sudden that Israel Ib is a married guy, although personally I figure Silk must know this all along, because it certainly is no mystery. In fact, Israel Ib is very much married, indeed, and his ever-loving wife is a big fat old doll whose family has plenty of potatoes.

The chances are Silk is sick and tired of looking at Israel Ib, and stays abroad so she will not have to look at his ugly kisser more than two or three times a year, which is about as often as Israel Ib can think up excuses to go over and see her. Then one winter we hear that Silk is coming home to stay, and it is the winter of 1930 when things are very tough, indeed.

It is close to Christmas when Silk lands one morning around eleven o'clock from the steamship, and it seems she is expecting Israel Ib to meet her at the dock, but Israel Ib is not present, and nobody else is there to tell her why Israel Ib is absent.

It seems that some of Silk's luggage is being held up by the customs guys, as she brings over enough merchandise of one kind and another to stock a department store, and she wishes to see Israel Ib to get this matter straightened out, so she hires a taxi and tells the jockey to take her to Israel Ib's jug, figuring to stop in a minute and give Israel Ib his instructions, and maybe a good rousting around for not meeting her.

Now Silk never before goes to Israel Ib's jug, which is deep down on the lower East Side where many citizens wear long whiskers and do not speak much English, and where there always seems to be a smell of herring around and about, and she is greatly surprised and much disgusted by her surroundings as she approaches the corner where Israel Ib's jug stands.

Furthermore, she is much surprised to find a big crowd in front of the jug, and this crowd is made up of many whiskers and old dolls wearing shawls over their heads, and kids of all sizes and shapes, and everybody in the crowd seems much excited, and there is plenty of moaning and groaning from one and all, and especially from an old doll who is standing in the doorway of a little store a couple of doors from the jug.

In fact, this old doll is making more racket than all the rest of the crowd put together, and at times is raising her voice to a scream and crying out in a strange language words that sound quite hostile.

Silk's taxi cannot get through the mob and a copper steps up and tells the driver he better make a detour, so Silk asks the copper why these people are raising such a rumpus in the street, instead of being home keeping warm, for it is colder than a blonde's heart, and there is plenty of ice around about.

'Why,' the copper says, 'do you not hear? This jug busts this morning and the guy who runs it, Israel Ib, is over in the Tombs, and the people are nervous because many of them have their potatoes in the jug. In fact,' the copper says, 'some of them, including the old doll over there in front of the store who is doing all the screeching, have their lifetime savings in this jug, and it looks as if they are ruined. It is very sad,' he says, 'because they are very, very poor people.'

And then tears come to his eyes, and he boffs an old guy with whiskers over the skull with his club because the old guy is moaning so loud the copper can scarcely make himself heard.

Now naturally all this is most surprising news to Silk, and while she is pretty much sored up because she cannot see Israel Ib to get her merchandise out of the customs, she has the taxi jockey take her away from these scenes right away, and up to her apartment in Park Avenue, which she has ready for her coming home. Then she sends out for the early editions of the evening papers and reads all about what a rapscallion Israel Ib is for letting his jug bust right in the poor people's faces.

It seems that Israel Ib is placed in the Tombs because somebody suspects something illegal about the busting, but of course nobody figures Israel Ib will be kept in the Tombs long on account of being a banker, and in fact there is already some talk that the parties who placed him there in the first place may find themselves in plenty of heat later on, because it is considered most discourteous to a banker to place him in the Tombs where the accommodations are by no means first class.

One of the papers has a story about Israel Ib's ever-loving wife taking it on the lam as soon as the news gets out about the jug busting and Israel Ib being in the Tombs, and about her saying he can get out of this predicament the best way he can, but that she will never help with as much as a thin dime of her dough and hinting pretty strong that Israel Ib's trouble is on account of him squandering the jug's scratch on a doll.

The story says she is going back to her people, and from the way the story reads it sounds as if the scribe who writes it figures this is one good break, at least, for Israel Ib.

Now these hints let out by Israel Ib's ever-loving wife about him squandering the jug's scratch on a doll are printed as facts in the morning papers the next morning, and maybe if Silk bothers to read these morning sheets she will think better of going down to Israel Ib's jug again, because her name is mentioned right out, and there are big pictures of her in the papers from her old days in the Follies.

But there Silk is in a taxi in front of the Bank of the Bridges at nine o'clock the next morning, and it seems her brain is buzzing with quite a large idea, although this idea does not come out until later.

There is already quite a crowd around the jug again, as it is always very difficult to make people who live on the lower East Side and wear whiskers and shawls understand about such matters as busted jugs. They are apt to hang around a busted jug for days at a time with their bank-books in their hands, and sometimes it takes as much as a week to convince such people that their potatoes are gone for good, and make them disperse to their homes and start saving more.

There is still much moaning and groaning, though not as much as the day before, and every now and then the old doll pops out of the little store and stands in the doorway and shakes her fist at the busted jug and hollers in a strange language. A short, greasy-looking guy with bristly whiskers and an old black derby hat jammed down over his ears is standing with a morning paper spread out in his hands, and a bunch of other guys are around him listening to him read what the paper has to say about the situation.

Just one copper is walking up and down now, and it is the copper who speaks to Silk the day before, and he seems to remember her as she gets out of the taxi and he walks over to her, while a lot of people stop moaning and groaning to take a gander at her, for it is by no means a common sight to see such a looking doll in this neighbourhood.

The copper no more than says good morning to Silk when the guy who is reading the paper stops reading and takes a peek at her, and then at her picture which is on the page in front of him. Then he points at the picture and points at Silk, and begins jabbering a blue streak to the guys around him. About this time the old doll peeps out of the store to shake her fist at Israel Ib's jug again and, hearing the jabbering, she joins the bunch around the guy with the paper.

She listens to the jabbering a while, peeking over the guy's shoulder at the picture, and then taking a good long look at Silk, and then all of a sudden the old doll turns and pops back into the store.

Now all the shawls and whiskers start gathering around Silk and the copper, and anybody can tell from the way they are looking that they are all sored up, and what they are sored up at is Silk, because naturally they figure out that she is the doll whose picture is in the morning paper and is therefore the doll who is responsible for Israel Ib's jug busting.

But of course the copper does not know that they are sored up at Silk, and figures they are gathering around just out of curiosity, as people will do when they see a copper talking to anybody. He is a young copper and naturally he does not wish to have an audience when he is speaking to such a looking doll as Silk, even if most of the audience cannot understand English, so as the crowd nudges closer he gets his club ready to boff a few skulls.

Just about then half a brickbat hits him under the right ear, and he begins wobbling about very loose at the hinges, and at the same minute all the shawls and whiskers take to pulling and hauling at Silk. There are about a hundred of the shawls and whiskers to begin with and more are coming up from every-which direction, and they are all yelling and screaming and punching and scratching at Silk.

She is knocked down two or three times, and many shawls and whiskers are walking up and down her person while she is on the ground, and she is bleeding here and there, and the chances are they will kill her as dead as a door-nail in their excitement if the old doll from the little store near the jug does not bob up all of a sudden with a mop handle in her duke and starts boffing the shawls and whiskers on their noggins.

In fact, the old doll plays a regular tune on these noggins with the mop handle, sometimes knocking a shawl or whiskers quite bow-legged, and soon clearing a path through the crowd to Silk and taking hold of Silk and dragging her off into the store just as the reserves and an ambulance arrive.

The young copper is still wobbling about from the brickbat and speaking of how he hears the birdies singing in the trees, although of course there are no birdies in this neighbourhood at such a time of year, and no trees either, and there are maybe half a dozen shawls and whiskers sitting on the pavement rubbing their noggins, and others are diving into doorways here and there, and there is much confusion generally.

So the ambulance takes Silk and some of the shawls and whiskers to a hospital and Professor D and Doc Daro visit her there a couple of hours later, finding her in bed somewhat plastered up in spots but in no danger, and naturally Professor D and Doc Daro wish to know what she is doing around Israel Ib's jug, anyway.

'Why,' Silk says, 'I am not able to sleep a wink all last night thinking of these poor people suffering on account of me taking Israel Ib's dough, although,' Silk says, 'of course I do not know it is wrong dough when I receive it. I do not know Israel Ib is clipping these poor people. But seeing them around the jug yesterday morning, I remember what happens to my poor mamma when the jug busts on her. I see her standing in front of the busted jug with me beside her, crying her eyes out, and my heart is very heavy,' Silk says. 'So I get to thinking,' she says, 'that it will be a very nice thing, indeed, if I am first to tell the poor souls who have their dough in Israel Ib's jug that they are going to get it back.'

'Wait a minute,' Doc Daro says. 'What do you mean – they are going to get their dough back?'

'Why,' Silk says, 'I consult with Judge Goldstein, who is my tongue, and a very good guy, at that, and fairly honest, last night, and Judge Goldstein tells me that I am worth in negotiable securities and real estate and jewellery, and one thing and another, about three million one hundred bobs, and a few odd cents.

'Judge Goldstein tells me,' Silk says, 'that such a sum will more than pay off all the depositors in Israel Ib's jug. In fact, Judge Goldstein tells me that what I have probably represents most of the deposits in the jug, and,' she says, 'I sign everything I own in this world over to Judge Goldstein to do this, although Judge Goldstein says there is no doubt I can beat any attempt to take my dough away from me if I wish to keep it.

'So,' Silk says, 'I am so happy to think these poor people will get their dough back that I cannot wait for Judge Goldstein to let it out. I wish to break the news to them myself, but,' Silk says, 'before I can say a word they hop on me and start giving me a pasting, and if it is not for the old doll with the mop handle maybe you will have to chip in to bury me, because I certainly do not have enough dough left to bury myself.'

Well, this is about all there is to this story, except that the Bank of the Bridges pays off one hundred per cent. on the dollar, and what is more Israel Ib is running it again, and doing very well, indeed, and his ever-loving wife returns to him, and everything is hotsy-totsy between them.

As for Silk, she is back on Broadway, and the last time I see her she is in love with a very legitimate guy who is in the hotel business, and while he does not strike me as having much brains, he has plenty of youth running for him, and Silk says it is the best break she ever gets in her life when Israel Ib's jug busts.

But anybody will tell you that the best break Silk ever gets is when the old doll on the lower East Side recognizes her from the photograph she has stuck up on the wall in the little store near Israel Ib's jug as the doll who once saves her son, Simeon Slotsky, from being placed in the pokey.

The Brain Goes Home

One night The Brain is walking me up and down Broadway in front of Mindy's Restaurant, and speaking of this and that, when along comes a red-headed raggedy doll selling apples at five cents per copy, and The Brain, being very fond of apples, grabs one out of her basket and hands her a five-dollar bill.

The red-headed raggedy doll, who is maybe thirty-odd and is nothing but a crow as far as looks are concerned, squints at the finnif, and says to The Brain like this:

'I do not have change for so much money,' she says, 'but I will go and get it in a minute.'

'You keep the change,' The Brain says, biting a big hunk out of the apple and taking my arm to start me walking again.

Well, the raggedy doll looks at The Brain again, and it seems to me that all of a sudden there are large tears in her eyes as she says:

'Oh, thank you, sir! Thank you, thank you, and God bless you, sir!'

And then she goes on up the street in a hurry, with her hands over her eyes and her shoulders shaking, and The Brain turns around very much astonished, and watches her until she is out of sight.

'Why, my goodness!' The Brain says. 'I give Doris Clare ten G's last night, and she does not make half as much fuss over it as this doll does over a pound note.'

'Well,' I say, 'maybe the apple dool needs a pound note more than Doris needs ten G's.'

'Maybe so,' The Brain says. 'And of course, Doris gives me much more in return than just an apple and a God bless me. Doris gives me her love. I guess,' The Brain says, 'that love costs me about as much dough as any guy that ever lives.'

'I guess it does,' I say, and the chances are we both guess right, because off-hand I figure that if The Brain gets out on three hundred G's per year for love, he is running his love business very economically indeed, because it is well known to one and all that The Brain has three different dolls, besides an ever-loving wife.

In fact, The Brain is sometimes spoken of by many citizens as the 'Love King,' but only behind his back, because The Brain likes to think his love affairs are a great secret to all but maybe a few, although the only guy I ever see in this town who does not know all about them is a guy who is deaf, dumb, and blind.

I once read a story about a guy by the name of King Solomon who lives a long time ago and who has a thousand dolls all at once, which is going in for dolls on a very large scale indeed, but I guarantee that all of King Solomon's dolls put together are not as expensive as any one of The Brain's dolls. The overhead on Doris Clare alone will drive an ordinary guy daffy, and Doris is practically frugal compared to Cynthia Harris and Bobby Baker.

Then there is Charlotte, who is The Brain's ever-loving wife and who has a society bug and needs plenty of coconuts at all times to keep her a going concern. I once hear The Brain tell Bobby Baker that his ever-loving wife is a bit of an invalid, but as a matter of fact there is never anything the matter with Charlotte that a few bobs will not cure, although of course this goes for nearly every doll in this world who is an invalid.

When a guy is knocking around Broadway as long as The Brain, he is bound to accumulate dolls here and there, but most guys accumulate one at a time, and when this one runs out on him, as Broadway dolls will do, he accumulates another, and so on, and so on, until he is too old to care about such matters as dolls, which is when he is maybe a hundred and four years old, although I hear of several guys who beat even this record.

But when The Brain accumulates a doll he seems to keep her accumulated, and none of them ever run out on him, and while this will be a very great nuisance to the average guy, it pleases The Brain no little because it makes him think he has a very great power over dolls.

'They are not to blame if they fall in love with me,' The Brain says to me one night. 'I will not cause one of them any sorrow for all the world.'

Well, of course, it is most astonishing to me to hear a guy as smart as The Brain using such language, but I figure he may really believe it, because The Brain thinks very good of himself at all times. However, some guys claim that the real reason The Brain keeps all his dolls is because he is too selfish to give them away, although personally I will not take any of them if The Brain throws in a cash bonus, except maybe Bobby Baker.

Anyway, The Brain keeps his dolls accumulated, and furthermore he spends plenty of dough on them, what with buying them automobiles and furs and diamonds and swell places to live in – especially swell places to live in. One time I tell The Brain he will save himself plenty if he hires a house and bunches his dolls together in one big happy family, instead of having them scattered all over town, but The Brain says this idea is no good.

'In the first place,' he says, 'they do not know about each other, except Doris and Cynthia and Bobby know about Charlotte, although she does not know about them. They each think they are the only one with me. So if I corral them all together they will be jealous of each other over my love. Anyway,' The Brain says, 'such an arrangement will be very immoral and against the law. No,' he says, 'it is better to have them in different spots, because think of the many homes it gives me to go to in case I wish to go home. In fact,' The Brain says, 'I guess I have more homes to go to than any other guy on Broadway.'

Well, this may be true, but what The Brain wants with a lot of different homes is a very great mystery on Broadway, because he seldom goes home, anyway, his idea in not going home being that something may happen in this town while he is at home that he is not in on. The Brain seldom goes anywhere in particular. He never goes out in public with any one of his dolls, except maybe once or twice a year with Charlotte, his ever-loving wife, and finally he even stops going with her because Doris Clare says it does not look good to Doris's personal friends.

The Brain marries Charlotte long before he becomes the biggest guy in gambling operations in the East, and a millionaire two or three times over, but he is never much of a hand to sit around home and chew the fat with his ever-loving wife, as husbands often do. Furthermore, when he is poor he has to live in a neighbourhood which is too far away for it to be convenient for him to go home, so finally he gets out of the habit of going there.

But Charlotte is not such a doll as cares to spend more than one or two years looking at the pictures on the wall, because it seems the pictures on the wall are nothing but pictures of cows in the meadows and houses covered with snow, so she does not go home any more than necessary, either, and has her own friends and is very happy indeed, especially after The Brain gets so he can send in right along.

I will say one thing about The Brain and his dolls: he never picks a crow. He has a very good eye for faces and shapes, and even Charlotte, his ever-loving wife, is not a crow, although she is

not as young as she used to be. As for Doris Clare, she is one of the
great beauties on the Ziegfeld roof in her day, and while her day is
by no means yesterday, or even the day before, Doris holds on
pretty well in the matter of looks. Giving her a shade the best of it,
I will say that Doris is thirty-two or -three, but she has plenty of
zing left in her, at that, and her hair remains very blonde, no
matter what.

In fact, The Brain does not care much if his dolls are blonde or
brunette, because Cynthia Harris's hair is as black as the inside of a
wolf, while Bobby Baker is betwixt and between, her hair being a
light brown. Cynthia Harris is more of a Johnny-come-lately than
Doris, being out of Mr. Earl Carroll's 'Vanities,' and I hear she
first comes to New York as Miss Somebody in one of these beauty
contests which she will win hands down if one of the judges does
not get a big wink from a Miss Somebody Else.

Of course, Cynthia is doing some winking herself at this time,
but it seems that she picks a guy to wink at thinking he is one of
the judges, when he is nothing but a newspaperman and has no say
whatever about the decision.

Well, Mr. Earl Carroll feels sorry for Cynthia, so he puts her in
the 'Vanities' and lets her walk around raw, and The Brain sees
her, and the next thing anybody knows she is riding in a big
foreign automobile the size of a rum chaser, and is chucking a
terrible swell.

Personally, I always consider Bobby Baker the smartest of all
The Brain's dolls, because she is just middling as to looks and she
does not have any of the advantages of life like Doris Clare and
Cynthia Harris, such as jobs on the stage where they can walk
around showing off their shapes to guys such as The Brain. Bobby
Baker starts off as nothing but a private secretary to a guy in Wall
Street, and naturally she is always wearing clothes, or anyway, as
many clothes as an ordinary doll wears nowadays, which is not so
many, at that.

It seems that The Brain once has some business with the guy
Bobby works for and happens to get talking to Bobby, and she tells
him how she always wishes to meet him, what with hearing
and reading about him, and how he is just as handsome and
romantic-looking as she always pictures him to herself.

Now I wish to say I will never call any doll a liar, being at all
times a genleman, and for all I know, Bobby Baker may really
think The Brain is handsome and romantic-looking, but personally

I figure if she is not lying to him, she is at least a little excited when she makes such a statement to The Brain. The best you can give The Brain at this time is that he is very well dressed.

He is maybe forty years old, give or take a couple of years, and he is commencing to get a little bunchy about the middle, what with sitting down at card-tables so much and never taking any exercise outside of walking guys such as me up and down in front of Mindy's for a few hours every night. He has a clean-looking face, always very white around the gills, and he has nice teeth and a nice smile when he wishes to smile, which is never at guys who owe him dough.

And I will say for The Brain he has what is called personality. He tells a story well, although he is always the hero of any story he tells, and he knows how to make himself agreeable to dolls in many ways. He has a pretty fair sort of education, and while dolls such as Cynthia and Doris and maybe Charlotte, too, will rather have a charge account at Cartier's than all the education in Yale and Harvard put together, it seems that Bobby Baker likes highbrow gab, so naturally she gets plenty of same from The Brain.

Well, pretty soon Bobby is riding around in a car bigger than Cynthia's, though neither is as big as Doris's car, and all the neighbours' children over in Flatbush, which is where Bobby hails from, are very jealous of her and running around spreading gossip about her, but keeping their eyes open for big cars themselves. Personally, I always figure The Brain lowers himself socially by taking up with a doll from Flatbush, especially as Bobby Baker soon goes in for literary guys, such as newspaper scribes and similar characters around Greenwich Village.

But there is no denying Bobby Baker is a very smart little doll, and in the four or five years she is one of The Brain's dolls, she gets more dough out of him than all the others put together, because she is always telling him how much she loves him, and saying she cannot do without him, while Doris Clare and Cynthia Harris sometimes forget to mention this more than once or twice a month.

Now what happens early one morning but a guy by the name of Daffy Jack hauls off and sticks a shiv in The Brain's left side. It seems that this is done at the request of a certain party by the name of Homer Swing, who owes The Brain plenty of dough in a gambling transaction, and who becomes very indignant when The Brain presses him somewhat for payment. It seems that Daffy Jack, who is considered a very good shiv artist, aims at The Brain's heart, but misses it by a couple of inches, leaving The Brain with a very bad cut in his side which calls for some stitching.

Big Nig, the crap shooter, and I are standing at Fifty-second Street and Seventh Avenue along about 2 a.m. speaking of not much, when The Brain comes stumbling out of Fifty-second Street, and falls in Big Nig's arms, practically ruining a brand-new topcoat which Big Nig pays sixty bucks for a few days back with the blood that is coming out of the cut. Naturally, Big Nig is indignant about this, but we can see that it is no time to be speaking to The Brain about such matters. We can see that The Brain is carved up quite some, and is in a bad way.

Of course, we are not greatly surprised at seeing The Brain in this condition, because for years he is practically no price around this town, what with this guy and that being anxious to do something or other to him, but we are never expecting to see him carved up like a turkey. We are expecting to see him with a few slugs in him, and both Big Nig and me are very angry to think that there are guys around who will use such instruments as a knife on anybody.

But while we are thinking it over, The Brain says to me like this:

'Call Hymie Weissberger, and Doc Frisch,' he says, 'and take me home.'

Naturally, a guy such as The Brain wishes his lawyer before he wishes his doctor, and Hymie Weissberger is The Brain's mouthpiece, and a very sure-footed guy, at that.

'Well,' I say, 'we better take you to a hospital where you can get good attention at once.'

'No,' The Brain says. 'I wish to keep this secret. It will be a bad thing for me right now to have this get out, and if you take me to a hospital they must report it to the coppers. Take me home.'

Naturally, I say which home, being somewhat confused about The Brain's homes, and he seems to study a minute as if this is a question to be well thought out.

'Park Avenue,' The Brain says finally, so Big Nig stops a taxicab, and we help The Brain into the cab and tell the jockey to take us to the apartment house on Park Avenue near Sixty-fourth where The Brain's ever-loving wife Charlotte lives.

When we get there, I figure it is best for me to go up first and break the news gently to Charlotte, because I can see what a shock it is bound to be to any ever-loving wife to have her husband brought home in the early hours of the morning all shivved up.

Well, the door man and the elevator guy in the apartment house give me an argument about going up to The Brain's apartment, saying a blow out of some kind is going on there, but after I explain to them that The Brain is sick, they let me go. A big fat butler comes to the door of the apartment when I ring, and I can see there are many dolls and guys in evening clothes in the apartment, and somebody is singing very loud.

The butler tries to tell me I cannot see Charlotte, but I finally convince him it is best, so by and by she comes to the door, and a very pleasant sight she is, at that, with jewellery all over her. I stall around awhile, so as not to alarm her too much, and then I tell her The Brain meets with an accident and that we have him outside in a cab, and ask her where we shall put him.

'Why,' she says, 'put him in a hospital, of course. I am entertaining some very important people to-night, and I cannot have them disturbed by bringing in a hospital patient. Take him to hospital, and tell him I will come and see him to-morrow and bring him some broth.'

I try to explain to her that The Brain does not need any broth, but a nice place to lie down in, but finally she gets very testy with me and shuts the door in my face, saying as follows:

'Take him to a hospital, I tell you. This is a ridiculous hour for him to be coming home, anyway. It is twenty years since he comes home so early.'

Then as I am waiting for the elevator, she opens the door again just a little bit and says:

'By the way, is he hurt bad?'

I say we do not know how bad he is hurt, and she shuts the door again, and I go back to the cab again, thinking what a heartless doll she is, although I can see where it will be very inconvenient for her to bust up her party, at that.

The Brain is lying back in the corner of the cab, his eyes half-closed, and by this time it seems that Big Nig stops the blood somewhat with a handkerchief, but The Brain acts somewhat weak to me. He sort of rouses himself when I climb in the cab, and when I tell him his ever-loving wife is not home he smiles a bit and whispers:

'Take me to Doris.'

Now Doris lives in a big apartment house away over on West Seventy-second Street near the Drive, and I tell the taxi jockey to go there while The Brain seems to slide off into a doze. Then Big

Nig leans over to me and says to me like this:

'No use taking him there,' Big Nig says. 'I see Doris going out to-night all dressed up in her ermine coat with this actor guy, Jack Walen, she is struck on. It is a very great scandal around and about the way they carry on. Let us take him to Cynthia,' Nig says. 'She is a very large-hearted doll who will be very glad to take him in.'

Now Cynthia Harris has a big suite of rooms that cost fifteen G's a year in a big hotel just off Fifth Avenue, Cynthia being a doll who likes to be downtown so if she hears of anything coming off anywhere she can get there very rapidly. When we arrive at the hotel I call her on the house 'phone and tell her I must see her about something very important, so Cynthia says for me to come up.

It is now maybe three-fifteen, and I am somewhat surprised to find Cynthia home, at that, but there she is, and looking very beautiful indeed in a négligée with her hair hanging down, and I can see that The Brain is no chump when it comes to picking them. She gives me a hello pleasant enough, but as soon as I explain what I am there for, her kisser gets very stern and she says to me like this:

'Listen,' she says, 'I got trouble enough around this joint, what with two guys getting in a fight over me at a little gathering I have here last night and the house copper coming to split them out, and I do not care to have any more. Suppose it gets out that The Brain is here? What will the newspapers print about me? Think of my reputation!'

Well, in about ten minutes I can see there is no use arguing with her, because she can talk faster than I can, and mostly she talks about what a knock it will be to her reputation if she takes The Brain in, so I leave her standing at the door in her négligée, still looking very beautiful, at that.

There is now nothing for us to do but take The Brain to Bobby Baker, who lives in a duplex apartment in Sutton Place over by the East River, where the swells set up a colony of nice apartments in the heart of an old tenement-house neighbourhood, and as we are on our way there with The Brain lying back in the cab just barely breathing, I say to Big Nig like this:

'Nig,' I say, 'when we get to Bobby's, we will carry The Brain in without asking her first and just dump him on her so she cannot refuse to take him in, although,' I say, 'Bobby Baker is a nice little doll, and I am pretty sure she will do anything she can for him, especially,' I say, 'since he pays fifty G's for this apartment we are going to.'

So when the taxicab stops in front of Bobby's house, Nig and I take The Brain out of the cab and lug him between us up to the door of Bobby's apartment, where I ring the bell. Bobby opens the door herself, and I happen to see a guy's legs zip into a room in the apartment behind her, although of course there is nothing wrong in such a sight, even though the guy's legs are in pink pyjamas.

Naturally, Bobby is greatly astonished to see us with The Brain dangling between us, but she does not invite us in as I explain to her that The Brain is stabbed and that his last words are for us to take him to his Bobby. Furthermore, she does not let me finish my story which will be very sad indeed, if she keeps on listening.

"If you do not take him away from here at once,' Bobby says, before I am down to the pathetic part, 'I will call the cops and you guys will be arrested on suspicion that you know something about how he gets hurt.'

Then she slams the door on us, and we lug The Brain back down the stairs into the street, because all of a sudden it strikes us that Bobby is right, and if The Brain is found in our possession all stabbed up, and he happens to croak, we are in a very tough spot, because the cops just naturally love to refuse to believe guys like Big Nig and me, no matter what we say.

Furthermore, the same idea must hit the taxicab jockey after we lift The Brain out of the cab, because he is nowhere to be seen, and there we are away over by the East River in the early morning, with no other taxis in sight, and a cop liable to happen along any minute.

Well, there is nothing for us to do but get away from there, so Big Nig and I start moving, with me carrying The Brain's feet, and Big Nig his head. We get several blocks away from Sutton Place, going very slow and hiding in dark doorways when we hear anybody coming, and now we are in a section of tenement houses, when all of a sudden up out of the basement of one of these tenements pops a doll.

She sees us before we can get in a dark place, and she seems to have plenty of nerve for a doll, because she comes right over to us and looks at Big Nig and me, and then looks at The Brain, who loses his hat somewhere along the line, so his pale face is plain to be seen by even the dim street light.

'Why,' the doll says, 'it is the kind gentleman who gives me the five dollars for the apple – the money that buys the medicine that saves my Joey's life. What is the matter?'

'Well,' I say to the doll, who is still raggedy and still red-headed, 'there is nothing much the matter except if we do not get him somewhere soon, this guy will up and croak on us.'

'Bring him into my house,' she says, pointing to the joint she just comes out of. 'It is not much of a place, but you can let him rest there until you get help. I am just going over here to a drug store to get some more medicine for Joey, although he is out of danger now, thanks to this gentleman.'

So we lug The Brain down the basement steps with the doll leading the way, and we follow her into a room that smells like a Chinese laundry and seems to be full of kids sleeping on the floor. There is only one bed in the room, and it is not much of a bed any way you take it, and there seems to be a kid in this bed, too, but the red-headed doll rolls this kid over to one side of the bed and motions us to lay The Brain alongside of the kid. Then she gets a wet rag and stars bathing The Brain's noggin.

He finally opens his eyes and looks at the red-headed raggedy doll, and she grins at him very pleasant. When I think things over afterwards, I figure The Brain is conscious of much of what is going on when we are packing him around, although he does not say anything, maybe because he is too weak. Anyway, he turns his head to Big Nig, and says to him like this:

'Bring Weissberger and Frisch as quick as you can,' he says. 'Anyway, get Weissberger. I do not know how bad I am hurt, and I must tell him some things.'

Well, The Brain is hurt pretty bad, as it turns out, and in fact he never gets well, but he stays in the basement dump until he dies three days later, with the red-headed raggedy doll nursing him alongside her sick kid Joey, because the croaker, old Doc Frisch, says it is no good moving The Brain, and may only make him pop off sooner. In fact, Doc Frisch is much astonished that The Brain lives at all, considering the way we lug him around.

I am present at The Brain's funeral at Wiggins's Funeral Parlours, like everybody else on Broadway, and I wish to say I never see more flowers in all my life. They are all over the casket and kneedeep on the floor, and some of the pieces must cost plenty, the price of flowers being what they are in this town nowadays. In fact, I judge it is the size and cost of the different pieces that makes me notice a little bundle of faded red carnations not much bigger than your fist that is laying alongside a pillow of violets the size of a horse blanket.

There is a small card tied to the carnations, and it says on this card, as follows: 'To a kind gentleman,' and it comes to my mind that out of all the thousands of dollars' worth of flowers there, these faded carnations represent the only true sincerity. I mention this to Big Nig, and he says the chances are I am right, but that even true sincerity is not going to do The Brain any good where he is going.

Anybody will tell you that for off-hand weeping at a funeral The Brain's ever-loving wife Charlotte does herself very proud indeed, but she is not one-two-seven with Doris Clare, Cynthia Harris, and Bobby Baker. In fact, Bobby Baker weeps so loud that there is some talk of heaving her out of the funeral altogether.

However, I afterwards hear that loud as they are at the funeral, it is nothing to the weep they all put on when it comes out that The Brain has Hymie Weissberger draw up a new will while he is dying and leaves all his dough to the red-headed raggedy doll, whose name seems to be O'Halloran, and who is the widow of a bricklayer and has five kids.

Well, at first all the citizens along Broadway say it is a wonderful thing for The Brain to do, and serves his ever-loving wife and Doris and Cynthia and Bobby just right; and from the way one and all speaks you will think they are going to build a monument to The Brain for his generosity to the red-headed raggedy doll.

But about two weeks after he is dead, I hear citizens saying the chances are the red-headed raggedy doll is nothing but one of The Brain's old-time dolls, and that maybe the kids are his and that he leaves them the dough because his conscience hurts him at the finish, for this is the way Broadway is. But personally I know it cannot be true, for if there is one thing The Brain never has it is a conscience.

Furthermore

Introduction by E. C. Bentley

When *More Than Somewhat* was published, an undertaking was given by all those concerned in the production that, if it was favourably received, a second volume of Damon Runyon's Broadway stories would appear in due course.

For my own part, I never doubted that the first volume would have a success, and an immediate one. In a fairly long experience I have hailed enthusiastically at their birth some new books which took a very long time to establish themselves in the place of honour that was theirs by right. But it seemed to me that for Damon Runyon in this country the hour had struck; and so it proved to be.

The book did better than even I had hoped. The critics welcomed it everywhere in varying notes of praise and joy. One of them called it 'easily the funniest book of the year.' A Scottish reviewer expressed the same feeling in his native idiom by saying that no one could read it 'without being impressed by Mr. Runyon's quality as a humorist,' and that Runyon's imaginary narrator was 'an amusing character.' Another – one of a number who succumbed to the infection of Runyonese – declared that any guy or doll who could finish the book without yelling for more 'deserved a bop on the snozzle and a month in the sneezer.' One scholarly writer pointed out a detail which had escaped myself – Runyon's debt to Homer, in telling use of the recurrent phrase and the fixed epithet; 'the ever-loving wife,' for instance, or 'the proud old Spanish nobleman' of one of the tales in the present volume. So true is it that we stand on the shoulders of those who have essayed the height before us.

Another critic's enthusiasm carried him to the length of saying, 'Harry the Horse is an angel' – which that cold-blooded ruffian would hardly have taken as a compliment after a lifetime spent in trying to be something entirely different. Then there was one who seasoned his admiration with the remark that Runyon's tough guys were, after all, just a lot of 'sentimentalists.' That is, I know, in these times a favourite way of referring to generous impulse or natural affection; and a very nauseating sort of cant it is, to my taste. But I must insist, in simple justice to the guys in question, that the recorded instances of their doing anything decent are not many. Howard Spring, I thought, went near to the root of the matter in speaking of them as 'jungle-dwellers, hateful and horrible men and women, who yet please us because they are alive and completely integrated.' Also, perhaps, because they are bold and vigorous. As a personage in a novel by John Masefield expresses it, 'Courageous energy is always valued and remembered, and though the highwaymen and others often used their energy wickedly, they still used it, and risked their lives to use it.' Surely that is why, in the words of a Runyon guy whom I have quoted before, many legitimate guys are much interested in the doings of tough guys, and consider them very romantic.

But not sentimental. If there are any who share the opinion of that reviewer who found them so, they may be recommended to read the story in this volume called *Sense of Humour*, and to ask themselves if they know of anything ghastlier in modern fiction.

And if the welcome given to *More Than Somewhat* by the Press was all that could have been wished, the same can be said of its reception by the reading public, which also has a certain importance. They have taken Runyon to their bosom, I am delighted to say. His stories are talked about everywhere. Many grateful letters have been received by the publishers, and a certain number have been addressed to myself from various parts of the Kingdom. Even now I am engaged in a courteous controversy with a philologist on the staff of the British Museum, who takes what I can only consider a rather fanciful view of certain elements in Runyonese. It is, by the way, not such an easy language to master as many people seem to think. It is full of subtleties; and if, as I am told, it is sometimes made the medium of conversation in University Common Rooms to-day, it is probably no more than a sort of pidgin Runyonese that is heard in those olive-groves of Academe. But there could be no sincerer compliment to an author whom we have taken so long to discover, and who very likely never gave a thought to the possibility of our discovering him at all; since his vast popularity in his own country might well be enough for any man.

So much, then, for the reception given to *More Than Somewhat*. An undertaking, as I said at the outset, was given. Breach of promise, as it was explained to Harry the Horse on a certain occasion, 'is when somebody promises to do something and fails to do this something'; and Harry, being familiar enough with 'a proposi-

tion of this nature,' was always ready to 'deal with it accordingly.'
But we have had no idea of ignoring our obligation, and so incur-
ring the righteous revenge of a thwarted public. *Furthermore* re-
deems our pledge. It has been planned to be as fully representative
of the best of Damon Runyon as the other volume was; and I wish
to say I hope that a good time will be had by one and all, and that
they will get a great bang out of the doings.

Madame La Gimp

One night I am passing the corner of Fiftieth Street and Broadway, and what do I see but Dave the Dude standing in a doorway talking to a busted-down old Spanish doll by the name of Madame La Gimp. Or rather Madame La Gimp is talking to Dave the Dude, and what is more he is listening to her, because I can hear him say yes, yes, as he always does when he is really listening to anybody, which is very seldom.

Now this is a most surprising sight to me, because Madame La Gimp is not such an old doll as anybody will wish to listen to, especially Dave the Dude. In fact, she is nothing but an old hay-bag, and generally somewhat ginned up. For fifteen years, or maybe sixteen, I see Madame La Gimp up and down Broadway, or sliding along through the Forties, sometimes selling newspapers, and sometimes selling flowers, and in all these years I seldom see her but what she seems to have about half a heat on from drinking gin.

Of course, nobody ever takes the newspapers she sells, even after they buy them off of her, because they are generally yesterday's papers, and sometimes last week's, and nobody ever wants her flowers, even after they pay her for them, because they are flowers such as she gets off an undertaker over in Tenth Avenue, and they are very tired flowers, indeed.

Personally, I consider Madame La Gimp nothing but an old pest, but kind-hearted guys like Dave the Dude always stake her to a few pieces of silver when she comes shuffling along putting on the moan about her tough luck. She walks with a gimp in one leg, which is why she is called Madame La Gimp, and years ago I hear somebody say Madame La Gimp is once a Spanish dancer, and a big shot on Broadway, but that she meets up with an accident which puts her out of the dancing dodge, and that a busted romance makes her become a gin-head.

I remember somebody telling me once that Madame La Gimp is quite a beauty in her day, and has her own servants, and all this and that, but I always hear the same thing about every bum on Broadway, male and female, including some I know are bums, in spades, right from taw, so I do not pay any attention to these stories.

Still, I am willing to allow that maybe Madame La Gimp is once a fair looker, at that, and the chances are has a fair shape, because once or twice I see her when she is not ginned up, and has her hair combed, and she is not so bad-looking, although even then if you put her in a claiming race I do not think there is any danger of anybody claiming her out of it.

Mostly she is wearing raggedy clothes, and busted shoes, and her grey hair is generally hanging down her face, and when I say she is maybe fifty years old I am giving her plenty the best of it. Although she is Spanish, Madame La Gimp talks good English, and in fact she can cuss in English as good as anybody I ever hear, barring Dave the Dude.

Well, anyway, when Dave the Dude sees me as he is listening to Madame La Gimp, he motions me to wait, so I wait until she finally gets through gabbing to him and goes gimping away. Then Dave the Dude comes over to me looking much worried.

'This is quite a situation,' Dave says. 'The old doll is in a tough spot. It seems that she once has a baby which she calls by the name of Eulalie, being it is a girl baby, and she ships this baby off to her sister in a little town in Spain to raise up, because Madame La Gimp figures a baby is not apt to get much raising-up off of her as long as she is on Broadway. Well, this baby is on her way here. In fact,' Dave says, 'she will land next Saturday and here it is Wednesday already.'

'Where is the baby's papa?' I ask Dave the Dude.

'Well,' Dave says, 'I do not ask Madame La Gimp this, because I do not consider it a fair question. A guy who goes around this town asking where babies' papas are, or even who they are, is apt to get the name of being nosey. Anyway, this has nothing whatever to do with the proposition, which is that Madame La Gimp's baby, Eulalie, is arriving here.

'Now,' Dave says, 'it seems that Madame La Gimp's baby, being now eighteen years old, is engaged to marry the son of a very proud old Spanish nobleman who lives in this little town in Spain, and it also seems that the very proud old Spanish nobleman, and his ever-loving wife, and the son, and Madame La Gimp's sister, are all with the baby. They are making a tour of the whole world, and will stop over here a couple of days just to see Madame La Gimp.'

'It is commencing to sound to me like a movie such as a guy is apt to see at a midnight show,' I say.

'Wait a minute,' Dave says, getting impatient. 'You are too gabby to suit me. Now it seems that the proud old Spanish nobleman does not wish his son to marry any lob, and one reason he is coming here is to look over Madame La Gimp, and see that she is okay. He thinks that Madame La Gimp's baby's own papa is dead, and that Madame La Gimp is now married to one of the richest and most aristocratic guys in America.'

'How does the proud old Spanish nobleman get such an idea as this?' I ask. 'It is a sure thing he never sees Madame La Gimp, or even a photograph of her as she is at present.'

'I will tell you how,' Dave the Dude says. 'It seems Madame La Gimp gives her baby the idea that such is the case in her letters to her. It seems Madame La Gimp does a little scrubbing business around a swell apartment hotel in Park Avenue that is called the Marberry, and she cops stationery there and writes her baby in Spain on this stationery, saying this is where she lives, and how rich and aristocratic her husband is. And what is more, Madame La Gimp has letters from her baby sent to her care of the hotel and gets them out of the employees' mail.'

'Why,' I say, 'Madame La Gimp is nothing but an old fraud to deceive people in this manner, especially a proud old Spanish nobleman. And,' I say, 'this proud old Spanish nobleman must be something of a chump to believe a mother will keep away from her baby all these years, especially if the mother has plenty of dough, although of course I do not know just how smart a proud old Spanish nobleman can be.'

'Well,' Dave says, 'Madame La Gimp tells me the thing that makes the biggest hit of all with the proud old Spanish nobleman is that she keeps her baby in Spain all these years because she wishes her raised up a true Spanish baby in every respect until she is old enough to know what time it is. But I judge the proud old Spanish nobleman is none too bright, at that,' Dave says, 'because Madame La Gimp tells me he always lives in his little town which does not even have running water in the bathrooms.

'But what I am getting at is this,' Dave says. 'We must have Madame La Gimp in a swell apartment in the Marberry with a rich and aristocratic guy for a husband by the time her baby gets here, because if the proud old Spanish nobleman finds out Madame La Gimp is nothing but a bum, it is a hundred to one he will cancel his son's engagement to Madame La Gimp's baby and break a lot of people's hearts, including his son's.

'Madame La Gimp tells me her baby is daffy about the young guy, and he is daffy about her, and there are enough broken hearts in this town as it is. I know how I will get the apartment, so you go and bring me Judge Henry G. Blake for a rich and aristocratic husband, or anyway for a husband.'

Well, I know Dave the Dude to do many a daffy thing, but never a thing as daffy as this. But I know there is no use arguing with him when he gets an idea, because if you argue with Dave the Dude too much he is apt to reach over and lay his Sunday punch on your snoot, and no argument is worth a punch on the snoot, especially from Dave the Dude.

So I go out looking for Judge Henry G. Blake to be Madame La Gimp's husband, although I am not so sure Judge Henry G. Blake will care to be anybody's husband, and especially Madame La Gimp's after he gets a load of her, for Judge Henry G. Blake is kind of a classy old guy.

To look at Judge Henry G. Blake, with his grey hair, and his nose glasses, and his stomach, you will think he is very important people, indeed. Of course, Judge Henry G. Blake is not a judge, and never is a judge, but they call him Judge because he looks like a judge, and talks slow, and puts in many long words, which very few people understand.

They tell me Judge Blake once has plenty of dough, and is quite a guy in Wall Street, and a high shot along Broadway, but he misses a few guesses at the market, and winds up without much dough, as guys generally do who miss guesses at the market. What Judge Henry G. Blake does for a living at this time nobody knows, because he does nothing much whatever, and yet he seems to be a producer in a small way at all times.

Now and then he makes a trip across the ocean with such as Little Manuel, and other guys who ride the tubs, and sits in with them on games of bridge, and one thing and another, when they need him. Very often when he is riding the tubs, Little Manuel runs into some guy he cannot cheat, so he has to call in Judge Henry G. Blake to outplay the guy on the level, although of course Little Manuel will much rather get a guy's dough by cheating him than by outplaying him on the level. Why this is, I do not know, but this is the way Little Manuel is.

Anyway, you cannot say Judge Henry G. Blake is a bum, especially as he wears good clothes, with a wing collar, and a derby hat, and most people consider him a very nice old man. Personally I never catch the judge out of line on any proposition whatever, and he always says hello to me, very pleasant.

It takes me several hours to find Judge Henry G. Blake, but finally I locate him in Derle's billiards-room playing a game of pool with a guy from Providence, Rhode Island. It seems the judge is playing the guy from Providence for five cents a ball, and the judge is about thirteen balls behind when I step into the joint, because naturally at five cents a ball the judge wishes the guy from Providence to win, so as to encourage him to play for maybe twenty-five cents a ball, the judge being very cute this way.

Well, when I step in I see the judge miss a shot anybody can make blindfolded, but as soon as I give him the office I wish to speak to him, the judge hauls off and belts in every ball on the table, bingity-bing, the last shot being a bank that will make Al de Oro stop and think, because when it comes to pool, the old judge is just naturally a curly wolf.

Afterwards he tells me he is very sorry I make him hurry up this way, because of course after the last shot he is never going to get the guy from Providence to play him pool even for fun, and the judge tells me the guy sizes up as a right good thing, at that.

Now Judge Henry G. Blake is not so excited when I tell him what Dave the Dude wishes to see him about, but naturally he is willing to do anything for Dave, because he knows that guys who are not willing to do things for Dave the Dude often have bad luck. The judge tells me that he is afraid he will not make much of a husband because he tries it before several times on his own hook and is always a bust, but as long as this time it is not to be anything serious, he will tackle it. Anyway, Judge Henry G. Blake says, being aristocratic will come natural to him.

Well, when Dave the Dude starts out on any proposition, he is a wonder for fast working. The first thing he does is to turn Madame La Gimp over to Miss Billy Perry, who is now Dave's ever-loving wife which he takes out of tap-dancing in Miss Missouri Martin's Sixteen Hundred Club, and Miss Billy Perry calls in Miss Missouri Martin to help.

This is water on Miss Missouri Martin's wheel, because if there is anything she loves it is to stick her nose in other people's business, no matter what it is, but she is quite a help at that, although at first they have a tough time keeping her from telling Waldo Winchester, the scribe, about the whole cat-hop, so he will put a story in the *Morning Item* about it, with Miss Missouri Martin's name in it. Miss Missouri Martin does not believe in ever overlooking any publicity bets on the layout.

Anyway, it seems that between them Miss Billy Perry and Miss Missouri Martin get Madame La Gimp dolled up in a lot of new clothes, and run her through one of these beauty joints until she comes out very much changed, indeed. Afterwards I hear Miss Billy Perry and Miss Missouri Martin have quite a few words, because Miss Missouri Martin wishes to paint Madame La Gimp's hair the same colour as her own, which is a high yellow, and buy her the same kind of dresses which Miss Missouri Martin wears herself, and Miss Missouri Martin gets much insulted when Miss Billy Perry says no, they are trying to dress Madame La Gimp to look like a lady.

They tell me Miss Missouri Martin thinks some of putting the slug on Miss Billy Perry for this crack, but happens to remember just in time that Miss Billy Perry is now Dave the Dude's ever-loving wife, and that nobody in this town can put the slug on Dave's ever-loving wife, except maybe Dave himself.

Now the next thing anybody knows, Madame La Gimp is in a swell eight- or nine-room apartment in the Marberry, and the way this comes about is as follows: It seems that one of Dave the Dude's most important champagne customers is a guy by the name of Rodney B. Emerson, who owns the apartment, but who is at his summer home in Newport, with his family, or anyway with his ever-loving wife.

This Rodney B. Emerson is quite a guy along Broadway, and a great hand for spending dough and looking for laughs, and he is very popular with the mob. Furthermore, he is obliged to Dave the Dude, because Dave sells him good champagne when most guys are trying to hand him the old phonus bolonus, and naturally Rodney B. Emerson appreciates this kind treatment.

He is a short, fat guy, with a round, red face, and a big laugh, and the kind of a guy Dave the Dude can call up at his home in Newport and explain the situation and ask for the loan of the apartment, which Dave does.

Well, it seems Rodney B. Emerson gets a big bang out of the idea, and he says to Dave the Dude like this:

'You not only can have the apartment, Dave, but I will come over and help you out. It will save a lot of explaining around the Marberry if I am there.'

So he hops right over from Newport, and joins in with Dave the Dude, and I wish to say Rodney B. Emerson will always be kindly remembered by one and all for his co-operation, and nobody will ever again try to hand him the phonus bolonus when he is buying champagne, even if he is not buying it off of Dave the Dude.

Well, it is coming on Saturday and the boat from Spain is due, so Dave the Dude hires a big town car, and puts his own driver, Wop Sam, on it, as he does not wish any strange driver tipping off anybody that it is a hired car. Miss Missouri Martin is anxious to go to the boat with Madame La Gimp, and take her jazz band, the Hi Hi Boys, from her Sixteen Hundred Club with her to make it a real welcome, but nobody thinks much of this idea. Only Madame La Gimp and her husband, Judge Henry G. Blake, and Miss Billy Perry go, though the judge holds out for some time for Little Manuel, because Judge Blake says he wishes somebody around to tip him off in case there are any bad cracks made about him as a husband in Spanish, and Little Manuel is very Spanish.

The morning they go to meet the boat is the first time Judge Henry G. Blake gets a load of his ever-loving wife, Madame La Gimp, and by this time Miss Billy Perry and Miss Missouri Martin give Madame La Gimp such a going-over that she is by no means the worst looker in the world. In fact, she looks first-rate, especially as she is off gin and says she is off it for good.

Judge Henry G. Blake is really quite surprised by her looks, as he figures all along she will turn out to be a crow. In fact, Judge Blake hurls a couple of shots into himself to nerve himself for the ordeal, as he explains it, before he appears to go to the boat. Between these shots, and the nice clothes, and the good cleaning-up Miss Billy Perry and Miss Missouri Martin give Madame La Gimp, she is really a pleasant sight to the judge.

They tell me the meeting at the dock between Madame La Gimp and her baby is very affecting indeed, and when the proud old Spanish nobleman and his wife, and their son, and Madame La Gimp's sister, all go into action, too, there are enough tears around there to float all the battleships we once sink for Spain. Even Miss Billy Perry and Judge Henry G. Blake do some first-class crying, although the chances are the judge is worked up to the crying more by the shots he takes for his courage than by the meeting.

Still, I hear the old judge does himself proud, what with kissing Madame La Gimp's baby plenty, and duking the proud old Spanish nobleman, and his wife, and son, and giving Madame La Gimp's sister a good strong hug that squeezes her tongue out.

It turns out that the proud old Spanish nobleman has white sideburns, and is entitled Conde de Something, so his ever-loving wife is the Condesa, and the son is a very nice-looking quiet young guy any way you take him, who blushes every time anybody looks at him. As for Madame La Gimp's baby, she is as pretty as they come, and many guys are sorry they do not get Judge Henry G. Blake's job as stepfather, because he is able to take a kiss at Madame La Gimp's baby on what seems to be very small excuse. I never see a nicer-looking young couple, and anybody can see they are very fond of each other, indeed.

Madame La Gimp's sister is not such a doll as I will wish to have sawed off on me, and is up in the paints as regards to age, but she is also very quiet. None of the bunch talk any English, so Miss Billy Perry and Judge Henry G. Blake are pretty much outsiders on the way uptown. Anyway, the judge takes the wind as soon as they reach the Marberry, because the judge is now getting a little tired of being a husband. He says he has to take a trip out to Pittsburgh to buy four or five coal-mines, but will be back the next day.

Well, it seems to me that everything is going perfect so far, and that it is good judgment to let it lay as it is, but nothing will do Dave the Dude but to have a reception the following night. I advise Dave the Dude against this idea, because I am afraid something will happen to spoil the whole cat-hop, but he will not listen to me, especially as Rodney B. Emerson is now in town and is a strong booster for the party, as he wishes to drink some of the good champagne he has planted in his apartment.

Furthermore, Miss Billy Perry and Miss Missouri Martin are very indignant at me when they hear about my advice, as it seems they both buy new dresses out of Dave the Dude's bank-roll when they are dressing up Madame La Gimp, and they wish to spring these dresses somewhere where they can be seen. So the party is on.

I get to the Marberry around nine o'clock and who opens the door of Madame La Gimp's apartment for me but Moosh, the door man from Miss Missouri Martin's Sixteen Hundred Club. Furthermore, he is in his Sixteen Hundred Club uniform, except he has a clean shave. I wish Moosh a hello, and he never raps to me but only bows, and takes my hat.

The next guy I see is Rodney B. Emerson in evening clothes, and the minute he sees me he yells out, 'Mister O. O. McIntyre.' Well, of course, I am not Mister O. O. McIntyre, and never put myself away as Mister O. O. McIntyre, and furthermore there is no resemblance whatever between Mister O. O. McIntyre and me, because I am a fairly good-looking guy, and I start to give Rodney B. Emerson an argument, when he whispers to me like this:

'Listen,' he whispers, 'we must have big names at this affair, so as to impress these people. The chances are they read the newspapers back there in Spain, and we must let them meet the folks they read about, so they will see Madame La Gimp is a real big shot to get such names to a party.'

Then he takes me by the arm and leads me to a group of people in a corner of the room, which is about the size of the Grand Central waiting-room.

'Mister O. O. McIntyre, the big writer!' Rodney B. Emerson says, and the next thing I know I am shaking hands with Mr. and Mrs. Conde, and their son, and with Madame La Gimp and her baby, and Madame La Gimp's sister, and finally with Judge Henry G. Blake, who has on a swallowtail coat, and does not give me much of a tumble. I figure the chances are Judge Henry G. Blake is getting a swelled head already, not to tumble up a guy who helps him get his job, but even at that I wish to say the old judge looks immense in his swallowtail coat, bowing and giving one and all the old castor-oil smile.

Madame La Gimp is in a low-neck black dress and is wearing a lot of Miss Missouri Martin's diamonds, such as rings and bracelets, which Miss Missouri Martin insists on hanging on her, although I hear afterwards that Miss Missouri Martin has Johnny Brannigan, the plain-clothes copper, watching these diamonds. I wonder at the time why Johnny is there, but figure it is because he is a friend of Dave the Dude's. Miss Missouri Martin is no sucker, even if she is kind-hearted.

Anybody looking at Madame La Gimp will bet you all the coffee in Java that she never lives in a cellar over in Tenth Avenue, and drinks plenty of gin in her day. She has her grey hair piled up high on her head, with a big Spanish comb in it, and she reminds me of a picture I see somewhere, but I do not remember just where. And her baby, Eulalie, in a white dress is about as pretty a little doll as you will wish to see, and nobody can blame Judge Henry G. Blake for copping a kiss off of her now and then.

Well, pretty soon I hear Rodney B. Emerson bawling, 'Mister Willie K. Vanderbilt,' and in comes nobody but Big Nig, and Rodney B. Emerson leads him over to the group and introduces him.

Little Manuel is standing alongside Judge Henry G. Blake, and he explains in Spanish to Mr. and Mrs. Conde and the others that 'Willie K. Vanderbilt' is a very large millionaire, and Mr. and Mrs. Conde seem much interested, anyway, though naturally Madame La Gimp and Judge Henry G. Blake are jerry to Big Nig, while Madame La Gimp's baby and the young guy are interested in nobody but each other.

Then I hear, 'Mister Al Jolson,' and in comes nobody but Tony Bertazzola, from the Chicken Club, who looks about as much like Al as I do like O. O. McIntyre, which is not at all. Next comes 'the Very Reverend John Roach Straton,' who seems to be Skeets Bolivar to me, then 'the Honourable Mayor James J. Walker,' and who is it but Good Time Charley Bernstein.

'Mister Otto H. Kahn,' turns out to be Rochester Red, and 'Mister Heywood Broun' is Nick the Greek, who asks me privately who Heywood Broun is, and gets very sore at Rodney B. Emerson when I describe Heywood Broun to him.

Finally there is quite a commotion at the door and Rodney B. Emerson announces, 'Mister Herbert Bayard Swope' in an extra loud voice which makes everybody look around, but it is nobody but the Pale Face Kid. He gets me to one side, too, and wishes to know who Herbert Bayard Swope is, and when I explain to him, the Pale Face Kid gets so swelled up he will not speak to Death House Donegan, who is only 'Mister William Muldoon.'

Well, it seems to me they are getting too strong when they announce, 'Vice-President of the United States, the Honourable Charles Curtis,' and in pops Guinea Mike, and I say as much to Dave the Dude, who is running around every which way looking after things, but he only says, 'Well, if you do not know it is Guinea Mike, will you know it is not Vice-President Curtis?'

But it seems to me all this is most disrespectful to our leading citizens, especially when Rodney B. Emerson calls, 'The Honourable Police Commissioner, Mister Grover A. Whalen,' and in pops Wild William Wilkins, who is a very hot man at this time, being wanted in several spots for different raps. Dave the Dude takes personal charge of Wild William and removes a rod from his pants pocket, because none of the guests are supposed to come rodded up, this being strictly a social matter.

I watch Mr. and Mrs. Conde, and I do not see that these names are making any impression on them, and I afterwards find out that they never get any newspapers in their town in Spain except a little local bladder which only prints the home news. In fact, Mr. and Mrs. Conde seem somewhat bored, although Mr. Conde cheers up no little and looks interested when a lot of dolls drift in. They are mainly dolls from Miss Missouri Martin's Sixteen Hundred Club, and the Hot Box, but Rodney B. Emerson introduces them as 'Sophie Tucker,' and 'Theda Bara,' and 'Jeanne Eagels,' and 'Helen Morgan,' and 'Aunt Jemima,' and one thing and another.

Well, pretty soon in comes Miss Missouri Martin's jazz band, the Hi Hi Boys, and the party commences getting up steam, especially when Dave the Dude gets Rodney B. Emerson to breaking out the old grape. By and by there is dancing going on, and a good time is being had by one and all, including Mr. and Mrs. Conde. In fact, after Mr. Conde gets a couple of jolts of the old grape, he turns out to be a pretty nice old skate, even if nobody can understand what he is talking about.

As for Judge Henry G. Blake, he is full of speed, indeed. By this time anybody can see that the judge is commencing to believe that all this is on the level and that he is really entertaining celebrities in his own home. You put a quart of good grape inside the old judge and he will believe anything. He soon dances himself plumb out of wind, and then I notice he is hanging around Madame La Gimp a lot.

Along about midnight, Dave the Dude has to go out into the kitchen and settle a battle there over a crap game, but otherwise everything is very peaceful. It seems that 'Herbert Bayard Swope,' 'Vice-President Curtis,' and 'Grover Whalen' get a little game going, when 'the Reverend John Roach Straton' steps up and cleans them in four passes, but it seems they soon discover that 'the Reverend John Roach Straton' is using tops on them, which are very dishonest dice, and so they put the slug on 'the Reverend John Roach Straton' and Dave the Dude has to split them out.

By and by I figure on taking the wind, and I look for Mr. and Mrs. Conde to tell them good night, but Mr. Conde and Miss Missouri Martin are still dancing, and Miss Missouri Martin is pouring conversation into Mr. Conde's ear by the bucketful, and while Mr. Conde does not savvy a word she says, this makes no difference to Miss Missouri Martin. Let Miss Missouri Martin do all the talking, and she does not care a whoop if anybody understands her.

Mrs. Conde is over in a corner with 'Herbert Bayard Swope,' or the Pale Face Kid, who is trying to find out from her by using hog

Latin and signs on her if there is any chance for a good twenty-one dealer in Spain, and of course Mrs. Conde is not able to make heads or tails of what he means, so I hunt up Madame La Gimp.

She is sitting in a darkish corner off by herself and I really do not see Judge Henry G. Blake leaning over her until I am almost on top of them, so I cannot help hearing what the judge is saying.

'I am wondering for two days,' he says, 'if by any chance you remember me. Do you know who I am?'

'I remember you,' Madame La Gimp says. 'I remember you – oh, so very well, Henry. How can I forget you? But I have no idea you recognize me after all these years.'

'Twenty of them now,' Judge Henry G. Blake says. 'You are beautiful then. You are still beautiful.'

Well, I can see the old grape is working first-class on Judge Henry G. Blake to make such remarks as this, although at that, in the half-light, with the smile on her face, Madame La Gimp is not so bad. Still, give me them carrying a little less weight for age.

'Well, it is all your fault,' Judge Henry G. Blake says. 'You go and marry that chile con carne guy, and look what happens!'

I can see there is no sense in me horning in on Madame La Gimp and Judge Henry G. Blake while they are cutting up old touches in this manner, so I think I will just say good-bye to the young people and let it go at that, but while I am looking for Madame La Gimp's baby, and her guy, I run into Dave the Dude.

'You will not find them here,' Dave says. 'By this time they are being married over at Saint Malachy's with my ever-loving wife and Big Nig standing up with them. We get the licence for them yesterday afternoon. Can you imagine a couple of young saps wishing to wait until they go plumb around the world before getting married?'

Well, of course, this elopement creates much excitement for a few minutes, but by Monday Mr. and Mrs. Conde and the young folks and Madame La Gimp's sister take a train for California to keep on going around the world, leaving us nothing to talk about but about old Judge Henry G. Blake and Madame La Gimp getting themselves married, too, and going to Detroit where Judge Henry G. Blake claims he has a brother in the plumbing business who will give him a job, although personally I think Judge Henry G. Blake figures to do a little booting on his own hook in and out of Canada. It is not like Judge Henry G. Blake to tie himself up to the plumbing business.

So there is nothing more to the story, except that Dave the Dude is around a few days later with a big sheet of paper in his duke and very, very indignant.

'If every single article listed here is not kicked back to the owners of the different joints in the Marberry that they are taken from by next Tuesday night, I will bust a lot of noses around this town,' Dave says. 'I am greatly mortified by such happenings at my social affairs, and everything must be returned at once. Especially,' Dave says, 'the baby grand piano that is removed from Apartment 9-D.'

Dancing Dan's Christmas

Now one time it comes on Christmas, and in fact it is the evening before Christmas, and I am in Good Time Charley Bernstein's little speakeasy in West Forty-seventh Street, wishing Charley a Merry Christmas and having a few hot Tom and Jerrys with him.

This hot Tom and Jerry is an old-time drink that is once used by one and all in this country to celebrate Christmas with, and in fact it is once so popular that many people think Christmas is invented only to furnish an excuse for hot Tom and Jerry, although of course this is by no means true.

But anybody will tell you that there is nothing that brings out the true holiday spirit like hot Tom and Jerry, and I hear that since Tom and Jerry goes out of style in the United States, the holiday spirit is never quite the same.

The reason hot Tom and Jerry goes out of style is because it is necessary to use rum and one thing and another in making Tom and Jerry, and naturally when rum becomes illegal in this country Tom and Jerry is also against the law, because rum is something that is very hard to get around town these days.

For a while some people try making hot Tom and Jerry without putting rum in it, but somehow it never has the same old holiday spirit, so nearly everybody finally gives up in disgust, and this is not surprising, as making Tom and Jerry is by no means child's play. In fact, it takes quite an expert to make good Tom and Jerry, and in the days when it is not illegal a good hot Tom and Jerry maker commands good wages and many friends.

Now of course Good Time Charley and I are not using rum in the Tom and Jerry we are making, as we do not wish to do anything illegal. What we are using is rye whisky that Good Time Charley gets on a doctor's prescription from a drug store, as we are personally drinking this hot Tom and Jerry and naturally we are not foolish enough to use any of Good Time Charley's own rye in it.

The prescription for the rye whisky comes from old Doc Moggs, who prescribes it for Good Time Charley's rheumatism in case Charley happens to get any rheumatism, as Doc Moggs says there is nothing better for rheumatism than rye whisky, especially if it is made up in a hot Tom and Jerry. In fact, old Doc Moggs comes around and has a few seidels of hot Tom and Jerry with us for his own rheumatism.

He comes around during the afternoon, for Good Time Charley and I start making this Tom and Jerry early in the day, so as to be sure to have enough to last us over Christmas, and it is now along towards six o'clock, and our holiday spirit is practically one hundred per cent.

Well, as Good Time Charley and I are expressing our holiday sentiments to each other over our hot Tom and Jerry, and I am trying to think up the poem about the night before Christmas and all through the house, which I know will interest Charley no little, all of a sudden there is a big knock at the front door, and when Charley opens the door who comes in carrying a large package under one arm but a guy by the name of Dancing Dan.

This Dancing Dan is a good-looking young guy, who always seems well-dressed, and he is called by the name of Dancing Dan because he is a great hand for dancing around and about with dolls in night clubs, and other spots where there is any dancing. In fact, Dan never seems to be doing anything else, although I hear rumours that when he is not dancing he is carrying on in a most illegal manner at one thing and another. But of course you can always hear rumours in this town about anybody, and personally I am rather fond of Dancing Dan as he always seems to be getting a great belt out of life.

Anybody in town will tell you that Dancing Dan is a guy with no Barnaby whatever in him, and in fact he has about as much gizzard as anybody around, although I wish to say I always question his judgment in dancing so much with Miss Muriel O'Neill, who works in the Half Moon night club. And the reason I question his judgment in this respect is because everybody knows that Miss Muriel O'Neill is a doll who is very well thought of by Heine Schmitz, and Heine Schmitz is not such a guy as will take kindly to anybody dancing more than once and a half with a doll that he thinks well of.

This Heine Schmitz is a very influential citizen of Harlem, where he has large interests in beer, and other business enterprises, and it is by no means violating any confidence to tell you that Heine Schmitz will just as soon blow your brains out as look at you. In fact, I hear sooner. Anyway, he is not a guy to monkey with and many citizens take the trouble to advise Dancing Dan that he is not only away out of line in dancing with Miss Muriel O'Neill, but that he is knocking his own price down to where he is no price at all.

But Dancing Dan only laughs ha-ha, and goes on dancing with Miss Muriel O'Neill any time he gets a chance, and Good Time Charley says he does not blame him, at that, as Miss Muriel O'Neill is so beautiful that he will be dancing with her himself no matter what, if he is five years younger and can get a Roscoe out as fast as in the days when he runs with Paddy the Link and other fast guys.

Well, anyway, as Dancing Dan comes in he weighs up the joint in one quick peek, and then he tosses the package he is carrying into a corner where it goes plunk, as if there is something very heavy in it, and then he steps up to the bar alongside of Charley and me and wishes to know what we are drinking.

Naturally we start boosting hot Tom and Jerry to Dancing Dan, and he says he will take a crack at it with us, and after one crack, Dancing Dan says he will have another crack, and Merry Christmas to us with it, and the first thing anybody knows it is a couple of hours later and we are still having cracks at the hot Tom and Jerry with Dancing Dan, and Dan says he never drinks anything so soothing in his life. In fact, Dancing Dan says he will recommend Tom and Jerry to everybody he knows, only he does not know anybody good enough for Tom and Jerry, except maybe Miss Muriel O'Neill, and she does not drink anything with drugstore rye in it.

Well, several times while we are drinking this Tom and Jerry, customers come to the door of Good Time Charley's little speakeasy and knock, but by now Charley is commencing to be afraid they will wish Tom and Jerry, too, and he does not feel we will have enough for ourselves, so he hangs out a sign which says 'Closed on Account of Christmas,' and the only one he will let in is a guy by the name of Ooky, who is nothing but an old rum-dum, and who is going around all week dressed like Santa Claus and carrying a sign advertising Moe Lewinsky's clothing joint around in Sixth Avenue.

This Ooky is still wearing his Santa Claus outfit when Charley lets him in, and the reason Charley permits such a character as Ooky in his joint is because Ooky does the porter work for Charley when he is not Santa Claus for Moe Lewinsky, such as sweeping out, and washing the glasses, and one thing and another.

Well, it is about nine-thirty when Ooky comes in, and his puppies are aching, and he is all petered out generally from walking up and down and here and there with his sign, for any time a guy is Santa Claus for Moe Lewinsky he must earn his dough. In fact, Ooky is so fatigued, and his puppies hurt him so much, that Dancing Dan and Good Time Charley and I all feel very sorry for him, and invite him to have a few mugs of hot Tom and Jerry with us, and wish him plenty of Merry Christmas.

But old Ooky is not accustomed to Tom and Jerry, and after about the fifth mug he folds up in a chair, and goes right to sleep on us. He is wearing a pretty good Santa Claus make-up, what with a nice red suit trimmed with white cotton, and a wig, and false nose, and long white whiskers, and a big sack stuffed with excelsior on his back, and if I do not know Santa Claus is not apt to be such a guy as will snore loud enough to rattle the windows, I will think Ooky is Santa Claus sure enough.

Well, we forget Ooky and let him sleep, and go on with our hot Tom and Jerry, and in the meantime we try to think up a few songs appropriate to Christmas, and Dancing Dan finally renders My Dad's Dinner Pail in a nice baritone and very loud, while I do first-rate with Will You Love Me in December – As You Do in May? But personally I always think Good Time Charley Bernstein is a little out of line trying to sing a hymn in Jewish on such an occasion, and it causes words between us.

While we are singing many customers come to the door and knock, and then they read Charley's sign, and this seems to cause some unrest among them, and some of them stand outside saying it is a great outrage, until Charley sticks his noggin out the door and threatens to bust somebody's beezer if they do not go on about their business and stop disturbing peaceful citizens.

Naturally the customers go away, as they do not wish their beezers busted, and Dancing Dan and Charley and I continue drinking our hot Tom and Jerry, and with each Tom and Jerry we are wishing one another a very Merry Christmas, and sometimes a very Happy New Year, although of course this does not go for Good Time Charley as yet, because Charley has his New Year separate from Dancing Dan and me.

By and by we take to waking Ooky up in his Santa Claus outfit and offering him more hot Tom and Jerry, and wishing him Merry Christmas, but Ooky only gets sore and calls us names, so we can see he does not have the right holiday spirit in him, and let him alone until along about midnight when Dancing Dan wishes to see how he looks as Santa Claus.

So Good Time Charley and I help Dancing Dan pull off Ooky's outfit and put it on Dan, and this is easy as Ooky only has this Santa Claus outfit on over his ordinary clothes, and he does not even wake up when we are undressing him of the Santa Claus uniform.

Well, I wish to say I see many a Santa Claus in my time, but I never see a better-looking Santa Claus than Dancing Dan, especially after he gets the wig and white whiskers fixed just right, and we put a sofa pillow that Good Time Charley happens to have around the joint for the cat to sleep on down his pants to give Dancing Dan a nice fat stomach such as Santa Claus is bound to have.

In fact, after Dancing Dan looks at himself in a mirror awhile he is greatly pleased with his appearance, while Good Time Charley is practically hysterical, although personally I am commencing to resent Charley's interest in Santa Claus, and Christmas generally, as he by no means has any claim on these matters. But then I remember Charley furnishes the hot Tom and Jerry, so I am more tolerant towards him.

'Well,' Charley finally says, 'it is a great pity we do not know where there are some stockings hung up somewhere, because then,' he says, 'you can go around and stuff things in these stockings, as I always hear this is the main idea of a Santa Claus. But,' Charley says, 'I do not suppose anybody in this section has any stockings hung up, or if they have,' he says, 'the chances are they are so full of holes they will not hold anything. Anyway,' Charley says, 'even if there are any stockings hung up we do not have anything to stuff in them, although personally,' he says, 'I will gladly donate a few pints of Scotch.'

Well, I am pointing out that we have no reindeer and that a Santa Claus is bound to look like a terrible sap if he goes around without any reindeer, but Charley's remarks seem to give Dancing Dan an idea, for all of a sudden he speaks as follows:

'Why,' Dancing Dan says, 'I know where a stocking is hung up. It is hung up at Miss Muriel O'Neill's flat over here in West Forty-ninth Street. This stocking is hung up by nobody but a party by the name of Gammer O'Neill, who is Miss Muriel O'Neill's grand-mamma,' Dancing Dan says. 'Gammer O'Neill is going on ninety-odd,' he says, 'and Miss Muriel O'Neill tells me she cannot hold out much longer, what with one thing and another, including being a little childish in spots.

'Now,' Dancing Dan says, 'I remember Miss Muriel O'Neill is telling me just the other night how Gammer O'Neill hangs up her stocking on Christmas Eve all her life, and,' he says, 'I judge from what Miss Muriel O'Neill says that the old doll always believes Santa Claus will come along some Christmas and fill the stocking full of beautiful gifts. But,' Dancing Dan says, 'Miss Muriel O'Neill tells me Santa Claus never does this, although Miss Muriel O'Neill personally always takes a few gifts home and pops them into the stocking to make Gammer O'Neill feel better.

'But, of course,' Dancing Dan says, 'these gifts are nothing much because Miss Muriel O'Neill is very poor, and proud, and also good, and will not take a dime off of anybody, and I can lick the guy who says she will, although,' Dancing Dan says, 'between me, and Heine Schmitz, and a raft of other guys I can mention, Miss Muriel O'Neill can take plenty.'

Well, I know that what Dancing Dan states about Miss Muriel O'Neill is quite true, and in fact it is a matter that is often dis-cussed on Broadway, because Miss Muriel O'Neill cannot get more than twenty bobs per week working in the Half Moon, and it is well known to one and all that this is no kind of dough for a doll as beautiful as Miss Muriel O'Neill.

'Now,' Dancing Dan goes on, 'it seems that while Gammer O'Neill is very happy to get whatever she finds in her stocking on Christmas morning, she does not understand why Santa Claus is not more liberal, and,' he says, 'Miss Muriel O'Neill is saying to me that she only wishes she can give Gammer O'Neill one real big

Christmas before the old doll puts her checks back in the rack.

'So,' Dancing Dan states, 'here is a job for us. Miss Muriel O'Neill and her grandmamma live all alone in this flat over in West Forty-ninth Street, and,' he says, 'at such an hour as this Miss Muriel O'Neill is bound to be working, and the chances are Gammer O'Neill is sound asleep, and we will just hop over there and Santa Claus will fill up her stocking with beautiful gifts.'

Well, I say, I do not see where we are going to get any beautiful gifts at this time of night, what with all the stores being closed, unless we dash into an all-night drug store and buy a few bottles of perfume and a bum toilet set as guys always do when they forget about their ever-loving wives until after store hours on Christmas Eve, but Dancing Dan says never mind about this, but let us have a few more Tom and Jerrys first.

So we have a few more Tom and Jerrys, and then Dancing Dan picks up the package he heaves into the corner, and dumps most of the excelsior out of Ooky's Santa Claus sack, and puts the bundle in, and Good Time Charley turns out all the lights but one, and leaves a bottle of Scotch on the table in front of Ooky for a Christmas gift, and away we go.

Personally, I regret very much leaving the hot Tom and Jerry, but then I am also very enthusiastic about going along to help Dancing Dan play Santa Claus, while Good Time Charley is practically overjoyed, as it is the first time in his life Charley is ever mixed up in so much holiday spirit. In fact, nothing will do Charley but that we stop in a couple of spots and have a few drinks to Santa Claus's health, and these visits are a big success, although everybody is much surprised to see Charley and me with Santa Claus, especially Charley, although nobody recognizes Dancing Dan.

But of course there are no hot Tom and Jerrys in these spots we visit, and we have to drink whatever is on hand, and personally I will always believe that the noggin I have on me afterwards comes of mixing the drinks we get in these spots with my Tom and Jerry.

As we go up Broadway, headed for Forty-ninth Street, Charley and I see many citizens we know and give them a large hello, and wish them Merry Christmas, and some of these citizens shake hands with Santa Claus, not knowing he is nobody but Dancing Dan, although later I understand there is some gossip among these citizens because they claim a Santa Claus with such a breath on him as our Santa Claus has is a little out of line.

And once we are somewhat embarrassed when a lot of little kids going home with their parents from a late Christmas party somewhere gather about Santa Claus with shouts of childish glee, and some of them wish to climb up Santa Claus's legs. Naturally, Santa Claus gets a little peevish, and calls them a few names, and one of the parents comes up and wishes to know what is the idea of Santa Claus using such language, and Santa Claus takes a punch at the parent, all of which is no doubt most astonishing to the little kids who have an idea of Santa Claus as a very kindly old guy. But of course they do not know about Dancing Dan mixing the liquor we get in the spots we visit with his Tom and Jerry, or they will understand how even Santa Claus can lose his temper.

Well, finally we arrive in front of the place where Dancing Dan says Miss Muriel O'Neill and her grandmamma live, and it is nothing but a tenement house not far back of Madison Square Garden, and furthermore it is a walk-up, and at this time there are no lights burning in the joint except a gas jet in the main hall, and by the light of this jet we look at the names on the letter-boxes, such as you always find in the hall of these joints, and we see that Miss Muriel O'Neill and her grandmamma live on the fifth floor.

This is the top floor, and personally I do not like the idea of walking up five flights of stairs, and I am willing to let Dancing Dan and Good Time Charley go, but Dancing Dan insists we must all go, and finally I agree because Charley is commencing to argue that the right way for us to do is to get on the roof and let Santa Claus go down a chimney, and is making so much noise I am afraid he will wake somebody up.

So up the stairs we climb and finally we come to a door on the top floor that has a little card in a slot that says O'Neill, so we know we reach our destination. Dancing Dan first tries the knob, and right away the door opens, and we are in a little two- or three-room flat, with not much furniture in it, and what furniture there is is very poor. One single gas jet is burning near a bed in a room just off the one the door opens into, and by this light we see a very old doll is sleeping on the bed, so we judge this is nobody but Gammer O'Neill.

On her face is a large smile, as if she is dreaming of something very pleasant. On a chair at the head of the bed is hung a long black stocking, and it seems to be such a stocking as is often patched and mended, so I can see what Miss Muriel O'Neill tells

Dancing Dan about her grandmamma hanging up her stocking is really true, although up to this time I have my doubts.

Well, I am willing to pack in after one gander at the old doll, especially as Good Time Charley is commencing to prowl around the flat to see if there is a chimney where Santa Claus can come down, and is knocking things over, but Dancing Dan stands looking down at Gammer O'Neill for a long time.

Finally he unslings the sack on his back, and takes out his package, and unties this package, and all of a sudden out pops a raft of big diamond bracelets, and diamond rings, and diamond brooches, and diamond necklaces, and I do not know what all else in the way of diamonds, and Dancing Dan and I begin stuffing these diamonds into the stocking and Good Time Charley pitches in and helps us.

There are enough diamonds to fill the stocking to the muzzle, and it is no small stocking, at that, and I judge that Gammer O'Neill has a pretty fair set of bunting sticks when she is young. In fact, there are so many diamonds that we have enough left over to make a nice little pile on the chair after we fill the stocking plumb up, leaving a nice diamond-studded vanity case sticking out the top where we figure it will hit Gammer O'Neill's eye when she wakes up.

And it is not until I get out in the fresh air again that all of a sudden I remember seeing large headlines in the afternoon papers about a five-hundred-G's stick-up in the afternoon of one of the biggest diamond merchants in Maiden Lane while he is sitting in his office, and I also recall once hearing rumours that Dancing Dan is one of the best lone-hand git-'em-up guys in the world.

Naturally I commence to wonder if I am in the proper company when I am with Dancing Dan, even if he is Santa Claus. So I leave him on the next corner arguing with Good Time Charley about whether they ought to go and find some more presents somewhere, and look for other stockings to stuff, and I hasten on home, and go to bed.

The next day I find I have such a noggin that I do not care to stir around, and in fact I do not stir around much for a couple of weeks.

Then one night I drop around to Good Time Charley's little speakeasy, and ask Charley what is doing.

'Well,' Charley says, 'many things are doing, and personally,' he says, 'I am greatly surprised I do not see you at Gammer O'Neill's wake. You know Gammer O'Neill leaves this wicked old world a couple of days after Christmas,' Good Time Charley says, 'and,' he says, 'Miss Muriel O'Neill states that Doc Moggs claims it is at least a day after she is entitled to go, but she is sustained,' Charley says, 'by great happiness on finding her stocking filled with beautiful gifts on Christmas morning.

'According to Miss Muriel O'Neill,' Charley says, 'Gammer O'Neill dies practically convinced that there is a Santa Claus, although of course,' he says, 'Miss Muriel O'Neill does not tell her the real owner of the gifts, an all-right guy by the name of Shapiro, leaves the gifts with her after Miss Muriel O'Neill notifies him of the finding of same.

'It seems,' Charley says, 'this Shapiro is a tender-hearted guy, who is willing to help keep Gammer O'Neill with us a little longer when Doc Moggs says leaving the gifts with her will do it.

'So,' Charley says, 'everything is quite all right, as the coppers cannot figure anything except that maybe the rascal who takes the gifts from Shapiro gets conscience stricken, and leaves them the first place he can, and Miss Muriel O'Neill receives a ten-G's reward for finding the gifts and returning them. And,' Charley says, 'I hear Dancing Dan is in San Francisco and is figuring on reforming and becoming a dancing teacher, so he can marry Miss Muriel O'Neill, and of course,' he says, 'we all hope and trust she never learns any details of Dancing Dan's career.'

Well, it is Christmas Eve a year later that I run into a guy by the name of Shotgun Sam, who is mobbed up with Heine Schmitz in Harlem, and who is a very, very obnoxious character indeed.

'Well, well, well,' Shotgun says, 'the last time I see you is another Christmas Eve like this, and you are coming out of Good Time Charley's joint, and,' he says, 'you certainly have your pots on.'

'Well, Shotgun,' I say, 'I am sorry you get such a wrong impression of me, but the truth is,' I say, 'on the occasion you speak of, I am suffering from a dizzy feeling in my head.'

'It is all right with me,' Shotgun says. 'I have a tip this guy Dancing Dan is in Good Time Charley's the night I see you, and Mockie Morgan and Gunner Jack and me are casing the joint, because,' he says, 'Heine Schmitz is all sored up at Dan over some doll, although of course,' Shotgun says, 'it is all right now, as Heine has another doll.

'Anyway,' he says, 'we never get to see Dancing Dan. We watch the joint from six-thirty in the evening until daylight Christmas morning, and nobody goes in all night but old Ooky the Santa Claus guy in his Santa Claus make-up, and,' Shotgun says, 'nobody comes out except you and Good Time Charley and Ooky.

'Well,' Shotgun says, 'it is a great break for Dancing Dan he never goes in or comes out of Good Time Charley's, at that, because,' he says, 'we are waiting for him on the second-floor front of the building across the way with some nice little sawed-offs, and are under orders from Heine not to miss.'

'Well, Shotgun,' I say, 'Merry Christmas.'

'Well, all right,' Shotgun says, 'Merry Christmas.'

Sense of Humour

One night I am standing in front of Mindy's restaurant on Broadway, thinking of practically nothing whatever, when all of a sudden I feel a very terrible pain in my left foot.

In fact, this pain is so very terrible that it causes me to leap up and down like a bullfrog, and to let out loud cries of agony, and to speak some very profane language, which is by no means my custom, although of course I recognize the pain as coming from a hot foot, because I often experience this pain before.

Furthermore, I know Joe the Joker must be in the neighbourhood, as Joe the Joker has the most wonderful sense of humour of anybody in this town, and is always around giving people the hot foot, and gives it to me more times than I can remember. In fact, I hear Joe the Joker invents the hot foot, and it finally becomes a very popular idea all over the country.

The way you give a hot foot is to sneak up behind some guy who is standing around thinking of not much, and stick a paper match in his shoe between the sole and the upper along about where his little toe ought to be, and then light the match. By and by the guy will feel a terrible pain in his foot, and will start stamping around, and hollering, and carrying on generally, and it is always a most comical sight and a wonderful laugh to one and all to see him suffer.

No one in the world can give a hot foot as good as Joe the Joker, because it takes a guy who can sneak up very quiet on the guy who is to get the hot foot, and Joe can sneak up so quiet many guys on Broadway are willing to lay you odds that he can give a mouse a hot foot if you can find a mouse that wears shoes. Furthermore, Joe the Joker can take plenty of care of himself in case the guy who gets the hot foot feels like taking the matter up, which sometimes happens, especially with guys who get their shoes made to order at forty bobs per copy and do not care to have holes burned in these shoes.

But Joe does not care what kind of shoes the guys are wearing when he feels like giving out hot foots, and furthermore, he does not care who the guys are, although many citizens think he makes a mistake the time he gives a hot foot to Frankie Ferocious. In fact, many citizens are greatly horrified by this action, and go around saying no good will come of it.

This Frankie Ferocious comes from over in Brooklyn, where he is considered a rising citizen in many respects, and by no means a guy to give hot foots to, especially as Frankie Ferocious has no sense of humour whatever. In fact, he is always very solemn, and nobody ever sees him laugh, and he certainly does not laugh when Joe the Joker gives him a hot foot one day on Broadway when Frankie Ferocious is standing talking over a business matter with some guys from the Bronx.

He only scowls at Joe, and says something in Italian, and while I do not understand Italian, it sounds so unpleasant that I guarantee I will leave town inside of the next two hours if he says it to me.

Of course Frankie Ferocious's name is not really Ferocious, but something in Italian like Feroccio, and I hear he originally comes from Sicily, although he lives in Brooklyn for quite some years, and from a modest beginning he builds himself up until he is a very large operator in merchandise of one kind and another, especially alcohol. He is a big guy of maybe thirty-odd, and he has hair blacker than a yard up a chimney, and black eyes, and black eyebrows, and a slow way of looking at people.

Nobody knows a whole lot about Frankie Ferocious, because he never has much to say, and he takes his time saying it, but everybody gives him plenty of room when he comes around, as there are rumours that Frankie never likes to be crowded. As far as I am concerned, I do not care for any part of Frankie Ferocious, because his slow way of looking at people always makes me nervous, and I am always sorry Joe the Joker gives him a hot foot, because I figure Frankie Ferocious is bound to consider it a most disrespectful action, and hold it against everybody that lives on the Island of Manhattan.

But Joe the Joker only laughs when anybody tells him he is out of line in giving Frankie the hot foot, and says it is not his fault if Frankie has no sense of humour. Furthermore, Joe says he will not only give Frankie another hot foot if he gets a chance, but that he will give hot foots to the Prince of Wales or Mussolini, if he catches them in the right spot, although Regret, the horse player, states that Joe can have twenty to one any time that he will not give Mussolini any hot foots and get away with it.

Anyway, just as I suspect, there is Joe the Joker watching me when I feel the hot foot, and he is laughing very heartily, and furthermore, a large number of other citizens are also laughing heartily, because Joe the Joker never sees any fun in giving people the hot foot unless others are present to enjoy the joke.

Well, naturally when I see who it is gives me the hot foot I join in the laughter, and go over and shake hands with Joe, and when I shake hands with him there is more laughter, because it seems Joe has a hunk of Limburger cheese in his duke, and what I shake hands with is this Limburger. Furthermore, it is some of Mindy's Limburger cheese, and everybody knows Mindy's Limburger is very squashy, and also very loud.

Of course I laugh at this, too, although to tell the truth I will laugh much more heartily if Joe the Joker drops dead in front of me, because I do not like to be made the subject of laughter on Broadway. But my laugh is really quite hearty when Joe takes the rest of the cheese that is not on my fingers and smears it on the steering-wheels of some automobiles parked in front of Mindy's, because I get to thinking of what the drivers will say when they start steering their cars.

Then I get talking to Joe the Joker, and I ask him how things are up in Harlem, where Joe and his younger brother, Freddy, and several other guys have a small organization operating in beer, and Joe says things are as good as can be expected considering business conditions. Then I ask him how Rosa is getting along, this Rosa being Joe the Joker's ever-loving wife, and a personal friend of mine, as I know her when she is Rosa Midnight and is singing in the old Hot Box before Joe hauls off and marries her.

Well, at this question Joe the Joker starts laughing, and I can see that something appeals to his sense of humour, and finally he speaks as follows:

'Why,' he says, 'do you not hear the news about Rosa? She takes the wind on me a couple of months ago for my friend Frankie Ferocious, and is living in an apartment over in Brooklyn, right near his house, although,' Joe says, 'of course you understand I am telling you this only to answer your question, and not to holler copper on Rosa.'

Then he lets out another large ha-ha, and in fact Joe the Joker keeps laughing until I am afraid he will injure himself internally. Personally, I do not see anything comical in a guy's ever-loving wife taking the wind on him for a guy like Frankie Ferocious, so when Joe the Joker quiets down a bit I ask him what is funny about the proposition.

'Why,' Joe says, 'I have to laugh every time I think of how the big greaseball is going to feel when he finds out how expensive Rosa is. I do not know how many things Frankie Ferocious has running for him in Brooklyn,' Joe says, 'but he better try to move himself in on the mint if he wishes to keep Rosa going.'

Then he laughs again, and I consider it wonderful the way Joe is able to keep his sense of humour even in such a situation as this, although up to this time I always think Joe is very daffy indeed about Rosa, who is a little doll, weighing maybe ninety pounds with her hat on and quite cute.

Now I judge from what Joe the Joker tells me that Frankie Ferocious knows Rosa before Joe marries her and is always pitching to her when she is singing in the Hot Box, and even after she is Joe's ever-loving wife, Frankie occasionally calls her up, especially when he commences to be a rising citizen of Brooklyn, although of course Joe does not learn about these calls until later. And about the time Frankie Ferocious commences to be a rising citizen of Brooklyn, things begin breaking a little tough for Joe the Joker, what with the depression and all, and he has to economize on Rosa in spots, and if there is one thing Rosa cannot stand it is being economized on.

Along about now, Joe the Joker gives Frankie Ferocious the hot foot, and just as many citizens state at the time, it is a mistake, for Frankie starts calling Rosa up more than somewhat, and speaking of what a nice place Brooklyn is to live in – which it is, at that – and between these boosts for Brooklyn and Joe the Joker's economy, Rosa hauls off and takes a subway to Borough Hall, leaving Joe a note telling him that if he does not like it he knows what he can do.

'Well, Joe,' I say, after listening to his story, 'I always hate to hear of these little domestic difficulties among my friends, but maybe this is all for the best. Still, I feel sorry for you, if it will do you any good,' I say.

'Do not feel sorry for me,' Joe says. 'If you wish to feel sorry for anybody, feel sorry for Frankie Ferocious, and,' he says, 'if you can spare a little more sorrow, give it to Rosa.'

And Joe the Joker laughs very hearty again and starts telling me about a little scatter that he has up in Harlem where he keeps a chair fixed up with electric wires so he can give anybody that sits down in it a nice jolt, which sounds very humorous to me, at that, especially when Joe tells me how they turn on too much juice one night and almost kill Commodore Jake.

Finally Joe says he has to get back to Harlem, but first he goes to the telephone in the corner cigar store and calls up Mindy's and imitates a doll's voice, and tells Mindy he is Peggy Joyce, or somebody, and orders fifty dozen sandwiches sent up at once to an apartment in West Seventy-second Street for a birthday party, although of course there is no such number as he gives, aɪ.d nobody there will wish fifty dozen sandwiches if there is such a number.

Then Joe gets in his car and starts off, and while he is waiting for the traffic lights at Fiftieth Street, I see citizens on the sidewalks making sudden leaps, and looking around very fierce, and I know Joe the Joker is plugging them with pellets made out of tin foil, which he fires from a rubber band hooked between his thumb and forefinger.

Joe the Joker is very expert with this proposition, and it is very funny to see the citizens jump, although once or twice in his life Joe makes a miscue and knocks out somebody's eye. But it is all in fun, and shows you what a wonderful sense of humour Joe has.

Well, a few days later I see by the papers where a couple of Harlem guys Joe the Joker is mobbed up with are found done up in sacks over in Brooklyn, very dead indeed, and the coppers say it is because they are trying to move in on certain business enterprises that belong to nobody but Frankie Ferocious. But of course the coppers do not say Frankie Ferocious puts these guys in the sacks, because in the first place Frankie will report them to Headquarters if the coppers say such a thing about him, and in the second place putting guys in sacks is strictly a St. Louis idea and to have a guy put in a sack properly you have to send to St. Louis for experts in this matter.

Now, putting a guy in a sack is not as easy as it sounds, and in fact it takes quite a lot of practice and experience. To put a guy in a sack properly, you first have to put him to sleep, because naturally no guy is going to walk into a sack wide awake unless he is a plumb sucker. Some people claim the best way to put a guy to sleep is to give him a sleeping powder of some kind in a drink, but the real experts just tap the guy on the noggin with a blackjack, which saves the expense of buying the drink.

Anyway, after the guy is asleep, you double him up like a pocketknife, and tie a cord or a wire around his neck and under his knees. Then you put him in a gunny sack, and leave him some place, and by and by when the guy wakes up and finds himself in the sack, naturally he wants to get out and the first thing he does is to try to straighten out his knees. This pulls the cord around his neck up so tight that after a while the guy is all out of breath.

So then when somebody comes along and opens the sack they find the guy dead, and nobody is responsible for this unfortunate situation, because after all the guy really commits suicide, because if he does not try to straighten out his knees he may live to a ripe old age, if he recovers from the tap on the noggin.

Well, a couple of days later I see by the papers where three Brooklyn citizens are scragged as they are walking peaceably along Clinton Street, the scragging being done by some parties in an automobile who seem to have a machine gun, and the papers state that the citizens are friends of Frankie Ferocious, and that it is rumoured the parties with the machine gun are from Harlem.

I judge by this that there is some trouble in Brooklyn, especially as about a week after the citizens are scragged in Clinton Street, another Harlem guy is found done up in a sack like a Virginia ham near Prospect Park, and now who is it but Joe the Joker's brother, Freddy, and I know Joe is going to be greatly displeased by this.

By and by it gets so nobody in Brooklyn will open as much as a sack of potatoes without first calling in the gendarmes, for fear a pair of No. 8 shoes will jump out at them.

Now one night I see Joe the Joker, and this time he is all alone, and I wish to say I am willing to leave him all alone, because something tells me he is hotter than a stove. But he grabs me as I am going past, so naturally I stop to talk to him, and the first thing I say is how sorry I am about his brother.

'Well,' Joe the Joker says, 'Freddy is always a kind of a sap. Rosa calls him up and asks him to come over to Brooklyn to see her. She wishes to talk to Freddy about getting me to give her a divorce,' Joe says, 'so she can marry Frankie Ferocious, I suppose. Anyway,' he says, 'Freddy tells Commodore Jake why he is going to see her. Freddy always likes Rosa, and thinks maybe he can patch it up between us. So,' Joe says, 'he winds up in a sack. They get him after he leaves her apartment. I do not claim Rosa will ask him to come over if she has any idea he will be sacked,' Joe says, 'but,' he says, 'she is responsible. She is a bad-luck doll.'

Then he starts to laugh, and at first I am greatly horrified, thinking it is because something about Freddy being sacked strikes his sense of humour, when he says to me, like this:

'Say,' he says, 'I am going to play a wonderful joke on Frankie Ferocious.'

'Well, Joe,' I say, 'you are not asking me for advice, but I am going to give you some free, gratis, and for nothing. Do not play any jokes on Frankie Ferocious, as I hear he has no more sense of humour than a nanny goat. I hear Frankie Ferocious will not laugh if you have Al Jolson, Eddie Cantor, Ed Wynn and Joe Cook telling him jokes all at once. In fact,' I say, 'I hear he is a tough audience.'

'Oh,' Joe the Joker says, 'he must have some sense of humour somewhere to stand for Rosa. I hear he is daffy about her. In fact, I understand she is the only person in the world he really likes, and trusts. But I must play a joke on him. I am going to have myself delivered to Frankie Ferocious in a sack.'

Well, of course I have to laugh at this myself, and Joe the Joker laughs with me. Personally, I am laughing just at the idea of anybody having themselves delivered to Frankie Ferocious in a sack, and especially Joe the Joker, but of course I have no idea Joe really means what he says.

'Listen,' Joe says, finally. 'A guy from St. Louis who is a friend of mine is doing most of the sacking for Frankie Ferocious. His name is Ropes McGonnigle. In fact,' Joe says, 'he is a very dear old pal of mine, and he has a wonderful sense of humour like me. Ropes McGonnigle has nothing whatever to do with sacking Freddy,' Joe says, 'and he is very indignant about it since he finds out Freddy is my brother, so he is anxious to help me play a joke on Frankie.

'Only last night,' Joe says, 'Frankie Ferocious sends for Ropes and tells him he will appreciate it as a special favour if Ropes will bring me to him in a sack. I suppose,' Joe says, 'that Frankie Ferocious hears from Rosa what Freddy is bound to tell her about my ideas on divorce. I have very strict ideas on divorce,' Joe says, 'especially where Rosa is concerned. I will see her in what's-this before I ever do her and Frankie Ferocious such a favour as giving her a divorce.

'Anyway,' Joe the Joker says, 'Ropes tells me about Frankie Ferocious propositioning him, so I send Ropes back to Frankie Ferocious to tell him he knows I am to be in Brooklyn to-morrow night, and furthermore, Ropes tells Frankie that he will have me in a sack in no time. And so he will,' Joe says.

'Well,' I say, 'personally, I see no percentage in being delivered to Frankie Ferocious in a sack, because as near as I can make out from what I read in the papers, there is no future for a guy in a sack that goes to Frankie Ferocious. What I cannot figure out,' I say, 'is where the joke on Frankie comes in.'

'Why,' Joe the Joker says, 'the joke is, I will not be asleep in the sack, and my hands will not be tied, and in each of my hands I will have a John Roscoe, so when the sack is delivered to Frankie Ferocious and I pop out blasting away, can you not imagine his astonishment?'

Well, I can imagine this, all right. In fact when I get to thinking of the look of surprise that is bound to come to Frankie Ferocious's face when Joe the Joker comes out of the sack I have to laugh, and Joe the Joker laughs right along with me.

'Of course,' Joe says, 'Ropes McGonnigle will be there to start blasting with me, in case Frankie Ferocious happens to have any company.'

Then Joe the Joker goes on up the street, leaving me still laughing, from thinking of how amazed Frankie Ferocious will be when Joe bounces out of the sack and starts throwing slugs around and about. I do not hear of Joe from that time to this, but I hear the rest of the story from very reliable parties.

It seems that Ropes McGonnigle does not deliver the sack himself, after all, but sends it by an expressman to Frankie Ferocious's home. Frankie Ferocious receives many sacks such as this in his time, because it seems that it is a sort of passion with him to personally view the contents of the sacks and check up on them before they are distributed about the city, and of course Ropes McGonnigle knows about this passion from doing so much sacking for Frankie.

When the expressman takes the sack into Frankie's house, Frankie personally lugs it down into his basement, and there he outs with a big John Roscoe and fires six shots into the sack, because it seems Ropes McGonnigle tips him off to Joe the Joker's plan to pop out of the sack and start blasting.

I hear Frankie Ferocious has a very strange expression on his pan and is laughing the only laugh anybody ever hears from him when the gendarmes break in and put the arm on him for murder, because it seems that when Ropes McGonnigle tells Frankie of Joe the Joker's plan, Frankie tells Ropes what he is going to do with his own hands before opening the sack. Naturally, Ropes speaks to Joe the Joker of Frankie's idea about filling the sack full of slugs, and Joe's sense of humour comes right out again.

So, bound and gagged, but otherwise as right as rain in the sack that is delivered to Frankie Ferocious, is by no means Joe the Joker, but Rosa.

Lillian

What I always say is that Wilbur Willard is nothing but a very lucky guy, because what is it but luck that has been teetering along Forty-ninth Street one cold snowy morning when Lillian is merowing around the sidewalk looking for her mamma?

And what is it but luck that has Wilbur Willard all mulled up to a million, what with him having been sitting out a few seidels of Scotch with a friend by the name of Haggerty in an apartment over in Fifty-ninth Street? Because if Wilbur Willard is not mulled up he will see Lillian as nothing but a little black cat, and give her plenty of room, for everybody knows that black cats are terribly bad luck, even when they are only kittens.

But being mulled up like I tell you, things look very different to Wilbur Willard, and he does not see Lillian as a little black kitten scrabbling around in the snow. He sees a beautiful leopard, because a copper by the name of O'Hara, who is walking past about then, and who knows Wilbur Willard, hears him say:

'Oh, you beautiful leopard!'

The copper takes a quick peek himself, because he does not wish any leopards running around his beat, it being against the law, but all he sees, as he tells me afterwards, is this rumpot ham, Wilbur Willard, picking up a scrawny little black kitten and shoving it in his overcoat pocket, and he also hears Wilbur say:

'Your name is Lillian.'

Then Wilbur teeters on up to his room on the top floor of an old fleabag in Eighth Avenue that is called the Hotel de Brussels, where he lives quite a while, because the management does not mind actors, the management of the Hotel de Brussels being very broad-minded, indeed.

There is some complaint this same morning from one of Wilbur's neighbours, an old burlesque doll by the name of Minnie Madigan, who is not working since Abraham Lincoln is assassinated, because she hears Wilbur going on in his room about a beautiful leopard, and calls up the clerk to say that an hotel which allows wild animals is not respectable. But the clerk looks in on Wilbur and finds him playing with nothing but a harmless-looking little black kitten, and nothing comes of the old doll's beef, especially as nobody ever claims the Hotel de Brussels is respectable anyway, or at least not much.

Of course when Wilbur comes out from under the ether next afternoon he can see Lillian is not a leopard, and in fact Wilbur is quite astonished to find himself in bed with a little black kitten, because it seems Lillian is sleeping on Wilbur's chest to keep warm. At first Wilbur does not believe what he sees, and puts it down to Haggerty's Scotch, but finally he is convinced, and so he puts Lillian in his pocket, and takes her over to the Hot Box night club and gives her some milk, of which it seems Lillian is very fond.

Now where Lillian comes from in the first place of course nobody knows. The chances are somebody chucks her out of a window into the snow, because people are always chucking kittens, and one thing and another, out of windows in New York. In fact, if there is one thing this town has plenty of, it is kittens, which finally grow up to be cats, and go snooping around ash cans, and mer-owing on roofs, and keeping people from sleeping good.

Personally, I have no use for cats, including kittens, because I never see one that has any too much sense, although I know a guy by the name of Pussy McGuire who makes a first-rate living doing nothing but stealing cats, and sometimes dogs, and selling them to old dolls who like such things for company. But Pussy only steals

Persian and Angora cats, which are very fine cats, and of course
Lillian is no such cat as this. Lillian is nothing but a black cat, and
nobody will give you a dime a dozen for black cats in this town, as
they are generally regarded as very bad jinxes.

Furthermore, it comes out in a few weeks that Wilbur Willard
can just as well name her Herman, or Sidney, as not, but Wilbur
sticks to Lillian, because this is the name of his partner when he is
in vaudeville years ago. He often tells me about Lillian Withington
when he is mulled up, which is more often than somewhat, for
Wilbur is a great hand for drinking Scotch, or rye, or bourbon, or
gin, or whatever else there is around for drinking, except water. In
fact, Wilbur Willard is a high-class drinking man, and it does no
good to tell him it is against the law to drink in this country,
because it only makes him mad, and he says to the dickens with the
law, only Wilbur Willard uses a much rougher word than dickens.

'She is like a beautiful leopard,' Wilbur says to me about Lillian
Withington. 'Black-haired, and black-eyed, and all ripply, like a
leopard I see in an animal act on the same bill at the Palace with us
once. We are headliners then,' he says, 'Willard and Withington,
the best singing and dancing act in the country.

'I pick her up in San Antonia, which is a spot in Texas,' Wilbur
says. 'She is not long out of a convent, and I just lose my old
partner, Mary McGee, who ups and dies on me of pneumonia
down there. Lillian wishes to go on the stage, and joins out with
me. A natural-born actress with a great voice. But like a leopard,'
Wilbur says. 'Like a leopard. There is cat in her, no doubt of this,
and cats and women are both ungrateful. I love Lillian Withington. I wish to marry her. But she is cold to me. She says she is not
going to follow the stage all her life. She says she wishes money,
and luxury, and a fine home and of course a guy like me cannot
give a doll such things.

'I wait on her hand and foot,' Wilbur says. 'I am her slave.
There is nothing I will not do for her. Then one day she walks in
on me in Boston very cool and says she is quitting me. She says she
is marrying a rich guy there. Well, naturally it busts up the act and
I never have the heart to look for another partner, and then I get to
belting that old black bottle around, and now what am I but a
cabaret performer?'

Then sometimes he will bust out crying, and sometimes I will
cry with him, although the way I look at it, Wilbur gets a pretty
fair break, at that, in getting rid of a doll who wishes things he

cannot give her. Many a guy in this town is tangled up with a doll who wishes things he cannot give her, but who keeps him tangled up just the same and busting himself trying to keep her quiet.

Wilbur makes pretty fair money as an entertainer in the Hot Box, though he spends most of it for Scotch, and he is not a bad entertainer, either. I often go to the Hot Box when I am feeling blue to hear him sing Melancholy Baby, and Moonshine Valley and other sad songs which break my heart. Personally, I do not see why any doll cannot love Wilbur, especially if they listen to him sing such songs as Melancholy Baby when he is mulled up good, because he is a tall, nice-looking guy with long eyelashes, and sleepy brown eyes, and his voice has a low moaning sound that usually goes very big with the dolls. In fact, many a doll does do some pitching to Wilbur when he is singing in the Hot Box, but somehow Wilbur never gives them a tumble, which I suppose is because he is thinking only of Lillian Withington.

Well, after he gets Lillian, the black kitten, Wilbur seems to find a new interest in life, and Lillian turns out to be right cute, and not bad-looking after Wilbur gets her fed up good. She is blacker than a yard up a chimney, with not a white spot on her, and she grows so fast that by and by Wilbur cannot carry her in his pocket any more, so he puts a collar on her and leads her round. So Lillian becomes very well known on Broadway, what with Wilbur taking her many places, and finally she does not even have to be led around by Wilbur, but follows him like a pooch. And in all the Roaring Forties there is no pooch that cares to have any truck with Lillian, for she will leap aboard them quicker than you can say scat, and scratch and bite them until they are very glad indeed to get away from her.

But of course the pooches in the Forties are mainly nothing but Chows, and Pekes, and Poms, or little woolly white poodles, which are led around by blonde dolls, and are not fit to take their own part against a smart cat. In fact, Wilbur Willard is finally not on speaking terms with any doll that owns a pooch between Times Square and Columbus Circle, and they are all hoping that both Wilbur and Lillian will go lay down and die somewhere. Furthermore, Wilbur has a couple of battles with guys who also belong to the dolls, but Wilbur is no sucker in a battle if he is not mulled up too much and leg-weary.

After he is through entertaining people in the Hot Box, Wilbur generally goes around to any speakeasies which may still be open, and does a little off-hand drinking on top of what he already drinks down in the Hot Box, which is plenty, and although it is considered very risky in this town to mix Hot Box liquor with any other, it never seems to bother Wilbur. Along towards daylight he takes a couple of bottles of Scotch over to his room in the Hotel de Brussels and uses them for a nightcap, so by the time Wilbur Willard is ready to slide off to sleep he has plenty of liquor of one kind and another inside him, and he sleeps pretty.

Of course nobody on Broadway blames Wilbur so very much for being such a rumpot, because they know about him loving Lillian Withington, and losing her, and it is considered a reasonable excuse in this town for a guy to do some drinking when he loses a doll, which is why there is so much drinking here, but it is a mystery to one and all how Wilbur stands off all this liquor without croaking. The cemeteries are full of guys who do a lot less drinking than Wilbur, but he never even seems to feel extra tough, or if he does he keeps it to himself and does not go around saying it is the kind of liquor you get nowadays.

He costs some of the boys around Mindy's plenty of dough one winter, because he starts in doing most of his drinking after hours in Good Time Charley's speakeasy, and the boys lay a price of four to one against him lasting until spring, never figuring a guy can drink very much of Good Time Charley's liquor and keep on living. But Wilbur Willard does it just the same, so everybody says the guy is naturally superhuman, and lets it go at that.

Sometimes Wilbur drops into Mindy's with Lillian following him on the look-out for pooches, or riding on his shoulder if the weather is bad, and the two of them will sit with us for hours chewing the rag about one thing and another. At such times Wilbur generally has a bottle on his hip and takes a shot now and then, but of course this does not come under the head of serious drinking with him. When Lillian is with Wilbur she always lays as close to him as she can get and anybody can see that she seems to be very fond of Wilbur, and that he is very fond of her, although he sometimes forgets himself and speaks of her as a beautiful leopard. But of course this is only a slip of the tongue, and anyway if Wilbur gets any pleasure out of thinking Lillian is a leopard, it is nobody's business but his own.

'I suppose she will run away from me some day,' Wilbur says, running his hand over Lillian's back until her fur crackles. 'Yes, although I give her plenty of liver and catnip, and one thing and another, and all my affection, she will probably give me the shake. Cats are like women, and women are like cats. They are both very ungrateful.'

'They are both generally bad luck,' Big Nig, the crap shooter, says. 'Especially cats, and most especially black cats.'

Many other guys tell Wilbur about black cats being bad luck, and advise him to slip Lillian into the North River some night with a sinker on her, but Wilbur claims he already has all the bad luck in the world when he loses Lillian Withington, and that Lillian, the cat, cannot make it any worse, so he goes on taking extra good care of her, and Lillian goes on getting bigger and bigger, until I commence thinking maybe there is some St. Bernard in her.

Finally I commence to notice something funny about Lillian. Sometimes she will be acting very loving towards Wilbur, and then again she will be very unfriendly to him, and will spit at him, and snatch at him with her claws, very hostile. It seems to me that she is all right when Willard is mulled up, but is as sad and fretful as he is himself when he is only a little bit mulled. And when Lillian is sad and fretful she makes it very tough indeed on the pooches in the neighbourhood of the Brussels.

In fact, Lillian takes to pooch-hunting, sneaking off when Wilbur is getting his rest, and running pooches bow-legged, especially when she finds one that is not on a leash. A loose pooch is just naturally cherry pie for Lillian.

Well, of course, this causes great indignation among the dolls who own the pooches, particularly when Lillian comes home one day carrying a Peke as big as she is herself by the scruff of the neck, and with a very excited blonde doll following her and yelling bloody murder outside Wilbur Willard's door when Lillian pops into Wilbur's room through a hole he cuts in the door for her, still lugging the Peke. But it seems that instead of being mad at Lillian and giving her a pasting for such goings on, Wilbur is somewhat pleased, because he happens to be still in a fog when Lillian arrives with the Peke, and is thinking of Lillian as a beautiful leopard.

'Why,' Wilbur says, 'this is devotion, indeed. My beautiful leopard goes off into the jungle and fetches me an antelope for dinner.'

Now of course there is no sense whatever to this, because a Peke is certainly not anything like an antelope, but the blonde doll outside Wilbur's door hears Wilbur mumble, and gets the idea that he is going to eat her Peke for dinner and the squawk she puts up is very terrible. There is plenty of trouble around the Brussels in chilling the blonde doll's beef over Lillian snagging her Peke, and what is more the blonde doll's ever-loving guy, who turns out to be a tough Ginney bootlegger by the name of Gregorio, shows up at the Hot Box the next night and wishes to put the slug on Wilbur Willard.

But Wilbur rounds him up with a few drinks and by singing Melancholy Baby to him, and before he leaves the Ginney gets very sentimental towards Wilbur, and Lillian, too, and wishes to give Wilbur five bucks to let Lillian grab the Peke again, if Lillian will promise not to bring it back. It seems Gregorio does not really care for the Peke, and is only acting quarrelsome to please the blonde doll and make her think he loves her dearly.

But I can see Lillian is having different moods, and finally I ask Wilbur if he notices it.

'Yes,' he says, very sad, 'I do not seem to be holding her love. She is getting very fickle. A guy moves on to my floor at the Brussels the other day with a little boy, and Lillian becomes very fond of this kid at once. In fact, they are great friends. Ah, well,' Wilbur says, 'cats are like women. Their affection does not last.'

I happen to go over to the Brussels a few days later to explain to a guy by the name of Crutchy, who lives on the same floor as Wilbur Willard, that some of our citizens do not like his face and that it may be a good idea for him to leave town, especially if he insists on bringing ale into their territory, and I see Lillian out in the hall with a youngster which I judge is the kid Wilbur is talking about. This kid is maybe three years old, and very cute, what with black hair, and black eyes, and he is woolling Lillian around the hall in a way that is most surprising, for Lillian is not such a cat as will stand for much woolling around, not even from Wilbur Willard.

I am wondering how anybody comes to take such a kid to a joint like the Brussels, but I figure it is some actor's kid, and that maybe there is no mamma for it. Later I am talking to Wilbur about this, and he says:

'Well, if the kid's old man is an actor, he is not working at it. He sticks close to his room all the time, and he does not allow the kid to go anywhere but in the hall, and I feel sorry for the little guy, which is why I allow Lillian to play with him.'

Now it comes on a very cold spell, and a bunch of us are sitting in Mindy's along towards five o'clock in the morning when we hear fire engines going past. By and by in comes a guy by the name of Kansas, who is named Kansas because he comes from Kansas, and who is a crap shooter by trade.

'The old Brussels is on fire,' this guy Kansas says.

'She is always on fire,' Big Nig says, meaning there is always plenty of hot stuff going on around the Brussels.

About this time who walks in but Wilbur Willard, and anybody can see he is just naturally floating. The chances are he comes from Good Time Charley's, and he is certainly carrying plenty of pressure. I never see Wilbur Willard mulled up more. He does not have Lillian with him, but then he never takes Lillian to Good Time Charley's, because Charley hates cats.

'Hey, Wilbur,' Big Nig says, 'your joint, the Brussels, is on fire.'

'Well,' Wilbur says, 'I am a little firefly, and I need a light. Let us go where there is fire.'

The Brussels is only a few blocks from Mindy's, and there is nothing else to do just then, so some of us walk over to Eighth Avenue with Wilbur teetering along ahead of us. The old shack is certainly roaring good when we get in sight of it, and the firemen are tossing water into it, and the coppers have the fire lines out to keep the crowd back, although there is not much of a crowd at such an hour in the morning.

'Is it not beautiful?' Wilbur Willard says, looking up at the flames. 'Is it not like a fairy palace all lighted up this way?'

You see, Wilbur does not realize the joint is on fire, although guys and dolls are running out of it every which way, most of them half dressed, or not dressed at all, and the firemen are getting out the life nets in case anybody wishes to hop out of the windows.

'It is certainly beautiful,' Wilbur says. 'I must get Lillian so she can see this.'

And before anybody has time to think, there is Wilbur Willard walking into the front door of the Brussels as if nothing happens. The firemen and the coppers are so astonished all they can do is holler at Wilbur, but he pays no attention whatever. Well, naturally everybody figures Wilbur is a gone gosling, but in about ten minutes he comes walking out of this same door through the fire and smoke as cool as you please, and he has Lillian in his arms.

'You know,' Wilbur says, coming over to where we are standing with our eyes popping out, 'I have to walk all the way up to my floor because the elevators seem to be out of commission. The service is getting terrible in this hotel. I will certainly make a strong beef to the management about it as soon as I pay something on my account.'

Then what happens but Lillian lets out a big mer-ow, and hops out of Wilbur's arms and skips past the coppers and the firemen with her back all humped up, and the next thing anybody knows she is tearing through the front door of the old hotel and making plenty of speed.

'Well, well,' Wilbur says, looking much surprised, 'there goes Lillian.'

And what does this daffy Wilbur Willard do but turn and go marching back into the Brussels again, and by this time the smoke is pouring out of the front doors so thick he is out of sight in a second. Naturally he takes the coppers and firemen by surprise, because they are not used to guys walking in and out of fires on them.

This time anybody standing around will lay you plenty of odds – two and a half and maybe three to one that Wilbur never shows up again, because the old Brussels is now just popping with fire and smoke from the lower windows, although there does not seem to be quite so much fire in the upper story. Everybody seems to be out of the joint, and even the firemen are fighting the blaze from the outside because the Brussels is so old and ramshackly there is no sense in them risking the floors.

I mean everybody is out of the joint except Wilbur Willard and Lillian, and we figure they are getting a good frying somewhere inside, although Feet Samuels is around offering to take thirteen to five for a few small bets that Lillian comes out okay, because Feet claims that a cat has nine lives and that is a fair bet at the price.

Well, up comes a swell-looking doll all heated up about something and pushing and clawing her way through the crowd up to the ropes and screaming until you can hardly hear yourself think, and about this same minute everybody hears a voice going ai-lee-hi-hee-hoo, like a Swiss yodeller, which comes from the roof of the Brussels, and looking up what do we see but Wilbur Willard standing up there on the edge of the roof, high above the fire and smoke, and yodelling very loud.

Under one arm he has a big bundle of some kind, and under the other he has the little kid I see playing in the hall with Lillian. As he stands up there going ai-lee-hi-hee-hoo, the swell-dressed doll near us begins yipping louder than Wilbur is yodelling, and the firemen rush over under him with a life net.

Wilbur lets go another ai-lee-hi-hee-hoo, and down he comes all spraddled out, with the bundle and the kid, but he hits the net sitting down and bounces up and back again for a couple of minutes before he finally settles. In fact, Wilbur is enjoying the bouncing, and the chances are he will be bouncing yet if the firemen do not drop their hold on the net and let him fall to the ground.

Then Wilbur steps out of the net, and I can see the bundle is a rolled-up blanket with Lillian's eyes peeking out of one end. He still has the kid under the other arm with his head stuck out in front, and his legs stuck out behind, and it does not seem to me that Wilbur is handling the kid as careful as he is handling Lillian. He stands there looking at the firemen with a very sneering look, and finally he says:

'Do not think you can catch me in your net unless I wish to be caught. I am a butterfly, and very hard to overtake.'

Then all of a sudden the swell-dressed doll who is doing so much hollering, piles on top of Wilbur and grabs the kid from him and begins hugging and kissing it.

'Wilbur,' she says, 'God bless you, Wilbur, for saving my baby! Oh, thank you, Wilbur, thank you! My wretched husband kidnaps and runs away with him, and it is only a few hours ago that my detectives find out where he is.'

Wilbur gives the doll a funny look for about half a minute and starts to walk away, but Lillian comes wiggling out of the blanket, looking and smelling pretty much singed up, and the kid sees Lillian and begins hollering for her, so Wilbur finally hands Lillian over to the kid. And not wishing to leave Lillian, Wilbur stands around somewhat confused, and the doll gets talking to him, and finally they go away together, and as they go Wilbur is carrying the kid, and the kid is carrying Lillian, and Lillian is not feeling so good from her burns.

Furthermore, Wilbur is probably more sober than he ever is before in years at this hour in the morning, but before they go I get a chance to talk some to Wilbur when he is still rambling somewhat, and I make out from what he says that the first time he goes to get Lillian he finds her in his room and does not see hide or hair of the little kid and does not even think of him, because he does not know what room the kid is in, anyway, having never noticed such a thing.

But the second time he goes up, Lillian is sniffing at the crack under the door of a room down the hall from Wilbur's and Wilbur says he seems to remember seeing a trickle of something like water coming out of the crack.

'And,' Wilbur says, 'as I am looking for a blanket for Lillian, and it will be a bother to go back to my room, I figure I will get one out of this room. I try the knob but the door is locked, so I kick it in, and walk in to find the room full of smoke, and fire is shooting through the windows very lovely, and when I grab a blanket off the bed for Lillian, what is under the blanket but the kid?

'Well,' Wilbur says, 'the kid is squawking, and Lillian is mer-owing, and there is so much confusion generally that it makes me nervous, so I figure we better go up on the roof and let the stink blow off us, and look at the fire from there. It seems there is a guy stretched out on the floor of the room alongside an upset table between the door and the bed. He has a bottle in one hand, and he is dead. Well, naturally there is no percentage in lugging a dead guy along, so I take Lillian and the kid and go up on the roof, and we just naturally fly off like humming birds. Now I must get a drink,' Wilbur says, 'I wonder if anybody has anything on their hip?'

Well, the papers are certainly full of Wilbur and Lillian the next day, especially Lillian, and they are both great heroes.

But Wilbur cannot stand the publicity very long, because he never has any time to himself for his drinking, what with the scribes and the photographers hopping on him every few minutes wishing to hear his story, and to take more pictures of him and Lillian, so one night he disappears, and Lillian disappears with him.

About a year later it comes out that he marries his old doll, Lillian Withington-Harmon, and falls into a lot of dough, and what is more he cuts out the liquor and becomes quite a useful citizen one way and another. So everybody has to admit that black cats are not always bad luck, although I say Wilbur's case is a little exceptional because he does not start out knowing Lillian is a black cat, but thinking she is a leopard.

I happen to run into Wilbur one day all dressed up in good clothes and jewellery and chucking quite a swell.

'Wilbur,' I say to him, 'I often think how remarkable it is the way Lillian suddenly gets such an attachment for the little kid and remembers about him being in the hotel and leads you back there a second time to the right room. If I do not see this come off with my own eyes, I will never believe a cat has brains enough to do such a thing, because I consider cats extra aumb.'

'Brains nothing,' Wilbur says. 'Lillian dues not have brains enough to grease a gimlet. And what is more, she has no more attachment for the kid than a jack rabbit. The time has come,' Wilbur says, 'to expose Lillian. She gets a lot of credit which is never coming to her. I will now tell you about Lillian, and nobody knows this but me.

'You see,' Wilbur says, 'when Lillian is a little kitten I always put a little Scotch in her milk, partly to help make her good and strong, and partly because I am never no hand to drink alone, unless there is nobody with me. Well, at first Lillian does not care so much for this Scotch in her milk, but finally she takes a liking to it, and I keep making her toddy stronger until in the end she will lap up a good big snort without any milk for a chaser, and yell for more. In fact, I suddenly realize that Lillian becomes a rumpot, just like I am in those days, and simply must have her grog, and it is when she is good and rummed up that Lillian goes off snatching Pekes, and acting tough generally.

'Now,' Wilbur says, 'the time of the fire is about the time I get home every morning and give Lillian her schnapps. But when I go into the hotel and get her the first time I forget to Scotch her up, and the reason she runs back into the hotel is because she is looking for her shot. And the reason she is sniffing at the kid's door is not because the kid is in there but because the trickle that is coming through the crack under the door is nothing but Scotch that is running out of the bottle in the dead guy's hand. I never mention this before because I figure it may be a knock to a dead guy's memory,' Wilbur says. 'Drinking is certainly a disgusting thing, especially secret drinking.'

'But how is Lillian getting along these days?' I ask Wilbur Willard.

'I am greatly disappointed in Lillian,' he says. 'She refuses to reform when I do, and the last I hear of her she takes up with Gregorio, the Ginney bootlegger, who keeps her well Scotched up all the time so she will lead his blonde doll's Peke a dog's life.'

Little Miss Marker

One evening along toward seven o'clock, many citizens are standing out on Broadway in front of Mindy's restaurant, speaking of one thing and another, and particularly about the tough luck they have playing the races in the afternoon, when who comes up the street with a little doll hanging on to his right thumb but a guy by the name of Sorrowful.

This guy is called Sorrowful because this is the way he always is about no matter what, and especially about the way things are with him when anybody tries to put the bite on him. In fact, if anybody who tries to put the bite on Sorrowful can listen to him for two minutes about how things are with him and not bust into tears, they must be very hard-hearted, indeed.

Regret, the horse player, is telling me that he once tries to put the bite on Sorrowful for a sawbuck, and by the time Sorrowful gets through explaining how things are with him, Regret feels so sorry for him that he goes out and puts the bite on somebody else for the saw and gives it to Sorrowful, although it is well known to one and all that Sorrowful has plenty of potatoes hid away somewhere.

He is a tall, skinny guy with a long, sad, mean-looking kisser, and a mournful voice. He is maybe sixty years old, give or take a couple of years, and for as long as I can remember he is running a handbook over in Forty-ninth Street next door to a chop-suey joint. In fact, Sorrowful is one of the largest handbook makers in this town.

Any time you see him he is generally by himself, because being by himself is not apt to cost him anything, and it is therefore a most surprising scene when he comes along Broadway with a little doll.

And there is much speculation among the citizens as to how this comes about, for no one ever hears of Sorrowful having any family, or relations of any kind, or even any friends.

The little doll is a very little doll indeed, the top of her noggin only coming up to Sorrowful's knee, although of course Sorrowful has very high knees, at that. Moreover, she is a very pretty little doll, with big blue eyes and fat pink cheeks, and a lot of yellow curls hanging down her back, and she has fat little legs and quite a large smile, although Sorrowful is lugging her along the street so fast that half the time her feet are dragging the sidewalk and she has a licence to be bawling instead of smiling.

Sorrowful is looking sadder than somewhat, which makes his face practically heart-rending, so he pulls up in front of Mindy's and motions us to follow him in. Anybody can see that he is worried about something very serious, and many citizens are figuring that maybe he suddenly discovers all his potatoes are counterfeit, because nobody can think of anything that will worry Sorrowful except money.

Anyway, four or five of us gather around the table where Sorrowful sits down with the little doll beside him, and he states a most surprising situation to us.

It seems that early in the afternoon a young guy who is playing the races with Sorrowful for several days pops into his place of business next door to the chop-suey joint, leading the little doll, and this guy wishes to know how much time he has before post in the first race at Empire.

Well, he only has about twenty-five minutes, and he seems very down-hearted about this, because he explains to Sorrowful that he has a sure thing in this race, which he gets the night before off a guy who is a pal of a close friend of Jockey Workman's valet.

The young guy says he is figuring to bet himself about a deuce on this sure thing, but he does not have such a sum as a deuce on him when he goes to bed, so he plans to get up bright and early in the morning and hop down to a spot on Fourteenth Street where he knows a guy who will let him have the deuce.

But it seems he oversleeps, and here it is almost post time, and it is too late for him to get to Fourteenth Street and back before the race is run off, and it is all quite a sad story indeed, although of course it does not make much impression on Sorrowful, as he is already sadder than somewhat himself just from thinking that somebody may beat him for a bet during the day, even though the races do not start anywhere as yet.

Well, the young guy tells Sorrowful he is going to try to get to Fourteenth Street and back in time to bet on the sure thing, because he says it will be nothing short of a crime if he has to miss such a wonderful opportunity.

'But,' he says to Sorrowful, 'to make sure I do not miss, you take my marker for a deuce, and I will leave the kid here with you as security until I get back.'

Now, ordinarily, asking Sorrowful to take a marker will be considered great foolishness, as it is well known to one and all that Sorrowful will not take a marker from Andrew Mellon. In fact, Sorrowful can almost break your heart telling you about the poor-houses that are full of bookmakers who take markers in their time.

But it happens that business is just opening up for the day, and Sorrowful is pretty busy, and besides the young guy is a steady customer for several days, and has an honest pan, and Sorrowful figures a guy is bound to take a little doll out of hock for a deuce. Furthermore, while Sorrowful does not know much about kids, he can see the little doll must be worth a deuce, at least, and maybe more.

So he nods his head, and the young guy puts the little doll on a chair and goes tearing out of the joint to get the dough, while Sorrowful marks down a deuce bet on Cold Cuts, which is the name of the sure thing. Then he forgets all about the proposition for a while, and all the time the little doll is sitting on the chair as quiet as a mouse, smiling at Sorrowful's customers, including the Chinks from the-chop-suey joint who come in now and then to play the races.

Well, Cold Cuts blows, and in fact is not even fifth, and along late in the afternoon Sorrowful suddenly realizes that the young guy never shows up again, and that the little doll is still sitting in the chair, although she is now playing with a butcher knife which one of the Chinks from the chop-suey joint gives her to keep her amused.

Finally it comes on Sorrowful's closing time, and the little doll is still there, so he can think of nothing else to do in this situation, but to bring her around to Mindy's and get a little advice from different citizens, as he does not care to leave her in his place of business alone, as Sorrowful will not trust anybody in there alone, not even himself.

'Now,' Sorrowful says, after giving us this long spiel, 'what are we to do about this proposition?'

Well, of course, up to this minute none of the rest of us know we are being cut in on any proposition, and personally I do not care for any part of it, but Big Nig, the crap shooter, speaks up as follows:

'If this little doll is sitting in your joint all afternoon,' Nig says, 'the best thing to do right now is to throw a feed into her, as the chances are her stomach thinks her throat is cut.'

Now this seems to be a fair sort of an idea, so Sorrowful orders up a couple of portions of ham hocks and sauerkraut, which is a very tasty dish in Mindy's at all times, and the little doll tears into it very enthusiastically, using both hands, although a fat old doll who is sitting at the next table speaks up and says this is terrible fodder to be tossing into a child at such an hour, and where is her mamma?

'Well,' Big Nig says to the old doll, 'I hear of many people getting a bust in the snoot for not minding their own business in this town, but you give off an idea, at that. Listen,' Big Nig says to the little doll, 'where is your mamma?'

But the little doll does not seem to know, or maybe she does not wish to make this information public, because she only shakes her head and smiles at Big Nig, as her mouth is too full of ham hocks and sauerkraut for her to talk.

'What is your name?' Big Nig asks, and she says something that Big Nig claims sounds like Marky, although personally I think she is trying to say Martha. Anyway it is from this that she gets the name we always call her afterward, which is Marky.

'It is a good monicker,' Big Nig says. 'It is short for marker, and she is certainly a marker unless Sorrowful is telling us a large lie. Why,' Big Nig says, 'this is a very cute little doll, at that, and pretty smart. How old are you, Marky?'

She only shakes her head again, so Regret, the horse player, who claims he can tell how old a horse is by its teeth, reaches over and sticks his finger in her mouth to get a peek at her crockery, but she seems to think Regret's finger is a hunk of ham hock and shuts down on it so hard Regret lets out an awful squawk. But he says that before she tries to cripple him for life he sees enough of her teeth to convince him she is maybe three, rising four, and this seems reasonable, at that. Anyway, she cannot be much older.

Well, about this time a guinea with a hand organ stops out in front of Mindy's and begins grinding out a tune while his ever-loving wife is passing a tambourine around among the citizens on the sidewalk and, on hearing this music, Marky slides off of her chair with her mouth still full of ham hock and sauerkraut, which she swallows so fast she almost chokes, and then she speaks as follows:

'Marky dance,' she says.

Then she begins hopping and skipping around among the tables, holding her little short skirt up in her hands and showing a pair of white panties underneath. Pretty soon Mindy himself comes along and starts putting up a beef about making a dance hall of his joint, but a guy by the name of Sleep-out, who is watching Marky with much interest, offers to bounce a sugar bowl off of Mindy's sconce if he does not mind his own business.

So Mindy goes away, but he keeps muttering about the white panties being a most immodest spectacle, which of course is great nonsense, as many dolls older than Marky are known to do dances in Mindy's, especially on the late watch, when they stop by for a snack on their way home from the night clubs and the speaks, and I hear some of them do not always wear white panties, either.

Personally, I like Marky's dancing very much, although of course she is no Pavlova, and finally she trips over her own feet and falls on her snoot. But she gets up smiling and climbs back on her chair and pretty soon she is sound asleep with her head against Sorrowful.

Well, now there is much discussion about what Sorrowful ought to do with her. Some claim he ought to take her to a police station, and others say the best thing to do is to put an ad. in the Lost and Found columns of the morning bladders, the same as people do when they find Angora cats, and Pekes, and other animals which they do not wish to keep, but none of these ideas seems to appeal to Sorrowful.

Finally he says he will take her to his own home and let her sleep there while he is deciding what is to be done about her, so Sorrowful takes Marky in his arms and lugs her over to a fleabag in West Forty-ninth Street where he has a room for many years, and afterward a bell hop tells me Sorrowful sits up all night watching her while she is sleeping.

Now what happens but Sorrowful takes on a great fondness for the little doll, which is most surprising, as Sorrowful is never before fond of anybody or anything, and after he has her overnight he cannot bear the idea of giving her up.

Personally, I will just as soon have a three-year-old baby wolf around me as a little doll such as this, but Sorrowful thinks she is the greatest thing that ever happens. He has a few inquiries made around and about to see if he can find out who she belongs to, and he is tickled silly when nothing comes of these inquiries, although nobody else figures anything will come of them anyway, as it is by no means uncommon in this town for little kids to be left sitting in chairs, or on doorsteps, to be chucked into orphan asylums by whoever finds them.

Anyway, Sorrowful says he is going to keep Marky, and his attitude causes great surprise, as keeping Marky is bound to be an expense, and it does not seem reasonable that Sorrowful will go to any expense for anything. When it commences to look as if he means what he says, many citizens naturally figure there must be an angle, and soon there are a great many rumours on the subject.

Of course one of these rumours is that the chances are Marky is Sorrowful's own offspring which is tossed back on him by the wronged mamma, but this rumour is started by a guy who does not know Sorrowful, and after he gets a gander at Sorrowful, the guy apologizes, saying he realizes that no wronged mamma will be daffy enough to permit herself to be wronged by Sorrowful. Personally, I always say that if Sorrowful wishes to keep Marky it is his own business, and most of the citizens around Mindy's agree with me.

But the trouble is Sorrowful at once cuts everybody else in on the management of Marky, and the way he talks to the citizens around Mindy's about her, you will think we are all personally responsible for her. As most of the citizens around Mindy's are bachelors, or are wishing they are bachelors, it is most inconvenient to them to suddenly find themselves with a family.

Some of us try to explain to Sorrowful that if he is going to keep Marky it is up to him to handle all her play, but right away Sorrowful starts talking so sad about all his pals deserting him and Marky just when they need them most that it softens all hearts, although up to this time we are about as pally with Sorrowful as a burglar with a copper. Finally every night in Mindy's is meeting night for a committee to decide something or other about Marky.

The first thing we decide is that the fleabag where Sorrowful lives is no place for Marky, so Sorrowful hires a big apartment in one of the swellest joints on West Fifty-ninth Street, overlooking Central Park, and spends plenty of potatoes furnishing it, although up to this time Sorrowful never sets himself back more than about ten bobs per week for a place to live and considers it extravagance, at that. I hear it costs him five G's to fix up Marky's bedroom alone, not counting the solid gold toilet set that he buys for her.

Then he gets her an automobile and he has to hire a guy to drive it for her, and finally when we explain to Sorrowful that it does not look right for Marky to be living with nobody but him and a chauffeur, Sorrowful hires a French doll with bobbed hair and red cheeks by the name of Mam'selle Fifi as a nurse for Marky, and this seems to be quite a sensible move, as it insures Marky plenty of company.

In fact, up to the time that Sorrowful hires Mam'selle Fifi, many citizens are commencing to consider Marky something of a nuisance and are playing the duck for her and Sorrowful, but after Mam'selle Fifi comes along you can scarcely get in Sorrowful's joint on Fifty-ninth Street, or around his table in Mindy's when he brings Marky and Mam'selle Fifi in to eat. But one night Sorrowful goes home early and catches Sleep-out guzzling Mam'selle Fifi, and Sorrowful makes Mam'selle Fifi take plenty of breeze, claiming she will set a bad example to Marky.

Then he gets an old tomato by the name of Mrs. Clancy to be Marky's nurse, and while there is no doubt Mrs. Clancy is a better nurse than Mam'selle Fifi and there is practically no danger of her setting Marky a bad example, the play at Sorrowful's joint is by no means as brisk as formerly.

You can see that from being closer than a dead heat with his potatoes, Sorrowful becomes as loose as ashes. He not only spends plenty on Marky, but he starts picking up checks in Mindy's and other spots, although up to this time picking up checks is something that is most repulsive to Sorrowful.

He gets so he will hold still for a bite, if the bite is not too savage and, what is more, a great change comes over his kisser. It is no longer so sad and mean looking, and in fact it is almost a pleasant sight at times, especially as Sorrowful gets so he smiles now and then, and has a big hello for one and all, and everybody says the Mayor ought to give Marky a medal for bringing about such a wonderful change.

Now Sorrowful is so fond of Marky that he wants her with him all the time, and by and by there is much criticism of him for having her around his handbook joint among the Chinks and the horse players, and especially the horse players, and for taking her around night clubs and keeping her out at all hours, as some people do not consider this a proper bringing-up for a little doll.

We hold a meeting in Mindy's on this proposition one night, and we get Sorrowful to agree to keep Marky out of his joint, but we know Marky is so fond of night clubs, especially where there is music, that it seems a sin and a shame to deprive her of this pleasure altogether, so we finally compromise by letting Sorrowful take her out one night a week to the Hot Box in Fifty-fourth

Street, which is only a few blocks from where Marky lives, and Sorrowful can get her home fairly early. In fact, after this Sorrowful seldom keeps her out any later than 2 a.m.

The reason Marky likes night clubs where there is music is because she can do her dance there, as Marky is practically daffy on the subject of dancing, especially by herself, even though she never seems to be able to get over winding up by falling on her snoot, which many citizens consider a very artistic finish, at that.

The Choo-Choo Boys' band in the Hot Box always play a special number for Marky in between the regular dances, and she gets plenty of applause, especially from the Broadway citizens who know her, although Henri, the manager of the Hot Box, once tells me he will just as soon Marky does not do her dancing there, because one night several of his best customers from Park Avenue, including two millionaires and two old dolls, who do not understand Marky's dancing, bust out laughing when she falls on her snoot, and Big Nig puts the slug on the guys, and is trying to put the slug on the old dolls, too, when he is finally headed off.

Now one cold, snowy night, many citizens are sitting around the tables in the Hot Box, speaking of one thing and another and having a few drams, when Sorrowful drops in on his way home, for Sorrowful has now become a guy who is around and about, and in and out. He does not have Marky with him, as it is not her night out and she is home with Mrs. Clancy.

A few minutes after Sorrowful arrives, a party by the name of Milk Ear Willie from the West Side comes in, this Milk Ear Willie being a party who is once a prize fighter and who has a milk ear, which is the reason he is called Milk Ear Willie, and who is known to carry a John Roscoe in his pants pocket. Furthermore, it is well known that he knocks off several guys in his time, so he is considered rather a suspicious character.

It seems that the reason he comes into the Hot Box is to shoot Sorrowful full of little holes, because he has a dispute with Sorrowful about a parlay on the races the day before, and the chances are Sorrowful will now be very dead if it does not happen that, just as Milk Ear outs with the old equalizer and starts taking dead aim at Sorrowful from a table across the room, who pops into the joint but Marky.

She is in a long nightgown that keeps getting tangled up in her bare feet as she runs across the dance floor and jumps into Sorrowful's arms, so if Milk Ear Willie lets go at this time he is apt to put

a slug in Marky, and this is by no means Willie's intention. So
Willie puts his rod back in his kick, but he is greatly disgusted and
stops as he is going out and makes a large complaint to Henri about
allowing children in a night club.

Well, Sorrowful does not learn until afterward how Marky saves
his life, as he is too much horrified over her coming four or five
blocks through the snow bare-footed to think of anything else, and
everybody present is also horrified and wondering how Marky finds
her way there. But Marky does not seem to have any good explanation for her conduct, except that she wakes up and discovers Mrs.
Clancy asleep and gets to feeling lonesome for Sorrowful.

About this time, the Choo-Choo Boys start playing Marky's
tune, and she slips out of Sorrowful's arms and runs out on the
dance floor.

'Marky dance,' she says.

Then she lifts her nightgown in her hands and starts hopping
and skipping about the floor until Sorrowful collects her in his
arms again, and wraps her in an overcoat and takes her home.

Now what happens but the next day Marky is sick from being
out in the snow bare-footed and with nothing on but her nightgown, and by night she is very sick indeed, and it seems that she
has pneumonia, so Sorrowful takes her to the Clinic hospital, and
hires two nurses and two croakers, and wishes to hire more, only
they tell him these will do for the present.

The next day Marky is no better, and the next night she is worse,
and the management of the Clinic is very much upset because it
has no place to put the baskets of fruit and candy and floral horseshoes and crates of dolls and toys that keep arriving every few
minutes. Furthermore, the management by no means approves of
the citizens who are tiptoeing along the hall on the floor where
Marky has her room, especially such as Big Nig, and Sleep-out,
and Wop Joey, and the Pale Face Kid and Guinea Mike and many
other prominent characters, especially as these characters keep trying to date up the nurses.

Of course I can see the management's point of view, but I wish
to say that no visitor to the Clinic ever brings more joy and cheer
to the patients than Sleep-out, as he goes calling in all the private
rooms and wards to say a pleasant word or two to the inmates, and
I never take any stock in the rumour that he is looking around to
see if there is anything worth picking up. In fact, an old doll from
Rockville Centre, who is suffering with yellow jaundice, puts up an

awful holler when Sleep-out is heaved from her room, because she says he is right in the middle of a story about a travelling salesman and she wishes to learn what happens.

There are so many prominent characters in and around the Clinic that the morning bladders finally get the idea that some well-known mob guy must be in the hospital full of slugs, and by and by the reporters come buzzing around to see what is what. Naturally they find out that all this interest is in nothing but a little doll, and while you will naturally think that such a little doll as Marky can scarcely be worth the attention of the reporters, it seems they get more heated up over her when they hear the story than if she is Jack Diamond.

In fact, the next day all the bladders have large stories about Marky, and also about Sorrowful and about how all these prominent characters of Broadway are hanging around the Clinic on her account. Moreover, one story tells about Sleep-out entertaining the other patients in the hospital, and it makes Sleep-out sound like a very large-hearted guy.

It is maybe three o'clock on the morning of the fourth day Marky is in the hospital that Sorrowful comes into Mindy's looking very sad, indeed. He orders a sturgeon sandwich on pumpernickel, and then he explains that Marky seems to be getting worse by the minute and that he does not think his doctors are doing her any good, and at this Big Nig, the cràp shooter, speaks up and states as follows:

'Well,' Big Nig says, 'if we are only able to get Doc Beerfeldt, the great pneumonia specialist, the chances are he will cure Marky like breaking sticks. But of course,' Nig says, 'it is impossible to get Doc Beerfeldt unless you are somebody like John D. Rockefeller, or maybe the President.'

Naturally, everybody knows that what Big Nig says is very true, for Doc Beerfeldt is the biggest croaker in this town, but no ordinary guy can get close enough to Doc Beerfeldt to hand him a ripe peach, let alone get him to go out on a case. He is an old guy, and he does not practise much any more, and then only among a few very rich and influential people. Furthermore, he has plenty of potatoes himself, so money does not interest him whatever, and anyway it is great foolishness to be talking of getting Doc Beerfeldt out at such an hour as this.

'Who do we know who knows Doc Beerfeldt?' Sorrowful says. 'Who can we call up who may have influence enough with him to get him to just look at Marky? I will pay any price,' he says. 'Think of somebody,' he says.

Well, while we are all trying to think, who comes in but Milk Ear Willie, and he comes in to toss a few slugs at Sorrowful, but before Milk Ear can start blasting Sleep-out sees him and jumps up and takes him off to a corner table, and starts whispering in Milk Ear's good ear.

As Sleep-out talks to him Milk Ear looks at Sorrowful in great surprise, and finally he begins nodding his head, and by and by he gets up and goes out of the joint in a hurry, while Sleep-out comes back to our table and says like this:

'Well,' Sleep-out says, 'let us stroll over to the Clinic. I just send Milk Ear Willie up to Doc Beerfeldt's house on Park Avenue to get the old Doc and bring him to the hospital. But, Sorrowful,' Sleep-out says, 'if he gets him, you must pay Willie the parlay you dispute with him, whatever it is. The chances are,' Sleep-out says, 'Willie is right. I remember once you out-argue me on a parlay when I know I am right.'

Personally, I consider Sleep-out's talk about sending Milk Ear Willie after Doc Beerfeldt just so much nonsense, and so does everybody else, but we figure maybe Sleep-out is trying to raise Sorrowful's hopes, and anyway he keeps Milk Ear from tossing these slugs at Sorrowful, which everybody considers very thoughtful of Sleep-out, at least, especially as Sorrowful is under too great a strain to be dodging slugs just now.

About a dozen of us walk over to the Clinic, and most of us stand around the lobby on the ground floor, although Sorrowful goes up to Marky's floor to wait outside her door. He is waiting there from the time she is first taken to the hospital, never leaving except to go over to Mindy's once in a while to get something to eat, and occasionally they open the door a little to let him get a peek at Marky.

Well, it is maybe six o'clock when we hear a taxi stop outside the hospital and pretty soon in comes Milk Ear Willie with another character from the West Side by the name of Fats Finstein, who is well known to one and all as a great friend of Willie's, and in between them they have a little old guy with a Vandyke beard, who does not seem to have on anything much but a silk dressing-gown and who seems somewhat agitated, especially as Milk Ear Willie and Fats Finstein keep prodding him from behind.

Now it comes out that this little old guy is nobody but Doc

Beerfeldt, the great pneumonia specialist, and personally I never see a madder guy, although I wish to say I never blame him much for being mad when I learn how Milk Ear Willie and Fats Finstein boff his butler over the noggin when he answers their ring, and how they walk right into old Doc Beerfeldt's bedroom and haul him out of the hay at the point of their Roscoes and make him go with them.

In fact, I consider such treatment most discourteous to a prominent croaker, and if I am Doc Beerfeldt I will start hollering copper as soon as I hit the hospital, and for all I know maybe Doc Beerfeldt has just such an idea, but as Milk Ear Willie and Fats Finstein haul him into the lobby who comes downstairs but Sorrowful. And the minute Sorrowful sees Doc Beerfeldt he rushes up to him and says like this:

'Oh Doc,' Sorrowful says, 'do something for my little girl. She is dying, Doc,' Sorrowful says. 'Just a little bit of a girl, Doc. Her name is Marky. I am only a gambler, Doc, and I do not mean anything to you or to anybody else, but please save the little girl.'

Well, old Doc Beerfeldt sticks out his Vandyke beard and looks at Sorrowful a minute, and he can see there are large tears in old Sorrowful's eyes, and for all I know maybe the Doc knows it has been many and many a year since there are tears in these eyes, at that. Then the Doc looks at Milk Ear Willie and Fats Finstein and the rest of us, and at the nurses and internes who are commencing to come running up from every which way. Finally, he speaks as follows:

'What is this?' he says. 'A child? A little child? Why,' he says, 'I am under the impression that these gorillas are kidnapping me to attend to some other sick or wounded gorilla. A child? This is quite different. Why do you not say so in the first place? Where is the child?' Doc Beerfeldt says, 'and,' he says, 'somebody get me some pants.'

We all follow him upstairs to the door of Marky's room and we wait outside when he goes in, and we wait there for hours, because it seems that even old Doc Beerfeldt cannot think of anything to do in this situation no matter how he tries. And along toward ten-thirty in the morning he opens the door very quietly and motions Sorrowful to come in, and then he motions all the rest of us to follow, shaking his head very sad.

There are so many of us that we fill the room around a little high

narrow bed on which Marky is lying like a flower against a white
wall, her yellow curls spread out over her pillow. Old Sorrowful
drops on his knees beside the bed and his shoulders heave quite
some as he kneels there, and I hear Sleep-out sniffing as if he has a
cold in his head. Marky seems to be asleep when we go in, but
while we are standing around the bed looking down at her, she
opens her eyes and seems to see us and, what is more, she seems to
know us, because she smiles at each guy in turn and then tries to
hold out one of her little hands to Sorrowful.

Now very faint, like from far away, comes a sound of music
through a half-open window in the room, from a jazz band that is
rehearsing in a hall just up the street from the hospital, and Marky
hears this music because she holds her head in such a way that
anybody can see she is listening, and then she smiles again at us
and whispers very plain, as follows:

'Marky dance.'

And she tries to reach down as if to pick up her skirt as she
always does when she dances, but her hands fall across her breast as
soft and white and light as snowflakes, and Marky never again
dances in this world.

Well, old Doc Beerfeldt and the nurses make us go outside at
once, and while we are standing there in the hall outside the door,
saying nothing whatever, a young guy and two dolls, one of them
old, and the other not so old, come along the hall much excited.
The young guy seems to know Sorrowful, who is sitting down
again in his chair just outside the door, because he rushes up to
Sorrowful and says to him like this:

'Where is she?' he says. 'Where is my darling child? You remember me?' he says. 'I leave my little girl with you one day while
I go on an errand, and while I am on this errand everything goes
blank, and I wind up back in my home in Indianapolis with my
mother and sister here, and recall nothing about where I leave my
child, or anything else.'

'The poor boy has amnesia,' the old doll says. 'The stories that
he deliberately abandons his wife in Paris and his child in New
York are untrue.'

'Yes,' the doll who is not old puts in. 'If we do not see the stories
in the newspapers about how you have the child in this hospital we
may never learn where she is. But everything is all right now. Of
course we never approve of Harold's marriage to a person of the
stage, and we only recently learn of her death in Paris soon after

their separation there and are very sorry. But everything is all right now. We will take full charge of the child.'

Now while all this gab is going on, Sorrowful never glances at them. He is just sitting there looking at Marky's door. And now as he is looking at the door a very strange thing seems to happen to his kisser, for all of a sudden it becomes the sad, mean-looking kisser that it is in the days before he ever sees Marky, and furthermore it is never again anything else.

'We will be rich,' the young guy says. 'We just learn that my darling child will be sole heiress to her maternal grandpapa's fortune, and the old guy is only a hop ahead of the undertaker right now. I suppose,' he says, 'I owe you something?'

And then Sorrowful gets up off his chair, and looks at the young guy and at the two dolls, and speaks as follows:

'Yes,' he says, 'you owe me a two-dollar marker for the bet you blow on Cold Cuts, and,' he says, 'I will trouble you to send it to me at once, so I can wipe you off my books.'

Now he walks down the hall and out of the hospital, never looking back again, and there is a very great silence behind him that is broken only by the sniffing of Sleep-out, and by some first-class sobbing from some of the rest of us, and I remember now that the guy who is doing the best job of sobbing of all is nobody but Milk Ear Willie.

Pick the Winner

What I am doing in Miami associating with such a character as Hot Horse Herbie is really quite a long story, and it goes back to one cold night when I am sitting in Mindy's restaurant on Broadway thinking what a cruel world it is, to be sure, when in comes Hot Horse Herbie and his ever-loving fiancée, Miss Cutie Singleton.

This Hot Horse Herbie is a tall, skinny guy with a most depressing kisser, and he is called Hot Horse Herbie because he can always tell you about a horse that is so hot it is practically on fire, a hot horse being a horse that is all readied up to win a race, although sometimes Herbie's hot horses turn out to be so cold they freeze everybody within fifty miles of them.

He is following the races almost since infancy, to hear him tell it. In fact, old Captain Duhaine, who has charge of the Pinkertons around the race tracks, says he remembers Hot Horse Herbie as a little child, and that even then Herbie is a hustler, but of course Captain Duhaine does not care for Hot Horse Herbie, because he claims Herbie is nothing but a tout, and a tout is something that is most repulsive to Captain Duhaine and all other Pinkertons.

A tout is a guy who goes around a race track giving out tips on the races, if he can find anybody who will listen to his tips, especially suckers, and a tout is nearly always broke. If he is not broke, he is by no means a tout, but a handicapper, and is respected by one and all, including the Pinkertons, for knowing so much about the races.

Well, personally, I have nothing much against Hot Horse Herbie, no matter what Captain Duhaine says he is, and I certainly have nothing against Herbie's ever-loving fiancée, Miss Cutie Singleton. In fact, I am rather in favour of Miss Cutie Singleton, because in all the years I know her, I wish to say I never catch Miss Cutie Singleton out of line, which is more than I can say of many other dolls I know.

She is a little, good-natured blonde doll, and by no means a crow, if you care for blondes, and some people say that Miss Cutie Singleton is pretty smart, although I never can see how this can be, as I figure a smart doll will never have any truck with a guy like Hot Horse Herbie, for Herbie is by no means a provider.

But for going on ten years, Miss Cutie Singleton and Hot Horse Herbie are engaged, and it is well known to one and all that they are to be married as soon as Herbie makes a scratch. In fact, they are almost married in New Orleans in 1928, when Hot Horse Herbie beats a good thing for eleven C's, but the tough part of it is the good thing is in the first race, and naturally Herbie bets the eleven C's right back on another good thing in the next race, and this good thing blows, so Herbie winds up with nothing but the morning line and is unable to marry Miss Cutie Singleton at this time.

Then again in 1929 at Churchill Downs, Hot Horse Herbie has a nice bet on Naishapur to win the Kentucky Derby, and he is so sure Naishapur cannot miss that the morning of the race he sends Miss Cutie Singleton out to pick a wedding ring. But Naishapur finishes second, so naturally Hot Horse Herbie is unable to buy the ring, and of course Miss Cutie Singleton does not wish to be married without a wedding ring.

They have another close call in 1931 at Baltimore when Hot Horse Herbie figures Twenty Grand a standout in the Preakness, and in fact is so sure of his figures that he has Miss Cutie Singleton go down to the city hall to find out what a marriage licence costs. But of course Twenty Grand does not win the Preakness, so the information Miss Cutie Singleton obtains is of no use to them and anyway Hot Horse Herbie says he can beat the price on marriage licences in New York.

However, there is no doubt but what Hot Horse Herbie and Miss Cutie Singleton are greatly in love, although I hear rumours that for a couple of years past Miss Cutie Singleton is getting somewhat impatient about Hot Horse Herbie not making a scratch as soon as he claims he is going to when he first meets up with her in Hot Springs in 1923.

In fact, Miss Cutie Singleton says if she knows Hot Horse Herbie is going to be so long delayed in making his scratch she will never consider becoming engaged to him, but will keep her job as a manicurist at the Arlington Hotel, where she is not doing bad, at that.

It seems that the past couple of years Miss Cutie Singleton is taking to looking longingly at the little houses in the towns they pass through going from one race track to another, and especially at little white houses with green shutters and yards and vines all around and about, and saying it must be nice to be able to live in such places instead of in a suitcase.

But of course Hot Horse Herbie does not put in with her on these ideas, because Herbie knows very well if he is placed in a little white house for more than fifteen minutes the chances are he will lose his mind, even if the house has green shutters.

Personally, I consider Miss Cutie Singleton somewhat ungrateful for thinking of such matters after all the scenery Hot Horse Herbie lets her see in the past ten years. In fact, Herbie lets her see practically all the scenery there is in this country, and some in Canada, and all she has to do in return for all this courtesy is to occasionally get out a little crystal ball and deck of cards and let on she is a fortune teller when things are going especially tough for Herbie.

Of course Miss Cutie Singleton cannot really tell fortunes, or she will be telling Hot Horse Herbie's fortune, and maybe her own, too, but I hear she is better than a raw hand at making people believe she is telling their fortunes, especially old maids who think they are in love, or widows who are looking to snare another husband and other such characters.

Well, anyway, when Hot Horse Herbie and his ever-loving fiancée come into Mindy's, he gives me a large hello, and so does Miss Cutie Singleton, so I hello them right back, and Hot Horse Herbie speaks to me as follows:

'Well,' Herbie says, 'we have some wonderful news for you. We are going to Miami,' he says, 'and soon we will be among the waving palms, and revelling in the warm waters of the Gulf Stream.'

Now of course this is a lie, because while Hot Horse Herbie is in Miami many times, he never revels in the warm waters of the Gulf Stream, because he never has time for such a thing, what with hustling around the race tracks in the daytime, and around the dog tracks and the gambling joints at night, and in fact I will lay plenty of six to five Hot Horse Herbie cannot even point in the direction of the Gulf Stream when he is in Miami, and I will give him three points, at that.

But naturally what he says gets me to thinking how pleasant it is in Miami in the winter, especially when it is snowing up north, and a guy does not have a flogger to keep himself warm, and I am commencing to feel very envious of Hot Horse Herbie and his ever-loving fiancée when he says like this:

'But,' Herbie says, 'our wonderful news for you is not about us going. It is about you going,' he says. 'We already have our railroad tickets,' he says, 'as Miss Cutie Singleton, my ever-loving fiancée here, saves up three C's for her hope chest the past summer, but when it comes to deciding between a hope chest and Miami, naturally she chooses Miami, because,' Herbie says, 'she claims she does not have enough hope left to fill a chest. Miss Cutie Singleton is always kidding,' he says.

'Well, now,' Herbie goes on, 'I just run into Mr. Edward Donlin, the undertaker, and it seems that he is sending a citizen of Miami back home to-morrow night, and of course you know,' he says, 'that Mr. Donlin must purchase two railroad tickets for this journey, and as the citizen has no one else to accompany him, I got to thinking of you. He is a very old and respected citizen of Miami,' Herbie says, 'although of course,' he says, 'he is no longer with us, except maybe in spirit.'

Of course such an idea is most obnoxious to me, and I am very indignant that Hot Horse Herbie can even think I will travel in this manner, but he gets to telling me that the old and respected citizen of Miami that Mr. Donlin is sending back home is a great old guy in his day, and that for all anybody knows he will appreciate having company on the trip, and about this time Big Nig, the crap shooter, comes into Mindy's leaving the door open behind him so that a blast of cold air hits me, and makes me think more than somewhat of the waving palms and the warm waters of the Gulf Stream.

So the next thing I know, there I am in Miami with Hot Horse Herbie, and it is the winter of 1931, and everybody now knows that this is the winter when the suffering among the horse players in Miami is practically horrible. In fact, it is worse than it is in the winter of 1930. In fact, the suffering is so intense that many citizens are wondering if it will do any good to appeal to Congress for relief for the horse players, but The Dancer says he hears Congress needs a little relief itself.

Hot Horse Herbie and his ever-loving fiancée, Miss Cutie Singleton, and me have rooms in a little hotel on Flagler Street, and while it is nothing but a fleabag, and we are doing the landlord a favour by living there, it is surprising how much fuss he makes any time anybody happens to be a little short of the rent. In fact, the landlord hollers and yells so much any time anybody is a little short of the rent that he becomes a very great nuisance to me, and I have half a notion to move, only I cannot think of any place to move to. Furthermore, the landlord will not let me move unless I pay him all I owe him, and I am not in a position to take care of this matter at the moment.

Of course I am not very dirty when I first come in as far as having any potatoes is concerned, and I start off at once having a little bad luck. It goes this way a while, and then it gets worse, and sometimes I wonder if I will not be better off if I buy myself a rope and end it all on a palm tree in the park on Biscayne Boulevard. But the only trouble with the idea is I do not have the price of a rope, and anyway I hear most of the palm trees in the park are already spoken for by guys who have the same notion.

And bad off as I am, I am not half as bad off as Hot Horse Herbie, because he has his ever-loving fiancée, Miss Cutie Singleton, to think of, especially as Miss Cutie Singleton is putting up quite a beef about not having any recreation, and saying if she only has the brains God gives geese she will break off their engagement at once and find some guy who can show her a little speed, and she seems to have no sympathy whatever for Hot Horse Herbie when he tells her how many tough snoots he gets beat at the track.

But Herbie is very patient with her, and tells her it will not be long now, because the law of averages is such that his luck is bound to change, and he suggests to Miss Cutie Singleton that she get the addresses of a few preachers in case they wish to locate one in a hurry. Furthermore, Hot Horse Herbie suggests to Miss Cutie Singleton that she get out the old crystal ball and her deck of cards, and hang out her sign as a fortune teller while they are waiting for the law of averages to start working for him, although personally I doubt if she will be able to get any business telling fortunes in Miami at this time because everybody in Miami seems to know what their fortune is already.

Now I wish to say that after we arrive in Miami I have very little truck with Hot Horse Herbie, because I do not approve of some of his business methods, and furthermore I do not wish Captain Duhaine and his Pinkertons at my hip all the time, as I never permit myself to get out of line in any respect, or anyway not much. But of course I see Hot Horse Herbie at the track every day, and one day I see him talking to the most innocent-looking guy I ever see in all my life.

He is a tall, spindling guy with a soft brown Vandyke beard, and soft brown hair, and no hat, and he is maybe forty-odd, and wears rumpled white flannel pants, and a rumpled sports coat, and big horn cheaters, and he is smoking a pipe that you can smell a block away. He is such a guy as looks as if he does not know what time it is, and furthermore he does not look as if he has a quarter, but I can see by the way Hot Horse Herbie is warming his ear that Herbie figures him to have a few potatoes.

Furthermore, I never know Hot Horse Herbie to make many bad guesses in this respect, so I am not surprised when I see the guy pull out a long flat leather from the inside pocket of his coat and weed Herbie a bank-note. Then I see Herbie start for the mutuels windows, but I am quite astonished when I see that he makes for a two-dollar window. So I follow Hot Horse Herbie to see what this is all about, because it is certainly not like Herbie to dig up a guy with a bank roll and then only promote him for a deuce.

When I get hold of Herbie and ask him what this means, he laughs, and says to me like this:

'Well,' he says, 'I am just taking a chance with the guy. He may be a prospect, at that,' Herbie says. 'You never can tell about people. This is the first bet he ever makes in his life, and furthermore,' Herbie says, 'he does not wish to bet. He says he knows one horse can beat another, and what of it? But,' Herbie says, 'I give him a good story, so he finally goes for the deuce. I think he is a college professor somewhere,' Herbie says, 'and he is only wandering around the track out of curiosity. He does not know a soul here. Well,' Herbie says, 'I put him on a real hot horse, and if he wins maybe he can be developed into something. You know,' Herbie says, 'they can never rule you off for trying.'

Well, it seems that the horse Herbie gives the guy wins all right and at a fair price, and Herbie lets it go at that for the time being, because he gets hold of a real good guy, and cannot be bothering with guys who only bet deuces. But every day the professor is at the track and I often see him wandering through the crowds, puffing at his old stinkaroo and looking somewhat bewildered.

I get somewhat interested in the guy myself, because he seems so much out of place, but I wish to say I never think of promoting him in any respect, because this is by no means my dodge, and finally one day I get to talking to him and he seems just as innocent as he looks. He is a professor at Princeton, which is a college in New Jersey, and his name is Woodhead, and he has been very sick, and is in Florida to get well, and he thinks the track mob is the greatest show he ever sees, and is sorry he does not study this business a little earlier in life.

Well, personally, I think he is a very nice guy, and he seems to have quite some knowledge of this and that and one thing and another, although he is so ignorant about racing that it is hard to believe he is a college guy.

Even if I am a hustler, I will just as soon try to hustle Santa Claus as Professor Woodhead, but by and by Hot Horse Herbie finds things getting very desperate indeed, so he picks up the professor again and starts working on him, and one day he gets him to go for another deuce, and then for a fin, and both times the horses Herbie gives him are winners, which Herbie says just goes to show you the luck he is playing in, because when he has a guy who is willing to make a bet for him, he cannot pick one to finish fifth.

You see, the idea is when Hot Horse Herbie gives a guy a horse he expects the guy to bet for him, too, or maybe give him a piece of what he wins, but of course Herbie does not mention this to Professor Woodhead as yet, because the professor does not bet enough to bother with, and anyway Herbie is building him up by degrees, although if you ask me, it is going to be slow work, and finally Herbie himself admits as much, and says to me like this:

'It looks as if I will have to blast,' Herbie says. 'The professor is a nice guy, but,' he says, 'he does not loosen so easy. Furthermore,' Herbie says, 'he is very dumb about horses. In fact,' he says, 'I never see a guy so hard to educate, and if I do not like him personally, I will have no part of him whatever. And besides liking him personally,' Herbie says, 'I get a gander into that leather he carries the other day, and what do I see,' he says, 'but some large, coarse notes in there back to back.'

Well, of course this is very interesting news, even to me, because large, coarse notes are so scarce in Miami at this time that if a guy runs into one he takes it to a bank to see if it is counterfeit before he changes it, and even then he will scarcely believe it.

I get to thinking that if a guy such as Professor Woodhead can be going around with large, coarse notes in his possession, I make a serious mistake in not becoming a college professor myself, and naturally after this I treat Professor Woodhead with great respect.

Now what happens one evening, but Hot Horse Herbie and his ever-loving fiancée, Miss Cutie Singleton, and me are in a little grease joint on Second Street putting on the old hot tripe à la Creole, which is a very pleasant dish, and by no means expensive, when who wanders in but Professor Woodhead.

Naturally Herbie calls him over to our table and introduces Professor Woodhead to Miss Cutie Singleton, and Professor Woodhead sits there with us looking at Miss Cutie Singleton with great interest, although Miss Cutie Singleton is at this time feeling somewhat peevish because it is the fourth evening hand running she has to eat tripe à la Creole, and Miss Cutie Singleton does not care for tripe under any circumstances.

She does not pay any attention whatever to Professor Woodhead, but finally Hot Horse Herbie happens to mention that the professor is from Princeton, and then Miss Cutie Singleton looks at the professor, and says to him like this:

'Where is this Princeton?' she says. 'Is it a little town?'

'Well,' Professor Woodhead says, 'Princeton is in New Jersey, and it is by no means a large town, but,' he says, 'it is thriving.'

'Are there any little white houses in this town?' Miss Cutie

Singleton asks. 'Are there any little white houses with green shutters and vines all around and about?'

'Why,' Professor Woodhead says, looking at her with more interest than somewhat, 'you are speaking of my own house,' he says. 'I live in a little white house with green shutters and vines all around and about, and,' he says, 'it is a nice place to live in, at that, although it is sometimes a little lonesome, as I live there all by myself, unless,' he says, 'you wish to count old Mrs. Bixby, who keeps house for me. I am a bachelor,' he says.

Well, Miss Cutie Singleton does not have much to say after this, although it is only fair to Miss Cutie Singleton to state that for a doll, and especially a blonde doll, she is never so very gabby, at that, but she watches Professor Woodhead rather closely, as Miss Cutie Singleton never before comes in contact with anybody who lives in a little white house with green shutters.

Finally we get through with the hot tripe à la Creole and walk around to the fleabag where Hot Horse Herbie and Miss Cutie Singleton and me are residing, and Professor Woodhead walks around with us. In fact, Professor Woodhead walks with Miss Cutie Singleton, while Hot Horse Herbie walks with me, and Hot Horse Herbie is telling me that he has the very best thing of his entire life in the final race at Hialeah the next day, and he is expressing great regret that he does not have any potatoes to bet on this thing, and does not know where he can get any potatoes.

It seems that he is speaking of a horse by the name of Breezing Along, which is owned by a guy by the name of Moose Tassell, who is a citizen of Chicago, and who tells Hot Horse Herbie that the only way Breezing Along can lose the race is to have somebody shoot him at the quarter pole, and of course nobody is shooting horses at the quarter pole at Hialeah, though many citizens often feel like shooting horses at the half.

Well, by this time we get to our fleabag, and we all stand there talking when Professor Woodhead speaks as follows:

'Miss Cutie Singleton informs me,' he says, 'that she dabbles somewhat in fortune telling. Well,' Professor Woodhead says, 'this is most interesting to me, because I am by no means sceptical of fortune telling. In fact,' he says, 'I make something of a study of the matter, and there is no doubt in my mind that certain human beings *do* have the faculty of foretelling future events with remarkable accuracy.'

Now I wish to say one thing for Hot Horse Herbie, and this is that he is a quick-thinking guy when you put him up against a situation that calls for quick thinking, for right away he speaks up and says like this:

'Why, Professor,' he says, 'I am certainly glad to hear you make this statement, because,' he says, 'I am a believer in fortune telling myself. As a matter of fact, I am just figuring on having Miss Cutie Singleton look into her crystal ball and see if she can make out anything on a race that is coming up to-morrow, and which has me greatly puzzled, what with being undecided between a couple of horses.'

Well, of course, up to this time Miss Cutie Singleton does not have any idea she is to look into any crystal ball for a horse, and furthermore, it is the first time in his life Hot Horse Herbie ever asks her to look into the crystal ball for anything whatever, except to make a few bobs for them to eat on, because Herbie by no means believes in matters of this nature.

But naturally Miss Cutie Singleton is not going to display any astonishment, and when she says she will be very glad to oblige, Professor Woodhead speaks up and says he will be glad to see this crystal gazing come off, which makes it perfect for Hot Horse Herbie.

So we all go upstairs to Miss Cutie Singleton's room, and the next thing anybody knows there she is with her crystal ball, gazing into it with both eyes.

Now Professor Woodhead is taking a deep interest in the proceedings, but of course Professor Woodhead does not hear what Hot Horse Herbie tells Miss Cutie Singleton in private, and as far as this is concerned neither do I, but Herbie tells me afterwards that he tells her to be sure and see a breeze blowing in the crystal ball. So by and by, after gazing into the ball a long time, Miss Cutie Singleton speaks in a low voice as follows:

'I seem to see trees bending to the ground under the force of a great wind,' Miss Cutie Singleton says. 'I see houses blown about by the wind,' she says. 'Yes,' Miss Cutie Singleton says, 'I see pedestrians struggling along and shivering in the face of this wind, and I see waves driven high on a beach and boats tossed about like paper cups. In fact,' Miss Singleton says, 'I seem to see quite a blow.'

Well, then, it seems that Miss Cutie Singleton can see no more, but Hot Horse Herbie is greatly excited by what she sees already, and he says like this:

'It means this horse Breezing Along,' he says. 'There can be no doubt about it. Professor,' he says, 'here is the chance of your lifetime. The horse will be not less than six to one,' he says. 'This is the spot to bet a gob, and,' he says, 'the place to bet it is downtown with a bookmaker at the opening price, because there will be a ton of money for the horse in the machines. Give me five C's,' Hot Horse Herbie says, 'and I will bet four for you, and one for me.'

Well, Professor Woodhead seems greatly impressed by what Miss Cutie Singleton sees in the crystal ball, but of course taking a guy from a finnif to five C's is carrying him along too fast, especially when Herbie explains that five C's is five hundred dollars, and naturally the professor does not care to bet any such money as this. In fact, the professor does not seem anxious to bet more than a sawbuck, tops, but Herbie finally moves him up to bet a yard, and of this yard twenty-five bobs is running for Hot Horse Herbie, as Herbie explains to the professor that a remittance he is expecting from his New York bankers fails him.

The next day Herbie takes the hundred bucks and bets it with Gloomy Gus downtown, for Herbie really has great confidence in the horse.

We are out to the track early in the afternoon and the first guy we run into is Professor Woodhead, who is very much excited. We speak to him, and then we do not see him again all day.

Well, I am not going to bother telling you the details of the race, but this horse Breezing Along is nowhere. In fact, he is so far back that I do not recollect seeing him finish, because by the time the third horse in the field crosses the line, Hot Horse Herbie and me are on our way back to town, as Herbie does not feel that he can face Professor Woodhead at such a time as this. In fact, Herbie does not feel that he can face anybody, so we go to a certain spot over on Miami Beach and remain there drinking beer until a late hour, when Herbie happens to think of his ever-loving fiancée, Miss Cutie Singleton, and how she must be suffering from lack of food, so we return to our fleabag so Herbie can take Miss Cutie Singleton to dinner.

But he does not find Miss Cutie Singleton. All he finds from her is a note, and in this note Miss Cutie Singleton says like this: 'Dear Herbie,' she says, 'I do not believe in long engagements any more, so Professor Woodhead and I are going to Palm Beach to be married to-night, and are leaving for Princeton, New Jersey, at once, where I am going to live in a little white house with green shutters and vines all around and about. Good-bye, Herbie,' the note says. 'Do not eat any bad fish. Respectfully, Mrs. Professor Woodhead.'

Well, naturally this is most surprising to Hot Horse Herbie, but I never hear him mention Miss Cutie Singleton or Professor Woodhead again until a couple of weeks later when he shows me a letter from the professor.

It is quite a long letter, and it seems that Professor Woodhead wishes to apologize, and naturally Herbie has a right to think that the professor is going to apologize for marrying his ever-loving fiancée, Miss Cutie Singleton, as Herbie feels he has an apology coming on this account.

But what the professor seems to be apologizing about is not being able to find Hot Horse Herbie just before the Breezing Along race to explain a certain matter that is on his mind.

'It does not seem to me,' the professor says, as near as I can remember the letter, 'that the name of your selection is wholly adequate as a description of the present Mrs. Professor Woodhead's wonderful vision in the crystal ball, so,' he says, 'I examine the programme further, and finally discover what I believe to be the name of the horse meant by the vision, and I wager two hundred dollars on this horse, which turns out to be the winner at ten to one, as you may recall. It is in my mind,' the professor says, 'to send you some share of the proceeds, inasmuch as we are partners in the original arrangement, but the present Mrs. Woodhead disagrees with my view, so all I can send you is an apology, and best wishes.'

Well, Hot Horse Herbie cannot possibly remember the name of the winner of any race as far back as this, and neither can I, but we go over to the Herald office and look at the files, and what is the name of the winner of the Breezing Along race but Mistral, and when I look in the dictionary to see what this word means, what does it mean but a violent, cold and dry northerly wind.

And of course I never mention to Hot Horse Herbie or anybody else that I am betting on another horse in this race myself, and the name of the horse I am betting on is Leg Show, for how do I know for certain that Miss Cutie Singleton is not really seeing in the crystal ball just such a blow as she describes?

Undertaker Song

Now this story I am going to tell you is about the game of football, a very healthy pastime for the young, and a great character builder from all I hear, but to get around to this game of football I am compelled to bring in some most obnoxious characters, beginning with a guy by the name of Joey Perhaps, and all I can conscientiously say about Joey is you can have him.

It is a matter of maybe four years since I see this Joey Perhaps until I notice him on a train going to Boston, Mass., one Friday afternoon. He is sitting across from me in the dining-car, where I am enjoying a small portion of baked beans and brown bread, and he looks over to me once, but he does not rap to me.

There is no doubt but what Joey Perhaps is bad company, because the last I hear of him he is hollering copper on a guy by the name of Jack Ortega, and as a result of Joey Perhaps hollering copper, this Jack Ortega is taken to the city of Ossining, N.Y., and placed in an electric chair, and given a very, very, very severe shock in the seat of his pants.

It is something about plugging a most legitimate business guy in the city of Rochester, N.Y., when Joey Perhaps and Jack Ortega are engaged together in a little enterprise to shake the guy down, but the details of this transaction are dull, sordid, and quite uninteresting, except that Joey Perhaps turns state's evidence and announces that Jack Ortega fires the shot which cools the legitimate guy off, for which service he is rewarded with only a small stretch.

I must say for Joey Perhaps that he looks good, and he is very well dressed, but then Joey is always particular about clothes, and he is quite a handy guy with the dolls in his day and, to tell the truth, many citizens along Broadway are by no means displeased when Joey is placed in the state institution, because they are generally pretty uneasy about their dolls when he is around.

Naturally, I am wondering why Joey Perhaps is on this train going to Boston, Mass., but for all I know maybe he is wondering the same thing about me, although personally I am making no secret about it. The idea is I am *en route* to Boston, Mass., to see a contest of skill and science that is to take place there this very Friday night between a party by the name of Lefty Ledoux and another party by the name of Pile Driver, who are very prominent middleweights.

Now ordinarily I will not go around the corner to see a contest of skill and science between Lefty Ledoux and Pile Driver, or anybody else, as far as that is concerned, unless they are using blackjacks and promise to hurt each other, but I am the guest on this trip of a party by the name of Meyer Marmalade, and I will go anywhere to see anything if I am a guest.

This Meyer Marmalade is really a most superior character, who is called Meyer Marmalade because nobody can ever think of his last name, which is something like Marmalodowski, and he is known far and wide for the way he likes to make bets on any sporting proposition, such as baseball, or horse races, or ice hockey, or contests of skill and science, and especially contests of skill and science.

So he wishes to be present at this contest in Boston, Mass., between Lefty Ledoux and Pile Driver to have a nice wager on Driver, as he has reliable information that Driver's manager, a party by the name of Koons, has both judges and the referee in the satchel.

If there is one thing Meyer Marmalade dearly loves, it is to have a bet on a contest of skill and science of this nature, and so he is going to Boston, Mass. But Meyer Marmalade is such a guy as loathes and despises travelling all alone, so when he offers to pay my expenses if I will go along to keep him company, naturally I am pleased to accept, as I have nothing on of importance at the moment and, in fact, I do not have anything on of importance for the past ten years.

I warn Meyer Marmalade in advance that if he is looking to take anything off of anybody in Boston, Mass., he may as well remain at home, because everybody knows that statistics show that the percentage of anything being taken off of the citizens of Boston, Mass., is less *per capita* than anywhere else in the United States, especially when it comes to contests of skill and science, but Meyer Marmalade says this is the first time they ever had two judges and a referee running against the statistics, and he is very confident.

Well, by and by I go from the dining-car back to my seat in another car, where Meyer Marmalade is sitting reading a detective magazine, and I speak of seeing Joey Perhaps to him. But Meyer Marmalade does not seem greatly interested, although he says to me like this:

'Joey Perhaps, eh?' he says. 'A wrong gee. A dead wrong gee. He must just get out. I run into the late Jack Ortega's brother, young Ollie, in Mindy's restaurant last week,' Meyer Marmalade says, 'and when we happen to get to talking of wrong gees, naturally Joey Perhaps's name comes up, and Ollie remarks he understands Joey Perhaps is about due out, and that he will be pleased to see him some day. Personally,' Meyer Marmalade says, 'I do not care for any part of Joey Perhaps at any price.'

Now our car is loaded with guys and dolls who are going to Boston, Mass., to witness a large football game between the Harvards and the Yales at Cambridge, Mass., the next day, and the reason I know this is because they are talking of nothing else.

So this is where the football starts getting into this story.

One old guy that I figure must be a Harvard from the way he talks seems to have a party all his own, and he is getting so much attention from one and all in the party that I figure he must be a guy of some importance, because they laugh heartily at his remarks, and although I listen very carefully to everything he says he does not sound so very humorous to me.

He is a heavy-set guy with a bald head and a deep voice, and anybody can see that he is such a guy as is accustomed to plenty of authority. I am wondering out loud to Meyer Marmalade who the guy can be, and Meyer Marmalade states as follows:

'Why,' he says, 'he is nobody but Mr. Phillips Randolph, who makes the automobiles. He is the sixth richest guy in this country,' Meyer says, 'or maybe it is the seventh. Anyway, he is pretty well up with the front runners. I spot his monicker on his suitcase, and then I ask the porter, to make sure. It is a great honour for us to be travelling with Mr. Phillips Randolph,' Meyer says, 'because of him being such a public benefactor and having so much dough, especially having so much dough.'

Well, naturally everybody knows who Mr. Phillips Randolph is, and I am surprised that I do not recognize his face myself from seeing it so often in the newspapers alongside the latest model automobile his factory turns out, and I am as much pleasured up as Meyer Marmalade over being in the same car with Mr. Phillips Randolph.

He seems to be a good-natured old guy, at that, and he is having a grand time, what with talking, and laughing, and taking a dram now and then out of a bottle, and when old Crip McGonnigle comes gimping through the car selling his football souvenirs, such as red and blue feathers, and little badges and pennants, and one thing and another, as Crip is doing around the large football games since Hickory Slim is a two-year-old, Mr. Phillips Randolph stops him and buys all of Crip's red feathers, which have a little white H on them to show they are for the Harvards.

Then Mr. Phillips Randolph distributes the feathers around among his party, and the guys and dolls stick them in their hats, or pin them on their coats, but he has quite a number of feathers left over, and about this time who comes through the car but Joey Perhaps, and Mr. Phillips Randolph steps out in the aisle and stops Joey and politely offers him a red feather, and speaks as follows:

'Will you honour us by wearing our colours?'

Well, of course Mr. Phillips Randolph is only full of good spirits, and means no harm whatever, and the guys and dolls in his party laugh heartily as if they consider his action very funny, but maybe because they laugh, and maybe because he is just naturally a hostile guy, Joey Perhaps knocks Mr. Phillips Randolph's hand down, and says like this:

'Get out of my way,' Joey says. 'Are you trying to make a sucker out of somebody?'

Personally, I always claim that Joey Perhaps has a right to reject the red feather, because for all I know he may prefer a blue feather, which means the Yales, but what I say is he does not need to be so impolite to an old guy such as Mr. Phillips Randolph, although of course Joey has no way of knowing at this time about Mr. Phillips Randolph having so much dough.

Anyway, Mr. Phillips Randolph stands staring at Joey as if he is greatly startled, and the chances are he is, at that, for the chances are nobody ever speaks to him in such a manner in all his life, and Joey Perhaps also stands there a minute staring back at Mr. Phillips Randolph, and finally Joey speaks as follows:

'Take a good peek,' Joey Perhaps says. 'Maybe you will remember me if you ever see me again.'

'Yes,' Mr. Phillips Randolph says, very quiet. 'Maybe I will. They say I have a good memory for faces. I beg your pardon for stopping you, sir. It is all in fun, but I am sorry,' he says.

Then Joey Perhaps goes on, and he does not seem to notice Meyer Marmalade and me sitting there in the car, and Mr. Phillips Randolph sits down, and his face is redder than somewhat, and all the joy is gone out of him, and out of his party, too. Personally, I am very sorry Joey Perhaps comes along, because I figure Mr.

Phillips Randolph will give me one of his spare feathers, and I will consider it a wonderful keepsake.

But now there is not much more talking, and no laughing whatever in Mr. Phillips Randolph's party, and he just sits there as if he is thinking, and for all I know he may be thinking that there ought to be a law against a guy speaking so disrespectfully to a guy with all his dough as Joey Perhaps speaks to him.

Well, the contest of skill and science between Lefty Ledoux and Pile Driver turns out to be something of a disappointment, and, in fact, it is a stinkeroo, because there is little skill and no science whatever in it, and by the fourth round the customers are scuffling their feet, and saying throw these bums out, and making other derogatory remarks, and furthermore it seems that this Koons does not have either one of the judges, or even as much as the referee, in the satchel, and Ledoux gets the duke by unanimous vote of the officials.

So Meyer Marmalade is out a couple of C's, which is all he can wager at the ringside, because it seems that nobody in Boston, Mass., cares a cuss about who wins the contest, and Meyer is much disgusted with life, and so am I, and we go back to the Copley Plaza Hotel, where we are stopping, and sit down in the lobby to meditate on the injustice of everything.

Well, the lobby is a scene of gaiety, as it seems there are a number of football dinners and dances going on in the hotel, and guys and dolls in evening clothes are all around and about, and the dolls are so young and beautiful that I get to thinking that this is not such a bad old world, after all, and even Meyer Marmalade begins taking notice.

All of a sudden, a very, very beautiful young doll who is about forty per cent. in and sixty per cent. out of an evening gown walks right up to us sitting there, and holds out her hand to me, and speaks as follows:

'Do you remember me?'

Naturally, I do not remember her, but naturally I am not going to admit it, because it is never my policy to discourage any doll who wishes to strike up an acquaintance with me, which is what I figure this doll is trying to do; then I see that she is nobody but Doria Logan, one of the prettiest dolls that ever hits Broadway, and about the same time Meyer Marmalade also recognizes her.

Doria changes no little since last I see her, which is quite some time back, but there is no doubt the change is for the better, because she is once a very rattle-headed young doll, and now she seems older, and quieter, and even prettier than ever. Naturally, Meyer Marmalade and I.are glad to see her looking so well, and we ask her how are tricks, and what is the good word, and all this and that, and finally Doria Logan states to us as follows:

'I am in great trouble,' Doria says. 'I am in terrible trouble, and you are the first ones I see that I can talk to about it.'

Well, at this, Meyer Marmalade begins to tuck in somewhat, because he figures it is the old lug coming up, and Meyer Marmalade is not such a guy as will go for the lug from a doll unless he gets something more than a story. But I can see Doria Logan is in great earnest.

'Do you remember Joey Perhaps?' she says.

'A wrong gee,' Meyer Marmalade says. 'A dead wrong gee.'

'I not only remember Joey Perhaps,' I say, 'but I see him on the train to-day.'

'Yes,' Doria says, 'he is here in town. He hunts me up only a few hours ago. He is here to do me great harm. He is here to finish ruining my life.'

'A wrong gee,' Meyer Marmalade puts in again. 'Always a hundred per cent. wrong gee.'

Then Doria Logan gets us to go with her to a quiet corner of the lobby, and she tells us a strange story, as follows, and also to wit:

It seems that she is once tangled up with Joey Perhaps, which is something I never know before, and neither does Meyer Marmalade, and, in fact, the news shocks us quite some. It is back in the days when she is just about sixteen and is in the chorus of Earl Carroll's Vanities, and I remember well what a standout she is for looks, to be sure.

Naturally, at sixteen, Doria is quite a chump doll, and does not know which way is south, or what time it is, which is the way all dolls at sixteen are bound to be, and she has no idea what a wrong gee Joey Perhaps is, as he is good-looking, and young, and seems very romantic, and is always speaking of love and one thing and another.

Well, the upshot of it all is the upshot of thousands of other cases since chump dolls commence coming to Broadway, and the first thing she knows, Doria Logan finds herself mixed up with a very bad character, and does not know what to do about it.

By and by, Joey Perhaps commences mistreating her no little, and finally he tries to use her in some nefarious schemes of his, and of course everybody along Broadway knows that most of Joey's schemes are especially nefarious, because Joey is on the shake almost since infancy.

Well, one day Doria says to herself that if this is love, she has all she can stand, and she hauls off and runs away from Joey Perhaps. She goes back to her people, who live in the city of Cambridge, Mass., which is the same place where the Harvards have their college, and she goes there because she does not know of any other place to go.

It seems that Doria's people are poor, and Doria goes to a business school and learns to be a stenographer, and she is working for a guy in the real estate dodge by the name of Poopnoodle, and doing all right for herself, and in the meantime she hears that Joey Perhaps gets sent away, so she figures her troubles are all over as far as he is concerned.

Now Doria Logan goes along quietly through life, working for Mr. Poopnoodle, and never thinking of love, or anything of a similar nature, when she meets up with a young guy who is one of the Harvards, and who is maybe twenty-one years old, and is quite a football player, and where Doria meets up with this guy is in a drug store over a banana split.

Well, the young Harvard takes quite a fancy to Doria and, in fact, he is practically on fire about her, but by this time Doria is going on twenty, and is no longer a chump doll, and she has no wish to get tangled up in love again.

In fact, whenever she thinks of Joey Perhaps, Doria takes to hating guys in general, but somehow she cannot seem to get up a real good hate on the young Harvard, because, to hear her tell it, he is handsome, and noble, and has wonderful ideals.

Now as time goes on, Doria finds she is growing pale, and is losing her appetite, and cannot sleep, and this worries her no little, as she is always a first-class feeder, and finally she comes to the conclusion that what ails her is that she is in love with the young Harvard, and can scarcely live without him, so she admits as much to him one night when the moon is shining on the Charles River, and everything is a dead cold set-up for love.

Well, naturally, after a little off-hand guzzling, which is quite permissible under the circumstances, the young guy wishes her to name the happy day, and Doria has half a notion to make it the following Monday, this being a Sunday night, but then she gets to thinking about her past with Joey Perhaps, and all, and she figures it will be bilking the young Harvard to marry him unless she has a small talk with him first about Joey, because she is well aware that many young guys may have some objection to wedding a doll with a skeleton in her closet, and especially a skeleton such as Joey Perhaps.

But she is so happy she does not wish to run the chance of spoiling everything by these narrations right away, so she keeps her trap closed about Joey, although she promises to marry the young Harvard when he gets out of college, which will be the following year, if he still insists, because Doria figures that by then she will be able to break the news to him about Joey very gradually, and gently, and especially gently.

Anyway, Doria says she is bound and determined to tell him before the wedding, even if he takes the wind on her as a consequence, and personally I claim this is very considerate of Doria, because many dolls never tell before the wedding, or even after. So Doria and the young Harvard are engaged, and great happiness prevails, when, all of a sudden, in pops Joey Perhaps.

It seems that Joey learns of Doria's engagement as soon as he gets out of the state institution, and he hastens to Boston, Mass., with an inside coat pocket packed with letters that Doria writes him long ago, and also a lot of pictures they have taken together, as young guys and dolls are bound to do, and while there is nothing much out of line about these letters and pictures, put them all together they spell a terrible pain in the neck to Doria at this particular time.

'A wrong gee,' Meyer Marmalade says. 'But,' he says, 'he is only going back to his old shakedown dodge, so all you have to do is to buy him off.'

Well, at this, Doria Logan laughs one of these little short dry laughs that go 'hah,' and says like this:

'Of course he is looking to get bought off, but,' she says, 'where will I get any money to buy him off? I do not have a dime of my own, and Joey is talking large figures, because he knows my fiancé's papa has plenty. He wishes me to go to my fiancé and make him get the money off his papa, or he threatens to personally deliver the letters and pictures to my fiancé's papa.

'You can see the predicament I am in,' Doria says, 'and you can see what my fiancé's papa will think of me if he learns I am once mixed up with a blackmailer such as Joey Perhaps.

'Besides,' Doria says, 'it is something besides money with Joey

Perhaps, and I am not so sure he will not double-cross me even if I can pay him his price. Joey Perhaps is very angry at me. I think,' she says, 'if he can spoil my happiness, it will mean more to him than money.'

Well, Doria states that all she can think of when she is talking to Joey Perhaps is to stall for time, and she tells Joey that, no matter what, she cannot see her fiancé until after the large football game between the Harvards and the Yales as he has to do a little football playing for the Harvards, and Joey asks her if she is going to see the game, and naturally she is.

And then Joey says he thinks he will look up a ticket speculator, and buy a ticket and attend the game himself, as he is very fond of football, and where will she be sitting, as he hopes and trusts he will be able to see something of her during the game, and this statement alarms Doria Logan no little, for who is she going with but her fiancé's papa, and a party of his friends, and she feels that there is no telling what Joey Perhaps may be up to.

She explains to Joey that she does not know exactly where she will be sitting, except that it will be on the Harvards' side of the field, but Joey is anxious for more details than this.

'In fact,' Doria says, 'he is most insistent, and he stands at my elbow while I call up Mr. Randolph at this very hotel, and he tells me the exact location of our seats. Then Joey says he will endeavour to get a seat as close to me as possible, and he goes away.'

'What Mr. Randolph?' Meyer says. 'Which Mr. Randolph?' he says. 'You do not mean Mr. Phillips Randolph, by any chance, do you?'

'Why, to be sure,' Doria says. 'Do you know him?'

Naturally, from now on Meyer Marmalade gazes at Doria Logan with deep respect, and so do I, although by now she is crying a little, and I am by no means in favour of crying dolls. But while she is crying, Meyer Marmalade seems to be doing some more thinking, and finally he speaks as follows:

'Kindly see if you can recall these locations you speak of.'

So here is where the football game comes in once more.

Only I regret to state that personally I do not witness this game, and the reason I do not witness it is because nobody wakes me up the next day in time for me to witness it, and the way I look at it, this is all for the best, as I am scarcely a football enthusiast.

So from now on the story belongs to Meyer Marmalade, and I will tell it to you as Meyer tells it to me.

It is a most exciting game [Meyer says]. The place is full of people, and there are bands playing, and much cheering, and more lovely dolls than you can shake a stick at, although I do not believe there are any lovelier present than Doria Logan.

It is a good thing she remembers the seat locations, otherwise I will never find her, but there she is surrounded by some very nice-looking people, including Mr. Phillips Randolph, and there I am two rows back of Mr. Phillips Randolph, and the ticket spec I get my seat off of says he cannot understand why everybody wishes to sit near Mr. Phillips Randolph to-day when there are other seats just as good, and maybe better, on the Harvards' side.

So I judge he has other calls similar to mine for this location, and a sweet price he gets for it, too, and I judge that maybe at least one call is from Joey Perhaps, as I see Joey a couple of rows on back up of where I am sitting, but off to my left on an aisle, while I am almost in a direct line with Mr. Phillips Randolph.

To show you that Joey is such a guy as attracts attention, Mr. Phillips Randolph stands up a few minutes before the game starts, peering around and about to see who is present that he knows, and all of a sudden his eyes fall on Joey Perhaps, and then Mr. Phillips Randolph proves he has a good memory for faces, to be sure, for he states as follows:

'Why,' he says, 'there is the chap who rebuffs me so churlishly on the train when I offer him our colours. Yes,' he says, 'I am sure it is the same chap.'

Well, what happens in the football game is much pulling and hauling this way and that, and to and fro, between the Harvards and the Yales without a tally right down to the last five minutes of play, and then all of a sudden the Yales shove the football down to within about three-eighths of an inch of the Harvards' goal line.

At this moment quite some excitement prevails. Then the next thing anybody knows, the Yales outshove the Harvards, and now the game is over, and Mr. Phillips Randolph gets up out of his seat, and I hear Mr. Phillips Randolph say like this:

'Well,' he says, 'the score is not so bad as it might be, and it is a wonderful game, and,' he says, 'we seem to make one convert to our cause, anyway, for see who is wearing our colours.'

And with this he points to Joey Perhaps, who is still sitting down, with people stepping around him and over him, and he is still smiling a little smile, and Mr. Phillips Randolph seems greatly pleased to see that Joey Perhaps has a big, broad crimson ribbon where he once wears his white silk muffler.

But the chances are Mr. Phillips Randolph will be greatly surprised if he knows that the crimson ribbon across Joey's bosom comes of Ollie Ortega planting a short knife in Joey's throat, or do I forget to mention before that Ollie Ortega is among those present?

I send for Ollie after I leave you last night, figuring he may love to see a nice football game. He arrives by 'plane this morning, and I am not wrong in my figuring. Ollie thinks the game is swell.

Well, personally, I will never forget this game, it is so exciting. Just after the tally comes off, all of a sudden, from the Yales in the stand across the field from the Harvards, comes a long-drawn-out wail that sounds so mournful it makes me feel very sad, to be sure. It starts off something like Oh-oh-oh-oh-oh, with all the Yales Oh-oh-oh-oh-oh-ing at once, and I ask a guy next to me what it is all about.

'Why,' the guy says, 'it is the Yales' "Undertaker Song." They always sing it when they have the other guy licked. I am an old Yale myself, and I will now personally sing this song for you.'

And with this the guy throws back his head, and opens his mouth wide and lets out a yowl like a wolf calling to its mate.

Well, I stop the guy, and tell him it is a very lovely song, to be sure, and quite appropriate all the way around, and then I hasten away from the football game without getting a chance to say good-bye to Doria, although afterwards I mail her the package of letters and pictures that Ollie gets out of Joey Perhaps's inside coat pocket during the confusion that prevails when the Yales make their tally, and I hope and trust that she will think the crimson streaks across the package are just a little touch of colour in honour of the Harvards.

But the greatest thing about the football game [Meyer Marmalade says] is I win two C's off of one of the Harvards sitting near me, so I am now practically even on my trip.

Butch Minds the Baby

One evening along about seven o'clock I am sitting in Mindy's restaurant putting on the gefillte fish, which is a dish I am very fond of, when in come three parties from Brooklyn wearing caps as follows: Harry the Horse, Little Isadore, and Spanish John.

Now these parties are not such parties as I will care to have much truck with, because I often hear rumours about them that are very discreditable, even if the rumours are not true. In fact, I hear that many citizens of Brooklyn will be very glad indeed to see Harry the Horse, Little Isadore and Spanish John move away from there, as they are always doing something that is considered a knock to the community, such as robbing people, or maybe shooting or stabbing them, and throwing pineapples, and carrying on generally.

I am really much surprised to see these parties on Broadway, as it is well known that the Broadway coppers just naturally love to shove such parties around, but there they are in Mindy's, and there I am, so of course I give them a very large hello, as I never wish to seem inhospitable, even to Brooklyn parties. Right away they come over to my table and sit down, and Little Isadore reaches out and spears himself a big hunk of my gefillte fish with his fingers, but I overlook this, as I am using the only knife on the table.

Then they all sit there looking at me without saying anything, and the way they look at me makes me very nervous indeed. Finally I figure that maybe they are a little embarrassed being in a high-class spot such as Mindy's, with legitimate people around and about, so I say to them, very polite:

'It is a nice night.'

'What is nice about it?' asks Harry the Horse, who is a thin man with a sharp face and sharp eyes.

Well, now that it is put up to me in this way, I can see there is nothing so nice about the night, at that, so I try to think of something else jolly to say, while Little Isadore keeps spearing at my gefillte fish with his fingers, and Spanish John nabs one of my potatoes.

'Where does Big Butch live?' Harry the Horse asks.

'Big Butch?' I say, as if I never hear the name before in my life, because in this man's town it is never a good idea to answer any question without thinking it over, as some time you may give the right answer to the wrong guy, or the wrong answer to the right guy. 'Where does Big Butch live?' I ask them again.

'Yes, where does he live?' Harry the Horse says, very impatient. 'We wish you to take us to him.'

'Now wait a minute, Harry,' I say, and I am now more nervous than somewhat. 'I am not sure I remember the exact house Big Butch lives in, and furthermore I am not sure Big Butch will care to have me bringing people to see him, especially three at a time, and especially from Brooklyn. You know Big Butch has a very bad disposition, and there is no telling what he may say to me if he does not like the idea of me taking you to him.'

'Everything is very kosher,' Harry the Horse says. 'You need not be afraid of anything whatever. We have a business proposition for Big Butch. It means a nice score for him, so you take us to him at once, or the chances are I will have to put the arm on somebody around here.'

Well, as the only one around there for him to put the arm on at this time seems to be me, I can see where it will be good policy for me to take these parties to Big Butch especially as the last of my gefillte fish is just going down Little Isadore's gullet, and Spanish John is finishing up my potatoes, and is donking a piece of rye-bread in my coffee, so there is nothing more for me to eat.

So I lead them over into West Forty-ninth Street, near Tenth Avenue, where Big Butch lives on the ground floor of an old brownstone-front house, and who is sitting out on the stoop but Big Butch himself. In fact, everybody in the neighbourhood is sitting out on the front stoops over there, including women and children, because sitting out on the front stoops is quite a custom in this section.

Big Butch is peeled down to his undershirt and pants, and he has no shoes on his feet, as Big Butch is a guy who loves his comfort. Furthermore, he is smoking a cigar, and laid out on the stoop beside him on a blanket is a little baby with not much clothes on. This baby seems to be asleep, and every now and then Big Butch fans it with a folded newspaper to shoo away the mosquitoes that wish to nibble on the baby. These mosquitoes come across the river from the Jersey side on hot nights and they seem to be very fond of babies.

'Hello, Butch,' I say, as we stop in front of the stoop.

'Sh-h-h-h!' Butch says, pointing at the baby, and making more noise with his shush than an engine blowing off steam. Then he gets up and tiptoes down to the sidewalk where we are standing, and I am hoping that Butch feels all right, because when Butch does not feel so good he is apt to be very short with one and all. He is a guy of maybe six foot two and a couple of feet wide, and he has big hairy hands and a mean look.

In fact, Big Butch is known all over this man's town as a guy you must not monkey with in any respect, so it takes plenty of weight off me when I see that he seems to know the parties from Brooklyn, and nods at them very friendly, especially at Harry the Horse. And right away Harry states a most surprising proposition to Big Butch.

It seems that there is a big coal company which has an office in an old building down in West Eighteenth Street, and in this office is a safe, and in this safe is the company pay roll of twenty thousand dollars cash money. Harry the Horse knows the money is there because a personal friend of his who is the paymaster for the company puts it there late this very afternoon.

It seems that the paymaster enters into a dicker with Harry the Horse and Little Isadore and Spanish John for them to slug him while he is carrying the pay roll from the bank to the office in the afternoon, but something happens that they miss connections on the exact spot, so the paymaster has to carry the sugar on to the office without being slugged, and there it is now in two fat bundles.

Personally it seems to me as I listen to Harry's story that the paymaster must be a very dishonest character to be making deals to hold still while he is being slugged and the company's sugar taken away from him, but of course it is none of my business, so I take no part in the conversation.

Well, it seems that Harry the Horse and Little Isadore and Spanish John wish to get the money out of the safe, but none of them knows anything about opening safes, and while they are standing around over in Brooklyn talking over what is to be done in this emergency Harry suddenly remembers that Big Butch is once in the business of opening safes for a living.

In fact, I hear afterwards that Big Butch is considered the best safe-opener east of the Mississippi River in his day, but the law finally takes to sending him to Sing Sing for opening these safes, and after he is in and out of Sing Sing three different times for opening safes Butch gets sick and tired of the place, especially as they pass what is called the Baumes Law in New York, which is a law that says if a guy is sent to Sing Sing four times hand running, he must stay there the rest of his life, without any argument about it.

So Big Butch gives up opening safes for a living, and goes into business in a small way, such as running beer, and handling a little Scoïch now and then, and becomes an honest citizen. Furthermore, he marries one of the neighbours' children over on the West Side by the name of Mary Murphy, and I judge the baby on this stoop comes of this marriage between Big Butch and Mary because I can see that it is a very homely baby, indeed. Still, I never see many babies that I consider rose geraniums for looks, anyway.

Well, it finally comes out that the idea of Harry the Horse and Little Isadore and Spanish John is to get Big Butch to open the coal company's safe and take the pay-roll money out, and they are willing to give him fifty per cent. of the money for his bother, taking fifty per cent. for themselves for finding the plant, and paying all the overhead, such as the paymaster, out of their bit, which strikes me as a pretty fair sort of deal for Big Butch. But Butch only shakes his head.

'It is old-fashioned stuff,' Butch says. 'Nobody opens pete boxes for a living any more. They make the boxes too good, and they are all wired up with alarms and are a lot of trouble generally. I am in a legitimate business now and going along. You boys know I cannot stand another fall, what with being away three times already, and in addition to this I must mind the baby. My old lady goes to Mrs. Clancy's wake to-night up in the Bronx, and the chances are she will be there all night, as she is very fond of wakes, so I must mind little John Ignatius Junior.'

'Listen, Butch,' Harry the Horse says, 'this is a very soft pete. It is old-fashioned, and you can open it with a toothpick. There are no wires on it, because they never put more than a dime in it before in years. It just happens they have to put the twenty G's in it to-night because my pal the paymaster makes it a point not to get back from the jug with the scratch in time to pay off to-day, especially after he sees we miss out on him. It is the softest touch you will ever know, and where can a guy pick up ten G's like this?'

I can see that Big Butch is thinking the ten G's over very seriously, at that, because in these times nobody can afford to pass up ten G's, especially a guy in the beer business, which is very, very tough just now. But finally he shakes his head again and says like this:

'No,' he says, 'I must let it go, because I must mind the baby. My old lady is very, very particular about this, and I dast not leave little John Ignatius Junior for a minute. If Mary comes home and finds I am not minding the baby she will put the blast on me plenty. I like to turn a few honest bobs now and then as well as anybody, but,' Butch says, 'John Ignatius Junior comes first with me.'

Then he turns away and goes back to the stoop as much as to say he is through arguing, and sits down beside John Ignatius Junior again just in time to keep a mosquito from carrying off one of John's legs. Anybody can see that Big Butch is very fond of this baby, though personally I will not give you a dime for a dozen babies, male and female.

Well, Harry the Horse and Little Isadore and Spanish John are very much disappointed, and stand around talking among themselves, and paying no attention to me, when all of a sudden Spanish John, who never has much to say up to this time, seems to have a bright idea. He talks to Harry and Isadore, and they get all pleasured up over what he has to say, and finally Harry goes to Big Butch.

'Sh-h-h-h!' Big Butch says, pointing to the baby as Harry opens his mouth.

'Listen, Butch,' Harry says in a whisper, 'we can take the baby with us, and you can mind it and work, too.'

'Why,' Big Butch whispers back, 'this is quite an idea indeed. Let us go into the house and talk things over.'

So he picks up the baby and leads us into his joint, and gets out some pretty fair beer, though it is needled a little, at that, and we sit around the kitchen chewing the fat in whispers. There is a crib in the kitchen, and Butch puts the baby in this crib, and it keeps on snoozing away first rate while we are talking. In fact, it is sleeping so sound that I am commencing to figure that Butch must give it some of the needled beer he is feeding us, because I am feeling a little dopey myself.

Finally Butch says that as long as he can take John Ignatius Junior with him he sees no reason why he shall not go and open the safe for them, only he says he must have five per cent. more to put in the baby's bank when he gets back, so as to round himself up with his ever-loving wife in case of a beef from her over keeping the baby out in the night air. Harry the Horse says he considers this extra five per cent. a little strong, but Spanish John, who seems to be a very square guy, says that after all it is only fair to cut the baby in if it is to be with them when making the score, and Little Isadore seems to think this is all right, too. So Harry the Horse gives in, and says five per cent. it is.

Well, as they do not wish to start out until after midnight, and as there is plenty of time, Big Butch gets out some more needled beer, and then he goes looking for the tools with which he opens safes, and which he says he does not see since the day John Ignatius Junior is born and he gets them out to build the crib.

Now this is a good time for me to bid one and all farewell, and what keeps me there is something I cannot tell you to this day, because personally I never before have any idea of taking part in a safe opening, especially with a baby, as I consider such actions very dishonourable. When I come to think over things afterwards, the only thing I can figure is the needled beer, but I wish to say I am really very much surprised at myself when I find myself in a taxi-cab along about one o'clock in the morning with these Brooklyn parties and Big Butch and the baby.

Butch has John Ignatius Junior rolled up in a blanket, and John is still pounding his ear. Butch has a satchel of tools, and what looks to me like a big flat book, and just before we leave the house Butch hands me a package and tells me to be very careful with it. He gives Little Isadore a smaller package, which Isadore shoves into his pistol pocket, and when Isadore sits down in the taxi something goes wa-wa, like a sheep, and Big Butch becomes very indignant because it seems Isadore is sitting on John Ignatius Junior's doll, which says 'Mamma' when you squeeze it.

It seems Big Butch figures that John Ignatius Junior may wish something to play with in case he wakes up, and it is a good thing for Little Isadore that the mamma doll is not squashed so it cannot say 'Mamma' any more, or the chances are Little Isadore will get a good bust in the snoot.

We let the taxicab go a block away from the spot we are headed for in West Eighteenth Street, between Seventh and Eighth Avenues, and walk the rest of the way two by two. I walk with Big Butch carrying my package, and Butch is lugging the baby and his satchel and the flat thing that looks like a book. It is so quiet down in West Eighteenth Street at such an hour that you can hear yourself think, and in fact I hear myself thinking very plain that I am a big sap to be on a job like this, especially with a baby, but I keep going just the same, which shows you what a very big sap I am, indeed.

There are very few people in West Eighteenth Street when we get there, and one of them is a fat guy who is leaning against a building almost in the centre of the block, and who takes a walk for himself as soon as he sees us. It seems that this fat guy is the watchman at the coal company's office and is also a personal friend of Harry the Horse, which is why he takes the walk when he sees us coming.

It is agreed before we leave Big Butch's house that Harry the Horse and Spanish John are to stay outside the place as lookouts, while Big Butch is inside opening the safe, and that Little Isadore is to go with Butch. Nothing whatever is said by anybody about where I am to be at any time, and I can see that, no matter where I am, I will still be an outsider, but, as Butch gives me the package to carry, I figure he wishes me to remain with him.

It is no bother at all getting into the office of the coal company, which is on the ground floor, because it seems the watchman leaves the front door open, this watchman being a most obliging guy, indeed. In fact, he is so obliging that by and by he comes back and lets Harry the Horse and Spanish John tie him up good and tight, and stick a handkerchief in his mouth and chuck him in an area-way next to the office, so nobody will think he has anything to do with opening the safe in case anybody comes around asking.

The office looks out on the street, and the safe that Harry the Horse and Little Isadore and Spanish John wish Big Butch to open is standing up against the rear wall of the office facing the street windows. There is one little electric light burning very dim over the safe so that when anybody walks past the place outside, such as a watchman, they can look in through the window and see the safe at all times, unless they are blind. It is not a tall safe, and it is not a big safe, and I can see Big Butch grin when he sees it, so I figure this safe is not much of a safe, just as Harry the Horse claims.

Well, as soon as Big Butch and the baby and Little Isadore and me get into the office, Big Butch steps over to the safe and unfolds what I think is the big flat book, and what is it but a sort of screen painted on one side to look exactly like the front of a safe. Big Butch stands this screen up on the floor in front of the real safe, leaving plenty of space in between, the idea being that the screen will keep anyone passing in the street outside from seeing Butch while he is opening the safe, because when a man is opening a safe he needs all the privacy he can get.

Big Butch lays John Ignatius Junior down on the floor on the blanket behind the phony safe front and takes his tools out of the satchel and starts to work opening the safe, while Little Isadore and me get back in a corner where it is dark, because there is not room for all of us back of the screen. However, we can see what Big Butch is doing, and I wish to say while I never before see a professional safe-opener at work, and never wish to see another, this Butch handles himself like a real artist.

He starts drilling into the safe around the combination lock, working very fast and very quiet, when all of a sudden what happens but John Ignatius Junior sits up on the blanket and lets out a squall. Naturally this is most disquieting to me, and personally I am in favour of beaning John Ignatius Junior with something to make him keep still, because I am nervous enough as it is. But the squalling does not seem to bother Big Butch. He lays down his tools and picks up John Ignatius Junior and starts whispering, 'There, there, there, my itty oddleums. Da-dad is here.'

Well, this sounds very nonsensical to me in such a situation, and it makes no impression whatever on John Ignatius Junior. He keeps on squalling, and I judge he is squalling pretty loud because I see Harry the Horse and Spanish John both walk past the window and look in very anxious. Big Butch jiggles John Ignatius Junior up and down and keeps whispering baby talk to him, which sounds very undignified coming from a high-class safe-opener, and finally Butch whispers to me to hand him the package I am carrying.

He opens the package, and what is in it but a baby's nursing bottle full of milk. Moreover, there is a little tin stew pan, and Butch hands the pan to me and whispers to me to find a water tap somewhere in the joint and fill the pan with water. So I go stumbling around in the dark in a room behind the office and bark my shins several times before I find a tap and fill the pan. I take it back to Big Butch, and he squats there with the baby on one arm, and gets a tin of what is called canned heat out of the package, and lights this canned heat with his cigar lighter, and starts heating the pan of water with the nursing bottle in it.

Big Butch keeps sticking his finger in the pan of water while it is heating, and by and by he puts the rubber nipple of the nursing bottle in his mouth and takes a pull at it to see if the milk is warm enough, just like I see dolls who have babies do. Apparently the milk is okay, as Butch hands the bottle to John Ignatius Junior, who grabs hold of it with both hands, and starts sucking on the business end. Naturally he has to stop squalling, and Big Butch goes to work on the safe again, with John Ignatius Junior sitting on the blanket, pulling on the bottle and looking wiser than a treeful of owls.

It seems the safe is either a tougher job than anybody figures, or Big Butch's tools are not so good, what with being old and rusty and used for building baby cribs, because he breaks a couple of drills and works himself up into quite a sweat without getting anywhere. Butch afterwards explains to me that he is one of the first guys in this country to open safes without explosives, but he says to do this work properly you have to know the safes so as to drill to the tumblers of the lock just right, and it seems that this particular safe is a new type to him, even if it is old, and he is out of practice.

Well, in the meantime, John Ignatius Junior finishes his bottle and starts mumbling again, and Big Butch gives him a tool to play with, and finally Butch needs this tool and tries to take it away from John Ignatius Junior, and the baby lets out such a squawk that Butch has to let him keep it until he can sneak it away from him, and this causes more delay.

Finally Big Butch gives up trying to drill the safe open, and he whispers to us that he will have to put a little shot in it to loosen up the lock, which is all right with us, because we are getting tired of hanging around and listening to John Ignatius Junior's glug-glugging. As far as I am personally concerned, I am wishing I am home in bed.

Well, Butch starts pawing through his satchel looking for something and it seems that what he is looking for is a little bottle of some kind of explosive with which to shake the lock on the safe up some, and at first he cannot find this bottle, but finally he discovers that John Ignatius Junior has it and is gnawing at the cork, and Butch has quite a battle making John Ignatius Junior give it up.

Anyway, he fixes the explosive in one of the holes he drills near the combination lock on the safe, and then he puts in a fuse, and just before he touches off the fuse Butch picks up John Ignatius Junior and hands him to Little Isadore, and tells us to go into the

room behind the office. John Ignatius Junior does not seem to care
for Little Isadore, and I do not blame him, at that, because he
starts to squirm around quite some in Isadore's arms and lets out a
squall, but all of a sudden he becomes very quiet indeed, and, while
I am not able to prove it, something tells me that Little Isadore has
his hand over John Ignatius Junior's mouth.

Well, Big Butch joins us right away in the back room, and sound
comes out of John Ignatius Junior again as Butch takes him from
Little Isadore, and I am thinking that it is a good thing for Isadore
that the baby cannot tell Big Butch what Isadore does to him.

'I put in just a little bit of a shot,' Big Butch says, 'and it will
not make any more noise than snapping your fingers.'

But a second later there is a big whoom from the office, and the
whole joint shakes, and John Ignatius laughs right out loud. The
chances are he thinks it is the Fourth of July.

'I guess maybe I put in too big a charge,' Big Butch says, and
then he rushes into the office with Little Isadore and me after him,
and John Ignatius Junior still laughing very heartily for a small
baby. The door of the safe is swinging loose, and the whole joint
looks somewhat wrecked, but Big Butch loses no time in getting his
dukes into the safe and grabbing out two big bundles of cash
money, which he sticks inside his shirt.

As we go into the street Harry the Horse and Spanish John
come running up much excited, and Harry says to Big Butch like
this:

'What are you trying to do,' he says, 'wake up the whole town?'

'Well,' Butch says, 'I guess maybe the charge is too strong, at
that, but nobody seems to be coming, so you and Spanish John
walk over to Eighth Avenue, and the rest of us will walk to
Seventh, and if you go along quiet, like people minding their own
business, it will be all right.'

But I judge Little Isadore is tired of John Ignatius Junior's
company by this time, because he says he will go with Harry the
Horse and Spanish John, and this leaves Big Butch and John
Ignatius Junior and me to go the other way. So we start moving,
and all of a sudden two cops come tearing around the corner toward which Harry and Isadore and Spanish John are going. The
chances are the cops hear the earthquake Big Butch lets off and are
coming to investigate.

But the chances are, too, that if Harry the Horse and the other
two keep on walking along very quietly like Butch tells them to, the

coppers will pass them up entirely, because it is not likely that coppers will figure anybody to be opening safes with explosives in this neighbourhood. But the minute Harry the Horse sees the coppers he loses his nut, and he outs with the old equalizer and starts blasting away, and what does Spanish John do but get his out, too, and open up.

The next thing anybody knows, the two coppers are down on the ground with slugs in them, but other coppers are coming from every which direction, blowing whistles and doing a little blasting themselves, and there is plenty of excitement, especially when the coppers who are not chasing Harry the Horse and Little Isadore and Spanish John start poking around the neighbourhood and find Harry's pal, the watchman, all tied up nice and tight where Harry leaves him, and the watchman explains that some scoundrels blow open the safe he is watching.

All this time Big Butch and me are walking in the other direction toward Seventh Avenue, and Big Butch has John Ignatius in his arms, and John Ignatius is now squalling very loud indeed. The chances are he is still thinking of the big whoom back there which tickles him so and is wishing to hear some more whooms. Anyway, he is beating his own best record for squalling, and as we go walking along Big Butch says to me like this:

'I dast not run,' he says, 'because if any coppers see me running they will start popping at me and maybe hit John Ignatius Junior, and besides running will joggle the milk up in him and make him sick. My old lady always warns me never to joggle John Ignatius Junior when he is full of milk.'

'Well, Butch,' I say, 'there is no milk in me, and I do not care if I am joggled up, so if you do not mind, I will start doing a piece of running at the next corner.'

But just then around the corner of Seventh Avenue toward which we are headed comes two or three coppers with a big fat sergeant with them, and one of the coppers, who is half-out of breath as if he has been doing plenty of sprinting, is explaining to the sergeant that somebody blows a safe down the street and shoots a couple of coppers in the getaway.

And there is Big Butch, with John Ignatius Junior in his arms and twenty G's in his shirt front and a tough record behind him, walking right up to them.

I am feeling very sorry, indeed, for Big Butch, and very sorry for myself, too, and I am saying to myself that if I get out of this I will never associate with anyone but ministers of the gospel as long as I live. I can remember thinking that I am getting a better break than Butch, at that, because I will not have to go to Sing Sing for the rest of my life, like him, and I also remember wondering what they will give John Ignatius Junior, who is still tearing off these squalls, with Big Butch saying, 'There, there, there, Daddy's itty woogleums.' Then I hear one of the coppers say to the fat sergeant:

'We better nail these guys. They may be in on this.'

Well, I can see it is good-bye to Butch and John Ignatius Junior and me, as the fat sergeant steps up to Big Butch, but instead of putting the arm on Butch, the fat sergeant only points at John Ignatius Junior and asks very sympathetic:

'Teeth?'

'No,' Big Butch says. 'Not teeth. Colic. I just get the doctor here out of bed to do something for him, and we are going to a drug store to get some medicine.'

Well, naturally I am very much surprised at this statement, because of course I am not a doctor, and if John Ignatius Junior has colic it serves him right, but I am only hoping they do not ask for my degree, when the fat sergeant says:

'Too bad. I know what it is. I got three of them at home. But,' he says, 'it acts more like it is teeth than colic.'

Then as Big Butch and John Ignatius Junior and me go on about our business I hear the fat sergeant say to the copper, very sarcastic:

'Yes, of course a guy is out blowing safes with a baby in his arms! You will make a great detective, you will!'

I do not see Big Butch for several days after I learn that Harry the Horse and Little Isadore and Spanish John get back to Brooklyn all right, except they are a little nicked up here and there from the slugs the coppers toss at them, while the coppers they clip are not damaged so very much. Furthermore, the chances are I will not see Big Butch for several years, if it is left to me, but he comes looking for me one night, and he seems to be all pleasured up about something.

'Say,' Big Butch says to me, 'you know I never give a copper credit for knowing any too much about anything, but I wish to say that this fat sergeant we run into the other night is a very, very smart duck. He is right about it being teeth that is ailing John Ignatius Junior, for what happens yesterday but John cuts his first tooth.'

The Hottest Guy in the World

I wish to say I am very nervous indeed when Big Jule pops into my hotel room one afternoon, because anybody will tell you that Big Jule is the hottest guy in the whole world at the time I am speaking about.

In fact, it is really surprising how hot he is. They wish to see him in Pittsburgh, Pa., about a matter of a mail truck being robbed, and there is gossip about him in Minneapolis, Minn., where somebody takes a fifty-G pay roll off a messenger in cash money, and slugs the messenger around somewhat for not holding still.

Furthermore, the Bankers' Association is willing to pay good dough to talk to Big Jule out in Kansas City, Mo., where a jug is knocked off by a stranger, and in the confusion the paying teller and the cashier, and the second vice-president are clouted about, and the day watchman is hurt, and two coppers are badly bruised, and over fifteen G's is removed from the counters, and never returned.

Then there is something about a department store in Canton, O., and a flour-mill safe in Toledo, and a grocery in Spokane, Wash., and a branch post office in San Francisco, and also something about a shooting match in Chicago, but of course this does not count so much, as only one party is fatally injured. However, you can see that Big Jule is really very hot, what with the coppers all over the country looking for him high and low. In fact, he is practically on fire.

Of course I do not believe Big Jule does all the things the coppers say, because coppers always blame everything no matter where it happens on the most prominent guy they can think of, and Big Jule is quite prominent all over the U.S.A. The chances are he does not do more than half these things, and he probably has a good alibi for the half he does do, at that, but he is certainly hot, and I do not care to have hot guys around me, or even guys who are only just a little bit warm.

But naturally I am not going to say this to Big Jule when he pops in on me, because he may think I am inhospitable, and I do not care to have such a rap going around and about on me, and furthermore, Jule may become indignant if he thinks I am inhospitable, and knock me on my potato, because Big Jule is quick to take offence

So I say hello to Big Jule, very pleasant, and ask him to have a chair by the window where he can see the citizens walking to and fro down in Eighth Avenue and watch the circus wagons moving into Madison Square Garden by way of the Forty-ninth Street side, for the circus always shows in the Garden in the spring before going out on the road. It is a little warm, and Big Jule takes off his coat, and I can see he has one automatic slung under his arm, and another sticking down in the waist-band of his pants, and I hope and trust that no copper steps into the room while Big Jule is there because it is very much against the law for guys to go around rodded up this way in New York City.

'Well, Jule,' I say, 'this is indeed a very large surprise to me, and I am glad to see you, but I am thinking maybe it is very foolish for you to be popping into New York just now, what with all the heat around here, and the coppers looking to arrest people for very little.'

'I know,' Jule says. 'I know. But they do not have so very much on me around here, no matter what people say, and a guy gets homesick for his old home town, especially a guy who is stuck away where I am for the past few months. I get homesick for the lights and the crowds on Broadway, and for the old neighbour-hood. Furthermore, I wish to see my Maw. I hear she is sick and may not live, and I wish to see her before she goes.'

Well, naturally anybody will wish to see their Maw under such circumstances, but Big Jule's Maw lives over in West Forty-ninth Street near Eleventh Avenue, and who is living in the very same block but Johnny Brannigan, the strong-arm copper, and it is a hundred to one if Big Jule goes nosing around his old neighbour-hood, Johnny Brannigan will hear of it, and if there is one guy Johnny Brannigan does not care for, it is Big Jule, although they are kids together.

But it seems that even when they are kids they have very little use for each other, and after they grow up and Johnny gets on the strong-arm squad, he never misses a chance to push Big Jule around, and sometimes trying to boff Big Jule with his blackjack, and it is well known to one and all that before Big Jule leaves town the last time, he takes a punch at Johnny Brannigan, and Johnny swears he will never rest until he puts Big Jule where he belongs, although where Big Jule belongs, Johnny does not say.

So I speak of Johnny living in the same block with Big Jule's Maw to Big Jule, but it only makes him mad.

'I am not afraid of Johnny Brannigan,' he says. 'In fact,' he says,

'I am thinking for some time lately that maybe I will clip Johnny Brannigan good while I am here. I owe Johnny Brannigan a clipping. But I wish to see my Maw first, and then I will go around and see Miss Kitty Clancy. I guess maybe she will be much surprised to see me, and no doubt very glad.'

Well, I figure it is a sure thing Miss Kitty Clancy will be surprised to see Big Jule, but I am not so sure about her being glad, because very often when a guy is away from a doll for a year or more, no matter how ever-loving she may be, she may get to thinking of someone else, for this is the way dolls are, whether they live on Eleventh Avenue or over on Park. Still, I remember hearing that this Miss Kitty Clancy once thinks very well of Big Jule, although her old man, Jack Clancy, who runs a speak-easy, always claims it is a big knock to the Clancy family to have such a character as Big Jule hanging around.

'I often think of Miss Kitty Clancy the past year or so,' Big Jule says, as he sits there by the window, watching the circus wagons, and the crowds. 'I especially think of her the past few months. In fact,' he says, 'thinking of Miss Kitty Clancy is about all I have to do where I am at, which is in an old warehouse on the Bay of Fundy outside of a town that is called St. John's, or some such, up in Canada, and thinking of Miss Kitty Clancy all this time, I find out I love her very much indeed.

'I go to this warehouse,' Big Jule says, 'after somebody takes a jewellery store in the town, and the coppers start in blaming me. This warehouse is not such a place as I will choose myself if I am doing the choosing, because it is an old fur warehouse, and full of strange smells, but in the excitement around the jewellery store, somebody puts a slug in my hip, and Leon Pierre carries me to the old warehouse, and there I am until I get well.

'It is very lonesome,' Big Jule says. 'In fact, you will be surprised how lonesome it is, and it is very, very cold, and all I have for company is a lot of rats. Personally, I never care for rats under any circumstances because they carry disease germs, and are apt to bite a guy when he is asleep, if they are hungry, which is what these rats try to do to me.

'The warehouse is away off by itself,' Jule says, 'and nobody ever comes around there except Leon Pierre to bring me grub and dress my hip, and at night it is very still, and all you can hear is the wind howling around outside, and the rats running here and there. Some of them are very, very large rats. In fact, some of them seem about the size of rabbits, and they are pretty fresh, at that. At first I am willing to make friends with these rats, but they seem very hostile, and after they take a few nips at me, I can see there is no use trying to be nice to them, so I have Leon Pierre bring me a lot of ammunition for my rods every day and I practise shooting at the rats.

'The warehouse is so far off there is no danger of anybody hearing the shooting,' Big Jule says, 'and it helps me pass the time away. I get so I can hit a rat sitting, or running, or even flying through the air, because these warehouse rats often leap from place to place like mountain sheep, their idea being generally to take a good nab at me as they fly past.

'Well, sir,' Jule says, 'I keep score on myself one day, and I hit fifty rats hand running without a miss, which I claim makes me the champion rat shooter of the world with a forty-five automatic, although of course,' he says, 'if anybody wishes to challenge me to a rat shooting match I am willing to take them on for a side bet. I get so I can call my shots on the rats, and in fact several times I say to myself, I will hit this one in the right eye, and this one in the left eye, and it always turns out just as I say, although sometimes when you hit a rat with a forty-five up close it is not always possible to tell afterwards just where you hit him, because you seem to hit him all over.

'By and by,' Jule says, 'I seem to discourage the rats somewhat, and they get so they play the chill for me, and do not try to nab me even when I am asleep. They find out that no rat dast poke his whiskers out at me or he will get a very close shave. So I have to look around for other amusement, but there is not much doing in such a place, although I finally find a bunch of doctor's books which turn out to be very interesting reading. It seems these books are left there by some croaker who retires there to think things over after experimenting on his ever-loving wife with a knife. In fact, it seems he cuts his ever-loving wife's head off, and she does not continue living, so he takes his books and goes to the warehouse and remains there until the law finds him, and hangs him up very high, indeed.

'Well, the books are a great comfort to me, and I learn many astonishing things about surgery, but after I read all the books there is nothing for me to do but think, and what I think about is Miss Kitty Clancy, and how much pleasure we have together walking around and about and seeing movie shows, and all this and that, until her old man gets so tough with me. Yes, I will be very glad to see Miss Kitty Clancy, and the old neighbourhood, and my Maw again.'

Well, finally nothing will do Big Jule but he must take a stroll over into his old neighbourhood, and see if he cannot see Miss Kitty Clancy, and also drop in on his Maw, and he asks me to go along with him. I can think of a million things I will rather do than take a stroll with Big Jule, but I do not wish him to think I am snobbish, because as I say, Big Jule is quick to take offence. Furthermore, I figure that at such an hour of the day he is less likely to run into Johnny Brannigan or any other coppers who know him than at any other time, so I say I will go with him, but as we start out, Big Jule puts on his rods.

'Jule,' I say, 'do not take any rods with you on a stroll, because somebody may happen to see them, such as a copper, and you know they will pick you up for carrying a rod in this town quicker than you can say Jack Robinson, whether they know who you are or not. You know the Sullivan law is very strong against guys carrying rods in this town.'

But Big Jule says he is afraid he will catch cold if he goes out without his rods, so we go down into Forty-ninth Street and start west toward Madison Square Garden, and just as we reach Eighth Avenue and are standing there waiting for the traffic to stop, so we can cross the street, I see there is quite some excitement around the Garden on the Forty-ninth Street side, with people running every which way, and yelling no little, and looking up in the air.

So I look up myself, and what do I see sitting up there on the edge of the Garden roof but a big ugly-faced monkey. At first I do not recognize it as a monkey, because it is so big I figure maybe it is just one of the prize-fight managers who stand around on this side of the Garden all afternoon waiting to get a match for their fighters, and while I am somewhat astonished to see a prize-fight manager in such a position, I figure maybe he is doing it on a bet. But when I take a second look I see that it is indeed a big monk, and an exceptionally homely monk at that, although personally I never see any monks I consider so very handsome, anyway.

Well, this big monk is holding something in its arms, and what it is I am not able to make out at first, but then Big Jule and I cross the street to the side opposite the Garden, and now I can see that the monk has a baby in its arms. Naturally I figure it is some kind of advertising dodge put on by the Garden to ballyhoo the circus, or maybe the fight between Sharkey and Risko which is coming off after the circus, but guys are still yelling and running up and down, and dolls are screaming until finally I realize that a most surprising situation prevails.

It seems that the big monk up on the roof is nobody but Bongo, who is a gorilla belonging to the circus, and one of the very few gorillas of any account in this country, or anywhere else, as far as this goes, because good gorillas are very scarce, indeed. Well, it seems that while they are shoving Bongo's cage into the Garden, the door becomes unfastened, and the first thing anybody knows, out pops Bongo, and goes bouncing along the street where a lot of the neighbours' children are playing games on the sidewalk, and a lot of Mammas are sitting out in the sun alongside baby buggies containing their young. This is a very common sight in side streets such as West Forty-ninth on nice days, and by no means unpleasant, if you like Mammas and their young.

Now what does this Bongo do but reach into a baby buggy which a Mamma is pushing past on the sidewalk on the Garden side of the street, and snatch out a baby, though what Bongo wants with this baby nobody knows to this day. It is a very young baby, and not such a baby as is fit to give a gorilla the size of Bongo any kind of struggle, so Bongo has no trouble whatever in handling it. Anyway, I always hear a gorilla will make a sucker out of a grown man in a battle, though I wish to say I never see a battle between a gorilla and a grown man. It ought to be a first-class drawing card, at that.

Well, naturally the baby's Mamma puts up quite a squawk about Bongo grabbing her baby, because no Mamma wishes her baby to keep company with a gorilla, and this Mamma starts in screaming very loud, and trying to take the baby away from Bongo, so what does Bongo do but run right up on the roof of the Garden by way of a big electric sign which hangs down on the Forty-ninth Street side. And there old Bongo sits on the edge of the roof with the baby in his arms, and the baby is squalling quite some, and Bongo is making funny noises, and showing his teeth as the folks commence gathering in the street below.

There is a big guy in his shirt-sleeves running through the crowd waving his hands, and trying to shush everybody, and saying 'Quiet, please' over and over, but nobody pays any attention to him. I figure this guy has something to do with the circus, and maybe with Bongo, too. A traffic copper takes a peek at the situation, and calls for the reserves from the Forty-seventh Street station, and somebody else sends for the fire truck down the street, and pretty soon cops are running from every direction, and the fire-engines are coming, and the big guy in his shirt-sleeves is more excited than ever.

'Quiet, please,' he says. 'Everybody keep quiet, because if Bongo becomes disturbed by the noise he will throw the baby down in the street. He throws everything he gets his hands on,' the guy says. 'He acquires this habit from throwing coco-nuts back in his old home country. Let us get a life net, and if you all keep quiet we may be able to save the baby before Bongo starts heaving it like a coco-nut.'

Well, Bongo is sitting up there on the edge of the roof about seven stories above the ground peeking down with the baby in his arms, and he is holding this baby just like a Mamma would, but anybody can see that Bongo does not care for the row below, and once he lifts the baby high above his head as if to bean somebody with it. I see Big Nig, the crap shooter, in the mob, and afterwards I hear he is around offering to lay seven to five against the baby, but everybody is too excited to bet on such a proposition, although it is not a bad price, at that.

I see one doll in the crowd on the sidewalk on the side of the street opposite the Garden who is standing perfectly still staring up at the monk and the baby with a very strange expression on her face, and the way she is looking makes me take a second gander at her, and who is it but Miss Kitty Clancy. Her lips are moving as she stands there staring up, and something tells me Miss Kitty Clancy is saying prayers to herself, because she is such a doll as will know how to say prayers on an occasion like this.

Big Jule sees her about the same time I do, and Big Jule steps up beside Miss Kitty Clancy, and says hello to her, and though it is over a year since Miss Kitty Clancy sees Big Jule she turns to him and speaks to him as if she is talking to him just a minute before. It is very strange indeed the way Miss Kitty Clancy speaks to Big Jule as if he has never been away at all.

'Do something, Julie,' she says. 'You are always the one to do something. Oh, please do something, Julie.'

Well, Big Jule never answers a word, but steps back in the clear of the crowd and reaches for the waistband of his pants, when I grab him by the arm and say to him like this:

'My goodness, Jule,' I say, 'what are you going to do?'

'Why,' Jule says, 'I am going to shoot this thieving monk before he takes a notion to heave the baby on somebody down here. For all I know,' Jule says, 'he may hit me with it, and I do not care to be hit with anybody's baby.'

'Jule,' I say, very earnestly, 'do not pull a rod in front of all these coppers, because if you do they will nail you sure, if only for having the rod, and if you are nailed you are in a very tough spot, indeed, what with being wanted here and there. Jule,' I say, 'you are hotter than a forty-five all over this country, and I do not wish to see you nailed. Anyway,' I say, 'you may shoot the baby instead of the monk, because anybody can see it will be very difficult to hit the monk up there without hitting the baby. Furthermore, even if you do hit the monk it will fall into the street, and bring the baby with it.'

'You speak great foolishness,' Jule says. 'I never miss what I shoot at. I will shoot the monk right between the eyes, and this will make him fall backwards, not forwards, and the baby will not be hurt because anybody can see it is no fall at all from the ledge to the roof behind. I make a study of such propositions,' Jule says, 'and I know if a guy is in such a position as this monk sitting on a ledge looking down from a high spot, his defensive reflexes tend backwards, so this is the way he is bound to fall if anything unexpected comes up on him, such as a bullet between the eyes. I read all about it in the doctor's books,' Jule says.

Then all of a sudden up comes his hand, and in his hand is one of his rods, and I hear a sound like ker-bap. When I come to think about it afterwards, I do not remember Big Jule even taking aim like a guy will generally do if he is shooting at something sitting, but old Bongo seems to lift up a little bit off the ledge at the crack of the gun, and then he keels over backwards, the baby still in his arms, and squalling more than somewhat, and Big Jule says to me like this:

'Right between the eyes, and I will bet on it,' he says, 'although it is not much of a target, at that.'

Well, nobody can figure what happens for a minute, and there is much silence except from the guy in his shirtsleeves who is expressing much indignation with Big Jule and saying the circus people will sue him for damages sure if he has hurt Bongo, because the monk is worth $100,000, or some such. I see Miss Kitty Clancy kneeling on the sidewalk with her hands clasped, and looking upwards, and Big Jule is sticking his rod back in his waistband again.

By this time some guys are out on the roof getting through from the inside of the building with the idea of heading Bongo off from that direction, and they let out a yell, and pretty soon I see one of them holding the baby up so everyone in the street can see it. A couple of other guys get down near the edge of the roof and pick up Bongo and show him to the crowd, as dead as a mackerel, and one of the guys puts a finger between Bongo's eyes to show where the bullet hits the monk, and Miss Kitty Clancy walks over to Big Jule and tries to say something to him, but only busts out crying very loud.

Well, I figure this is a good time for Big Jule and me to take a walk, because everybody is interested in what is going on up on the roof, and I do not wish the circus people to get a chance to serve a summons in a damage suit on Big Jule for shooting the valuable monk. Furthermore, a couple of coppers in harness are looking Big Jule over very critically, and I figure they are apt to put the old sleeve on Jule any second.

All of a sudden a slim young guy steps up to Big Jule and says to him like this:

'Jule,' he says, 'I want to see you,' and who is it but Johnny Brannigan. Naturally Big Jule starts reaching for a rod, but Johnny starts him walking down the street so fast Big Jule does not have time to get in action just then.

'No use getting it out, Jule,' Johnny Brannigan says. 'No use, and no need. Come with me, and hurry.'

Well, Big Jule is somewhat puzzled because Johnny Brannigan is not acting like a copper making a collar, so he goes along with Johnny, and I follow after him, and half-way down the block Johnny stops a Yellow short, and hustles us into it and tells the driver to keep shoving down Eighth Avenue.

'I am trailing you ever since you get in town, Jule,' Johnny Brannigan says. 'You never have a chance around here. I am going over to your Maw's house to put the arm on you, figuring you are sure to go there, when the thing over by the Garden comes off. Now I am getting out of this cab at the next corner, and you go on and see your Maw, and then screw out of town as quick as you can, because you are red hot around here, Jule.

'By the way,' Johnny Brannigan says, 'do you know it is my kid you save, Jule? Mine and Kitty Clancy's? We are married a year ago to-day.'

Well, Big Jule looks very much surprised for a moment, and then he laughs, and says like this: 'Well, I never know it is Kitty Clancy's, but I figure it for yours the minute I see it because it looks like you.'

'Yes,' Johnny Brannigan says, very proud, 'everybody says he does.'

'I can see the resemblance even from a distance,' Big Jule says. 'In fact,' he says, 'it is remarkable how much you look alike. But,' he says, 'for a minute, Johnny, I am afraid I will not be able to pick out the right face between the two on the roof, because it is very hard to tell the monk and your baby apart.'

The Lemon Drop Kid

I am going to take you back a matter of four or five years ago to an August afternoon and the race track at Saratoga, which is a spot in New York state very pleasant to behold, and also to a young guy by the name of The Lemon Drop Kid, who is called The Lemon Drop Kid because he always has a little sack of lemon drops in the side pocket of his coat, and is always munching at same, a lemon drop being a breed of candy that is relished by many, although personally I prefer peppermints.

On this day I am talking about, The Lemon Drop Kid is looking about for business, and not doing so good for himself, at that, as The Lemon Drop Kid's business is telling the tale, and he is finding it very difficult indeed to discover citizens who are willing to listen to him tell the tale.

And of course if a guy whose business is telling the tale cannot find anybody to listen to him, he is greatly handicapped, for the tale such a guy tells is always about how he knows something is doing in a certain race, the idea of the tale being that it may cause the citizen who is listening to it to make a wager on this certain race, and if the race comes out the way the guy who is telling the tale says it will come out, naturally the citizen is bound to be very grateful to the guy, and maybe reward him liberally.

Furthermore, the citizen is bound to listen to more tales, and a guy whose business is telling the tale, such as The Lemon Drop

Kid, always has tales to tell until the cows come home, and generally they are long tales, and sometimes they are very interesting and entertaining, according to who is telling them, and it is well known to one and all that nobody can tell the tale any better than The Lemon Drop Kid.

But old Cap Duhaine and his sleuths at the Saratoga track are greatly opposed to guys going around telling the tale, and claim that such guys are nothing but touts, and they are especially opposed to The Lemon Drop Kid, because they say he tells the tale so well that he weakens public confidence in horse racing. So they are casing The Lemon Drop Kid pretty close to see that he does not get some citizen's ear and start telling him the tale, and finally The Lemon Drop Kid is greatly disgusted and walks up the lawn towards the head of the stretch.

And while he is walking, he is eating lemon drops out of his pocket, and thinking about how much better off he will be if he puts in the last ten years of his life at some legitimate dodge, instead of hop-scotching from one end of the country to the other telling the tale, although just off-hand The Lemon Drop Kid cannot think of any legitimate dodge at which he will see as much of life as he sees around the race tracks since he gets out of the orphan asylum in Jersey City where he is raised.

At the time this story starts out, The Lemon Drop Kid is maybe twenty-four years old, and he is a quiet little guy with a low voice, which comes of keeping it confidential when he is telling the tale, and he is nearly always alone. In fact, The Lemon Drop Kid is never known to have a pal as long as he is around telling the tale, although he is by no means an unfriendly guy, and is always speaking to everybody, even when he is in the money.

But it is now a long time since The Lemon Drop Kid is in the money, or seems to have any chance of being in the money, and the landlady of the boarding-house in Saratoga where he is residing is becoming quite hostile, and making derogatory cracks about him, and also about most of her other boarders, too, so The Lemon Drop Kid is unable to really enjoy his meals there, especially as they are very bad meals to start with.

Well, The Lemon Drop Kid goes off by himself up the lawn and stands there looking out across the track, munching a lemon drop from time to time, and thinking what a harsh old world it is, to be sure, and how much better off it will be if there are no sleuths whatever around and about.

It is a day when not many citizens are present at the track, and the only one near The Lemon Drop Kid seems to be an old guy in a wheel chair, with a steamer rug over his knees, and a big, sleepy-looking stove lid who appears to be in charge of the chair.

This old guy has a big white mouser, and big white bristly eyebrows, and he is a very fierce-looking old guy, indeed, and anybody can tell at once that he is nothing but a curmudgeon, and by no means worthy of attention. But he is a familiar spectacle at the race track at Saratoga, as he comes out nearly every day in a limousine the size of a hearse, and is rolled out of the limousine in his wheel chair on a little runway by the stove lid, and pushed up to this spot where he is sitting now, so he can view the sport of kings without being bothered by the crowds.

It is well known to one and all that his name is Rarus P. Griggsby, and that he has plenty of potatoes, which he makes in Wall Street, and that he is closer than the next second with his potatoes, and furthermore, it is also well known that he hates everybody in the world, including himself, so nobody goes anywhere near him if they can help it.

The Lemon Drop Kid does not realize he is standing so close to Rarus P. Griggsby, until he hears the old guy growling at the stove lid, and then The Lemon Drop Kid looks at Rarus P. Griggsby very sympathetic and speaks to him in his low voice as follows:

'Gout?' he says.

Now of course The Lemon Drop Kid knows who Rarus P. Griggsby is, and under ordinary circumstances The Lemon Drop Kid will not think of speaking to such a character, but afterwards he explains that he is feeling so despondent that he addresses Rarus P. Griggsby just to show he does not care what happens. And under ordinary circumstances, the chances are Rarus P. Griggsby will start hollering for the gendarmes if a stranger has the gall to speak to him, but there is so much sympathy in The Lemon Drop Kid's voice and eyes, that Rarus P. Griggsby seems to be taken by surprise, and he answers like this:

'Arthritis,' Rarus P. Griggsby says. 'In my knees,' he says. 'I am not able to walk a step in three years.'

'Why,' The Lemon Drop Kid says, 'I am greatly distressed to hear this. I know just how you feel, because I am troubled from infancy with this same disease.'

Now of course this is strictly the old ackamarackus, as The Lemon Drop Kid cannot even spell arthritis, let alone have it, but he makes the above statement just by way of conversation, and furthermore he goes on to state as follows:

'In fact,' The Lemon Drop Kid says, 'I suffer so I can scarcely think, but one day I find a little remedy that fixes me up as right as rain, and I now have no trouble whatsoever.'

And with this, he takes a lemon drop out of his pocket and pops it into his mouth, and then he hands one to Rarus P. Griggsby in a most hospitable manner, and the old guy holds the lemon drop between his thumb and forefinger and looks at it as if he expects it to explode right in his pan, while the stove lid gazes at The Lemon Drop Kid with a threatening expression.

'Well,' Rarus P. Griggsby says, 'personally I consider all cures fakes. I have a standing offer of five thousand dollars to anybody that can cure me of my pain, and nobody even comes close so far. Doctors are also fakes,' he says. 'I have seven of them, and they take out my tonsils, and all my teeth, and my appendix, and they keep me from eating anything I enjoy, and I only get worse. The waters here in Saratoga seem to help me some, but,' he says, 'they do not get me out of this wheel chair, and I am sick and tired of it all.'

Then, as if he comes to a quick decision, he pops the lemon drop into his mouth, and begins munching it very slow, and after a while he says it tastes just like a lemon drop to him, and of course it is a lemon drop all along, but The Lemon Drop Kid says this taste is only to disguise the medicine in it.

Now, by and by, The Lemon Drop Kid commences telling Rarus P. Griggsby the tale, and afterwards The Lemon Drop Kid says he has no idea Rarus P. Griggsby will listen to the tale, and that he only starts telling it to him in a spirit of good clean fun, just to see how he will take it, and he is greatly surprised to note that Rarus P. Griggsby is all attention.

Personally, I find nothing unusual in this situation, because I often see citizens around the race tracks as prominent as Rarus P. Griggsby, listening to the tale from guys who do not have as much as a seat in their pants, especially if the tale has any larceny in it, because it is only human nature to be deeply interested in larceny.

And the tale The Lemon Drop Kid tells Rarus P. Griggsby is that he is a brother of Sonny Saunders, the jock, and that Sonny tells him to be sure and be at the track this day to bet on a certain horse in the fifth race, because it is nothing but a boat race, and everything in it is as stiff as a plank, except this certain horse.

Now of course this is all a terrible lie, and The Lemon Drop Kid is taking a great liberty with Sonny Saunders's name, especially as Sonny does not have any brothers, anyway, and even if Sonny knows about a boat race the chances are he will never tell The Lemon Drop Kid, but then very few guys whose business is telling the tale ever stop to figure they may be committing perjury.

So The Lemon Drop Kid goes on to state that when he arrives at the track he has fifty bobs pinned to his wishbone to bet on this certain horse, but unfortunately he gets a tip on a real good thing in the very first race, and bets his fifty bobs right then and there, figuring to provide himself with a larger taw to bet on the certain horse in the fifth, but the real good thing receives practically a criminal ride from a jock who does not know one end of a horse from the other, and is beat a very dirty snoot, and there The Lemon Drop Kid is with the fifth race coming up, and an absolute cinch in it, the way his tale goes, but with no dough left to bet on it.

Well, personally I do not consider this tale as artistic as some The Lemon Drop Kid tells, and in fact The Lemon Drop Kid himself never rates it among his masterpieces, but old Rarus P. Griggsby listens to the tale quite intently without saying a word, and all the time he is munching the lemon drop and smacking his lips under his big white mouser, as if he greatly enjoys this delicacy, but when The Lemon Drop Kid concludes the tale, and is standing there gazing out across the track with a very sad expression on his face, Rarus P. Griggsby speaks as follows:

'I never bet on horse races,' Rarus P. Griggsby says. 'They are too uncertain. But this proposition you present sounds like finding money, and I love to find money. I will wager one hundred dollars on your assurance that this certain horse cannot miss.'

And with this, he outs with a leather so old that The Lemon Drop Kid half expects a cockroach to leap out at him, and produces a C note which he hands to The Lemon Drop Kid, and as he does so, Rarus P. Griggsby inquires:

'What is the name of this certain horse?'

Well, of course this is a fair question, but it happens that The Lemon Drop Kid is so busy all afternoon thinking of the injustice of the sleuths that he never even bothers to look up this particular race beforehand, and afterwards he is quite generally criticized for slovenliness in this matter, for if a guy is around telling the tale about a race, he is entitled to pick out a horse that has at least some kind of a chance.

But of course The Lemon Drop Kid is not expecting the opportunity of telling the tale to arise, so the question finds him unprepared, as off-hand he cannot think of the name of a horse in the race, as he never consults the scratches, and he does not wish to mention the name of some plug that may be scratched out, and lose the chance to make the C note. So as he seizes the C note from Rarus P. Griggsby and turns to dash for the bookmakers over in front of the grandstand, all The Lemon Drop Kid can think of to say at this moment is the following:

'Watch Number Two,' he says.

And the reason he says No. 2, is he figures there is bound to be a No. 2 in the race, while he cannot be so sure about a No. 7 or a No. 9 until he looks them over, because you understand that all The Lemon Drop Kid states in telling the tale to Rarus P. Griggsby about knowing of something doing in this race is very false.

And of course The Lemon Drop Kid has no idea of betting the C note on anything whatever in the race. In the first place, he does not know of anything to bet on, and in the second place he needs the C note, but he is somewhat relieved when he inquires of the first bookie he comes to, and learns that No. 2 is an old walrus by the name of The Democrat, and anybody knows that The Democrat has no chance of winning even in a field of mud turtles.

So The Lemon Drop Kid puts the C note in his pants pocket, and walks around and about until the horses are going to the post, and you must not think there is anything dishonest in his not betting this money with a bookmaker, as The Lemon Drop Kid is only taking the bet himself, which is by no means unusual, and in fact it is so common that only guys like Cap Duhaine and his sleuths think much about it.

Finally The Lemon Drop Kid goes back to Rarus P. Griggsby, for it will be considered most ungenteel for a guy whose business is telling the tale to be absent when it comes time to explain why the tale does not stand up, and about this time the horses are turning for home, and a few seconds later they go busting past the spot where Rarus P. Griggsby is sitting in his wheel chair, and what is in front to the wire by a Salt Lake City block but The Democrat with No. 2 on his blanket.

Well, old Rarus P. Griggsby starts yelling and waving his hands, and making so much racket that he is soon the centre of attention, and when it comes out that he bets a C note on the winner, nobody blames him for cutting up these didoes, for the horse is a twenty to one shot, but all this time The Lemon Drop Kid only stands there looking very, very sad and shaking his head, until finally Rarus P. Griggsby notices his strange attitude.

'Why are you not cheering over our winning this nice bet?' he says. 'Of course I expect to declare you in,' he says. 'In fact I am quite grateful to you.'

'But,' The Lemon Drop Kid says, 'we do not win. Our horse runs a jolly second.'

'What do you mean, second?' Rarus P. Griggsby says. 'Do you not tell me to watch Number Two, and does not Number Two win?'

'Yes,' The Lemon Drop Kid says, 'what you state is quite true, but what I mean when I say watch Number Two is that Number Two is the only horse I am afraid of in the race, and it seems my fear is well founded.'

Now at this, old Rarus P. Griggsby sits looking at The Lemon Drop Kid for as long as you can count up to ten, if you count slow, and his mouser and eyebrows are all twitching at once, and anybody can see that he is very much perturbed, and then all of a sudden he lets out a yell and to the great amazement of one and all he leaps right out of his wheel chair and makes a lunge at The Lemon Drop Kid.

Well, there is no doubt that Rarus P. Griggsby has murder in his heart, and nobody blames The Lemon Drop Kid when he turns and starts running away at great speed, and in fact he has such speed that finally his feet are throwing back little stones off the gravel paths of the race track with such velocity that a couple of spectators who get hit by these stones think they are shot.

For a few yards, old Rarus P. Griggsby is right at The Lemon Drop Kid's heels, and furthermore Rarus P. Griggsby is yelling and swearing in a most revolting manner. Then some of Cap Duhaine's sleuths come running up and they take after The Lemon Drop Kid too, and he has to have plenty of early foot to beat them to the race-track gates, and while Rarus P. Griggsby does not figure much in the running after the first few jumps, The Lemon Drop Kid seems to remember hearing him cry out as follows:

'Stop, there! Please stop!' Rarus P. Griggsby cries. 'I wish to see you.'

But of course The Lemon Drop Kid is by no means a chump, and he does not even slacken up, let alone stop, until he is well beyond the gates, and the sleuths are turning back, and what is more, The Lemon Drop Kid takes the road leading out of Saratoga instead of going back to the city, because he figures that Saratoga may not be so congenial to him for a while.

In fact, The Lemon Drop Kid finds himself half-regretting that he ever tells the tale to Rarus P. Griggsby as The Lemon Drop Kid likes Saratoga in August, but of course such a thing as happens to him in calling a winner the way he does is just an unfortunate accident, and is not apt to happen again in a lifetime.

Well, The Lemon Drop Kid keeps on walking away from Saratoga for quite some time, and finally he is all tuckered out and wishes to take the load off his feet. So when he comes to a small town by the name of Kibbsville, he sits down on the porch of what seems to be a general store and gas station, and while he is sitting there thinking of how nice and quiet and restful this town seems to be, with pleasant shade trees, and white houses all around and about, he sees standing in the doorway of a very little white house across the street from the store, in a gingham dress, the most beautiful young doll that ever lives, and I know this is true, because The Lemon Drop Kid tells me so afterwards.

This doll has brown hair hanging down her back, and her smile is so wonderful that when an old pappy guy with a goatee comes out of the store to sell a guy in a flivver some gas, The Lemon Drop Kid hauls off and asks him if he can use a clerk.

Well, it seems that the old guy can, at that, because it seems that a former clerk, a guy by the name of Pilloe, recently lays down and dies on the old guy from age and malnutrition, and so this is how The Lemon Drop Kid comes to be planted in Kibbsville, and clerking in Martin Potter's store for the next couple of years, at ten bobs per week.

And furthermore, this is how The Lemon Drop Kid meets up with Miss Alicia Deering, who is nobody but the beautiful little doll that The Lemon Drop Kid sees standing in the doorway of the little house across the street.

She lives in this house with her papa, her mamma being dead a long time, and her papa is really nothing but an old bum who dearly loves his applejack, and who is generally around with a good heat on. His first name is Jonas, and he is a house painter by trade, but he seldom feels like doing any painting, as he claims he never really recovers from a terrible backache he gets when he is in the Spanish-American War with the First New York, so Miss Alicia Deering supports him by dealing them off her arm in the Commercial Hotel.

But although The Lemon Drop Kid now works for a very great old skinflint who even squawks about The Lemon Drop Kid's habit of filling his side pocket now and then with lemon drops out of a jar on the shelf in the store, The Lemon Drop Kid is very happy, for the truth of the matter is he loves Miss Alicia Deering, and it is the first time in his life he ever loves anybody, or anything. And furthermore, it is the first time in his life The Lemon Drop Kid is living quietly, and in peace, and not losing sleep trying to think of ways of cheating somebody.

In fact, The Lemon Drop Kid now looks back on his old life with great repugnance, for he can see that it is by no means the proper life for any guy, and sometimes he has half a mind to write to his former associates who may still be around telling the tale, and request them to mend their ways, only The Lemon Drop Kid does not wish these old associates to know where he is.

He never as much as peeks at a racing sheet nowadays, and he spends all his spare time with Miss Alicia Deering, which is not so much time, at that, as old Martin Potter does not care to see his employees loafing between the hours of 6 a.m. and 10 p.m., and neither does the Commercial Hotel. But one day in the spring, when the apple blossoms are blooming in these parts, and the air is chock-a-block with perfume, and the grass is getting nice and green, The Lemon Drop Kid speaks of his love to Miss Alicia Deering, stating that it is such a love that he can scarcely eat.

Well, Miss Alicia Deering states that she reciprocates this love one hundred per cent., and then The Lemon Drop Kid suggests they get married up immediately, and she says she is in favour of the idea, only she can never think of leaving her papa, who has no one else in all this world but her, and while this is a little more extra weight than The Lemon Drop Kid figures on picking up, he says his love is so terrific he can even stand for her papa, too.

So they are married, and go to live in the little house across the street from Martin Potter's store with Miss Alicia Deering's papa.

When he marries Miss Alicia Deering, The Lemon Drop Kid has a bank roll of one hundred and eighteen dollars, including the C note he takes off of Rarus P. Griggsby, and eighteen bobs that he saves out of his salary from Martin Potter in a year, and three nights after the marriage, Miss Alicia Deering's papa sniffs out where The Lemon Drop Kid plants his roll and sneezes same. Then he goes on a big applejack toot, and spends all the dough.

But in spite of everything, including old man Deering, The

Lemon Drop Kid and Miss Alicia Deering are very, very happy in
the little house for about a year, especially when it seems that Miss
Alicia Deering is going to have a baby, although this incident com-
pels her to stop dealing them off the arm at the Commercial Hotel,
and cuts down their resources.

Now one day, Miss Alica Deering comes down with a great
illness, and it is such an illness as causes old Doc Abernathy, the
local croaker, to wag his head, and to state that it is beyond him,
and that the only chance for her is to send her to a hospital in New
York City where the experts can get a crack at her. But by this
time, what with all his overhead, The Lemon Drop Kid is as clean
as a jaybird, and he has no idea where he can get his dukes on any
money in these parts, and it will cost a couple of C's, for low, to do
what Doc Abernathy suggests.

Finally, The Lemon Drop Kid asks old Martin Potter if he can
see his way clear to making him an advance on his salary, which
still remains ten bobs per week, but Martin Potter laughs, and says
he not only cannot see his way clear to doing such a thing, but that
if conditions do not improve he is going to cut The Lemon Drop
Kid off altogether. Furthermore, about this time the guy who owns
the little house drops around and reminds The Lemon Drop Kid
that he is now in arrears for two months' rent, amounting in all to
twelve bobs, and if The Lemon Drop Kid is not able to meet this
obligation shortly, he will have to vacate.

So one way and another The Lemon Drop Kid is in quite a
quandary, and Miss Alicia Deering is getting worse by the minute,
and finally The Lemon Drop Kid hoofs and hitch-hikes a matter
of maybe a hundred and fifty miles to New York City, with the
idea of going out to Belmont Park, where the giddy-aps are now
running, figuring he may be able to make some kind of a scratch
around there, but he no sooner lights on Broadway than he runs
into a guy he knows by the name of Short Boy, and this Short Boy
pulls him into a doorway, and says to him like this:

'Listen, Lemon Drop,' Short Boy says, 'I do not know what it is
you do to old Rarus P. Griggsby, and I do not wish to know, but it
must be something terrible, indeed, as he has every elbow around
the race tracks laying for you for the past couple of years. You
know Rarus P. Griggsby has great weight around these tracks, and
you must commit murder the way he is after you. Why,' Short Boy
says, 'only last week over in Maryland, Whitey Jordan, the track
copper, asks me if ever I hear of you, and I tell him I understand

you are in Australia. Keep away from the tracks,' Short Boy says, 'or you will wind up in the clink.'

So The Lemon Drop Kid hoofs and hitch-hikes back to Kibbs-ville, as he does not wish to become involved in any trouble at this time, and the night he gets back home is the same night a masked guy with a big six pistol in his duke steps into the lobby of the Commercial Hotel and sticks up the night clerk and half a dozen citizens who are sitting around in the lobby, including old Jonas Deering, and robs the damper of over sixty bobs, and it is also the same night that Miss Alicia Deering's baby is born dead, and old Doc Abernathy afterwards claims that it is all because the experts cannot get a crack at Miss Alica Deering a matter of about twelve hours earlier.

And it is along in the morning after this night, around four bells, that Miss Alicia Deering finally opens her eyes, and see The Lemon Drop Kid sitting beside her bed in the little house, crying very hard, and it is the first time The Lemon Drop Kid is levelling with his crying since the time one of the attendants in the orphans' asylum in Jersey City gives him a good belting years before.

Then Miss Alicia Deering motions to The Lemon Drop Kid to bend down so she can whisper to him, and what Miss Alicia Deering whispers, soft and low, is the following:

'Do not cry, Kid,' she whispers. 'Be a good boy after I am gone, Kid, and never forget I love you, and take good care of poor papa.'

And then Miss Alicia Deering closes her eyes for good and all, and The Lemon Drop Kid sits there beside her, watching her face until some time later he hears a noise at the front door of the little house, and he opens the door to find old Sheriff Higginbotham waiting there, and after they stand looking at each other a while, the sheriff speaks as follows:

'Well, son,' Sheriff Higginbotham says, 'I am sorry, but I guess you will have to come along with me. We find the vinegar barrel spigot wrapped in tin foil that you use for a gun in the back yard here where you throw it last night.'

'All right,' The Lemon Drop Kid says. 'All right, Sheriff. But how do you come to think of me in the first place?'

'Well,' Sheriff Higginbotham says, 'I do not suppose you recall doing it, and the only guy in the hotel lobby that notices it is nobody but your papa-in-law, Jonas Deering, but,' he says, 'while you are holding your home-made pistol with one hand last night, you reach into the side pocket of your coat with the other hand and take out a lemon drop and pop it into your mouth.'

I run into The Lemon Drop Kid out on the lawn at Hialeah in Miami last winter, and I am sorry to see that the twoer he does in Auburn leaves plenty of lines in his face, and a lot of grey in his hair.

But of course I do not refer to this, nor do I mention that he is the subject of considerable criticism from many citizens for turning over to Miss Alicia Deering's papa a purse of three C's that we raise to pay a mouthpiece for his defence.

Furthermore, I do not tell The Lemon Drop Kid that he is also criticized in some quarters for his action while in the sneezer at Auburn in sending the old guy the few bobs he is able to gather in by making and selling knick-knacks of one kind and another to visitors, until finally Jonas Deering saves him any more bother by up and passing away of too much applejack.

The way I look at it, every guy knows his own business best, so I only duke The Lemon Drop Kid, and say I am glad to see him, and we are standing there carving up a few old scores, when all of a sudden there is a great commotion and out of the crowd around us on the lawn comes an old guy with a big white mouser, and bristly white eyebrows, and as he grabs The Lemon Drop Kid by the arm, I am somewhat surprised to see that it is nobody but old Rarus P. Griggsby, without his wheel chair, and to hear him speak as follows:

'Well, well, well, well, well!' Rarus P. Griggsby says to The Lemon Drop Kid. 'At last I find you,' he says. 'Where are you hiding all these years? Do you not know I have detectives looking for you high and low because I wish to pay you the reward I offer for anybody curing me of my arthritis? Yes,' Rarus P. Griggsby says, 'the medicine you give me at Saratoga which tastes like a lemon drop, works fine, although,' he says, 'my seven doctors all try to tell me it is nothing but their efforts finally getting in their work, while the city of Saratoga is attempting to cut in and claim credit for its waters.

'But,' Rarus P. Griggsby says, 'I know it is your medicine, and if it is not your medicine, it is your scallawaggery that makes me so hot that I forget my arthritis, and never remember it since, so it is all one and the same thing. Anyway, you now have forty-nine hundred dollars coming from me, for of course I must hold out the hundred out of which you swindle me,' he says.

Well, The Lemon Drop Kid stands looking at Rarus P. Griggsby and listening to him, and finally The Lemon Drop Kid begins to laugh in his low voice, ha-ha-ha-ha-ha, but somehow there does not seem to be any laughter in the laugh, and I cannot bear to hear it, so I move away leaving Rarus P. Griggsby and The Lemon Drop Kid there together.

I look back only once, and I see The Lemon Drop Kid stop laughing long enough to take a lemon drop out of the side pocket of his coat and pop it into his mouth, and then he goes on laughing, ha-ha-ha-ha-ha.

What, No Butler?

To look at Ambrose Hammer, the newspaper scribe, you will never suspect that he has sense enough to pound sand in a rat hole, but Ambrose is really a pretty slick guy. In fact, Ambrose is a great hand for thinking, and the way I find this out makes quite a story.

It begins about seven o'clock one May morning when I am standing at the corner of Fiftieth Street and Broadway, and along comes Ambrose with his neck all tied up as if he has a sore throat, and he gives me a large hello in a hoarse tone of voice.

Then we stand there together, speaking of the beautiful sunrise, and one thing and another, and of how we wish we have jobs that will let us enjoy the daylight more, although personally I do not have any job to begin with, and if there is one thing I hate and despise it is the daylight, and the chances are this goes for Ambrose, too.

In fact, in all the years I know Ambrose, I never catch him out in the daylight more than two or three times, and then it is when we are both on our way home and happen to meet up as we do this morning I am talking about. And always Ambrose is telling me what a tough life he leads, and how his nerves are all shot to pieces, although I hear the only time Ambrose's nerves really bother him is once when he goes to Florida for a vacation, and has a nervous breakdown from the quiet that is around and about those parts.

This Ambrose Hammer is a short, chubby guy, with big, round, googly eyes, and a very innocent expression, and in fact it is this innocent expression that causes many guys to put Ambrose away as slightly dumb, because it does not seem possible that a guy who is around Broadway as long as Ambrose can look so innocent unless he is dumb.

He is what is called a dramatic critic by trade, and his job is to write pieces for the paper about the new plays that somebody is always producing on Broadway, and Ambrose's pieces are very interesting, indeed, as he loves to heave the old harpoon into actors if they do not act to suit him, and as it will take a combination of Katherine Cornell, Jimmy Durante and Lillian Gish to really suit Ambrose, he is generally in there harpooning away very good.

Well, while we are standing on the corner boosting the daylight, who comes along but a plain-clothes copper by the name of Marty Kerle, and he stops to give us a big good morning. Personally, I have no use for coppers, even if they are in plain clothes, but I believe in being courteous to them at all times, so I give Marty a big good morning right back at him, and ask him what he is doing out and about at such an hour, and Marty states as follows:

'Why,' Marty says, 'some doll who claims she is housekeeper for Mr. Justin Veezee just telephones the station that she finds Mr. Justin Veezee looking as if he is very dead in his house over here in West Fifty-sixth Street, and I am going there to investigate this rumour. Maybe,' Marty says, 'you will wish to come along with me.'

'Mr. Justin Veezee?' Ambrose Hammer says. 'Why, my goodness gracious, this cannot be true, because I hear he is in the Club Soudan only a few hours ago watching the Arabian acrobatic dancer turn flip-flops, and one thing and another, although personally,' Ambrose says, 'I do nct think she is any more Arabian than Miss Ethel Barrymore.'

But of course if Mr. Justin Veezee is dead, it is a nice item of news for Ambrose Hammer to telephone in to his paper, so he tel's Marty he will be delighted to go with him, for one, and I decide to go too, as I will rather be looking at a dead guy than at guys hurrying to work at such an hour.

Furthermore, I am secretly hoping that the housekeeper does not make any mistake, as I can think of nothing nicer than seeing Mr. Justin Veezee dead, unless maybe it is two or three Mr. Justin Veezees dead, for personally I consider Mr. Justin Veezee nothing but an old stinker.

In fact, everybody in this town considers Mr. Justin Veezee nothing but an old stinker, because for many years he is along Broadway, in and out, and up and down, and always he is on the grab for young dolls such as work in night clubs and shows, and especially young dolls who do not have brains enough to realize that Mr. Justin Veezee is nothing but an old stinker. And of course there is always a fresh crop of such dolls coming to Broadway every year, and in fact it is getting so nowadays that there are several crops per year.

But although it is well known to one and all that Mr. Justin Veezee is nothing but an old stinker, nobody ever dasts speak of this matter out loud, as Mr. Justin Veezee has plenty of potatoes, which come down to him from his papa, and it is considered very disrespectful along Broadway to speak of a guy with plenty of potatoes as an old stinker, even if he is as tight with his potatoes as Mr. Justin Veezee, which is very, very, very, very tight, indeed.

Now, the house in West Fifty-sixth Street where Mr. Justin Veezee lives in between Fifth and Sixth Avenues, and is once the private home of the Veezee family when there is quite a raft of Veezees around, but it seems that these Veezees all die off one by one, except Mr. Justin Veezee, and so he finally turns the old home into an apartment house.

It is a very nice-looking building, maybe four or five stories high, with apartments on each floor, and Mr. Justin Veezee's apartment is on the first floor above the street, and takes in the whole floor, although this does not mean so much space at that, as the house is very narrow.

It is one of these apartment houses where you push a button at the front door on the street floor, and this push rings a bell in the apartment you are after, and then somebody in the apartment pushes a button up there, and this unlocks the front door, and you walk up the stairs to where you are going, as there is no elevator, and no doorman, either.

Well, anyway, it is in the front room of Mr. Justin Veezee's apartment that we see Mr. Justin Veezee himself. He is sitting straight up in a big easy-chair beside a table on which there is a stack of these pictures called etchings, and he has on evening clothes, and his eyes are wide open and bugging out of his head, as if he is totally amazed at something he sees, and the chances are he is, at that.

There is no doubt whatever but that Mr. Justin Veezee is very dead, indeed, and Marty Kerle says we are not to touch anything until the medical examiner has a peek, although by the time he says this, Ambrose Hammer is looking the etchings over with great interest, as Ambrose is such a guy as dearly loves to look at works of art.

The housekeeper who calls up the station is present when we arrive, but she turns out to be nothing but an old tomato by the name of Mrs. Swanson, who does not live in Mr. Justin Veezee's house, but who comes every morning at an early hour to clean up the joint. And this Mrs. Swanson states that she finds Mr. Justin Veezee just as he is when she comes in on this particular morning, although she says that usually he is in the hay pounding his ear at such an hour.

She thinks maybe he falls asleep in the chair, and tries to roust him out, but as Mr. Justin Veezee does not say aye, yes, or no, she figures the chances are he is dead, and so she gives the gendarmes a buzz.

'Well,' I say to Ambrose Hammer, 'this is a most ghastly scene, indeed. In fact, Mr. Justin Veezee looks worse dead than he does alive, which I will never consider possible. The chances are this guy dies of old age. He must be fifty, if he is a day,' I say.

'No,' Ambrose says, 'he does not die of old age. The way I look at it, this is a case of homicide. Somebody gets in here and cools off Mr. Justin Veezee, and it is a very dirty trick if you ask me, because,' Ambrose says, 'they do not give Mr. Justin Veezee a chance to change into something more comfortable than a dinner jacket.'

Well, Ambrose says he will look around and see if he can locate any clues, and while he is snooping around the joint in comes a guy from the medical examiner's office and takes a gander at Mr. Justin Veezee. And the guy states at once that Mr. Justin Veezee is positively dead, although nobody is giving him any argument on this point, and he further states that what kills Mr. Justin Veezee is nothing but a broken neck.

Right away this broken neck becomes a very great mystery, because it does not stand to reason that a guy can break his own neck sitting down, unless maybe he is practising to be a contortionist, and nobody figures it possible that Mr. Justin Veezee is practising to be a contortionist at his age.

Furthermore, the medical guy finds certain marks on Mr. Justin Veezee's neck which he claims show that somebody grabs Mr. Justin Veezee by the guzzle and cracks his neck for him as if he is nothing but a goose, and the medical guy says it must be somebody with very strong dukes to play such a prank on Mr. Justin Veezee.

Well, Ambrose Hammer seems to be all heated up about this whole matter, although personally I cannot see where it is any of his put-in. The way I look at it, Mr. Justin Veezee is no price any way you take him when he is alive and kicking, and his death does not change the betting any as far as I am concerned, because I know from the things I see of Mr. Justin Veezee, and the things I hear of him, that he is still an old stinker, in spades.

Ambrose tells me that he is certainly going to solve this mystery in the interests of justice, and I tell him that the only way to solve a murder mystery is to suspect everybody in town, beginning with the old tomato who discovers the remains of Mr. Justin Veezee, and winding up with the gendarmes who investigate the case.

'But,' I say to Ambrose Hammer, 'you do not pin the foul deed on any of these parties, but on the butler, because this is the way these things are done in all the murder-mystery movies and plays I ever see, and also in all the murder-mystery books I ever read.'

Well, at this Marty Kerle, the plain-clothes copper, states that the only trouble with my idea is that there is no butler connected with Mr. Justin Veezee's establishment in any way, shape, manner, or form, and when I tell Ambrose that maybe we can hire a butler to double in murder for us, Ambrose becomes very indignant, and speaks to me as follows:

'No butler commits this murder,' Ambrose says, 'and, further-more, I do not consider your remarks in good taste, no matter if you are joking, or what. I am convinced that this crime is the work of nobody but a doll, because of certain clues I encounter in my survey of the premises.'

But Ambrose will not tell me what these clues are, and person-ally I do not care, because the way I look at it, even if some doll does give Mr. Justin Veezee the business, it is only retribution for what Mr. Justin Veezee does to other dolls in his time.

Well, the scragging of Mr. Justin Veezee is a very great sensa-tion, and the newspapers make quite a lot of it, because there is no doubt but what it is the greatest mystery in this town in several weeks. Furthermore, anybody that ever as much as speaks to Mr. Justin Veezee in the past twenty years becomes very sorry for it when the newspapers commence printing their names and pictures, and especially any dolls who have any truck with Mr. Justin Veezee in the past, for naturally the newspaper scribes and the gendarmes are around asking them where they are at such and such an hour on such and such a date, and it is quite amazing how few guys and dolls can remember this off-hand, especially dolls.

In fact, pretty soon the scragging of Mr. Justin Veezee becomes one of the most embarrassing propositions that ever comes off east of the Mississippi River, and many citizens are thinking of going out and scragging somebody else just to take the attention of the scribes and the gendarmes away from Mr. Justin Veezee.

As near as anybody can find out, the last party to see Mr. Justin Veezee alive the morning he is scragged is a red-headed doll at the Club Soudan by the name of Sorrel-top, and who is by no means a bad-looking doll, if you like them red-headed. This Sorrel-top is in charge of the check-room where one and all are supposed to check their hats and coats on entering the Club Soudan, and to tip Sorrel-top a shilling or two when they go out for keeping cases on these articles.

It seems that Sorrel-top always remembers when Mr. Justin Veezee leaves the Club Soudan, because he never stakes her to as much as a thin dime when he calls for his kady, and naturally Sorrel-top is bound to remember such a guy, especially as he is the only guy in the United States of America who dasts pass up Sorrel-top in this manner.

So she remembers that Mr. Justin Veezee leaves the Club Soudan on the morning in question around three bells, and the chances are he walks home, as none of the taxi jockeys who hang out in front of the Club Soudan remember seeing him, and, anyway, it is only a few blocks from the club to Mr. Justin Veezee's house, and it is a cinch he is never going to pay money to ride in a taxi just a few blocks.

Now it comes out that there are only two entrances to Mr. Justin Veezee's apartment, and one entrance is the front door, but the other entrance is a back door, but the back door is locked and barred on the inside when Mr. Justin Veezee is found, while the front door is locked with a patent snap lock, and Mrs. Swanson, the old tomato who does the housekeeping for Mr. Justin Veezee, states that she and Mr. Justin Veezee have the only two keys in the world to this lock that she knows of, although of course the parties who live in the other apartments in the house have keys to the street door, and so has the old tomato.

Furthermore, the windows of Mr. Justin Veezee's apartment are all locked on the inside, and there seems to be no way whatever that anybody except Mr. Justin Veezee and the old tomato can get in this apartment, and the gendarmes begin looking at the old tomato very suspiciously, indeed, until she digs up a milkman by the name of Schmalz, who sees her going into the apartment house about six-thirty in the morning, and then sees her a few minutes later come tearing out of the joint yelling watch, murder, police, and the medical guys say there is no chance she can guzzle Mr. Justin Veezee in this time, unless she is a faster worker than anybody they ever hear of in all their days.

Anyway, nobody can figure a motive for the old tomato to guzzle Mr. Justin Veezee, although a couple of the newspaper scribes try to make out that maybe she is an ever-loving sweetheart of Mr. Justin Veezee in the long ago, and that he does her dirt. Personally, I consider this proposition reasonable enough, because it is a sure thing that if the old tomato is ever Mr. Justin Veezee's sweetheart, he is just naturally bound to do her dirt. But the old tomato seems so depressed over losing a customer for her housekeeping that finally nobody pays any more attention to her, and one and all go looking around for someone else who may have a motive for giving Mr. Justin Veezee the business.

Well, it comes out that there are a large number of parties, including both male and female, in this part of the country who figure to have a motive for giving Mr. Justin Veezee the business, but they are all able to prove they are some place else when this matter comes off, so the mystery keeps getting more mysterious by the minute, especially as the gendarmes say there is no chance that robbery is the motive, because Mr. Justin Veezee has all his jewellery on him and plenty of potatoes in his pockets when he is found, and nothing in the apartment seems disturbed.

Furthermore, they find no finger-prints around and about, except some that turn out to belong to Ambrose Hammer, and at that Ambrose has a tough time explaining that he makes these finger-prints after Mr. Justin Veezee is found, and not before. They find most of Ambrose's finger-prints on the etchings, and personally I am glad I am not around fingering anything while I am in the joint, as the gendarmes may not listen to my explanations as easy as they listen to Ambrose.

Well, I do not see Ambrose for several nights, but it seems that this is because there are some shows opening around town and Ambrose is busy harpooning the actors. Finally one night he comes looking for me, and he states that as I am with him when he starts working on the mystery of who gives Mr. Justin Veezee the business, it is only fair that I be present when he exposes the party who commits this dastardly deed. And, Ambrose says, the hour now arrives, and although I do my best to show Ambrose that there can be no percentage for him in hollering copper on anybody in this matter, nothing will do but I must go with him.

And where does he take me but to the Club Soudan, and as it is early in the evening there are very few customers in the joint when we arrive, as the Club Soudan does not heat up good until along about midnight. Furthermore, I judge that the customers are strangers in the city, as they seem to be partaking of food, and nobody who is not a stranger in the city will think of partaking of food in the Club Soudan, although the liquor there is by no means bad.

Well, Ambrose and I get to talking to a character by the name of Flat-wheel Walter, who has a small piece of the joint, and who is called by this name because he walks with a gimp on one side, and by and by Ambrose asks for the Arabian acrobatic dancer, and Flat-wheel says she is at this time in her dressing-room making up for her dance. So Ambrose takes me up a flight of stairs to a little room, which is one of several little rooms along a hallway, and sure enough, there is this Arabian acrobatic dancer making up.

And the way she is making up is by taking off her clothes, because it seems that an Arabian acrobatic dancer cannot dance with anything on except maybe a veil or two, and personally I am somewhat embarrassed by the spectacle of a doll taking off her clothes to make up, especially an Arabian. But Ambrose Hammer does not seem to mind, as he is greatly calloused to such scenes because of his experience with the modern stage, and, anyway, the Arabian manages to get a few veils around her before I can really find any grounds for complaint. But I wish to say that I am greatly surprised when I hear this Arabian dancer speak in very good English, and in fact with a Brooklyn accent, and as follows:

'Oh, Ambrose,' she says, 'I am so glad to see you again.'

With this she makes out as if to put her arms around Ambrose Hammer, but then she remembers just in time that if she does this she will have to let go her hold of the veils and, anyway, Ambrose pulls away from her and stands looking at her with a very strange expression on his kisser.

Well, I will say one thing for Ambrose Hammer, and this is that he is at all times very gentlemanly, and he introduces me to the

Arabian acrobatic dancer, and I notice that he speaks of her as Miss Cleghorn, although I remember that they bill her in lights in front of the Club Soudan as Illah-Illah, which is maybe her first name.

Now Ambrose gazes at Miss Cleghorn most severely, and then he speaks:

'The game is up,' Ambrose says. 'If you wish to confess to me and this party, well and good, otherwise you will tell your story to the gendarmes. I know you kill Mr. Justin Veezee, and,' Ambrose says, 'while you may have an excellent excuse, it is against the law.'

Well, at this Miss Cleghorn turns very pale, indeed, and begins trembling so she almost forgets to hold on to her veils, and then she sits down in a chair and breathes so hard you will think she just finishes a tough tenth round. Naturally, I am somewhat surprised by Ambrose's statement, because up to this time I am not figuring Miss Cleghorn as such a doll as will harm a flea, although of course I will never lay a price against this proposition on any doll without having something of a line on her.

'Yes,' Ambrose says, speaking very severely, indeed, to Miss Cleghorn, 'you make an appointment to go to Mr. Justin Veezee's apartment the other morning after you get through with your Arabian acrobatic dancing here, to look at his etchings. I am surprised you fall for etchings, but I am glad you do, at that, because it gives me my first clue. No guy is hauling out etchings at four o'clock in the morning to look at them by himself,' Ambrose says. 'It is one of the oldest build-ups of a doll in the world,' he says.

'Well,' Ambrose goes on, 'you look at Mr. Justin Veezee's etchings. They are very bad. In fact, they are terrible. But never mind this. Presently you struggle. You are very strong on account of your Arabian acrobatic dancing. Yes,' Ambrose says, 'you are very, very, very strong. In this struggle you break Mr. Justin Veezee's neck, and now he is extremely dead. It is all very sad,' Ambrose says.

Now, I wish to state that I am greatly mortified at being present at this scene, because if I know what Ambrose Hammer says he knows about Miss Cleghorn, I will keep my trap closed, especially as there is no reward offered for any information leading to the apprehension of the party who gives Mr. Justin Veezee the business, but Ambrose is undoubtedly a very law-abiding guy, and the chances are he feels he is only doing his duty in this matter, and, furthermore, he may get a nice item for his paper out of it.

But when he tells Miss Cleghorn that she is guilty of this un-ladylike conduct toward Mr. Justin Veezee, she gets up out of her chair, still holding on to her veils, and speaks to Ambrose Hammer like this:

'No, Ambrose,' she says, 'you are wrong. I do not kill Mr. Justin Veezee. I admit I go to his apartment, but not to see his etchings. I go there to have a bite to eat with him, because Mr. Justin Veezee swears to me that his housekeeper will be present, and I do not know he is deceiving me until after I arrive there. Mr. Justin Veezee gets out his etchings later when he can think of nothing else. But even Mr. Justin Veezee is not so old-fashioned as to believe any doll will go to his apartment just to look at etchings nowadays. I admit we struggle, but,' Miss Cleghorn says, 'I do not kill him.'

'Well,' Ambrose says, 'if you do not think Mr. Justin Veezee is dead, a dollar will win you a trip around the world.'

'Yes,' Miss Cleghorn says, 'I know he is dead. He is dead when I leave the apartment. I am very, very sorry for this, but I tell you again I do not kill him.'

'Well,' Ambrose says, 'then who does kill Mr. Justin Veezee?'

'This I will never, never tell,' Miss Cleghorn says.

Now, naturally, Ambrose Hammer becomes very indignant at this statement, and he tells Miss Cleghorn that if she will not tell him she will have to tell the gendarmes, and she starts in to cry like I do not know what, when all of a sudden the door of the dressing-room opens, and in comes a big, stout-built, middle-aged-looking guy, who does not seem any too well dressed, and who speaks as follows:

'Pardon the intrusion, gentlemen,' the guy says, 'but I am wait-ing in the next room and cannot help overhearing your conversa-tion. I am waiting there because Miss Cleghorn is going to draw enough money off her employers to get me out of this part of the country. My name,' the guy says, 'is Riggsby. I am the party who kills Mr. Justin Veezee.'

Well, naturally Ambrose Hammer is greatly surprised by these remarks, and so am I, but before either of us can express ourselves, the guy goes on like this:

'I am a roomer in the humble home of Mrs. Swanson in Ninth Avenue,' he says. 'I learn all about Mr. Justin Veezee from her. I sneak her key to the street door of Mr. Justin Veezee's house, and her key to the door of Mr. Justin Veezee's apartment one day and get copies of them made, and put the originals back before she misses them. I am hiding in Mr. Justin Veezee's apartment the other morning waiting to stick him up.

'Well,' the guy says, 'Mr. Justin Veezee comes in alone, and I am just about to step out on him and tell him to get them up, when in comes Miss Cleghorn, although of course I do not know at the time who she is. I can hear everything they say, and I see at once from their conversation that Miss Cleghorn is there under false pretences. She finally wishes to leave, and Mr. Justin Veezee attacks her. She fights valiantly, and in just a straightaway hand-to-hand struggle, I will relish a small bet on her against Mr. Justin Veezee, or any other guy. But Mr. Justin Veezee picks up a bronze statuette and is about to bean her with it, so,' the middle-aged guy says, 'I step into it.

'Well,' he says, 'I guess maybe I am a little rougher with Mr. Justin Veezee than I mean to be, because I find myself putting a nice flying-mare hold on him and hurling him across the room. I fear the fall injures him severely. Anyway, when I pick him up he seems to be dead. So I sit him up in a chair, and take a bath towel and wipe out any chance of finger-prints around and about, and then escort Miss Cleghorn to her home.

'I do not intend to kill Mr. Justin Veezee,' the middle-aged-looking guy says. 'I only intend to rob him, and I am very sorry he is no longer with us, especially as I cannot now return and carry out my original plan. But,' he says, 'I cannot bear to see you hand Miss Cleghorn over to the law, although I hope and trust she will never be so foolish as to go visiting the apartments of such characters as Mr. Justin Veezee again.'

'Yes,' Ambrose Hammer says to Miss Cleghorn, 'why do you go there in the first place?'

Well, at this Miss Cleghorn begins crying harder than ever, and between sobs she states to Ambrose Hammer as follows:

'Oh, Ambrose,' she says, 'it is because I love you so. You do not come around to see me for several nights, and I accept Mr. Justin Veezee's invitation hoping you will hear of it, and become jealous.'

So of course there is nothing for Ambrose Hammer to do but take her in his arms and start whispering to her in such terms as guys are bound to whisper under these circumstances, and I motion the middle-aged-looking guy to go outside, as I consider this scene far too sacred for a stranger to witness.

Then about this time, Miss Cleghorn gets a call to go downstairs and do a little Arabian acrobatic dancing for the customers of the Club Soudan, and so she leaves us without ever once forgetting in all this excitement to keep a hold on her veils, although I am watching at all times to remind her in case her memory fails her in this respect.

And then I ask Ambrose Hammer something that is bothering me no little, and this is how he comes to suspect in the first place that Miss Cleghorn may know something about the scragging of Mr. Justin Veezee, even allowing that the etchings give him a clue that a doll is present when the scragging comes off. And I especially wish to know how he can ever figure Miss Cleghorn even as much as an outside chance of scragging Mr. Justin Veezee in such a manner as to break his neck.

'Why,' Ambrose Hammer says, 'I will gladly tell you about this, but only in strict confidence. The last time I see Miss Cleghorn up to to-night is the night I invite her to my own apartment to look at etchings, and they are better etchings than Mr. Justin Veezee shows her, at that. And,' Ambrose says, 'maybe you remember I am around with my neck tied up for a week.'

Well, the middle-aged-looking guy is waiting for us outside the Club Soudan when we come out, and Ambrose Hammer stakes him to half a C and tells him to go as far as he can on this, and I shake hands with him, and wish him luck, and as he is turning to go, I say to him like this:

'By the way, Mr. Riggsby,' I say, 'what is your regular occupation, anyway, if I am not too nosey?'

'Oh,' he says, 'until the depression comes on, I am for years rated one of the most efficient persons in my line in this town. In fact, I have many references to prove it. Yes,' he says, 'I am considered an exceptionally high-class butler.'

The Three Wise Guys

One cold winter afternoon I am standing at the bar in Good Time Charley's little drum in West Forty-ninth Street, partaking of a mixture of rock candy and rye whisky, and this is a most surprising thing for me to be doing, as I am by no means a rum-pot, and very seldom indulge in alcoholic beverages in any way, shape, manner, or form.

But when I step into Good Time Charley's on the afternoon in question, I am feeling as if maybe I have a touch of grippe coming on, and Good Time Charley tells me that there is nothing in this world as good for a touch of grippe as rock candy and rye whisky, as it assassinates the germs at once.

It seems that Good Time Charley always keeps a stock of rock candy and rye whisky on hand for touches of the grippe, and he gives me a few doses immediately, and in fact Charley takes a few doses with me, as he says there is no telling but what I am scattering germs of my touch of the grippe all around the joint, and he must safeguard his health. We are both commencing to feel much better when the door opens, and who comes in but a guy by the name of Blondy Swanson.

This Blondy Swanson is a big, six-foot-two guy, with straw-coloured hair, and pink cheeks, and he is originally out of Harlem, and it is well known to one and all that in his day he is the largest puller on the Atlantic seaboard. In fact, for upwards of ten years, Blondy is bringing wet goods into New York from Canada, and one place and another, and in all this time he never gets a fall, which is considered a phenomenal record for an operator as extensive as Blondy.

Well, Blondy steps up alongside me at the bar, and I ask him if he cares to have a few doses of rock candy and rye whisky with me and Good Time Charley, and Blondy says he will consider it a privilege and a pleasure, because, he says, he always has something of a sweet tooth. So we have these few doses, and I say to Blondy Swanson that I hope and trust that business is thriving with him.

'I have no business,' Blondy Swanson says, 'I retire from business.'

Well, if J. Pierpont Morgan, or John D. Rockefeller, or Henry Ford step up and tell me they retire from business, I will not be more astonished than I am by this statement from Blondy Swanson, and in fact not as much. I consider Blondy's statement the most important commercial announcement I hear in many years, and naturally I ask him why he makes such a decision, and what is to become of thousands of citizens who are dependent on him for merchandise.

'Well,' Blondy says, 'I retire from business because I am one hundred per cent American citizen. In fact,' he says, 'I am a patriot. I serve my country in the late war. I am cited at Château-Thierry. I always vote the straight Democratic ticket, except,' he says, 'when we figure it better to elect some Republican. I always stand up when the band plays the Star Spangled Banner. One year I even pay an income tax,' Blondy says.

And of course I know that many of these things are true, although I remember hearing rumours that if the draft officer is along half an hour later than he is, he will not see Blondy for heel dust, and that what Blondy is cited for at Château-Thierry is for not robbing the dead.

But of course I do not speak of these matters to Blondy Swanson, because Blondy is not such a guy as will care to listen to rumours, and may become indignant, and when Blondy is indignant he is very difficult to get along with.

'Now,' Blondy says, 'I am a bootie for a long time, and supply very fine merchandise to my trade, as everybody knows, and it is a respectable business, because one and all in this country are in favour of it, except the prohibitionists. But,' he says, 'I can see into the future, and I can see that one of these days they are going to repeal the prohibition law, and then it will be most unpatriotic to be bringing in wet goods from foreign parts in competition with home industry. So I retire,' Blondy says.

'Well, Blondy,' I say, 'your sentiments certainly do you credit, and if we have more citizens as high-minded as you are, this will be a better country.'

'Furthermore,' Blondy says, 'there is no money in booting any more. All the booties in this country are broke. I am broke myself,' he says. 'I just lose the last piece of property I own in the world, which is the twenty-five-G home I build in Atlantic City, figuring to spend the rest of my days there with Miss Clarabelle Cobb, before she takes a runout powder on me. Well,' Blondy says, 'if I only listen to Miss Clarabelle Cobb, I will now be an honest clerk in a gents' furnishing store, with maybe a cute little apartment up around One Hundred and Tenth Street, and children running all around and about.'

And with this, Blondy sighs heavily, and I sigh with him, because the romance of Blondy Swanson and Miss Clarabelle Cobb is well known to one and all on Broadway.

It goes back a matter of anyway six years when Blondy Swanson is making money so fast he can scarcely stop to count it, and at this time Miss Clarabelle Cobb is the most beautiful doll in this town, and many citizens almost lose their minds just gazing at her when she is a member of Mr. Georgie White's 'Scandals,' including Blondy Swanson.

In fact, after Blondy Swanson sees Miss Clarabelle Cobb in just one performance of Mr. Georgie White's 'Scandals,' he is never quite the same guy again. He goes to a lot of bother meeting up with Miss Clarabelle Cobb, and then he takes to hanging out around Mr. Georgie White's stage door, and sending Miss Clarabelle Cobb ten-pound boxes of candy, and floral horseshoes, and wreaths, and also packages of trinkets, including such articles as diamond bracelets, and brooches, and vanity cases, for there is no denying that Blondy is a fast guy with a dollar.

But it seems that Miss Clarabelle Cobb will not accept any of these offerings, except the candy and the flowers, and she goes so far as to return a sable coat that Blondy sends her one very cold day, and she is openly criticized for this action by some of the other dolls in Mr. Georgie White's 'Scandals,' for they say that after all there is a limit even to eccentricity.

But Miss Clarabelle Cobb states that she is not accepting valuable offerings from any guy, and especially a guy who is engaged in trafficking in the demon rum, because she says that his money is nothing but blood money that comes from breaking the law of the land, although, as a matter of fact, this is a dead wrong rap against Blondy Swanson, as he never handles a drop of rum in his life, but only Scotch, and furthermore he keeps himself pretty well straightened out with the law.

The idea is, Miss Clarabelle Cobb comes of very religious people back in Akron, Ohio, and she is taught from childhood that rum is a terrible thing, and personally I think it is myself, except in cocktails, and furthermore, the last thing her mamma tells her when she leaves for New York is to beware of any guys who come around offering her diamond bracelets and fur coats, because her mamma says such guys are undoubtedly snakes in the grass, and probably on the make.

But while she will not accept his offerings, Miss Clarabelle Cobb does not object to going out with Blondy Swanson now and then, and putting on the chicken Mexicaine, and the lobster Newburg, and other items of this nature, and any time you put a good-looking young guy and a beautiful doll together over the chicken

Mexicaine and the lobster Newburg often enough, you are apt to have a case of love on your hands.

And this is what happens to Blondy Swanson and Miss Clarabelle Cobb, and in fact they become in love more than somewhat, and Blondy Swanson is wishing to marry Miss Clarabelle Cobb, but one night over a batch of lobster Newburg, she says to him like this:

'Blondy,' she says, 'I love you, and,' she says, 'I will marry you in a minute if you get out of trafficking in rum. I will marry you if you are out of the rum business, and do not have a dime, but I will never marry you as long as you are dealing in rum, no matter if you have a hundred million.'

Well, Blondy says he will get out of the racket at once, and he keeps saying this every now and then for a year or so, and the chances are that several times he means it, but when a guy is in this business in those days as strong as Blondy Swanson it is not so easy for him to get out, even if he wishes to do so. And then one day Miss Clarabelle Cobb has a talk with Blondy, and says to him as follows:

'Blondy,' she says, 'I still love you, but you care more for your business than you do for me. So I am going back to Ohio,' she says. 'I am sick and tired of Broadway, anyhow. Some day when you are really through with the terrible traffic you are now engaged in, come to me.'

And with this, Miss Clarabelle Cobb takes plenty of outdoors on Blondy Swanson, and is seen no more in these parts. At first Blondy thinks she is only trying to put a little pressure on him, and will be back, but as the weeks become months, and the months finally count up into years, Blondy can see that she is by no means clowning with him. Furthermore, he never hears from her, and all he knows is she is back in Akron, Ohio.

Well, Blondy is always promising himself that he will soon pack in on hauling wet goods, and go look up Miss Clarabelle Cobb and marry her, but he keeps putting it off, and putting it off, until finally one day he hears that Miss Clarabelle Cobb marries some legitimate guy in Akron, and this is a terrible blow to Blondy, indeed, and from this day he never looks at another doll again, or anyway not much.

Naturally, I express my deep sympathy to Blondy about being broke, and I also mention that my heart bleeds for him in his loss of Miss Clarabelle Cobb, and we have a few doses of rock candy and rye whisky on both propositions, and by this time Good Time Charley runs out of rock candy, and anyway it is a lot of bother for him to be mixing it up with the rye whisky, so we have the rye whisky without the rock candy, and personally I do not notice much difference.

Well, while we are standing there at the bar having our rye whisky without the rock candy, who comes in but an old guy by the name of The Dutchman, who is known to one and all as a most illegal character in every respect. In fact, The Dutchman has no standing whatever in the community, and I am somewhat surprised to see him appear in Good Time Charley's, because The Dutchman is generally a lammie from some place, and the gendarmes everywhere are always anxious to have a chat with him. The last I hear of The Dutchman he is in college somewhere out West for highway robbery, although afterwards he tells me it is a case of mistaken identity. It seems he mistakes a copper in plain clothes for a groceryman.

The Dutchman is an old-fashioned-looking guy of maybe fifty-odd, and he has grey hair, and a stubby grey beard, and he is short, and thickset, and always good-natured, even when there is no call for it, and to look at him you will think there is no more harm in him than there is in a preacher, and maybe not as much.

As The Dutchman comes in, he takes a peek all around and about as if he is looking for somebody in particular, and when he sees Blondy Swanson he moves up alongside Blondy and begins whispering to Blondy until Blondy pulls away and tells him to speak freely.

Now The Dutchman has a very interesting story, and it goes like this: It seems that about eight or nine months back The Dutchman is mobbed up with a party of three very classy heavy guys who make quite a good thing of going around knocking off safes in small-town jugs, and post offices, and stores in small towns, and taking the money, or whatever else is valuable in these safes. This is once quite a popular custom in this country, although it dies out to some extent of late years because they improve the brand of safes so much it is a lot of bother knocking them off, but it comes back during the depression when there is no other way of making money, until it is a very prosperous business again. And of course this is very nice for old-time heavy guys, such as The Dutchman, because it gives them something to do in their old age.

Anyway, it seems that this party The Dutchman is with goes

over into Pennsylvania one night on a tip from a friend and knocks off a safe in a factory office, and gets a pay roll amounting to maybe fifty G's. But it seems that while they are making their getaway in an automobile, the gendarmes take out after them, and there is a chase, during which there is considerable blasting back and forth.

Well, finally in this blasting, the three guys with The Dutchman get cooled off, and The Dutchman also gets shot up quite some, and he abandons the automobile out on an open road, taking the money, which is in a gripsack, with him, and he somehow manages to escape the gendarmes by going across country, and hiding here and there.

But The Dutchman gets pretty well petered out, what with his wounds, and trying to lug the gripsack, and one night he comes to an old deserted barn, and he decides to stash the gripsack in this barn, because there is no chance he can keep lugging it around much longer. So he takes up a few boards in the floor of the barn, and digs a nice hole in the ground underneath and plants the gripsack there, figuring to come back some day and pick it up.

Well, The Dutchman gets over into New Jersey one way and another, and lays up in a town by the name of New Brunswick until his wounds are healed, which requires considerable time as The Dutchman cannot take it nowadays as good as he can when he is younger.

Furthermore, even after The Dutchman recovers and gets to thinking of going after the stashed gripsack, he finds he is about half out of confidence, which is what happens to all guys when they commence getting old, and he figures that it may be a good idea to declare somebody else in to help him, and the first guy he thinks of is Blondy Swanson, because he knows Blondy Swanson is a very able citizen in every respect.

'Now, Blondy,' The Dutchman says, 'if you like my proposition, I am willing to cut you in for fifty per cent, and fifty per cent of fifty G's is by no means pretzels in these times.'

'Well, Dutchman,' Blondy says, 'I will gladly assist you in this enterprise on the terms you state. It appeals to me as a legitimate proposition, because there is no doubt this dough is coming to you, and from now on I am strictly legit. But in the meantime, let us have some more rock candy and rye whisky, without the rock candy, while we discuss the matter further.'

But it seems that The Dutchman does not care for rock candy

and rye whisky, even without the rock candy, so Blondy Swanson and me and Good Time Charley continue taking our doses, and Blondy keeps getting more enthusiastic about The Dutchman's proposition until finally I become enthusiastic myself, and I say I think I will go along as it is an opportunity to see new sections of the country, while Good Time Charley states that it will always be the great regret of his life that his business keeps him from going, but that he will provide us with an ample store of rock candy and rye whisky, without the rock candy, in case we run into any touches of the grippe.

Well, anyway, this is how I come to be riding around in an old can belonging to The Dutchman on a very cold Christmas Eve with The Dutchman and Blondy Swanson, although none of us happen to think of it being Christmas Eve until we notice that there seems to be holly wreaths in windows here and there as we go bouncing along the roads, and finally we pass a little church that is all lit up, and somebody opens the door as we are passing, and we see a big Christmas tree inside the church, and it is a very pleasant sight, indeed, and in fact it makes me a little homesick, although of course the chances are I will not be seeing any Christmas trees even if I am home.

We leave Good Time Charley's along mid-afternoon, with The Dutchman driving this old can of his, and all I seem to remember about the trip is going through a lot of little towns so fast they seem strung together, because most of the time I am dozing in the back seat.

Blondy Swanson is riding in the front seat with The Dutchman and Blondy also cops a little snooze now and then as we are going along, but whenever he happens to wake up he pokes me awake, too, so we can take a dose of rock candy and rye whisky, without the rock candy. So in many respects it is quite an enjoyable journey.

I recollect the little church because we pass it right after we go busting through a pretty fair-sized town, and I hear The Dutchman say the old barn is now only a short distance away, and by this time it is dark, and colder than a deputy sheriff's heart, and there is snow on the ground, although it is clear overhead, and I am wishing I am back in Mindy's restaurant wrapping myself around a nice T-bone steak, when I hear Blondy Swanson ask The Dutchman if he is sure he knows where he is going, as this seems to be an untravelled road, and The Dutchman states as follows:

'Why,' he says, 'I know I am on the right road. I am following the big star you see up ahead of us, because I remember seeing this star always in front of me when I am going along the road before.'

So we keep following the star, but it turns out that it is not a star at all, but a light shining from the window of a ramshackle old frame building pretty well off to one side of the road and on a rise of ground, and when The Dutchman sees this light, he is greatly nonplussed, indeed, and speaks as follows :

'Well,' he says, 'this looks very much like my barn, but my barn does not call for a light in it. Let us investigate this matter before we go any farther.'

So The Dutchman gets out of the old can, and slips up to one side of the building and peeks through the window, and then he comes back and motions for Blondy and me to also take a peek through this window, which is nothing but a square hole cut in the side of the building with wooden bars across it, but no window-panes, and what we behold inside by the dim light of a lantern hung on a nail on a post is really most surprising.

There is no doubt whatever that we are looking at the inside of a very old barn, for there are several stalls for horses, or maybe cows, here and there, but somebody seems to be living in the barn, as we can see a table, and a couple of chairs, and a tin stove, in which there is a little fire, and on the floor in one corner is what seems to be a sort of a bed.

Furthermore, there seems to be somebody lying on the bed and making quite a fuss in the way of groaning and crying and carrying on generally in a loud tone of voice, and there is no doubt that it is the voice of a doll, and anybody can tell that this doll is in some distress.

Well, here is a situation, indeed, and we move away from the barn to talk it over.

The Dutchman is greatly discouraged, because he gets to thinking that if this doll is living in the barn for any length of time, his plant may be discovered. He is willing to go away and wait a while, but Blondy Swanson seems to be doing quite some thinking, and finally Blondy says like this :

'Why,' Blondy says, 'the doll in this barn seems to be sick, and only a bounder and a cad will walk away from a sick doll, especially,' Blondy says, 'a sick doll who is a total stranger to him. In fact, it will take a very large heel to do such a thing. The idea is for us to go inside and see if we can do anything for this sick doll,' Blondy says.

Well, I say to Blondy Swanson that the chances are the doll's ever-loving husband, or somebody, is in town, or maybe over to the nearest neighbours digging up assistance, and will be back in a jiffy, and that this is no place for us to be found.

'No,' Blondy says, 'it cannot be as you state. The snow on the ground is anyway a day old. There are no tracks around the door of this old joint, going or coming, and it is a cinch if anybody knows there is a sick doll here, they will have plenty of time to get help before this. I am going inside and look things over,' Blondy says.

Naturally, The Dutchman and I go too, because we do not wish to be left alone outside, and it is no trouble whatever to get into the barn, as the door is unlocked, and all we have to do is walk in. And when we walk in with Blondy Swanson leading the way, the doll on the bed on the floor half-raises up to look at us, and although the light of the lantern is none too good, anybody can see that this doll is nobody but Miss Clarabelle Cobb, although personally I see some changes in her since she is in Mr. Georgie White's 'Scandals.'

She stays half-raised up on the bed looking at Blondy Swanson for as long as you can count ten, if you count fast, then she falls back and starts crying and carrying on again, and at this The Dutchman kneels down on the floor beside her to find out what is eating her.

All of a sudden The Dutchman jumps up and speaks to us as follows :

'Why,' he says, 'this is quite a delicate situation, to be sure. In fact,' he says, 'I must request you guys to step outside. What we really need for this case is a doctor, but it is too late to send for one. However, I will endeavour to do the best I can under the circumstances.'

Then The Dutchman starts taking off his overcoat, and Blondy Swanson stands looking at him with such a strange expression on his kisser that The Dutchman laughs out loud, and says like this:

'Do not worry about anything, Blondy,' The Dutchman says. 'I am maybe a little out of practice since my old lady put her checks back in the rack, but she leaves eight kids alive and kicking, and I bring them all in except one, because we are seldom able to afford a croaker.'

So Blondy Swanson and I step out of the barn and after a while The Dutchman calls us and we go back into the barn to find he has a big fire going in the stove, and the place nice and warm.

Miss Clarabelle Cobb is now all quieted down, and is covered with The Dutchman's overcoat, and as we come in The Dutchman tiptoes over to her and pulls back the coat and what do we see but a baby with a noggin no bigger than a crab apple and a face as wrinkled as some old pappy guy's, and The Dutchman states that it is a boy, and a very healthy one, at that.

'Furthermore,' The Dutchman says, 'the mamma is doing as well as can be expected. She is as strong a doll as ever I see,' he says, 'and all we have to do now is send out a croaker when we go through town just to make sure there are no complications. But,' The Dutchman says, 'I guarantee the croaker will not have much to do.'

Well, the old Dutchman is as proud of this baby as if it is his own, and I do not wish to hurt his feelings, so I say the baby is a darberoo, and a great credit to him in every respect, and also to Miss Clarabelle Cobb, while Blondy Swanson just stands there looking at it as if he never sees a baby before in his life, and is greatly astonished.

It seems that Miss Clarabelle Cobb is a very strong doll, just as The Dutchman states, and in about an hour she shows signs of being wide awake, and Blondy Swanson sits down on the floor beside her, and she talks to him quite a while in a low voice, and while they are talking The Dutchman pulls up the floor in another corner of the barn, and digs around underneath a few minutes, and finally comes up with a gripsack covered with dirt, and he opens this gripsack and shows me it is filled with lovely, large coarse bank-notes.

Later Blondy Swanson tells The Dutchman and me the story of Miss Clarabelle Cobb, and parts of this story are rather sad. It seems that after Miss Clarabelle Cobb goes back to her old home in Akron, Ohio, she winds up marrying a young guy by the name of Joseph Hatcher, who is a book-keeper by trade, and has a pretty good job in Akron, so Miss Clarabelle Cobb and this Joseph Hatcher are as happy as anything together for quite a spell.

Then about a year before the night I am telling about Joseph Hatcher is sent by his firm to these parts where we find Miss Clarabelle Cobb, to do the book-keeping in a factory there, and one night a few months afterwards, when Joseph Hatcher is staying after hours in the factory office working on his books, a mob of wrong gees breaks into the joint, and sticks him up, and blows open the safe, taking away a large sum of money and leaving Joseph Hatcher tied up like a turkey.

When Joseph Hatcher is discovered in this predicament the next morning, what happens but the gendarmes put the sleeve on him, and place him in the pokey, saying the chances are Joseph Hatcher is in and in with the safe-blowers, and that he tips them off the dough is in the safe, and it seems that the guy who is especially fond of this idea is a guy by the name of Ambersham, who is manager of the factory, and a very hard-hearted guy, at that.

And now, although this is eight or nine months back, there is Joseph Hatcher still in the pokey awaiting trial, and it is seven to five anywhere in town that the judge throws the book at him when he finally goes to bat, because it seems from what Miss Clarabelle Cobb tells Blondy Swanson that nearly everybody figures Joseph Hatcher is guilty.

But of course Miss Clarabelle Cobb does not put in with popular opinion about her ever-loving Joe, and she spends the next few months trying to spring him from the pokey, but she has no potatoes, and no way of getting any potatoes, so things go from bad to worse with Miss Clarabelle Cobb.

Finally, she finds herself with no place to live in town, and she happens to run into this old barn, which is on an abandoned property owned by a doctor in town by the name of Kelton, and it seems that he is a kind-hearted guy, and he gives her permission to use it any way she wishes. So Miss Clarabelle moves into the barn, and the chances are there is many a time when she wishes she is back in Mr. Georgie White's 'Scandals.'

Now The Dutchman listens to this story with great interest, especially the part about Joseph Hatcher being left tied up in the factory office, and finally The Dutchman states as follows:

'Why, my goodness,' The Dutchman says, 'there is no doubt but what this is the very same young guy we are compelled to truss up the night we get this gripsack. As I recollect it, he wishes to battle for his employer's dough, and I personally tap him over the coco with a blackjack.

'But,' he says, 'he is by no means the guy who tips us off about the dough being there. As I remember it now, it is nobody but the guy whose name you mention in Miss Clarabelle Cobb's story. It is this guy Ambersham, the manager of the joint, and come to think of it, he is supposed to get his bit of this dough for his trouble, and it is only fair that I carry out this agreement as the executor of the estate of my late comrades, although,' The Dutchman says, 'I do not approve of his conduct towards this Joseph Hatcher. But,' he says, 'the first thing for us to do is to get a doctor out here to Miss Clarabelle Cobb, and I judge the doctor for us to get is this Doc Kelton she speaks of.'

So The Dutchman takes the gripsack and we get into the old can and head back the way we come, although before we go I see Blondy Swanson bend down over Miss Clarabelle Cobb, and while I do not wish this to go any farther, I will take a paralysed oath I see him plant a small kiss on the baby's noggin, and I hear Miss Clarabelle Cobb speak as follows:

'I will name him for you, Blondy,' she says. 'By the way, Blondy, what is your right name?'

'Olaf,' Blondy says.

It is now along in the early morning and not many citizens are stirring as we go through town again, with Blondy in the front seat again holding the gripsack on his lap so The Dutchman can drive, but finally we find a guy in an all-night lunch counter who knows where Doc Kelton lives, and this guy stands on the running-board of the old can and guides us to a house in a side street, and after pounding on the door quite a spell, we roust the Doc out and Blondy goes inside to talk with him.

He is in there quite a spell, but when he comes out he says everything is okay, and that Doc Kelton will go at once to look after Miss Clarabelle Cobb, and take her to a hospital, and Blondy states that he leaves a couple of C's with the Doc to make sure Miss Clarabelle Cobb gets the best of care.

'Well,' The Dutchman says, 'we can afford a couple of C's out of what we have in this gripsack, but,' he says, 'I am still wondering if it is not my duty to look up this Ambersham, and give him his bit.'

'Dutchman,' Blondy says, 'I fear I have some bad news for you. The gripsack is gone. This Doc Kelton strikes me as a right guy in every respect, especially,' Blondy says, 'as he states to me that he always half-suspects there is a wrong rap in on Miss Clarabelle Cobb's ever-loving Joe, and that if it is not for this guy Ambersham agitating all the time other citizens may suspect the same thing, and it will not be so tough for Joe.

'So,' Blondy says, 'I tell Doc Kelton the whole story, about Ambersham and all, and I take the liberty of leaving the gripsack with him to be returned to the rightful owners, and Doc Kelton says if he does not have Miss Clarabelle Cobb's Joe out of the sneezer, and this Ambersham on the run out of town in twenty-four hours, I can call him a liar. But,' Blondy says, 'let us now proceed on our way, because I only have Doc Kelton's word that he will give us twelve hours' leeway before he does anything except attend to Miss Clarabelle Cobb, as I figure you need this much time to get out of sight, Dutchman.'

Well, The Dutchman does not say anything about all this news for a while, and seems to be thinking the situation over, and while he is thinking he is giving his old can a little more gas than he intends, and she is fairly popping along what seems to be the main drag of the town when a gendarme on a motor-cycle comes up alongside us, and motions The Dutchman to pull over to the kerb.

He is a nice-looking young gendarme, but he seems somewhat hostile as he gets off his motor-cycle, and walks up to us very slow, and asks us where the fire is.

Naturally, we do not say anything in reply, which is the only thing to say to a gendarme under these circumstances, so he speaks as follows:

'What are you guys carrying in this old skillet, anyway?' he says. 'Stand up, and let me look you guys over.'

And then as we stand up, he peeks into the front and back of the car, and under our feet, and all he finds is a bottle which once holds some of Good Time Charley's rock candy and rye whisky without the rock candy, but which is now very empty, and he holds this bottle up, and sniffs at the nozzle, and asks what is formerly in this bottle, and I tell him the truth when I tell him it is once full of medicine, and The Dutchman and Blondy Swanson nod their heads in support of my statement. But the gendarme takes another sniff, and then he says like this:

'Oh,' he says, very sarcastic, 'wise guys, eh? Three wise guys, eh? Trying to kid somebody, eh? Medicine, eh?' he says. 'Well, if it is not Christmas Day I will take you in and hold you just on suspicion. But I will be Santa Claus to you, and let you go ahead, wise guys.'

And then after we get a few blocks away, The Dutchman speaks as follows:

'Yes,' he says, 'that is what we are, to be sure. We are wise guys. If we are not wise guys, we will still have the gripsack in this car for the copper to find. And if the copper finds the gripsack, he will wish to take us to the jail house for investigation, and if he wishes to take us there I fear he will not be alive at this time, and we will be in plenty of heat around and about, and personally,' The Dutchman says, 'I am sick and tired of heat.'

And with this The Dutchman puts a large Betsy back in a holster under his left arm, and turns on the gas, and as the old can begins leaving the lights of the town behind, I ask Blondy if he happens to notice the name of this town.

'Yes,' Blondy says, 'I notice it on a signboard we just pass. It is Bethlehem, Pa.'

A Very Honourable Guy

Off and on I know Feet Samuels a matter of eight or ten years, up and down Broadway, and in and out, but I never have much truck with him because he is a guy I consider no dice. In fact, he does not mean a thing.

In the first place, Feet Samuels is generally broke, and there is no percentage in hanging around brokers. The way I look at it, you are not going to get anything off a guy who has not got anything. So while I am very sorry for brokers, and am always willing to hope that they get hold of something, I do not like to be around them. Long ago an old-timer who knows what he is talking about says to me:

'My boy,' he says, 'always try to rub up against money, for if you rub up against money long enough, some of it may rub off on you.'

So in all the years I am around this town, I always try to keep in with the high shots and guys who carry these large coarse banknotes around with them, and I stay away from small operators and chisellers and brokers. And Feet Samuels is one of the worst brokers in this town, and has been such as long as I know him.

He is a big heavy guy with several chins and very funny feet, which is why he is called Feet. These feet are extra large feet, even for a big guy, and Dave the Dude says Feet wears violin-cases for shoes. Of course this is not true, because Feet cannot get either of his feet in a violin-case, unless it is a case for a very large violin, such as a 'cello.

I see Feet one night in the Hot Box, which is a night club, dancing with a doll by the name of Hortense Hathaway, who is in Georgie White's 'Scandals,' and what is she doing but standing on Feet's feet as if she is on sled runners, and Feet never knows it. He only thinks the old gondolas are a little extra heavy to shove around this night, because Hortense is no invalid. In fact, she is a good rangy welterweight.

She has blonde hair and plenty to say, and her square monicker is Annie O'Brien, and not Hortense Hathaway at all. Furthermore, she comes from Newark, which is in New Jersey, and her papa is a taxi jockey by the name of Skush O'Brien, and a very rough guy, at that, if anybody asks you. But of course the daughter of a taxi jockey is as good as anybody else for Georgie White's 'Scandals' as long as her shape is okay, and nobody ever hears any complaint from the customers about Hortense on this proposition.

She is what is called a show girl, and all she has to do is to walk around and about Georgie White's stage with only a few light bandages on, and everybody considers her very beautiful, especially from the neck down, although personally I never care much for Hortense because she is very fresh to people. I often see her around the night clubs, and when she is in these deadfalls Hortense generally is wearing quite a number of diamond bracelets and fur wraps, and one thing and another, so I judge she is not doing bad for a doll from Newark, New Jersey.

Of course Feet Samuels never knows why so many other dolls besides Hortense are wishing to dance with him, but gets to thinking maybe it is because he has the old sex appeal, and he is very sore indeed when Henri, the head waiter at the Hot Box, asks him to please stay off the floor except for every tenth dance, because Feet's feet take up so much room when he is on the floor that only two other dancers can work out at the same time, it being a very small floor.

I must tell you more about Feet's feet, because they are very remarkable feet indeed. They go off at different directions under him, very sharp, so if you see Feet standing on a corner it is very difficult to tell which way he is going, because one foot will be headed one way, and the other foot the other way. In fact, guys around Mindy's restaurant often make bets on the proposition as to which way Feet is headed when he is standing still.

What Feet Samuels does for a living is the best he can, which is the same thing many other guys in this town do for a living. He hustles some around the race tracks and crap games and prize fights, picking up a few bobs here and there as a runner for the bookmakers, or scalping bets, or steering suckers, but he is never really in the money in his whole life. He is always owing and always paying off, and I never see him but what he is troubled with the shorts as regards to dough.

The only good thing you can say about Feet Samuels is he is very honourable about his debts, and what he owes he pays when he can. Anybody will tell you this about Feet Samuels, although of course it is only what any hustler such as Feet must do if he wishes to protect his credit and keep in action. Still, you will be surprised how many guys forget to pay.

It is because Feet's word is considered good at all times that he is nearly always able to raise a little dough, even off The Brain, and The Brain is not an easy guy for anybody to raise dough off of. In fact, The Brain is very tough about letting people raise dough off of him.

If anybody gets any dough off of The Brain he wishes to know right away what time they are going to pay it back, with certain interest, and if they say at five-thirty Tuesday morning, they better not make it five-thirty-one Tuesday morning, or The Brain will consider them very unreliable and never let them have any money again. And when a guy loses his credit with The Brain he is in a very tough spot indeed in this town, for The Brain is the only man who always has dough.

Furthermore, some very unusual things often happen to guys who get money off of The Brain and fail to kick it back just when they promise, such as broken noses and sprained ankles and other injuries, for The Brain has people around him who seem to resent guys getting dough off of him and not kicking it back. Still, I know of The Brain letting some very surprising guys have dough, because he has a bug that he is a wonderful judge of guys' characters, and that he is never wrong on them, although I must say that no guy who gets dough off of The Brain is more surprising than Feet Samuels.

The Brain's right name is Armand Rosenthal, and he is called The Brain because he is so smart. He is well known to one and all in this town as a very large operator in gambling, and one thing and another, and nobody knows how much dough The Brain has, except that he must have plenty, because no matter how much dough is around, The Brain sooner or later gets hold of all of it. Some day I will tell you more about The Brain, but right now I wish to tell you about Feet Samuels.

It comes on a tough winter in New York, what with nearly all hands who have the price going to Miami and Havana and New Orleans, leaving the brokers behind. There is very little action of any kind in town with the high shots gone, and one night I run into Feet Samuels in Mindy's, and he is very sad indeed. He asks me if I happen to have a finnif on me, but of course I am not giving finnifs to guys like Feet Samuels, and finally he offers to compromise with me for a deuce, so I can see things must be very bad with Feet for him to come down from five dollars to two.

'My rent is away overdue for the shovel and broom,' Feet says, 'and I have a hard-hearted landlady who will not listen to reason. She says she will give me the wind if I do not lay something on the line at once. Things are never so bad with me,' Feet says, 'and I am thinking of doing something very desperate.'

I cannot think of anything very desperate for Feet Samuels to do, except maybe go to work, and I know he is not going to do such a thing no matter what happens. In fact, in all the years I am around Broadway I never know any broker to get desperate enough to go to work.

I once hear Dave the Dude offer Feet Samuels a job riding rum between here and Philly at good wages, but Feet turns it down because he claims he cannot stand the open air, and anyway Feet says he hears riding rum is illegal and may land a guy in the pokey. So I know whatever Feet is going to do will be nothing difficult.

'The Brain is still in town,' I say to Feet. 'Why do you not put the lug on him? You stand okay with him.'

'There is the big trouble,' Feet says. 'I owe The Brain a C note already, and I am supposed to pay him back by four o'clock Monday morning, and where I am going to get a hundred dollars I do not know, to say nothing of the other ten I must give him for interest.'

'What are you figuring on doing?' I ask, for it is now a Thursday, and I can see Feet has very little time to get together such a sum.

'I am figuring on scragging myself,' Feet says, very sad. 'What good am I to anybody? I have no family and no friends, and the world is packing enough weight without me. Yes, I think I will scrag myself.'

'It is against the law to commit suicide in this man's town,' I say, 'although what the law can do to a guy who commits suicide I am never able to figure out.'

'I do not care,' Feet says. 'I am sick and tired of it all. I am especially sick and tired of being broke. I never have more than a few quarters to rub together in my pants pocket. Everything I try turns out wrong. The only thing that keeps me from scragging myself at once is the C note I owe The Brain, because I do not wish to have him going around after I am dead and gone saying I am no good. And the toughest thing of all,' Feet says, 'is I am in love. I am in love with Hortense.'

'Hortense?' I say, very much astonished indeed. 'Why, Hortense is nothing but a big—'

'Stop!' Feet says. 'Stop right here! I will not have her called a big boloney or whatever else big you are going to call her, because I love her. I cannot live without her. In fact,' Feet says, 'I do not wish to live without her.'

'Well,' I say, 'what does Hortense think about you loving her?'

'She does not know it,' Feet says. 'I am ashamed to tell her, because naturally if I tell her I love her, Hortense will expect me to buy her some diamond bracelets, and naturally I cannot do this. But I think she likes me more than somewhat, because she looks at me in a certain way. But,' Feet says, 'there is some other guy who likes her also, and who is buying her diamond bracelets and what goes with them, which makes it very tough on me. I do not know who the guy is, and I do not think Hortense cares for him so much, but naturally any doll must give serious consideration to a guy who can buy her diamond bracelets. So I guess there is nothing for me to do but scrag myself.'

Naturally I do not take Feet Samuels serious, and I forget about his troubles at once, because I figure he will wiggle out some way, but the next night he comes into Mindy's all pleasured up, and I figure he must make a scratch somewhere, for he is walking like a man with about sixty-five dollars on him.

But it seems Feet only has an idea, and very few ideas are worth sixty-five dollars.

'I am laying in bed thinking this afternoon,' Feet says, 'and I get to thinking how I can raise enough dough to pay off The Brain, and maybe a few other guys, and my landlady, and leave a few bobs over to help bury me. I am going to sell my body.'

Well, naturally I am somewhat bewildered by this statement, so I ask Feet to explain, and here is his idea: He is going to find some doctor who wishes a dead body and sell his body to this doctor for as much as he can get, his body to be delivered after Feet scrags himself, which is to be within a certain time.

'I understand,' Feet says, 'that these croakers are always looking for bodies to practise on, and that good bodies are not easy to get nowadays.'

'How much do you figure your body is worth?' I ask.

'Well,' Feet says, 'a body as big as mine ought to be worth at least a G.'

'Feet,' I say, 'this all sounds most gruesome to me. Personally I do not know much about such a proposition, but I do not believe if doctors buy bodies at all that they buy them by the pound. And I do not believe you can get a thousand dollars for your body, especially while you are still alive, because how does a doctor know if you will deliver your body to him?'

'Why,' Feet says, very indignant, 'everybody knows I pay what I owe. I can give The Brain for reference, and he will okay me with anybody for keeping my word.'

Well, it seems to me that there is very little sense to what Feet Samuels is talking about, and anyway I figure that maybe he blows his topper, which is what often happens to brokers, so I pay no more attention to him. But on Monday morning, just before four o'clock, I am in Mindy's, and what happens but in walks Feet with a handful of money, looking much pleased.

The Brain is also there at the table where he always sits facing the door so nobody can pop in on him without him seeing them first, because there are many people in this town that The Brain likes to see first if they are coming in where he is. Feet steps up to the table and lays a C note in front of the Brain and also a sawbuck, and The Brain looks up at the clock and smiles and says:

'Okay, Feet, you are on time.'

It is very unusual for The Brain to smile about anything, but afterwards I hear he wins two C's off of Manny Mandelbaum, who bets him Feet will not pay off on time, so The Brain has a smile coming.

'By the way, Feet,' The Brain says, 'some doctor calls me up to-day and asks me if your word is good, and you may be glad to know I tell him you are one hundred per cent. I put the okay on you because I know you never fail to deliver on a promise. Are you sick, or something?'

'No,' Feet says, 'I am not sick. I just have a little business deal on with the guy. Thanks for the okay.'

Then he comes over to the table where I am sitting, and I can see he still has money left in his duke. Naturally I am anxious to know where he makes the scratch, and by and by he tells me.

'I put over the proposition I am telling you about,' Feet says. 'I sell my body to a doctor over on Park Avenue by the name of Bodeeker, but I do not get a G for it as I expect. It seems bodies are not worth much right now because there are so many on the market, but Doc Bodeeker gives me four C's on thirty days' delivery.

'I never know it is so much trouble selling a body before,' Feet says. 'Three doctors call the cops on me when I proposition them, thinking I am daffy, but Doc Bodeeker is a nice old guy and is glad to do business with me, especially when I give The Brain as reference. Doc Bodeeker says he is looking for a head shaped just like mine for years, because it seems he is a shark on heads. But,' Feet says, 'I got to figure out some way of scragging myself besides jumping out a window, like I plan, because Doc Bodeeker does not wish my head mussed up.'

'Well,' I say, 'this is certainly most ghastly to me and does not sound legitimate. Does The Brain know you sell your body?'

'No,' Feet says, 'Doc Bodeeker only asks him over the phone if my word is good, and does not tell him why he wishes to know, but he is satisfied with The Brain's okay. Now I am going to pay my landlady, and take up a few other markers here and there, and feed myself up good until it is time to leave this bad old world behind.'

But it seems Feet Samuels does not go to pay his landlady right away. Where he goes is to Johnny Crackow's crap game downtown, which is a crap game with a $500 limit where the high shots seldom go, but where there is always some action for a small operator. And as Feet walks into the joint it seems that Big Nig is trying to make four with the dice, and everybody knows that four is a hard point for Big Nig, or anybody else, to make.

So Feet Samuels looks on a while watching Big Nig trying to make four, and a guy by the name of Whitey offers to take two to one for a C note that Big Nig makes this four, which is certainly more confidence than I will ever have in Big Nig. Naturally Feet hauls out a couple of his C notes at once, as anybody must do who has a couple of C notes, and bets Whitey two hundred to a hundred that Big Nig does not make the four. And right away Big Nig outs with a seven, so Feet wins the bet.

Well, to make a long story short, Feet stands there for some time betting guys that other guys will not make four, or whatever it is they are trying to make with the dice, and the first thing anybody knows Feet Samuels is six G's winner, and has the crap game all crippled up. I see him the next night up in the Hot Box, and this big first baseman, Hortense, is with him, sliding around on Feet's feet, and a blind man can see that she has on at least three more diamond bracelets than ever before.

A night or two later I hear of Feet beating Long George Mc-Cormack, a high shot from Los Angeles, out of eighteen G's playing a card game that is called low ball, and Feet Samuels has no more licence to beat a guy like Long George playing low ball than I have to lick Jack Dempsey. But when a guy finally gets his rushes in gambling nothing can stop him for a while; and this is the way it is with Feet. Every night you hear of him winning plenty of dough at this or that.

He comes into Mindy's one morning, and naturally I move over to his table at once, because Feet is now in the money and is a guy anybody can associate with freely. I am just about to ask him how things are going with him, although I know they are going pretty good, when in pops a fierce-looking old guy with his face all covered with grey whiskers that stick out every which way, and whose eyes peek out of these whiskers very wild indeed. Feet turns pale as he sees the guy, but nods at him, and the guy nods back and goes out.

'Who is the Whiskers?' I ask Feet. 'He is in here the other morning looking around, and he makes people very nervous because nobody can figure who he is or what his dodge may be.'

'It is old Doc Bodeeker,' Feet says. 'He is around checking up on me to make sure I am still in town. Say, I am in a very hot spot one way and another.'

'What are you worrying about?' I ask. 'You got plenty of dough and about two weeks left to enjoy yourself before this Doc Bodeeker forecloses on you.'

'I know,' Feet says, very sad. 'But now I get this dough things do not look as tough to me as formerly, and I am very sorry I make the deal with the doctor. Especially,' Feet says, 'on account of Hortense.'

'What about Hortense?' I ask.

'I think she is commencing to love me since I am able to buy her more diamond bracelets than the other guy,' Feet says. 'If it is not for this thing hanging over me, I will ask her to marry me, and maybe she will do it, at that.'

'Well, then,' I say, 'why do you not go to old Whiskers and pay him his dough back, and tell him you change your mind about selling your body, although of course if it is not for Whiskers's buying your body you will not have all this dough.'

'I do go to him,' Feet says, and I can see there are big tears in his eyes. 'But he says he will not cancel the deal. He says he will not take the money back; what he wants is my body, because I have such a funny-shaped head. I offer him four times what he pays me, but he will not take it. He says my body must be delivered to him promptly on March first.'

'Does Hortense know about this deal?' I ask.

'Oh, no, no!' Feet says. 'And I will never tell her, because she will think I am crazy, and Hortense does not care for crazy guys. In fact, she is always complaining about the other guy who buys her the diamond bracelets, claiming he is a little crazy, and if she thinks I am the same way the chances are she will give me the breeze.'

Now this is a situation, indeed, but what to do about it I do not know. I put the proposition up to a lawyer friend of mine the next day, and he says he does not believe the deal will hold good in court, but of course I know Feet Samuels does not wish to go to court, because the last time Feet goes to court he is held as a material witness and is in the Tombs ten days.

The lawyer says Feet can run away, but personally I consider this a very dishonourable idea after The Brain putting the okay on Feet with old Doc Bodeeker, and anyway I can see Feet is not going to do such a thing as long as Hortense is around. I can see that one hair of her head is stronger than the Atlantic cable with Feet Samuels.

A week slides by, and I do not see so much of Feet, but I hear of him murdering crap games and short card players, and winning plenty, and also going around the night clubs with Hortense, who finally has so many bracelets there is no more room on her arms, and she puts a few of them on her ankles, which are not bad ankles to look at, at that, with or without bracelets.

Then goes another week, and it just happens I am standing in front of Mindy's about four-thirty one morning and thinking that

Feet's time must be up and wondering how he makes out with old Doc Bodeeker, when all of a sudden I hear a ploppity-plop coming up Broadway, and what do I see but Feet Samuels running so fast he is passing taxis that are going thirty-five miles an hour like they are standing still. He is certainly stepping along.

There are no traffic lights and not much traffic at such an hour in the morning, and Feet passes me in a terrible hurry. And about twenty yards behind him comes an old guy with grey whiskers, and I can see it is nobody but Doc Bodeeker. What is more, he has a big long knife in one hand, and he seems to be reaching for Feet at every jump with the knife.

Well, this seems to me a most surprising spectacle, and I follow them to see what comes of it, because I can see at once that Doc Bodeeker is trying to collect Feet's body himself. But I am not much of a runner, and they are out of my sight in no time, and only that I am able to follow them by ear through Feet's feet going ploppity-plop I will never trail them.

They turn east into Fifty-fourth Street off Broadway, and when I finally reach the corner I see a crowd halfway down the block in front of the Hot Box, and I know this crowd has something to do with Feet and Doc Bodeeker even before I get to the door to find that Feet goes on in while Doc Bodeeker is arguing with Soldier Sweeney, the door man, because as Feet passes the Soldier he tells the Soldier not to let the guy who is chasing him in. And the Soldier, being a good friend of Feet's, is standing the doc off.

Well, it seems that Hortense is in the Hot Box waiting for Feet, and naturally she is much surprised to see him come in all out of breath, and so is everybody else in the joint, including Henri, the head waiter, who afterwards tells me what comes off there, because you see I am out in front.

'A crazy man is chasing me with a butcher knife,' Feet says to Hortense. 'If he gets inside I am a goner. He is down at the door trying to get in.'

Now I will say one thing for Hortense, and this is she has plenty of nerve, but of course you will expect a daughter of Skush O'Brien to have plenty of nerve. Nobody ever has more moxie than Skush. Henri, the head waiter, tells me that Hortense does not get excited, but says she will just have a little peek at the guy who is chasing Feet.

The Hot Box is over a garage, and the kitchen windows look down into Fifty-fourth Street, and while Doc Bodeeker is arguing with Soldier Sweeney, I hear a window lift, and who looks out but Hortense. She takes one squint and yanks her head in quick, and Henri tells me afterwards she shrieks:

'My Lord, Feet! This is the same daffy old guy who sends me all the bracelets, and who wishes to marry me!'

'And he is the guy I sell my body to,' Feet says, and then he tells Hortense the story of his deal with Doc Bodeeker.

'It is all for you, Horty,' Feet says, although of course this is nothing but a big lie, because it is all for The Brain in the beginning. 'I love you, and I only wish to get a little dough to show you a good time before I die. If it is not for this deal I will ask you to be my ever-loving wife.'

Well, what happens but Hortense plunges right into Feet's arms, and gives him a big kiss on his ugly mush, and says to him like this:

'I love you too, Feet, because nobody ever makes such a sacrifice as to hock their body for me. Never mind the deal. I will marry you at once, only we must first get rid of this daffy old guy downstairs.'

Then Hortense peeks out of the window again and hollers down at old Doc Bodeeker. 'Go away,' she says. 'Go away, or I will chuck a moth in your whiskers, you old fool.'

But the sight of her only seems to make old Doc Bodeeker a little wilder than somewhat, and he starts struggling with Soldier Sweeney very ferocious, so the Soldier takes the knife away from the doc and throws it away before somebody gets hurt with it.

Now it seems Hortense looks around the kitchen for something to chuck out the window at old Doc Bodeeker, and all she sees is a nice new ham which the chef just lays out on the table to slice up for ham sandwiches. This ham is a very large ham, such as will last the Hot Box a month, for they slice the ham in their ham sandwiches very, very thin up at the Hot Box. Anyway, Hortense grabs up the ham and runs to the window with it and gives it a heave without even stopping to take aim.

Well, this ham hits the poor old Doc Bodeeker kerbowie smack dab on the noggin. The doc does not fall down, but he commences staggering around with his legs bending under him like he is drunk.

I wish to help him, because I feel sorry for a guy in such a spot as this, and what is more I consider it a dirty trick for a doll such as Hortense to slug anybody with a ham.

Well, I take charge of the old doc and lead him back down Broadway and into Mindy's, where I set him down and get him a cup of coffee and a Bismarck herring to revive him, while quite a number of citizens gather about him very sympathetic.

'My friends,' the old doc says finally, looking around, 'you see in me a broken-hearted man. I am not a crack-pot, although of course my relatives may give you an argument on this proposition. I am in love with Hortense. I am in love with her from the night I first see her playing the part of a sunflower in "Scandals." I wish to marry her, as I am a widower of long standing, but somehow the idea of me marrying anybody never appeals to my sons and daughters.

'In fact,' the doc says, dropping his voice to a whisper, 'sometimes they even talk of locking me up when I wish to marry somebody. So naturally I never tell them about Hortense, because I fear they may try to discourage me. But I am deeply in love with her and send her many beautiful presents, although I am not able to see her often on account of my relatives. Then I find out Hortense is carrying on with this Feet Samuels.

'I am desperately jealous,' the doc says, 'but I do not know what to do. Finally Fate sends this Feet to me offering to sell his body. Of course, I am not practising for years, but I keep an office on Park Avenue just for old times' sake, and it is to this office he comes. At first I think he is crazy, but he refers me to Mr. Armand Rosenthal, the big sporting man, who assures me that Feet Samuels is all right.

'The idea strikes me that if I make a deal with Feet Samuels for his body as he proposes, he will wait until the time comes to pay his obligation and run away, and,' the doc says, 'I will never be troubled by his rivalry for the affections of Hortense again. But he does not depart. I do not reckon on the holding power of love.

'Finally in a jealous frenzy I take after him with a knife, figuring to scare him out of town. But it is too late. I can see now Hortense loves him in return, or she will not drop a scuttle of coal on me in his defence as she does.

'Yes, gentlemen,' the old doc says, 'I am broken-hearted. I also seem to have a large lump on my head. Besides, Hortense has all my presents, and Feet Samuels has my money, so I get the worst of it all around. I only hope and trust that my daughter Eloise, who is Mrs. Sidney Simmons Bragdon, does not hear of this, or she may be as mad as she is the time I wish to marry the beautiful cigarette girl in Jimmy Kelley's.'

Here Doc Bodeeker seems all busted up by his feelings and starts to shed tears, and everybody is feeling very sorry for him indeed, when up steps The Brain, who is taking everything in.

'Do not worry about your presents and your dough,' The Brain says. 'I will make everything good, because I am the guy who okays Feet Samuels with you. I am wrong on a guy for the first time in my life, and I must pay, but Feet Samuels will be very, very sorry when I find him. Of course, I do not figure on a doll in the case, and this always makes quite a difference, so I am really not a hundred per cent. wrong on the guy, at that.

'But,' The Brain says, in a very loud voice so everybody can hear, 'Feet Samuels is nothing but a dirty welsher for not turning in his body to you as per agreement, and as long as he lives he will never get another dollar or another okay off of me, or anybody I know. His credit is ruined for ever on Broadway.'

But I judge that Feet and Hortense do not care. The last time I hear of them they are away over in New Jersey where not even The Brain's guys dast to bother them on account of Skush O'Brien, and I understand they are raising chickens and children right and left, and that all of Hortense's bracelets are now in Newark municipal bonds, which I am told are not bad bonds, at that.

Princess O'Hara

Now of course Princess O'Hara is by no means a regular princess, and in fact she is nothing but a little red-headed doll, with plenty of freckles, from over in Tenth Avenue, and her right name is Maggie, and the only reason she is called Princess O'Hara is as follows:

She is the daughter of King O'Hara, who is hacking along Broadway with one of these old-time victorias for a matter of maybe twenty-five years, and every time King O'Hara gets his pots on, which is practically every night, rain or shine, he is always bragging that he has the royal blood of Ireland in his veins, so somebody starts calling him King, and this is his monicker as long as I can remember, although probably what King O'Hara really has in his veins is about ninety-eight per cent. alcohol.

Well, anyway, one night about seven or eight years back, King O'Hara shows up on his stand in front of Mindy's restaurant on Broadway with a spindly-legged, little doll about ten years of age on the seat beside him, and he says that this little doll is nobody but his daughter, and he is taking care of her because his old lady is not feeling so good, and right away Last Card Louie, the gambler, reaches up and dukes the little doll and says to her like this:

'If you are the daughter of the King, you must be the princess,' Last Card Louie says. 'How are you, Princess?'

So from this time on, she is Princess O'Hara, and afterwards for several years she often rides around in the early evening with the King, and sometimes when the King has his pots on more than somewhat, she personally drives Goldberg, which is the King's horse, although Goldberg does not really need much driving as he knows his way along Broadway better than anybody. In fact, this Goldberg is a most sagacious old pelter, indeed, and he is called Goldberg by the King in honour of a Jewish friend by the name of Goldberg, who keeps a delicatessen store in Tenth Avenue.

At this time, Princess O'Hara is as homely as a mud fence, and maybe homelier, what with the freckles, and the skinny gambs, and a few buck teeth, and she does not weigh more than sixty pounds, sopping wet, and her red hair is down her back in pigtails, and she giggles if anybody speaks to her, so finally nobody speaks to her much, but old King O'Hara seems to think well of her, at that.

Then by and by she does not seem to be around with the King any more, and when somebody happens to ask about her, the King says his old lady claims the Princess is getting too grown-up to be shagging around Broadway, and that she is now going to public school. So after not seeing her for some years, everybody forgets that King O'Hara has a daughter, and in fact nobody cares a cuss.

Now King O'Hara is a little shrivelled-up old guy with a very red beezer, and he is a most familiar spectacle to one and all on Broadway as he drives about with a stove-pipe hat tipped so far over to one side of his noggin that it looks as if it is always about to fall off, and in fact the King himself is always tipped so far over to one side that it seems to be a sure thing that he is going to fall off.

The way the King keeps himself on the seat of his victoria is really most surprising, and one time Last Card Louie wins a nice bet off a gambler from St. Louis by the name of Olive Street Oscar, who takes eight to five off of Louie that the King cannot drive them through Central Park without doing a Brodie off the seat. But of course Louie is betting with the best of it, which is the way he always dearly loves to bet, because he often rides through Central Park with King O'Hara, and he knows the King never falls off, no matter how far over he tips.

Personally, I never ride with the King very much, as his victoria is so old I am always afraid the bottom will fall out from under me, and that I will run myself to death trying to keep up, because the King is generally so busy singing Irish come-all-yeez up on his seat that he is not apt to pay much attention to what his passengers are doing.

There are quite a number of these old victorias left in this town, a victoria being a low-neck, four-wheeled carriage with seats for four or five people, and they are very popular in the summer-time with guys and dolls who wish to ride around and about in Central Park taking the air, and especially with guys and dolls who may wish to do a little off-hand guzzling while taking the air.

Personally, I consider a taxicab much more convenient and less expensive than an old-fashioned victoria if you wish to get to some place, but of course guys and dolls engaged in a little off-hand guzzling never wish to get any place in particular, or at least not soon. So these victorias, which generally stand around the entrances to the Park, do a fair business in the summer-time, because it seems that no matter what conditions are, there are always guys and dolls who wish to do a little off-hand guzzling.

But King O'Hara stands in front of Mindy's because he has many regular customers among the citizens of Broadway, who do not go in for guzzling so very much, unless a case of guzzling comes up, but who love to ride around in the Park on hot nights just to cool themselves out, although at the time I am now speaking of, things are so tough with one and all along Broadway that King O'Hara has to depend more on strangers for his trade.

Well, what happens one night, but King O'Hara is seen approaching Mindy's, tipping so far over to one side of his seat that Olive Street Oscar, looking to catch even on the bet he loses before, is offering to take six to five off of Last Card Louie that this time the King goes plumb off, and Louie is about to give it to him, when the old King tumbles smack-dab into the street, as dead as last

Tuesday, which shows you how lucky Last Card Louie is, because nobody ever figures such a thing to happen to the King, and even Goldberg, the horse, stops and stands looking at him very much surprised, with one hind hoof in the King's stovepipe hat. The doctors state that King O'Hara's heart just naturally hauls off and quits working on him, and afterwards Regret, the horse player, says the chances are the King probably suddenly remembers refusing a drink somewhere.

A few nights later, many citizens are out in front of Mindy's, and Big Nig, the crap shooter, is saying that things do not look the same around there since King O'Hara puts his checks back in the rack, when all of a sudden up comes a victoria that anybody can see is the King's old rattletrap, especially as it is being pulled by Goldberg.

And who is on the driver's seat, with King O'Hara's bunged-up old stovepipe hat sitting jack-deuce on her noggin, but a red-headed doll of maybe eighteen or nineteen with freckles all over her pan, and while it is years since I see her, I can tell at once that she is nobody but Princess O'Hara, even though it seems she changes quite some.

In fact, she is now about as pretty a little doll as anybody will wish to see, even with the freckles, because the buck teeth seem to have disappeared, and the gambs are now filled out very nicely, and so has the rest of her. Furthermore, she has a couple of blue eyes that are most delightful to behold, and a smile like six bits, and all in all, she is a pleasing scene.

Well, naturally, her appearance in this manner causes some comment, and in fact some citizens are disposed to criticize her as being unladylike, until Big Nig, the crap shooter, goes around among them very quietly stating that he will knock their ears down if he hears any more cracks from them, because it seems that Big Nig learns that when old King O'Hara dies, all he leaves in this world besides his widow and six kids is Goldberg, the horse, and the victoria, and Princess O'Hara is the eldest of these kids, and the only one old enough to work, and she can think of nothing better to do than to take up her papa's business where he leaves off.

After one peek at Princess O'Hara, Regret, the horse player, climbs right into the victoria, and tells her to ride him around the Park a couple of times, although it is well known to one and all that it costs two bobs per hour to ride in anybody's victoria, and the only dough Regret has in a month is a pound note that he just borrows off of Last Card Louie for eating money. But from this time on, the chances are Regret will be Princess O'Hara's best customer if he can borrow any more pound notes, but the competition gets too keen for him, especially from Last Card Louie, who is by this time quite a prominent character along Broadway, and in the money, although personally I always say you can have him, as Last Card Louie is such a guy as will stoop to very sharp practice, and in fact he often does not wait to stoop.

He is called Last Card Louie because in his youth he is a great hand for riding the tubs back and forth between here and Europe and playing stud poker with other passengers, and the way he always gets much strength from the last card is considered quite abnormal, especially if Last Card Louie is dealing. But of course Last Card Louie no longer rides the tubs as this occupation is now very old-fashioned, and anyway Louie has more profitable interests that require his attention, such as a crap game, and one thing and another.

There is no doubt but what Last Card Louie takes quite a fancy to Princess O'Hara, but naturally he cannot spend all his time riding around in a victoria, so other citizens get a chance to patronize her now and then, and in fact I once take a ride with Princess O'Hara myself, and it is a very pleasant experience, indeed, as she likes to sing while she is driving, just as old King O'Hara does in his time.

But what Princess O'Hara sings is not Irish come-all-yeez but Kathleen Mavourneen, and My Wild Irish Rose, and Asthore, and other such ditties, and she has a loud contralto voice, and when she lets it out while driving through Central Park in the early hours of the morning, the birds in the trees wake up and go tweet-tweet, and the coppers on duty for blocks around stand still with smiles on their kissers, and the citizens who live in the apartment houses along Central Park West and Central Park South come to their windows to listen.

Then one night in October, Princess O'Hara does not show up in front of Mindy's, and there is much speculation among one and all about this absence, and some alarm, when Big Nig, the crap shooter, comes around and says that what happens is that old Goldberg, the horse, is down with colic, or some such, so there is Princess O'Hara without a horse.

Well, this news is received with great sadness by one and all, and there is some talk of taking up a collection to buy Princess O'Hara another horse, but nobody goes very far with this idea because things are so tough with everybody, and while Big Nig mentions that maybe Last Card Louie will be glad to do something large in this matter, nobody cares for this idea, either, as many citizens are displeased with the way Last Card Louie is pitching to Princess O'Hara, because it is well known that Last Card Louie is nothing but a wolf when it comes to young dolls, and anyway about now Regret, the horse player, speaks up as follows:

'Why,' Regret says, 'it is great foolishness to talk of wasting money buying a horse, even if we have any money to waste, when the barns up at Empire City are packed at this time with crocodiles of all kinds. Let us send a committee up to the track,' Regret says, 'and borrow a nice horse for Princess O'Hara to use until Goldberg is back on his feet again.'

'But,' I say to Regret, 'suppose nobody wishes to lend us a horse?'

'Why,' Regret says, 'I do not mean to ask anybody to lend us a horse. I mean let us borrow one without asking anybody. Most of these horse owners are so very touchy that if we go around asking them to lend us a horse to pull a hack, they may figure we are insulting their horses, so let us just get the horse and say nothing whatever.'

Well, I state that this sounds to me like stealing, and stealing is something that is by no means upright and honest, and Regret has to admit that it really is similar to stealing, but he says what of it, and as I do not know what of it, I discontinue the argument. Furthermore, Regret says it is clearly understood that we will return any horse we borrow when Goldberg is hale and hearty again, so I can see that after all there is nothing felonious in the idea, or anyway, not much.

But after much discussion, it comes out that nobody along Broadway seems to know anything about stealing a horse. There are citizens who know all about stealing diamond necklaces, or hot stoves, but when it comes to horses, everybody confesses themselves at a loss. It is really amazing the amount of ignorance there is on Broadway about stealing horses.

Then finally Regret has a bright idea. It seems that a rodeo is going on at Madison Square Garden at this time, a rodeo being a sort of wild west show with bucking broncos, and cowboys, and all this and that, and Regret seems to remember reading when he is a young squirt that stealing horses is a very popular pastime out in the wild west.

So one evening Regret goes around to the Garden and gets to talking to a cowboy in leather pants with hair on them, and he asks this cowboy, whose name seems to be Laramie Pink, if there are any expert horse stealers connected with the rodeo. Moreover, Regret explains to Laramie Pink just why he wants a good horse stealer, and Pink becomes greatly interested and wishes to know if the loan of a nice bucking bronco, or a first-class cow pony will be of any assistance, and when Regret says he is afraid not, Laramie Pink says like this:

'Well,' he says, 'of course horse stealing is considered a most antique custom out where I come from, and in fact it is no longer practised in the best circles, but,' he says, 'come to think of it, there is a guy with this outfit by the name of Frying Pan Joe, who is too old to do anything now except mind the cattle, but who is said to be an excellent horse stealer out in Colorado in his day. Maybe Frying Pan Joe will be interested in your proposition,' Laramie Pink says.

So he hunts up Frying Pan Joe, and Frying Pan Joe turns out to be a little old pappy guy with a chin whisker, and a sad expression, and a wide-brimmed cowboy hat, and when they explain to him that they wish him to steal a horse, Frying Pan Joe seems greatly touched, and his eyes fill up with tears, and he speaks as follows:

'Why,' Frying Pan Joe says, 'your idea brings back many memories to me. It is a matter of over twenty-five years since I steal a horse, and the last time I do this it gets me three years in the calabozo. Why,' he says, 'this is really a most unexpected order, and it finds me all out of practice, and with no opportunity to get myself in shape. But,' he says, 'I will put forth my best efforts on this job for ten dollars, as long as I do not personally have to locate the horse I am to steal. I am not acquainted with the ranges hereabouts, and will not know where to go to find a horse.'

So Regret, the horse player, and Big Nig, the crap shooter, and Frying Pan Joe go up to Empire this very same night, and it turns out that stealing a horse is so simple that Regret is sorry he does not make the tenner himself, for all Frying Pan Joe does is to go to the barns where the horses live at Empire, and walk along until he comes to a line of stalls that do not seem to have any watchers around in the shape of stable hands at the moment. Then Frying Pan Joe just steps into a stall and comes out leading a horse, and if anybody sees him, they are bound to figure he has a right to do this, because of course not even Sherlock Holmes is apt to think of anybody stealing a horse around this town.

Well, when Regret gets a good peek at the horse, he sees right away it is not just a horse that Frying Pan Joe steals. It is Gallant Godfrey, one of the greatest handicap horses in this country, and the winner of some of the biggest stakes of the year, and Gallant Godfrey is worth twenty-five G's if he is worth a dime, and when Regret speaks of this, Frying Pan Joe says it is undoubtedly the most valuable single piece of horseflesh he ever steals, although he claims that once when he is stealing horses along the Animas River in Colorado, he steals two hundred horses in one batch that will probably total up more.

They take Gallant Godfrey over to Eleventh Avenue, where Princess O'Hara keeps Goldberg in a little stable that is nothing but a shack, and they leave Gallant Godfrey there alongside old Goldberg, who is groaning and carrying on in a most distressing manner, and then Regret and Big Nig shake hands with Frying Pan Joe and wish him good-bye.

So there is Princess O'Hara with Gallant Godfrey hitched up to her victoria the next night, and the chances are it is a good thing for her that Gallant Godfrey is a nice tame old dromedary, and does not mind pulling a victoria at all, and in fact he seems to enjoy it, although he likes to go along at a gallop instead of a slow trot, such as the old skates that pull these victorias usually employ.

And while Princess O'Hara understands that this is a borrowed horse, and is to be returned when Goldberg is well, nobody tells her just what kind of a horse it is, and when she gets Goldberg's harness on Gallant Godfrey his appearance changes so that not even the official starter is apt to recognize him if they come face to face.

Well, I hear afterwards that there is great consternation around Empire when it comes out that Gallant Godfrey is missing, but they keep it quiet as they figure he just wanders away, and as he is engaged in certain large stakes later on, they do not wish it made public that he is absent from his stall. So they have guys looking for him high and low, but of course nobody thinks to look for a high-class race-horse pulling a victoria.

When Princess O'Hara drives the new horse up in front of Mindy's, many citizens are anxious to take the first ride with her, but before anybody has time to think, who steps up but Ambrose Hammer, the newspaper scribe, who has a foreign-looking young guy with him, and Ambrose states as follows:

'Get in, Georges,' Ambrose says. 'We will take a spin through the Park and wind up at the Casino.'

So away they go, and from this moment begins one of the greatest romances ever heard of on Broadway, for it seems that the foreign-looking young guy that Ambrose Hammer calls Georges takes a wonderful liking to Princess O'Hara right from taw, and the following night I learn from Officer Corbett, the motor-cycle cop who is on duty in Central Park, that they pass him with Ambrose Hammer in the back seat of the victoria, but with Georges riding on the driver's seat with Princess O'Hara.

And moreover, Officer Corbett states that Georges is wearing King O'Hara's old stovepipe hat, while Princess O'Hara is singing Kathleen Mavourneen in her loud contralto in such a way as nobody ever hears her sing before.

In fact, this is the way they are riding along a little later in the week, and when it is coming on four bells in the morning. But this time, Princess O'Hara is driving north on the street that is called Central Park West because it borders the Park on the west, and the reason she is taking this street is because she comes up Broadway through Columbus Circle into Central Park West, figuring to cross over to Fifth Avenue by way of the transverse at Sixty-sixth Street, a transverse being nothing but a roadway cut through the Park from Central Park West to the Avenue.

There are several of these transverses, and why they do not call them roads, or streets, instead of transverses, I do not know, except maybe it is because transverse sounds more fancy. These transverses are really like tunnels without any roofs, especially the one at Sixty-sixth Street, which is maybe a quarter of a mile long and plenty wide enough for automobiles to pass each other going in different directions, but once a car is in the transverse there is no way it can get out except at one end or the other. There is no such thing as turning off to one side anywhere between Central Park West and the Avenue, because the Sixty-sixth Street transverse is a deep cut with high sides, or walls.

Well, just as Princess O'Hara starts to turn Gallant Godfrey into the transverse, with the foreign-looking young guy beside her on the driver's seat, and Ambrose Hammer back in the cushions, and half-asleep, and by no means interested in the conversation that is going on in front of him, a big beer truck comes rolling along Central Park West, going very slow.

And of course there is nothing unusual in the spectacle of a beer truck at this time, as beer is now very legal, but just as this beer truck rolls alongside Princess O'Hara's victoria, a little car with two guys in it pops out of nowhere, and pulls up to the truck, and one of the guys requests the jockey of the beer truck to stop.

Of course Princess O'Hara and her passengers do not know at the time that this is one of the very first cases of histing a truckload of legal beer that comes off in this country, and that they are really seeing history made, although it all comes out later. It also comes out later that one of the parties committing this historical deed is nobody but a guy by the name of Fats O'Rourke, who is considered one of the leading characters over on the west side, and the reason he is histing this truckload of beer is by no means a plot against the brewing industry, but because it is worth several C's, and Fats O'Rourke can use several C's very nicely at the moment.

It comes out that the guy with him is a guy by the name of Joe the Blow Fly, but he is really only a fink in every respect, a fink being such a guy as is extra nothing, and many citizens are somewhat surprised when they learn that Fats O'Rourke is going around with finks.

Well, if the jockey of the beer truck does as he is requested without any shilly-shallying, all that will happen is he will lose his beer. But instead of stopping the truck, the jockey tries to keep right on going, and then all of a sudden Fats O'Rourke becomes very impatient and outs with the old thing, and gives it to the jockey, as follows: Bang, bang.

By the time Fats O'Rourke lets go, The Fly is up on the seat of the truck and grabs the wheel just as the jockey turns it loose and falls back on the seat, and Fats O'Rourke follows The Fly up there, and then Fats O'Rourke seems to see Princess O'Hara and her customers for the first time, and he also realizes that these parties witness what comes off with the jockey, although otherwise Central Park West is quite deserted, and if anybody in the apartment houses along there hears the shots the chances are they figure it must be nothing but an automobile backfiring.

And in fact The Fly has the beer truck backfiring quite some at this moment as Fats O'Rourke sees Princess O'Hara and her customers, and only somebody who happens to observe the flashes from Fats O'Rourke's duke, or who hears the same buzzes that

Princess O'Hara, and the foreign-looking young guy, and Ambrose Hammer hear, can tell that Fats is emptying that old thing at the victoria.

The chances are Fats O'Rourke will not mind anybody witnessing him histing a legal beer truck, and in fact he is apt to welcome their testimony in later years when somebody starts disputing his claim to being the first guy to hist such a truck, but naturally Fats does not wish to have spectators spying on him when he is giving it to somebody, as very often spectators are apt to go around gossiping about these matters, and cause dissension.

So he takes four cracks at Princess O'Hara and her customers, and it is a good thing for them that Fats O'Rourke is never much of a shot. Furthermore, it is a good thing for them that he is now out of ammunition because of course Fats O'Rourke never figures that it is going to take more than a few shots to hist a legal beer truck, and afterwards there is little criticism of Fats' judgment, as everybody realizes that it is a most unprecedented situation.

Well, by now, Princess O'Hara is swinging Gallant Godfrey into the transverse, because she comes to the conclusion that it is no time to be loitering in this neighbourhood, and she is no sooner inside the walls of the transverse than she knows this is the very worst place she can go, as she hears a rumble behind her, and when she peeks back over her shoulder she sees the beer truck coming lickity-split, and what is more, it is coming right at the victoria.

Now Princess O'Hara is no chump, and she can see that the truck is not coming right at the victoria by accident, when there is plenty of room for it to pass, so she figures that the best thing to do is not to let the truck catch up with the victoria if she can help it, and this is very sound reasoning, indeed, because Joe the Blow Fly afterwards says that what Fats O'Rourke requests him to do is to sideswipe the victoria with the truck and squash it against the side of the transverse, Fats O'Rourke's idea being to keep Princess O'Hara and her customers from speaking of the transaction with the jockey of the truck.

Well, Princess O'Hara stands up in her seat, and tells Gallant Godfrey to giddap, and Gallant Godfrey is giddapping very nicely, indeed, when she looks back and sees the truck right at the rear wheel of the victoria, and coming like a bat out of what-is-this. So she grabs up her whip and gives Gallant Godfrey a good smack across the vestibule, and it seems that if there is one thing Gallant Godfrey hates and despises it is a whip. He makes a lunge that pulls the victoria clear of the truck, just as The Fly drives it up alongside the victoria and is bearing over for the squash, with Fats O'Rourke yelling directions at him, and from this lunge, Gallant Godfrey settles down to running.

While this is going on, the foreign-looking young guy is standing up on the driver's seat of the victoria beside Princess O'Hara, whooping and laughing, as he probably figures it is just a nice, friendly little race. But Princess O'Hara is not laughing, and neither is Ambrose Hammer.

Now inside the next hundred yards, Joe the Blow Fly gets the truck up alongside again, and this time it looks as if they are gone goslings when Princess O'Hara gives Gallant Godfrey another smack with the whip, and the chances are Gallant Godfrey comes to the conclusion that Westrope is working on him in a stretch run, as he turns on such a burst of speed that he almost runs right out of his collar and leaves the truck behind by anyway a length and a half.

And it seems that just as Gallant Godfrey turns on, Fats O'Rourke personally reaches over and gives the steering-wheel of the beer truck a good twist, figuring that the squashing is now a cinch, and the next thing anybody knows the truck goes smack-dab into the wall with a loud kuh-boom, and turns over all mussed up, with beer kegs bouncing around very briskly, and some of them popping open and letting the legal beer leak out.

In the meantime, Gallant Godfrey goes tearing out of the transverse into Fifth Avenue and across Fifth Avenue so fast that the wheels of Princess O'Hara's victoria are scarcely touching the ground, and a copper who sees him go past afterwards states that what Gallant Godfrey is really doing is flying, but personally I always consider this an exaggeration.

Anyway, Gallant Godfrey goes two blocks beyond Fifth Avenue before Princess O'Hara can get him to whoa-up, and there is still plenty of run in him, although by this time Princess O'Hara is plumb worn out, and Ambrose Hammer is greatly fatigued, and only the foreign-looking young guy seems to find any enjoyment in the experience, although he is not so jolly when he learns that the coppers take two dead guys out of the truck, along with Joe the Blow Fly, who lives just long enough to relate the story.

Fats O'Rourke is smothered to death under a stack of kegs of legal beer, which many citizens consider a most gruesome finish, indeed, but what kills the jockey of the truck is the bullet in his heart, so the smash-up of the truck does not make any difference to him one way or the other, although of course if he lives, the chances are his employers will take him to task for losing the beer.

I learn most of the details of the race through the transverse from Ambrose Hammer, and I also learn from Ambrose that Princess O'Hara and the foreign-looking young guy are suffering from the worst case of love that Ambrose ever witnesses, and Ambrose Hammer witnesses some tough cases of love in his day. Furthermore, Ambrose says they are not only in love but are planning to get themselves married up as quickly as possible.

'Well,' I say, 'I hope and trust this young guy is all right, because Princess O'Hara deserves the best. In fact,' I say, 'a Prince is not too good for her.'

'Well,' Ambrose says, 'a Prince is exactly what she is getting. I do not suppose you can borrow much on it in a hock shop in these times, but the title of Prince Georges Latour is highly respected over in France, although,' he says, 'I understand the proud old family does not have as many potatoes as formerly. But he is a nice young guy, at that, and anyway, what is money compared to love?'

Naturally, I do not know the answer to this, and neither does Ambrose Hammer, but the very same day I run into Princess O'Hara and the foreign-looking young guy on Broadway, and I can see the old love light shining so brightly in their eyes that I get to thinking that maybe money does not mean so much alongside of love, at that, although personally, I will take a chance on the money.

I stop and say hello to Princess O'Hara, and ask her how things are going with her, and she says they are going first class.

'In fact,' she says, 'it is a beautiful world in every respect. Georges and I are going to be married in a few days now, and are going to Paris, France, to live. At first I fear we will have a long wait, because of course I cannot leave my mamma and the rest of the children unprovided for. But,' Princess O'Hara says, 'what happens but Regret sells my horse to Last Card Louie for a thousand dollars, so everything is all right.

'Of course,' Princess O'Hara says, 'buying my horse is nothing but an act of great kindness on the part of Last Card Louie as my horse is by no means worth a thousand dollars, but I suppose Louie does it out of his old friendship for my papa. I must confess,' she says, 'that I have a wrong impression of Louie, because the last time I see him I slap his face thinking he is trying to get fresh with me. Now I realize it is probably only his paternal interest in me, and I am very sorry.'

Well, I know Last Card Louie is such a guy as will give you a glass of milk for a nice cow, and I am greatly alarmed by Princess O'Hara's statement about the sale, for I figure Regret must sell Gallant Godfrey, not remembering that he is only a borrowed horse and must be returned in good order, so I look Regret up at once and mention my fears, but he laughs and speaks to me as follows:

'Do not worry,' he says. 'What happens is that Last Card Louie comes around last night and hands me a G note and says to me like this: "Buy Princess O'Hara's horse off of her for me, and you can keep all under this G that you get it for."

'Well,' Regret says, 'of course I know that old Last Card is thinking of Gallant Godfrey, and forgets that the only horse that Princess O'Hara really owns is Goldberg, and the reason he is thinking of Gallant Godfrey is because he learns last night about us borrowing the horse for her. But as long as Last Card Louie refers just to her horse, and does not mention any names, I do not see that it is up to me to go into any details with him. So I get him a bill of sale for Princess O'Hara's horse, and I am waiting ever since to hear what he says when he goes to collect the horse and finds it is nothing but old Goldberg.'

'Well,' I say to Regret, 'it all sounds most confusing to me, because what good is Gallant Godfrey to Last Card Louie when he is only a borrowed horse, and is apt to be recognized anywhere except when he is hitched to a victoria? And I am sure Last Card Louie is not going into the victoria business.'

'Oh,' Regret says, 'this is easy. Last Card Louie undoubtedly sees the same ad. in the paper that the rest of us see, offering a reward of ten G's for the return of Gallant Godfrey and no questions asked, but of course Last Card Louie has no way of knowing that Big Nig is taking Gallant Godfrey home long before Louie comes around and buys Princess O'Hara's horse.'

Well, this is about all there is to tell, except that a couple of weeks later I hear that Ambrose Hammer is in the Clinic Hospital very ill, and I drop around to see him because I am very fond of Ambrose Hammer no matter if he is a newspaper scribe.

He is sitting up in bed in a nice private room, and he has on blue silk pyjamas with his monogram embroidered over his heart, and there is a large vase of roses on the table beside him, and a nice-looking nurse holding his hand, and I can see that Ambrose Hammer is not doing bad, although he smiles very feebly at me when I come in.

Naturally I ask Ambrose Hammer what ails him, and after he takes a sip of water out of a glass that the nice-looking nurse holds up to his lips, Ambrose sighs, and in a very weak voice he states as follows:

'Well,' Ambrose says, 'one night I get to thinking about what will happen to us in the transverse if we have old Goldberg hitched to Princess O'Hara's victoria instead of one of the fastest race horses in the world, and I am so overcome by the thought that I have what my doctor claims is a nervous breakdown. I feel terrible,' Ambrose says.

Social Error

When Mr. Ziegfeld picks a doll she is apt to be above the average when it comes to looks, for Mr. Ziegfeld is by no means a chump at picking dolls. But when Mr. Ziegfeld picks Miss Midgie Muldoon, he beats his own best record, or anyway ties it. I never see a better-looking doll in my life, although she is somewhat smaller than I like them. I like my dolls big enough to take a good hold on, and Miss Midgie Muldoon is only about knee-high to a Pomeranian. But she is very cute, and I do not blame Handsome Jack Maddigan for going daffy about her.

Now most any doll on Broadway will be very glad indeed to have Handsome Jack Maddigan give her a tumble, so it is very surprising to one and all when Miss Midgie Muldoon plays the chill for Handsome Jack, especially when you figure that Miss Midgie Muldoon is nothing but a chorus doll, while Handsome Jack is quite a high shot in this town. But one night in the Hot Box when Handsome Jack sends word to Miss Midgie Muldoon, by Miss Billy Perry, who is Dave the Dude's wife, that he will like to meet up with her, Miss Midgie Muldoon sends word back to Handsome Jack that she is not meeting up with tough guys.

Well, naturally this crack burns Handsome Jack up quite some. But Dave the Dude says never mind, and furthermore Dave says

Miss Midgie Muldoon's crack serves Handsome Jack right for sitting around shooting off his mouth, and putting himself away as a tough guy, because if there is anything Dave hates it is a guy letting on he is tough, no matter how tough he really is, and Handsome Jack is certainly such a guy.

He is a big tall blond guy who comes up out of what they call Hell's Kitchen over on the West Side, and if he has a little more sense the chances are he will be as important a guy as Dave the Dude himself in time, instead of generally working for Dave, but Handsome Jack likes to wear very good clothes, and drink, and sit around a lot, and also do plenty of talking, and no matter how much dough he makes he never seems able to hold much of anything.

Personally, I never care to have any truck with Handsome Jack because he always strikes me as a guy who is a little too quick on the trigger to suit me, and I always figure the best you are going to get out of being around guys who are quick on the trigger is the worst of it, and so any time I see Handsome Jack I give him the back of my neck. But there are many people in this world such as Basil Valentine who love to be around these characters.

This Basil Valentine is a little guy who wears horn cheaters and writes articles for the magazines, and is personally a very nice little guy, and as harmless as a water snake, but he cannot have a whole lot of sense, or he will not be hanging out with Handsome Jack and other such characters.

If a guy hangs out with tough guys long enough he is apt to get to thinking maybe he is tough himself, and by and by other people may get the idea he is tough, and the first thing you know along comes some copper in plain clothes, such as Johnny Brannigan, of the strong-arm squad, and biffs him on the noggin with a blackjack just to see how tough he is. As I say, Basil Valentine is a very harmless guy, but after he is hanging out with Handsome Jack a while, I hear Basil talking very tough to a bus boy, and the chances are he is building himself up to talk tough to a waiter, and then maybe to a head waiter, and finally he may consider himself tough enough to talk tough to anybody.

I can show you many a guy who is supposed to be strictly legitimate sitting around with guys who are figured as tough guys, and why this is I do not know, but I am speaking to Waldo Winchester, the newspaper scribe, about the proposition one night, and Waldo Winchester, who is a half-smart guy in many respects, says it is what is called an underworld complex. Waldo Winchester says many legitimate people are much interested in the doings of tough guys, and consider them very romantic, and he says if I do not believe it look at all the junk the newspapers print making heroes out of tough guys.

Waldo Winchester says the underworld complex is a very common complex and that Basil Valentine has it, and so has Miss Harriet Mackyle, or she will not be all the time sticking her snoot into joints where tough guys hang out. This Miss Harriet Mackyle is one of these rich dolls who wears snaky-looking evening clothes, and has her hair cut like a boy's, with her ears sticking out, and is always around the night traps, generally with some guy with a little moustache, and a way of talking like an Englishman, and come to think of it I do see her in tough joints more than somewhat, saying hello to different parties such as nobody in their right minds will say hello to, including such as Red Henry, who is just back from Dannemora, after being away for quite a spell for taking things out of somebody's safe and blowing the safe open to take these things.

In fact, I see Miss Harriet Mackyle dancing one night in the Hearts and Flowers club, which is a very tough joint indeed, and who is she dancing with but Red Henry, and when I ask Waldo Winchester what he makes of this proposition, he says it is part of the underworld complex he is talking about. He says Miss Harriet Mackyle probably thinks it smart to tell her swell friends she dances with a safe-blower, although personally if I am going to dance with a safe-blower at all, which does not seem likely, I will pick me out a nicer safe-blower than Red Henry, because he is such a guy as does not take a bath since he leaves Dannemora, and he is back from Dannemora for several months.

One party who does not seem to have much of Waldo Winchester's underworld complex as far as I can see is Miss Midgie Muldoon, because I never see her around any night traps except such as the Hot Box and the Sixteen Hundred club, which are considered very nice places, and reasonably safe for anybody who does not get too far out of line, and Miss Midgie Muldoon is always with very legitimate guys such as Buddy Donaldson, the song writer, or Walter Gumble, who plays the trombone in Paul Whiteman's band, or maybe sometimes with Paul Hawley, the actor.

Furthermore, when she is around such places, Miss Midgie Muldoon minds her own business quite a bit, and always looks right past Handsome Jack Maddigan, which burns Jack up all the more. It is the first time Handsome Jack ever runs into a doll who does not seem excited about him, and he does not know what to make of such a situation.

Well, what happens but Dave the Dude comes to me one day and says to me like this: 'Listen,' Dave says, 'this doll Miss Harriet Mackyle is one of my best customers for high-grade merchandise, and is as good as wheat in the bin, and she is asking a favour of me. She is giving a party Sunday night in her joint over on Park Avenue, and she wishes me to invite some of the mob, so go around and tell about a dozen guys to be there all dressed, and not get too fresh, because a big order of Scotch and champagne goes with the favour.'

Now such a party is by no means unusual, although generally it is some swell guy who gives it rather than a doll, and he gets Broadway guys to be there to show his pals what a mixer he is. Waldo Winchester says it is to give colour to things, though where the colour comes in I do not know, for Broadway guys, such as will go to a party like this, are apt to just sit around and say nothing, and act very gentlemanly, because they figure they are on exhibition like freaks, and the only way you can get them to such parties in the first place is through some such connection as Miss Harriet Mackyle has with Dave the Dude.

Anyway, I go around and about and tell a lot of guys what Dave the Dude wishes them to do, and among others I tell Handsome Jack, who is tickled to death by the invitation, because if there is anything Jack loves more than anything else it is to be in a spot where he can show off some. Furthermore, Handsome Jack has a sneaking idea Miss Harriet Mackyle is red hot for him because she sometimes gives him the old eye when she sees him around the Sixteen Hundred club, and other spots, but then she does the same thing to Big Nig, and a lot of other guys I can mention, because that is just naturally the way Miss Harriet Mackyle is. But of course I do not speak of this to Handsome Jack. Basil Valentine is with Jack when I invite him, so I tell Basil to come along, too, because I do not wish him to think I am a snob.

It turns out that Basil is one of the very first guys to show up Sunday night at Miss Harriet Mackyle's apartment, where I am already on hand to help get in the Scotch and champagne, and to make Miss Harriet Mackyle acquainted with such of the mob as I invite, although I find we are about lost in the shuffle of guys with little moustaches, and dolls in evening clothes that leave plenty of them sticking out here and there. It seems everybody on Broadway is there, as well as a lot of Park Avenue, and Mr. Ziegfeld is especially well represented, and among his people I see Miss Midgie Muldoon, although I have to stand on tiptoe to see her on account of the guys with little moustaches around her, and their interest in Miss Midgie Muldoon proves that they are not such saps as they look, even if they do wear little moustaches.

It is a very large apartment, and the first thing I notice is a big green parrot swinging in a ring hung from the ceiling in a corner of what seems to be the main room, and the reason I notice this parrot is because it is letting out a squawk now and then, and yelling different words, such as Polly wants a cracker. There are also a lot of canary birds hung around the joint, so I judge Miss Harriet Mackyle loves animals, as well as peculiar people, such as she has for guests.

I am somewhat surprised to see Red Henry all dressed up in evening clothes moving around among the guests. I do not invite Red Henry, so I suppose Miss Harriet Mackyle invites him, or he hears rumours of the party, and just crashes in, but personally I consider it very bad taste on Red Henry's part to show himself in such a spot, and so does everybody else that knows him, although he seems to be minding his own business pretty well.

Finally when the serious drinking is under way, and a good time is being had by one and all, Miss Harriet Mackyle comes over to me and says to me like this: 'Now tell me about your different friends, so I can tell my other guests. They will be thrilled to death meeting these bad characters.'

'Well,' I say, 'you see the little guy over there staring at you as if you are a ghost, or some such? Well, he is nobody but Bad Basil Valentine, who will kill you as quick as you can say scat, and maybe quicker. He is undoubtedly the toughest guy here tonight, or anywhere else in this man's town for that matter. Yes, ma'am, Bad Basil Valentine is one dead tough mug,' I say, 'although he is harmless-looking at this time. Bad Basil kills many a guy in his day. In fact, Miss Mackyle,' I say, 'Bad Basil can scarcely sleep good any night he does not kill some guy.'

'My goodness!' Miss Harriet Mackyle says, looking Basil over very carefully. 'He does not look so bad at first glance, although now that I examine him closely I believe I do detect a sinister gleam in his eye.'

Well, Miss Harriet Mackyle can hardly wait until she gets away from me, and the next I see of her she has Basil Valentine surrounded and is almost chewing his ear off as she gabs to him, and anybody can see that Basil is all pleasured up by this attention. In fact, Basil is snagged if ever I see a guy snagged, and personally I do not blame him, because Miss Harriet Mackyle may not look a million, but she has a couple, and you can see enough of her in her evening clothes to know that nothing about her is phony.

The party is going big along towards one o'clock when all of a sudden in comes Handsome Jack Maddigan with half a heat on, and in five minutes he is all over the joint, drinking everything that is offered him, and making a fast play for all the dolls, and talking very loud. He is sored up more than somewhat when he finds Miss Harriet Mackyle does not give him much of a tumble, because he figures she will be calling him on top the minute he blows in, but Miss Harriet Mackyle is too busy with Basil Valentine finding out from Basil how he knocks off six of Al Capone's mob out in Chicago one time when he is out there on a pleasure trip.

Well, while feeling sored up about Miss Harriet Mackyle passing him up for Basil Valentine, and not knowing how it comes Basil is in so stout with her, Handsome Jack bumps into Red Henry, and Red Henry makes some fresh crack to Jack about Basil moving in on him, which causes Handsome Jack to hit Red Henry on the chin, and knock him half into the lap of Miss Midgie Muldoon, who is sitting in a chair with a lot of little moustaches around her.

Naturally this incident causes some excitement for a moment. But the way Miss Midgie Muldoon takes it is very surprising. She just sort of dusts Red Henry off her, and stands up no bigger than a demi-tasse, and looks Handsome Jack right in the eye very cool, and says: 'Ah, a parlour tough guy.' Then she walks away, leaving Handsome Jack with his mouth open, because he does not know up to this moment that Miss Midgie Muldoon is present.

Well, somebody heaves Red Henry out of the joint, and the party continues, but I see Handsome Jack wandering around looking very lonesome, and with not much speed left compared to what he brings in. Somehow I figure Handsome Jack is looking for Miss Midgie Muldoon, but she keeps off among the little moustaches, and finally Handsome Jack takes to belting the old grape right freely to get his zing back. He gets himself pretty well organized, and when he suddenly comes upon Miss Midgie Muldoon standing

by herself for a moment, he is feeling very brisk indeed, and he says
to her like this: 'Hello, Beautiful, are you playing the hard-to-get
for me?' But Miss Midgie Muldoon only looks him in the eye
again and says: 'Ah, the parlour tough guy! Go away, tough guy.
I do not like tough guys.'

Well, this is not so encouraging when you come to think of it,
but Handsome Jack is a guy who will never be ruled off for not
trying with the dolls, and he is just about to begin giving her a
little more work, when all of a sudden a voice goes 'Ha-ha-ha,' and
then it says: 'Hello, you fool!'

Now of course it is nothing but the parrot talking, and it says
again: 'Ha-ha-ha. Hello, you fool!' Of course, the parrot, whose
name turns out to be Polly, does not mean Handsome Jack, but of
course Handsome Jack does not know the parrot does not mean
him, and naturally he feels very much insulted. Furthermore, he
has plenty of champagne inside him. So all of a sudden he outs
with the old equalizer and lets go at Polly, and the next minute
there are green feathers flying all over the joint, and poor old
Mister, or maybe Missus, Polly is stretched out as dead as a door-
nail, and maybe deader.

Well, I never see a doll carry on like Miss Harriet Mackyle does
when she finds out her Polly is a goner, and what she says to
Handsome Jack is really very cutting, and quite extensive, and the
chances are Handsome Jack will finally haul off and smack Miss
Harriet Mackyle in the snoot, only he realizes he is already guilty
of a very grave social error in shooting the parrot, and he does not
wish to make it any worse.

Anyway, Miss Midgie Muldoon is standing looking at Handsome Jack out of her great big round beautiful eyes with what
Waldo Winchester, the scribe, afterwards tells me is plenty of
scorn, and it looks to me as if Handsome Jack feels worse about
Miss Midgie Muldoon's looks than he does about what Miss
Harriet Mackyle is saying to him. But Miss Midgie Muldoon never
opens her mouth. She just keeps looking at him for quite a spell,
and then finally walks away, and it looks to me as if she is ready to
bust out crying any minute, maybe because she feels sorry for
Polly.

Well, naturally Handsome Jack's error busts up the party,
because Miss Harriet Mackyle does not wish to take any chances on
Handsome Jack starting in to pot her canaries, so we all go away
leaving Miss Harriet Mackyle weeping over what she can find of

Polly, and Basil Valentine crying with her, which I consider very chummy of Basil, at that.

A couple of nights later Basil comes into Mindy's restaurant, where I happen to be sitting with Handsome Jack, and anybody can tell that Basil is much worried about something.

'Jack,' he says, 'Miss Harriet Mackyle is very, very, very angry about you shooting Polly. In fact, she hates you, because Polly is a family heirloom.'

'Well,' Jack says, 'tell her I apologize, and will get her a new parrot as soon as I get the price. You know I am broke now. Tell her I am very sorry, although,' Jack says, 'her parrot has no right to call me a fool, and I leave this to everybody.'

'Miss Harriet Mackyle is after me every day to shoot you, Jack,' Basil says. 'She thinks I am a very tough guy, and that I will shoot anybody on short notice, and she wishes me to shoot you. In fact, she is somewhat displeased because I do not shoot you when you shoot poor Polly, but of course I explain to her I do not have a gun at the moment. Now Miss Harriet Mackyle says if I do not shoot you she will not love me, and I greatly wish to have Miss Harriet Mackyle love me, because I am practically daffy about her. So,' Basil says, 'I am wondering how much you will take to hold still and let me shoot you, Jack?'

'Why,' Handsome Jack says, very much astonished, 'you must be screwy.'

'Of course I do not mean to really shoot you, Jack,' Basil says. 'I mean to maybe shoot you with a blank cartridge, so Miss Harriet Mackyle will think I am shooting you sure enough, which will make her very grateful to me. I am thinking that maybe I can pay you one thousand five hundred dollars for such a job, although this sum represents nearly my life savings.'

'Why,' Handsome Jack says, 'your proposition sounds very reasonable, at that. I am just wondering where I can get hold of a few bobs to send Miss Midgie Muldoon a bar pin, or some such, and see if I cannot round myself up with her. She is still playing plenty of chill for me. You better make it two grand while you are about it.'

Well, Basil Valentine finally agrees to pay the two grand. Furthermore, Basil promises to put the dough up in advance with Dave the Dude, or some other reliable party, as this is rather an unusual business deal, and naturally Handsome Jack wishes to have his interests fully protected.

Well, the thing comes off a few nights later in the Hot Box, and it is all pretty well laid out in advance. It is understood that Basil is to bring Miss Harriet Mackyle into the Hot Box after regular hours when there are not apt to be any too many people around, and to find Handsome Jack there. Basil is to out with a gun and take a crack at Handsome Jack, and Handsome Jack is to let on he is hit, and Basil is to get Miss Harriet Mackyle out of the joint in the confusion.

Handsome Jack promises to lay low a few weeks afterwards so it will look as if he is dead, and Basil figures that in the meantime Miss Harriet Mackyle will be so grateful to him that she will love him very much indeed, and maybe marry him, which is really the big idea with Basil.

It is pretty generally known to one and all what is coming off, and quite a number of guys drift into the Hot Box during the night, including Dave the Dude, who seems to be getting quite a bang out of the situation. But who also bobs up very unexpectedly but Miss Midgie Muldoon with Buddy Donaldson, the song writer.

Handsome Jack is all upset by Miss Midgie Muldoon being there, but she never as much as looks at him. So Handsome Jack takes to drinking Scotch more than somewhat, and everybody commences to worry about whether he will hold still for Basil Valentine to shoot him, even with a blank cartridge. The Hot Box closes at three o'clock in the morning, and everybody is always turned out except the regulars. So by three-thirty there are only about a dozen guys and dolls in the joint when in comes Basil Valentine and Miss Harriet Mackyle.

Handsome Jack happens to be standing with his back to the door and not far from the table where Miss Midgie Muldoon and this Buddy Donaldson are sitting when Basil and Miss Harriet Mackyle come in, and right away Basil sings out, his voice wobbling no little: 'Handsome Jack Maddigan, your time has come!' At this Handsome Jack turns around, and there is Basil Valentine tugging a big rod out of the hind pocket of his pants.

The next thing anybody knows, there is a scream, and a doll's voice cries: 'Jack! Look out, Jack!' and out of her seat and over to Handsome Jack Maddigan bounces Miss Midgie Muldoon, and just as Basil finally raises the rod and turns it on, Miss Midgie Muldoon plants herself right in front of Jack and stretches out her arms on either side of her as if to shield him.

Well, the gun goes bingo in Basil's hand, but instead of falling like he is supposed to do, Handsome Jack stands there with his mouth open looking at Miss Midgie Muldoon, not knowing what to make of her jumping between him and the gun, and it is a good thing he does not fall, at that, because he is able to catch Miss Midgie Muldoon as she starts to keel over. At first we think maybe it is only a faint, but she has on a low-neck dress, and across her left shoulder there slowly spreads a red smear, and what is this red smear but blood, and as Handsome Jack grabs her she says to him like this: 'Hold me, dear, I am hurt.'

Now this is most unexpected, indeed, and is by no means a part of the play. Basil Valentine is standing by the door with the rod in his duke looking quite astonished, and making no move to get Miss Harriet Mackyle out of the joint as he is supposed to the minute he fires, and Miss Harriet Mackyle is letting out a few off-hand screams which are very piercing, and saying she never thinks that Basil will take her seriously and really plug anybody for her, although she also says she appreciates his thoughtfulness, at that.

You can see Basil is standing there wondering what goes wrong, when Dave the Dude, who is a fast thinker under all circumstances, takes a quick peek at Miss Midgie Muldoon, and then jumps across the room and nails Basil. 'Why,' Dave says to Basil, 'you are nothing but a rascal. You mean to kill him after all. You do not shoot a blank, you throw a slug, and you get Miss Midgie Muldoon with it in the shoulder.'

Well, Basil is a pretty sick-looking toad as Dave the Dude takes hold of him, and Miss Harriet Mackyle is putting on a few extra yips when Basil says: 'My goodness, Dave,' he says. 'I never know this gun is really loaded. In fact, I forget all about getting a gun of my own until the last minute, and am looking around for one when Red Henry comes along and says he will lend me his. I explain to him how the whole proposition is a joke, and tell him I must have blanks, and he kindly takes the lead out of the cartridges in front of my own eyes and makes them blank.'

'The chances are Red Henry works a quick change on you,' Dave the Dude says. 'Red Henry is very angry at Jack for hitting him on the chin.'

Then Dave takes the rod out of Basil's hand and breaks it open, and sure enough there are enough real slugs in it to sink a rowboat and no blanks whatever, which surprises Basil Valentine no little.

'Now,' Dave says, 'get away from here before Jack realizes what happens, and keep out of sight until you hear from me, because if Miss Midgie Muldoon croaks it may cause some gossip. Furthermore,' Dave says, 'take this squawking doll with you.'

Well, you can see that Dave the Dude is pretty much steamed up, and he remains steamed up until it comes out that Miss Midgie Muldoon is only a little bit shot, and is by no means in danger of dying. We take her over to the Polyclinic Hospital, and a guy there digs the bullet out of her shoulder, and we leave her there with Handsome Jack holding her tight in his arms, and swearing he will never be tough again, but will get her a nice little home on Basil Valentine's two grand, and find himself a job, and take no more part in his old life, all of which seems to sound fair enough.

It is a couple of years before we hear of Miss Harriet Mackyle again, and then she is Mrs. Basil Valentine, and is living in Naples over in Italy, and the people there are very much surprised because Mrs. Basil Valentine never lets Mr. Basil Valentine associate with guys over ten years old, and never lets him handle anything more dangerous than a niblick.

So this is about all there is to the story, except that when Handsome Jack Maddigan and Miss Midgie Muldoon stand up to be married by Father Leonard, Dave the Dude sizes them up for a minute, and then turns to me and says like this:

'Look,' Dave says, 'and tell me where does Miss Midgie Muldoon's shoulder come up to on Jack's left side.'

'Well,' I say, 'her shoulder comes just up to Jack's heart.'

'So you see,' Dave says, 'it is just as well for Jack she stops Basil's bullet, at that.'

Take It Easy

Tight Shoes

All this begins the day a young character by the name of Rupert Salsinger sells Hymie Minsk, the horse player, a pair of shoes that are too tight.

This Rupert Salsinger works in Bilby's shoe store on Broadway, near Mindy's restaurant, and Hymie stops in there on his way to the Belmont race track early one afternoon, and buys the shoes.

Now Hymie is in pretty much of a hurry, as he knows of a right good thing in the first race at Belmont, so he tells Rupert Salsinger to kindly get out a pair of shoes, size $8\frac{1}{2}$D, and make haste about it.

Well, Rupert Salsinger takes one look at Hymie's dogs, and he can see that Hymie can no more wear an $8\frac{1}{2}$D than he can fly, for Hymie has large, flat Bronx feet that can cover as much ground as there is between second and third when Hymie is just standing still.

So Rupert Salsinger gets out a measuring gadget, and puts one of Hymie's feet in it, and tells Hymie that what he really needs is a $10\frac{1}{4}$EE, but Hymie immediately becomes very indignant, as he is extremely sensitive about the size of his feet, and he says he knows what size shoes he wears, and if Rupert Salsinger does not care to give him what he wants, he will take his custom elsewhere.

Now if old man Bilby is personally present, he will know enough to give Hymie his usual $10\frac{1}{4}$EE's, and tell him they are $8\frac{1}{2}$D's and Hymie will go on about his business, and think nothing more of it, but Rupert Salsinger is new to Bilby's store, and furthermore he is a very honest and conscientious young character, and does not believe in skull-duggery even about a pair of shoes, so he outs with some $8\frac{1}{2}$D's and shows Hymie the mark in them, and Hymie puts them on, and says they are just the right size, and away he goes to the race track.

Well, the good thing in the first race blows, and right away Hymie commences to notice that his shoes seem full of feet, for there is nothing like a loser in the first race for making a guy notice his feet. Then Hymie gets five more losers in a row, so by the time the races are over his feet are almost killing him.

In fact, anybody will tell you that six losers in a row will make a guy's feet hurt, even if he is barefooted, so a pair of tight shoes on such an occasion is practically murder in the first degree. Hymie has to take his shoes off in the train going back to New York to rest his feet, and one and all are most sympathetic with him, because they realize how keenly he must be suffering between the tight shoes and the six losers, and especially the six losers.

Well, Hymie Minsk goes right up to Bilby's shoe store in the tight shoes, and what does he do but use these shoes to kick Rupert Salsinger in the pants all the way from Bilby's store to Fifty-third Street, three blocks away, and the chances are he will be kicking Rupert Salsinger to this very day, if one foot does not finally connect with a book by Karl Marx, which Rupert is wearing in his hip pocket, and which almost breaks Hymie's big toe, it being a very solid book.

But everybody agrees that Hymie does the right thing, especially when Hymie explains that the shoes hurt his feet so at the track that he does not really know what he is doing after the first race, and his pain causes him to bet on horses that he has no right to consider in any manner, shape or form whatever. In fact, everybody agrees that Rupert is a very dangerous character to have on Broadway, as he may take to selling tight shoes to horse players generally, and thus cause untold suffering among them, besides upsetting their figures on the horse races.

Furthermore, when Rupert Salsinger gets back to the shoe store old man Bilby pays him off and fires him, and also personally takes a few kicks at Rupert Salsinger's pants himself as Rupert is going out the door, and old man Bilby's aim is much better than Hymie's, and he does not hit the volume of Karl Marx even once.

So there Rupert Salsinger is without a position, and with only half a week's wages consisting of about seven slugs in his pocket, and as it is the first position Rupert has since the depression sets in, he is downcast no little, especially as he is hoping to save enough money in this position to justify him in asking Miss Minnie Schultz, who lives over on Tenth Avenue, to be his bride.

He is in love with Miss Minnie Schultz for several years, and expects to one day ask her to marry him, but Rupert Salsinger is such a conscientious young character that he will never think of making such a request until he becomes a provider, and anyway, Miss Minnie Schultz's papa, who keeps a delicatessen store, by no means approves of Rupert Salsinger, because Rupert is always so thoughtful and studious, and also always so much out of a position.

In fact, Miss Minnie Schultz's papa considers Rupert nothing but a bum, and he wishes his daughter to marry an entirely different character by the name of Gus Schmelk, who runs a delicatessen store right across the street from the Schultz store, and is giving Miss Minnie Schultz's papa such tough competition that her papa figures it will be a nice business deal for her to marry Gus Schmelk and combine the stores.

But Miss Minnie Schultz is rather fond of Rupert Salsinger, as he ¸s tall and thin, and has thick black hair, and a very serious expression, and wears spectacles, and is really much better than a raw hand when it comes to making love, even though he is so conservative about speaking of marriage.

Well, anyway, Rupert Salsinger goes up Broadway feeling very sad and blue, and finally he stops in the Bridle Grill, and steps up to the bar and calls for a glass of beer, and while he is drinking this beer, he gets to thinking what a cruel world it is to be sure, so he calls for another beer, with a little rye whisky on the side, for while Rupert Salsinger is by no means a rum-dum, he feels that this is an occasion that calls for a few drams, anyway.

It is now along about eight bells in the evening, and not many cash customers are in the Bridle Grill, when all of a sudden in comes a tall, good-looking young fellow in evening clothes, including a high hat, and an opera cape, lined with white silk, and who is this young fellow but Calvin Colby, who is known far and wide as a great pain in the neck to his loving parents.

He is also known as a character who likes to get around and, in fact, Calvin Colby's only occupation is getting around. His people are as rich as mud, and to tell the truth, richer, and what is more they are in the Social Register and, in fact, Calvin Colby is in the Social Register himself until the publishers come upon his name one day and see that it is a typographical error.

He is often in the newspapers, because it is really remarkable how Calvin Colby's automobiles can spill dolls up against telegraph poles along the Boston Post Road, when he happens to strike these obstacles, and the dolls are always suing Calvin Colby for breaking their legs, or spoiling their complexions. It finally gets so there is talk of taking Calvin's driving licence away from him before he shatters all the telegraph poles along the Boston Post Road.

He is without doubt strictly a Hoorah Henry, and he is generally figured as nothing but a lob as far as ever doing anything useful in this world is concerned, although everybody admits that he has a nice disposition, and is as good a right guard as ever comes out of Yale.

Calvin Colby is undoubtedly slightly mulled when he enters the Bridle Grill, and he steps up to the bar alongside Rupert Salsinger, and calls for an old-fashioned cocktail, and after he inhales this, he calls for three more of the same, one right after the other, and about this time, Rupert Salsinger, who is standing there thinking of the wrongs he suffers at the feet of Hymie Minsk and old man Bilby, lets out a terrible sigh, as follows:

'Hah-ah-ah-hah.'

Well, at this, Calvin Colby gazes at Rupert Salsinger in surprise, as Rupert's sigh sounds very much like wind escaping from a punctured tyre, and Calvin speaks to Rupert like this:

'What is eating you?' Calvin says. 'Have a drink,' he says.

Naturally, Rupert has a drink, because it is very seldom in his life that he gets a drink for nothing, and this time he calls for an old-fashioned, too, as he is tired of beer and rye whisky, and moreover he figures it will be polite to drink the same as his host, and then he says to Calvin Colby:

'Comrade,' he says, 'this is an awful world. There is no justice.'

'Well,' Calvin Colby says, 'I never give the matter much thought, because personally I never have any occasion for justice. But,' he says, 'you may be right. Have a drink.'

So they have this second drink, and also quite a few other drinks, and presently they are as friendly as a new bride and groom, and Rupert Salsinger tells Calvin Colby about the shoes, and Hymie Minsk, and old man Bilby, and also about Miss Minnie Schultz, and when he gets to Miss Minnie Schultz, he sheds tears all over Calvin Colby's white pique vest.

Well, Calvin Colby is practically petrified with horror to think of what Rupert Salsinger suffers, although he does not consider Rupert's tears over Miss Minnie Schultz quite manly, as Calvin Colby personally never experiences love, and regards dolls as only plaintiffs, but he admits that his soul seethes with indignation at the idea of Miss Minnie Schultz's papa wishing to force her into a marriage with Gus Schmelk. In fact, Calvin Colby says that while he does not know this Gus Schmelk he is willing to make a little wager that he is nothing but a bounder and a cad.

Now it seems that Calvin Colby is all dressed up to go somewhere, but by this time he cannot remember where, and he suggests to Rupert Salsinger that they take a little stroll and see if the old-fashioneds are up to standard in other parts of the city.

So they leave the Bridle Grill, and the bartender is not sorry to see them depart, at that, as they are making him work too hard, and they walk north on Broadway, arm-in-arm, stopping here and there to have a few drinks, and all the time Calvin Colby is talking about the great injustice that has been done Rupert Salsinger.

By and by they come to Columbus Circle, and in Columbus Circle there are many little groups of citizens, and each group is gathered around a guy standing on a box making a speech, so there are maybe ten different groups, and ten different guys making speeches, although each guy is only talking to his own group, but they are all talking at once, so they make quite a racket.

Now of course all this is a very familiar scene to anybody that ever goes through Columbus Circle in the evening, but it seems that Calvin Colby never before witnesses such a thing, as he does not visit Columbus Circle since infancy, and he is greatly astonished at what he beholds, and asks Rupert Salsinger what is the meaning of this.

Well, it seems that Rupert Salsinger knows all about the matter, and in fact it seems that Rupert Salsinger often takes part in these meetings personally when he has nothing else to do, and he explains to Calvin Colby that each of the speakers has a message of some kind to deliver to the people about one thing and another, and they are delivering them in Columbus Circle because it is a sort of public forum, and the coppers are not permitted to bother anybody with a message here, although they may run them bowlegged if they try to deliver any message anywhere else.

Now Calvin Colby becomes greatly interested in this proposition and he listens in here and there on different groups, but he is unable to make heads or tails of what the speakers are talking about, except that most of them are weighing in the sacks on the rich, and on the government, and on this and that, and finally Calvin Colby says to Rupert Salsinger, like this:

'Why,' Calvin Colby says, 'the trouble with these parties is they are all over the layout. They are scattering their play too much. What we need here is a little centralization of ideas. Get me a box,' Calvin says.

Well, all the boxes around and about are occupied, but by this time, what with the beer, and the old-fashioneds, and all, Rupert Salsinger is a character of great determination, and he goes up to one speaker and yanks the box right from under him without saying aye, yes, or no, and this action leaves the speaker flat in Columbus Circle, but it seems that the speaker is about all out of ideas, anyway, and cannot think of anything more to say, so he does not mind losing his box as much as you might expect.

Then Rupert takes the box and plants it right in the centre of all the groups, and Calvin Colby gets up on the box and begins letting out loud yells to attract attention. Naturally Calvin Colby can out-yell any of the speakers in Columbus Circle, because he is fresh, and furthermore he is full of old-fashioneds, and it is well known that there is nothing like old-fashioneds to help anybody yell.

Well, everyone in the Circle turns at once to see what the yelling is about and when they see a party in evening clothes, with a high hat and a white-lined opera cape on, naturally they are somewhat impressed, and they leave all the other speakers and gather around Calvin Colby.

Some think at first that maybe he is selling a patent medicine, or ballyhooing a dance hall with forty hostesses, and they expect to see his shirt bosom light up with an ad on it, as they cannot figure any other reason for anybody in such a make-up to be in Columbus Circle, but when Calvin Colby finally gets a big crowd around him, including not only the citizens who are listening to the other speakers, but many characters, male and female, who happen to be passing along the sidewalks and hear his yells, he speaks to them as follows, and to wit:

'Comrades,' Calvin Colby says, 'when I think of all the injustice in this world it almost makes me bust right out crying. My heart bleeds. I am very sad. All humanity cries out "Justice, justice," but what is the answer; Nothing, comrades,' he says.

Now at this point somebody back in the crowd pegs an egg at Calvin Colby's high hat, and cries out in a loud, coarse voice:

'Look at the daffydill.'

The egg just misses Calvin Colby's hat and continues on and strikes a member of the Communist party on the chin, and the member of the Communist party is slightly irritated, as he says he can use the egg for breakfast if it does not break when it meets his chin.

Well, naturally this interruption annoys Calvin Colby no little, and he stops a moment and tries to see who it is that is guilty of such uncouth conduct, and then he says:

'Comrades,' he says, 'if the jerk who just hurls the aforesaid remark and egg at me will kindly hold still until I reach him, I will guarantee to yank one of his arms off and beat his brains out with it.'

At this the crowd cheers Calvin Colby quite some, and there are cries for him to continue his address, although Calvin Colby has half a notion to stop right there and go to work on the party who pegs the egg, because such a course promises more fun for Calvin Colby than making a speech, but finally he resumes as follows:

'No, comrades,' he says, 'there is no justice, and to prove it I wish to present to you my friend, my pal, my comrade, Mr. Rupert Salsinger, who will now address you.'

So he makes room for Rupert Salsinger on the box, and Rupert puts on a really wonderful speech, because it seems that Rupert is not only a natural-born speaker, but he knows extracts from great speeches by such characters as Father Coughlin, Patrick Henry, F. D. Roosevelt, Abraham Lincoln and Robert Ingersoll, and he drops in these extracts here and there as he goes along, and they are very effective.

He tells of his own personal experiences with representatives of the capitalistic system, and while he does not mention them by name, he undoubtedly means Hymie Minsk and old man Bilby, and Rupert's remarks about his own suffering touch every heart, and there are cries of pity and rage from all parts of the crowd, although Rupert himself afterward admits that maybe he does give Hymie and old man Bilby a shade the worst of it in his statements.

By the time Rupert finishes, his audience is greatly excited, and Calvin Colby is sitting on the edge of the box half asleep, so Rupert wakes him up to make some more remarks, but now Calvin Colby is slightly bored by his surroundings and wishes to get away from this spot, and all he can think of to say is as follows:

'Comrades,' he says, 'let us stop talking, and go into action. The cry,' he says, 'is forward!'

And with this, Calvin Colby starts off down Broadway, walking in the middle of the street, and all he is thinking of at the moment is to remove himself from Columbus Circle, and Rupert starts off with him, but all the other citizens present fall in behind them, so there they are leading a big march.

There are only a few hundred citizens behind them when they start, but before they go two blocks this number increases to several thousand, because naturally the spectacle of a character in a high hat and a white-lined opera cape leading a procession down Broadway is most intriguing to one and all who behold same, and everybody wishes to find out what it means.

Of course Calvin and Rupert Salsinger have no idea where they are going when they start off, and when they arrive at Fiftieth and Broadway, Calvin Colby is getting sick and tired of walking, and wishes one of his cars will come along and pick him up, and furthermore he is yearning for a few old-fashioned cocktails.

In fact, Calvin Colby is getting ready to cop a sneak on his followers, when Rupert Salsinger points out old man Bilby's shoe store, which of course is closed at this hour, as the seat of much of the injustice to him, and the member of the Communist party, who is in the procession, still thinking about the loss of the egg, hears what Rupert says, and steps over on the sidewalk and kicks in old man Bilby's door.

Well, in five minutes old man Bilby's shoe store is a total wreck, and everybody has a pair of shoes, including many characters who are never in the procession at all, and are by no means entitled to same. There is great confusion, and some of the shoes get all mixed up in this confusion, and in fact for weeks afterward parties are around Broadway with odd shoes trying to match them up.

Naturally the commotion brings out a number of officers of the law, who go around inquiring what is coming off here, and when they are unable to learn what is coming off, they start slapping citizens right and left with their nightsticks, and the result is a great deal of new business for the near-by hospitals.

But this part of it no longer interests Calvin Colby and Rupert Salsinger, who retire from the scene and go elsewhere, but not before Rupert Salsinger gets into the store and picks out a pair of shoes for himself and carries them off under his arm.

Well, by and by the reporters from the newspapers arrive on the scene and start getting interviews here and there about the goings-on, and it seems from the stories in the papers the next morning that the reporters learn that it is all the upshot of a great new movement for social justice organized by Rupert Salsinger, a famous young student of such matters, and supported by Calvin Colby, the well-known young multimillionaire thinker, although of course it is a big surprise to Rupert Salsinger to learn that he is famous, and a much bigger surprise to Calvin Colby to hear that he is a thinker, and in fact this sounds like libel to Calvin Colby, when he gets around to reading it.

But it seems that what the newspapers see in this movement for social justice led by such young characters as Rupert Salsinger and Calvin Colby, more than anything else, is a revolution of youth against the old order, and in fact the papers make it a matter of great importance and by 8 a.m. the next morning the reporters and photographers from the afternoon bladders are almost breaking down the doors of Calvin Colby's apartment on Park Avenue to interview him and take his picture.

Naturally, Calvin Colby is still in the hay at such an hour, and he does not wake up until 1.30 p.m. and by this time he does not remember about the movement for social justice, and in fact he will be greatly nonplussed to find himself sleeping with such a character as Rupert Salsinger if it is not for the fact that Calvin Colby is accustomed to finding himself sleeping with all kinds of characters.

He wakes Rupert Salsinger up and asks him what about a little of the hair of the dog that bites them, but Rupert is very ill, and all he can bear is a little straight Scotch, and then Rupert commences to recall vaguely some of the events of the night before, when Calvin Colby's butler brings in the morning papers, and tells them that fifty reporters and photographers are still waiting outside to see Calvin Colby, and that they are getting fretful, and that moreover Calvin Colby's loving parents are calling up every few minutes, wishing to know what he means by becoming a thinker.

Then Calvin Colby commences remembering a few things himself, and he worries no little about how he is going to explain to his loving parents. Naturally he cannot face reporters and photographers while he is in such a state of mind, so he gives Rupert Salsinger a little more straight Scotch, and lends Rupert a dressing-gown, and sends him out to see the reporters and photographers.

Well, Rupert Salsinger gives them quite an interview, and in fact he repeats as much of the speech he makes in Columbus Circle as he can remember, including the extracts from the speeches of F. D. Roosevelt and Abraham Lincoln, and he tells them that he and Calvin Colby will continue this movement for social justice until the bad place freezes over, if necessary, because by now the straight Scotch is working very good in Rupert Salsinger, and he is by no means at any loss for words.

Now Rupert Salsinger is a very serious-minded young character and by no means a chump, and he sees that all this publicity may lead somewhere, so what does he do in the next few days but organize the American Amalgamation for Social Justice, with himself as president, and Calvin Colby as treasurer, and Calvin Colby's loving parents are so proud of their son becoming prominent at something else besides spilling dolls out of his automobiles that they donate five thousand slugs to the cause.

Furthermore, they settle with old man Bilby for the wrecking of his shoe store, and the loss of his shoes, including the pair taken away by Rupert Salsinger, although of course nobody but Rupert knows about these shoes, and he does not mention the matter publicly.

But Calvin Colby is getting sick and tired of all this business, because the reporters are always after him for interviews, and it is commencing to interfere with his occupation of getting around, especially as Rupert Salsinger is always after him, too, telling him to do this and that, and one thing and another, and Calvin Colby is delighted when Rupert announces himself as a candidate for Congress on the Social Justice ticket, because Calvin figures that with Rupert in Congress he will not bother him any more, and he can resume getting around just where he leaves off.

Well, it seems that about the time Rupert Salsinger makes his announcement, Tammany Hall is greatly dissatisfied with the character who already represents it in Congress from Rupert's district, because he often votes in a manner that is by no means to the interest of this splendid organization, so somebody from the Hall has a talk with Rupert Salsinger, and reports that he is an honest, clean, upright young character, who is by no means sore at Tammany, or at least not so sore that he can never get over it.

Then it seems that Tammany quietly passes the word around Rupert Salsinger's district to vote for this honest, clean, upright young character, and such a word means that Rupert is 1 to 20 in the betting to be elected, even on a platform for social justice, and about this time Rupert begins thinking more than somewhat of Miss Minnie Schultz, and of how much he loves her.

Rupert is so busy that it is quite a spell since he finds leisure to get over to Tenth Avenue to see Miss Minnie Schultz and he requests Calvin Colby, as a personal favour, to step over and explain to Miss Minnie Schultz why he cannot appear before her in person.

So Calvin Colby goes over to Tenth Avenue and locates Miss Minnie Schultz at her papa's delicatessen store, and explains to her about Rupert, and Calvin Colby is greatly surprised to notice that Miss Minnie Schultz is very beautiful.

He notices that she has taffy-coloured hair, and big blue eyes, and a lovely speaking voice, and hands like the ears of little tiny white rabbits, and feet like little tiny mice, and a complexion like Grade-A milk, and a shape that is wonderful to behold, and great intelligence, and charm, and in fact Miss Minnie Schultz is the first doll Calvin Colby ever beholds that he does not figure a plaintiff.

He also notices a character skulking in the background of Miss Minnie Schultz whose name seems to be Gus Schmelk, and whose features seem to be very familiar to Calvin Colby, and also very distasteful, especially as this Gus Schmelk seems to be on very friendly terms with Miss Minnie Schultz, and in fact in the presence of Calvin Colby he gives her a pat on the pistol pocket, causing Calvin Colby's blood to boil out of loyalty to Rupert Salsinger.

However, Miss Minnie Schultz seems quite interested in hearing about Rupert, and says she hopes and trusts he is enjoying the best of health, and that he will come to see her soon, though she realizes from what she reads in the papers how busy he is, and she also says that she is personally as well and as happy as can be expected, and that business in her papa's delicatessen store is picking up.

Well, Calvin Colby reports much of the above situation to Rupert Salsinger, especially about Gus Schmelk, and tells Rupert that Gus impresses him as a low, degraded character, who will steal another's doll without any compunction of conscience whatever, and in fact Calvin Colby says to Rupert like this:

'If I am you,' he says, 'I will dispense with this social justice for a while and look after my interests with Miss Minnie Schultz. It is seldom in my career,' Calvin says, 'that I see such a shape as Miss Minnie Schultz possesses.'

Well, Rupert Salsinger sighs, and says he realizes that Calvin Colby's statements are only too true, especially about Gus Schmelk, and also about Miss Minnie Schultz's shape, but Rupert says he feels that social justice must come first with him above all else, even Miss Minnie Schultz's shape.

Then Rupert says to Calvin Colby:

'Comrade,' he says, 'I realize that you loathe and despise all characters of a female nature, but,' he says, 'I am going to ask you to make a great sacrifice for me. I will deem it an act of fealty to our cause, and of personal friendship,' Rupert says, 'if you will occasionally go over to Tenth Avenue and do anything you can to protect me in that direction from vipers in my bosom and snakes in the grass.'

There are tears in Rupert's eyes as he makes this request, and naturally Calvin Colby promises to assist him in this emergency, and presently between looking after Rupert's interests with Miss Minnie Schultz and signing cheques as treasurer of the American Amalgamation for Social Justice for Rupert's campaign, Calvin Colby finds little time for his occupation of getting around.

Now in the meantime, in spite of being so busy, Rupert Salsinger finds himself brooding no little over Miss Minnie Schultz and Gus Schmelk, and finally one day he decides that he can spare a couple of hours to go over to Tenth Avenue and see Miss Minnie Schultz and present his proposal of marriage to her in person, so he calls her up and requests an interview with her, and it seems she can tell by the tone of his voice what is on his chest, and she says all right but to be sure and get over in an hour.

So Rupert Salsinger puts everything else aside, and dresses himself up in a new suit of clothes which he purchases from the treasury of the Amalgamated Association for Social Justice as part of his campaign expenses, and puts on the new shoes that he secures at old man Bilby's shoe store, and starts out from Calvin Colby's residence on Park Avenue, where Rupert is living ever since the first night he lands there.

Well, Rupert is passing the corner of Fiftieth Street and Broadway when who does he see standing in front of Mindy's restaurant but Hymie Minsk, the horse player, and then Rupert suddenly remembers that while social justice is going forward very nicely in most quarters that he never really gets justice from Hymie Minsk.

So Rupert Salsinger steps up behind Hymie, and takes him by the nape of the neck and kicks Hymie's pants up the street to Fifty-third, using his new shoes for this purpose, and, what is more, doing a much better job on Hymie than Hymie does on him, as Hymie has no books whatsoever in his hip pocket to slow up Rupert's kicking.

When he finally lets Hymie go with a final kick in the pants, Rupert starts across Fifty-third Street towards Tenth Avenue, but after he goes a couple of blocks he notices that his feet are giving him great pain, and he realizes that his new shoes must be too tight for him, and what with his walking, and the extra exertion of kicking Hymie Minsk's pants, these shoes are commencing to pinch his puppies quite some.

The pain finally becomes so great that Rupert sits down on the steps of a school house and takes off his shoes to let his feet stop aching, and he sits there for anyway fifteen minutes, when it occurs to him that the hour Miss Minnie Schultz mentions is up, so he tries to put the shoes back on his feet again, but it seems his feet swell up to such an extent that the shoes will not go on again, so Rupert resumes his journey in his stocking feet, but carrying the shoes in his hand.

When he arrives in sight of the delicatessen store conducted by Miss Minnie Schultz's papa, he sees Miss Minnie Schultz standing on the sidewalk out in front, and he also sees Gus Schmelk walking across the street, and disappearing inside his own store, which is a scene that is most odious to Rupert Salsinger although he does not see a large automobile with Calvin Colby in it just going around the corner.

Well, Rupert Salsinger hastens forward with a glad smile, and he tips his hat with the hand which is not carrying the shoes, and he says to Miss Minnie Schultz like this:

'Minnie,' Rupert says, 'I love you with all my heart and soul, and now that my future is open before me, bright and shining, I wish you to be my wife, and never mind what your papa says to the contrary about Gus Schmelk. He is strictly a wrong gee. I mean Gus Schmelk,' Rupert says. 'Let us be married at once, and my friend, my pal, my comrade, Mr. Calvin Colby, will stand up with us as my best man.'

'Rupert,' Miss Minnie Schultz says, 'if you are here fifteen minutes ago, I will undoubtedly accept you. When you call me on the telephone and make an appointment for an interview with me, I say to myself, I wait all these years for Rupert to speak, and now I will give him just one more hour of my life, and not one minute more, for another is requesting my hand. On the expiration of the hour to the dot,' Miss Minnie Schultz says, 'I pledge myself to him. Rupert,' she says, 'as far as I am personally concerned you are a goner.'

Naturally, Rupert Salsinger is greatly vexed to hear this news, and in fact he is so vexed that he takes the tight shoes that are the cause of his tardiness, and throws them as far as he can, and as straight as he can, which is plumb across the street and through the plate-glass window of Gus Schmelk's delicatessen store.

The next thing anybody knows, Rupert Salsinger is hastening up Tenth Avenue in his stocking feet, and Gus Schmelk is right behind him calling him names of such a crude nature that Miss Minnie Schultz retires to her papa's delicatessen store, although this does not prevent her from seeing a character leave Gus Schmelk's store with Rupert's tight shoes under his arm, and it does not prevent her from recognizing this character as the member of the Communist party.

Well, I see in the papers that Congressman Rupert Salsinger is going to marry some society doll in Washington, who is a widow with plenty of money left to her by her late husband, but I do not believe Rupert will be any happier than Calvin Colby, who is very busy at this time opening the twenty-second branch of the Schultz-Colby Delicatessen Stores, Inc., and who is greatly pleased over being married to Miss Minnie Schultz.

But although Gus Schmelk's store is in the new combination, and Gus himself is a member of the Board of Directors of same, Calvin Colby never really forgets that Gus Schmelk is the party who almost ruins his high hat with an egg in Columbus Circle the night Calvin makes the public address.

Lonely Heart

It seems that one spring day, a character by the name of Nicely-Nicely Jones arrives in a ward in a hospital in the City of Newark, N.J., with such a severe case of pneumonia that the attending physician, who is a horse player at heart, and very absent-minded, writes 100, 40 and 10 on the chart over Nicely-Nicely's bed.

It comes out afterward that what the physician means is that it is 100 to 1 in his line that Nicely-Nicely does not recover at all, 40 to 1 that he will not last a week, and 10 to 1 that if he does get well he will never be the same again.

Well, Nicely-Nicely is greatly discouraged when he sees this price against him, because he is personally a chalk eater when it comes to price, a chalk eater being a character who always plays the short-priced favourites, and he can see that such a long shot as he is has very little chance to win. In fact, he is so discouraged that he does not even feel like taking a little of the price against him to show.

Afterward there is some criticism of Nicely-Nicely among the citizens around Mindy's restaurant on Broadway, because he does not advise them of this marker, as these citizens are always willing to bet that what Nicely-Nicely dies of will be over-feeding and never anything small like pneumonia, for Nicely-Nicely is known far and wide as a character who dearly loves to commit eating.

But Nicely-Nicely is so discouraged that he does not as much as send them word that he is sick, let alone anything about the price. He just pulls the covers up over his head and lies there waiting for the finish and thinking to himself what a tough thing it is to pass away of pneumonia, and especially in Newark, N.J., and nobody along Broadway knows of his predicament until Nicely-Nicely appears in person some months later and relates this story to me.

So now I will tell you about Nicely-Nicely Jones, who is called Nicely-Nicely because any time anybody asks him how he is feeling, or how things are going with him, he always says nicely, nicely, in a very pleasant tone of voice, although generally this is by no means the gospel truth, especially about how he is going.

He is a character of maybe forty-odd, and he is short, and fat, and very good-natured, and what he does for a livelihood is the best he can, which is an occupation that is greatly overcrowded at all times along Broadway.

Mostly, Nicely-Nicely follows the races, playing them whenever he has anything to play them with, but anyway following them, and the reason he finds himself in Newark, N.J., in the first place is because of a business proposition in connection with the races. He hears of a barber in Newark, N.J., who likes to make a wager on a sure thing now and then, and Nicely-Nicely goes over there to tell him about a sure thing that is coming up at Pimlico the very next Tuesday.

Nicely-Nicely figures that the barber will make a wager on this sure thing and cut him in on the profits, but it seems that somebody else gets to the barber the week before with a sure thing that is coming up a Monday, and the barber bets on this sure thing, and the sure thing blows, and now the barber will have to shave half of Newark, N.J., to catch even.

Nicely-Nicely always claims that the frost he meets when he approaches the barber with his sure thing gives him a cold that results in the pneumonia I am speaking of, and furthermore that his nervous system is so disorganized by the barber chasing him nine blocks with a razor in his hand that he has no vitality left to resist the germs.

But at that it seems that he has enough vitality left to beat the pneumonia by so far the attending physician is somewhat embarrassed, although afterward he claims that he makes a mistake in chalking up the 100, 40 and 10 on Nicely-Nicely's chart. The attending physician claims he really means the character in the bed next to Nicely-Nicely, who passes away of lockjaw the second day after Nicely-Nicely arrives.

Well, while he is convalescing in the hospital of this pneumonia, Nicely-Nicely has a chance to do plenty of thinking, and what he thinks about most is the uselessness of the life he leads all these years, and how he has nothing to show for same except some high-class knowledge of race horses, which at this time is practically a drug on the market.

There are many other patients in the same ward with Nicely-Nicely, and he sees their ever-loving wives, and daughters, and maybe their sweet-peas visiting them, and hears their cheerful chatter, and he gets to thinking that here he is without chick or child, and no home to go to, and it just about breaks his heart.

He gets to thinking of how he will relish a soft, gentle, loving hand on his brow at this time, and finally he makes a pass at one of the nurses, figuring she may comfort his lonely hours, but what she lays on his brow is a beautiful straight right cross, and furthermore she hollers watch, murder, police, and Nicely-Nicely has to pretend he has a relapse and is in a delirium to avoid being mistreated by the internes.

As Nicely-Nicely begins getting some of his strength back, he takes to thinking, too, of such matters as food, and when Nicely-Nicely thinks of food it is generally very nourishing food, such as a nice double sirloin, smothered with chops, and thinking of these matters, and of hamburgers, and wiener schnitzel and goulash with noodles, and lamb stew, adds to his depression, especially when they bring him the light diet provided for invalids by the hospital.

He takes to reading to keep himself from thinking of his favourite dishes, and of his solitary life, and one day in a bundle of old magazines and newspapers that they give him to read, he comes upon a bladder that is called the *Matrimonial Tribune*, which seems to be all about marriage, and in this *Matrimonial Tribune* Nicely-Nicely observes an advertisement that reads as follows:

LONELY HEART

Widow of middle age, no children, cheerful companion, neat, excellent cook, owner of nice farm in Central New Jersey, wishes to meet home-loving gentleman of not more than fifty who need not necessarily be possessed of means but who will appreciate warm, tender companionship and pleasant home. Object, matrimony. Address Lonely Heart, this paper.

Well, Nicely-Nicely feels romance stirring in his bosom as he reads these lines, because he is never married, and has no idea that marriage is as described in this advertisement. So what does he do but write a letter to Lonely Heart in care of the *Matrimonial Tribune* stating that he is looking for a warm, tender companionship, and a pleasant home, and an excellent cook, especially an excellent cook, all his life, and the next thing he knows he is gazing into what at first seems to be an old-fashioned round cheese, but which he finally makes out as the face of a large Judy seated at his bedside.

She is anywhere between forty and fifty-five years of age, and she is as big and rawboned as a first baseman, but she is by no means a crow. In fact, she is rather nice-looking, except that she has a pair of eyes as pale as hens' eggs, and these eyes never change expression.

She asks Nicely-Nicely as many questions as an assistant district attorney, and especially if he has any money, and does he have any relatives, and Nicely-Nicely is able to state truthfully that he is all out of both, although she does not seem to mind. She wishes to know about his personal habits, and Nicely-Nicely says they are all good, but of course he does not mention his habit of tapping out any time a 4-to-5 shot comes along, which is as bad a habit as anybody can have, and finally she says she is well satisfied with him and will be pleased to marry him when he is able to walk.

She has a short, sharp voice that reminds Nicely-Nicely of a tough starter talking to the jockeys at the post, and she never seems to smile, and, take her all around, the chances are she is not such a character as Nicely-Nicely will choose as his ever-loving wife if he has the pick of a herd, but he figures that she is not bad for an off-hand draw.

So Nicely-Nicely and the Widow Crumb are married, and they go to live on her farm in Central New Jersey, and it is a very nice little farm, to be sure, if you care for farms, but it is ten miles from the nearest town, and in a very lonesome country, and furthermore there are no neighbours handy, and the Widow Crumb does not have a telephone or even a radio in her house.

In fact, about all she has on this farm are a couple of cows, and a horse, and a very old joskin with a chin whisker and rheumatism and a mean look, whose name seems to be Harley something, and who also seems to be the Widow Crumb's hired hand. Nicely-Nicely can see at once that Harley has no use for him, but afterward he learns that Harley has no use for anybody much, not even himself.

Well, it comes on supper-time the first night. Nicely-Nicely is there and he is delighted to observe that the Widow Crumb is making quite an uproar in the kitchen with the pots and pans, and this uproar is music to Nicely-Nicely's ears as by now he is in the mood to put on the hot meat very good, and he is wondering if the Widow Crumb is as excellent a cook as she lets on in her advertisement.

It turns out that she is even better. It turns out that she is as fine a cook as ever straddles a skillet, and the supper she spreads for Nicely-Nicely is too good for a king. There is round steak hammered flat and fried in a pan, with thick cream gravy, and hot biscuits, and corn on the cob, and turnip greens, and cottage-fried potatoes, and lettuce with hot bacon grease poured over it, and apple-pie, and coffee, and I do not know what all else, and Nicely-Nicely almost founders himself, because it is the first time since he leaves the hospital that he gets a chance to move into real food.

Harley, the old joskin, eats with them, and Nicely-Nicely notices that there is a fourth place set at the table, and he figures that maybe another hired hand is going to show up, but nobody appears to fill the vacant chair, and at first Nicely-Nicely is glad of it, as it gives him more room in which to eat.

But then Nicely-Nicely notices that the Widow Crumb loads the plate at the vacant place with even more food than she does any of the others, and all through the meal Nicely-Nicely keeps expecting someone to come in and knock off these victuals. Nobody ever appears, however, and when they are through eating, the Widow Crumb clears up the extra place the same as the others, and scrapes the food off the plate into a garbage pail.

Well, of course, Nicely-Nicely is somewhat perplexed by this proceeding, but he does not ask any questions, because where he comes from only suckers go around asking questions. The next morning at breakfast, and again at dinner, and in fact at every meal put on the table the extra place is fixed, and the Widow Crumb goes through the same performance of serving the food to this place, and afterward throwing it away, and while Nicely-Nicely commences thinking it is a great waste of excellent food, he keeps his trap closed.

Now being the Widow Crumb's husband is by no means a bad dodge, as she is anything but a gabby Judy, and will go all day long without saying more than a few words, and as Nicely-Nicely is a character who likes to chat this gives him a chance to do all the talking, although she never seems to be listening to him much. She seldom asks him to do any work, except now and then to help the old joskin around the barn, so Nicely-Nicely commences to figure this is about as soft a drop-in as anybody can wish.

The only drawback is that sometimes the Widow Crumb likes to sit on Nicely-Nicely's lap of an evening, and as he does not have much lap to begin with, and it is getting less every day under her feeding, this is quite a handicap, but he can see that it comes of her affectionate nature, and he bears up the best he can.

One evening after they are married several months, the Widow Crumb is sitting on what is left of Nicely-Nicely's lap, and she puts her arms around his neck, and speaks to him as follows:

'Nicely,' she says, 'do you love me?'

'Love you?' Nicely-Nicely says. 'Why, I love you like anything. Maybe more. You are a wonderful cook. How can I help loving you?' he says.

'Well,' the Widow Crumb says, 'do you ever stop to consider that if anything happens to you, I will be left here lone and lorn, because you do not have any means with which to provide for me after you are gone?'

'What do you mean after I am gone?' Nicely-Nicely says. 'I am not going anywhere.'

'Life is always a very uncertain proposition,' the Widow Crumb says. 'Who can say when something is apt to happen to you and take you away from me, leaving me without a cent of life insurance?'

Naturally, Nicely-Nicely has to admit to himself that what she says is very true, and of course he never gives the matter a thought before, because he figures from the way the Widow Crumb feeds him that she must have some scratch of her own stashed away somewhere, although this is the first time the subject of money is ever mentioned between them since they are married.

'Why,' Nicely-Nicely says, 'you are quite right, and I will get my life insured as soon as I get enough strength to go out and raise a few dibs. Yes, indeed,' Nicely-Nicely says, 'I will take care of this situation promptly.'

Well, the Widow Crumb says there is no sense in waiting on a matter as important as this, and that she will provide the money for the payment of the premiums herself, and for Nicely-Nicely to forget about going out to raise anything, as she cannot bear to have him out of her sight for any length of time, and then she gets to telling Nicely-Nicely what she is going to give him for breakfast, and he forgets about the insurance business.

But the next thing Nicely-Nicely knows, a thin character with a nose like a herring comes out from town, and there is another character with him who has whiskers that smell of corn whisky, but who seems to be a doctor, and in practically no time at all Nicely-Nicely's life is insured for five thousand dollars, with double indemnity if he gets used up by accident, and Nicely-Nicely is greatly pleased by this arrangement because he sees that he is now worth something for the first time in his career, although everybody on Broadway claims it is a terrible overlay by the insurance company when they hear the story.

Well, several months more go by, and Nicely-Nicely finds life on the farm very pleasant and peaceful as there is nothing much for him to do but eat and sleep, and he often finds himself wondering how he ever endures his old life, following the races and associating with the low characters of the turf.

He gets along first class with the Widow Crumb and never has a cross word with her, and he even makes friends with the old joskin, Harley, by helping him with his work, although Nicely-Nicely is really not fitted by nature for much work, and what he likes best at the farm is the eating and sleeping, especially the eating.

For a while he finds it difficult to get as much sleep as he requires, because the Widow Crumb is a great hand for staying up late reading books in their bedroom by kerosene lamp, and at the same time eating molasses candy which she personally manufactures, and sometimes she does both in bed, and the molasses candy bothers Nicely-Nicely no little until he becomes accustomed to it.

Once he tries reading one of her books to put himself to sleep after she dozes off ahead of him, but he discovers that it is all about nothing but spiritualism, and about parties in this life getting in touch with characters in the next world, and Nicely-Nicely has no interest whatever in matters of this nature, although he personally knows a character by the name of Spooks McGurk who claims to be a spiritualist, and who makes a nice thing of it in connection with tips on the races, until a race-track fuzz catches up with him.

Nicely-Nicely never discusses the books with the Widow Crumb, because in the first place he figures it is none of his business, and in the second place, the more she reads the better chance he has of getting to sleep before she starts snoring, because it seems that as a snorer the Widow Crumb is really all-America material, although of course Nicely-Nicely is too much of a gentleman to make an issue of this.

She gives him three meals every day, and every meal is better than the last, and finally Nicely-Nicely is as fat as a goose, and can scarcely wobble. But he notices that the Widow Crumb never once fails to set the fourth place that nobody ever fills, and furthermore he suddenly commences to notice that she always puts the best cuts of meat, and the best of everything else on the plate at this place, even though she throws it all away afterward.

Well, this situation preys on Nicely-Nicely's mind, as he cannot bear to see all this good fodder going to waste, so one morning he gets hold of old Harley and puts the siphon on him, because by this time Harley talks freely with Nicely-Nicely, although Nicely-Nicely can see that Harley is somewhat simple in spots and his conversation seldom makes much sense.

Anyway, he asks Harley what the Widow Crumb's idea is about the extra place at the table, and Harley says like this: 'Why,' he says, 'the place is for Jake.'

'Jake who?' Nicely-Nicely says.

'I do not recall his other name,' Harley says. 'He is her third or fourth husband, I do not remember which. Jake is the only one the Widow Crumb ever loves, although she does not discover this until after Jake departs. So,' Harley says, 'in memory of Jake she always sets his place at the table, and gives him the best she has. She misses Jake and wishes to feel that he is still with her.'

'What happens to Jake?' Nicely-Nicely says.

'Arsenic,' Harley says. 'Jake departs ten years ago.'

Well, of course all this is news to Nicely-Nicely, and he becomes very thoughtful to be sure, because in all the time he is married to her the Widow Crumb does not crack to him about her other husbands, and in fact Nicely-Nicely has no idea there is ever more than one.

'What happens to the others?' he says. 'Do they depart the same as Jake?'

'Yes,' Harley says, 'they all depart. One by one. I remember Number Two well. In fact, you remind me of him. Carbon monoxide,' Harley says. 'A charcoal stove in his room. It is most ingenious. The coroner says Number Three commits suicide by hanging himself with a rope in the barn loft. Number Three is small and weak, and it is no trouble whatever to handle him.

'Then comes Jake,' Harley says, 'unless Jake is Number Three and the hanging item is Number Four. I do not remember exactly. But the Widow Crumb never employs arsenic or other matters of this nature again. It is too slow. Jake lingers for hours. Besides,' Harley says, 'she realizes it may leave traces if anybody happens to get nosy.

'Jake is a fine-looking character,' Harley says. 'But a ne'er-do-well. He is a plumber from Salt Lake City, Utah, and has a hearty laugh. He is always telling funny stories. He is a great eater, even better than you, and he loves beans the way the Widow Crumb cooks them, with bacon and tomatoes. He suffers no little from the arsenic. He gets it in his beans. Number Five comes upon a black widow spider in his bed. He is no good. I mean Number Five.'

Well, by this time, Nicely-Nicely is very thoughtful to be sure, because what Harley says is commencing to sound somewhat disquieting.

'Number Six steps on a plank in the doorway of the house that drops a two-hundred-pound keystone on his head,' Harley says. 'The Widow Crumb personally figures this out herself. She is very bright. It is like a figure-4 trap, and has to be very accurate. An inch one way or the other, and the stone misses Number Six. I remember he has a big wen on the back of his neck. He is a carpenter from Keokuk, Iowa,' Harley says.

'Why,' Nicely-Nicely says, 'do you mean to say that the Widow Crumb purposely arranges to use up husbands in the manner you describe?'

'Oh, sure,' Harley says. 'Why do you suppose she marries them? It is a good living to her because of the insurance,' he says, 'although,' he says, 'to show you how bright she is, she does not insure Number Five for a dime, so people can never say she is making a business of the matter. He is a total loss to her, but it quiets talk. I am wondering,' Harley says, 'what she will think up for you.'

Well, Nicely-Nicely now commences to wonder about this, too, and he hopes and trusts that whatever she thinks up it will not be a black widow spider, because if there is one thing Nicely-Nicely despises, it is insects. Furthermore, he does not approve of hanging, or of dropping weights on people.

After giving the matter much thought, he steps into the house and mentions to the Widow Crumb that he will like to pay a little visit to town, figuring that if he can get to town, she will never see him again for heel dust.

But he finds that the Widow Crumb is by no means in favour of the idea of him visiting the town. In fact, she says it will bring great sorrow to her if he absents himself from her side more than two minutes, and moreover, she points out that it is coming on winter, and that the roads are bad, and she cannot spare the horse for such a trip just now.

Well, Nicely-Nicely says he is a fair sort of walker and, in fact, he mentions that he once walks from Saratoga Springs to Albany to avoid a bookmaker who claims there is a slight difference between them, but the Widow Crumb says she will not hear of him trying to walk to town because it may develop varicose veins in his legs.

In fact, Nicely-Nicely can see that the subject of his leaving the farm is very distasteful to her in every respect, and the chances are he will feel quite flattered by her concern for him if he does not happen to go into the house again a little later this same afternoon, and find her cleaning a double-barrelled shotgun.

She says she is thinking of going rabbit hunting, and wishes him to keep her company, saying it may take his mind off the idea of a visit to town; but she goes out of the room for a minute, and Nicely-Nicely picks up one of the shotgun shells she lays out on a table, and notices that it is loaded with buckshot.

So he tells her he guesses he will not go, as he is not feeling so good, and in fact he is not feeling so good, at that, because it seems that Nicely-Nicely is a rabbit hunter from infancy, and he never before hears of anyone hunting these creatures with buckshot. Then the Widow Crumb says all right, she will postpone her hunting until he feels better, but Nicely-Nicely cannot help noticing that she loads the shotgun and stands it in a corner where it is good and handy.

Well, Nicely-Nicely now sits down and gives this general situation some serious consideration, because he is now convinced that the Widow Crumb is unworthy of his companionship as a husband. In fact, Nicely-Nicely makes up his mind to take steps at his earliest convenience to sue her for divorce on the grounds of in-compatibility, but in the meantime he has to think up a means of getting away from her, and while he is thinking of this phase of the problem, she calls him to supper.

It is now coming on dark, and she has the lamps lit and the table set when Nicely-Nicely goes into the dining-room, and a fire is going in the base burner, and usually this is a pleasant and com-forting scene to Nicely-Nicely, but to-night he does not seem to find it as attractive as usual.

As he sits down at the table he notices that Harley is not present at the moment, though his place at the table is laid, and as a rule Harley is Johnny-at-the-rat-hole when it comes time to scoff, and moreover he is a pretty good doer at that. The fourth place that nobody ever occupies is also laid as usual, and now that he knows who this place is for, Nicely-Nicely notes that it is more neatly laid than his own, and that none of the china at this place is chipped, and that the bread and butter, and the salt and pepper, and the vinegar cruet and the bottle of Worcestershire sauce are handier to it than to any other place, and naturally his feelings are deeply wounded.

Then the Widow Crumb comes out of the kitchen with two plates loaded with spare-ribs and sauerkraut, and she puts one plate in front of Nicely-Nicely, and the other at Jake's place, and she says to Nicely-Nicely like this:

'Nicely,' she says, 'Harley is working late down at the barn, and when you get through with your supper, you can go down and call him. But,' she says, 'go ahead and eat first.'

Then she returns to the kitchen, which is right next to the dining-room with a swinging door in between, and Nicely-Nicely now observes that the very choicest spare-ribs are on Jake's plate, and also the most kraut, and this is really more than Nicely-Nicely can bear, for if there is one thing he adores it is spare-ribs, so he gets to feeling very moody to be sure about this discrimination, and he turns to Jake's place, and in a very sarcastic tone of voice he speaks out loud as follows:

'Well,' he says, 'it is pretty soft for you, you big lob, living on the fat of the land around here.'

Now of course what Nicely-Nicely is speaking is what he is thinking, and he does not realize that he is speaking out loud until the Widow Crumb pops into the dining-room carrying a bowl of salad, and looking all around and about.

'Nicely,' she says, 'do I hear you talking to someone?'

Well, at first Nicely-Nicely is about to deny it, but then he takes another look at the choice spare-ribs on Jake's plate, and he figures that he may as well let her know that he is on to her playing Jake for a favourite over him, and maybe cure her of it, for by this time Nicely-Nicely is so vexed about the spare-ribs that he almost forgets about leaving the farm, and is thinking of his future meals, so he says to the Widow Crumb like this:

'Why, sure,' he says. 'I am talking to Jake.'

'Jake?' she says. 'What Jake?'

And with this she starts looking all around and about again, and Nicely-Nicely can see that she is very pale, and that her hands are shaking so that she can scarcely hold the bowl of salad, and there is no doubt but what she is agitated no little, and quite some.

'What Jake?' the Widow Crumb says again.

Nicely-Nicely points to the empty chair, and says:

'Why, Jake here,' he says. 'You know Jake. Nice fellow, Jake.'

Then Nicely-Nicely goes on talking to the empty chair as follows:

'I notice you are not eating much to-night, Jake,' Nicely-Nicely says. 'What is the matter, Jake? The food cannot disagree with you, because it is all picked out and cooked to suit you, Jake. The best is none too good for you around here, Jake,' he says.

Then he lets on that he is listening to something Jake is saying in reply, and Nicely-Nicely says is that so, and I am surprised, and what do you think of that, and tut-tut, and my-my, just as if Jake is talking a blue streak to him, although, of course, Jake is by no means present.

Now Nicely-Nicely is really only being sarcastic in this conversation for the Widow Crumb's benefit, and naturally he does not figure that she will take it seriously, because he knows she can see Jake is not there, but Nicely-Nicely happens to look at her while he is talking, and he observes that she is still standing with the bowl of salad in her hands, and looking at the empty chair with a most unusual expression on her face, and in fact, it is such an unusual expression that it makes Nicely-Nicely feel somewhat uneasy, and he readies himself up to dodge the salad bowl at any minute.

He commences to remember the loaded shotgun in the corner, and what Harley gives him to understand about the Widow Crumb's attitude towards Jake, and Nicely-Nicely is sorry he ever brings Jake's name up, but it seems that Nicely-Nicely now finds that he cannot stop talking to save his life with the Widow Crumb standing there with the unusual expression on her face, and then he remembers the books she reads in her bed at night, and he goes on as follows:

'Maybe the pains in your stomach are just indigestion, Jake,' he says. 'I have stomach trouble in my youth myself. You are suffering terribly, eh, Jake? Well, maybe a little of the old bicarb will help you, Jake. Oh,' Nicely-Nicely says, 'there he goes.'

And with this he jumps up and runs to Jake's chair and lets on that he is helping a character up from the floor, and as he stoops over and pretends to be lifting this character, Nicely-Nicely grunts no little, as if the character is very heavy, and the grunts are really on the level with Nicely-Nicely as he is now full of spare-ribs, because he never really stops eating while he is talking, and stooping is not easy for him.

At these actions the Widow Crumb lets out a scream and drops the bowl of salad on the floor.

'I will help you to bed, Jake,' he says. 'Poor Jake. I know your stomach hurts, Jake. There now, Jake,' he says, 'take it easy. I know you are suffering horribly, but I will get something for you to ease the pain. Maybe it is the sauerkraut,' Nicely-Nicely says.

Then when he seems to get Jake up on his legs, Nicely-Nicely pretends to be assisting him across the floor towards the bedroom and all the time he is talking in a comforting tone to Jake, although you must always remember that there really is no Jake.

Now, all of a sudden, Nicely-Nicely hears the Widow Crumb's voice, and it is nothing but a hoarse whisper that sounds very strange in the room, as she says like this:

'Yes,' she says, 'it is Jake. I see him. I see him as plain as day.'

Well, at this Nicely-Nicely is personally somewhat startled, and he starts looking around and about himself, and it is a good thing for Jake that Nicely-Nicely is not really assisting Jake or Jake will find himself dropped on the floor, as the Widow Crumb says:

'Oh, Jake,' she says, 'I am so sorry. I am sorry for you in your suffering. I am sorry you ever leave me. I am sorry for everything. Please forgive me, Jake,' she says. 'I love you.'

Then the Widow Crumb screams again and runs through the swinging door into the kitchen and out the kitchen door and down the path that leads to the barn about two hundred yards away, and it is plain to be seen that she is very nervous. In fact, the last Nicely-Nicely sees of her before she disappears in the darkness down the path, she is throwing her hands up in the air, and letting out little screams, as follows: eee-eee-eee, and calling out old Harley's name.

Then Nicely-Nicely hears one extra loud scream, and after this there is much silence, and he figures that now is the time for him to take his departure, and he starts down the same path towards the barn, but figuring to cut off across the fields to the road that leads to the town when he observes a spark of light bobbing up and down on the path ahead of him, and presently he comes upon old Harley with a lantern in his hand.

Harley is down on his knees at what seems to be a big, round hole in the ground, and this hole is so wide it extends clear across the path, and Harley is poking his lantern down the hole, and when he sees Nicely-Nicely, he says:

'Oh,' he says, 'there you are. I guess there is some mistake here,' he says. 'The Widow Crumb tells me to wait in the barn until after supper and she will send you out after me, and,' Harley says, 'she also tells me to be sure and remove the cover of this old well as soon as it comes on dark. And,' Harley says, 'of course, I am expecting to find you in the well at this time, but who is in there but the Widow Crumb. I hear her screech as she drops in. I judge she must be hastening along the path and forgets about telling me to remove the cover of the well,' Harley says. 'It is most confusing,' he says.

Then he pokes his lantern down the well again, and leans over and shouts as follows:

'Hello, down there,' Harley shouts. 'Hello, hello, hello.'

But all that happens is an echo comes out of the well like this: Hello. And Nicely-Nicely observes that there is nothing to be seen down the well, but a great blackness.

'It is very deep, and dark, and cold down there,' Harley says. 'Deep, and dark, and cold, and half full of water. Oh, my poor baby,' he says.

Then Harley busts out crying as if his heart will break, and in fact he is so shaken by his sobs that he almost drops the lantern down the well.

Naturally Nicely-Nicely is somewhat surprised to observe these tears because personally he is by no means greatly distressed by the Widow Crumb being down the well, especially when he thinks of how she tries to put him down the well first, and finally he asks Harley why he is so downcast, and Harley speaks as follows:

'I love her,' Harley says. 'I love her very, very, very much. I am her Number One husband, and while she divorces me thirty years ago when it comes out that I have a weak heart, and the insurance companies refuse to give me a policy, I love her just the same. And now,' Harley says, 'here she is down a well.'

And with this he begins hollering into the hole some more, but the Widow Crumb never personally answers a human voice in this life again and when the story comes out, many citizens claim this is a right good thing, to be sure.

So Nicely-Nicely returns to Broadway, and he brings with him the sum of eleven hundred dollars, which is what he has left of the estate of his late ever-loving wife from the sale of the farm, and one thing and another, after generously declaring old Harley in for fifty per cent of his bit when Harley states that the only ambition he has left in life is to rear a tombstone to the memory of the Widow Crumb, and Nicely-Nicely announces that he is through with betting on horses, and other frivolity, and will devote his money to providing himself with food and shelter, and maybe a few clothes.

Well, the chances are Nicely-Nicely will keep his vow, too, but what happens the second day of his return, but he observes in the entries for the third race at Jamaica a horse by the name of Apparition, at 10 to 1 in the morning line, and Nicely-Nicely considers this entry practically a message to him, so he goes for his entire bundle on Apparition.

And it is agreed by one and all along Broadway who knows Nicely-Nicely's story that nobody in his right mind can possibly ignore such a powerful hunch as this, even though it loses, and Nicely-Nicely is again around doing the best he can.

The Brakeman's Daughter

It is coming on spring in Newark, New Jersey, and one nice afternoon I am standing on Broad Street with a guy from Cleveland, Ohio, by the name of The Humming Bird, speaking of this and that, and one thing and another, when along comes a very tasty-looking young doll.

In fact, she is a doll with black hair, and personally I claim there is nothing more restful to the eye than a doll with black hair, because it is even money, or anyway 9 to 10, that it is the natural colour of the hair, as it seems that dolls will change the colour of their hair to any colour but black, and why this is nobody knows, except that it is just the way dolls are.

Well, besides black hair, this doll has a complexion like I do not know what, and little feet and ankles, and a way of walking that is very pleasant to behold. Personally, I always take a gander at a doll's feet and ankles before I start handicapping her, because the way I look at it, the feet and ankles are the big tell in the matter of class, although I wish to state that I see some dolls in my time who have large feet and big ankles, but who are by no means bad.

But this doll I am speaking of is 100 per cent in every respect, and as she passes, The Humming Bird looks at her, and she looks at The Humming Bird, and it is just the same as if they hold a two hours' conversation on the telephone, for they are both young, and it is spring, and the way language can pass between young guys and young dolls in the spring without them saying a word is really most surprising, and, in fact, it is practically uncanny.

Well, I can see that The Humming Bird is somewhat confused for a minute, while the young doll seems to go right off into a trance, and she starts crossing the street against the lights, which is not only unlawful in Newark, New Jersey, but most indiscreet, and she is about to be run down and mashed like a turnip by one of Big False Face's beer trucks when The Humming Bird hops out into the street and yanks her out of danger, while the jockey looking back and yelling words you will scarcely believe are known to anybody in Newark, New Jersey.

Then The Humming Bird and the young doll stand on the sidewalk chewing the fat for a minute or two, and it is plain to be seen that the doll is very much obliged to The Humming Bird, and it is also plain to be seen that The Humming Bird will give anyway four bobs to have the jockey of the beer truck where he can talk to him quietly.

Finally the doll goes on across the street, but this time she keeps her head up and watches where she is going, and The Humming Bird comes back to me, and I ask him if he finds out who she is, and does he date her up, or what? But in answer to my questions, The Humming Bird states to me as follows:

'To tell the truth,' The Humming Bird says, 'I neglect these details, because,' he says, 'I am already dated up to go out with Big False Face to-night to call on a doll who is daffy to meet me. Otherwise,' he says, 'I will undoubtedly make arrangements to see more of this pancake I just save from rack and ruin.

'But,' The Humming Bird says, 'Big Falsy tells me I am going to meet the most wonderful doll in the world, and one that is very difficult to meet, so I cannot be picking up any excess at this time. In fact,' he says, 'Big Falsy tells me that every guy in this town will give his right leg for the privilege of meeting the doll in question, but she will have no part of them. But it seems that she sees me talking to Big Falsy on the street yesterday, and now nothing will do but she must meet up with me personally. Is it not remarkable,' The Humming Bird says, 'the way dolls go for me?'

Well, I say it is, for I can see that The Humming Bird is such a guy as thinks he has something on the dolls, and for all I know maybe he has, at that, for he has plenty of youth, and good looks, and good clothes, and a nice line of gab, and all these matters are given serious consideration by the dolls, especially the youth.

But I cannot figure any doll that Big False Face knows being such a doll as the one The Humming Bird just yanks out the way of the beer truck, and in fact I do not see how any doll whatever can have any truck with a guy as ugly as Big False Face. But then of course Big False Face is now an important guy in the business world, and has plenty of potatoes, and of course potatoes are also something that is taken into consideration by the dolls.

Big False Face is in the brewery business, and he controls a number of breweries in different spots on the Atlantic seaboard, and especially in New Jersey, and the reason The Humming Bird is in Newark, New Jersey, at this time, is because Big False Face gets a very huge idea in connection with these breweries.

It seems that they are breweries that Big False Face takes over during the past ten years when the country is trying to get along without beer, and the plants are laying idle, and Big False Face opens up these plants and puts many guys to work, and turns out plenty of beer, and thus becomes quite a philanthropist in his way, especially to citizens who like their beer, although up to the time he gets going good as a brewer, Big False Face is considered a very humble character, indeed.

He comes from the lower East Side of New York, and he is called Big False Face from the time he is very young, because he has a very large and a very homely kisser, and on this kisser there is always a castor-oil smile that looks as if it is painted on. But this smile is strictly a throw-off, and Big False Face is often smiling when he is by no means amused at anything, though I must say for him that he is generally a very light-hearted guy.

In his early youth, it is Big False Face's custom to stand chatting with strangers to the city around the railroad stations and ferryboat landings, and smiling very genially at them, and in this way Big False Face learns much about other parts of the country. But it seems that while he is chatting with these strangers, friends of Big False Face search the strangers' pockets, sometimes removing articles from these pockets such as watches, and lucky pieces, and keepsakes of one kind and another, including money.

Of course it is all in fun, but it seems that some of the strangers become greatly annoyed when they find their pockets empty, and go out of their way to mention the matter to the gendarmes. Well, after the gendarmes hear some little mention from strangers about their pockets being searched while they are chatting with a guy with a large, smiling kisser, the gendarmes take to looking around for such a guy.

Naturally, they finally come upon Big False Face, for at the time I am speaking of, it is by no means common to find guys with smiles on their kissers on the lower East Side, and, especially, large smiles. So what happens but Big False Face is sent to college in his youth by the gendarmes, and the place where the college is located is Auburn, New York, where they teach him that it is very, very wrong to smile at strangers while their pockets are being searched.

After Big False Face is in college for several years, the warden sends for him one day and gives him a new suit of clothes, and a railroad ticket, and a few bobs, and plenty of sound advice, and tells him to go back home again, and afterward Big False Face says he is only sorry he can never remember the advice, as he has no doubt it will be of great value to him in his subsequent career.

Well, later on, Big False Face takes a post-graduate course at Ossining, and also at Dannemora, and by the time he is through with all this, he finds that conditions change throughout the country, and that his former occupation is old-fashioned, and by no means genteel, so Big False Face has to think up something else to do. And while he is thinking, he drives a taxicab and has his station in front of the Pekin restaurant on Broadway, which is a real hot spot at this time.

Then one night a sailor off U.S. battleship hires Big False Face to take him riding in Central Park, and it seems that somewhere on this ride the sailor loses his leather containing a month's salary, and he hops out of the taxicab and starts complaining to a gendarme, making quite a mountain out of nothing but a molehill, for anybody knows that if the sailor does not lose his leather in the taxicab he is bound to spend it at ten cents a clip dancing with the dolls in the Flowerland dance hall, or maybe taking boat rides on the lagoon in the park.

Well, Big False Face can see an argument coming up, and rather than argue, he retires from the taxicab business at once, leaving his taxicab right there in the park, and going over into New Jersey, and Big False Face always says that one of the regrets of his life is he never collects the taxi fare off the sailor.

In New Jersey, Big False Face secures a position with the late Crowbar Connolly, riding loads down out of Canada, and then he is with the late Hands McGovern, and the late Dark Tony de More, and also the late Lanky-lank Watson, and all this time Big False Face is advancing step by step in the business world, for he has a great personality and is well liked by one and all.

Naturally, many citizens are jealous of Big False Face, and sometimes when they are speaking of him they speak of the days of his youth when he is on the whiz, as if this is something against him, but I always say it is very creditable of Big False Face to rise from such a humble beginning to a position of affluence in the business world.

Personally, I consider Big False Face a remarkable character, especially when he takes over the idle breweries, because it is at a time when everybody is going around saying that if they can only have beer everything will be all right. So Big False Face starts turning out beer that tastes very good indeed, and if everything is not all right, it is by no means his fault.

You must remember that at the time he starts turning out his beer, and for years afterward, Big False Face is being most illegal and quite against the law, and I claim that the way he is able to hide several breweries, each covering maybe half a block of ground, from the gendarmes all these years is practically magical, and proves that what I say about Big False Face being a remarkable character is very true.

Well, when Congress finally gets around to saying that beer is all right again, Big False Face is a well-established, going concern, and has a fair head-start on the old-fashioned brewers who come back into the business again, but Big False Face is smart enough to know that he will be able to keep ahead of them only by great enterprise and industry, because it seems that certain parties are bound and determined to make it tough on the brewers who supply this nation with beer when beer is illegal, such as Big False Face, forgetting all the hardships and dangers that these brewers face through the years to give the American people their beer, and all the bother they are put to in hiding breweries from the gendarmes.

In fact, these certain parties are making it so tough that Big False Face himself has to write twice before he can get permits for his breweries, and naturally this annoys Big False Face no little, as he hates to write letters.

Furthermore, he hears this condition prevails all over the country, so Big False Face gets to thinking things over, and he decides that the thing to do is to organize the independent brewers like himself into an association to protect their interests.

So he calls a meeting in Newark, New Jersey, of all these brewers and this is how it comes that The Humming Bird is present, for The Humming Bird represents certain interests around Cleveland, Ohio, and furthermore The Humming Bird is personally regarded as a very able young guy when it comes to breweries.

Well, the only reason I am in Newark, New Jersey, at this time is because a guy by the name of Abie Schumtzenheimer is a delegate representing a New York brewery, and this Abie is a friend of mine, and after the meeting lasts three days he sends for me to come over and play pinochle with him because he cannot make heads or tails of what they are all talking about.

And anyway Abie does not care much, because the brewery he represents is going along for nearly twelve years, and is doing all the business it can handle, and any time it fails to do all the business it can handle, Abie will be around asking a lot of people why.

So Abie's brewery does not care if it enters any association or not, but of course Abie cannot disregard an invitation from such a guy as Big False Face. So there he is, and by and by there I am, and in this way I meet up with The Humming Bird, and, after watching the way he goes darting around and about, especially if a doll happens to pop up in his neighbourhood, I can understand why they call him The Humming Bird.

But, personally, I do not mind seeing a young guy displaying an interest in dolls, and, in fact, if a young guy does not display such an interest in dolls, I am apt to figure there is something wrong with him. And anyway what is the use of being young if a guy does not display an interest in dolls?

Well, there are delegates to the meeting from as far west as Chicago, and most of them seem to be greatly interested in Big False Face's proposition, especially a delegate from South Chicago who keeps trying to introduce a resolution to sue the government for libel for speaking of brewers who supply the nation with beer after prohibition sets in as racket guys and wildcatters.

The reason the meeting lasts so long is partly because Big False Face keeps making motions for recesses so he can do a little entertaining, for if there is one thing Big False Face loves, it is to entertain, but another reason is that not all the delegates are willing to join Big False Face's association, especially certain delegates who are operating in Pennsylvania.

These delegates say it is nothing but a scheme on the part of Big False Face to nab the business on them, and in fact it seems that there is much resentment among these delegates against Big False Face, and especially on the part of a guy by the name of Cheeks Sheracki, who comes from Philadelphia, Pennsylvania, and I wish to state that if there is one guy in the United States I will not care to have around resenting me it is Cheeks Sheracki, for nobody knows how many guys Cheeks cools off in his time, not even himself.

But Big False Face does not seem to notice anybody resenting him and he is putting on entertainment for the delegates right and left, including a nice steak dinner on the evening of the day I am speaking of, and it is at this dinner that I state to Big False Face that I hear he is taking The Humming Bird out in society.

'Yes,' Big False Face says, 'I am going to take The Humming Bird to call on the brakeman's daughter.'

Well, when I hear this, I wish to say I am somewhat surprised, because the brakeman's daughter is nothing but a practical joke, and, furthermore, it is a practical joke that is only for rank suckers, and The Humming Bird does not look to be such a sucker to me.

In fact, when Big False Face speaks of the brakeman's daughter, I take a gander at The Humming Bird figuring to see some expression on his kisser that will show he knows what the brakeman's daughter is, but instead The Humming Bird is only looking quite eager, and then I get to thinking about what he tells me in the afternoon about Big False Face taking him to see a doll who is daffy to meet him, and I can see that Big False Face is working on him with the brakeman's daughter for some time.

And I also get to thinking that a lot of smarter guys than The Humming Bird will ever be, no matter how smart he gets, fall for the brakeman's daughter joke, including Big False Face himself. In fact, Big False Face falls for it in the spring of 1928 at Hot Springs, Arkansas, and ever since it is his favourite joke, and it becomes part of his entertainment of all visitors to Newark, New Jersey, unless of course they happen to be visitors who are jerry to the brakeman's daughter into quite a well-known institution in Newark, New Jersey, and the way the brakeman's daughter joke goes is as follows:

The idea is Big False Face picks out some guy that he figures is a little doll-dizzy, and the way Big False Face can rap to a doll-dizzy guy is really quite remarkable.

Then he starts telling this guy about the brakeman's daughter, who is the most beautiful doll that ever steps in shoe leather, to hear Big False Face tell it. In fact, I once hear Big False Face telling a sucker about how beautiful the brakeman's daughter is, and I find myself wishing to see her, although of course I know there is no such thing as the brakeman's daughter.

Furthermore, everybody around Big False Face starts putting in a boost for the brakeman's daughter, stating to the sucker that she is so lovely that guys are apt to go silly just looking at her. But it seems that the brakeman's daughter has a papa who is a brakeman on the Central, and who is the orneriest guy in the world when it comes to his daughter, and who will not let anybody get close enough to her to hand her a slice of fruit cake.

In fact, this brakeman is so ornery he will shoot you setting if he catches you fooling around his daughter, the way Big False Face and other citizens of Newark, New Jersey, state the situation to the sucker, and everybody is afraid of the brakeman, including guys who are not supposed to be afraid of anything in this world.

But it seems that Big False Face is acquainted with the brakeman's daughter, and knows the nights the brakeman has to be out on his run, and on these nights the brakeman's daughter is home alone, and on such a night Big False Face occasionally calls on her, and sometimes takes a friend. But Big False Face and everybody else says that it is a dangerous proposition, because if the brakeman ever happens to come home unexpectedly and find callers with his daughter, he is pretty sure to hurt somebody.

Well, the chances are the sucker wishes to call on the brakeman's daughter, no matter what, especially as Big False Face generally lets on that the brakeman's daughter sees the sucker somewhere and is very anxious to meet him, just as he lets on to The Humming Bird, so finally some night Big Falsy takes the sucker to the house where the brakeman's daughter lives, making their approach to the house very roundabout, and mysterious, and sneaky.

Then the minute Big Falsy knocks on the door, out pops a guy from somewhere roaring at them in a large voice, and Big False Face yells that it is the brakeman's daughter's papa himself, and starts running, telling the sucker to follow, although as a rule this is by no means necessary. And when the sucker starts running, he commences to hear shots, and naturally he figures that the old brakeman is popping at him with a Betsy, but what he really hears is incandescent light bulbs going off around him and sometimes they hit him if the bulb-thrower has good control.

Now, the house Big False Face generally uses is an old empty residence pretty well out in a suburb of Newark, New Jersey, and it sits away off by itself in a big yard near a piece of woods, and when he starts running, Big False Face always runs into this woods, and naturally the sucker follows him. And pretty soon Big False Face loses the sucker in the woods, and doubles back and goes on downtown and leaves the sucker wandering around in the woods for maybe hours.

Then when the sucker finally makes his way back to his hotel, he always finds many citizens gathered to give him the ha-ha, and to make him buy refreshments for one and all, and the sucker tries to make out that he is greatly amused himself, although the chances are he is so hot you can fry an egg on any part of him.

The biggest laugh that Big False Face ever gets out of the brakeman's daughter joke is the time he leaves a guy from Brooklyn by the name of Rocco Scarpati in the woods one cold winter night, and Rocco never does find his way out, and freezes as stiff as a starched shirt. And of course Big False Face has quite a time explaining to Rocco's Brooklyn friends that Rocco is not cooled off by other means than freezing.

Well, now the way I tell it, you say to yourself how can anybody be sucker enough to fall for such a plant as this? But Big False Face's record with the brakeman's daughter joke in Newark, New

Jersey, includes a congressman, a justice of the peace, three G-guys, eighteen newspaper scribes, five prize fighters, and a raft of guys from different parts of the country, who are such guys as the ordinary citizen will hesitate about making merry with.

In fact, I hear Big False Face is putting the feel on Cheeks Sheracki with reference to the brakeman's daughter until he finds out Cheeks knows this joke as well as he does himself, and then Big False Face discovers The Humming Bird, and no one is talking stronger for the brakeman's daughter with The Humming Bird than Cheeks.

Well, anyway, along about nine o'clock on the night in question, Big False Face tells The Humming Bird that the brakeman is now well out on his run on the Central so they get in Big False Face's car and start out, and I notice that, as they get in the car, Big False Face gives The Humming Bird a quick fanning, as Big False Face does not care to take chances on a sucker having that certain business on him.

The Humming Bird is all sharpened up for this occasion, and furthermore he is quite excited, and one and all are telling him what a lucky guy he is to get to call on the brakeman's daughter, but anybody can see from the way The Humming Bird acts that he feels that it is really the brakeman's daughter who is having the luck.

It seems that Cheeks Sheracki and a couple of his guys from Philadelphia go out to the house in advance to heave the incandescent bulbs and do the yelling, and personally I sit up playing pinochle with Abie Schumtzenheimer waiting to hear what comes off, although Abie says it is all great foolishness, and by no means worthy of grown guys. But Abie admits he will be glad to see the brakeman's daughter himself, if she is as beautiful as Big False Face claims.

Well, when they come within a couple of blocks of the empty house in the suburbs of Newark, New Jersey, Big False Face tells his driver, a guy by the name of Ears Acosta, who afterwards informs me on several points in this transaction, to pull up and wait there, and then Big False Face and The Humming Bird get out of the car and Big False Face leads the way up the street and into the yard.

This yard is filled with big trees and shrubbery, but the moon is shining somewhat, and it is easy enough to make out objects around and about, but there are no lights in the house, and it is so quiet you can hear your watch tick in your pocket, if you happen to have a watch.

Well, Big False Face has The Humming Bird by the coat sleeve, and he tiptoes through the gate and up a pathway, and The Humming Bird tiptoes right with him, and every now and then Big False Face stops and listens, and the way Big False Face puts this on is really wonderful, because he does it so often he can get a little soul into his work.

Now, The Humming Bird has plenty of moxie from all I hear, but naturally seeing the way Big False Face is acting makes him feel a little nervous, because The Humming Bird knows that Big False Face is as game as they come, and he figures that any situation that makes Big False Face act as careful as all this must be a very dangerous situation, indeed.

When they finally get up close to the house, The Humming Bird sees there is a porch, and Big False Face tiptoes up on this porch, still leading The Humming Bird by the coat sleeve, and then Big False Face knocks softly on the door, and lets out a little low whistle, and, just as The Humming Bird is commencing to notice that this place seems to be somewhat deserted, all of a sudden a guy comes busting around the corner of the house.

This guy is making a terrible racket, what with yelling and swearing, and among other things he yells as follows:

'Ah-ha!' the guy yells, 'now I have you dead to rights!'

And with this, something goes pop, and then something goes pop-pop, and Big False Face says to The Humming Bird like this:

'My goodness,' Big False Face says, 'it is the brakeman! Run!' he says. 'Run for your life!'

Then Big False Face turns and runs, and The Humming Bird is about to turn and run with him because The Humming Bird figures if a guy like Big False Face can afford to run there can be no percentage in standing still himself, but before he can move the door of the house flies open and The Humming Bird feels himself being yanked inside the joint, and he puts up his dukes and gets ready to do the best he can until he is overpowered. Then he hears a doll's voice going like this:

'Sh-h-h-h!' the doll's voice goes. 'Sh-h-h-h!'

So The Humming Bird sh-h-h-h's, and the racket goes on outside a while with a guy still yelling, and much pop-pop-popping away. Then the noise dies out, and all is still, and by the moonlight that is coming through a window on which there is no curtain,

The Humming Bird can see a lot of furniture scattered around and about the room, but some of it is upside-down and none of it is arranged in any order.

Furthermore, The Humming Bird can now also see that the doll who pulls him into the house and gives him the sh-h-h-h is nobody but the black-haired doll he hauls out of the way of the beer truck in the afternoon, and naturally The Humming Bird is somewhat surprised to see her at this time.

Well, the black-haired doll smiles at The Humming Bird and finally he forgets his nervousness to some extent, and in fact drops his dukes which he still has up ready to sell his life dearly, and by and by the black-haired doll says to him like this:

'I recognize you through the window in the moonlight,' she says. 'As I see you coming up on the porch, I also see some parties lurking in the shrubbery, and,' she says, 'I have a feeling they are seeking to do you harm, so I pull you inside the house. I am glad to see you again,' she says.

Well, Big False Face does not show up in his accustomed haunts to laugh at the joke on The Humming Bird, but Ears Acosta returns with disquieting news such as causes many citizens to go looking for Big False Face, and they find him face downward on the path just inside the gateway, and when they turn him over the old castor-oil smile is still on his kisser, and even larger than ever, as if Big False Face is greatly amused by some thought that hits him all of a sudden.

And Big False Face is extremely dead when they find him, as it seems that some of the incandescent bulbs that go pop-popping around him are really sawed-off shotguns, and it also seems that Cheeks Sheracki and his guys from Philadelphia are such careless shots that they tear off half the gate with their slugs, so it is pretty lucky for The Humming Bird that he is not running with Big False Face for this gate at the moment, or in fact anywhere near him.

And back in the house, while they are lugging Big False Face away, The Humming Bird and the black-haired doll are sitting on an overturned sofa in the parlour with the moonlight streaming through the window on which there is no curtain and spilling all over them as The Humming Bird is telling her how much he loves her, and how he hopes and trusts she feels the same towards him, for they are young, and it is spring in Newark, New Jersey.

'Well,' The Humming Bird says, 'so you are the brakeman's

daughter, are you? Well,' he says, 'I wish to state that they do not overboost you a nickel's worth when they tell me you are the most beautiful doll in all this world, and I am certainly tickled to find you.'

'But how do you learn my new address so soon?' the black-haired doll says. 'We just move in here this morning, although,' she says, 'I guess it is a good thing for you we do not have time to put up any window shades. And what do you mean,' the black-haired doll says, 'by calling me the brakeman's daughter? My papa is one of the oldest and best known conductors anywhere on the Erie,' she says.

Cemetery Bait

One pleasant morning in early April, a character by the name of Gentleman George wakes up to find himself in a most embarrassing predicament.

He wakes up to find himself in a cell in the state penitentiary at Trenton, N.J., and while a cell in a state penitentiary is by no means a novelty to George, and ordinarily will cause him no confusion whatever, the trouble is this particular cell is what is known as the death house.

Naturally, George is very self-conscious about this, as it is only the second time in his life he ever finds himself in such a house, and the first time is so far back in his youth that it leaves scarcely any impression on him, especially as he is commuted out of it in less than sixty days.

Well, George sits there on the side of the cot in his cell this pleasant April morning, thinking what a humiliating circumstance this is to a proud nature such as his, when all of a sudden he remembers that on the morrow he is to be placed in Mister Edison's rocking-chair in the room adjoining his cell, and given a very severe shock in the seat of his breeches.

On remembering this George becomes very thoughtful to be sure, and sighs to himself as follows: Heigh-ho, heigh-ho, heigh-ho. And then he sends for me to come and see him, although George is well aware that I have no use for penitentiaries, or their environs, and consider them a most revolting spectacle.

In fact, I have such a repugnance for penitentiaries that I never even glance at them in passing, because I am afraid that peepings may be catchings, but of course in a situation such as this I can scarcely deny the call of an old friend.

They let me talk to George through the bars of his cell, and naturally I am somewhat perturbed to observe him in this plight, although I can see that his surroundings are clean and sanitary, and that the hacks seem kindly disposed towards him, except one big doorknob who is inclined to be somewhat churlish because George just beats him in a game of two-handed pinochle.

Furthermore, I can see that George is in pretty fair physical condition, although a little stouter than somewhat, and that he looks as if he is getting some rest.

He is at this time about forty-five years of age, is known far and wide as the handsomest and most genteel character on Broadway. His brown hair now has some grey in it along the edges, and there are lines of care in his face, and, of course, George is not dressed as fashionably as usual.

In fact, his clothes need pressing, and he can stand a haircut, and a shave, and when I mention this to George he says he understands they are going to give him all the haircutting he requires before morning, and maybe a close shave, too.

In the old days, Gentleman George is very prominent in the jewellery trade with Tommy Entrata and his associates, and anybody will tell you that Tommy and his crowd are the best in the country, because they pursue strictly business methods, and are very high-principled.

They generally work with a character by the name of Lou Adolia, who is a private fuzz often employed by big insurance companies that make a speciality of insuring jewellery for wealthy female parties, a fuzz being a way of saying a detective, although the chances are Lou Adolia cannot really find his hip pocket with both hands.

But when Tommy Entrata and his associates come into possession of jewellery belonging to these wealthy female parties, they notify Lou Adolia, and he arranges with the insurance companies to pay a certain sum for the return of the merchandise, and no beefs, and everybody is satisfied, especially the insurance companies, because, of course, if they do not get the goods back, the companies will have to pay the full amount of the insurance.

As Tommy Entrata is generally very reasonable in his fees on jewellery that comes into his possession, it really is a most economical arrangement for the insurance companies, and for everybody else concerned, and it is also very nice for Lou Adolia, as he always gets a reward from the companies, and sometimes a piece of what Tommy Entrata collects.

Then a piece always goes to the stout fellow in the city in which Tommy Entrata and his associates are operating, the stout fellow being the local fix, because, of course, you understand that in a business as large as this carried on by Tommy Entrata it is necessary to take care of all angles. So the stout fellow looks after the local law to see that it does not interfere with Tommy Entrata any more than is absolutely necessary.

To tell the truth, when Tommy Entrata and his associates go into a town, it is generally as well-organized from top to bottom as Standard Oil, and Tommy not only has a complete roster of all the local jewellery owners, and what they are insured for, from Lou Adolia, but also a few diagrams as to where this jewellery is located, and Tommy never fails to make ample provision for one and all in the town who may be concerned before he turns a wheel. In fact, I hear that in a spot up in the North-west Tommy once even declares the mayor and the commissioner of public safety in on one of his transactions, just out of the goodness of his heart, and this unselfishness in his business operations makes Tommy highly respected far and wide.

Anyway, Gentleman George is one of Tommy Entrata's experts in the matter of coming into possession of jewellery, and Tommy appreciates George no little, as George is strictly a lone hand at his work, and he never carries that thing on him, and considers all forms of violence most revolting, so he never gets into trouble, or at least not much.

I am telling you all this so you will understand that Tommy Entrata conducts his business in a high-class, conservative manner, and personally I consider him a great boon to a community, because he teaches people the value of insurance, and now I will return to Gentleman George in his cell in the death house in Trenton, N.J.

'Well,' George says, 'there you are, and here I am, and you are the only friend that comes to see me since the judge mentions the date that now becomes of some importance in my life, and which is in fact to-morrow. And now I wish to tell you a story, which will be the truth, the whole truth, and nothing but the truth, and the object of this story is to show that I once perform a great service to the public.'

At this, I become uneasy, because I am afraid it may be a tedious story, and I do not care to remain in such surroundings listening to reminiscence, so I request George to epitomize as much as possible, and to omit all reference to low characters and sordid situations, and then George states as follows, and to wit, viz.:

In the winter of 1935, I am going southward by train on business bent, and the reason I do not reveal my destination at this time is because I do not wish to be recalled as ever hollering copper, even on a city, but I will say that it is a certain winter resort spot about as far below the Mason & Dixon's line as you can get before you start swimming, and a very pleasant spot it is, at that.

The first night out on the train, I go into the diner and partake of a fish that is on the menu, because the steward of the diner weighs in with a strong shill for this fish, and the next thing I know I am back in my compartment as sick as anything, and maybe a little bit sicker.

To tell the truth, I am so sick that I think I am going to pass away, and this thought disturbs me no little, as Tommy Entrata is looking forward to my arrival with keen interest, and I know that he is apt to take my passing away as a personal affront.

Well, while I am lying in my berth as sick as stated, all of a sudden the door of my compartment opens, and a pair of specs and a short, scrubby, grey tash appear, and behind the specs and the tash is a stern-looking character of maybe fifty-odd who speaks to me in a gruff voice, as follows:

'See here, now,' he says, 'what is all this runting and grunting about? Are you sick?'

'Well,' I say, 'if I am not sick, I will do until an invalid comes along.'

And then I start retching again, and in between retches, I mention the dining-car fish, and I tell the stern-looking character that if he will kindly get the dining-car steward to step into my compartment for just one minute I will die happy.

'You speak great nonsense,' the stern-looking character says. 'You are not going to die, although,' he says, 'who knows but what you may be better off if you do? Not enough people know when to die. What ails you is ptomaine poisoning, and I will take charge of this situation myself because I will be unable to sleep in this car with you scrooning and mooning all night.

'I once get the same thing myself in Gloucester, Mass.' he says. 'You will expect fish to be all right in Gloucester, Mass. If I remember,' he says, 'it is mackerel in my case.'

Then he rings for the porter, and pretty soon he has the train secretary, and the Pullman conductor, and even a couple of other passengers running in and out of my compartment getting him this, and that, and one thing and another, and dosing me with I do not know what, and sick as I am, I can see that this stern-looking character is accustomed to having people step around when he speaks.

Well, for a while I am thinking that the best break I can get is to pass away without any further lingering; then, by and by, I commence feeling better, and finally I doze off to sleep. But I seem to remember the stern-looking character mentioning that he is going to the same place that I am, and that he is just returning from a hunting-trip in Canada, and I also seem to recall him telling me what a wonderful shot he is with any kind of fire-arms.

Afterward, however, I figure I must dream all this because the next morning the stern-looking character just glances in on me once and asks how I feel in a tone of voice that indicates he does not care much one way or the other, and after this I do not see hide or hair of him, and I can see that he does not mean to make a friendship of the matter.

In fact, when I am getting off the train at my destination, I suddenly remember that I do not even know the stern-looking character's name, and I am sorry about this, as so few people in the world are ever good to me that I wish to cherish the names of those who are. But, of course, I now have no time for sentiment, as duty calls me, and I do not bother to inquire around and about with reference to the stern-looking character.

I telephone Tommy Entrata, and make a meet with him for dinner in a night-club that is called by the name of the Bath and Sail Club, although there is no bathing connected with it whatever, and no sailing either, for that matter, and while I am waiting there for Tommy, I observe at another table the most beautiful Judy I see in many a day, and you know very well that few better judges of beauty ever live than yours sincerely, G. George.

She is young, and has hair the colour of straw, and she is dressed in a gorgeous white evening gown, and she has plenty of junk on her in the way of diamonds, and she seems to be waiting for someone and I find myself regretting that it is not me. I am so impressed by her that I call Emil, the head-waiter, and question him, because Emil is an old friend of mine, and I know he always has a fund of information on matters such as this.

'Emil,' I say, 'who is the lovely pancake over there by the window?'

'Cemetery bait,' Emil says, so I know he means she is married, and has a husband who is selfish about her, and naturally I cast no sheep's eyes in her direction, especially as Tommy Entrata comes in about now and takes me to a private room where we have a nice dinner, and discuss my business in this city.

It is in pursuit of this business, at the hour of 1 a.m. on a warm Sunday morning, that I am making a call at the residence of a character by the name of Colonel Samuel B. Venus, and am in the boudoir of his ever-loving wife, and a beautiful room it is, at that, with the windows on one side looking out over the sea waves, and the windows on the other side overlooking a patio of whispering palm-trees.

The moon is shining down on this scene, and it is so lovely that I stand at the front windows a few moments looking out over the water before I start seeking the small can, or safe, that I know is concealed in a clothes closet in the room unless the butler in the Venus house is telling a terrible falsehood and accepting money from us under false pretences for this information and for admitting me to the premises.

Of course, Colonel Samuel B. Venus's ever-loving wife is not present in her boudoir at this hour, and neither is Colonel Samuel B. Venus, and in fact I afterward learn that the only way Colonel Samuel B. Venus can get in there is on a writ of habeas corpus, but this has nothing to do with my story.

My information is that Colonel Samuel B. Venus is a very wealthy character of maybe sixty years of age, come next grass, and that his ever-loving wife is less than half of that, and has some of the finest jewellery in this country, including pearls, diamonds, star rubies, emeralds, and I do not know what all else, and I am given to understand that Colonel Samuel B. Venus leaves the night before on a fishing-trip, and that Mrs. Colonel Samuel B. Venus is out somewhere wearing only a couple of pounds of her jewels, so the rest of her stuff is bound to be in the little can in her boudoir.

Well, the little can is in the closet just where the butler reports, and I observe that it is such a can as I will be able to open with a toothpick if necessary, although, of course, I bring along my regular can-opener, which is a tool for cutting open safes that I personally invent, as you perhaps remember, although I never think to get a patent on it from the government, and I am about to start operations when I hear voices, and two characters, male and female, enter the boudoir.

So there I am in the closet among a lot of dresses and coats, and all this and that, and, what is more, I leave the closet door open a little when I go in, as I figure I may require a little air, and I am now afraid to close the door for fear of making a noise, and the best I can make of this situation is that I am a gone gosling. To tell the truth, it is one of the few times in my life that I regret I do not have that thing on me, just for self-defence.

I can see right away from the way she talks that the female character must be Mrs. Colonel Samuel B. Venus, but the character with her is by no means her husband, and naturally I am greatly scandalized to think that a married broad will bring a party not her husband into her boudoir with her at such an hour, and I am wondering what on earth the world is coming to.

But although I listen keenly, there seems to be no goings-on, and in fact all they are doing is talking, so I figure the character with Mrs. Colonel Samuel B. Venus must be a character without any imagination whatever.

Finally, when I judge from their conversation that they are looking at the view of the sad sea waves, I cop a quick peek, and I see that Mrs. Colonel Samuel B. Venus is nobody but the blonde I admire at the Bath and Sail Club, and while this surprises me no little, it does not surprise me half as much as the fact that the character with her is a party by the name of Count Tomaso, who is known far and wide as a most unworthy character. In fact, Count Tomaso is regarded in some circles as a 22-carat fink, a fink being a character who is lower than a mudcat's vest pocket.

He is a small, slim-built character, with dark hair greased down on his head, and he wears a monocle, and seems very foreign in every respect. In fact, Count Tomaso claims to belong to the Italian nobility, but he is no more a count than I am, and to tell the truth, he is nothing but a ginzo out of Sacramento, and his right name is Carfarelli.

For a matter of twenty years or more, this Count Tomaso is on the socket, which is a way of saying his dodge is blackmail, and of course there is little or no class to such a dodge as this. He generally pitches to foolish old married Judys, and gets them wedged in with letters, and one thing and another, and then puts the shake on them.

Personally, I rarely criticize anybody else's methods of earning a livelihood, but I can never approve of the shake, although I must admit that from what I hear of Count Tomaso, he really is an artist in his line, and can nine those old phlugs in first-class style when he is knuckling.

I only hope and trust that his presence in Mrs. Colonel Samuel B. Venus's boudoir does not mean that Count Tomaso is trespassing in any way upon my affairs, as I can see where this will produce complications, and it is always my policy to avoid complications, so I remain very quiet, with a firm grip on my can-opener in case Mrs. Colonel Samuel B. Venus or Count Tomaso happens to come to the closet.

But it seems to be nothing but a social visit, as I can hear her getting out some liquor, and after a couple of drinks they begin speaking of nothing much in particular, including the weather. Presently the conversation becomes quite dull, for it is all about love and conversation about love always bores me no little unless I am making the conversation myself, although I can see that Mrs. Colonel Samuel B. Venus is better than a raw hand in conversation of this nature.

I am so bored that I put down my can-opener and am about to doze off among the dresses, when all of a sudden the conversation takes a very unusual turn, to be sure, for Mrs. Colonel Samuel B. Venus says to Count Tomaso like this:

'I know you love me,' she says, 'and I love you madly in return, but what good will it do us? I am married to a character old enough to be my father and, although he does not know it, I hate and despise him. But even if I tell him this, I know he will never give me a divorce, and, besides, if I do get a divorce, he is sure to put me off with a mere pittance. I am bound to him as long as he lives,' she says. 'As long as he lives, Tomaso.'

Well, Count Tomaso says this is certainly a sad state of affairs, and seems to be taking another drink, and she goes on as follows:

'Of course,' she says, 'if he passes away, Tomaso, I will marry you the next day, or anyway' she says, 'as soon as my mourning goes out of style. Then we can go all over the world and enjoy our love, because I know his will leaves me all his vast fortune. I am afraid it is wicked,' she says, 'but sometimes I wish an accident will befall him.'

Now I can see that what is coming off here is that Mrs. Colonel Samuel B. Venus is giving Count Tomaso a hint in a roundabout way to cause an accident to befall Colonel Samuel B. Venus, and thinks I to myself there in the closet, it is a pretty how-do-you-do if such goings-on are tolerated in society circles, and I am glad I am not in society. To tell the truth, I consider Mrs. Colonel Samuel B. Venus's attitude most unbecoming.

Well, they converse at some length about various forms of accidents that they hear of, but they seem unable to arrive at any definite conclusion, and I am almost sorry I am unable to join in the discussion and offer a few original ideas of my own, when Mrs. Colonel Samuel B. Venus says:

'Well,' she says, 'we are sailing next week on the *Castilla* for New York, and you can come on the same ship. New York is a better place for accidents than down here, because they are not apt to attract so much attention there. But, Tomaso,' she says, 'be very careful the Colonel does not see you on the trip, as he has been hearing things here, and he is terribly jealous, and has a violent temper, and, furthermore, he always has deadly weapons around, and he claims he is a wonderful marksman.

'Oh, Tomaso,' she says, 'is it not awful to be yoked to an old character who thinks of nothing but hunting, and fishing, and business, when I love you so much?'

Well, Tomaso says it is, indeed, and does she have a few dibs on her to tide him over the week-end, and it seems she has, and then there is a little offhand billing and cooing that I consider very bad taste in her under her own roof, and finally they go out of the boudoir.

As soon as they depart, I turn to my own business of opening the little can and removing the jewellery, which I deliver to Tommy Entrata, who gives it to Lou Adolia, and this is the time that Lou Adolia gets eighty thousand dollars from the insurance companies for the return of the goods, and then disappears with all the sugar, and without as much as saying, aye, yes or no to anybody.

But I am getting ahead of my story.

A couple of days later, I am reclining on the beach with Tommy Entrata, taking a little sun for my complexion, when who comes along in a bathing-suit which displays a really remarkable shape but Mrs. Colonel Samuel B. Venus, and who is with her but the stern-looking character who doctors me up on the train, and at first I have half a notion to jump up and say hello to him and thank him for his kindness to me about the fish, but he looks right through me as if he never sees me before in his life, and I can see that he does not remember me, or if he does, he does not care to make anything of it.

So I do not give him a blow, because the way I look at it, the fewer people you know in this world, the better you are off. But I ask Tommy Entrata who the stern-looking character is, and I am somewhat surprised when Tommy says:

'Why,' he says, 'he is Colonel Samuel B. Venus, the party you knock off the other night, but,' Tommy says, 'let us not speak of that now. Colonel Samuel B. Venus is a most irascible character, and he is making quite a chirp about matters, and it is very fortunate for us that he and his wife are sailing for New York, because the stout fellow is getting nervous about the outcry.

'By the way,' Tommy says, 'I do not wish to seem inhospitable in suggesting your departure from these pleasant scenes, but it may be a good idea for you to take it on the Jesse Owens until the beef is chilled. There are many nightingales in these parts,' he says, 'and they will sing to the law on very slight provocation, for instance such a character as Count Tomaso. I notice him around here nuzzling up to Mrs. Colonel Samuel B. Venus, and while the chances are he is on a business mission of his own, Count Tomaso knows you, and it is always my opinion that he is a singer, at heart.'

Well, I do not mention the incident in Mrs. Colonel Samuel B. Venus's boudoir to Tommy Entrata, because in the first place I do not consider it any of his business, and in the second place I know Tommy is not apt to be interested in such a matter, but I get to thinking about the conversation between Mrs. Colonel Samuel B. Venus and Count Tomaso, and I also get to thinking about Colonel Samuel B. Venus being so nice to me in connection with the bad fish.

And thinks I, as long as I must take my departure, anyway, a little sea voyage may be beneficial to my health, and I will go on the *Castilla* myself, and will look up Count Tomaso and admonish him that I will hold him personally responsible if any accident happens to Colonel Samuel B. Venus, as I feel that it is only fair to do what I can to discharge my debt of gratitude to Colonel Samuel B. Venus concerning the fish.

So when the *Castilla* sails a few days later, I am a passenger, and, furthermore, I have a nice cabin on the same deck as Colonel Samuel B. Venus and his ever-loving wife, because I always believe in travelling with the best people, no matter what.

I see Colonel Samuel B. Venus, and I also see Mrs. Colonel Samuel B. Venus on the first day out, and I observe that Colonel Samuel B. Venus is looking sterner than ever, and also that Mrs. Colonel Samuel B. Venus is growing lovelier by the hour, but never do I see Count Tomaso, although I am pretty sure he does not miss the boat.

I figure that he is taking Mrs. Colonel Samuel B. Venus's advice about keeping out of sight of Colonel Samuel B. Venus.

I do not bother to go looking for Count Tomaso on the *Castilla* to admonish him about Colonel Samuel B. Venus, because I figure I am bound to catch up with him getting off the boat in New York, and that in the meantime Colonel Samuel B. Venus is safe from accident, especially as it comes up stormy at sea after we are a few hours out, and Colonel Samuel B. Venus and his ever-loving wife seem to be keeping close to their cabin, and in fact so is everybody else.

Well, the storm keeps getting worse, and it is sleety and cold all around and about, and the sea is running higher than somewhat, and now one night off the Jersey coast when I am sleeping as peacefully as anything, I am awakened by a great to-do and it seems that the *Castilla* is on fire.

Naturally, I do not care to be toasted in my cabin, so I don my clothes, and pop out into the passageway and start for the nearest exit, when I remember that in moments of confusion many characters, male and female, are apt to forget articles of one kind and another that may come in handy to somebody such as me later on, for instance bits of jewellery, and other portable merchandise.

So I try various doors as I go along the passageway, and all of them are open and unoccupied, as the *Castilla* is an old-time vessel with cabin doors that lock with keys, and not with snap locks, and, just as I suspect, I find numerous odds and ends in the way of finger-rings, and bracelets and clips and pins and necklaces, and watches, and gold cigarette-cases, and even a few loose bundles of ready scratch, so I am very glad, indeed, that I am gifted with foresight.

Finally I come to one door that seems to be locked, and I remember that this is the cabin occupied by Colonel Samuel B.

Venus and his ever-loving wife, and after first knocking at the door and receiving no reply, I figure they hastily depart and carelessly lock the door after them, and I also figure that I am bound to garner something of more than ordinary value there.

So I kick the door in, and who is in the cabin on a bed, all trussed up like a goose, with a towel tied across his mouth to keep him from hollering out loud, but Colonel Samuel B. Venus, in person.

Naturally, I am somewhat surprised at this spectacle, and also somewhat embarrassed to have Colonel Samuel B. Venus find me kicking in his door, but of course this is no time for apologies, so I take a quick swivel about the cabin to see if there are any articles lying around that I may be able to use. I am slightly disappointed to note that there appears to be nothing, and I am about to take my departure, when all of a sudden I remember my debt of gratitude to Colonel Samuel B. Venus, and I realize that it will be most unkind to leave him in this predicament to be barbecued like a steer without being able to move hand or foot.

So I out with my pocket chiv, and cut him loose, and I also remove the towel, and as soon as he can talk, Colonel Samuel B. Venus issues a statement to me, in a most severe tone of voice, as follows:

'They try to murder me,' he says. 'My own wife, Cora, and a character in a white polo coat with a little cap to match. When the alarm of fire is sounded,' Colonel Samuel B. Venus says, 'she starts screaming, and he comes banging up against our door, and she unlocks it and lets him in before I have time to think, and then he knocks me down with something, I do not know what.'

'The chances are,' I say, 'it is a blunt instrument.'

'You may be right,' Colonel Samuel B. Venus says. 'Anyway, after he knocks me down, my own wife, Cora, picks up one of my shoes and starts belting me over the head with the heel, and then she helps the character in the polo coat and the little cap to match tie me up as you find me.'

'It is a scurvy trick,' I say.

'I am half unconscious,' Colonel Samuel B. Venus says, 'but I remember hearing my own wife, Cora, remark that the fire is a wonderful break for them, and will save them a lot of bother in New York. And then before they leave, she hits me another belt on the head with the shoe. I fear,' Colonel Samuel B. Venus says, 'that my own wife, Cora, is by no means the ever-loving helpmeet I think. In fact,' he says, 'I am now wondering about the overdose of sleeping powders she gives me in London, England, in 1931, and about the bomb in my automobile in Los Angeles, Cal., in 1933.'

'Well, well, well,' I say, 'let us let bygones be bygones, and get off this tub, as it seems to be getting hotter than a ninth-inning finish around here.'

But Colonel Samuel B. Venus remains very testy about the incident he just describes, and he fumbles around under a pillow on the bed on which I find him, and outs with that thing, and opens the cylinder as if to make sure it is loaded, and says to me like this:

'I will shoot him down like a dog,' he says. 'I mean the character in the white polo coat and the little cap to match. He undoubtedly leads my poor little wife, Cora, astray in this, although,' he says, 'I do not seem to recall him anywhere in the background of the overdose and the bomb matters. But she is scarcely more than a child and does not know right from wrong. He is the one who must die,' Colonel Samuel B. Venus says. 'I wonder who he is?' he says.

Well, of course I know Colonel Samuel B. Venus must be talking about Count Tomaso, but I can see that Count Tomaso is a total stranger to him, and while I am by no means opposed to Colonel Samuel B. Venus's sentiments with reference to Count Tomaso, I do not approve of his spirit of forgiveness towards Mrs. Colonel Samuel B. Venus, because I figure that as long as she is around and about, Colonel Samuel B. Venus will always be in danger of accidents.

But I do not feel that this is a time for argument, so I finally get him to go up on the deck with me, and as soon as we are on deck, Colonel Samuel B. Venus leaves me and starts running every which way as if he is looking for somebody.

There seems to be some little agitation on deck, what with smoke and flame coming out of the *Castilla* amidships, and many characters, male and female, running up and down, and around and about, and small children crying.

Some of the crew are launching lifeboats, and then getting into these boats themselves, and pulling away from the burning ship without waiting for any passengers, which strikes me as most discourteous on the part of the sailors and which alarms many passengers so they start chucking themselves over the rail into the sea trying to catch up with the boats.

Well, this scene is most distasteful to me, so I retire from the

general mêlée, and go looking elsewhere about the ship, figuring I
may find an opportunity to ease myself quietly into a boat before
all the seats are taken by sailors, and finally I come upon a group
trying to launch a big life raft over the rail, and about this time I
observe Colonel Samuel B. Venus standing against the rail with
that thing in his hand, and peering this way and that.

And then I notice a boat pulling away from the ship, and in the
stern of the boat I see a character in a white polo coat, and a little
cap to match, and I call the attention of Colonel Samuel B. Venus
to same.

The boat is so overcrowded that it is far down in the water, but
the waves, which are running very high, are carrying it away in
long lunges, and it is fully one hundred yards off, and is really
visible to the naked eye by the light of the flames from the *Castilla*
only when it rises a moment to the top of a wave, and Colonel
Samuel B. Venus looks for some time before he sees what I wish
him to see.

'I spot him now,' he says. 'I recognize the white polo coat and
the little cap to match.'

And with this, he ups with that thing and goes tooty-toot-toot
out across the water three times, and the last I see of the white polo
coat and the little cap to match they are folding up together very
gently just as a big wave washes the boat off into the darkness
beyond the light of the burning ship.

By this time the raft is in the water, and I take Colonel Samuel
B. Venus and chuck him down on to the raft, and then I jump
after him, and as the raft is soon overcrowded, I give the foot to a
female character who is on the raft before anybody else and ease
her off into the water.

As this female character disappears in the raging sea, I am not
surprised to observe that she is really nobody but Count Tomaso,
as I seem to remember seeing Count Tomaso making Mrs. Colonel
Samuel B. Venus change clothes with him at the point of a
knife.

Well, some of the boats get ashore, and some do not, and in one
that does arrive, they find the late Mrs. Colonel Samuel B. Venus,
and everybody is somewhat surprised to note that she is in male
garments with a white polo coat and a little cap to match.

I wish to call attention to the public service I render in easing
Count Tomaso off the raft, because here is a character who is
undoubtedly a menace to the sanctity of the American home.

And I take pride in the fact that I discharge my debt of gratitude to Colonel Samuel B. Venus, and it is not my fault that he permits himself to be so overcome by his experience on the ship and on the raft that he turns out to be a raving nut, and never has the pleasure of learning that his aim is still so good that he can put three slugs in a moving target within the span of a baby's hand.

'Why, George,' I say to Gentleman George, 'then you are the victim of a great wrong, and I will see the governor, or somebody, in your behalf at once. They cannot do this to you, when according to your own story, you are not directly connected with the matter of Mrs. Colonel Samuel B. Venus, and it is only a case of mistaken identity, at best.'

'Oh, pshaw!' Gentleman George says. 'They are not taking the severe measures they contemplate with me because of anything that happens to Mrs. Colonel Samuel B. Venus.

'They are vexed with me,' George says, 'because one night I take Lou Adolia's automobile out on the salt meadows near Secaucus, N.J., and burn it to a crisp, and it seems that I forget to remove Lou Adolia first from same.'

'Well, George,' I say, '*bon voyage.*'

'The same to you,' George says, 'and many of them.'

It Comes Up Mud

Personally, I never criticize Miss Beulah Beauregard for breaking her engagement to Little Alfie, because from what she tells me she becomes engaged to him under false pretences, and I do not approve of guys using false pretences on dolls, except, of course, when nothing else will do.

It seems that Little Alfie promises to show Miss Beulah Beauregard the life of Riley following the races with him when he gets her to give up a first-class job displaying her shape to the customers in the 900 Club, although Miss Beulah Beauregard frankly admits that Little Alfie does not say what Riley, and afterward Little Alfie states that he must be thinking of Four-eyes Riley when he makes the promise, and everybody knows that Four-eyes Riley is nothing but a bum, in spades.

Anyway, the life Little Alfie shows Miss Beulah Beauregard after they become engaged is by no means exciting, according to what she tells me, as Little Alfie is always going around the race tracks with one or two crocodiles that he calls race horses, trying to win a few bobs for himself, and generally Little Alfie is broke and struggling, and Miss Beulah Beauregard says this is no existence for a member of a proud old Southern family such as the Beauregards.

In fact, Miss Beulah Beauregard often tells me that she has half a mind to leave Little Alfie and return to her ancestral home in Georgia, only she can never think of any way of getting there without walking, and Miss Beulah Beauregard says it always makes her feet sore to walk very far, although the only time anybody ever hears of Miss Beulah Beauregard doing much walking is the time she is shell-roaded on the Pelham Parkway by some Yale guys when she gets cross with them.

It seems that when Little Alfie is first canvassing Miss Beulah Beauregard to be his fiancée he builds her up to expect diamonds and furs and limousines and one thing and another, but the only diamond she ever sees is an engagement hoop that Little Alfie gives her as the old convincer when he happens to be in the money for a moment, and it is a very small diamond, at that, and needs a high north light when you look at it.

But Miss Beulah Beauregard treasures this diamond very highly just the same, and one reason she finally breaks off her engagement to Little Alfie is because he borrows the diamond one day during the Hialeah meeting at Miami without mentioning the matter to her, and hocks it for five bobs which he bets on an old caterpillar of his by the name of Governor Hicks to show.

Well, the chances are Miss Beulah Beauregard will not mind Little Alfie's borrowing the diamond so much if he does not take the twenty-five bobs he wins when Governor Hicks drops in there in the third hole and sends it to Colonel Matt Winn in Louisville to enter a three-year-old of his by the name of Last Hope in the Kentucky Derby, this Last Hope being the only other horse Little Alfie owns at this time.

Such an action makes Miss Beulah Beauregard very indignant indeed, because she says a babe in arms will know Last Hope cannot walk a mile and a quarter, which is the Derby distance, let alone run so far, and that even if Last Hope can run a mile and a quarter, he cannot run it fast enough to get up a sweat.

In fact, Miss Beulah Beauregard and Little Alfie have words over this proposition, because Little Alfie is very high on Last Hope and will not stand for anybody insulting this particular horse, not even his fiancée, although he never seems to mind what anybody says about Governor Hicks, and, in fact, he often says it himself.

Personally, I do not understand what Little Alfie sees in Last Hope, because the horse never starts more than once or twice since it is born, and then has a tough time finishing last, but Little Alfie says the fifty G's that Colonel Winn gives to the winner of the Kentucky Derby is just the same as in the jug in his name, especially if it comes up mud on Derby Day, for Little Alfie claims that Last Hope is bred to just naturally eat mud.

Well, Miss Beulah Beauregard says there is no doubt Little Alfie blows his topper, and that there is no percentage in her remaining engaged to a crack-pot, and many citizens put in with her on her statement because they consider entering Last Hope in the Derby very great foolishness, no matter if it comes up mud or what, and right away Tom Shaw offers 1,000 to 1 against the horse in the future book, and everybody says Tom is underlaying the price at that.

Miss Beulah Beauregard states that she is very discouraged by the way things turn out, and that she scarcely knows what to do, because she fears her shape changes so much in the four or five years she is engaged to Little Alfie that the customers at the 900 Club may not care to look at it any more, especially if they have to pay for this privilege, although personally I will pay any reasonable cover charge to look at Miss Beulah Beauregard's shape any time, if it is all I suspect. As far as I can see it is still a very nice shape indeed, if you care for shapes.

Miss Beulah Beauregard is at this time maybe twenty-five or twenty-six, and is built like a first baseman, being tall and rangy. She has hay-coloured hair, and blue eyes, and lots of health, and a very good appetite. In fact, I once see Miss Beulah Beauregard putting on the fried chicken in the Seven Seas Restaurant in a way that greatly astonishes me, because I never knew before that members of proud old Southern families are such hearty eaters. Furthermore, Miss Beulah Beauregard has a very Southern accent, which makes her sound quite cute, except maybe when she is a little excited and is putting the zing on somebody, such as Little Alfie.

Well, Little Alfie says he regrets exceedingly that Miss Beulah Beauregard sees fit to break their engagement, and will not be with him when he cuts up the Derby dough, as he is planning a swell wedding for her at French Lick after the race, and even has a list all made out of the presents he is going to buy her, including another diamond, and now he has all this bother of writing out the list for nothing.

Furthermore, Little Alfie says he is so accustomed to having Miss Beulah Beauregard as his fiancée that he scarcely knows what to do without her, and he goes around with a very sad puss, and is generally quite low in his mind, because there is no doubt that Little Alfie loves Miss Beulah Beauregard more than somewhat.

But other citizens are around stating that the real reason Miss Beulah Beauregard breaks her engagement to Little Alfie is because a guy by the name of Mr. Paul D. Veere is making a powerful play for her, and she does not wish him to know that she has any truck with a character such as Little Alfie, for of course Little Alfie is by no means anything much to look at, and, furthermore, what with hanging out with his horses most of the time, he never smells like any rose geranium.

It seems that this Mr. Paul D. Veere is a New York banker, and he has a little moustache, and plenty of coco-nuts, and Miss Beulah Beauregard meets up with him one morning when she is displaying her shape on the beach at the Roney Plaza for nothing, and it also seems that there is enough of her shape left to interest Mr. Paul D. Veere no little.

In fact, the next thing anybody knows, Mr. Paul D. Veere is taking Miss Beulah Beauregard here and there, and around and about, although at this time Miss Beulah Beauregard is still engaged to Little Alfie, and the only reason Little Alfie does not notice Mr. Paul D. Veere at first is because he is busy training Last Hope to win the Kentucky Derby, and hustling around trying to get a few bobs together every day to stand off the overhead, including Miss Beulah Beauregard, because naturally Miss Beulah Beauregard cannot bear the idea of living in a fleabag, such as the place where Little Alfie resides, but has to have a nice room at the Roney Plaza.

Well, personally, I have nothing against bankers as a class, and in fact I never meet up with many bankers in my life, but somehow I do not care for Mr. Paul D. Veere's looks. He looks to me like a stony-hearted guy, although, of course, nobody ever sees any banker who does not look stony-hearted, because it seems that being bankers just naturally makes them look this way.

But Mr. Paul D. Veere is by no means an old guy, and the chances are he speaks of something else besides horses to Miss Beulah Beauregard, and furthermore he probably does not smell like horses all the time, so nobody can blame Miss Beulah Beauregard for going around and about with him, although many citizens claim she is a little out of line in accepting Mr. Paul D. Veere's play while she is still engaged to Little Alfie. In fact, there is great indignation in some circles about this, as many citizens feel that Miss Beulah Beauregard is setting a bad example to other fiancées.

But after Miss Beulah Beauregard formally announces that their engagement is off, it is agreed by one and all that she has a right to do as she pleases, and that Little Alfie himself gets out of line in what happens at Hialeah a few days later when he finally notices that Miss Beulah Beauregard seems to be with Mr. Paul D. Veere, and on very friendly terms with him, at that. In fact, Little Alfie comes upon Mr. Paul D. Veere in the act of kissing Miss Beulah Beauregard behind a hibiscus bush out near the paddock, and this scene is most revolting to Little Alfie as he never cares for hibiscus, anyway.

He forgets that Miss Beulah Beauregard is no longer his fiancée, and tries to take a punch at Mr. Paul D. Veere, but he is stopped by a number of detectives, who are greatly horrified at the idea of anybody taking a punch at a guy who has as many coco-nuts as Mr. Paul D. Veere, and while they are expostulating with Little Alfie, Miss Beulah Beauregard disappears from the scene and is observed no more in Miami. Furthermore, Mr. Paul D. Veere also disappears, but of course nobody minds this very much, and, in fact, his disappearance is a great relief to all citizens who have fiancées in Miami at this time.

But it seems that before he disappears Mr. Paul D. Veere calls on certain officials of the Jockey Club and weighs in the sacks on Little Alfie, stating that he is a most dangerous character to have loose around a race track, and naturally the officials are bound to listen to a guy who has as many coco-nuts as Mr. Paul D. Veere.

So a day or two later old Cap Duhaine, the head detective

around the race track, sends for Little Alfie and asks him what he thinks will become of all the prominent citizens such as bankers if guys go around taking punches at them and scaring them half to death, and Little Alfie cannot think of any answer to this conundrum off-hand, especially as Cap Duhaine then asks Little Alfie if it will be convenient for him to take his two horses elsewhere.

Well, Little Alfie can see that Cap Duhaine is hinting in a polite way that he is not wanted around Hialeah any more, and Little Alfie is a guy who can take a hint as well as the next guy, especially when Cap Duhaine tells him in confidence that the racing stewards do not seem able to get over the idea that some scalawag slips a firecracker into Governor Hicks the day old Governor Hicks runs third, because it seems from what Cap Duhaine says that the stewards consider it practically supernatural for Governor Hicks to run third anywhere, any time.

So there Little Alfie is in Miami, as clean as a jaybird, with two horses on his hands, and no way to ship them to any place where horses are of any account, and it is quite a predicament indeed, and causes Little Alfie to ponder quite some. And the upshot of his pondering is that Little Alfie scrapes up a few bobs here and there, and a few oats, and climbs on Governor Hicks one day and boots him in the slats and tells him to giddyup, and away he goes out of Miami, headed north, riding Governor Hicks and leading Last Hope behind him on a rope.

Naturally, this is considered a most unusual spectacle by one and all who witness it and, in fact, it is the first time anybody can remember a horse owner such as Little Alfie riding one of his own horses off in this way, and Gloomy Gus is offering to lay plenty of 5 to 1 that Governor Hicks never makes Palm Beach with Little Alfie up, as it is well known that the old Governor has bum legs and is half out of wind and is apt to pig it any time.

But it seems that Governor Hicks makes Palm Beach all right with Little Alfie up and going so easy that many citizens are around asking Gloomy for a price against Jacksonville. Furthermore, many citizens are now saying that Little Alfie is a pretty smart guy, at that, to think of such an economical idea, and numerous other horse owners are looking their stock over to see if they have anything to ride up north themselves.

Many citizens are also saying that Little Alfie gets a great break when Miss Beulah Beauregard runs out on him, because it takes plenty of weight off him in the way of railroad fare and one thing and another; but it seems Little Alfie does not feel this way about the matter at all.

It seems that Little Alfie often thinks about Miss Beulah Beauregard as he goes jogging along to the north, and sometimes he talks to Governor Hicks and Last Hope about her, and especially to Last Hope, as Little Alfie always considers Governor Hicks somewhat dumb. Also Little Alfie sometimes sings sad love songs right out loud as he is riding along, although the first time he starts to sing he frightens Last Hope and causes him to break loose from the lead rope and run away, and Little Alfie is an hour catching him. But after this Last Hope gets so he does not mind Little Alfie's voice so much, except when Little Alfie tries to hit high C.

Well, Little Alfie has a very nice ride, at that, because the weather is fine and the farmers along the road feed him and his horses, and he has nothing whatever to worry about except a few saddle galls, and about getting to Kentucky for the Derby in May, and here it is only late in February, and anyway Little Alfie does not figure to ride any farther than maybe Maryland where he is bound to make a scratch so he can ship from there.

Now, one day Little Alfie is riding along a road through a stretch of piny woods, a matter of maybe ninety-odd miles north of Jacksonville, which puts him in the State of Georgia, when he passes a half-ploughed field on one side of the road near a ramshackly old house and beholds a most unusual scene:

A large white mule hitched to a plough is sitting down in the field and a tall doll in a sunbonnet and a gingham dress is standing beside the mule crying very heartily.

Naturally, the spectacle of a doll in distress, or even a doll who is not in distress, is bound to attract Little Alfie's attention, so he tells Governor Hicks and Last Hope to whoa, and then he asks the doll what is eating her, and the doll looks up at him out of her sunbonnet, and who is this doll but Miss Beulah Beauregard.

Of course Little Alfie is somewhat surprised to see Miss Beulah Beauregard crying over a mule, and especially in a sunbonnet, so he climbs down off of Governor Hicks to inquire into this situation, and right away Miss Beulah Beauregard rushes up to Little Alfie and chucks herself into his arms and speaks as follows:

'Oh, Alfie,' Miss Beulah Beauregard says, 'I am so glad you find me. I am thinking of you day and night, and wondering if you forgive me. Oh, Alfie, I love you,' she says. 'I am very sorry I go away with Mr. Paul D. Veere. He is nothing but a great rapscallion,' she says. 'He promises to make me his ever-loving wife when he gets me to accompany him from Miami to his shooting-lodge on the Altamaha River, twenty-five miles from here, although,' she says, 'I never know before he has such a lodge in these parts.

'And,' Miss Beulah Beauregard says, 'the very first day I have to pop him with a pot of cold cream and render him half unconscious to escape his advances. Oh, Alfie,' she says, 'Mr. Paul D. Veere's intentions towards me are by no means honourable. Furthermore,' she says, 'I learn he already has an ever-loving wife and three children in New York.'

Well, of course Little Alfie is slightly perplexed by this matter and can scarcely think of anything much to say, but finally he says to Miss Beulah Beauregard like this:

'Well,' he says, 'but what about the mule?'

'Oh,' Miss Beulah Beauregard says, 'his name is Abimelech, and I am ploughing with him when he hauls off and sits down and refuses to budge. He is the only mule we own,' she says, 'and he is old and ornery, and nobody can do anything whatever with him when he wishes to sit down. But,' she says, 'my papa will be very angry because he expects me to get this field all ploughed up by supper-time. In fact,' Miss Beulah Beauregard says, 'I am afraid my papa will be so angry he will give me a whopping, because he by no means forgives me as yet for coming home, and this is why I am shedding tears when you come along.'

Then Miss Beulah Beauregard begins crying again as if her heart will break, and if there is one thing Little Alfie hates and despises it is to see a doll crying, and especially Miss Beulah Beauregard, for Miss Beulah Beauregard can cry in a way to wake the dead when she is going good, so Little Alfie holds her so close to his chest he ruins four cigars in his vest pocket, and speaks to her as follows:

'Tut, tut,' Little Alfie says. 'Tut, tut, tut, tut, tut,' he says. 'Dry your eyes and we will just hitch old Governor Hicks here to the plough and get this field ploughed quicker than you can say scat, because,' Little Alfie says, 'when I am a young squirt, I am the best plougher in Columbia County, New York.'

Well, this idea cheers Miss Beulah Beauregard up no little, and so Little Alfie ties Last Hope to a tree and takes the harness off Abimelech, the mule, who keeps right on sitting down as if he does not care what happens, and puts the harness on Governor Hicks and hitches Governor Hicks to the plough, and the way the old Governor carries on when he finds out they wish him to pull a plough is really most surprising. In fact, Little Alfie has to get a club and reason with Governor Hicks before he will settle down and start pulling the plough.

It turns out that Little Alfie is a first-class plougher, at that, and while he is ploughing, Miss Beulah Beauregard walks along with him and talks a blue streak, and Little Alfie learns more things from her in half an hour than he ever before suspects in some years, and especially about Miss Beulah Beauregard herself.

It seems that the ramshackly old house is Miss Beulah Beauregard's ancestral home, and that her people are very poor, and live in these piny woods for generations, and that their name is Benson and not Beauregard at all, this being nothing but a name that Miss Beulah Beauregard herself thinks up out of her own head when she goes to New York to display her shape.

Furthermore, when they go to the house it comes out that Miss Beulah Beauregard's papa is a tall, skinny old guy with a goatee, who can lie faster than Little Alfie claims Last Hope can run. But it seems that the old skeezicks takes quite an interest in Last Hope when Little Alfie begins telling him what a great horse this horse is, especially in the mud, and how he is going to win the Kentucky Derby.

In fact, Miss Beulah Beauregard's papa seems to believe everything Little Alfie tells him, and as he is the first guy Little Alfie ever meets up with who believes anything he tells about anything whatever, it is a privilege and a pleasure for Little Alfie to talk to him. Miss Beulah Beauregard also has a mamma who turns out to be very fat, and full of Southern hospitality, and quite handy with a skillet.

Then there is a grown brother by the name of Jeff, who is practically a genius, as he knows how to disguise skimmin's so it makes a person only a little sick when they drink it, this skimmin's being a drink which is made from skimmings that come to the top on boiling sugar cane, and generally it tastes like gasoline, and is very fatal indeed.

Now, the consequences are Little Alfie finds this place very pleasant, and he decides to spend a few weeks there, paying for his keep with the services of Governor Hicks as a plough horse, especially as he is now practically engaged to Miss Beulah Beauregard all over again and she will not listen to him leaving without her. But they have no money for her railroad fare, and Little Alfie becomes very indignant when she suggests she can ride Last Hope on north while he is riding Governor Hicks, and wishes to know if she thinks a Derby candidate can be used for a truck horse.

Well, this almost causes Miss Beulah Beauregard to start breaking the engagement all over again, as she figures it is a dirty crack about her heft, but her papa steps in and says they must remain until Governor Hicks get through with the ploughing anyway, or he will know the reason why. So Little Alfie stays and he puts in all his spare time training Last Hope and wondering who he can write to for enough dough to send Miss Beulah Beauregard north when the time comes.

He trains Last Hope by walking him and galloping him along the country roads in person, and taking care of him as if he is a baby, and what with this work, and the jog up from Miami, Last Hope fills out very strong and hearty, and anybody must admit that he is not a bad-looking beetle, though maybe a little more leggy than some like to see.

Now, it comes a Sunday, and all day long there is a very large storm with rain and wind that takes to knocking over big trees, and one thing and another, and no one is able to go outdoors much. So late in the evening Little Alfie and Miss Beulah Beauregard and all the Bensons are gathered about the stove in the kitchen drinking skimmin's, and Little Alfie is telling them all over again about how Last Hope will win the Kentucky Derby, especially if it comes up mud, when they hear a hammering at the door.

When the door is opened, who comes in but Mr. Paul D. Veere, sopping wet from head to foot, including his little moustache, and limping so he can scarcely walk, and naturally his appearance nonplusses Miss Beulah Beauregard and Little Alfie, who can never forget that Mr. Paul D. Veere is largely responsible for the saddle galls he gets riding up from Miami.

In fact, several times since he stops at Miss Beulah Beauregard's ancestral home, Little Alfie thinks of Mr. Paul D. Veere, and every time he thinks of him he is in favour of going over to Mr. Paul D. Veere's shooting-lodge on the Altamaha and speaking to him severely.

But Miss Beulah Beauregard always stops him, stating that the proud old Southern families in this vicinity are somewhat partial to the bankers and other rich guys from the North who have shooting-lodges around and about in the piny woods, and especially on the Altamaha, because these guys furnish a market to the local citizens for hunting guides, and corn liquor, and one thing and another.

Miss Beulah Beauregard says if a guest of the Bensons speaks to Mr. Paul D. Veere severely, it may be held against the family, and it seems that the Benson family cannot stand any more beefs against it just at this particular time. So Little Alfie never goes, and here all of a sudden is Mr. Paul D. Veere right in his lap.

Naturally, Little Alfie steps forward and starts winding up a large right hand with the idea of parking it on Mr. Paul D. Veere's chin, but Mr. Paul D. Veere seems to see that there is hostility afoot, and he backs up against the wall, and raises his hand, and speaks as follows:

'Folks,' Mr. Paul D. Veere says, 'I just go into a ditch in my automobile half a mile up the road. My car is a wreck,' he says, 'and my right leg seems so badly hurt I am just barely able to drag myself here. Now, folks,' he says, 'it is almost a matter of life and death with me to get to the station at Tillinghast in time to flag the Orange Blossom Special. It is the last train to-night to Jacksonville, and I must be in Jacksonville before midnight so I can hire an aeroplane and get to New York by the time my bank opens at ten o'clock in the morning. It is about ten hours by plane from Jacksonville to New York,' Mr. Paul D. Veere says, 'so if I can catch the Orange Blossom, I will be able to just about make it!'

Then he goes on speaking in a low voice and states that he receives a telephone message from New York an hour or so before at his lodge telling him he must hurry home, and right away afterward, while he is trying to telephone the station at Tillinghast to make sure they will hold the Orange Blossom until he gets there, no matter what, all the telephone and telegraph wires around and about go down in the storm.

So he starts for the station in his car, and just as it looks as if he may make it, his car runs smack-dab into a ditch and Mr. Paul D. Veere's leg is hurt so there is no chance he can walk the rest of the way to the station, and there Mr. Paul D. Veere is.

'It is a very desperate case, folks,' Mr. Paul D. Veere says. 'Let me take your automobile, and I will reward you liberally.'

Well, at this Miss Beulah Beauregard's papa looks at a clock on the kitchen wall and states as follows:

'We do not keep an automobile, neighbour,' he says, 'and anyway,' he says, 'it is quite a piece from here to Tillinghast and the Orange Blossom is due in ten minutes, so I do not see how you can possibly make it. Rest your hat, neighbour,' Miss Beulah Beauregard's papa says, 'and have some skimmin's, and take things easy, and I will look at your leg and see how bad you are bunged up.'

Well, Mr. Paul D. Veere seems to turn as pale as a pillow as he hears this about the time, and then he says:

'Lend me a horse and buggy,' he says. 'I must be in New York in person in the morning. No one else will do but me,' he says, and as he speaks these words he looks at Miss Beulah Beauregard and then at Little Alfie as if he is speaking to them personally, although up to this time he does not look at either of them after he comes into the kitchen.

'Why, neighbour,' Miss Beulah Beauregard's papa says, 'we do not keep a buggy, and even if we do keep a buggy we do not have time to hitch up anything to a buggy. Neighbour,' he says, 'you are certainly on a bust if you think you can catch the Orange Blossom now.'

'Well, then,' Mr. Paul D. Veere says, very sorrowful, 'I will have to go to jail.'

Then he flops himself down in a chair and covers his face with his hands, and he is a spectacle such as is bound to touch almost any heart, and when she sees him in this state Miss Beulah Beauregard begins crying because she hates to see anybody as sorrowed up as Mr. Paul D. Veere, and between sobs she asks Little Alfie to think of something to do about the situation.

'Let Mr. Paul D. Veere ride Governor Hicks to the station,' Miss Beauregard says. 'After all,' she says, 'I cannot forget his courtesy in sending me half-way here in his car from his shooting-lodge after I pop him with the pot of cold cream, instead of making me walk as those Yale guys do the time they red-light me.'

'Why,' Little Alfie says, 'it is a mile and a quarter from the gate out here to the station. I know,' he says, 'because I get a guy in an automobile to clock it on his meter one day last week, figuring to give Last Hope a workout over the full Derby route pretty soon. The road must be fetlock deep in mud at this time, and,' Little Alfie says, 'Governor Hicks cannot as much as stand up in the mud. The only horse in the world that can run fast enough through this mud to make the Orange Blossom is Last Hope, but,' Little Alfie says, 'of course I'm not letting anybody ride a horse as valuable as Last Hope to catch trains.'

Well, at this Mr. Paul D. Veere lifts his head and looks at Little Alfie with great interest and speaks as follows:

'How much is this valuable horse worth?' Mr. Paul D. Veere says.

'Why,' Little Alfie says, 'he is worth anyway fifty G's to me, because,' he says, 'this is the sum Colonel Winn is giving to the winner of the Kentucky Derby, and there is no doubt whatever that Last Hope will be this winner, especially,' Little Alfie says, 'if it comes up mud.'

'I do not carry any such large sum of money as you mention on my person,' Mr. Paul D. Veere says, 'but,' he says, 'if you are willing to trust me, I will give you my IOU for same, just to let me ride your horse to the station. I am once the best amateur steeplechase rider in the Hunts Club,' Mr. Paul D. Veere says, 'and if your horse can run at all there is still a chance for me to keep out of jail.'

Well, the chances are Little Alfie will by no means consider extending a lone of credit for fifty G's to Mr. Paul D. Veere or any other banker, and especially a banker who is once an amateur steeplechase jock, because if there is one thing Little Alfie does not trust it is an amateur steeplechase jock, and furthermore Little Alfie is somewhat offended because Mr. Paul D. Veere seems to think he is running a livery stable.

But Miss Beulah Beauregard is now crying so loud nobody can scarcely hear themselves think, and Little Alfie gets to figuring what she may say to him if he does not rent Last Hope to Mr. Paul D. Veere at this time and it comes out later that Last Hope does not happen to win the Kentucky Derby after all. So he finally says all right, and Mr. Paul D. Veere at once outs with a little gold pencil and a notebook, and scribbles off a marker for fifty G's to Little Alfie.

And the next thing anybody knows, Little Alfie is leading Last Hope out of the barn and up to the gate with nothing on him but a bridle as Little Alfie does not wish to waste time saddling, and as he is boosting Mr. Paul D. Veere on to Last Hope Little Alfie speaks as follows:

'You have three minutes left,' Little Alfie says. 'It is almost a straight course, except for a long turn going into the last quarter. Let this fellow run,' he says. 'You will find plenty of mud all the way, but,' Little Alfie says, 'this is a mud-running fool. In fact,' Little Alfie says, 'you are pretty lucky it comes up mud.'

Then he gives Last Hope a smack on the hip and away goes Last Hope lickity-split through the mud and anybody can see from the way Mr. Paul D. Veere is sitting on him that Mr. Paul D. Veere knows what time it is when it comes to riding. In fact, Little Alfie himself says he never sees a better seat anywhere in his life, especially for a guy who is riding bareback.

Well, Little Alfie watches them go down the road in a gob of mud, and it will always be one of the large regrets of Little Alfie's life that he leaves his split-second super in hock in Miami, because he says he is sure Last Hope runs the first quarter through the mud faster than any quarter is ever run before in this world. But of course Little Alfie is more excited than somewhat at this moment, and the chances are he exaggerates Last Hope's speed.

However, there is no doubt that Last Hope goes over the road very rapidly, indeed, as a coloured party who is out squirrel hunting comes along a few minutes afterward and tells Little Alfie that something goes past him on the road so fast he cannot tell exactly what it is, but he states that he is pretty sure it is old Henry Devil himself, because he smells smoke as it passes him, and hears a voice yelling hi-yah. But of course the chances are this voice is nothing but the voice of Mr. Paul D. Veere yelling words of encouragement to Last Hope.

It is not until the station-master at Tillinghast, a guy by the name of Asbury Potts, drives over to Miss Beulah Beauregard's ancestral home an hour later that Little Alfie hears that as Last Hope pulls up at the station and Mr. Paul D. Veere dismounts with so much mud on him that nobody can tell if he is a plaster cast or what, the horse is gimping as bad as Mr. Paul D. Veere himself, and Asbury Potts says there is no doubt Last Hope bows a tendon, or some such, and that if they are able to get him to the races again he will eat his old wool hat.

'But, personally,' Asbury Potts says as he mentions this sad news, 'I do not see what Mr. Paul D. Veere's hurry is, at that, to be pushing a horse so hard. He has fifty-seven seconds left by my watch when the Orange Blossom pulls in right on time to the dot,' Asbury Potts says.

Well, at this Little Alfie sits down and starts figuring, and finally he figures that Last Hope runs the mile and a quarter in around 2.03 in the mud, with maybe one hundred and sixty pounds up, for Mr. Paul D. Veere is no feather duster, and no horse ever runs a mile and a quarter in the mud in the Kentucky Derby as fast as this, or anywhere else as far as anybody knows, so Little Alfie claims that this is practically flying.

But of course few citizens ever accept Little Alfie's figures as strictly official, because they do not know if Asbury Potts's watch is properly regulated for timing race horses, even though Asbury Potts is 100 per cent right when he says they will never be able to get Last Hope to the races again.

Well, I meet up with Little Alfie one night this summer in Mindy's Restaurant on Broadway, and it is the first time he is observed in these parts in some time, and he seems to be looking very prosperous, indeed, and after we get to cutting up old touches, he tells me the reason for this prosperity.

It seems that after Mr. Paul D. Veere returns to New York and puts back in his bank whatever it is that it is advisable for him to put back, or takes out whatever it is that seems best to take out, and gets himself all rounded up so there is no chance of his going to jail, he remembers that there is a slight difference between him and Little Alfie, so what does Mr. Paul D. Veere do but sit down and write out a cheque for fifty G's to Little Alfie to take up his IOU, so Little Alfie is nothing out on account of losing the Kentucky Derby, and, in fact, he is stone rich, and I am glad to hear of it, because I always sympathize deeply with him in his bereavement over the loss of Last Hope. Then I ask Little Alfie what he is doing in New York at this time, and he states to me as follows:

'Well,' Little Alfie says, 'I will tell you. The other day,' he says, 'I get to thinking things over, and among other things I get to thinking that after Last Hope wins the Kentucky Derby, he is a sure thing to go on and also win the Maryland Preakness, because,' Little Alfie says, 'the Preakness is a sixteenth of a mile shorter than the Derby, and a horse that can run a mile and a quarter in the mud in around 2.03 with a brick house on his back is bound to make anything that wears hair look silly at a mile and three-sixteenths, especially,' Little Alfie says, 'if it comes up mud.

'So,' Little Alfie says, 'I am going to call on Mr. Paul D. Veere and see if he does not wish to pay me the Preakness stake, too, because,' he says, 'I am building the finest house in South Georgia at Last Hope, which is my stock farm where Last Hope himself is on public exhibition, and I can always use a few bobs here and there.'

'Well, Alfie,' I say, 'this seems to me to be a very fair proposition, indeed, and,' I say, 'I am sure Mr. Paul D. Veere will take care of it as soon as it is called to his attention, as there is no doubt you and Last Hope are of great service to Mr. Paul D. Veere. By the way, Alfie,' I say, 'whatever becomes of Governor Hicks?'

'Why,' Little Alfie says, 'do you know Governor Hicks turns out to be a terrible disappointment to me as a plough horse? He learns how to sit down from Abimelech, the mule, and nothing will make him stir, not even the same encouragement I give him the day he drops down there third at Hialeah.

'But,' Little Alfie says, 'my ever-loving wife is figuring on using the old Governor as a saddle-horse for our twins, Beulah and Little Alfie, Junior, when they get old enough, although,' he says, 'I tell her the Governor will never be worth a dime in such a way especially,' Little Alfie says, 'if it comes up mud.'

The Big Umbrella

Now No. 23 is a very high-class trap which is patronized only by the better element of rumpots in New York, and what I am doing in these unusual surroundings with Spider McCoy, the fight manager, is something that requires a job of telling.

This No. 23 is a spot where wealthy characters assemble on an afternoon and evening to sit around tables or stand at the bar guzzling old-fashioneds, and Scotches, and other delicacies of this nature, and there are always many swell-looking Judys present, so it is generally a scene of great gaiety, but it is certainly about the last place you will ever expect to find Spider McCoy and me.

But there we are, and the reason we are there starts in front of Mindy's restaurant on Broadway, when I observe Spider McCoy walking along the street following close behind a tall young character of most unique appearance in many respects.

This tall young character cannot be more than twenty-one years of age, and he is maybe six feet two inches tall and must weigh around one hundred and ninety pounds. He has shoulders like the back of a truck, and he has blond hair, and pink cheeks, and is without doubt as good-looking as any male character has a right to be without causing comment.

He is wearing a pair of striped pants, and a cut-away coat, and a white vest, and a high hat, and in fact he is dressed as if he just comes from a high-toned wedding such as you see in pictures in the Sunday blats, and this is by no means a familiar costume in

front of Mindy's, so naturally the tall young character attracts no
little attention, and many citizens wonder what he is advertising.

Well, as soon as he sees me, Spider McCoy beckons me to join
him, and as I fall into step with him behind the tall young character, Spider McCoy says to me:

'Sh-h-h-h!' Spider McCoy says. 'Here is without doubt the next
heavy-weight champion of the whole world. I just see him kiss the
jockey of a short down the street with a right-hand shot that is
positively a lily. It does not travel more than three inches. The
jockey takes a run at this party quite ferocious and, bap, down he
goes as still as a plank under his own cab. It is the best natural
right hand I ever see. He reminds me of Jack Dempsey,' Spider
McCoy says. 'Also Gene Tunney.'

Well, it is very seldom I see Spider McCoy but what he is speaking of some guy who is the next heavy-weight champion of the
world, and they nearly always remind him of Jack Dempsey and
Gene Tunney, and sometimes of Max Schmeling, so I am about to
go about my business when Spider grabs me by the arm and com-
pels me to accompany him.

'Who is the guy, Spider?' I say.

'What difference does it make who a guy is that can punch like
he can?' Spider says. 'All I know is he is the next heavy-weight
champion of the world if he gets in the proper hands, such as
mine. The broads will go crazy about his looks and the way he
dresses. He will be a wonderful card,' Spider says. 'You can see by
the way he carries himself that he is a natural fighter. He is loose
and light on his feet,' he says. 'Chances are there is plenty of
animal in him. I like my fighters to have plenty of animal in them,
especially,' Spider says, 'my heavy-weights.'

'Well, Spider,' I say, 'from the way your heavy-weights I see
knock off that hot meat on you, there is plenty of animal in them.
But,' I say, 'how do you know this party wishes to be a fighter,
anyway? Maybe he has other plans in life.'

'We will find out,' Spider McCoy says. 'We will tail him until
we learn where he hangs out so I can make a connection with him.
Look at his chest development,' Spider says. 'Look at his small
waist-line,' he says. 'Look at the shape of his head.'

So we follow the tall young character until he leads us into No.
23, and I notice that Sammy the doorman gives him a very small
hello, and I figure the tall young character cannot be anybody
much, because when anybody is anybody much, Sammy the door-

man gives them a very large hello, indeed. In fact, Sammy's hello to the tall young character is almost as small as the hello he gives us, and this is practically unnoticeable.

Well, I know Sammy the doorman from back down the years when he is not working in a joint as classy as No. 23, and to tell the truth I know him when he is nothing but a steer for a bust-out joint in West Forty-third, a bust-out joint being a joint where they will cheat your eyeballs out at cards, and dice, and similar devices. So I ask Sammy who the tall young character is, and Sammy says:

'Oh,' he says, 'he is one of these ex-kings. He comes from some nickel country over in Europe. A dictator gives him the foot off the throne and then chases him out of the country and takes personal charge of matters. His name is Jonas. I mean the ex-king,' Sammy says. 'They are getting to be quite a nuisance around.'

'Is this ex-king holding anything?' I say.

'Nothing,' Sammy says. 'Not a quarter. The hotel where he is stopping catches him out to a society tea the other afternoon and puts a hickey in his keyhole and now he cannot get at his other clothes and has to go around the way you see him. The chances are,' Sammy says, 'he is in here looking to cadge a drink or a bite to eat.'

Well, Spider McCoy is looking the joint over to see if he can find anybody he knows to introduce him to the ex-king, but when I tell him what Sammy says, Spider at once eases himself up alongside the ex-king and begins talking to him, because Spider knows that when guys are not holding anything they are willing to talk to anybody.

He is somewhat surprised to find that the ex-king speaks English and seems to be a nice, pleasant young character and the chances are he is by no means high-toned even when he is holding something, so pretty soon Spider is buying him Scotches, although this is by no means a dram that Spider approves of for fighters unless they buy them themselves, and finally Spider says to him like this:

'I see you tag that taxi jockey over on Broadway,' Spider says. 'I never see a more beautiful right in my born days. It reminds me something of Georges Carpentier's right, only,' Spider says, 'Georges always pulls his just a little before shooting to get more leverage, and you just barely move yours. Why,' Spider says, 'the more I think of it, the more I am amazed. What does the guy do to vex you?'

'Why,' the ex-king says, 'he does not do anything to vex me. I am quite unvexed at the time. It is almost inadvertent. The taxi-driver gets off his seat and starts to run after a passenger that fails to settle his account with him, and he is about to collide with me there on the sidewalk, so,' he says, 'I just put out my right hand to ward him off, and he runs into it with his chin and knocks himself unconscious. I must look him up some day and express my regrets. But,' he says, 'I will never think of deliberately striking anybody without serious provocation.'

Well, at this, Spider McCoy is somewhat nonplussed, because he can now see that what he takes for the ex-king's natural punch is merely an accident that may not happen if it is on purpose, and furthermore, the ex-king's expressions are scarcely the expressions of anybody with much animal in them, and Spider is commencing to regret the purchase of the Scotches for the ex-king. In fact, I can see that Spider is reaching a state of mind that may cause him to take a pop at the ex-king for grossly deceiving him.

But Spider McCoy cannot look at six feet two and one hundred and ninety pounds of anybody under thirty without becoming most avaricious, and so after a couple of more Scotches, he begins feeling the ex-king's muscles, which causes the ex-king to laugh quite heartily, as it seems he is a little ticklish in spots, and finally Spider says:

'Well,' he says, 'there is undoubtedly great natural strength here, and all it needs is to be properly developed. Why,' Spider says, 'the more I think of you knocking a guy out by just letting him run into your hand, the more impressed I am. In fact,' he says, 'I can scarcely get over it. How do you feel about becoming a profes-sional?'

'A professional what?' the ex-king says.

'A professional boxer,' Spider says. 'It is a name we have in this country for prize-fighters.'

'I never give such a matter a thought,' the ex-king says. 'What is the idea?'

'The idea is money,' Spider McCoy says. 'I hear of other ideas for professional boxing, but,' he says, 'I do not approve of them, your Majesty.'

'Call me Jonas,' the ex-king says. 'Do you mean to tell me I can make money out of boxing? Well, I will feel right kindly towards anything I can make money out of. I find,' he says, 'that money seems to be somewhat necessary in this country.'

So then Spider McCoy explains to him how he can make a ton of money by winning the heavy-weight championship of the world and that all he requires to do this is to have Spider for his manager. Furthermore, Spider explains that all he will ask for being the manager is 33⅓ per cent of the ex-king's earnings, with the expenses off the top, which means before they cut up anything.

Well, the ex-king listens very intently and keeps nodding his head to show that he understands, and finally he says:

'In the meantime,' he says, 'do I eat?'

'The best, your Majesty,' Spider says.

'Call me Jonas,' the ex-king says again. 'All right, then,' Jonas says, 'I will become heavy-weight champion of the world as you say, and make a ton of money, and then I snap my fingers at Dictator Poltafuss, the dirty rat.'

'The big heel,' Spider says.

So Spider McCoy takes Jonas to his home, which is an apartment in West Fiftieth Street, where his orphan niece, Miss Margie Grogan, keeps house for him, and bosses him around no little, and quite some, and I go with them to lend moral support to Spider, because by this time he is slightly Scotched up, and he always likes to have a little moral support when he goes home Scotched.

His niece, Miss Margie Grogan, is a Judy of maybe twenty, and if you like them small, and lively, and with huckleberry hair, and blue eyes, and freckles on the nose, and plenty of temper, she is all right. In fact, I hear some say that Margie is extra all right, but those who say this are younger than I am and maybe not such good judges. Personally, I like them with more heft and less temper.

It is not a large apartment where Spider McCoy lives, but it is a neat and clean little joint, at that, for Margie is without doubt a good all-round housekeeper. Furthermore, she is much better than a raw hand with a skillet, and she comes flying out of the kitchen with her face red and her hair all tousled up to meet Spider, but when she sees Jonas behind him she stops, and speaks as follows:

'Good grief,' Margie says, 'another big umbrella.'

'What do you mean, umbrella?' Spider says.

'Why,' Margie says, 'something that folds up. I never know you to bring home any other kind.'

'This is no umbrella,' Spider says. 'This is the next heavy-weight champion of the world.'

'No,' Margie says, 'it cannot be, for two months you tell me that somebody called Ben Robbins is the next heavy-weight champion of the world.'

'Ben Robbins is nothing but a bum,' Spider says.

'So I find out,' Margie says. 'Well,' she says, 'come on in, you and your next heavy-weight champion of the world. We are about to put on the corned beef and.'

Then Spider introduces Jonas to her, and right away Jonas grabs her hand and lifts it to his lips, and this astonishes Margie no little, and afterward she tells me that she regrets for a moment that she just recently sticks her hand in a pot of boiled onions, and the chances are Jonas does too.

But Miss Margie Grogan is by no means in favour of prize-fighters in any manner, shape or form, because all they ever mean to her is an extra plate, and more cooking, and it is plain to be seen that though he seems to be an expert hand-kisser, Jonas is no more welcome than any of the others that Spider brings home, and he brings them home too often to suit Margie.

The ones he brings home are always heavy-weight prospects, for while Spider McCoy manages a number of fighters, he never gets excited about anything but a heavy-weight, and this is the way all fight managers are. A fight manager may have a light-weight champion of the world, but he will get more heated up about some sausage who scarcely knows how to hold his hands up if he is a heavy-weight.

Personally, I consider it most remarkable that Margie is able to spot Jonas as one of Spider's heavy-weight prospects in a high hat and a cut-away coat, but Margie says it is a sixth sense with her. She says Spider once brings home a party with a beard half-way down to his waist, but that as soon as she opens the door she pegs him as a heavy-weight prospect that Spider does not yet have time to get shaved.

But she says she is so fond of Spider that she takes them all in, and feeds them up good, and the only time she ever bars anybody on him is the time Spider brings home a big widow he finds in Mickey Walker's bar and claims he is going to make her the only female contender for the heavy-weight title in the world. Miss Margie Grogan says she has to draw the line somewhere on Uncle Spider's prospects.

Well, from now on, Spider has Jonas in the gymnasium for several hours every day, teaching how to box, and anybody will tell you that Spider is as good a teacher as there is in the world, especially of a punch that is called the one-two, although this punch is really two punches. It is a left jab followed through fast with a right cross, and it is considered quite a gravy punch if properly put on.

Jonas lives in a spare room in Spider's apartment, and takes his meals there, and Spider tells me everything will be very nice indeed for them all, if Margie does not happen to take more of a dislike than somewhat to Jonas, especially when she learns that he is once a king and gets the old hoovus-groovus from a dictator.

Margie tells Spider McCoy that it proves there must be anyway a trace of umbrella in a character who lets anybody run him out of his own country, and Spider says the only reason he does not give her an argument on the matter is that he is not sure but what she is right, though not because Jonas lets himself get run out.

'I do not figure this in at all,' Spider says. 'I sometimes let myself get run out of places, and I do not think there is umbrella in me, or anyway not much. But,' he says, 'a young heavy-weight prospect is a peculiar proposition. You can find out in the gymnasium if he can box, if he is fast, and if he can punch, but you cannot find out if he can take a punch and if he is dead game until you see him boffed around good in the ring.

'And,' Spider says, 'this is what you must find out before you know if you have a heavy-weight contender, or just a heavy-weight. This Jonas looks great in the gym, but,' he says, 'sometimes I wonder about him. I do not know why I wonder, but I remember I wonder the same way about Ben Robbins, who is such a gymnasium marvel that I turn down twenty thousand for his contract. Then,' Spider says, 'I put him with this punching-bag, Joe Grosher, in Newark, and my guy geeks it the first good smack he gets. Somehow,' Spider says, 'Jonas has a certain look in his eyes that reminds me of Ben Robbins.'

'Well,' I says, 'if you are not sure about him, why not chuck him in with somebody the same as you do Ben, and find out if he can fight, or what?'

'Look,' Spider McCoy says, 'I will never find out anything more about this guy than I know now, if the offers I am getting keep on coming in. I will not have to find out,' he says. 'We must have a hundred propositions right now, and I am going to commence taking some.'

Naturally the blats make quite an uproar when they discover that an ex-king is training to be a fighter, and they are full of stories and pictures about Jonas every day, and of course Spider does not discourage this publicity because it is responsible for the offers of matches for Jonas from all over the country.

But the matches Spider finally commences accepting are not the matches the promoters offer, because the promoters offer opponents who may have no respect for royalty, and may try to knock Jonas's brains out. The matches Spider accepts have his own personal supervision, and they are much better for Jonas than what the promoters might think up.

These matches are with sure-footed watermen, who plunge in swiftly and smoothly when Jonas waves at them, and while everybody knows these matches are strictly tank jobs, nobody cares, especially the customers who almost break down the doors of the clubs where Jonas appears, trying to get in. The customers are so greatly pleased to be permitted to observe an ex-king in short pants that they scarcely pause for their change at the box-office windows.

Of course Spider does not tell Jonas that these contests are dipsy-doos and Jonas thinks he really is belting out these porter-houses, and as he is getting pretty nice money for the work, he feels very well, indeed. Anybody will tell you that it helps build up a young fighter's confidence to let him see a few people take naps in front of him as he is coming along, though Jonas is slightly bewildered the night at the Sun Casino when a generally very reliable waterboy by the name of Charley Drunckley misses his cue and falls down before Jonas can hit him.

The boxing commission is somewhat bewildered, too, and asks a few questions that nobody tries to answer, and Spider McCoy explains to Jonas that he hits so fast he cannot notice his punches landing himself, but even then Jonas continues to look somewhat bewildered.

He continues living at Spider McCoy's apartment, because Spider is by no means sucker enough to let Jonas get very far away from him, what with so many unscrupulous characters around the boxing game who are always looking to steal somebody's fighter, especially a fighter who is worth his weight in platinum, like Jonas, but from what I hear Miss Margie Grogan continues to play plenty of ice for him.

She goes to see him fight once, because everybody else in town is trying to go, but Margie is pretty cute, and she can spot a tank job as far as anybody, and while she knows very well that it is Spider McCoy and not Jonas who is responsible for these half-Gainors that are going on, she tells Spider that if Jonas is not a big umbrella he will be fighting somebody who can really fight.

'Over my dead body,' Spider says. 'If I ever hear of anybody that can really fight trying to fight my Jonas, I will cause trouble. And Margie,' Spider says, 'do not call Jonas an umbrella in my presence. It hurts my feelings.'

But Jonas is a great disappointment to Spider in some respects, especially about publicity angles. Spider wishes to get a tin crown made for him to wear going into the ring, but Jonas will not listen to this, and what is more he will not stand for as much as a monocle, because he claims he does not know how to keep one in his eye.

Well, the dough is rolling in on Spider and Jonas just with tank acts, but some of the boxing scribes are commencing to say Jonas ought to meet real competition, and I tell Spider myself it may be a good idea to see if Jonas really can fight.

'Yes,' Spider says, 'I am sometimes tempted myself. He shapes up so good that I get to thinking maybe he is the makings, at that. But I think I will let well enough alone.

'Anyway,' Spider says, 'what a sap I will be to throw him in with competition as long as the suckers will pay to see him as he is. I can go on with him indefinitely this way,' Spider says, 'but one smack on the chops may finish us up for good. Yes,' he says, 'I think I will let well enough alone.'

Now, one day a chunky guy with a big moustache and his hair cut short comes to see Jonas and has a long talk with him, and Jonas tells Spider that this guy is from his home country over in Europe, and that he is sent by the dictator who runs Jonas off, and his cabinet, who wish Jonas to return home to talk to them about certain matters, which may include a proposition for him to be king again, and Jonas says it sounds like a fair sort of proposition, at that.

'Why,' Spider says, 'nobody can talk business with you now. I am your manager, and all propositions must come to me first. Is there any chance of us making any real dough out of your going back to being king?'

Well, Jonas says it is by no means definite that he is to be king again, but that there is something in the air, and as he now has plenty of dough, and it is safe for him to return, he wishes to go home a while if only to pick up a few belongings that he does not have time to collect the last time he departs.

Furthermore, nothing will do but Spider must go with him, and

Spider says this means Miss Margie Grogan will have to go, too, because she is practically his right arm in business, and every other way, and Jonas says he thinks this is an excellent idea. He says Margie looks to him as if a sea voyage will do her good, and when Spider mentions this opinion to Margie, she says she wishes the big umbrella will stop looking at her to see how she looks, but that she will go just to spite him, and so they sail away.

Well, it is some months before I see Spider McCoy again, and then I run into him on Broadway one afternoon, and he is all dressed up in striped pants, and white spats, and a cut-away coat, and a high hat, and before I can start asking questions he says to me like this:

'Come with me to number twenty-three,' he says. 'I am on a meet there with somebody, and I will tell you all.'

So from now on for a while this is Spider McCoy's story:

Well [Spider says] we have a most satisfactory journey in every respect. Going over on the boat, what happens what with the moon and the stars, and the music, and dancing, and all this and that, but Margie and Jonas get so they are on slightly better terms, and this makes things more pleasant for me, as they are together quite a bit, and this gives me time to catch up on my drinking, which I neglect no little when I am so busy looking after Jonas's interests.

He gets a wonderful reception when we reach his old home country, what with bands and soldiers, and one thing and another, but I am surprised to find that none of the natives hear of me as his manager. In fact, it seems that his reputation there rests entirely on once being king, and they never hear of his accomplishments in the ring, which consist of eighteen consecutive k.o.'s. This really hurts my feelings after all my work with him in the gym and the trouble I go to in picking his opponents.

Personally, his country does not strike me as much of a country, and in fact it strikes me as nothing but a sort of double Jersey City, and the natives speak a language of their own, and the scenery is filled with high hills, and take it all around, I do not consider it anything to get excited about, but it is plain to be seen that Jonas is glad to get back there.

Well, we are not there more than a few hours before we get a line on what is doing, and what is doing is that the people wish Jonas to be king again, and they are making life a burden for this Dictator Poltafuss, and his cabinet, and Poltafuss figures it will be a good scheme to put Jonas back, all right, but first he wishes to discuss certain terms of his own with Jonas.

The very afternoon of the day we arrive there is a cabinet meeting in the palace, which is a building quite similar to a county court-house, and Jonas is invited to this meeting. They do not invite me, but naturally as Jonas's manager, I insist on going to protect his interests, and in fact I consider it quite unethical for them to be inviting my fighter to discuss terms of any kind and not including me, and then Jonas requests Margie to also accompany him.

The cabinet meeting is in a big room with high windows overlooking a public square and in this square a large number of natives of Jonas's country gather while the meeting is in progress, and talk among themselves in their own language.

There must be thirty characters of one kind and another sitting around a big table when we enter the room, and I figure they are the cabinet, and it does not take me long to pick Dictator Poltafuss. He is sitting at the head of the table and he is wearing a uniform with about four pounds of medals on his chest, and he has short black whiskers, and a fierce eye, and anybody can see that he is built from the ground up.

He is as big as a Russian wrestler, and looks to me as if he may be a tough character in every respect. A solid-looking Judy in a black dress is sitting in a chair behind him with some knitting in her hands, and she does not seem to be paying much attention to what is going on.

Well, as we enter the room and Jonas sees Poltafuss, a look comes into Jonas's eyes that is without doubt the same look I sometimes see in the gymnasium and in the ring, and which is the look that makes me wonder about him and keeps me from ever putting him in without knowing his opponent's right name and address, and, thinks I to myself, he is afraid of the guy with the sassafras. Thinks I to myself, Margie is right. He is a big umbrella.

Poltafuss begins talking very fast to Jonas, and in their own language, and after he gets through, Jonas does a lot of talking in the same language, and finally Jonas turns to us, and in our language he tells us what Poltafuss says to him and what he says to Poltafuss, and what Poltafuss says is really somewhat surprising.

'He says,' Jonas says, 'that I will be returned to the throne if I first marry his sister. She is the chromo sitting behind him. I tell him she is older than he is, and has a big nose, and a moustache.

He says,' Jonas says, 'that she is only a year older, which puts her shading forty, and that a big horn indicates character, and a moustache is good luck.

'Then,' Jonas says, 'I tell him the real reason I will not marry her, which is because I am going to marry someone else.'

'Wait a minute, Jonas,' I say. 'You mustn't never tell a lie, even to be king. You know you are not going to marry anybody. I do not permit my fighters to marry,' I say. 'It takes their mind off their business.'

'Yes,' Jonas says, 'I am going to marry Miss Margie Grogan. We fix it up on the ship.'

Then all of a sudden Poltafuss jumps up and says to Margie in English like this:

'Why,' he says, 'the idea is ridiculous. He cannot marry you. He is of royal blood. You are of common stock,' he says.

'Look, Jonas,' Margie says, 'are you going to stand here and hear me insulted? If you are, I am leaving right now,' she says.

Then she starts for the door, and Jonas runs after her and grabs her by the arm and says:

'But, Margie,' he says, 'what can I do?'

'Well,' Margie says, 'you can boff this big ape for one thing, as any gentleman is bound to do, unless,' she says, 'there is even more umbrella in you than ever I suspect.'

'Why, yes,' Jonas says. 'To be sure, and certainly,' he says.

And with this he walks over to Poltafuss, but old Polty hears what Margie says, and as Jonas gets near him, he lets go a big right hand that starts down around China and bangs Jonas on the chin, and Jonas goes down.

Well, I thinks to myself, I am only glad this does not occur at the Garden some night when the joint is packed. Then I hear Margie's voice saying like this:

'Get up, Jonas,' Margie says. 'Get up and steady yourself.'

'It is no use, Margie,' I say. 'You are right, he is an umbrella.'

'You are a liar,' Margie says.

'Margie,' I say, 'remember you are speaking to your Uncle Spider.'

I am still thinking of how disrespectfully Margie addresses me, when I notice that Jonas is up on his feet, and as he gets up he sticks out his left in time to drive it through Poltafuss's whiskers, as Poltafuss rushes at him. This halts Polty for an instant, then he comes on again swinging both hands. He is strictly a wild thrower, but he hits like a steer kicking when he lands, and he has Jonas down three times in as many minutes, and every time I figure Jonas will remain there and doze off, but Margie says get up, and Jonas gets up, and when he gets up he has sense enough to stick his left in Poltafuss's beard.

There seems to be some slight confusion among the members of the cabinet as the contest opens, and I take a good strong grip on a big chair, just in case of fire or flood, but I wish to say I never witness a finer spirit of fair play than is exhibited by the members of the cabinet. They stand back against the wall and give Jonas and Poltafuss plenty of elbow-room, and they seem to be enjoying the affair no little. In fact, the only spectator present who does not seem to be enjoying it is Poltafuss's sister, who does not get up out of her chair to get a better view, and furthermore does not stop her knitting, so I can see she is by no means a fight fan.

Pretty soon Jonas's left-hand sticking has Poltafuss's nose bleeding and then one eye begins to close, and I find myself getting very much interested, because I now see what I am looking for all my life, which is a dead game heavy-weight, and I can see that I will no longer have to be worrying about who I put Jonas in with. I see the next heavy-weight champion of the world as sure as I am standing there, and I now begin coaching Jonas in person.

'Downstairs, Jonas,' I say. 'In the elly-bay, Jonas,' I say.

So Jonas hits Poltafuss a left hook in the stomach, and Polty goes oof.

'The old one-two, Jonas,' I say, and Jonas stabs Poltafuss's nose with a long left, then follows through with a right cross, just as I educate him to do, and this right-hand cross lands on Polty's chin, among the whiskers, and down he goes as stiff as a board on his face, and when they fall in this manner, you may proceed at once to the pay-off window.

The next thing I know, Margie is in Jonas's arms, dabbing at his bloody face with a little handkerchief, and shedding tears, and a member of the cabinet that I afterward learn is the secretary of war is at one of the windows yelling down to the natives in the square and they are yelling back at him, and later someone tells me that what he yells is that the king just flattens Poltafuss and what they are yelling back is long live the king.

'Spider,' Jonas says, 'I never have any real confidence in myself before, but I have now. I just lick the party who can lick any six guys in my country all at once and with one hand tied behind him.

Spider,' he says, 'I know now I will be heavy-weight champion of the world.'

Well, Poltafuss is sitting up on the floor holding his nose with both hands, and looking somewhat dishevelled, but at this he puts his hands down long enough to speak as follows:

'No,' he says, 'you will be king, and your sweetheart there will be queen.'

And this is the way it turns out [Spider says] and Jonas and Poltafuss get along very nicely indeed together afterward, except once at a cabinet meeting when King Jonas has to flatten Poltafuss again to make him agree to some unemployment measure.

'But, Spider,' I say, as Spider McCoy finishes his story, 'you do not state what becomes of the dictator's sister.'

'Well,' Spider says, 'I will tell you. It seems to me that the dictator's sister gets a rough deal, one way and another, especially,' he says, 'as her beezer is by no means as big as some people think.

'So,' Spider says, 'while I will always regret blowing the next heavy-weight champion of the world, I console myself with the thought that I get a wonderful and ever-loving wife, and if you will wait a few minutes longer, I will introduce you to the former Miss Sofia Poltafuss, now Mrs. Spider McCoy.'

For a Pal

For a matter of maybe fifteen years or more, Little Yid and Blind Benny are pals, and this is considered a very good thing for Benny because he is as blind as a bat, and maybe blinder, while Yid can see as good as anybody and sometimes better.

So Little Yid does the seeing for Benny, explaining in his own way to Benny just what he sees, such as a horse race or a baseball game or a prize fight or a play or a moving picture or anything else, for Yid and Blind Benny are great hands for going around and about wherever anything is coming off, no matter what, and up to the time this doll Mary Marble comes into their lives they are as happy as two pups in a basket.

How Benny comes to go blind I do not know, and nobody else along Broadway seems to know either, and in fact nobody cares, although I once hear Regret, the horse player, say it is probably in sympathy with the judges at the race track, Regret being such a guy as claims all these judges are very blind indeed. But of course Regret is sore at these race-track judges because they always call the wrong horse for him in the close finishes.

Little Yid tells me that Blind Benny is once a stick man in a gambling joint in Denver, and a very good stick man, at that, and one night a fire comes off in a flop house on Larimer Street, and Blind Benny, who is not blind at this time, runs into the fire to haul out an old guy who has more smoke in him than somewhat, and a rush of flames burns Benny's eyes so bad he loses his sight.

Well, this may be the true story of how Benny comes to go blind, but I know Little Yid likes Benny so much that he is not going to give Benny the worst of any story he tells about him, and for all anybody knows maybe Benny really goes into the fire to search for the old guy. Personally, I do not believe in taking too much stock in any story you hear on Broadway about anything.

But there is no doubt about Blind Benny being blind. His eyelids are tacked down tight over his eyes, and there is no chance that he is faking, because many guys keep close tab on him for years and never catch him peeping once.

Furthermore, several guys send Benny to eye specialists at different times to see if they can do anything about his eyes, and all these specialists say he is one of the blindest guys they ever examine. Regret says maybe it is a good thing, at that, because Benny is so smart as a blind guy that the chances are if he can see he will be too smart to live.

He is especially smart when it comes to playing such games as pinochle. In fact, Benny is about as good a single-handed pinochle player as there is in this town, and there are many first-rate pinochle players in this town, if anybody asks you.

Benny punches little holes in the cards so he can tell which is which by feeling them, and the only way anybody can beat him is to cheat him, and it is considered most discourteous to cheat a blind guy, especially as Benny is always apt to catch a guy at cheating and put up an awful beef.

He is a tall, skinny guy with a thin face, and is by no means bad-looking, while Little Yid is about knee high to a snake, and they look like a father and his little boy as they go along the street with

Little Yid hanging on to Blind Benny's arm and giving him the right steer.

Of course it is by no means an uncommon thing on Broadway for citizens to steer these blind guys across the street, although if the blind guys have any sense they will keep their dukes on their tin cups while they are being steered, but it is a most unusual proposition in this town for anybody to go steering a blind guy around for fifteen years the way Little Yid steers Blind Benny, as Blind Benny is a guy who takes plenty of steering.

In fact, one time Yid has to be away from business for a week, and he leaves Blind Benny with a committee of guys, and every day one of these guys has to steer Benny around wherever he wishes to go, which is wherever there is anything going on, and Benny wears the whole committee plumb out before Yid gets back, as Benny is certainly a guy who likes to go around and about. Furthermore, he is so unhappy while Yid is away that he becomes a great nuisance, because it seems that none of the committee can see things as good as Yid for him, or explain them so he can understand them.

Personally, I will not care to have Little Yid do my seeing for me, even if I am blind, because I listen to him telling what he sees to Blind Benny many times, and it seems to me Little Yid is often somewhat cock-eyed in his explanations.

Furthermore, I will hate to be explaining things to Blind Benny, because he is always arguing about what is taking place, and giving you his opinions of it, even though he cannot see. In fact, although he cannot see a lick, Blind Benny is freer with his opinions than guys who can see from here to Europe.

It is a very interesting sight to watch Little Yid and Blind Benny at the race track, for they are both great hands for playing the horses and, in fact, Benny is a better handicapper than a lot of guys who have two good eyes and a pair of spectacles to do their handicapping with.

At night they get the form sheet and sit up in their room with Yid reading off the past performances and the time trials, and all this and that, and with Blind Benny doping the horses from what Yid reads, and picking the ones he figures ought to win the next day. They always have a big argument over each horse, and Yid will tell Blind Benny he is daffy to be picking whatever horse it is he picks, and Benny will tell Yid he is out of his mind to think anything else can beat this horse, and they will holler and yell at each other for hours.

But they always wind up very friendly, and they always play the horse Benny picks, for Yid has much confidence in Benny's judgment, although he hollers and yells at him more than somewhat when one of his picks loses. They sit up in the grandstand during every race and Yid will explain to Benny what is doing in the race, and generally he manages to mention that the horse they are betting on is right up there and going easy, even though it may be laying back of the nine ball, for Yid believes in making Blind Benny feel good at all times.

But when a horse they are betting on is really in the running, especially in the stretch, Yid starts to root him home, and Benny roots right along with him as if he can see, and rocks back and forth in his seat, and pounds with his cane, and yells, 'Come on with him, Jock,' the same as anybody with two good eyes.

I am telling you all this about Little Yid and Benny to show you that they are very close friends indeed. They live together and eat together and argue together, and nobody ever hears of a nicer friendship on Broadway, although naturally some citizens figure for a while that one or the other must have some angle in this friendship, as it is practically uncanny for a friendship to last all these years on Broadway.

Blind Benny has some kind of an income from his people out West who are sorry about him being blind, and Little Yid has a piece of a small factory run by a couple of his brothers over in Hoboken where they make caps such as some citizens wear on their heads, and it seems this factory does very well, and the brothers are willing to send Little Yid his piece without him being around the factory very much, as they do not seem to consider him any boost to a cap factory.

So Yid and Blind Benny have all the money they need to go along, what with making a little scratch now and then on the races, and they never seem to care for any company but their own and are very happy and contented with each other. In all the years they are together Yid is never known to more than say hello to a doll, and of course Blind Benny cannot see dolls, anyway, which many citizens claim is a great break for Benny, so Yid and Benny are carrying no weight in this respect.

Now one night it seems that Ike Jacobs, the ticket spec, has a pair of Chinese duckets on the opening of a new play by the name of Red Hot Love, a Chinese ducket being a complimentary ducket that is punched full of holes like Chinese money, and which you do not have to pay for, and Ike gives these duckets to Little Yid and Blind Benny, which is considered very large-hearted of Ike, at that.

So when the curtain goes up on Red Hot Love, Yid and Benny are squatted right down in front among many well-known citizens who are all dressed up in evening clothes, because this Red Hot Love has a bunch of swell actors in it, and is expected to be first-class.

Naturally, when the play begins, Yid has to give Blind Benny a little information about what is doing, otherwise Benny cannot appreciate the thing. So Yid starts off in a whisper, but any time Yid starts explaining anything to Benny he always winds up getting excited, and talking so loud you can hear him down at the Battery.

Of course Blind Benny can follow the play as good as anybody if there is plenty of gab on the stage, but he likes to know what actors are doing the gabbing, and what they look like, and what the scenery looks like, and other details that he cannot see, and Little Yid is telling him in such a voice as causes some of the citizens around to say shush-shush. But Little Yid and Blind Benny are accustomed to being shushed in theatres, so they do not pay much attention.

Well, Red Hot Love is one of these problem plays, and neither Little Yid nor Blind Benny can make much of it, although they are no worse off than anybody else around them, at that. But Little Yid tries to explain to Blind Benny what it is all about, and Benny speaks out loud as follows:

'It sounds to me like a rotten play.'

'Well,' Little Yid says, 'maybe the play is not so rotten, but the acting is.'

There is much shushing from one and all around them, and the actors are giving them the bad eye from the stage, because the actors can hear what they say, and are very indignant, especially over this crack about acting.

Well, the next thing anybody knows down the aisle come a couple of big guys who put the arm on Little Yid and Blind Benny and give them the old heave-o out of the joint, as you are not supposed to speak out loud in a theatre about any bad acting that is going on there, no matter how bad it is.

Anyway, as Little Yid and Blind Benny are being prodded up the aisle by the big guys, Blind Benny states as follows:

'I still claim,' he says, 'that it sounds like a rotten play.'

'Well,' Little Yid says, 'the acting certainly is.'

There is much applause as Yid and Benny are getting the heave-o, and many citizens claim it is because the customers are glad to see them heaved, but afterward it comes out that what many of the customers are really applauding is the statements by Little Yid and Benny.

Well, Yid and Benny do not mind getting the heave-o so much, as they are heaved out of many better theatres than this in their time, but they are very indignant when the box office refuses to give them back the admission price, although of course their duckets do not cost them anything in the first place and they are a little out of line in trying to collect.

They are standing on the sidewalk saying what an outrage it is when all of a sudden out of the theatre pops this doll by the name of Mary Marble, and her face is very red, and she is also very indignant, because it seems that in the second act of the play there are some very coarse cracks led out on the stage, and it seems that Mary Marble is such a doll as believes that cracks of this nature are only fit for married people to hear, and she is by no means married.

Of course Little Yid and Blind Benny do not know at the time that she is Mary Marble, and in fact they do not know her from Adam's off ox as she marches up to them and speaks as follows:

'Gentlemen,' she says, 'I wish to compliment you on your judgment of the affair inside. I hear what you say as you are getting ejected,' she says, 'and I wish to state that you are both right. It is a rotten play, and the acting is rotten.'

Now off this meeting, what happens but Mary Marble gets to going around with Little Yid and Blind Benny whenever she can spare time from her job, which is managing a little joint on Broadway where they sell stockings such as dolls wear on their legs, except in summer-time, although even when they wear these stockings you cannot tell if a doll has anything on her legs unless you pinch them, the stockings that dolls wear nowadays being very thin, indeed.

Furthermore, whenever she is with them, it is now Mary Marble who does most of the explaining to Blind Benny of what is going on, because Mary Marble is such a doll as is just naturally bound to do all the explaining necessary when she is around.

When it comes to looks, Mary Marble is practically no dice.

In fact, if she is not the homeliest doll on Broadway, I will guarantee she is no worse than a dead-heat with the homeliest. She has a large beezer and large feet, and her shape is nothing whatever to speak of, and Regret, the horse player, says they never need to be afraid of entering Mary Marble in a claiming race at any price. But of course Regret is such a guy as will not give you a counterfeit dime for any doll, no matter what she looks like.

Mary Marble is maybe twenty-five years old – although Regret says he will lay 6 to 5 against her being any better than twenty-eight – and about all she has running for her, anyway you take her, is a voice that is soft and gentle and very nice, indeed, except that she is fond of using it more than somewhat.

She comes from a little town over in Pennsylvania, and is pretty well educated, and there is no doubt whatever that she is unusually respectable, because such a looking doll as Mary Marble has no excuse for being anything but respectable on Broadway. In fact, Mary Marble is so respectable that many citizens figure there must be an angle, but it is agreed by one and all that she is perfectly safe with Little Yid and Blind Benny, no matter what.

And now at night instead of always doping the horse, Little Yid and Blind Benny will often sit up in their room talking about nothing much but Mary Marble, and Benny asks Yid a million questions over and over again.

'Tell me, Yid,' Blind Benny will say, 'what does Mary look like?'
'She is beautiful,' Yid always says.

Well, of course, this is practically perjury, and many citizens figure that Yid tells Blind Benny this very large lie because he has an idea Benny wishes to hear only the best about Mary Marble, although it comes out afterward that Little Yid thinks Mary Marble beautiful, at that.

'She is like an angel,' he says.

'Yes, yes,' Blind Benny says, 'tell me more.'

And Little Yid keeps on telling him, and if Mary Marble is only one-eighth as good-looking as Yid tells, Ziegfeld and Georgie White and Earl Carroll will be breaking each other's legs trying to get to her first.

'Well,' Blind Benny often says, after Little Yid gets through telling him about Mary Marble, 'she is just as I picture her to myself, Yid,' he says. 'I never care so much about not being able to see until now, and even now all I wish to see is Mary.'

The idea seems to be that Blind Benny is in love with Mary Marble, and the way Little Yid is always boosting her it is no wonder. In fact, the chances are a lot of other citizens will be in love with Mary Marble if they listen to Yid telling Blind Benny about her, and never get a gander at her personally.

But Blind Benny does not mention right out that he is in love with Mary Marble, and it may be that he does not really know what is eating him, which is often the case with guys who are in love. All Blind Benny knows is that he likes to be with Mary Marble and to listen to her explaining things to him, and, what is more, Mary Marble seems to like to be with Blind Benny, and to explain things to him, although as far as this goes Mary Marble is such a doll as likes to be explaining things to anybody any time she gets a chance.

Now Little Yid and Blind Benny are still an entry at all times, even when Mary Marble is with them, but many citizens see that Little Yid is getting all sorrowed up, and they figure it is because he feels Blind Benny is gradually drifting away from him after all these years, and everybody sympathizes with Little Yid no little, and there is some talk of getting him another blind guy to steer around in case Blind Benny finally leaves him for good.

Then it comes on a Saturday night when Little Yid says he must go over to Hoboken to see his brothers about the cap business and, as Mary Marble has to work in the stocking joint Saturday nights, Little Yid asks Blind Benny to go with him.

Of course Blind Benny does not care two cents about the cap business, but Little Yid explains to him that he knows a Dutchman's in Hoboken where there is some very nice real beer, and if there is one thing Blind Benny likes more than somewhat it is nice real beer, especially as it seems that since they become acquainted with Mary Marble he seldom gets nice real beer, as Mary Marble is a terrible knocker against such matters as nice real beer.

So they start for Hoboken, and Little Yid sees his brothers about the cap business, and then he takes Blind Benny to a Dutchman's to get the nice real beer, only it turns out that the beer is not real, and by no means nice, being all needled up with alky, and full of headaches, and one thing and another. But of course Little Yid and Blind Benny are not going around complaining about beer even if it is needled, as, after all, needled beer is better than no beer whatever.

They sit around the Dutchman's quite a while, although it turns out that the Dutchman is nothing but a Polack, and then they nab a late ferryboat for home, as Little Yid says he wishes to ride on a ferryboat to get the breeze. As far as Blind Benny is concerned, he does not care how they go as long as he can get back to New York to meet up with Mary Marble when she is through work.

There are not many citizens on the ferryboat with them, because it is getting on towards midnight, and at such an hour anybody who lives in Jersey is home in bed. In fact, there are not over four or five other passengers on the ferryboat with Little Yid and Blind Benny, and these passengers are all dozing on the benches in the smoking-room with their legs stuck out in front of them.

Now if you know anything about a ferryboat you know that they always hook big gates across each end of such a boat to keep automobiles and trucks and citizens and one thing and another from going off these ends into the water when the ferryboat is travelling back and forth, as naturally it will be a great nuisance to other boats in the river to have things falling off the ferryboats and clogging up the stream.

Well, Little Yid is away out on the end of the ferryboat up against the gate enjoying the breeze, and Blind Benny is leaning against the rail just outside the smoking-room door where Little Yid plants him when they get on the boat, and Blind Benny is smoking a big heater that he gets at the Dutchman's and maybe thinking of Mary Marble, when all of a sudden Little Yid yells like this:

'Oh, Benny,' he yells, 'come here.'

Naturally Benny turns and goes in the direction of the voice and Little Yid's voice comes from the stern, and Blind Benny keeps following his beezer in the direction of the voice, expecting to feel Little Yid's hand stopping him any minute, and the next thing he knows he is walking right off the ferryboat into the river.

Of course Blind Benny cannot continue walking after he hits the water, so he sinks at once, making a sound like glug-glug as he goes down. It is in the fall of the year, and the water is by no means warm, so as Benny comes up for air he naturally lets out a loud squawk, but by this time the ferryboat is quite some jumps away from him, and nobody seems to see him, or even hear him.

Now Blind Benny cannot swim a lick, so he sinks again with a glug-glug. He comes up once more, and this time he does not squawk so loud, but he sings out, very distinct, as follows: 'Goodbye, Pal Yid.'

All of a sudden there is quite a splash in the water near the ferryboat, and Little Yid is swimming for Blind Benny so fast the chances are he will make a sucker of Johnny Weissmuller if Johnny happens to be around, for Little Yid is a regular goldfish when it comes to water, although he is not much of a hand for going swimming without provocation.

He has to dive for Blind Benny, for by this time Blind Benny is going down for the third time, and everybody knows that a guy is only allowed three downs when he is drowning. In fact, Blind Benny is almost down where the crabs live before Little Yid can get a fistful of his collar. At first Little Yid's idea is to take Blind Benny by the hair, but he remembers in time that Benny does not have much hair, so he compromises on the collar.

And being a little guy, Yid has quite a job getting Benny to the top and keeping him there. By this time the ferryboat is almost at its dock on the New York side, and nobody on board seems to realize that it is shy a couple of passengers, although of course the ferryboat company is not going to worry about that as it collects the fares in advance.

But it is a pretty lucky break for Little Yid and Blind Benny that a tugboat happens along and picks them up, or Yid may be swimming around the North River to this day with Blind Benny by the nape of the neck going glug-glug.

The captain of the tugboat is a kind old guy with whiskers by the name of Deusenberg, and he is very sorry indeed to see them in such a situation, so after he hauls them on board the tugboat, and spreads them out on bunks to let them dry, he throws a couple of slugs of gin into Little Yid and Blind Benny, it being gin of such a nature that they are half sorry they do not go ahead and drown before they meet up with it.

Then the captain unloads them at Forty-second Street on the New York side, and by this time, between the water and the gin, Blind Benny is very much fagged out, indeed, and in bad shape generally, so Little Yid puts him in a cab and takes him to a hospital.

Well, for several days Blind Benny is not better than even money to get well, because after they get the water out of him they still have to contend with the gin, and Mary Marble is around carrying on quite some, and saying she does not see how Little Yid can be so careless as to let Benny walk off the end of a ferryboat when there are gates to prevent such a thing, or how he can let Benny drink tugboat gin, and many citizens do not see either, especially about the gin.

As for Little Yid, he is looking very sad, and is at the hospital at all times, and finally, one day when Blind Benny is feeling all right again, Little Yid sits down beside his bed, and speaks to him as follows:

'Benny,' Little Yid says, 'I will now make a confession to you, and I will then go away somewhere and knock myself off. Benny,' he says, 'I let you fall into the river on purpose. In fact,' Little Yid says, 'I unhook the gate across the passageway and call you, figuring you will follow the sound of my voice and walk on off the boat into the water.

'I am very sorry about this,' Little Yid says, 'but, Benny,' he says, 'I love Mary Marble more than somewhat, although I never before mention this to a soul. Not even to Mary Marble, because,' Little Yid says, 'I know she loves you, as you love her. I love her,' Little Yid says, 'from the night we first meet, and this love winds up by making me a little daffy.

'I get to thinking,' Little Yid says, 'that with you out of the way Mary Marble will turn to me and love me instead. But,' he says, starting to shed large tears, 'when I hear your voice from the water saying "Good-bye, Pal Yid," my heart begins to break, and I must jump in after you. So now you know, and I will go away and shoot myself through the head if I can find somebody to lend me a Roscoe, because I am no good.'

'Why,' Blind Benny says, 'Pal Yid, what you tell me about leading me into the river is no news to me. In fact,' he says, 'I know it the minute I hit the water because, although I am blind, I see many things as I am going down, and I see very plain that you must do this thing on purpose, because I know you are close enough around to grab me if you wish.

'I know, of course,' Blind Benny says, 'that there is bound to be a gate across the end of the boat because I often fix this gate when we are leaving Hoboken. So,' he says, 'I see that you must unhook this gate. I see that for some reason you wish to knock me off, although I do not see the reason, and the chances are I will never see it unless you tell me now, so I do not put up more of a holler and maybe attract the attention of the other guys on the boat. I am willing to let it all go as it lays.'

'My goodness,' Little Yid says, 'this is most surprising to me, indeed. In fact,' he says, 'I scarcely know what to say, Benny. In fact,' he says, 'I cannot figure out why you are willing to go without putting up a very large beef.'

'Well, Pal Yid,' Benny says, reaching out and taking Little Yid by the hand, 'I am so fond of you that I figure if my being dead is going to do you any good, I am willing to die, even though I do not know why. Although,' Benny says, 'it seems to me you can think up a nicer way of scragging me than by drowning, because you know I loathe and despise water. Now then,' he says, 'as for Mary Marble, if you—'

But Little Yid never lets Blind Benny finish this, because he cuts in and speaks as follows:

'Benny,' he says, 'if you are willing to die for me, I can certainly afford to give up a doll for you, especially,' he says, 'as my people tell me only yesterday that if I marry anybody who is not of my religion, which is slightly Jewish, they will chop me off at the pants' pocket. You take Mary Marble,' he says, 'and I will stake you to my blessing, and maybe a wedding present.'

So the upshot of the whole business is Mary Marble is now Mrs. Blind Benny, and Blind Benny seems to be very happy, indeed, although some citizens claim the explanations he gets nowadays of whatever is going on are much shorter than when he is with Little Yid, while Little Yid is over in Hoboken in the cap racket with his brothers, and he never sees Blind Benny any more, as Mary Marble still holds the gin against him.

Personally, I always consider Little Yid's conduct in this matter very self-sacrificing, and furthermore I consider him a very great hero for rescuing Blind Benny from the river, and I am saying as much only the other day to Regret the horse player.

'Yes,' Regret says, 'it sounds very self-sacrificing, indeed, and maybe Little Yid is a hero, at that, but,' Regret says, 'many citizens are criticizing him no little for sawing off such a crow as Mary Marble on a poor blind guy.'

Big Shoulders

One night I am sitting in Mindy's Restaurant on Broadway partaking of some delicious gefillte fish when a very beautiful young Judy comes in and sits down at my table and starts in sobbing as if her little heart will break.

I am about to call a waiter and have her chucked out of the place as her sobbing interferes with my enjoyment of the gefillte fish, when I observe that she is nobody but Zelma Bodinski, the daughter of Blooch Bodinski, a character who is well known to one and all along Broadway as a small operator in betting matters.

Well, every time I see Zelma Bodinski, she always makes me think I am looking at a ghost, because she is a dead ringer for her mama, Zelma O'Dare, who once does a hot wiggle in the old Garden Café on Seventh Avenue a matter of some twenty-odd years back, and who confirms a general suspicion that she is none too bright by marrying Blooch Bodinski and going to live in the Bronx.

However, as near as anybody can figure out, they get along together pretty well down through the years, because all Zelma O'Dare ever says is yes and no, and this is enough for Blooch, who does not understand many longer words, anyway, and when Zelma finally dies of influenza, she leaves him this daughter, who looks so much like her the chances are Blooch never misses the original.

This Blooch Bodinski is a short, fat, scary-looking little character who wears a derby hat and loud clothes when he marries Zelma O'Dare, and who always has a sad expression, and he does not change much in appearance as he grows older, except maybe to look sadder.

He comes up out of Essex Street to Broadway, and he does this and that, and one thing and another, to make a living, until finally he gets to taking bets on prize fights and baseball games, and scalping the bets. That is, if somebody gives Blooch a bet on a proposition, right away he hustles around and gets somebody else to take it off his hands, generally at a shade better price than Blooch gives in the first place.

Besides, he knocks off five per cent on a winning bet as his commission for his trouble, so he really is nothing but a sort of middleman, or broker, though what he calls himself is a betting commissioner. He never risks anything on his own account, no matter what, because Blooch is a very careful character by nature, and about as loose as concrete with his money.

So it gets around that you can always place a bet on almost any proposition through Blooch Bodinski, and that he is an honest character and always pays off, and by and by Blooch opens an office and goes grinding and chiselling along in a modest way for quite a spell, making a few dibs here and there, and having Zelma O'Dare stash them away in a jug uptown against a rainy day.

I hear Blooch has quite a package planted when the jug fails and he is knocked out and has to start all over again, and there is a rumour around and about that things are none too good for Blooch at the time I am speaking of. He still has his office, and his credit remains A1 with the trade all over the country, and anybody will accept a commission from Blooch because they know he never offers any bets he cannot guarantee, but the trouble is most of his old customers are also pretty well out of money, and new customers are scarce.

Anyway, here is Blooch Bodinski's daughter sobbing in Mindy's Restaurant, so naturally I ask her what ails her, and Zelma looks at me out of her big, black, wet eyes that are blacker than ever, what with the tears making the mascara run, and she says to me like this:

'It is Poppa,' she says. 'Poppa wishes me to marry Jake Applebaum, the druggist, and I hate druggists, especially when they are Jake Applebaum. Poppa wishes me to marry Jake because he owes Jake ten thousand dollars borrowed money, and Jake is getting tough about it.'

'Jake Applebaum already has ten thousand dollars,' I say. 'Twice,' I say. 'Maybe five or ten times. Jake Applebaum is fatter than a goose when it comes to money. Besides,' I say, 'Jake Applebaum is not hard to take. He is by no means bad-looking. He has a kind heart, unless you are asking him for dough. In fact, somebody tells me that you and Jake are almost an entry.'

'Yes,' she says, 'I promised to marry him six months back. This is why he lends Poppa the ten thousand, which Poppa needs for the overhead. Up to yesterday, I practically love Jake Applebaum. Then I meet Charley.'

Well, I do not ask her Charley who, as I figure it may be one of those knock-knock things, and anyway, I can see that if I just let her talk I will get the whole story. I am thinking of the difference between her and her mama, Zelma O'Dare, who never makes a longer speech than to say she will have another rye high, but who foals a chatter-box.

'Charley is a Yale,' Zelma says. 'He is very handsome and full of fun and not like Jake Applebaum, who only thinks of betting on something when he is not thinking of his drugstore.'

'Jake makes a nice bet, at that,' I say. 'But where do you meet this Charley and what happens?'

'He comes into Poppa's office yesterday,' Zelma says. 'You know

I am working in Poppa's office since last summer because Poppa cannot afford a regular office girl just now. I wish you could see his eyes. They are blue-grey. I am glad the baseball season is over because I get sick and tired of sitting there all day long telephoning bets on the Giants and the Yankees and the Cubs and Joe Louis, to Brad Cross in Fort Worth, and Dutch Ambrose in Omaha, and Izzy Harter in Indianapolis. They get awfully fresh with you. I mean the people in Izzy Harter's office.'

'You are speaking of Charley's eyes,' I say.

'Oh, yes,' Zelma says. 'He wishes to make a small bet on the Yales to beat the Princetons to-morrow. Somebody sends him to Poppa's office thinking we take football bets. Poppa is not there, so he talks to me. I tell him we not only do not take football bets but that it makes Poppa mad to even mention them, because he thinks football is silly. Poppa says football is nothing but a lot of big shoulders, and zing-boom-bah, and that anybody who bets on such a matter is a sucker.

'Well,' Zelma says, 'Charley says Poppa is wrong, and that he is making a big mistake not to take football bets. He says football is the coming big-betting proposition of this country. He talks to me four hours. He is a poor boy and works his way through college. This is his last year. He says I look like Mona Lisa, and he likes my shape.'

'Well,' I say, 'the bloke is no chump about some things, anyway, although I cannot say much for his idea of betting on the Yales to beat the Princetons. The Princetons are one-to-four favourites in the betting.'

'Yes,' Zelma says, 'Charley says it is a wonderful opportunity for everybody to get rich betting on the Yales. He says he is only sorry he does not have more than ten dollars to bet on them. He says they cannot possibly lose. He says he personally dopes the game for the Yales to win. I ask him if he is certain, and he crosses his heart and hopes to die if it is not the truth. I am going to tell Poppa about it as soon as I get back to the office. Just think,' Zelma says, 'Poppa can win enough money on this game to pay Jake Apple-baum back and then give me some so Charley and I can get married and go into business.'

'Just a minute,' I say. 'Does Charley ask you to marry him already?'

'Why, sure,' Zelma says. 'Do I not tell you we talk four hours? What else is there to talk about so long? He goes on to Princeton to the game, and he is coming back here as soon as he can and take me to dinner. He plays substitute in the game, and he simply has to be there. But now I must go back to the office and tell Poppa what a wonderful opportunity this is for him.'

Well, I figure that listening to Blooch Bodinski when he is propositioned to bet his own money on something, and especially a football game, will make Broadway history, so I tell Zelma I wish to see her papa about a little business matter, and I go with her to Blooch's office, which at this time is a rat-hole in an old building in West Forty-ninth Street, with just a desk and a couple of chairs and only one telephone in it, and as we come in, Blooch is slamming the receiver back on the hook and talking out loud to himself.

'Big shoulders!' Blooch is saying to himself. 'Zing-boom-bah, eight to five.' Then he sees me, and he says to me like this: 'Baseball, yes,' Blooch says. 'Prize fights, yes. Hockey, yes. Elections, yes. Big shoulders, no. Fifty times a day they call asking for prices on Mr. Minnesota, or Mr. Wisconsin, or somebody. I am about crazy. What do I know about prices on the big shoulders?'

'Why, Poppa,' Zelma says, 'Charley says it is your duty to hire college parties who can handicap the games for you, and get out your own prices and make your own book. Charley says most of the betting figures on the football games are a joke, and that if he is in the business he can get rich taking bets at his own prices and then catching the other fellows out of line and laying the bets off to them at their odds.'

Well, Blooch Bodinski looks at her for a minute without saying a word, and Zelma goes right ahead as follows:

'Charley says football betting is in its infancy,' she says. 'But the big thing is about the Yales to-morrow,' she says. 'Charley says they cannot possibly lose to the Princetons, and you can make yourself well off for life by betting on them.'

'Charley?' Blooch says. 'Charley what?'

At this Zelma pauses to think, but she is never much of a hand at thinking, just like her mama, Zelma O'Dare, so she soon gives it up and says like this: 'I forget what,' she says. 'Maybe he never tells me. Anyway, you are to bet on the Yales. Charley says they are like wheat in the bin.'

Well, Blooch finally shakes his head and looks at me and says: 'Yes, I am crazy. The big shoulders get me at last. What are the Yales?' he says.

'They are four to one,' I say.

Well, at this, Blooch drops his head on the desk and groans, and
I can see that he is overcome at the idea that anybody in this whole
world thinks he will bet on a 4-to-1 shot, but Zelma pays no attention to him and goes right on gabbing.

'Charley says college football and Presidential elections are the
only things it is safe to bet on,' she says. 'Charley says they are the
only propositions that give you a dead-square rattle. Charley says
nobody can cheat you in college football or Presidential elections.'

Blooch raises his head and sits there looking at her as if he never
sees her before in his life, and moreover he acts as if he does not
hear a word she says for a while. But finally, when Zelma has to
stop for breath, he holds up one hand to keep her from starting off
again and says like this:

'My own daughter,' he says, 'she wishes me to bet my own
dough on something. The whole world is crazy. Listen,' Blooch
says. 'For nearly thirty years I grind along in this town and never
do I risk a single dib of my own on a bet. I take it off the top, or I
take it off the bottom. Always something for nothing is my motto.
And if ever I do bet it will not be on the big shoulders, and what is
more, Jake Applebaum is in here a little while ago about you standing him up last night, so,' Blooch says, 'never you mind about
somebody called Charley.'

'He loves me,' Zelma says.

'So he tells me,' Blooch says.

'I mean Charley loves me,' Zelma says.

Then all of a sudden Zelma begins sobbing again, and I wish to
say that when it comes to a job of sobbing she is much better than a
raw hand, and between sobs she says she works hard all summer in
this dirty old office, taking the insults of people over the telephone,
and she never gets to go anywhere or see anything, and she wishes
she is dead, and if her poppa loves her as he claims he does, he will
take her to see the Yales and the Princetons play, even if he refuses
a chance to bet on an absolutely sure thing like the Yales.

Well, I can see that these tears make Blooch Bodinski very uneasy, and he says there, there, and now, now, and my, my to Zelma,
but she only sobs all the harder, and says for two cents she will
pitch herself off the new Tri-Boro bridge, and finally Blooch is
almost crying himself, and he pats Zelma on the head with his hand
and says to her like this:

'Why,' Blooch says, 'I remember hearing Jake Applebaum say he
is going to this very game, and I know he will be glad to take you. I

will call Jake up at once if you will just stop crying.'

Now I claim Zelma is sobbing right up there around the record from the beginning, but when Blooch says this she turns on a notch higher and says it shows her that her poppa does not love her at all to wish to shove her off on Jake Applebaum when she has only one desire in the world and this is to be with her only parent, so finally Blooch says all right, he will go around to Jack's ticket office and see if he can buy some tickets to the game, on condition that I go along.

Well, naturally, Zelma has no reason to bar me, so there we are the next morning taking a special train to Princeton, and I remember seeing Jake Applebaum at a distance in the Pennsylvania Station before we start, but he does not see us, and I also remember that Zelma seems to manoeuvre us around so we do not make the same train that Jake does, or connect with him when we hit Princeton.

Blooch dozes most of the way, because it seems he is awake most of the night worrying about the way Zelma is acting towards Jake Applebaum, and I sit in a seat with Zelma and listen to her talk about Charley. I also listen to what some of the other characters in our Pullman are saying, and although most of them seem to be Yales, I judge that they figure this game is just a breeze for the Princetons, and I say as much to Zelma.

'No,' she says, 'they are wrong. Charley says the Yales are a cinch. Charley says the handicapping of football teams so you can determine the winner of a game is an exact science and not mere guesswork as many people may think, and,' Zelma says, 'Charley says he applies scientific methods to handicapping this game, and he makes it close but certain for the Yales.'

She places so much faith in what Charley says that I am wondering if maybe I am making a mistake in not taking advantage of the price, for if there is anything I dearly love it is a long shot, and in football 4 to 1 is a very long shot indeed, and they do not often get down there in front. Then I remember that some handicappers who are maybe about as smart as Charley make this price, so I decide I am just as well off keeping my dough in my kick, although I do not speak of this to Zelma.

Blooch wakes up when our special pulls into Princeton, and we get off and start walking to the football yard with the rest of the crowd, and I am thinking that these scenes must be quite a novelty to him, when we pass a bunch of characters who are offering to buy or sell tickets to the game, and who are what is known as ticket hustlers, and a couple of old characters among them give Blooch a blow, and he stops to talk to them. When he joins us again, Blooch is smiling, and he says to me like this:

'I hustle duckets with those parties among these same crowds over twenty years ago,' he says. 'They remember old Blooch. I am a champion in those days, too.'

He livens up quite some after this and begins taking an interest in his surroundings and talking about the good old days, but as near as I can make out, Blooch's good old days are about the same as everybody else's good old days, and most of the time he is half starving.

Well, by this time Zelma is paying no attention whatever to us, but is looking all around and about, and I can see that she is hoping she may get a swivel at Charley, but naturally he is not to be seen, so she does the next best thing and takes to looking at other young characters who are quite numerous all over the place, and they look right back at her, if anybody asks you, and personally I do not blame them. She is the prettiest thing that ever steps in shoe leather this particular day, what with her eyes shining, and her cheeks red with excitement, and all this and that.

Our seats in the football stadium are not so good because they are right behind the goal-posts at one end of the field, and close to the ground, and we are not able to see a whole lot of the game, especially when the ball is in the middle of the field or down towards the other end, and Zelma is disappointed no little and Blooch is saying he will see Jack when he gets home about this, but personally I do not care where we are as long as we are at a football game, because football is one of my favourite dishes. Even Blooch partakes of the general excitement when we get settled down, and the bands play, and the young characters in the stands begin letting out cheers.

Zelma keeps watching the Yales' bench trying to locate Charley, but we are too far away for her to see good, and anyway, the game gets going and takes her attention, especially as right away the Princetons start running all over the Yales in a most disquieting manner.

I can see in about two plays why the Princetons are 1-to-4 favourites, and I say to Zelma like this:

'I am afraid Charley is wrong,' I say. 'This looks as if it may be murder.'

'Never fear,' Zelma says. 'Charley gives me his word the Yales will win.

'Where are the big shoulders?' Blooch says. 'These parties are a lot of midgets.'

Well, all of a sudden the Yales commence playing better football, and instead of running over them, the Princetons now have a tough time keeping from getting run over themselves, and the game goes this way and that way, and nothing happens in the way of a score, and the Yales in the stands are in quite a hubbub, and are singing Boolaboola and I do not know what all else, and Zelma is jumping up and down and shrieking, 'Charley is right!'

All the time she is trying to locate Charley on the field or on the side lines, but there seems to be no Charley, and I am commencing to wonder if some character does not play a joke on her.

She is somewhat downhearted when the second half starts and Charley remains invisible, although she is still confident that the Yales will win. Personally, I figure a tie is about the answer.

Well, it is getting on towards the end of the game, and the goal in front of us belongs at this time to the Princetons, and the Yales start a march that winds up with them losing the ball on downs on the Princetons' one-inch line, and everybody is half insane, especially Zelma, and even Blooch Bodinski is saying out loud to the Yales: 'Come on, big shoulders!'

But it is no go, and it is coming on dark when the Yales lose the ball, and one of the Yales gets hurt on the last play, and there is a substitution, and when they line up again one of the Princetons goes back behind his own goal to kick out of danger, and he is standing just a short distance from where we are sitting waiting for the pass.

Then, just as the ball is flipped to the Princeton back of the line, Zelma Bodinski lets out a shriek like a steam whistle, because it seems that she just spots the last Yale substitute, and she screams as follows: 'Char-lee!'

Well, afterward I read what the reporters say about the darkness and the slippery ball and all this and that, but it seems to me that I see the Princeton character back of the line jump at the scream and half turn his head, and the next thing anybody knows he drops the football out of his hands, and then as all the Yales are coming at him, he falls on it behind his own goal for what is called a safety, and this means two points against the Princetons.

And a few seconds later the whistle blows, and there the Princetons are, licked by the Yales by a score of two to nothing, which is very discouraging to the Princetons, to be sure. Naturally, there are some great goings-on over this business among the Yales, and nobody is more delighted than Zelma Bodinski, and I hear her saying to Blooch like this:

'Well,' Zelma says, 'now everything is all right. Jake Applebaum is paid off, and we have all the money we need. I am glad, because it proves Charley is right.'

'What do you mean Jake Applebaum is paid off?' Blooch says. 'And what do you mean we have all the money we need? If you do not marry Jake, we will be on relief in a month.'

'Oh,' Zelma says, 'I forget to tell you. This morning before we leave New York, I go to the office and call up Dutch Ambrose and Brad Cross and Izzy Harter and bet them two thousand dollars each in your name on Yale at four to one. Then I happen to have a date with Jake Applebaum the night before, and I tell him you have a commission of two thousand dollars from out of town to place on the Yales at the best price you can get, and Jake says he will lay five to one, because it is just the same as finding the two thousand in the street.

'So,' Zelma says, 'we pay off Jake and win twenty-four thousand in cash. Even if we lose,' she says, 'the most we can lose is eight thousand dollars, but I know that Charley says there is no chance of our losing. I will always believe Charley all my life, no matter what.'

Well, Blooch stands there as if he is thinking this over, and there is a very strange expression on his face, and about this time who comes up but Jake Applebaum, and it is plain to be seen that Jake is very angry, and he shakes his finger in Zelma Bodinski's beautiful face and says to her like this:

'See here,' Jake says. 'I hear all about you this morning when I am at breakfast in Mindy's. I hear all about you being in love with a Yale by the name of Charley, and now I know why you are jerking me around. But do not forget your old man owes me plenty, and I will make him hard to catch.'

Naturally, Jake's statement is most uncouth, and Zelma is starting to turn on the sobs, when a large young character in football clothes approaches, and I can see that he is nobody but the Princeton who fumbles the ball, and I can also see that he seems to be slightly perturbed as he says to us like this:

'Where is the pancake who sings out Charley over here? My name is Charley.'

Well, personally, I do not care for his attitude, and I do not think it shows proper college training for him to be speaking of pancakes, but before I can decide what to do about the situation, Jake Applebaum steps forward and says:

'Oh, so you are Charley, are you, you snake in the grass? Well, my lady friend here that you try to steal from me is the one who sings out. Why?' Jake says. 'What do you wish to make of it?'

'Only this!' the football character says, and then he lets go as neat a left hook as ever I could wish to behold and stretches Jake as flat as a pancake, and immediately disappears in the dusk.

We leave Jake there and start walking back to the railroad, and all this time Blooch never says a word but seems to be thinking of something, and finally he turns to Zelma and speaks as follows:

'You mean to say I stand to lose eight thousand of my own money on a four-to-one shot in this game?' Blooch says.

'Yes, Poppa,' Zelma says, 'you can figure it in such a way. But Charley says—'

Then without finishing she lets out a scream, because Blooch falls in a dead faint and starts rolling down a little hill, and the chances are he will be rolling yet if a big blond young character does not come leaping out of the dusk to grab him and set him on his pins again and shake him out of his faint. At the sight of this young character Zelma lets out another scream and says like this:

'Char-lee!'

So now Blooch Bodinski has a big suite of offices, and fifty telephones, and he calls himself the Flannagan Brokerage Company and makes the biggest football book in this country, and everybody along Broadway is pretty jealous about this, although Mindy, the restaurant man, says: 'Well, you must give Blooch credit for digging up Charley Flannagan, the best football handicapper in the world, for a son-in-law.'

And every time Blooch looks at Charley he nods his head to show he approves him, and sometimes Blooch says out loud: 'Big shoulders!'

That Ever-Loving Wife of Hymie's

If anybody ever tells me I will wake up some morning to find myself sleeping with a horse, I will consider them very daffy indeed, especially if they tell me it will be with such a horse as old Mahogany, for Mahogany is really not much horse. In fact, Mahogany is nothing but an old bum, and you can say it again, and many horse players wish he is dead ten thousand times over.

But I will think anybody is daffier still if they tell me I will wake up some morning to find myself sleeping with Hymie Banjo Eyes, because as between Mahogany and Hymie Banjo Eyes to sleep with, I will take Mahogany every time, even though Mahogany snores more than somewhat when he is sleeping. But Mahogany is by no means as offensive to sleep with as Hymie Banjo Eyes, as Hymie not only snores when he is sleeping, but he hollers and kicks around and takes on generally.

He is a short, pudgy little guy who is called Hymie Banjo Eyes because his eyes bulge out as big and round as banjos, although his right name is Weinstein, or some such, and he is somewhat untidy-looking in spots, for Hymie Banjo Eyes is a guy who does not care if his breakfast gets on his vest, or what. Furthermore, he gabs a lot and thinks he is very smart, and many citizens consider him a pest, in spades. But personally I figure Hymie Banjo Eyes as very harmless, although he is not such a guy as I will ordinarily care to have much truck with.

But there I am one morning waking up to find myself sleeping with both Mahogany and Hymie, and what are we sleeping in but a horse car bound for Miami, and we are passing through North Carolina in a small-time blizzard when I wake up, and Mahogany is snoring and shivering, because it seems Hymie cops the poor horse's blanket to wrap around himself, and I am half frozen and wishing I am back in Mindy's Restaurant on Broadway, where all is bright and warm, and that I never see either Mahogany or Hymie in my life.

Of course it is not Mahogany's fault that I am sleeping with him and Hymie, and in fact, for all I know, Mahogany may not consider me any bargain whatever to sleep with. It is Hymie's fault for digging me up in Mindy's one night and explaining to me how wonderful the weather is in Miami in the winter-time, and how we can go there for the races with his stable and make plenty of potatoes for ourselves, although of course I know when Hymie is speaking of his stable he means Mahogany, for Hymie never has more than one horse at any one time in his stable.

Generally it is some broken-down lizard that he buys for about the price of an old wool hat and patches up the best he can, as Hymie Banjo Eyes is a horse trainer by trade, and considering the kind of horses he trains he is not a bad trainer, at that. He is very good indeed at patching up cripples and sometimes winning races with them until somebody claims them on him or they fall down dead, and then he goes and gets himself another cripple and starts all over again.

I hear he buys Mahogany off a guy by the name of O'Shea for a hundred bucks, although the chances are if Hymie waits a while the guy will pay him at least two hundred to take Mahogany away and hide him, for Mahogany has bad legs and bum feet, and is maybe nine years old, and does not win a race since the summer of 1924, and then it is an accident. But anyway, Mahogany is the stable Hymie Banjo Eyes is speaking of taking to Miami when he digs me up in Mindy's.

'And just think,' Hymie says, 'all we need to get there is the price of a drawing-room on the Florida Special.'

Well, I am much surprised by this statement, because it is the first time I ever hear of a horse needing a drawing-room, especially such a horse as Mahogany, but it seems the drawing-room is not to be for Mahogany, or even for Hymie or me. It seems it is to be for Hymie's ever-loving wife, a blonde doll by the name of 'Lasses, which he marries out of some night-club where she is what is called an adagio dancer.

It seems that when 'Lasses is very young somebody once says she is just as sweet as Molasses, and this is how she comes to get the name of 'Lasses, although her right name is Maggie Something, and I figure she must change quite a lot since they begin calling her 'Lasses because at the time I meet her she is sweet just the same as green grapefruit.

She has a partner in the adagio business by the name of Donaldo, who picks her up and heaves her around the night-club as if she is nothing but a baseball, and it is very thrilling indeed to see Donaldo giving 'Lasses a sling as if he is going to throw her plumb away, which many citizens say may not be a bad idea, at that, and then catching her by the foot in mid-air and hauling her back to him.

But one night it seems that Donaldo takes a few slugs of gin before going into this adagio business, and he muffs 'Lasses' foot, although nobody can see how this is possible, because 'Lasses' foot is no more invisible than a box car, and 'Lasses keeps on sailing through the air. She finally sails into Hymie Banjo Eyes' stomach as he is sitting at a table pretty well back, and this is the way Hymie and 'Lasses meet, and a romance starts, although it is nearly a week before Hymie recovers enough from the body beating he takes off 'Lasses to go around and see her.

The upshot of the romance is 'Lasses and Hymie get married, although up to the time Donaldo slings her into Hymie's stomach, 'Lasses is going around with Brick McCloskey, the bookmaker, and is very loving with him indeed, but they have a row about something and are carrying the old torch for each other when Hymie happens along.

Some citizens say the reason 'Lasses marries Hymie is because she is all sored up on Brick and that she acts without thinking, as dolls often do, especially blonde dolls, although personally I figure Hymie takes all the worst of the situation, as 'Lasses is not such a doll as any guy shall marry without talking it over with his lawyer. 'Lasses is one of these little blondes who is full of short answers, and personally I will just as soon marry a porcupine. But Hymie loves her more than somewhat, and there is no doubt Brick McCloskey is all busted up because 'Lasses takes this run-out powder on him, so maybe after all 'Lasses has some kind of appeal which I cannot notice off-hand.

'But,' Hymie explains to me when he is speaking to me about this trip to Miami, ' 'Lasses is not well, what with nerves and one thing and another, and she will have to travel to Miami along with her Pekingese dog, Sooey-pow, because,' Hymie says, 'it will make her more nervous than somewhat if she has to travel with anybody else. And of course,' Hymie says, 'no one can expect 'Lasses to travel in anything but a drawing-room on account of her health.'

Well, the last time I see 'Lasses she is making a sucker of a big sirloin in Bobby's Restaurant, and she strikes me as a pretty healthy doll, but of course I never examine her close, and anyway, her health is none of my business.

'Now,' Hymie says, 'I get washed out at Empire, and I am pretty much in hock here and there and have no dough to ship my stable to Miami, but,' he says, 'a friend of mine is shipping several horses there and he has a whole car, and he will kindly let me have room in one end of the car for my stable, and you and I can ride in there, too.

'That is,' Hymie says, 'we can ride in there if you will dig up the price of a drawing-room and the two tickets that go with it so 'Lasses' nerves will not be disturbed. You see,' Hymie says, 'I happen to know you have two hundred and fifty bucks in the jug over here on the corner, because one of the tellers in the jug is a friend of mine, and he tips me off you have this sugar, even though,' Hymie says, 'you have it in there under another name.'

Well, a guy goes up against many daffy propositions as he goes along through life, and the first thing I know I am waking up, like I tell you, to find myself sleeping with Mahogany and Hymie, and as I lay there in the horse car slowly freezing to death, I get to thinking of 'Lasses in a drawing-room on the Florida Special, and I hope and trust that she and the Peke are sleeping nice and warm.

The train finally runs out of the blizzard and the weather heats up somewhat, so it is not so bad riding in the horse car, and Hymie and I pass the time away playing two-handed pinochle. Furthermore, I get pretty well acquainted with Mahogany, and I find he is personally not such a bad old pelter as many thousands of citizens think.

Finally we get to Miami, and at first it looks as if Hymie is going to have a tough time finding a place to keep Mahogany, as all the stable room at the Hialeah track is taken by cash customers, and Hymie certainly is not a cash customer and neither is Mahogany. Personally, I am not worried so much about stable room for Mahogany as I am about stable room for myself, because I am now down to a very few bobs and will need same to eat on.

Naturally, I figure Hymie Banjo Eyes will be joining his everloving wife 'Lasses, as I always suppose a husband and wife are an entry, but Hymie tells me 'Lasses is parked in the Roney Plaza over on Miami Beach, and that he is going to stay with Mahogany, because it will make her very nervous to have people around her, especially people who are training horses every day, and who may not smell so good.

Well, it looks as if we will wind up camping out with Mahogany under a palm-tree, although many of the palm-trees are already taken by other guys camping out with horses, but finally Hymie finds a guy who has a garage back of his house right near the race track, and having no use for this garage since his car blows away in the hurricane of 1926, the guy is willing to let Hymie keep Mahogany in the garage. Furthermore, he is willing to let Hymie sleep in the garage with Mahogany, and pay him now and then.

So Hymie borrows a little hay and grain, such as horses love to eat, off a friend who has a big string at the track, and moves into the garage with Mahogany, and about the same time I run into a guy by the name of Pottsville Legs, out of Pottsville, Pa., and he has a room in a joint downtown, and I move in with him, and it is no worse than sleeping with Hymie Banjo Eyes and Mahogany, at that.

I do not see Hymie for some time after this, but I hear of him getting Mahogany ready for a race. He has the old guy out galloping on the track every morning, and who is galloping him but Hymie himself, because he cannot get any stable-boys to do the galloping for him, as they do not wish to waste their time. However, Hymie rides himself when he is a young squirt, so galloping Mahogany is not such a tough job for him, except that it gives him a terrible appetite, and it is very hard for him to find anything to satisfy this appetite with, and there are rumours around that Hymie is eating most of Mahogany's hay and grain.

In the meantime, I am going here and there doing the best I can, and this is not so very good, at that, because never is there such a terrible winter in Miami or so much suffering among the horse players. In the afternoon I go out to the race track, and in the evening I go to the dog tracks, and later to the gambling joints trying to pick up a few honest bobs, and wherever I go I seem to see Hymie's ever-loving wife 'Lasses, and she is always dressed up more than somewhat, and generally she is with Brick McCloskey, for Brick shows up in Miami figuring to do a little business in bookmaking at the track.

When they turn off the books there and put in the mutuels, Brick still does a little booking to big betters who do not wish to put their dough in the mutuels for fear of ruining a price, for Brick is a very large operator at all times. He is not only a large operator, but he is a big, good-looking guy, and how 'Lasses can ever give him the heave-o for such a looking guy as Hymie Banjo Eyes is always a great mystery to me. But then this is the way blondes are.

Of course Hymie probably does not know 'Lasses is running around with Brick McCloskey, because Hymie is too busy getting Mahogany ready for a race to make such spots as 'Lasses and Brick are apt to be, and nobody is going to bother to tell him, because so many ever-loving wives are running around with guys who are not their ever-loving husbands in Miami this winter that nobody considers it any news.

Personally, I figure 'Lasses' running around with Brick is a pretty fair break for Hymie, at that, as it takes plenty of weight off him in the way of dinners, and maybe breakfasts for all I know, although it seems to me 'Lasses cannot love Hymie as much as Hymie thinks to be running around with another guy. In fact, I am commencing to figure 'Lasses does not care for Hymie Banjo Eyes whatever.

Well, one day I am looking over the entries, and I see where Hymie has old Mahogany in a claiming race at a mile and an eighth, and while it is a cheap race, there are some pretty fair hides in it. In fact, I can figure at least eight out of the nine that are entered to beat Mahogany by fourteen lengths.

Well, I go out to Hialeah very early, and I step around to the garage where Mahogany and Hymie are living, and Hymie is sitting out in front of the garage on a bucket looking very sad, and Mahogany has his beezer stuck out through the door of the garage, and he is looking even sadder than Hymie.

'Well,' I say to Hymie Banjo Eyes, 'I see the big horse goes to-day.'

'Yes,' Hymie says, 'the big horse goes to-day if I can get ten bucks for the jockey fee, and if I can get a jock after I get the fee. It is a terrible situation,' Hymie says. 'Here I get Mahogany all readied up for the race of his life in a spot where he can win by as far as from here to Palm Beach and grab a purse worth six hundred fish, and me without as much as a sawbuck to hire one of these hop-toads that are putting themselves away as jocks around here.'

'Well,' I say, 'why do you not speak to 'Lasses, your ever-loving wife, about this situation? I see 'Lasses playing the wheel out at Hollywood last night,' I say, 'and she has a stack of cheques in front of her a greyhound cannot hurdle, and,' I say, 'it is not like 'Lasses to go away from there without a few bobs off such a start.'

'Now there you go again,' Hymie says, very impatient indeed. 'You are always making cracks about 'Lasses, and you know very well it will make the poor little doll very nervous if I speak to her about such matters as a sawbuck, because 'Lasses needs all the sawbucks she can get hold of to keep herself and Sooey-pow at the

Roney Plaza. By the way,' Hymie says, 'how much scratch do you have on your body at this time?'

Well, I am never any hand for telling lies, especially to an old friend such as Hymie Banjo Eyes, so. I admit I have a ten-dollar note, although naturally I do not mention another tenner which I also have in my pocket, as I know Hymie will wish both of them. He will wish one of my tenners to pay the jockey fee, and he will wish the other to bet on Mahogany, and I am certainly not going to let Hymie throw my dough away betting it on such an old crocodile as Mahogany, especially in a race which a horse by the name of Side Burns is a sure thing to win.

In fact, I am waiting patiently for several days for a chance to bet on Side Burns. So I hold out one sawbuck on Hymie, and then I go over to the track and forget all about him and Mahogany until the sixth race is coming up, and I see by the jockey board that Hymie has a jock by the name of Scroon riding Mahogany, and while Mahogany is carrying only one hundred pounds, which is the light-weight of the race, I will personally just as soon have Paul Whiteman up as Scroon. Personally I do not think Scroon can spell 'horse,' for he is nothing but a dizzy little guy who gets a mount about once every Pancake Tuesday. But of course Hymie is not a guy who can pick and choose his jocks, and the chances are he is pretty lucky to get anybody to ride Mahogany.

I see by the board where it tells you the approximate odds that Mahogany is 40 to 1, and naturally nobody is paying any attention to such a horse, because it will not be good sense to pay any attention to Mahogany in this race, what with it being his first start in months, and Mahogany not figuring with these horses, or with any horses, as far as this is concerned. In fact, many citizens think Hymie Banjo Eyes is either crazy, or is running Mahogany in this race for exercise, although nobody who knows Hymie will figure him to be spending dough on a horse just to exercise him.

The favourite in the race is this horse named Side Burns, and from the way they are playing him right from taw you will think he is Twenty Grand. He is even money on the board, and I hope and trust that he will finally pay as much as this, because at even money I consider him a very sound investment, indeed. In fact, I am willing to take 4 to 5 for my dough, and will consider it money well found, because I figure this will give me about eighteen bobs to bet on Tony Joe in the last race, and anybody will tell you that you can go to sleep on Tony Joe winning, unless something happens.

There is a little action on several other horses in the race, but of course there is none whatever for Mahogany and the last time I look he is up to fifty. So I buy my ticket on Side Burns, and go out to the paddock to take a peek at the horses, and I see Hymie Banjo Eyes in there saddling Mahogany with his jockey, this dizzy Scroon, standing alongside him in Hymie's colours of red, pink and yellow, and making wise-cracks to the guys in the next stall about Mahogany.

Hymie Banjo Eyes sees me and motions me to come into the paddock, so I go in and give Mahogany a pat on the snoot, and the old guy seems to remember me right away, because he rubs his beezer up and down my arm and lets out a little snicker. But it seems to me the old plug looks a bit peaked, and I can see his ribs very plain indeed, so I figure maybe there is some truth in the rumour about Hymie sharing Mahogany's hay and grain, after all.

Well, as I am standing there, Hymie gives this dizzy Scroon his riding instructions, and they are very short, for all Hymie says is as follows:

'Listen,' Hymie says, 'get off with this horse and hurry right home.'

And Scroon looks a little dizzier than somewhat and nods his head, and then turns and tips a wink to Kurtsinger, who is riding the horse in the next stall.

Well, finally the post bugle goes, and Hymie walks back with me to the lawn as the horses are coming out on the track, and Hymie is speaking about nothing but Mahogany.

'It is just my luck,' Hymie says, 'not to have a bob or two to bet on him. He will win this race as far as you can shoot a rifle, and the reason he will win this far,' Hymie says, 'is because the track is just soft enough to feel nice and soothing to his sore feet. Furthermore,' Hymie says, 'after lugging my one hundred and forty pounds around every morning for two weeks, Mahogany will think it is Christmas when he finds nothing but this Scroon's one hundred pounds on his back.

'In fact,' Hymie says, 'if I do not need the purse money, I will not let him run to-day, but will hide him for a bet. But,' he says, ' 'Lasses must have five yards at once, and you know how nervous she will be if she does not get the five yards. So I am letting Mahogany run,' Hymie says, 'and it is a pity.'

'Well,' I say, 'why do you not promote somebody to bet on him for you?'

'Why,' Hymie says, 'if I ask one guy I ask fifty. But they all think I am out of my mind to think Mahogany can beat such horses as Side Burns and the rest. Well,' he says, 'they will be sorry. By the way,' he says, 'do you have a bet down of any kind?'

Well, now, I do not wish to hurt Hymie's feelings by letting him know I bet on something else in the race, so I tell him I do not play this race at all, and he probably figures it is because I have nothing to bet with after giving him the sawbuck. But he keeps on talking as we walk over in front of the grandstand, and all he is talking about is what a tough break it is for him not to have any dough to bet on Mahogany. By this time the horses are at the post a little way up the track, and as we are standing there watching them, Hymie Banjo Eyes goes on talking, half to me and half to himself, but out loud.

'Yes,' he says, 'I am the unluckiest guy in all the world. Here I am,' he says, 'with a race that is a kick in the pants for my horse at fifty to one, and me without a quarter to bet. It is certainly a terrible thing to be poor,' Hymie says. 'Why,' he says, 'I will bet my life on my horse in this race, I am so sure of winning. I will bet my clothes. I will bet all I ever hope to have. In fact,' he says, 'I will even bet my ever-loving wife, this is how sure I am.'

Now of course this is only the way horse players rave when they are good and heated up about the chances of a horse, and I hear such conversations as this maybe a million times, and never pay any attention to it whatever, but as Hymie makes this crack about betting his ever-loving wife, a voice behind us says as follows:

'Against how much?'

Naturally, Hymie and I look around at once, and who does the voice belong to but Brick McCloskey. Of course I figure Brick is kidding Hymie Banjo Eyes, but Brick's voice is as cold as ice as he says to Hymie like this:

'Against how much will you bet your wife your horse wins this race?' he says. 'I hear you saying you are sure this old buzzard meat you are running will win,' Brick says, 'so let me see how sure you are. Personally,' Brick says, 'I think they ought to prosecute you for running a broken-down hound like Mahogany on the ground of cruelty to animals, and furthermore,' Brick says, 'I think they ought to put you in an insane asylum if you really believe your old dog has a chance. But I will give you a bet,' he says. 'How much do you wish me to lay against your wife?'

Well, this is very harsh language indeed, and I can see that Brick is getting something off his chest he is packing there for some time. The chances are he is putting the blast on poor Hymie Banjo Eyes on account of Hymie grabbing 'Lasses from him, and of course Brick McCloskey never figures for a minute that Hymie will take his question seriously. But Hymie answers like this:

'You are a price-maker,' he says. 'What do you lay?'

Now this is a most astonishing reply, indeed, when you figure that Hymie is asking what Brick will bet against Hymie's ever-loving wife 'Lasses, and I am very sorry to hear Hymie ask, especially as I happen to turn around and find that nobody but 'Lasses herself is listening in on the conversation, and the chances are her face will be very white, if it is not for her make-up, 'Lasses being a doll who goes in for make-up more than somewhat.

'Yes,' Brick McCloskey says, 'I am a price-maker, all right, and I will lay you a price. I will lay you five C's against your wife that your plug does not win,' he says.

Brick looks at 'Lasses as he says this, and 'Lasses looks at Brick, and personally I will probably take a pop at a guy who looks at my ever-loving wife in such a way, if I happen to have any ever-loving wife, and maybe I will take a pop at my ever-loving wife, too, if she looks back at a guy in such a way, but of course Hymie is not noticing such things as looks at this time, and in fact he does not see 'Lasses as yet. But he does not hesitate in answering Brick.

'You are a bet,' says Hymie. 'Five hundred bucks against my ever-loving wife 'Lasses. It is a chiseller's price such as you always lay,' he says, 'and the chances are I can do better if I have time to go shopping around but as it is,' he says, 'it is like finding money and I will not let you get away. But be ready to pay cash right after the race, because I will not accept your paper.'

Well, I hear of many a strange bet on horse races, but never before do I hear of a guy betting his ever-loving wife, although to tell you the truth I never before hear of a guy getting the opportunity to bet his wife on a race. For all I know, if bookmakers take wives as a steady thing there will be much action in such matters at every track.

But I can see that both Brick McCloskey and Hymie Banjo Eyes are in dead earnest, and about this time 'Lasses tries to cop a quiet sneak, and Hymie sees her and speaks to her as follows:

'Hello, Baby,' Hymie says. 'I will have your five yards for you in a few minutes and five more to go with it, as I am just about to clip a sucker. Wait here with me, Baby,' Hymie says.

'No,' 'Lasses says, 'I am too nervous to wait here. I am going down by the fence to root your horse in,' she says, but as she goes away I see another look pass between her and Brick McCloskey.

Well, all of a sudden Cassidy gets the horses in a nice line and lets them go, and as they come busting down past the stand the first time who is right there on top but old Mahogany, with this dizzy Scroon kicking at his skinny sides and yelling in his ears. As they make the first turn, Scroon has Mahogany a length in front, and he moves him out another length as they hit the back side.

Now I always like to watch the races from a spot away up the lawn, as I do not care to have anybody much around me when the tough finishes come along in case I wish to bust out crying, so I leave Hymie Banjo Eyes and Brick McCloskey still glaring at each other and go to my usual place, and who is standing there, too, all by herself but 'Lasses. And about this time the horses are making the turn into the stretch and Mahogany is still on top, but something is coming very fast on the outside. It looks as if Mahogany is in a tough spot, because halfway down the stretch the outside horse nails him and looks him right in the eye, and who is it but the favourite, Side Burns.

They come on like a team, and I am personally giving Side Burns a great ride from where I am standing, when I hear a doll yelling out loud, and who is the doll but 'Lasses, and what is she yelling but the following:

'Come on with him, jock!'

Furthermore, as she yells, 'Lasses snaps her fingers like a crap shooter and runs a couple of yards one way and then turns and runs a couple of yards back the other way, so I can see that 'Lasses is indeed of a nervous temperament, just as Hymie Banjo Eyes is always telling me, although up to this time I figure her nerves are the old alzo.

'Come on!' 'Lasses yells again. 'Let him roll!' she yells. 'Ride him, boy!' she yells. 'Come on with him, Frankie!'

Well, I wish to say that 'Lasses' voice may be all right if she is selling tomatoes from door to door, but I will not care to have her using it around me every day for any purpose whatever, because she yells so loud I have to move off a piece to keep my ear-drums from being busted wide open. She is still yelling when the horses go past the finish line, the snozzles of old Mahogany and Side Burns so close together that nobody can hardly tell which is which.

In fact, there is quite a wait before the numbers go up, and I can see 'Lasses standing there with her programme all wadded up in her fist as she watches the board, and I can see she is under a very terrible nervous strain indeed, and I am very sorry I go around thinking her nerves are the old alzo. Pretty soon the guy hangs out No. 9, and No. 9 is nobody but old Mahogany, and at this I hear 'Lasses screech, and all of a sudden she flops over in a faint, and somebody carries her under the grandstand to revive her, and I figure her nerves bog down entirely, and I am sorrier than ever for thinking bad thoughts of her.

I am also very, very sorry I do not bet my sawbuck on Mahogany, especially when the board shows he pays $102, and I can see where Hymie Banjo Eyes is right about the weight and all, but I am glad Hymie wins the purse and also the five C's off of Brick McCloskey and that he saves his ever-loving wife, because I figure Hymie may now pay me back a few bobs.

I do not see Hymie or Brick or 'Lasses again until the races are over, and then I hear of a big row going on under the stand, and go to see what is doing, and who is having the row but Hymie Banjo Eyes and Brick McCloskey. It seems that Hymie hits Brick a clout on the beezer that stretches Brick out, and it seems that Hymie hits Brick this blow because as Brick is paying Hymie the five C's he makes the following crack:

'I do not mind losing the dough to you, Banjo Eyes,' Brick says, 'but I am sore at myself for overlaying the price. It is the first time in all the years I am booking that I make such an overlay. The right price against your wife,' Brick says, 'is maybe two dollars and a half.'

Well, as Brick goes down with a busted beezer from Hymie's punch, and everybody is much excited, who steps out of the crowd around them and throws her arms around Hymie Banjo Eyes but his ever-loving wife 'Lasses, and as she kisses Hymie smack-dab in the mush, 'Lasses says as follows:

'My darling Hymie,' she says, 'I hear what this big flannel-mouth says about the price on me, and,' she says, 'I am only sorry you do not cripple him for life. I know now I love you, and only you, Hymie,' she says, 'and I will never love anybody else. In fact,' 'Lasses says, 'I just prove my love for you by almost wrecking my nerves in rooting Mahogany home. I am still weak,' she says, 'but I have strength enough left to go with you to the Sunset Inn for a nice dinner, and you can give me my money then. Furthermore,' 'Lasses says, 'now that we have a few bobs, I think you better find another place for Mahogany to stay, as it does not look nice for my husband to be living with a horse.'

Well, I am going by the jockey house on my way home, thinking how nice it is that Hymie Banjo Eyes will no longer have to live with Mahogany, and what a fine thing it is to have a loyal, ever-loving wife such as 'Lasses, who risks her nerves rooting for her husband's horse, when I run into this dizzy Scroon in his street clothes, and wishing to be friendly, I say to him like this:

'Hello, Frankie,' I say. 'You put up a nice ride to-day.'

'Where do you get this "Frankie"?' Scroon says. 'My name is Gus.'

'Why,' I say, commencing to think of this and that, 'so it is, but is there a jock called Frankie in the sixth race with you this afternoon?'

'Sure,' Scroon says. 'Frankie Madeley. He rides Side Burns, the favourite; and I make a sucker of him in the stretch run.'

But of course I never mention to Hymie Banjo Eyes that I figure his ever-loving wife roots herself into a dead faint for the horse that will give her to Brick McCloskey, because for all I know she may think Scroon's name is Frankie, at that.

Neat Strip

Now this Rose Viola is twenty years old and is five feet five inches tall in her high-heeled shoes, and weighs one hundred and twenty pounds, net, and has a twenty-six waist, and a thirty-six bust, and wears a four and one-half shoe.

Moreover, she has a seven-inch ankle, and an eleven-inch calf, and the reason I know all these intimate details is because a friend of mine by the name of Rube Goldstein has Rose Viola in a burlesque show and advertises her as the American Venus, and he always prints these specifications in his ads.

But of course Rube Goldstein has no way of putting down in figures how beautiful Rose Viola is, because after all any pancake may have the same specifications and still be a rutabaga. All Rube can do is to show photographs of Rose Viola and after you see these photographs and then see Rose Viola herself you have half a mind to look the photographer up and ask him what he means by so grossly underestimating the situation.

She has big blue eyes, and hair the colour of sunup, and further-more this colour is as natural as a six and five. Her skin is as white and as smooth as ivory and her teeth are like rows of new corn on the cob and she has a smile that starts slow and easy on her lips and in her eyes and seems to sort of flow over the rest of her face until any male characters observing same are wishing there is a murder handy that they can commit for her.

Well, I suppose by this time you are saying to yourself what is such a darberoo doing in a burlesque turkey, for burlesque is by no means an intellectual form of entertainment, and the answer to this question is that Rube Goldstein pays Rose Viola four hundred dollars per week, and this is by no means tin.

And the reason Rube Goldstein pays her such a sum is not be-cause Rube is any philanthropist but because Rose Viola draws like a flaxseed poultice, for besides her looks she has that certain some-thing that goes out across the footlights and hits every male character present smack-dab in the kisser and makes him hate to go home and gaze upon his ever-loving wife. In fact, I hear that for three weeks after Rose Viola plays a town the percentage of missing husbands appals the authorities.

It seems that the first time Rube Goldstein sees Rose Viola is in the city of Baltimore, Md., where his show is playing the old Gaiety, and one of Rube's chorus Judys, a sod widow who is with him nearly thirteen years and raises up three sons to manhood under him, runs off and marries a joskin from over on the eastern shore.

Naturally, Rube considers this a dirty trick, as he is so accus-tomed to seeing this Judy in his chorus that he feels his show will never look the same to him again; but the same night the widow is missing, Rose Viola appears before him asking for a situation.

Rube tells me he is greatly surprised at such a looking Judy seeking a place in a burlesque show and he explains to Rose Viola that it is a very tough life, to be sure, and that the pay is small, and that she will probably do better for herself if she gets a job dealing them off her arm in a beanery, or some such, but she requests Rube to kindly omit the alfalfa and give her a job, and Rube can see at once by the way she talks that she has personality.

So he hires her at twenty-five slugs per week to start with and raises her to half a C and makes her a principal the second night when he finds eighteen blokes lined up at the stage door after the show looking to date her up. In three weeks she is his star and he is three-sheeting her as if she is Katherine Cornell.

She comes out on the stage all dressed up in a beautiful evening gown and sings a little song, and as soon as she begins singing you wonder, unless you see her before, what she really is, as you can see by her voice that she is scarcely a singer by trade.

Her voice is not at all the same as Lily Pons's and in fact it is more like an old-fashioned coffee grinder, and about the time you commence to figure that she must be something like a magician and will soon start pulling rabbits out of a hat, Rose Viola begins to dance.

It is not a regular dance, to be sure. It is more of a hop and a skip and a jump back and forth across the stage, and as she is hopping and skipping and jumping, Rose Viola is also feeling around for zippers here and there about her person, and finally the evening gown disappears and she seems to be slightly dishabille but in a genteel manner, and then you can see by her shape that she is indeed a great artist.

Sometimes she will come down off the stage and work along the centre aisle, and this is when the audience really enjoys her most, as she will always stop before some bald-headed old character in an aisle seat where bald-headed characters are generally found, and will pretend to make a great fuss over him, singing to him, and maybe kissing him on top of the bald head and leaving the print of her lips in rouge there, which sometimes puts bald-headed characters to a lot of bother explaining when they get home.

She has a way of laughing and talking back to an audience and keeping it in good humour while she is working, although outside the theatre Rose Viola is very serious, and seldom has much to say. In fact, Rose Viola has so little to say that there are rumours in some quarters that she is a trifle dumb, but personally I would not mind being dumb myself at four hundred boffoes per week.

Well, it seems that a character by the name of Newsbaum, who runs a spot called the Pigeon Club, hears of Rose Viola, and he goes to see her one night at the old Mid Theatre on Broadway where Rube's show is playing a New York engagement, and this Newsbaum is such a character as is always looking for novelties for his club and he decides that Rose Viola will go good there.

So he offers her a chance to double at his club, working there after she gets through with her regular show, and Rube Goldstein advises her to take it, as Rube is very fond of Rose and he says this may be a first step upward in her career because the Pigeon Club is patronized only by very high-class rumpots.

So Rose Viola opens one night at the Pigeon Club, and she is working on the dance floor close to the tables, and doing the same act she does in burlesque, when a large young character who is sitting at one of the front tables with a bunch of other young characters, including several nice-looking Judys, reaches out and touches Rose Viola with the end of a cigarette in a spot she just unzippers.

Now of course this is all in a spirit of fun, but it is something that never happens in a burlesque house, and naturally Rose is startled no little, and quite some, and in addition to this she is greatly pained, as it seems that it is the lighted end of the cigarette that the large young character touches her with.

So she begins letting out screams, and these screams attract the attention of Rube Goldstein, who is present to see how she gets along at her opening, and although Rube is nearly seventy years old, and is fat and slow and sleepy-looking, he steps forward and flattens the large young character with a dish of chicken à la king, which he picks up off a near-by table.

Well, it seems that the large young character is nobody but a character by the name of Mr. Choicer, who has great sums of money, and a fine social position, and this incident creates some little confusion, especially as old Rube Goldstein also flattens Newsbaum with another plate, this one containing lobster Newberg, when Newsbaum comes along complaining about Rube ruining his chinaware and also one of his best-paying customers.

Then Rube puts his arm around Rose Viola and makes her get dressed and leads her out of the Pigeon Club and up to Mindy's Restaurant on Broadway, where I am personally present to observe much of what follows.

They sit down at my table and order up a couple of oyster stews, and Rose Viola is still crying at intervals, especially when she happens to rub the spot where the lighted cigarette hits, and Rube Goldstein is saying that for two cents he will go back to the Pigeon Club and flatten somebody again, when all of a sudden the door opens and in comes a young character in dinner clothes.

He is without a hat, and he is looking rumpled up no little, and on observing him, Rose Viola lets out a small cry, and Rube Goldstein picks up his bowl of oyster stew and starts getting to his feet, for it seems that they both recognize the young character as one of the characters at Mr. Choicer's table in the Pigeon Club.

This young character rushes up in great excitement, and grabs Rube's arm before Rube can let fly with the oyster stew, and he holds Rube down in his chair, and looks at Rose Viola and speaks to her as follows:

'Oh,' he says, 'I search everywhere for you after you leave the Pigeon Club. I wish to beg your pardon for what happens there. I am ashamed of my friend Mr. Choicer. I will never speak to him again as long as I live. He is a scoundrel. Furthermore, he is in bad shape from the chicken à la king. Oh,' the young character says, 'please forgive me for ever knowing him.'

Well, all the time he is talking, he is holding Rube Goldstein down and looking at Rose Viola, and she is looking back at him, and in five minutes more they do not know Rube Goldstein and me are in the restaurant, and in fact they are off by themselves at another table so the young character can make his apologies clearer, and Rube Goldstein is saying to me that after nearly seventy years he comes to the conclusion that the Judys never change.

So, then, this is the beginning of a wonderful romance, and in fact it is love at first sight on both sides, and very pleasant to behold, at that.

It seems that the name of the young character is Daniel Frame, and that he is twenty-six years of age, and in his last year in law school at Yale, and that he comes to New York for a week-end visit and runs into his old college chum, Mr. Choicer, and now here he is in love.

I learn these details afterward from Rose Viola, and I also learn that this Daniel Frame is an only child, and lives with his widowed mother in a two-story white colonial house with ivy on the walls, and a yard around it, just outside the city of Manchester, N.H.

I learn that his mother has an old poodle dog by the name of Rags, and three servants, and that she lives very quietly, and never goes anywhere much except maybe to church and that the moonlight is something wonderful up around Manchester, N.H.

Furthermore, I learn that Daniel Frame comes of the best people in New England, and that he likes ski-ing, and Benny Goodman's band, and hates mufflers around his neck, and is very fond of popovers for breakfast, and that his eyes are dark brown, and that he is six feet even and weighs one hundred and eighty pounds and that he never goes to a dentist in his life.

I also learn that the ring he wears on the little finger of his left hand is his family crest, and that he sings baritone with a glee club, and the chances are I will learn plenty more about Daniel Frame if I care to listen any further to Rose Viola.

'He wishes to marry me,' Rose says. 'He wishes to take me to the white colonial house outside of Manchester, N.H., where we can raise Sealyham terriers, and maybe children. I love Sealyham terriers,' she says. 'They are awfully cute. Daniel wishes me to quit burlesque entirely. He sees me work at the Mid the other night and he thinks I am wonderful, but,' Rose says, 'he says it worries him constantly to think of me out there on that stage running the risk of catching colds.

'Another thing,' Rose Viola says, 'Daniel wishes me to meet his mother, but he is afraid she will be greatly horrified if she finds out the way I am exposed to the danger of catching colds. He says,' Rose says, 'that his mother is very strict about such things.'

Personally, I consider Daniel Frame a very wishy-washy sort of character, and by no means suitable to a strong personality such as Rose Viola, but when I ask Rube Goldstein what he thinks about it, Rube says to me like this:

'Well,' he says, 'I think it will be a fine thing for her to marry this young character, although,' Rube says, 'from what he tells her of his mother, I do not see how they are going to get past her. I know these old New England broads,' he says. 'They consider burlesque anything but a worthy amusement. Still,' he says, 'I have no kick coming about the male characters of New England. They are always excellent customers of mine.'

'Why,' I say, 'Rose Viola is a fine artist, and does not need such a thing as marriage.'

'Yes,' Rube says, 'she is the finest artist in her line I ever see but one. Laura Legayo is still tops with me. She retires on me away back yonder before you ever see one of my shows. But,' he says, 'if Rose marries this young character, she will have a home, and a future. Rose needs a future.

'This burlesque business is about done around here for a while,' Rube says. 'I can see the signs. The blats are beefing, and the cops are complaining about this and that, and one thing and another. They have no soul for art, and besides we are the easiest marks around when the reformers start rousing the cops for anything whatever.

'It is always this way with burlesque,' Rube says. 'It is up and down. It is on the way down now, and Rose may not still be young enough by the time it goes up again. Yes,' he says, 'Rose needs a future.'

Well, it seems that old Rube is a pretty good guesser, because a couple of nights later he gets an order from the police commissioner that there must be no more of this and that, and one thing and another, in his show, and what is more the police commissioner puts cops in all the burlesque houses to see that his order is obeyed.

At first Rube Goldstein figures that he may as well close down his New York run at once, and move to some city that is more hospitable to art, but he is wedged in at the Mid on a contract to pay rent for a few weeks longer, so while he is trying to think what is the best thing to do, he lets the show go on just the same, but omitting this and that, and one thing and another, so as not to offend the police commissioner in case he comes around looking for offence, or the cop the commissioner places on duty in the Mid, who is a character by the name of Halligan.

So there is Rose Viola out on the stage of the Mid doing her number in full costume without ever reaching for as much as a single zipper, and I can see what Rube Goldstein means when he says Rose needs a future, because looking at Rose in full costume really becomes quite monotonous after a while.

To tell the truth, the only one who seems to appreciate Rose in full costume is Daniel Frame when he comes down from Yale one week-end and finds her in this condition. In fact, Daniel Frame is really quite delighted with her.

'It is wonderful,' he says. 'It is especially wonderful because I tell my mother all about you, and she is talking of coming down from Manchester, N.H., to see you perform, and I have been worrying myself sick over her beholding you out there in danger of catching colds. I know she will be greatly pleased with you now, because,' he says, 'you look so sweet and modest and so well dressed.'

Naturally, as long as he is pleased, Rose Viola is pleased too, except that she suffers somewhat from the heat, for there is no doubt but what Rose is greatly in love with him and she scarcely ever talks about anything else, and does not seem to care if her art suffers from the change.

Now it comes on another Saturday night and I am backstage at the Mid talking to Rube Goldstein and he is telling me that he is greatly surprised to find business holding up so good. The house is packed to the doors, and I tell Rube that maybe he is wrong all these years and that the public appreciates art even when it has clothes on, but Rube says he thinks not. He says he thinks it is more likely that the customers are just naturally optimists.

Rose Viola is on the stage in full costume singing her song when all of a sudden somebody in the back of the audience lets out a yell of fire and this is an alarming cry in any theatre, to be sure, and especially in a spot like the Mid as it is an old house, and about as well fixed to stand off a fire as a barrel of grease. Then a duty fireman by the name of Rossoffsky, who is always on duty in the Mid when a show is on, comes rushing backstage and says it is a fire all right.

It seems that a cafeteria next door to the Mid is blazing inside and the flames are eating their way through the theatre wall at the front of the house by the main entrance, and in fact when the alarm is raised the whole wall is blazing on both sides, and it is a most disturbing situation, to be sure.

Well, the audience in the Mid is composed mostly of male characters, because male characters always appreciate burlesque much more than females or children, and these male characters now rise from their seats and start looking for the exits nearest to them, but by now they are shut off from the main entrance by the fire.

So they commence looking for other exits, and there are several of these, but it seems from what Rossoffsky says afterward that these exits are not used for so long that nobody figures it will ever be necessary to use them again, and the doors do not come open so easy, especially with so many trying to open them at once.

Then the male characters begin fighting with each other for the privilege of opening the doors, and also of getting out through the doors after they are opened, and this results in some confusion. In fact, it is not long before the male characters are fighting all over the premises, and knocking each other down, and stepping on each other's faces in a most discourteous manner.

While it is well known to one and all that a burlesque theatre is no place to take an ever-loving wife to begin with, it seems that some of these male characters have their wives with them, and these wives start screaming, but of course they are among the first knocked down and stepped on, so not much is heard of them until afterward.

A few of the male characters are smart enough to leap up on the

stage and high-tail it out of there by the back way, but most of
them are so busy fighting on the floor of the theatre that they do
not think of this means of exit, and it is just as well that they do
not think of it all at once, at that, as there is but one narrow stage
door, and a rush will soon pile them up like jack-rabbits there.

The orchestra quits playing and the musicians are dropping
their instruments and getting ready to duck under the stage and
Rose Viola is standing still in the centre of the stage with her
mouth open, looking this way and that in some astonishment and
alarm, when all of a sudden a tall, stern-looking old Judy with
white hair, and dressed in grey, stands up on a seat in the front
row right back of the orchestra leader, and says to Rose Viola like
this:

'Quick,' she says. 'Go into your routine.'

Well, Rose Viola still stands there as if she cannot figure out
what the old Judy is talking about, and the old Judy makes
motions at her with her hands, and then slowly unbuttons a little
grey jacket she is wearing, and tosses it aside, and Rose gets the
idea.

Now the stern-looking old Judy looks over to the orchestra
leader, who is a character by the name of Butwell, and who is with
Rube Goldstein's burlesque show since about the year one, and says
to him:

'Hit 'er, Buttsy.'

Well, old Buttsy takes a look at her, and then he takes another
look, and then he raises his hand, and his musicians settle back in
their chairs, and as Buttsy lets his hand fall, they start playing Rose
Viola's music, and the tall, stern-looking old Judy stands there on
the seat in the front row pointing at the stage and hollering so loud
her voice is heard above all the confusion of the male characters at
their fighting.

'Look, boys,' she hollers.

And there on the stage is Rose Viola doing her hop, skip and a
jump back and forth and feeling for the zippers here and there
about her person, and finding same.

Now, on hearing the old Judy's voice, and on observing the
scene on the stage, the customers gradually stop fighting with each
other and begin easing themselves back into the seats, and paying
strict attention to Rose Viola's performance, and all this time the
wall behind them is blazing, and it is hotter than one hundred and
six in the shade, and smoke is pouring into the Mid, and anybody

will tell you that Rose Viola's feat of holding an audience against a house fire is really quite unsurpassed in theatrical history.

The tall, stern-looking old Judy remains standing on the seat in the front row until there are cries behind her to sit down, because it seems she is obstructing the view of some of those back of her, so finally she takes her seat, and Rose Viola keeps right on working.

By this time the fire department arrives and has the situation in the cafeteria under control, and the fire in the wall extinguished, and a fire captain and a squad of men come into the Mid, because it seems that rumours are abroad that a great catastrophe takes place in the theatre. In fact, the captain and his men are greatly alarmed because they cannot see a thing inside the Mid when they first enter on account of the smoke, and the captain sings out as follows:

'Is everybody dead in here?'

Then he sees through the smoke what is going on there on the stage, and he stops and begins enjoying the scene himself, and his men join him, and a good time is being had by one and all until all of a sudden Rose Viola keels over in a faint from her exertions. Rube orders the curtain down but the audience, including the firemen, remain for some time afterward in the theatre, hoping they may get an encore.

While I am standing near the stage door in readiness to take it on the Jesse Owens out of there in case the fire gets close, who comes running up all out of breath but Daniel Frame.

'I just get off the train from New Haven,' he says. 'I run all the way from the station on hearing a report that the Mid is on fire. Is anybody hurt?' he says. 'Is Rose safe?'

Well, I suggest that the best way to find out about this is to go inside and see, so we enter together, and there among the scenery we find Rube Goldstein and a bunch of actors still in their make-ups gathered about Rose Viola, who is just getting to her feet and looking somewhat nonplussed.

At this same moment, Halligan, the cop stationed in the Mid, comes backstage, and pushes his way through the bunch around Rose Viola and taps her on the shoulder and says to her:

'You are under arrest,' Halligan says. 'I guess I will have to take you, too, Mr. Goldstein,' he says.

'My goodness,' Daniel Frame says. 'What is Miss Viola under arrest for?'

'For putting on that number out there just now,' Halligan says.

'It's a violation of the police commissioner's order.'

'Heavens and earth,' Daniel Frame says. 'Rose, do not tell me you are out there to-night running the risk of catching cold, as before?'

'Yes,' Rose says.

'Oh, my goodness,' Daniel Frame says, 'and all the time my mother is sitting out there in the audience. I figure this week is a great time for her to see you perform, Rose,' he says. 'I cannot get down from New Haven in time to go with her, but I send her alone to see you, and I am to meet her after the theatre with you and introduce you to her. What will she think?'

'Well,' Halligan says, 'I have plenty of evidence against this party. In fact, I see her myself. Not bad,' he says. 'Not bad.'

Rose Viola is standing there looking at Daniel Frame in a sad way, and Daniel Frame is looking at Rose Viola in even a sadder way, when Rossoffsky, the fireman, shoves his way into the gathering, and says to Halligan:

'Copper,' he says, 'I overhear your remarks. Kindly take a walk,' he says. 'If it is not for this party putting on that number out there, the chances are there will be a hundred dead in the aisles from the panic. In fact,' he says, 'I remember seeing you yourself knock over six guys trying to reach an exit before she starts dancing. She is a heroine,' he says. 'That is what she is, and I will testify to it in court.'

At this point who steps in through the stage door but the tall, stern-looking old Judy in grey, and when he sees her, Daniel Frame runs up to her and says:

'Oh, Mother,' he says, 'I am so mortified. Still,' he says, 'I love her just the same.'

But the old Judy scarcely notices him because by this time Rube Goldstein is shaking both of her hands and then over Rube's shoulder she sees Rose Viola, and she says to Rose like this:

'Well, miss,' she says, 'that is a right neat strip you do out there just now, although,' she says, 'you are mighty slow getting into it. You need polishing in spots, and then you will be okay. Rube,' she says, 'speaking of neat strips, who is the best you ever see?'

'Well,' Rube Goldstein says, 'if you are talking of the matter as art, I will say that thirty years ago, if they happen to be holding any competitions anywhere, I will be betting on you against the world, Laura.'

Bred for Battle

One night a guy by the name of Bill Corum, who is one of these sport scribes, gives me a Chinee for a fight at Madison Square Garden, a Chinee being a ducket with holes punched in it like old-fashioned Chink money, to show that it is a free ducket, and the reason I am explaining to you how I get this ducket is because I do not wish anybody to think I am ever simple enough to pay out my own potatoes for a ducket to a fight, even if I have any potatoes.

Personally, I will not give you a bad two-bit piece to see a fight anywhere, because the way I look at it, half the time the guys who are supposed to do the fighting go in there and put on the old do-se-do, and I consider this a great fraud upon the public, and I do not believe in encouraging dishonesty.

But of course I never refuse a Chinee to such events, because the way I figure it, what can I lose except my time, and my time is not worth more than a bob a week the way things are. So on the night in question I am standing in the lobby of the Garden with many other citizens, and I am trying to find out if there is any skull-duggery doing in connection with the fight, because any time there is any skullduggery doing I love to know it, as it is something worth knowing in case a guy wishes to get a small wager down.

Well, while I am standing there, somebody comes up behind me and hits me an awful belt on the back, knocking my wind plumb out of me, and making me very indignant indeed. As soon as I get a little of my wind back again, I turn around figuring to put a large blast on the guy who slaps me, but who is it but a guy by the name of Spider McCoy, who is known far and wide as a manager of fighters.

Well, of course I do not put the blast on Spider McCoy, because he is an old friend of mine, and furthermore, Spider McCoy is such a guy as is apt to let a left hook go at anybody who puts the blast on him, and I do not believe in getting in trouble, especially with good left-hookers.

So I say hello to Spider, and am willing to let it go at that, but Spider seems glad to see me, and says to me like this:

'Well, well, well, well, well!' Spider says.

'Well,' I say to Spider McCoy, 'how many wells does it take to make a river?'

'One, if it is big enough,' Spider says, so I can see he knows the answer all right. 'Listen,' he says, 'I just think up the greatest proposition I ever think of in my whole life, and who knows but what I can interest you in same.'

'Well, Spider,' I say, 'I do not care to hear any propositions at this time, because it may be a long story, and I wish to step inside and see the impending battle. Anyway,' I say, 'if it is a proposition involving financial support, I wish to state that I do not have any resources whatever at this time.'

'Never mind the battle inside,' Spider says. 'It is nothing but a tank job, anyway. And as for financial support,' Spider says, 'this does not require more than a pound note, tops, and I know you have a pound note because I know you put the bite on Overcoat Obie for this amount not an hour ago. Listen,' Spider McCoy says, 'I know where I can place my hands on the greatest heavy-weight prospect in the world to-day, and all I need is the price of car-fare to where he is.'

Well, off and on, I know Spider McCoy twenty years, and in all this time I never know him when he is not looking for the greatest heavy-weight prospect in the world. And as long as Spider knows I have the pound note, I know there is no use trying to play the duck for him, so I stand there wondering who the stool pigeon can be who informs him of my financial status.

'Listen,' Spider says, 'I just discover that I am all out of line in the way I am looking for heavy-weight prospects in the past. I am always looking for nothing but plenty of size,' he says. 'Where I make my mistake is not looking for blood lines. Professor D just smartens me up,' Spider says.

Well, when he mentions the name of Professor D, I commence taking a little interest, because it is well known to one and all that Professor D is one of the smartest old guys in the world. He is once a professor in a college out in Ohio, but quits this dodge to handicap the horses, and he is a first-rate handicapper, at that. But besides knowing how to handicap the horses, Professor D knows many other things, and is highly respected in all walks of life, especially on Broadway.

'Now then,' Spider says, 'Professor D calls my attention this afternoon to the fact that when a guy is looking for a race horse, he does not take just any horse that comes along, but he finds out if the horse's papa is able to run in his day, and if the horse's mamma can get out of her own way when she is young. Professor

D shows me how a guy looks for speed in a horse's breeding away back to its great-great-great-great-grandpa and grand-mamma,' Spider McCoy says.

'Well,' I say, 'anybody knows this without asking Professor D. In fact,' I say, 'you even look up a horse's parents to see if they can mud before betting on a plug to win in heavy going.'

'All right,' Spider says, 'I know all this myself, but I never think much about it before Professor D mentions it. Professor D says if a guy is looking for a hunting dog he does not pick a Pekingese pooch, but he gets a dog that is bred to hunt from away back yonder, and if he is after a game chicken he does not take a Plymouth Rock out of the back-yard.

'So then,' Spider says, 'Professor D wishes to know if when I am looking for a fighter, if I do not look for one who comes of fighting stock. Professor D wishes to know,' Spider says, 'why I do not look for some guy who is bred to fight, and when I think this over, I can see the professor is right.

'And then all of a sudden,' Spider says, 'I get the largest idea I ever have in all my life. Do you remember a guy I have about twenty years back by the name of Shamus Mulrooney, the Fighting Harp?' Spider says. 'A big, rough, tough heavy-weight out of Newark?'

'Yes,' I say, 'I remember Shamus very well indeed. The last time I see him is the night Pounder Pat O'Shea almost murders him in the old Garden,' I say. 'I never see a guy with more ticker than Shamus, unless maybe it is Pat.'

'Yes,' Spider says, 'Shamus has plenty of ticker. He is about through the night of the fight you speak of, otherwise Pat will never lay a glove on him. It is not long after this fight that Shamus packs in and goes back to brick-laying in Newark, and it is also about this same time,' Spider says, 'that he marries Pat O'Shea's sister, Bridget.

'Well, now,' Spider says, 'I remember they have a boy who must be around nineteen years old now, and if ever a guy is bred to fight it is a boy by Shamus Mulrooney out of Bridget O'Shea, because,' Spider says, 'Bridget herself can lick half the heavy-weights I see around nowadays if she is half as good as she is the last time I see her. So now you have my wonderful idea. We will go to Newark and get this boy and make him heavy-weight champion of the world.'

'What you state is very interesting indeed, Spider,' I say. 'But,' I say, 'how do you know this boy is a heavy-weight?'

'Why,' Spider says, 'how can he be anything else but a heavy-weight, what with his papa as big as a house, and his mamma weighing maybe a hundred and seventy pounds in her step-ins? Although of course,' Spider says, 'I never see Bridget weigh in in such manner.

'But,' Spider says, 'even if she does carry more weight than I will personally care to spot a doll, Bridget is by no means a pelican when she marries Shamus. In fact,' he says, 'she is pretty good-looking. I remember their wedding well, because it comes out that Bridget is in love with some other guy at the time, and this guy comes to see the nuptials, and Shamus runs him all the way from Newark to Elizabeth, figuring to break a couple of legs for the guy if he catches him. But,' Spider says, 'the guy is too speedy for Shamus, who never has much foot anyway.'

Well, all that Spider says appeals to me as a very sound business proposition, so the upshot of it is I give him my pound note to finance his trip to Newark.

Then I do not see Spider McCoy again for a week, but one day he calls me up and tells me to hurry over to the Pioneer gymnasium to see the next heavy-weight champion of the world, Thunderbolt Mulrooney.

I am personally somewhat disappointed when I see Thunderbolt Mulrooney, and especially when I find out his first name is Raymond and not Thunderbolt at all, because I am expecting to see a big, fierce guy with red hair and a chest like a barrel, such as Shamus Mulrooney has when he is in his prime. But who do I see but a tall, pale-looking young guy with blond hair and thin legs.

Furthermore, he has pale blue eyes, and a far-away look in them, and he speaks in a low voice, which is nothing like the voice of Shamus Mulrooney. But Spider seems satisfied with Thunderbolt, and when I tell him Thunderbolt does not look to me like the next heavy-weight champion of the world, Spider says like this:

'Why,' he says, 'the guy is nothing but a baby, and you must give him time to fill out. He may grow to be bigger than his papa. But you know,' Spider says, getting indignant as he thinks about it, 'Bridget Mulrooney does not wish to let this guy be the next heavy-weight champion of the world. In fact,' Spider says, 'she kicks up an awful row when I go to get him, and Shamus finally has to speak to her severely. Shamus says he does not know if I can ever make a fighter of this guy because Bridget coddles him until he is nothing but a mush-head, and Shamus says he is sick and tired of seeing the guy sitting around the house doing nothing but reading and playing the zither.'

'Does he play the zither yet?' I ask Spider McCoy.

'No,' Spider says, 'I do not allow my fighters to play zithers. I figure it softens them up. This guy does not play anything at present. He seems to be in a daze most of the time, but of course everything is new to him. He is bound to come out okay, because,' Spider says, 'he is certainly bred right. I find out from Shamus that all the Mulrooneys are great fighters back in the old country,' Spider says, 'and furthermore he tells me Bridget's mother once licks four Newark cops who try to stop her from pasting her old man, so,' Spider says, 'this lad is just naturally steaming with fighting blood.'

Well, I drop around to the Pioneer once or twice a week after this, and Spider McCoy is certainly working hard with Thunderbolt Mulrooney. Furthermore, the guy seems to be improving right along, and gets so he can box fairly well and punch the bag, and all this and that, but he always has that far-away look in his eyes, and personally I do not care for fighters with far-away looks.

Finally one day Spider calls me up and tells me he has Thunderbolt Mulrooney matched in a four-round preliminary bout at the St. Nick with a guy by the name of Bubbles Browning, who is fighting almost as far back as the first battle of Bull Run, so I can see Spider is being very careful in matching Thunderbolt. In fact I congratulate Spider on his carefulness.

'Well,' Spider says, 'I am taking this match just to give Thunderbolt the feel of the ring. I am taking Bubbles because he is an old friend of mine, and very deserving, and furthermore,' Spider says, 'he gives me his word he will not hit Thunderbolt very hard and will become unconscious the instant Thunderbolt hits him. You know,' Spider says, 'you must encourage a young heavy-weight, and there is nothing that encourages one so much as knocking somebody unconscious.'

Now of course it is nothing for Bubbles to promise not to hit anybody very hard because even when he is a young guy, Bubbles cannot punch his way out of a paper bag, but I am glad to learn that he also promises to become unconscious very soon, as naturally I am greatly interested in Thunderbolt's career, what with owning a piece of him, and having an investment of one pound in him already.

So the night of the fight, I am at the St. Nick very early, and many other citizens are there ahead of me, because by this time Spider McCoy gets plenty of publicity for Thunderbolt by telling the boxing scribes about his wonderful fighting blood lines, and everybody wishes to see a guy who is bred for battle, like Thunderbolt.

I take a guest with me to the fight by the name of Harry the Horse, who comes from Brooklyn, and as I am anxious to help Spider McCoy all I can, as well as to protect my investment in Thunderbolt, I request Harry to call on Bubbles Browning in his dressing-room and remind him of his promise about hitting Thunderbolt.

Harry the Horse does this for me, and furthermore he shows Bubbles a large revolver and tells Bubbles that he will be compelled to shoot his ears off if Bubbles forgets his promise, but Bubbles says all this is most unnecessary, as his eyesight is so bad he cannot see to hit anybody, anyway.

Well, I know a party who is a friend of the guy who is going to referee the preliminary bouts, and I am looking for this party to get him to tell the referee to disqualify Bubbles in case it looks as if he is forgetting his promise and is liable to hit Thunderbolt, but before I can locate the party, they are announcing the opening bout, and there is Thunderbolt in the ring looking very far away indeed, with Spider McCoy behind him.

It seems to me I never see a guy who is so pale all over as Thunderbolt Mulrooney, but Spider looks down at me and tips me a large wink, so I can see that everything is as right as rain, especially when Harry the Horse makes motions at Bubbles Browning like a guy firing a large revolver at somebody, and Bubbles smiles, and also winks.

Well, when the bell rings, Spider gives Thunderbolt a shove towards the centre, and Thunderbolt comes out with his hands up, but looking more far away than somewhat, and something tells me that Thunderbolt by no means feels the killer instinct such as I love to see in fighters. In fact, something tells me that Thunderbolt is not feeling enthusiastic about this proposition in any way, shape, manner, or form.

Old Bubbles almost falls over his own feet coming out of his corner, and he starts bouncing around making passes at Thunderbolt, and waiting for Thunderbolt to hit him so he can become unconscious. Naturally, Bubbles does not wish to become unconscious without getting hit, as this may look suspicious to the public.

Well, instead of hitting Bubbles, what does Thunderbolt Mulrooney do but turn around and walk over to a neutral corner, and lean over the ropes with his face in his gloves, and bust out crying. Naturally, this is a most surprising incident to one and all, and especially to Bubbles Browning.

The referee walks over to Thunderbolt Mulrooney and tries to turn him around, but Thunderbolt keeps his face in his gloves and sobs so loud that the referee is deeply touched and starts sobbing with him. Between the sobs he asks Thunderbolt if he wishes to continue the fight, and Thunderbolt shakes his head, although as a matter of fact no fight whatever starts so far, so the referee declares Bubbles Browning the winner, which is a terrible surprise to Bubbles.

Then the referee puts his arm around Thunderbolt and leads him over to Spider McCoy, who is standing in his corner with a very strange expression on his face. Personally, I consider the entire spectacle so revolting that I go out into the air, and stand around a while expecting to hear any minute that Spider McCoy is in the hands of the gendarmes on a charge of mayhem.

But it seems that nothing happens, and when Spider finally comes out of the St. Nick, he is only looking sorrowful because he just hears that the promoter declines to pay him the fifty bobs he is supposed to receive for Thunderbolt's services, the promoter claiming that Thunderbolt renders no service.

'Well,' Spider says, 'I fear this is not the next heavy-weight champion of the world after all. There is nothing in Professor D's idea about blood lines as far as fighters are concerned, although,' he says, 'it may work out all right with horses and dogs, and one thing and another. I am greatly disappointed,' Spider says, 'but then I am always being disappointed in heavy-weights. There is nothing we can do but take this guy back home, because,' Spider says, 'the last thing I promise Bridget Mulrooney is that I will personally return him to her in case I am not able to make him heavy-weight champion, as she is afraid he will get lost if he tries to find his way home alone.'

So the next day, Spider McCoy and I take Thunderbolt Mulrooney over to Newark and to his home, which turns out to be a nice little house in a side street with a yard all round and about, and Spider and I are just as well pleased that old Shamus Mul-

rooney is absent when we arrive, because Spider says that Shamus
is just such a guy as will be asking a lot of questions about the fifty
bobbos that Thunderbolt does not get.

Well, when we reach the front door of the house, out comes a
big, fine-looking doll with red cheeks, all excited, and she takes
Thunderbolt in her arms and kisses him, so I know this is Bridget
Mulrooney, and I can see she knows what happens, and in fact I
afterward learn that Thunderbolt telephones her the night before.

After a while she pushes Thunderbolt into the house and stands
at the door as if she is guarding it against us entering to get him
again, which of course is very unnecessary. And all this time
Thunderbolt is sobbing no little, although by and by the sobs die
away, and from somewhere in the house comes the sound of music
I seem to recognize as the music of a zither.

Well, Bridget Mulrooney never says a word to us as she stands in
the door, and Spider McCoy keeps staring at her in a way that I
consider very rude indeed. I am wondering if he is waiting for a
receipt for Thunderbolt, but finally he speaks as follows:

'Bridget,' Spider says, 'I hope and trust that you will not consider me too fresh, but I wish to learn the name of the guy you are
going around with just before you marry Shamus. I remember him
well,' Spider says, 'but I cannot think of his name, and it bothers
me not being able to think of names. He is a tall, skinny, stoop-
shouldered guy,' Spider says, 'with a hollow chest and a soft voice,
and he loves music.'

Well, Bridget Mulrooney stands there in the doorway, staring
back at Spider, and it seems to me that the red suddenly fades out
of her cheeks, and just then we hear a lot of yelling, and around the
corner of the house comes a bunch of five or six kids, who seem to
be running from another kid.

This kid is not very big, and is maybe fifteen or sixteen years old,
and he has red hair and many freckles, and he seems very mad at
the other kids. In fact, when he catches up with them he starts
belting away at them with his fists and before anybody can as much
as say boo, he has three of them on the ground as flat as pancakes,
while the others are yelling bloody murder.

Personally, I never see such wonderful punching by a kid,
especially with his left hand, and Spider McCoy is also much impressed, and is watching the kid with great interest. Then Bridget
Mulrooney runs out and grabs the freckle-faced kid with one hand
and smacks him with the other hand and hauls him, squirming

and kicking, over to Spider McCoy and says to Spider like this:

'Mr. McCoy,' Bridget says, 'this is my youngest son, Terence, and though he is not a heavy-weight, and will never be a heavy-weight, perhaps he will answer your purpose. Suppose you see his father about him sometime,' she says, 'and hoping you will learn to mind your own business, I wish you a very good day.'

Then she takes the kid into the house under her arm and slams the door in our kissers, and there is nothing for us to do but walk away. And as we are walking away, all of a sudden Spider McCoy snaps his fingers as guys will do when they get an unexpected thought, and says like this:

'I remember the guy's name,' he says. 'It is Cedric Tilbury, and he is a floor-walker in Hamburgher's department store, and,' Spider says, 'how he can play the zither!'

I see in the papers the other day where Jimmy Johnston, the match-maker at the Garden, matches Tearing Terry Mulrooney, the new sensation of the light-weight division, to fight for the championship, but it seems from what Spider McCoy tells me that my investment with him does not cover any fighters in his stable except maybe heavy-weights.

And it also seems that Spider McCoy is not monkeying with heavy-weights since he gets Tearing Terry.

Too Much Pep

It is really surprising how many wicked people there are in this world, and especially along East 114th Street up in Harlem.

Of course I do not say that all the wicked people in the world are along East 114th Street, because some of them are on East 115th Street, and maybe on East 116th Street, too, but the wicked people on East 114th Street are wickeder than somewhat, especially Ignazio Vardarelli and his mob.

This Ignazio Vardarelli is called Ignaz the Wolf, and he is an Italian party from Calabria, with a noggin shaped like the little end of an ice-cream cone, and a lot of scars on his face which make him look very fierce. All his mob are also Italians, and most of them have noggins shaped like Ignaz', and some of them have even more scars on their kissers, and therefore look even fiercer than he does, which is very, very fierce, indeed.

Now Ignaz the Wolf is a guy who never works, and neither does anybody else in his mob, and what they do for a living is very simple, and I do not mind saying I am sorry I never have the nerve to invent something as easy, because after all work is a great bother.

In Harlem there are a great many Italians, and among them are quite a lot of Moustache Petes, who are old-time Italians with large black moustaches, and who have little stores in cellars and such places and sell spaghetti, and macaroni and cheeses, and other articles of which Italian persons are very fond. I like spaghetti myself now and then, and also pasta fagiole, and broccoli, cooked with garlic, which is very good for the old stomach.

In fact, it is because I like such things that I come to hear about Ignazio Vardarelli, because I often go to a spot in Harlem where a guy can get good Italian food, especially devil-fish fixed a certain way, and maybe a little red wine which the guy who owns the joint makes right in his own cellar by walking up and down in his bare feet in a tub of grapes. In fact, one time when the guy has very painful corns on his feet, and cannot walk up and down in the tub of grapes, I take off my shoes and walk for him, but whoever sells him the grapes leaves a big rock among them, and I get a bad stone bruise from it on my heel.

There are always some very nice Italian people sitting around and about this joint, and I love to listen to them eat spaghetti, and talk, though I do not understand much of what they are saying because Italian is one language I never learn. In fact, I never learn any other language except English, and a very little bit of Yiddish, because a guy who lives in New York can get around most any-where on these two languages, with a few signs mixed up with them.

Anyway, I have a lot of very good friends among the Italians, and I never speak of them as wops, or guineas, or dagoes, or grease-balls, because I consider this most disrespectful, like calling Jewish people mockies, or Heebs, or geese. The way I look at it, if a guy is respectful to one and all, why, one and all will be respectful to him, and anyway, there are many Italians, and Jewish people too, who are apt to haul off and knock you bowlegged if you call them such names.

Well, these Moustache Petes I am talking about are very industrious, and very saving, and most of them have a few bobs laid away for a rainy day, so when Ignaz the Wolf feels that he needs a little money to take care of his overhead, he picks out some Moustache Pete that he figures is able to contribute and writes him a nice letter about as follows:

'Dear Joe' (or maybe Tony, for most Italians are called Joe or Tony), 'please call and see me with five hundred dollars. Yours sincerely, Ignazio.'

Then Ignazio waits two or three days, and if Joe or Tony does not show up with the five yards, or whatever it is that Ignazio asks for, Ignazio writes him another letter, which is a sort of follow-up letter, the same as any business concern sends out to a customer, and this follow-up letter is about as follows:

'Dear Joe' (or Tony), 'I am sorry to hear you have a headache. I figure you must have a headache, because you do not call to see me with the five hundred dollars. I hope and trust you get over this headache very soon, as I am waiting for the five hundred. With kindest regards, I am yours truly, Ignazio.'

He puts a black mark on this letter, and shoves it under Joe or Tony's door, and then he waits a couple of days more. By this time Ignaz the Wolf is naturally getting a little bit impatient, because he is a good business man, and business men like to see their letters receive prompt attention. If he gets no answer from Joe or Tony, there is nothing else for Ignaz the Wolf to do but put a little bomb under the joint where the Moustache Pete lives to remind him of the letter, and very few of Ignaz's customers wait any longer to settle after the first bomb.

So Ignaz the Wolf and his mob do very well for themselves and are able to wear good clothes, and jewellery, and sit around eating spaghetti and drinking dago red and having a nice time generally, and everybody that sees them says hello, very pleasant, even including the Moustache Petes, although of course the chances are they are not on the level with their hellos and secretly hope that Ignaz falls over dead.

Personally, I never hear much of Ignaz the Wolf until I run into a young Italian guy in the Harlem eating-joint by the name of Marco Sciarra, or some such, who is a very legitimate guy up in Harlem, being in the artichoke business with his old man. It seems that the artichoke business is a first-class business in Harlem, though personally I will not give you ten cents for all the artichokes you can pack in the Hudson tubes, as I consider them a very foolish fruit any way you look at them. But Marco and his old man do very good with artichokes, and in fact they do so well that Marco is able to play plenty of horses, which is how I come to get acquainted with him, because it is well known to one and all that I am one of the greatest horse players in New York, and will be a very rich guy if it is not for crooked jockeys riding the horses different from the way I dope them.

Anyway, one night Marco somehow starts beefing about Ignaz the Wolf and his mob, and finally he lets it out that Ignaz is trying to put the arm on him and his old man for five G's, for no reason except that Ignaz seems to need it.

Now Marco is born and raised right here in this man's town, and he is quite an all-round guy in many respects, and he is certainly not the kind of guy anybody with any sense will figure a chump. He is not the kind of a guy a smart guy will figure to hold still for five G's for no reason, and the chances are Ignaz the Wolf is not thinking of Marco in the first place. The chances are he is thinking more of Marco's old man, who is a Moustache Pete in every way.

Furthermore, if it is left to the old man, he will kick in the five G's to Ignaz without a yip, just to avoid trouble, but Marco can see where he can use any stray five G's himself to pay off a few bookmakers. Anyway, Marco tells me he will see Ignaz in the place where Ignaz is a sure thing to go some day before he will give up five G's, or any part of five G's, and I say I do not blame him, for five G's is plenty of sugar, even if you do not have it.

This is the last I see of Marco for a couple of weeks. Then one day I happen to be in Harlem, so I go over to his place of business on East 114th Street. The Marcos have an office on the ground floor of a two-story building, and live upstairs, and when I get there I notice that the glass in all the windows seems to be out, and that things are generally upset.

Well, when I find Marco he explains to me that somebody puts a fifteen-dollar bomb in the joint the night before, and while Marco does not say right out that Ignaz the Wolf does this, he says he is willing to lay 8 to 5 and take Ignaz against the field, because it seems he sends word to Ignaz that he need not expect the five G's he is looking for.

Then Marco explains to me that the fifteen-dollar bomb is only meant as a sort of convincer, and that according to the rules Ignaz will next put a thirty-two-dollar bomb in the joint, which will be a little more powerful than the fifteen-dollar bomb. In fact, Marco says, the thirty-two-dollar bomb will be powerful enough to lift them out of their beds upstairs a foot to a foot and a half. But finally, if the five G's is not paid to Ignaz the Wolf in the meantime, he will put a fifty-dollar bomb under them, and this bomb will practically ruin everything in the neighbourhood, including the neighbours.

Well, naturally I am very indignant about the whole proposition, but Marco says it is only fair to Ignaz the Wolf to say he writes them a couple of very polite letters before he makes a move, and does nothing whatever underhand before sending the bomb.

'But my old man is now very much displeased with Ignaz,' Marco says. 'He is even more displeased than I am. It takes quite a little to displease my old man, but when he is displeased, he is certainly greatly displeased, indeed. In fact,' Marco says, 'my old man and other Italian citizens of Harlem hold a meeting to-day, and they come to the conclusion that it is for the best interests of the community to have Ignaz put in his place before he cleans everybody out. So they are going to put Ignaz in his place.'

'Well,' I say, 'what is Ignaz's place?'

'Ignaz's place is six feet underground,' Marco says, 'and this is where the citizens are going to put him.'

'Why, Marco,' I say, 'this is most horrifying, indeed, although personally I am in favour of it. But,' I say, 'I do not think Ignaz will care to be put in his place, and as he is well mobbed I do not see how it can be brought about without somebody getting in trouble. I hope and trust, Marco,' I say, 'that neither you or your old man are going to get tangled up in this proposition.'

'No,' Marco says, 'we will not get tangled up. In fact, nobody in Harlem will get tangled up, because they are sending to Sicily for a certain party to put Ignaz in his place. They are sending for Don Pep'.'

Well, I finally make out from what Marco tells me that at this meeting many of the old-fashioned Italians of Harlem are present, with their moustaches sticking right out straight with indignation, and it is the opinion of one and all that Ignaz shall be put in his place as quickly as possible. But Marco says there is quite a difference of opinion as to who shall put Ignaz in his place, and the meeting lasts a long time, and there is plenty of argument.

It seems that all of these old-timers know of some party back in Italy that they figure is just the one to put Ignaz in his place, and they get up and make speeches about their guys as if they are delegates to a convention boosting candidates for a nice nomination.

Marco says an old Moustache Pete by the name of Bianchini, who is a shoemaker, almost carries the meeting in favour of a guy by the name of Corri, who, it seems, makes a great showing putting parties in their places around Napoli, and who is favourably remembered by many of the citizens present. Marco says old Bianchini is a good speaker and he talks for almost an hour telling about how this guy puts parties in their places by slipping a little short rope around their necks, and guzzling them before they have time to say Jack Robinson, and it is commencing to look as if Corri is the guy, when Marco's old man steps forward and raises his hand to stop all of this cheering for Corri.

'I will not take up much of your time in presenting the name of my choice,' Marco says his old man says. 'It is a name that is well known to many of you older delegates. It is the name of one who has made history at putting parties in their places, the name of a celebrated citizen of Sicily, experienced and skilful in his calling – a name that is above reproach. I give you, fellow citizens, the name of "Don Pep'"', of Siracusa.'

Well, at this everybody becomes very enthusiastic, Marco says, and also their blood runs cold, because it seems that Don Pep' is for many years the outstanding man in all Italy at putting parties in their places. All the old-timers know of him by reputation, and some of them even see him when they are young guys back in the old country, while Marco's old man knows him personally.

It seems that Don Pep' has a record like a prize fighter, and Marco's old man reads this record to the meeting, as follows:

Milan, 1899, 2 men
Venice, 1904, 1 man
Naples, 1909, 3 men
Rome, 1913, 1 man
Genoa, 1921, 2 men, 4 horses
Nice, 1928, 1 man

Well, when the thing comes to a vote, Don Pep' gets all the votes but one, old Bianchini sticking to Corri, and the meeting adjourns with everybody satisfied that Ignaz the Wolf is to be put in his place in first-class style.

Now getting Don Pep' over to this country to put Ignaz in his

place is going to cost something, so Marco, seeing a chance to turn
a few honest bobs, propositions his old man to get Ignaz put in his
place for about half of what Don Pep' will cost, Marco figuring
that he can find a couple of guys downtown who are willing to
work cheap, but his old man refuses to listen to him. His old man
says this business must be transacted in a dignified way, and under
the old-fashioned rules, though Marco says he does not see what
difference it makes if a guy is to be put in his place whether it is
under the old-fashioned rules or the new no-foul system, especially
as nobody explains the old-fashioned rules, or seems to know what
they are.

Personally, if I am planning to get a guy put in his place I will
not go around telling people about it. In fact, I will keep it a very
great secret for fear the guy may hear of it and take steps, but these
Moustache Petes make no bones whatever about sending for Don
Pep', and everybody in the neighbourhood knows it, including
Ignaz the Wolf and his mob. I figure that maybe the Moustache
Petes want Ignaz to know it, thinking he may decide to haul ashes
out of Harlem before anything happens to him, but Ignaz is a
pretty bold guy one way and another, and he only laughs about
Don Pep'. Ignaz says Don Pep' is old stuff, and may go in Italy
years ago, but not in the U.S.A. in these times.

Naturally, I am greatly interested in Don Pep', and I make
Marco promise to tell me when he arrives. I love to look at a top-
notcher in any line, and I judge from Don Pep's record that he is a
champion of the world. So some weeks later when I get a telephone
call from Marco that Don Pep' is here, I hurry up to Harlem and
meet Marco, and he promises to show me Don Pep' after it gets
dark, because it seems Don Pep' moves around only at night.

He is living in the basement of a tenement house in East 114th
Street with an old Sicilian by the name of Sutari, who is a real
Moustache Pete and who has a shoe-shining joint downtown. He is
a nice old man, and a good friend of mine, though afterward I hear
he is a tough guy back in his old home town in Sicily.

Well, when I get a peek at Don Pep', I almost bust out laughing,
for what is he but a little old man wearing a long black coat that
trails the ground, and a funny flat black hat with a low crown and
a stiff brim. He looks to me like somebody out of a play, especially
as he has long white hair and bushy white whiskers all over his face
like a poodle dog.

But when I get close to him, I do not feel so much like laughing, because he raises his head and stares at me through the whiskers and I see a pair of black eyes like a snake's eyes, with a look in them such as gives me the shivers all over. Personally, I never see such a look in anybody's eyes before in my life, and I am very glad indeed to walk briskly away from Don Pep'.

I peek back over my shoulder, and Don Pep' is standing there with his head bowed on his chest, as harmless-looking as a rabbit, and I feel like laughing again at the idea of such an old guy being brought all the way from Sicily to put Ignaz the Wolf in his place. Then I think of those eyes, and start shivering harder than ever, and Marco shivers with me and explains to me what happens when Don Pep' first arrives, and since.

It seems that Marco's old man and a lot of other Moustache Petes meet Don Pep' at the boat that brings him from Sicily, and they are wishing to entertain him, but Don Pep' says he is not here for pleasure, and all they can do for him is to show him the guy he is to put in his place. Well, naturally, nobody wishes to put the finger on Ignaz the Wolf in public, because Ignaz may remember same, and feel hurt about it, so they give Don Pep' a description of Ignaz, and his address, which is a cigar store on East 114th Street, where Ignaz and his mob always hang out.

A few hours later when Ignaz is sitting in the cigar store playing klob with some of his mob, in comes Don Pep', all bundled up in his black coat, though it is a warm night, at that. He has a way of walking along very slow, and he is always tap-tapping on the sidewalk ahead of him with a big cane, like a blind man, but his feet never make a sound.

Well, naturally Ignaz the Wolf jumps up when such a strange-looking party bobs in on him, for Ignaz can see that this must be Don Pep', the guy who is coming to put him in his place, and knowing where his place is, Ignaz is probably on the look-out for Don Pep', anyway. So Ignaz stands there with his cards in his hand staring at Don Pep', and Don Pep' walks right up to him, and shoots his head up out of his cloak collar like a turtle and looks Ignaz in the eye.

He never says one word to Ignaz, and while Ignaz tries to think of something smart to say to Don Pep', he cannot make his tongue move a lick. He is like a guy who is hypnotized. The other guys at the table sit there looking at Ignaz and Don Pep', and never making a wrong move, though on form any one of them figures to out with the old equalizer and plug Don Pep'. Finally, after maybe three minutes hand running of looking at Ignaz, Don Pep' suddenly makes a noise with his mouth like a snake hissing, and then he turns and walks out of the joint, tap-tapping with his cane ahead of him.

After he is gone, Ignaz comes up for air, and starts explaining why he does not do something about Don Pep', but even Ignaz's own mobsters figure the old guy runs something of a sandy on Ignaz. What puzzles them no little is that Don Pep' makes no move to put Ignaz in his place then and there, as long as he comes all the way from Sicily to do it.

But two nights later, when Ignaz the Wolf is again playing klob in the cigar store, who pops in but old Don Pep', and once more he stands looking Ignaz in the eye and never saying as much as howdy. This time Ignaz manages to get a few words out but Don Pep' never answers him, and winds up his looking at Ignaz with that same hissing sound, like a snake. After this Ignaz does not keep his old hours around the cigar store, but he starts in getting very tough with the Moustache Petes, and writing them very stiff business notes about sending in their contributions.

Well, it seems that the citizens around and about get very independent after Don Pep' arrives, and commence paying no attention to Ignaz's notes, and even take to giving Ignaz's collectors the old ha-ha, in Italian, which burns Ignaz up quite some. He complains that Don Pep' is hurting his business, and lets it out here and there that after he takes care of Don Pep' he is going to make his old customers very sorry that they ignore him. But somehow Ignaz does not put any more bombs around, except a few fifteen-dollar ones on guys who do not count much.

In the meantime, old Don Pep' goes walking up and down the streets, his whiskers down in his cloak collar, no matter how warm it gets, and the citizens lift their hats to him as he passes by. In fact, I lift my own lid one evening when he passes me, because I feel that a guy with his record is entitled to much respect. But knowing Ignaz the Wolf, I figure it is only a question of time when we will be walking slow behind the old guy, especially as he does not seem to be making any kind of move to put Ignaz in his place, per agreement.

Always late at night Don Pep' stands in front of an areaway between the tenement house where he lives and the house next door, leaning up against a sort of iron grating that walls off the areaway from the street. It happens that no light shines on the areaway, so all you see as you pass by is a sort of outline of Don Pep' against the grating, and now and then a little glow as he puffs at a cigarette through his whiskers. He is certainly a strange-looking old crocodile, and I often wonder what he is thinking about as he stands there.

I can see now how smart the Moustache Petes are in making no secret of what Don Pep' is here for, because the publicity he gets keeps Ignaz the Wolf from doing anything to him. Naturally if anything drastic happens to Don Pep', the coppers will figure Ignaz responsible, and the coppers in this town are waiting for several years to find something drastic that Ignaz is responsible for.

But there is no doubt Ignaz the Wolf is getting sick and tired of Don Pep', especially since business is so bad, so one night the thing that is a sure thing to happen comes off. An automobile tears past the spot where Don Pep' is standing, as usual, in front of the areaway, and out of this automobile comes a big blooey-blooey, with four guys letting go with sawed-off shotguns at once.

As the automobile cuts in close to the kerb, this puts the gunners only the distance across the sidewalk from Don Pep', so there is little chance that four guys using shotguns are going to miss, especially as the shotguns are loaded with buckshot, which scatters nice and wide.

Well, there are very few citizens around the spot at this hour, and they start running away lickity-split as soon as they hear the first blooey, because the citizens of this part of Harlem know that a blooey is never going to do anybody much good. But before they start running, some of the citizens see old Don Pep' fold up in a little black pile in front of the areaway as the automobile tears on down the street, with Ignaz the Wolf sitting back in it laughing very heartily. I will say one thing for Ignaz, that when it comes down to cases, he is always ready to go out on his own jobs himself, although this is mainly because he wishes to see that the jobs are well done.

Ten minutes later, Ignaz is walking into the cigar store so as to be playing klob and looking very innocent when the coppers come around to speak to him about the matter of Don Pep'. And he is no sooner inside the joint than right at his heels steps nobody in all this world but Don Pep', who has a licence to be laying up against the areaway grating as dead as a doornail.

Well, old Don Pep' is huddled up in his cape and whiskers as usual, but he seems to be stepping spryer than somewhat, and as Ignaz the Wolf turns around and sees him and lets out a yell, thinking he is seeing a ghost, Don Pep' closes in on him and grabs Ignaz as if he is giving him a nice hearty hug. Ignaz the Wolf screams once very loud, and the next thing anybody knows he is stretched out on the floor as stiff as a board and Don Pep' is stepping out of the cigar store.

Nobody ever sees Don Pep' again as far as I know, although the coppers still have the straw-stuffed black suit, and the black hat and cape, as well as the false whiskers with which Sutari, the shoe shiner, fixes up a phony Don Pep' to lean against the areaway grating for Ignaz the Wolf and his gunners to waste their buckshot on, because it seems from what Sutari says that Don Pep' carries two outfits of clothes for just such a purpose. Personally, I consider this very deceitful of Don Pep', but nobody else seems to see anything wrong in it.

Well, when the croakers examine Ignaz's body they do not find a mark of any kind on him, and they are greatly puzzled indeed, because naturally they expect to find a knife or maybe a darning-needle sticking in him. But there is nothing whatever to show what makes Ignaz the Wolf die, and Marco tells me afterward that his old man and all the other Moustache Petes are laughing very heartily at the idea that Don Pep' uses any such articles.

Marco tells me his old man says if the croakers have any sense they will see at once that Ignaz the Wolf dies of heart disease, and Marco says his old man claims anybody ought to know this heart disease is caused by fright because Don Pep' is putting guys in their places in such a way for many years. Furthermore, Marco says his old man states that this is according to the old-fashioned rules, and very dignified, though if you ask me I think it is a dirty trick to scare a guy to death.

Baseball Hattie

It comes on spring-time, and the little birdies are singing in the trees in Central Park, and the grass is green all around and about, and I am at the Polo Grounds on the opening day of the baseball season, when who do I behold but Baseball Hattie. I am somewhat surprised at this spectacle, as it is years since I see Baseball Hattie, and for all I know she long ago passes to a better and happier world.

But there she is, as large as life, and in fact twenty pounds larger, and when I call the attention of Armand Fibleman, the gambler, to her, he gets up and tears right out of the joint as if he sees a ghost, for if there is one thing Armand Fibleman loathes and despises, it is a ghost.

I can see that Baseball Hattie is greatly changed, and to tell the truth, I can see that she is getting to be nothing but an old bag. Her hair that is once as black as a yard up a stove-pipe is grey, and she is wearing gold-rimmed cheaters, although she seems to be pretty well dressed and looks as if she may be in the money a little bit, at that.

But the greatest change in her is the way she sits there very quiet all afternoon, never once opening her yap, even when many of the customers around her are claiming that Umpire William Klem is Public Enemy No. 1 to 16 inclusive, because they think he calls a close one against the Giants. I am wondering if maybe Baseball Hattie is stricken dumb somewhere back down the years, because I can remember when she is usually making speeches in the grandstand in favour of hanging such characters as Umpire William Klem when they call close ones against the Giants. But Hattie just sits there as if she is in a church while the public clamour goes on about her, and she does not as much as cry out robber, or even you big bum at Umpire William Klem.

I see many a baseball bug in my time, male and female, but without doubt the worst bug of them all is Baseball Hattie, and you can say it again. She is most particularly a bug about the Giants, and she never misses a game they play at the Polo Grounds, and in fact she sometimes bobs up watching them play in other cities, which is always very embarrassing to the Giants, as they fear the customers in these cities may get the wrong impression of New York womanhood after listening to Baseball Hattie a while.

The first time I ever see Baseball Hattie to pay any attention to her is in Philadelphia, a matter of twenty-odd years back, when the Giants are playing a series there, and many citizens of New York, including Armand Fibleman and myself, are present, because the Philadelphia customers are great hands for betting on baseball games in those days, and Armand Fibleman figures he may knock a few of them in the creek.

Armand Fibleman is a character who will bet on baseball games from who-laid-the-chunk, and in fact he will bet on anything whatever, because Armand Fibleman is a gambler by trade and has been such since infancy. Personally, I will not bet you four dollars on a baseball game, because in the first place I am not apt to have four dollars, and in the second place I consider horse races a much sounder investment, but I often go around and about with Armand Fibleman, as he is a friend of mine, and sometimes he gives me a little piece of one of his bets for nothing.

Well, what happens in Philadelphia but the umpire forfeits the game in the seventh innings to the Giants by a score of nine to nothing when the Phillies are really leading by five runs, and the reason the umpire takes this action is because he orders several of the Philadelphia players to leave the field for calling him a scoundrel and a rat and a snake in the grass, and also a baboon, and they refuse to take their departure, as they still have more names to call him.

Right away the Philadelphia customers become infuriated in a manner you will scarcely believe, for ordinarily a Philadelphia baseball customer is as quiet as a lamb, no matter what you do to him, and in fact in those days a Philadelphia baseball customer is only considered as somebody to do something to.

But these Philadelphia customers are so infuriated that they not only chase the umpire under the stand, but they wait in the street outside the baseball orchard until the Giants change into their street clothes and come out of the clubhouse. Then the Philadelphia customers begin pegging rocks, and one thing and another, at the Giants, and it is a most exciting and disgraceful scene that is spoken of for years afterward.

Well, the Giants march along towards the North Philly station to catch a train for home, dodging the rocks and one thing and another the best they can, and wondering why the Philadelphia gendarmes do not come to the rescue, until somebody notices several gendarmes among the customers doing some of the throwing themselves, so the Giants realize that this is a most inhospitable community, to be sure.

Finally all of them get inside the North Philly station and are safe, except a big, tall, left-handed pitcher by the name of Haystack Duggeler, who just reports to the club the day before and who finds himself surrounded by quite a posse of these infuriated Philadelphia customers, and who is unable to make them understand that he is nothing but a rookie, because he has a Missouri accent, and besides, he is half paralysed with fear.

One of the infuriated Philadelphia customers is armed with a brickbat and is just moving forward to maim Haystack Duggeler with this instrument, when who steps into the situation but Baseball Hattie, who is also on her way to the station to catch a train, and who is greatly horrified by the assault on the Giants.

She seizes the brickbat from the infuriated Philadelphia customer's grasp, and then tags the customer smack-dab between the eyes with his own weapon, knocking him so unconscious that I afterward hear he does not recover for two weeks, and that he remains practically an imbecile the rest of his days.

Then Baseball Hattie cuts loose on the other infuriated Philadelphia customers with language that they never before hear in those parts, causing them to disperse without further ado, and after the last customer is beyond the sound of her voice, she takes Haystack Duggeler by the pitching arm and personally escorts him to the station.

Now out of this incident is born a wonderful romance between Baseball Hattie and Haystack Duggeler, and in fact it is no doubt love at first sight, and about this period Haystack Duggeler begins burning up the league with his pitching, and at the same time giving Manager Mac plenty of headaches, including the romance with Baseball Hattie, because anybody will tell you that a left-hander is tough enough on a manager without a romance, and especially a romance with Baseball Hattie.

It seems that the trouble with Hattie is she is in business up in Harlem, and this business consists of a boarding-and-rooming-house where ladies and gentlemen board and room, and personally I never see anything out of line in the matter, but the rumour somehow gets around, as rumours will do, that in the first place it is not a boarding-and-rooming-house, and in the second place that the ladies and gentlemen who room and board there are by no means ladies and gentlemen, and especially ladies.

Well, this rumour becomes a terrible knock to Baseball Hattie's social reputation. Furthermore, I hear Manager Mac sends for her and requests her to kindly lay off his ball-players, and especially off a character who can make a baseball sing high C like Haystack Duggeler. In fact, I hear Manager Mac gives her such a lecture on her civic duty to New York and to the Giants that Baseball Hattie sheds tears, and promises she will never give Haystack another tumble the rest of the season.

'You know me, Mac,' Baseball Hattie says. 'You know I will cut off my nose rather than do anything to hurt your club. I sometimes figure I am in love with this big bloke, but,' she says, 'maybe it is only gas pushing up around my heart. I will take something for it. To hell with him, Mac!' she says.

So she does not see Haystack Duggeler again, except at a distance, for a long time, and he goes on to win fourteen games in a row, pitching a no-hitter and four two-hitters among them, and hanging up a reputation as a great pitcher, and also as a 100-percent. heel.

Haystack Duggeler is maybe twenty-five at this time, and he comes to the big league with more bad habits than anybody in the history of the world is able to acquire in such a short time. He is especially a great rumpot, and after he gets going good in the league, he is just as apt to appear for a game all mulled up as not.

He is fond of all forms of gambling, such as playing cards and shooting craps, but after they catch him with a deck of readers in a poker game and a pair of tops in a crap game, none of the Giants will play with him any more, except of course when there is nobody else to play with.

He is ignorant about many little things, such as reading and writing and geography and mathematics, as Haystack Duggeler himself admits he never goes to school any more than he can help, but he is so wise when it comes to larceny that I always figure they must have great tutors back in Haystack's old home town of Booneville, Mo.

And no smarter jobbie ever breathes than Haystack when he is out there pitching. He has so much speed that he just naturally throws the ball past a batter before he can get the old musket off his shoulder, and along with his hard one, Haystack has a curve like the letter Q. With two ounces of brains, Haystack Duggeler will be the greatest pitcher that ever lives.

Well, as far as Baseball Hattie is concerned, she keeps her word about not seeing Haystack, although sometimes when he is mulled up he goes around to her boarding-and-rooming-house, and tries to break down the door.

On days when Haystack Duggeler is pitching, she is always in her favourite seat back of third, and while she roots hard for the Giants no matter who is pitching, she puts on extra steam when Haystack is bending them over, and it is quite an experience to hear her crying lay them in there, Haystack, old boy, and strike this big tramp out, Haystack, and other exclamations of a similar nature, which please Haystack quite some, but annoy Baseball Hattie's neighbours back of third base, such as Armand Fibleman, if he happens to be betting on the other club.

A month before the close of his first season in the big league, Haystack Duggeler gets so ornery that Manager Mac suspends him, hoping maybe it will cause Haystack to do a little thinking, but naturally Haystack is unable to do this, because he has nothing to think with. About a week later, Manager Mac gets to noticing how he can use a few ball games, so he starts looking for Haystack Duggeler, and he finds him tending bar on Eighth Avenue with his uniform hung up back of the bar as an advertisement.

The baseball writers speak of Haystack as eccentric, which is a polite way of saying he is a screwball, but they consider him a most unique character and are always writing humorous stories about him, though any one of them will lay you plenty of 9 to 5 that Haystack winds up an umbay. The chances are they will raise their price a little, as the season closes and Haystack is again under suspension with cold weather coming on and not a dime in his pants' pockets.

It is some time along in the winter that Baseball Hattie hauls off and marries Haystack Duggeler, which is a great surprise to one and all, but not nearly as much of a surprise as when Hattie closes her boarding-and-rooming-house and goes to live in a little apartment with Haystack Duggeler up on Washington Heights.

It seems that she finds Haystack one frosty night sleeping in a hallway, after being around slightly mulled up for several weeks, and she takes him to her home and gets him a bath and a shave and a clean shirt and two boiled eggs and some toast and coffee and a shot or two of rye whisky, all of which is greatly appreciated by Haystack, especially the rye whisky.

Then Haystack proposes marriage to her and takes a paralysed oath that if she becomes his wife he will reform, so what with loving Haystack anyway, and with the fix commencing to request more dough off the boarding-and-rooming-house business than the business will stand, Hattie takes him at his word, and there you are.

The baseball writers are wondering what Manager Mac will say when he hears these tidings, but all Mac says is that Haystack cannot possibly be any worse married than he is single-o, and then Mac has the club office send the happy couple a little paper money to carry them over the winter.

Well, what happens but a great change comes over Haystack Duggeler. He stops bending his elbow and helps Hattie cook and wash the dishes, and holds her hand when they are in the movies, and speaks of his love for her several times a week, and Hattie is as happy as nine dollars' worth of lettuce. Manager Mac is so delighted at the change in Haystack that he has the club office send over more paper money, because Mac knows that with Haystack in shape he is sure of twenty-five games, and maybe the pennant.

In late February, Haystack reports to the training camp down South still as sober as some judges, and the other ball-players are so impressed by the change in him that they admit him to their poker game again. But of course it is too much to expect a man to alter his entire course of living all at once, and it is not long before Haystack discovers four nines in his hand on his own deal and breaks up the game.

He brings Baseball Hattie with him to the camp, and this is undoubtedly a slight mistake, as it seems the old rumour about her boarding-and-rooming-house business gets around among the ever-loving wives of the other players, and they put on a large chill for her. In fact, you will think Hattie has the smallpox.

Naturally, Baseball Hattie feels the frost, but she never lets on, as it seems she runs into many bigger and better frosts than this in her time. Then Haystack Duggeler notices it, and it seems that it makes him a little peevish towards Baseball Hattie, and in fact it is said that he gives her a slight pasting one night in their room, partly because she has no better social standing and partly because he is commencing to cop a few sneaks on the local corn now and then, and Hattie chides him for same.

Well, about this time it appears that Baseball Hattie discovers that she is going to have a baby, and as soon as she recovers from her astonishment, she decides that it is to be a boy who will be a great baseball player, maybe a pitcher, although Hattie admits she is willing to compromise on a good second baseman.

She also decides that his name is to be Derrill Duggeler, after his paw, as it seems Derrill is Haystack's real name, and he is only called Haystack because he claims he once makes a living stacking hay, although the general opinion is that all he ever stacks is cards.

It is really quite remarkable what a belt Hattie gets out of the idea of having this baby, though Haystack is not excited about the matter. He is not paying much attention to Baseball Hattie by now, except to give her a slight pasting now and then, but Hattie is so happy about the baby that she does not mind these pastings.

Haystack Duggeler meets up with Armand Fibleman along in midsummer. By this time, Haystack discovers horse racing and is always making bets on the horses, and naturally he is generally broke, and then I commence running into him in different spots with Armand Fibleman, who is now betting higher than a cat's back on baseball games.

It is late August, and the Giants are fighting for the front end of the league, and an important series with Brooklyn is coming up, and everybody knows that Haystack Duggeler will work in anyway two games of the series, as Haystack can generally beat Brooklyn just by throwing his glove on the mound. There is no doubt but what he has the old Indian sign on Brooklyn, and the night before the first game, which he is sure to work, the gamblers along Broadway are making the Giants 2-to-1 favourites to win the game.

This same night before the game, Baseball Hattie is home in her little apartment on Washington Heights waiting for Haystack to come in and eat a delicious dinner of pigs' knuckles and sauerkraut, which she personally prepares for him. In fact, she hurries home right after the ball game to get this delicacy ready, because Haystack tells her he will surely come home this particular night, although Hattie knows he is never better than even money to keep his word about anything.

But sure enough, in he comes while the pigs' knuckles and sauerkraut are still piping hot, and Baseball Hattie is surprised to see Armand Fibleman with him, as she knows Armand backwards and forwards and does not care much for him, at that. However, she can say the same thing about four million other characters in this town, so she makes Armand welcome, and they sit down and put on the pigs' knuckles and sauerkraut together, and a pleasant time is enjoyed by one and all. In fact, Baseball Hattie puts herself out to entertain Armand Fibleman, because he is the first guest Haystack ever brings home.

Well, Armand Fibleman can be very pleasant when he wishes, and he speaks very nicely to Hattie. Naturally, he sees that Hattie is expecting, and in fact he will have to be blind not to see it, and he seems greatly interested in this matter and asks Hattie many questions, and Hattie is delighted to find somebody to talk to about what is coming off with her, as Haystack will never listen to any of her remarks on the subject.

So Armand Fibleman gets to hear all about Baseball Hattie's son, and how he is to be a great baseball player, and Armand says is that so, and how nice, and all this and that, until Haystack Duggeler speaks up as follows and to wit:

'Oh, daggone her son!' Haystack says. 'It is going to be a girl, anyway, so let us dismiss this topic and get down to business. Hat,' he says, 'you fan yourself into the kitchen and wash the dishes, while Armand and me talk.'

So Hattie goes into the kitchen, leaving Haystack and Armand sitting there talking, and what are they talking about but a proposition for Haystack to let the Brooklyn club beat him the next day so Armand Fibleman can take the odds and clean up a nice little gob of money, which he is to split with Haystack.

Hattie can hear every word they say, as the kitchen is next door to the dining-room where they are sitting, and at first she thinks they are joking, because at this time nobody ever even as much as thinks of skullduggery in baseball, or anyway, not much.

It seems that at first Haystack is not in favour of the idea, but Armand Fibleman keeps mentioning money that Haystack owes him for bets on the horse races, and he asks Haystack how he expects to continue betting on the races without fresh money, and Armand also speaks of the great injustice that is being done Haystack by the Giants in not paying him twice the salary he is getting, and how the loss of one or two games is by no means such a great calamity.

Well, finally Baseball Hattie hears Haystack say all right, but he wishes a thousand dollars then and there as a guarantee, and Armand Fibleman says this is fine, and they will go downtown and he will get the money at once, and now Hattie realizes that maybe they are in earnest, and she pops out of the kitchen and speaks as follows:

'Gentlemen,' Hattie says, 'you seem to be sober, but I guess you are drunk. If you are not drunk, you must both be daffy to think of such a thing as phenagling around with a baseball game.'

'Hattie,' Haystack says, 'kindly close your trap and go back in the kitchen, or I will give you a bust in the nose.'

And with this he gets up and reaches for his hat, and Armand

Fibleman gets up too, and Hattie says like this:

'Why, Haystack,' she says, 'you are not really serious in this matter, are you?'

'Of course I am serious,' Haystack says. 'I am sick and tired of pitching for starvation wages, and besides, I will win a lot of games later on to make up for the one I lose to-morrow. Say,' he says, 'these Brooklyn bums may get lucky to-morrow and knock me loose from my pants, anyway, no matter what I do, so what difference does it make?'

'Haystack,' Baseball Hattie says, 'I know you are a liar and a drunkard and a cheat and no account generally, but nobody can tell me you will sink so low as to purposely toss off a ball game. Why, Haystack, baseball is always on the level. It is the most honest game in all this world. I guess you are just ribbing me, because you know how much I love it.'

'Dry up!' Haystack says to Hattie. 'Furthermore, do not expect me home again to-night. But anyway, dry up.'

'Look, Haystack,' Hattie says, 'I am going to have a son. He is your son and my son, and he is going to be a great ball-player when he grows up, maybe a greater pitcher than you are, though I hope and trust he is not left-handed. He will have your name. If they find out you toss off a game for money, they will throw you out of baseball and you will be disgraced. My son will be known as the son of a crook, and what chance will he have in baseball? Do you think I am going to allow you to do this to him, and to the game that keeps me from going nutty for marrying you?'

Naturally, Haystack Duggeler is greatly offended by Hattie's crack about her son being maybe a greater pitcher than he is, and he is about to take steps, when Armand Fibleman stops him. Armand Fibleman is commencing to be somewhat alarmed at Baseball Hattie's attitude, and he gets to thinking that he hears that people in her delicate condition are often irresponsible, and he fears that she may blow a whistle on this enterprise without realizing what she is doing. So he undertakes a few soothing remarks to her.

'Why, Hattie,' Armand Fibleman says, 'nobody can possibly find out about this little matter, and Haystack will have enough money to send your son to college, if his markers at the race track do not take it all. Maybe you better lie down and rest a while,' Armand says.

But Baseball Hattie does not as much as look at Armand, though she goes on talking to Haystack. 'They always find out thievery, Haystack,' she says, 'especially when you are dealing with a fink like Fibleman. If you deal with him once, you will have to deal with him again and again, and he will be the first to holler copper on you, because he is a stool pigeon in his heart.'

'Haystack,' Armand Fibleman says, 'I think we better be going.'

'Haystack,' Hattie says, 'you can go out of here and stick up somebody or commit a robbery or a murder, and I will still welcome you back and stand by you. But if you are going out to steal my son's future, I advise you not to go.'

'Dry up!' Haystack says. 'I am going.'

'All right, Haystack,' Hattie says, very calm.' 'But just step into the kitchen with me and let me say one little word to you by yourself, and then I will say no more.'

Well, Haystack Duggeler does not care for even just one little word more, but Armand Fibleman wishes to get this disagreeable scene over with, so he tells Haystack to let her have her word, and Haystack goes into the kitchen with Hattie, and Armand cannot hear what is said, as she speaks very low, but he hears Haystack laugh heartily and then Haystack comes out of the kitchen, still laughing, and tells Armand he is ready to go.

As they start for the door, Baseball Hattie outs with a long-nosed .38-calibre Colt's revolver, and goes root-a-toot-toot with it, and the next thing anybody knows, Haystack is on the floor yelling bloody murder, and Armand Fibleman is leaving the premises without bothering to open the door. In fact, the landlord afterward talks some of suing Haystack Duggeler because of the damage Armand Fibleman does to the door. Armand himself afterward admits that when he slows down for a breather a couple of miles down Broadway he finds splinters stuck all over him.

Well, the doctors come, and the gendarmes come, and there is great confusion, especially as Baseball Hattie is sobbing so she can scarcely make a statement, and Haystack Duggeler is so sure he is going to die that he cannot think of anything to say except oh-oh-oh, but finally the landlord remembers seeing Armand leave with his door, and everybody starts questioning Hattie about this until she confesses that Armand is there all right, and that he tries to bribe Haystack to toss off a ball game, and that she then suddenly finds herself with a revolver in her hand, and everything goes black before her eyes, and she can remember no more until somebody is sticking a bottle of smelling salts under her nose.

Naturally, the newspaper reporters put two and two together, and what they make of it is that Hattie tries to plug Armand Fibleman for his rascally offer, and that she misses Armand and gets Haystack, and right away Baseball Hattie is a great heroine, and Haystack is a great hero, though nobody thinks to ask Haystack how he stands on the bribe proposition, and he never brings it up himself.

And nobody will ever offer Haystack any more bribes, for after the doctors get through with him he is shy a left arm from the shoulder down, and he will never pitch a baseball again, unless he learns to pitch right-handed.

The newspapers make quite a lot of Baseball Hattie protecting the fair name of baseball. The National League plays a benefit game for Haystack Duggeler and presents him with a watch and a purse of twenty-five thousand dollars, which Baseball Hattie grabs away from him, saying it is for her son, while Armand Fibleman is in bad with one and all.

Baseball Hattie and Haystack Duggeler move to the Pacific Coast, and this is all there is to the story, except that one day some years ago, and not long before he passes away in Los Angeles, a respectable grocer, I run into Haystack when he is in New York on a business trip, and I say to him like this:

'Haystack,' I say, 'it is certainly a sin and a shame that Hattie misses Armand Fibleman that night and puts you on the shelf. The chances are that but for this little accident you will hang up one of the greatest pitching records in the history of baseball. Personally,' I say, 'I never see a better left-handed pitcher.'

'Look,' Haystack says. 'Hattie does not miss Fibleman. It is a great newspaper story and saves my name, but the truth is she hits just where she aims. When she calls me into the kitchen before I start out with Fibleman, she shows me a revolver I never before know she has, and says to me, "Haystack," she says, "if you leave with this weasel on the errand you mention, I am going to fix you so you will never make another wrong move with your pitching arm. I am going to shoot it off for you."

'I laugh heartily,' Haystack says. 'I think she is kidding me, but I find out different. By the way,' Haystack says, 'I afterward learn that long before I meet her, Hattie works for three years in a shooting gallery at Coney Island. She is really a remarkable broad,' Haystack says.

I guess I forget to state that the day Baseball Hattie is at the

Polo Grounds she is watching the new kid sensation of the big leagues, Derrill Duggeler, shut out Brooklyn with three hits.

He is a wonderful young left-hander.

Situation Wanted

One evening in the summer of 1936 I am passing in front of Mindy's restaurant on Broadway when the night manager suddenly opens the door and throws a character in a brown suit at me.

Fortunately, the character just misses me, and hits a yellow short that is standing at the kerb, and dents a mudguard, because he is a little character, and the night manager of Mindy's can throw that kind with an incurve.

Naturally, I am greatly vexed, and I am thinking of stepping into Mindy's and asking the night manager how dare he hurl missiles of this nature at me, when I remember that the night manager does not care for me, either, and in fact he hates me from head to foot, and does not permit me in Mindy's except on Fridays, because of course he does not have the heart to keep me from enjoying my chicken soup with matzoth dumplings once a week.

So I let the incident pass, and watch the jockey of the yellow short nail the character in the brown suit with a left hook that knocks him right under my feet, and then, as he gets up and dusts himself off with his hands and starts up the street, I see that he is nobody but a character by the name of Asleep, who is called by this name because he always goes around with his eyes half closed, and looking as if he is dozing off.

Well, here is a spectacle that really brings tears to my eyes, as I can remember when just a few years back the name of Asleep strikes terror to the hearts of one and all on Broadway, and everywhere else in this town for that matter, because in those days he is accounted one of the greatest characters in his line in the world, and in fact he is generally regarded as a genius.

Asleep's line is taking care of anybody that somebody wishes taken care of, and at one time he is the highest-priced character in the business. For several years along in the late 'twenties, he handles all of the late Dave the Dude's private business when Dave the Dude is at war with the late Big Moey, and when somebody finally takes care of Dave the Dude himself, Asleep is with Moey for quite a while.

In six or seven years, the chances are Asleep takes care of scores of characters of one kind and another, and he never looks for any publicity or glory. In fact, he is always a most retiring character, who goes about very quietly, minding his own affairs, and those who know him think very well of him indeed.

The bladders print many unkind stories about Asleep when he is finally lumbered in 1931 and sent to college, and some of them call him a torpedo, and a trigger, and I do not know what all else, and these names hurt Asleep's feelings, especially as they seem to make him out no better than a ruffian. In fact, one bladder speaks of him as a killer, and this title causes Asleep to wince more than anything else.

He is in college at Dannemora from 1931 until the late spring of 1936, and although I hear he is back, this is the first time I see him in person, and I hasten to overtake him to express my sympathy with him on his treatment by the night manager of Mindy's and also by the jockey of the yellow short, and to deplore the lack of respect now shown on Broadway for a character such as Asleep.

He seems glad to see me, and he accepts my expressions gratefully, and we go into the Bridle Grill and have a couple of drinks and then Asleep says to me like this:

'I only go into Mindy's seeking a situation,' he says. 'I hear Benny Barker, the bookie, is in there, and I understand that he has a disagreement with another bookie by the name of Jersey Cy down at Aqueduct, and that Jersey Cy punches Benny's beezer for him. So,' Asleep says, 'I figure Benny will wish to have Cy taken care of immediately and that it will be a nice quick pickup for me, because in the old days when Benny is a bootie, he is one of my best customers.

'It is the first time I see Benny since I get back,' Asleep says, 'but instead of being glad to see me, he seems very distant to me, and the minute I begin canvassing him for the business, he turns as white as one of Mindy's napkins, and in fact whiter, and says for me to get out of there, or he will call the law.

'Benny says he will never even dream of such a thing as having anybody taken care of, and,' Asleep says, 'when I start to remind him of a couple of incidents back down the years, he carries on in a way you will never believe. I even offer to cut my fee for him,' Asleep says, 'but Benny only gets more excited, and keeps yelling no, no, no, until the night manager appears, and you see for yourself what happens to me. I am publicly embarrassed,' he says.

'Well, Sleeps,' I say, 'to tell the truth, I am somewhat amazed that you do not out with that thing and resent these familiarities.'

But Asleep seems somewhat horrified at this suggestion, and he sets his glass down, and gazes at me a while in pained silence, and finally he says:

'Why,' he says, 'I hope and trust that you do not think I will ever use that thing except for professional purposes, and when I am paid for same. Why,' he says, 'in all my practice, covering a matter of nearly ten years, I never lift a finger against as much as a flea unless it is a business proposition, and I am not going to begin now.'

Well, I remember that this is indeed Asleep's reputation in the old days, and that a midget can walk up to him and tweak his ear without running any risk, and of course I am bound to respect his ethics, although I am sorry he cannot see his way clear to making an exception in the case of the night manager of Mindy's.

'I do not understand the way times change since I am in college,' Asleep says. 'Nobody around here wishes anybody taken care of any more. I call on quite a number of old customers of mine before I visit Benny Barker, but they have nothing for me, and none of them suggests that I call again. I fear I am *passé*,' Asleep says. 'Yet I am the one who first brings the idea to Brooklyn of putting them in the sack. I originate picking them off in barber chairs. I am always first and foremost with innovations in my business, and now there is no business.

'It is a tough break for me,' Asleep says, 'just when I happen to need a situation more than at any other time in my life. I simply must make good,' he says, 'because I am in love and wish to be married. I am in love with Miss Anna Lark, who dances behind bubbles over in the Starlight Restaurant. Yes,' he says, 'Miss Anna Lark is my sweet-pea, and she loves me as dearly as I love her, or anyway,' he says, 'she so states no longer ago than two hours.'

'Well,' I say, 'Miss Anna Lark has a shape that is a lulu. Even behind bubbles,' I say, and this is a fact that is well known to one and all on Broadway, but I do not consider it necessary to mention to Asleep that it is also pretty well known along Broadway that

Benny Barker, the bookie, is deeply interested in Miss Anna Lark, and, to tell the truth, is practically off his onion about her, because I am by no means a chirper.

'I often notice her shape myself,' Asleep says. 'In fact, it is one of the things that starts our romance before I go away to college. It seems to me it is better then than it is now, but,' he says, 'a shape is not everything in this life, although I admit it is never any knock. Miss Anna Lark waits patiently for me all the time I am away, and once she writes me a screeve, so you can see that this is undoubtedly true love.

'But,' Asleep says, 'Miss Anna Lark now wishes to abandon the bubble dodge, and return to her old home in Miami, Florida, where her papa is in the real-estate business. Miss Anna Lark feels that there is no future behind bubbles, especially,' he says, 'since she recently contracts arthritis in both knees from working in drafty night-clubs. And she wishes me to go to Miami, Florida, too, and perhaps engage in the real-estate business like her papa, and acquire some scratch so we can be married, and raise up children, and all this and that, and be happy ever after.

'But,' Asleep says, 'it is very necessary for me to get hold of a taw to make a start, and at this time I do not have as much as two white quarters to rub together in my pants' pocket, and neither has Miss Anna Lark, and from what I hear, the same thing goes for Miss Anna Lark's papa, and with conditions in my line what they are, I am greatly depressed, and scarcely know which way to turn.'

Well, naturally, I feel very sorry for Asleep, but I can offer no suggestions of any value at the moment, and in fact the best I can do is to stake him to a few dibs for walk-about money, and then I leave him in the Bridle Grill looking quite sad and forlorn, to be sure.

I do not see Asleep for several months after this, and am wondering what becomes of him, and I watch the bladders for news of happenings that may indicate he finally gets a break, but nothing of interest appears, and then one day I run into him at Broadway and Forty-sixth Street.

He is all sharpened up in new clothes, and a fresh shave, and he is carrying a suitcase, and looks very prosperous, indeed, and he seems happy to see me, and leads me around into Dinty Moore's, and sits me down at a table, and orders up some drinks, and then he says to me like this:

'Now,' he says, 'I will tell you what happens. After you leave me in the Bridle Grill, I sit down and take to reading one of the evening bladders, and what I read about is a war in a place by the name of Spain, and from what I read, I can see that it is a war between two different mobs living in this Spain, each of which wishes to control the situation. It reminds me of Chicago the time Big Moey sends me out to Al.

'Thinks I to myself,' Asleep says, 'where there is a war of this nature, there may be employment for a character of my experience, and I am sitting there pondering this matter when who comes in looking for me but Benny Barker, the bookie.

'Well,' Asleep says, 'Benny states that he gets to thinking of me after I leave Mindy's, and he says he remembers that he really has a soft place in his heart for me, and that while he has no business for me any more, he will be glad to stake me to go wherever I think I may find something, and I remember what I am just reading in the evening bladder, and I say all right, Spain.

' "Where is this Spain?" Benny Barker asks.

'Well,' Asleep says, 'of course I do not know where it is myself, so we inquire of Professor D, the educated horse player, and he says it is to hell and gone from here. He says it is across the sea, and Benny Barker says he will arrange my passage there at once, and furthermore that he will give me a thousand slugs in ready, and I can pay him back at my convenience. Afterward,' Asleep says, 'I recall that Benny Barker seems greatly pleased that I am going far away, but I figure his conscience hurts him for the manner in which he rebuffs me in Mindy's, and he wishes to round himself up with me.

'So I go to this Spain,' Asleep says, 'and now,' he says, 'if you wish to hear any more, I will be glad to oblige.'

Well, I tell Asleep that if he will keep calling the waiter at regular intervals, he may proceed, and Asleep proceeds as follows:

I go to this Spain seeking employment, and you will scarcely believe the trouble and inconvenience I am put to in getting there. I go by way of a ship that takes me to France, which is a place I remember somewhat, because I visit there in my early youth, in 1918, with the 77th Division, and which is a nice place, at that, especially the *Folies-Bergère*, and I go across France and down to a little jerk-water town just over the border from this Spain, and who do I run into sitting in front of a small gin-mill in the town but a Spanish character by the name of Manuel something.

He is once well known along Broadway as a heavy-weight fighter, and he is by no means a bad fighter in his day, and he now has a pair of scrambled ears to prove it. Furthermore, he is bobbing slightly, and seems to have a few marbles in his mouth, but he is greatly pleased to see me.

Manuel speaks English very good, considering the marbles, and he tells me he is personally in the fighting in this Spain for several weeks, but he is unable to find out what he is fighting about, so finally he gets tired, and is over in France taking a recess, and when I tell him I am going to this Spain, and what for, he says he has no doubt I will do very nice for myself, because of course Manuel knows my reputation in the old days in New York.

Furthermore, he says he will go with me, and act as my manager, and maybe take a piece of my earnings, just as his American managers do with him when he is active in the ring, and when I ask him what he calls a piece, he says 65 per cent. is the way his American managers always slice him, but naturally I do not agree to any such terms. Still, I can see that Manuel is such a character as may come in handy to me, what with knowing how to speak Spanish, as well as English, so I say I will look out for him very nicely when the time comes for a settlement, and this satisfies him.

We go across the border into this Spain by night, and Manuel says he will lead me to a spot where the fighting is very good, and by and by we come to a fair-sized town, with houses, and steeples, and all this and that, and which has a name I do not remember, and which I cannot pronounce, even if I do remember it.

Manuel says we are now in the war, and in fact I can hear shooting going on although it does not seem to be interfering with public business in the town, as many characters, male and female, are walking around and about, and up and down, and back and forth, and none of them seem to be disturbed by anything much.

But Manuel and I follow the sound of the shooting, and finally we come upon a large number of characters behind a breastworks made out of sandbags, and they all have rifles in their hands, and are shooting now and then at a big stone building on a high hill about three blocks away, and from this building also comes a lot of firing, and there are occasional bur-ur-ur-ups on both sides that I recognize as machine-guns, and bullets are zinging about the sandbags quite some.

Well, Manuel says this is some of the war, but all the characters behind the sandbags seem to be taking things easy, and in fact some are sitting in chairs and firing their rifles from a rest over the bags while so seated, and thinks I to myself, this is a very leisurely war, to be sure.

But about two blocks from the breastworks, and on a rise of ground almost as high as the hill the building is on, there is a field-gun, and this is also firing on the building about every fifteen minutes, and I can see that it seems to be doing some real damage, at that, what with knocking off pieces of the architecture, and punching holes in the roof, although now and then it lets go a shell that misses the mark in a way that will never be tolerated by the character who commands the battery I serve with in France.

Many of the characters behind the sandbags seem to know Manuel, who appears to be a famous character in this Spain, and they stop shooting, and gather about him, and there is much conversation among them, which of course I do not understand, so after a while I request Manuel to pay more attention to me and to kindly explain the situation I find here.

Well, Manuel says the building on the hill is an old castle and that it is being held by a lot of Spanish characters, male and female, who are as mad at the characters behind the sandbags as the Republicans are mad at the Democrats in my country, and maybe madder. Manuel says the characters in the castle represent one side of the war in this Spain, and the characters behind the sandbags represent the other side, although Manuel does not seem to know which is which, and naturally I do not care.

'Well,' I say to Manuel, 'this is a good place to start business. Tell them who I am,' I say, 'and ask them how much they will give me for taking care of these parties in the castle.'

So Manuel makes quite a speech, and while I do not understand what he is saying, I can see that he is putting me away with them very good, because they are gazing at me with great interest and respect. When he concludes his speech they give me a big cheer and crowd around me shaking hands, and I see Manuel talking with some characters who seem to be the mains in this situation, and they are listening eagerly to his remarks, and nodding their heads, and Manuel says to me like this:

'Well,' Manuel says, 'I tell them you are the greatest American gangster that ever lives, and that they undoubtedly see you often in the movies, and they are in favour of your proposition one hundred per cent. They are anxious to see how you operate,' Manuel says, 'because they wish to install similar methods in this country when things get settled down.'

'Kindly omit referring to me as a gangster,' I say. 'It is a most uncouth word, and besides I never operate with a gang in my life.'

'Well, all right,' Manuel says, 'but it is a word they understand. However,' he says, 'the trouble here is they do not have much *dinero*, which is money. In fact, they say the best they can offer you to take care of the parties in the castle is two pesetas per head.'

'How much is two pesetas?' I ask.

'The last time I am here, it is about forty cents in your language,' Manuel says.

Naturally, I am very indignant at this offer, because in my time I get as high as twenty thousand dollars for taking care of a case, and never less than five hundred, except once when I do a favour for one-fifty, but Manuel claims it is not such a bad offer as it sounds, as he says that at the moment two pesetas is by no means alfalfa in this Spain, especially as there are maybe four hundred heads in the castle, counting everything.

Manuel says it really is an exceptional offer as the characters behind the sandbags are anxious to conclude the siege because certain friends of the parties in the castle are arriving in a near-by town, and anyway, sitting behind these sandbags is getting most monotonous to one and all. Furthermore, Manuel says, when they are not sitting behind the sandbags, these characters are required to work every day digging a tunnel into the hill under the castle, and they regard this work as most enervating.

Manuel says the idea of the tunnel is to plant dynamite under the castle and blow it up.

'But you see,' Manuel says, 'digging is no work for proud souls such as Spaniards, so if you can think of some other way of taking care of these parties in the castle, it will be a great relief to my friends here.'

'To the dickens with these skinflints,' I say. 'Let us go to the castle and see what the parties there will give us for taking care of these cheap skates behind the sandbags. Never,' I say, 'will I accept such a reduction.'

Well, Manuel tells the mains behind the sandbags that I will take their offer under consideration, but that I am so favourably disposed towards it that I am going into the castle and examine the surroundings, and this pleases them no little, so Manuel ties his handkerchief on a stick and says this is a flag of truce and will get us into the castle safe and sound, and we set out.

Presently characters appear at the windows, and at holes in the walls of the castle, and Manuel holds a conversation with them in the Spanish language, and by and by they admit us to the castle yard, and one character with whiskers leads us into the building and down stone steps until we arrive in what seems to be a big basement far underground.

And in this basement I behold a very unusual scene to be sure. There are many characters present, male and female, also numerous small children, and they seem to be living in great confusion, but they are greatly interested in us when we appear, especially a tall, thin elderly character with white hair, and a white tash, and a white goatee, who seems to be a character of some authority.

In fact, Manuel says he is nobody but a character by the name of General Pedro Vega, and that this castle is his old family home, and that he is leader of these other characters in the basement.

I can see at once that Manuel and the general are old friends, because they make quite a fuss over meeting up in this manner, and then Manuel introduces me, and delivers another speech about me, explaining what a wonderful character I am. When he gets through, the general turns to me, and in very good English he speaks as follows:

'I am very glad to meet you, Señor Asleep,' he says. 'I once live in your country a couple of years,' he says. 'I live in your Miami, Florida.'

Well, I am glad to find somebody who can talk English, so I can do my own negotiating, and in a few words I state my proposition to the general to take care of the characters behind the sandbags, and call for his bid on same.

'Alas,' the general says, 'money is something we do not have. If you are offering to take care of the enemy at one centavo each,' he says, 'we still cannot pay. I am most regretful. It will be a big convenience to have you take care of the enemy, because we can then escape from this place and join our friends in a near-by city. Our food runs low,' he says. 'So does our ammunition. Some of our females and children are ill. The longer we remain here the worse it gets.

'If I do not know the calibre of the enemy,' he says, 'I will gladly surrender. But,' he says, 'we will then all be backed up against a wall and executed. It is better that we die here.'

Well, being backed up against a wall strikes me as a most undesirable fate, to be sure, but of course it is nothing to me, and all I am thinking of is that this is a very peculiar country where nobody has any scratch, and it is commencing to remind me of home. And I am also thinking that the only thing I can do is to accept the two pesetas per head offered by the characters behind the sandbags when a very beautiful young Judy, with long black hair hanging down her back, approaches and speaks to me at some length in the Spanish language. Manuel says:

'She says,' he says, ' "Oh, sir, if you can help us escape from this place you will earn my undying gratitude." She says,' Manuel says, ' "I am in love with a splendid young character by the name of Señor José Valdez, who is waiting for me with our friends in the near-by town. We are to be married as soon as the cruel war is over," she says,' Manuel says. 'It seems to be a most meritorious case,' Manuel says.

Now naturally this statement touches my heart no little, because I am in love myself, and besides the young Judy begins weeping, and if there is one thing I cannot stand it is female tears, and in fact my sweet-pea, Miss Anna Lark, can always make me do almost anything she wishes by breaking out crying. But of course business is business in this case, and I cannot let sentiment interfere, so I am about to bid one and all farewell when General Pedro Vega says:

'Wait!'

And with this he disappears into another part of the basement, but is back pretty soon with a small black tin box, and out of this box he takes a batch of papers, and hands them to me, and says:

'Here are the deeds to some property in your Miami, Florida,' he says. 'I pay much money for it in 1925. They tell me at the time I am lucky to get the property at the price, but,' he says, 'I will be honest with you. It is unimproved property, and all I ever get out of it so far is notices that taxes are due, which I always pay promptly. But now I fear I will never get back to your Miami, Florida, again, and if you will take care of enough of the enemy for us to escape, the deeds are yours. This is all I have to offer.'

Well, I say I will take the deeds and study them over and let him know my answer as soon as possible, and then I retire with Manuel, but what I really study more than anything else is the matter of the beautiful young Judy who yearns for her sweet-pea, and there is no doubt but what my studying of her is a point in favour of General Vega's proposition in my book, although I also do some strong studying of the fact that taking care of these characters in the castle is a task that will be very tough.

So after we leave the castle, I ask Manuel if he supposes there is a telegraph office in operation in town, and he says of course there is, or how can the newspaper scribes get their thrilling stories of the war out, so I get him to take me there, and I send a cablegram addressed to Mr. Lark, real estate, Miami, Florida, U.S.A., which reads as follows:

IS FIFTY ACRES LANDSCRABBLE SECTION ANY ACCOUNT

Then there is nothing for me to do but wait around until I get an answer, and this takes several days, and I devote this period to seeing the sights with Manuel, and I wish to say that some of the sights are very interesting. Finally, I drop around to the telegraph office, and sure enough there is a message there for me, collect, which says like this:

LANDSCRABBLE SECTION GREAT POSSIBILITIES STOP WHY LARK

Now I do not know Mr. Lark personally, and he does not know me, and the chances are he never even hears of me before, but I figure that if he is half as smart as his daughter, Miss Anna Lark, his judgment is worth following, so I tell Manuel it looks as if the deal with General Vega is on, and I begin giving my undivided attention to the case.

I can see at once that the key to the whole situation as far as I am concerned is the field-piece on the hill, because there are really too many characters behind the sandbags for me to take care of by myself, or even with the assistance of Manuel, and of course I do not care to get Manuel involved in my personal business affairs any more than I can help.

However, at my request he makes a few innocent inquiries among the characters behind the sandbags, and he learns that there are always seven characters on the hill with the gun, and that they sleep in little home-made shelters made of boards, and canvas, and tin, and one thing and another, and that these shelters are scattered over the top of the hill, and the top of the hill is maybe the width of a baseball diamond.

But I can observe for myself that they do no firing from the hilltop after sundown, and they seldom show any lights, which is maybe because they do not wish to have any aeroplanes come along and drop a few hot apples on them.

Manuel says that the characters behind the sandbags are asking about me, and he says they are so anxious to secure my services that he will not be surprised if I cannot get three pesetas per head, and I can see that Manuel thinks I am making a mistake not to dicker with them further.

But I tell him I am now committed to General Vega, and I have Manuel obtain a twelve-inch file for me in the city, and also some corks out of wine bottles, and I take the file and hammer it down, and smooth it out, and sharpen it up nicely, and I make a handle for it out of wood, according to my own original ideas, and I take the corks, and burn them good, and I find a big piece of black cloth and make myself a sort of poncho out of this by cutting a hole in the centre for my head to go through.

Then I wait until it comes on a night to suit me, and it is a dark night, and rainy, and blowy, and I black up my face and hands with the burnt cork, and slip the black cloth over my clothes, and put my file down the back of my neck where I can reach it quickly, and make my way very quietly to the foot of the hill on which the field-gun is located.

Now in the darkness, I begin crawling on my hands and knees, and wiggling along on my stomach up the hill, and I wish to state that it is a monotonous task because I can move only a few feet at a clip, and there are many sharp rocks in my path, and once an insect of some nature crawls up my pant leg and gives me a severe nip.

The hill is maybe as high as a two-story building, and very steep, and it takes me over an hour to wiggle my way to the top, and sometimes I pause *en route* and wonder if it is worth it. And then I think of the beautiful young Judy in the castle, and of the property in Miami, Florida, and of Miss Anna Lark, and I keep on wiggling.

Well, just as Manuel reports, there is a sentry on duty on top of the hill, and I can make out his shape in the darkness leaning on his rifle, and this sentry is a very large character, and at first I figure that he may present difficulties, but when I wiggle up close to him I observe that he seems to be dozing, and it is quiet as can be on the hilltop.

The sentry is really no trouble at all, and then I wiggle my way slowly along in and out of the little shelters, and in some shelters there is but one character, and in others two, and in one, three, and it is these three that confuse me somewhat, as they are three more than the seven Manuel mentions in his census of the scene, and I will overlook them entirely if one of them does not snore more than somewhat.

Personally, I will always say that taking care of these ten characters one after the other, and doing it so quietly that not one of them ever wakes up, is the high spot of my entire career, especially when you consider that I am somewhat rusty from lack of experience, and that my equipment is very crude.

Well, when morning dawns, there I am in charge of the hilltop, and with a field-gun at my disposal, and I discover that it is nothing but a French 75, with which I am quite familiar, and by and by Manuel joins me, and while the characters behind the sandbags are enjoying their breakfast, and the chances are, not thinking of much, I plant four shells among them so fast I ruin their morning meal, because, if I do say it myself, I am better than a raw hand with a French 75.

Then I remember that the characters who are boring under the castle are perhaps inside the tunnel at this time, so I peg away at the hole in the hill until the front of it caves in and blocks up the hole very neatly, and Manuel afterward claims that I wedged in the entire night-shift.

Well, of course these proceedings are visible to the occupants of the castle, and it is not long before I see General Pedro Vega come marching out of the castle with the whole kit and caboodle, of characters, male and female, and small children behind him, and they are laughing and shouting, and crying and carrying on no little.

And the last I see of them as they go hurrying off in the direction of the near-by town where their friends are located, the beautiful young Judy is bringing up the rear and throwing kisses at me and waving a flag, and I ask Manuel to kindly identify this flag for me so I will always remember which side of the war in this Spain it is that I assist.

But Manuel says his eyesight is bad ever since the night Jim Sharkey sticks a thumb in his eye in the fifth round in Madison Square Garden, and from this distance he cannot tell whose flag it is, and in fact, Manuel says, he does not give a Spanish cuss-word.

'And there you are,' Asleep says to me in Dinty Moore's.

'So,' I say, 'you are now back in New York looking for business again?'

'Oh, no,' Asleep says. 'I now reside in Miami, Florida, and I am going to marry Miss Anna Lark next month. I am doing very well for myself, too,' he says. 'You see, we turn the property that I get from General Vega into a cemetery, and I am now selling lots in same for our firm which is headed by Miss Anna Lark's papa. Manuel is our head grave-digger, and we are all very happy,' Asleep says.

Well, afterward I hear that the first lot Asleep sells is to the family of the late Benny Barker, the bookie, who passes away during the race meeting in Miami, Florida, of pneumonia, superinduced by lying out all night in a ditch full of water near the home of Miss Anna Lark, although I also understand that the fact that Benny is tied up in a sack in the ditch is considered a slight contributing cause of his last illness.

A Piece of Pie

On Boylston Street, in the city of Boston, Mass., there is a joint where you can get as nice a broiled lobster as anybody ever slaps a lip over, and who is in there one evening partaking of this tidbit but a character by the name of Horse Thief and me.

This Horse Thief is called Horsey for short, and he is not called by this name because he ever steals a horse but because it is the consensus of public opinion from coast to coast that he may steal one if the opportunity presents.

Personally, I consider Horsey a very fine character, because any time he is holding anything he is willing to share his good fortune with one and all, and at this time in Boston he is holding plenty. It is the time we make the race meeting at Suffolk Down, and Horsey gets to going very good, indeed, and in fact he is now a character of means, and is my host against the broiled lobster.

Well, at a table next to us are four or five characters who all seem to be well-dressed, and stout-set, and red-faced, and prosperous-looking, and who all speak with the true Boston accent, which consists of many ah's and very few r's. Characters such as these are familiar to anybody who is ever in Boston very much, and they are bound to be politicians, retired cops, or contractors, because Boston is really quite infested with characters of this nature.

I am paying no attention to them, because they are drinking local ale, and talking loud, and long ago I learn that when a Boston character is engaged in aleing himself up, it is a good idea to let him alone, because the best you can get out of him is maybe a boff on the beezer. But Horsey is in there on the old Ear-ie, and very much interested in their conversation, and finally I listen myself just to hear what is attracting his attention, when one of the characters speaks as follows:

'Well,' he says, 'I am willing to bet ten thousand dollars that he can outeat anybody in the United States any time.'

Now at this, Horsey gets right up and steps over to the table and bows and smiles in a friendly way on one and all, and says:

'Gentlemen,' he says, 'pardon the intrusion, and excuse me for billing in, but,' he says, 'do I understand you are speaking of a great eater who resides in your fair city?'

Well, these Boston characters all gaze at Horsey in such a hostile manner that I am expecting any one of them to get up and request him to let them miss him, but he keeps on bowing and smiling, and they can see that he is a gentleman, and finally one of them says:

'Yes,' he says, 'we are speaking of a character by the name of Joel Duffle. He is without doubt the greatest eater alive. He just wins a unique wager. He bets a character from Bangor, Me., that he can eat a whole window display of oysters in this very restaurant, and he not only eats all the oysters but he then wishes to wager that he can also eat the shells, but,' he says, 'it seems that the character from Bangor, Me., unfortunately taps out on the first proposition and has nothing with which to bet on the second.'

'Very interesting,' Horsey says. 'Very interesting, if true, but,' he says, 'unless my ears deceive me, I hear one of you state that he is willing to wager ten thousand dollars on this eater of yours against anybody in the United States.'

'Your ears are perfect,' another of the Boston characters says. 'I state it, although,' he says, 'I admit it is a sort of figure of speech. But I state it all right,' he says, 'and never let it be said that a Conway ever pigs it on a betting proposition.'

'Well,' Horsey says, 'I do not have a tenner on me at the moment, but,' he says, 'I have here a thousand dollars to put up as a forfeit that I can produce a character who will outeat your party for ten thousand, and as much more as you care to put up.'

And with this, Horsey outs with a bundle of coarse notes and tosses it on the table, and right away one of the Boston characters, whose name turns out to be Carroll, slaps his hand on the money and says:

'Bet.'

Well, now this is prompt action to be sure, and if there is one thing I admire more than anything else, it is action, and I can see that these are characters of true sporting instincts and I commence wondering where I can raise a few dibs to take a piece of Horsey's proposition, because of course I know that he has nobody in mind to do the eating for his side but Nicely-Nicely Jones.

And knowing Nicely-Nicely Jones, I am prepared to wager all the money I can possibly raise that he can outeat anything that walks on two legs. In fact, I will take a chance on Nicely-Nicely against anything on four legs, except maybe an elephant, and at that he may give the elephant a photo finish.

I do not say that Nicely-Nicely is the greatest eater in all history, but what I do say is he belongs up there as a contender. In fact, Professor D, who is a professor in a college out West before he turns to playing the horses for a livelihood, and who makes a study of history in his time, says he will not be surprised but what Nicely-Nicely figures one-two.

Professor D says we must always remember that Nicely-Nicely eats under the handicaps of modern civilization, which require that an eater use a knife and fork, or anyway a knife, while in the old days eating with the hands was a popular custom and much faster. Professor D says he has no doubt that under the old rules Nicely-Nicely will hang up a record that will endure through the ages, but of course maybe Professor D overlays Nicely-Nicely somewhat.

Well, now that the match is agreed upon, naturally Horsey and the Boston characters begin discussing where it is to take place, and one of the Boston characters suggests a neutral ground, such as New London, Conn., or Providence, R.I., but Horsey holds out for New York, and it seems that Boston characters are always ready to visit New York, so he does not meet with any great opposition on this point.

They all agree on a date four weeks later so as to give the principals plenty of time to get ready, although Horsey and I know that this is really unnecessary as far as Nicely-Nicely is concerned, because one thing about him is he is always in condition to eat.

This Nicely-Nicely Jones is a character who is maybe five feet eight inches tall, and about five feet nine inches wide, and when he is in good shape he will weigh upward of two hundred and eighty-three pounds. He is a horse player by trade, and eating is really just a hobby, but he is undoubtedly a wonderful eater even when he is not hungry.

Well, as soon as Horsey and I return to New York, we hasten to Mindy's restaurant on Broadway and relate the bet Horsey makes in Boston, and right away so many citizens, including Mindy himself, wish to take a piece of the proposition that it is oversubscribed by a large sum in no time.

Then Mindy remarks that he does not see Nicely-Nicely Jones for a month of Sundays, and then everybody present remembers that they do not see Nicely-Nicely around lately, either, and this leads to a discussion of where Nicely-Nicely can be, although up to this moment if nobody sees Nicely-Nicely but once in the next ten years it will be considered sufficient.

Well, Willie the Worrier, who is a bookmaker by trade, is among those present, and he remembers that the last time he looks for Nicely-Nicely hoping to collect a marker of some years' standing, Nicely-Nicely is living at the Rest Hotel in West Forty-ninth Street, and nothing will do Horsey but I must go with him over to the Rest to make inquiry for Nicely-Nicely, and there we learn that he leaves a forwarding address away up on Morningside Heights in care of somebody by the name of Slocum.

So Horsey calls a short, and away we go to this address, which turns out to be a five-story walk-up apartment, and a card downstairs shows that Slocum lives on the top floor. It takes Horsey and me ten minutes to walk up the five flights as we are by no means accustomed to exercise of this nature, and when we finally reach a door marked Slocum, we are plumb tuckered out, and have to sit down on the top step and rest a while.

Then I ring the bell at this door marked Slocum, and who appears but a tall young Judy with black hair who is without doubt beautiful, but who is so skinny we have to look twice to see her, and when I ask her if she can give me any information about a party named Nicely-Nicely Jones, she says to me like this:

'I guess you mean Quentin,' she says. 'Yes,' she says, 'Quentin is here. Come in, gentlemen.'

So we step into an apartment, and as we do so a thin, sickly looking character gets up out of a chair by the window, and in a weak voice says good evening. It is a good evening, at that, so Horsey and I say good evening right back at him, very polite, and then we stand there waiting for Nicely-Nicely to appear, when the beautiful skinny young Judy says:

'Well,' she says, 'this is Mr. Quentin Jones.'

Then Horsey and I take another swivel at the thin character, and we can see that it is nobody but Nicely-Nicely, at that, but the way he changes since we last observe him is practically shocking to us both, because he is undoubtedly all shrunk up. In fact, he looks as if he is about half what he is in his prime, and his face is pale and thin, and his eyes are away back in his head, and while we both shake hands with him it is some time before either of us is able to speak. Then Horsey finally says:

'Nicely,' he says, 'can we have a few words with you in private on a very important proposition?'

Well, at this, and before Nicely-Nicely can answer aye, yes, or no, the beautiful skinny young Judy goes out of the room and slams a door behind her, and Nicely-Nicely says:

'My fiancée, Miss Hilda Slocum,' he says. 'She is a wonderful character. We are to be married as soon as I lose twenty pounds more. It will take a couple of weeks longer,' he says.

'My goodness gracious, Nicely,' Horsey says. 'What do you mean lose twenty pounds more? You are practically emaciated now. Are you just out of a sick bed, or what?'

'Why,' Nicely-Nicely says, 'certainly I am not out of a sick bed. I am never healthier in my life. I am on a diet. I lose eighty-three pounds in two months, and am now down to two hundred. I feel great,' he says. 'It is all because of my fiancée, Miss Hilda Slocum. She rescues me from gluttony and obesity, or anyway,' Nicely-Nicely says, 'this is what Miss Hilda Slocum calls it. My, I feel good. I love Miss Hilda Slocum very much,' Nicely-Nicely says. 'It is a case of love at first sight on both sides the day we meet in the subway. I am wedged in one of the turnstile gates, and she kindly pushes on me from behind until I wiggle through. I can see she has a kind heart, so I date her up for a movie that night and propose to her while the newsreel is on. But,' Nicely-Nicely says, 'Hilda tells me at once that she will never marry a fat slob. She says I must put myself in her hands and she will reduce me by scientific methods and then she will become my ever-loving wife, but not before.

'So,' Nicely-Nicely says, 'I come to live here with Miss Hilda Slocum and her mother, so she can supervise my diet. Her mother is thinner than Hilda. And I surely feel great,' Nicely-Nicely says. 'Look,' he says.

And with this, he pulls out the waistband of his pants, and shows enough spare space to hide War Admiral in, but the effort seems to be a strain on him, and he has to sit down in his chair again.

'My goodness gracious,' Horsey says. 'What do you eat, Nicely?'

'Well,' Nicely-Nicely says, 'I eat anything that does not contain starch, but,' he says, 'of course everything worth eating contains starch, so I really do not eat much of anything whatever. My fiancée, Miss Hilda Slocum, arranges my diet. She is an expert dietician and runs a widely known department in a diet magazine by the name of *Let's Keep House.*'

Then Horsey tells Nicely-Nicely of how he is matched to eat against this Joel Duffle, of Boston, for a nice side bet, and how he has a forfeit of a thousand dollars already posted for appearance, and how many of Nicely-Nicely's admirers along Broadway are looking to win themselves out of all their troubles by betting on him, and at first Nicely-Nicely listens with great interest, and his eyes are shining like six bits, but then he becomes very sad, and says:

'It is no use, gentlemen,' he says. 'My fiancée, Miss Hilda Slocum, will never hear of me going off my diet even for a little while. Only yesterday I try to talk her into letting me have a little pumpernickel instead of toasted whole wheat bread, and she says if I even think of such a thing again, she will break our engagement. Horsey,' he says, 'do you ever eat toasted whole wheat bread for a month hand running? Toasted?' he says.

'No,' Horsey says. 'What I eat is nice, white French bread, and corn muffins, and hot biscuits with gravy on them.'

'Stop,' Nicely-Nicely says. 'You are eating yourself into an early grave, and, furthermore,' he says, 'you are breaking my heart. But,' he says, 'the more I think of my following depending on me in this emergency, the sadder it makes me feel to think I am unable to oblige them. However,' he says, 'let us call Miss Hilda Slocum in on an outside chance and see what her reactions to your proposition are.'

So we call Miss Hilda Slocum in, and Horsey explains our predicament in putting so much faith in Nicely-Nicely only to find him dieting, and Miss Hilda Slocum's reactions are to order Horsey and me out of the joint with instructions never to darken her door again, and when we are a block away we can still hear her voice speaking very firmly to Nicely-Nicely.

Well, personally, I figure this ends the matter, for I can see that Miss Hilda Slocum is a most determined character, indeed, and the chances are it does end it, at that, if Horsey does not happen to get a wonderful break.

He is at Belmont Park one afternoon, and he has a real good thing in a jump race, and when a brisk young character in a hard straw hat and eyeglasses comes along and asks him what he likes, Horsey mentions this good thing, figuring he will move himself in for a few dibs if the good thing connects.

Well, it connects all right, and the brisk young character is very grateful to Horsey for his information, and is giving him plenty of much-obliges, and nothing else, and Horsey is about to mention that they do not accept much-obliges at his hotel, when the brisk young character mentions that he is nobody but Mr. McBurgle and that he is the editor of the *Let's Keep House* magazine, and for Horsey to drop in and see him any time he is around his way.

Naturally, Horsey remembers what Nicely-Nicely says about Miss Hilda Slocum working for this *Let's Keep House* magazine, and he relates the story of the eating contest to Mr. McBurgle and asks him if he will kindly use his influence with Miss Hilda Slocum to get her to release Nicely-Nicely from his diet long enough for the contest. Then Horsey gives Mr. McBurgle a tip on another winner, and Mr. McBurgle must use plenty of influence on Miss Hilda Slocum at once, as the next day she calls Horsey up at his hotel before he is out of bed, and speaks to him as follows:

'Of course,' Miss Hilda Slocum says, 'I will never change my attitude about Quentin, but,' she says, 'I can appreciate that he feels very bad about you gentlemen relying on him and having to disappoint you. He feels that he lets you down, which is by no means true, but it weighs upon his mind. It is interfering with his diet.

'Now,' Miss Hilda Slocum says, 'I do not approve of your contest, because,' she says, 'it is placing a premium on gluttony, but I have a friend by the name of Miss Violette Shumberger who may answer your purpose. She is my dearest friend from childhood, but it is only because I love her dearly that this friendship endures. She is extremely fond of eating,' Miss Hilda Slocum says. 'In spite of my pleadings, and my warnings, and my own example, she persists in food. It is disgusting to me but I finally learn that it is no use arguing with her.

'She remains my dearest friend,' Miss Hilda Slocum says, 'though she continues her practice of eating, and I am informed that she is phenomenal in this respect. In fact,' she says, 'Nicely-Nicely tells me to say to you that if Miss Violette Shumberger can perform the eating exploits I relate to him from hearsay she is a lily. Good-bye,' Miss Hilda Slocum says. 'You cannot have Nicely-Nicely.'

Well, nobody cares much about this idea of a stand-in for Nicely-Nicely in such a situation, and especially a Judy that no one ever hears of before, and many citizens are in favour of pulling out of the contest altogether. But Horsey has his thousand-dollar forfeit to think of, and as no one can suggest anyone else, he finally arranges a personal meet with the Judy suggested by Miss Hilda Slocum.

He comes into Mindy's one evening with a female character who is so fat it is necessary to push three tables together to give her room for her lap, and it seems that this character is Miss Violette Shumberger. She weighs maybe two hundred and fifty pounds, but she is by no means an old Judy, and by no means bad-looking. She has a face the size of a town clock and enough chins for a fire escape, but she has a nice smile and pretty teeth, and a laugh that is so hearty it knocks the whipped cream off an order of strawberry shortcake on a table fifty feet away and arouses the indignation of a customer by the name of Goldstein who is about to consume same.

Well, Horsey's idea in bringing her into Mindy's is to get some kind of line on her eating form, and she is clocked by many experts when she starts putting on the hot meat, and it is agreed by one and all that she is by no means a selling-plater. In fact, by the time she gets through, even Mindy admits she has plenty of class, and the upshot of it all is Miss Violette Shumberger is chosen to eat against Joel Duffle.

Maybe you hear something of this great eating contest that comes off in New York one night in the early summer of 1937. Of course eating contests are by no means anything new, and in fact they are quite an old-fashioned pastime in some sections of this country, such as the South and East, but this is the first big public contest of the kind in years, and it creates no little comment along Broadway.

In fact, there is some mention of it in the blats, and it is not a
frivolous proposition in any respect, and more dough is wagered on
it than any other eating contest in history, with Joel Duffle a 6 to 5
favourite over Miss Violette Shumberger all the way through.

This Joel Duffle comes to New York several days before the
contest with the character by the name of Conway, and requests a
meet with Miss Violette Shumberger to agree on the final details
and who shows up with Miss Violette Shumberger as her coach
and adviser but Nicely-Nicely Jones. He is even thinner and more
peaked-looking than when Horsey and I see him last, but he says
he feels great, and that he is within six pounds of his marriage to
Miss Hilda Slocum.

Well, it seems that his presence is really due to Miss Hilda
Slocum herself, because she says that after getting her dearest
friend Miss Violette Shumberger into this jackpot, it is only fair to
do all she can to help her win it, and the only way she can think of
is to let Nicely-Nicely give Violette the benefit of his experience
and advice.

But afterward we learn that what really happens is that this
editor, Mr. McBurgle, gets greatly interested in the contest, and
when he discovers that in spite of his influence, Miss Hilda Slocum
declines to permit Nicely-Nicely to personally compete, but puts in
a pinch eater, he is quite indignant and insists on her letting
Nicely-Nicely school Violette.

Furthermore we afterward learn that when Nicely-Nicely returns to the apartment on Morningside Heights after giving
Violette a lesson, Miss Hilda Slocum always smells his breath to see
if he indulges in any food during his absence.

Well, this Joel Duffle is a tall character with stooped shoulders,
and a sad expression, and he does not look as if he can eat his way
out of a tea shoppe, but as soon as he commences to discuss the
details of the contest, anybody can see that he knows what time it
is in situations such as this. In fact, Nicely-Nicely says he can tell
at once from the way Joel Duffle talks that he is a dangerous
opponent, and he says while Miss Violette Shumberger impresses
him as an improving eater, he is only sorry she does not have more
seasoning.

This Joel Duffle suggests that the contest consist of twelve
courses of strictly American food, each side to be allowed to pick
six dishes, doing the picking in rotation, and specifying the weight
and quantity of the course selected to any amount the contestant

making the pick desires, and each course is to be divided for eating exactly in half, and after Miss Violette Shumberger and Nicely-Nicely whisper together a while, they say the terms are quite satisfactory.

Then Horsey tosses a coin for the first pick, and Joel Duffle says heads, and it is heads, and he chooses, as the first course, two quarts of ripe olives, twelve bunches of celery, and four pounds of shelled nuts, all this to be split fifty-fifty between them. Miss Violette Shumberger names twelve dozen cherry-stone clams as the second course, and Joel Duffle says two gallons of Philadelphia pepper-pot soup as the third.

Well, Miss Violette Shumberger and Nicely-Nicely whisper together again, and Violette puts in two five-pound striped bass, the heads and tails not to count in the eating, and Joel Duffle names a twenty-two pound roast turkey. Each vegetable is rated as one course, and Miss Violette Shumberger asks for twelve pounds of mashed potatoes with brown gravy. Joel Duffle says two dozen ears of corn on the cob, and Violette replies with two quarts of lima beans. Joel Duffle calls for twelve bunches of asparagus cooked in butter, and Violette mentions ten pounds of stewed new peas.

This gets them down to the salad, and it is Joel Duffle's play, so he says six pounds of mixed green salad with vinegar and oil dressing, and now Miss Violette Shumberger has the final selection, which is the dessert. She says it is a pumpkin pie, two feet across, and not less than three inches deep.

It is agreed that they must eat with knife, fork or spoon, but speed is not to count, and there is to be no time limit, except they cannot pause more than two consecutive minutes at any stage, except in case of hiccoughs. They can drink anything, and as much as they please, but liquids are not to count in the scoring. The decision is to be strictly on the amount of food consumed, and the judges are to take account of anything left on the plates after a course, but not of loose chewings on bosom or vest up to an ounce. The losing side is to pay for the food, and in case of a tie they are to eat it off immediately on ham and eggs only.

Well, the scene of this contest is the second-floor dining-room of Mindy's restaurant, which is closed to the general public for the occasion, and only parties immediately concerned in the contest are admitted. The contestants are seated on either side of a big table in the centre of the room, and each contestant has three waiters.

No talking and no rooting from the spectators is permitted, but of course in any eating contest the principals may speak to each other if they wish, though smart eaters never wish to do this, as talking only wastes energy, and about all they ever say to each other is please pass the mustard.

About fifty characters from Boston are present to witness the contest, and the same number of citizens of New York are admitted, and among them is this editor, Mr. McBurgle, and he is around asking Horsey if he thinks Miss Violette Shumberger is as good a thing as the jumper at the race track.

Nicely-Nicely arrives on the scene quite early, and his appearance is really most distressing to his old friends and admirers, as by this time he is shy so much weight that he is a pitiful scene, to be sure, but he tells Horsey and me that he thinks Miss Violette Shumberger has a good chance.

'Of course,' he says, 'she is green. She does not know how to pace herself in competition. But,' he says, 'she has a wonderful style. I love to watch her eat. She likes the same things I do in the days when I am eating. She is a wonderful character, too. Do you ever notice her smile?' Nicely-Nicely says.

'But,' he says, 'she is the dearest friend of my fiancée, Miss Hilda Slocum, so let us not speak of this. I try to get Hilda to come to see the contest, but she says it is repulsive. Well, anyway,' Nicely-Nicely says, 'I manage to borrow a few dibs, and am wagering on Miss Violette Shumberger. By the way,' he says, 'if you happen to think of it, notice her smile.'

Well, Nicely-Nicely takes a chair about ten feet behind Miss Violette Shumberger, which is as close as the judges will allow him, and he is warned by them that no coaching from the corners will be permitted, but of course Nicely-Nicely knows this rule as well as they do, and furthermore by this time his exertions seem to have left him without any more energy.

There are three judges, and they are all from neutral territory. One of these judges is a party from Baltimore, Md., by the name of Packard, who runs a restaurant, and another is a party from Providence, R.I., by the name of Croppers, who is a sausage manufacturer. The third judge is an old Judy by the name of Mrs. Rhubarb, who comes from Philadelphia, and once keeps an actors' boarding-house, and is considered an excellent judge of eaters.

Well, Mindy is the official starter, and at 8.30 p.m. sharp, when there is still much betting among the spectators, he outs with his watch, and says like this:

'Are you ready, Boston? Are you ready, New York?'

Miss Violette Shumberger and Joel Duffle both nod their heads, and Mindy says commence, and the contest is on, with Joel Duffle getting the jump at once on the celery and olives and nuts.

It is apparent that this Joel Duffle is one of these rough-and-tumble eaters that you can hear quite a distance off, especially on clams and soups. He is also an eyebrow eater, an eater whose eyebrows go up as high as the part in his hair as he eats, and this type of eater is undoubtedly very efficient.

In fact, the way Joel Duffle goes through the groceries down to the turkey causes the Broadway spectators some uneasiness, and they are whispering to each other that they only wish the old Nicely-Nicely is in there. But personally, I like the way Miss Violette Shumberger eats without undue excitement, and with great zest. She cannot keep close to Joel Duffle in the matter of speed in the early stages of the contest, as she seems to enjoy chewing her food, but I observe that as it goes along she pulls up on him, and I figure this is not because she is stepping up her pace, but because he is slowing down.

When the turkey finally comes on, and is split in two halves right down the middle, Miss Violette Shumberger looks greatly disappointed, and she speaks for the first time as follows:

'Why,' she says, 'where is the stuffing?'

Well, it seems that nobody mentions any stuffing for the turkey to the chef, so he does not make any stuffing, and Miss Violette Shumberger's disappointment is so plain to be seen that the confidence of the Boston characters is somewhat shaken. They can see that a Judy who can pack away as much fodder as Miss Violette Shumberger has to date, and then beef for stuffing, is really quite an eater.

In fact, Joel Duffle looks quite startled when he observes Miss Violette Shumberger's disappointment, and he gazes at her with great respect as she disposes of her share of the turkey, and the mashed potatoes, and one thing and another in such a manner that she moves up on the pumpkin pie on dead even terms with him. In fact, there is little to choose between them at this point, although the judge from Baltimore is calling the attention of the other judges to a turkey leg that he claims Miss Violette Shumberger does not clean as neatly as Joel Duffle does his, but the other judges dismiss this as a technicality.

Then the waiters bring on the pumpkin pie, and it is without doubt quite a large pie, and in fact it is about the size of a manhole cover, and I can see that Joel Duffle is observing this pie with a strange expression on his face, although to tell the truth I do not care for the expression on Miss Violette Shumberger's face, either.

Well, the pie is cut in two dead centre, and one half is placed before Miss Violette Shumberger and the other half before Joel Duffle, and he does not take more than two bites before I see him loosen his waistband and take a big swig of water, and thinks I to myself, he is now down to a slow walk, and the pie will decide the whole heat, and I am only wishing I am able to wager a little more dough on Miss Violette Shumberger. But about this moment, and before she as much as touches her pie, all of a sudden Violette turns her head and motions to Nicely-Nicely to approach her, and as he approaches, she whispers in his ear.

Now at this, the Boston character by the name of Conway jumps up and claims a foul and several other Boston characters join him in this claim, and so does Joel Duffle, although afterwards even the Boston characters admit that Joel Duffle is no gentleman to make such a claim against a lady.

Well, there is some confusion over this, and the judges hold a conference, and they rule that there is certainly no foul in the actual eating that they can see, because Miss Violette Shumberger does not touch her pie so far.

But they say that whether it is a foul otherwise all depends on whether Miss Violette Shumberger is requesting advice on the contest from Nicely-Nicely and the judge from Providence, R.I., wishes to know if Nicely-Nicely will kindly relate what passes between him and Violette so they may make a decision.

'Why,' Nicely-Nicely says, 'all she asks me is can I get her another piece of pie when she finishes the one in front of her.'

Now at this, Joel Duffle throws down his knife, and pushes back his plate with all but two bites of his pie left on it, and says to the Boston characters like this:

'Gentlemen,' he says, 'I am licked. I cannot eat another mouthful. You must admit I put up a game battle, but,' he says, 'it is useless for me to go on against this Judy who is asking for more pie before she even starts on what is before her. I am almost dying as it is, and I do not wish to destroy myself in a hopeless effort. Gentlemen,' he says, 'she is not human.'

Well, of course this amounts to throwing in the old napkin and Nicely-Nicely stands up on his chair, and says:

'Three cheers for Miss Violette Shumberger!'

Then Nicely-Nicely gives the first cheer in person, but the effort overtaxes his strength, and he falls off the chair in a faint just as Joel Duffle collapses under the table, and the doctors at the Clinic Hospital are greatly baffled to receive, from the same address at the same time, one patient who is suffering from undernourishment, and another patient who is unconscious from over-eating.

Well, in the meantime, after the excitement subsides, and wagers are settled, we take Miss Violette Shumberger to the main floor in Mindy's for a midnight snack, and when she speaks of her wonderful triumph, she is disposed to give much credit to Nicely-Nicely Jones.

'You see,' Violette says, 'what I really whisper to him is that I am a goner. I whisper to him that I cannot possibly take one bite of the pie if my life depends on it, and if he has any bets down to try and hedge them off as quickly as possible.

'I fear,' she says, 'that Nicely-Nicely will be greatly disappointed in my showing, but I have a confession to make to him when he gets out of the hospital. I forget about the contest,' Violette says, 'and eat my regular dinner of pig's knuckles and sauerkraut an hour before the contest starts and,' she says, 'I have no doubt this tends to affect my form somewhat. So,' she says, 'I owe everything to Nicely-Nicely's quick thinking.'

It is several weeks after the great eating contest that I run into Miss Hilda Slocum on Broadway and it seems to me that she looks much better nourished than the last time I see her, and when I mention this she says:

'Yes,' she says, 'I cease dieting. I learn my lesson,' she says. 'I learn that male characters do not appreciate anybody who tries to ward off surplus tissue. What male characters wish is substance. Why,' she says, 'only a week ago my editor, Mr. McBurgle, tells me he will love to take me dancing if only I get something on me for him to take hold of. I am very fond of dancing,' she says.

'But,' I say, 'what of Nicely-Nicely Jones? I do not see him around lately.'

'Why,' Miss Hilda Slocum says, 'do you not hear what this cad does? Why, as soon as he is strong enough to leave the hospital, he elopes with my dearest friend, Miss Violette Shumberger, leaving me a note saying something about two souls with but a single thought. They are down in Florida running a barbecue stand, and,' she says, 'the chances are, eating like seven mules.'

'Miss Slocum,' I say, 'can I interest you in a portion of Mindy's chicken fricassee?'

'With dumplings?' Miss Hilda Slocum says. 'Yes,' she says, 'you can. Afterwards I have a date to go dancing with Mr. McBurgle. I am crazy about dancing,' she says.

A Job for the Macarone

When the last race meeting of the winter season closes in Miami and it is time for one and all to move on to Maryland, I take a swivel at the weather reports one day and I observe that it is still down around freezing in those parts.

So thinks I to myself, I will remain in the sunny southland a while longer and continue enjoying the balmy breezes, and the ocean bathing, and all this and that, until the weather settles up yonder, and also until I acquire a blow stake, for at this time my bank-roll is worn down to a nubbin and, in fact, I do not have enough ready to get myself as far as Jax, even by walking.

Well, while waiting around Miami, trying to think of some way of making a scratch, I spend my evenings in the Shark Fin Grill, which is a little scatter on Biscayne Boulevard near the docks that is conducted by a friend of mine by the name of Chesty Charles.

He is called by this name because he has a chest like a tub and he walks with it stuck out in front of him, and the reason Charles keeps his chest out is because if he pulls it in, his stomach will take its place, only farther down, and Charles does not wish his stomach to show in this manner, as he likes to think he has a nice shape.

At the time I am speaking of, Chesty Charles is not as young as he used to be, and he wishes to go along very quiet and avoiding undue excitement, but anybody can see that he is such a character as observes a few things in his time. In fact, anybody can see that he is such a character as is around and about no little and quite some before he settles down to conducting the Shark Fin Grill.

The reason Charles calls his place the Shark Fin Grill is because it sounds nice, although, of course, Charles does not really grill anything there, and, personally, I think the name is somewhat confusing to strangers.

In fact, one night a character with a beard, from Rumson, New Jersey, comes in and orders a grilled porterhouse; and when he learns he cannot get same, he lets out a chirp that Charles has no right to call his place a grill when he does not grill anything and claims that Charles is obtaining money under false pretences.

It finally becomes necessary for Charles to tap him on the pimple with a beer mallet, and afterward the constables come around, saying what is going on here, and what do you mean by tapping people with beer mallets, and the only way Charles can wiggle out of it is by stating that the character with the beard claims that Mae West has no sex appeal. So the constables go away saying Charles does quite right and one of them has half a mind to tap the character himself with something.

Well, anyway, one night I am in the Shark Fin Grill playing rummy with Charles and there is nobody else whatever in the joint, because, by this time, the quiet season is on in Miami and Charles's business thins out more than somewhat; and just as I beat Charles a pretty good score, who comes in but two characters in sport shirts, and one of them has that thing in his hand and he says to us like this:

'Reach,' he says. 'This is a stick-up. No beefs, now,' he says.

Well, Chesty Charles and me raise our hands as high as possible, and, in fact, I am only sorry I cannot raise mine higher than possible, and Chesty Charles says: 'No beefs,' he says. 'But,' he says, 'boys, you are on an awful bust. All you are liable to get around this drum is fleas. If there is any dough here I will be using it myself,' Chesty says.

'Well,' one of the characters says, 'we will have a look at your damper, anyway. Maybe you overlook a few coarse notes here and there.'

So one character keeps that thing pointed at Chesty Charles and me, and the other goes through the cash register, but, just as Charles says, there is nothing in it. Then the character comes over and gives Charles and me a fanning, but all he finds is eighty cents on Charles, and he seems inclined to be a little vexed at the scarcity of ready between us and he acts as if he is thinking of clouting us around some for our shortage, as these git-'em-up characters will sometimes do if they are vexed, when all of a sudden Charles looks at one of the characters and speaks as follows:

'Why,' Chesty Charles says, 'do my eyes deceive me, or do I behold The Macarone, out of Kansas City?'

'Why, yes,' the character says. 'Why, hello, Chesty,' he says. 'Meet my friend Willie,' he says. 'He is out of Kansas City too. Why, I never expect to find you in such a joint as this, Chesty,' he says. 'Especially a joint where there is so little dough.'

'Well,' Chesty Charles says, 'you ought to drop around when the season is on. Things are livelier then. But,' he says, 'sit down and let's have a talk. I am glad to see you, Mac,' he says.

So they sit down and Chesty Charles puts out a bottle of Scotch and some glasses and we become quite sociable, to be sure, and presently The Macarone is explaining that Willie and him have been over in Havana all winter, working with a pay-off mob out of Indianapolis, Indiana, that has a store there, but that business is rotten, and they are now *en route* north and just stop over in Miami to pick up a few dibs, if possible, for walk-about money.

The Macarone seems to be quite an interesting character in many respects and I can see that he and Charles know each other from several places. The Macarone is maybe around forty and he is tall and black-looking, but the character he calls Willie is younger and by no means gabby, and, in fact, he scarcely has a word to say. We sit there quite a while drinking Scotches and speaking of this and that, and finally Chesty Charles says to The Macarone:

'Mac,' he says, 'come to think of it, I may be able to drop something in your lap, at that. Only last night a character is in here with a right nice proposition, but,' Chesty says, 'it is not in my line, so it does not interest me.'

'Chesty,' The Macarone says, 'any proposition that is not in your line must be a very unusual proposition indeed. Let me hear this one,' he says.

'Well,' Chesty says, 'it is a trifle unusual, but,' he says, 'it seems quite sound, and I only regret that I cannot handle it in person. I am froze in here with this business and I do not feel free to engage in any outside enterprises. The character I refer to,' he says, 'is Mr. Cleeburn T. Box, who lives on a big estate over here on the bay front with his nephew. Mr. Cleeburn T. Box wishes to quit these earthly scenes,' Chesty says. 'He is sick and tired of living. His nerves are shot to pieces. He cannot eat. He is in tough shape.

'But,' Chesty says, 'he finds he does not have the nerve to push himself off. So he wishes to find some good reliable party to push him off, for which service he will pay five thousand dollars cash money. He will deposit the dough with me,' Chesty says. 'He realizes that I am quite trustworthy. It is a soft touch, Mac,' he says. 'Of course,' he says, 'I am entitled to the usual twenty-five per cent. commission for finding the plant.'

'Well,' The Macarone says, 'this Mr. Box must be quite an eccentric character. But,' he says, 'I can understand his reluctance about pushing himself off. Personally, I will not care to push myself off. However,' he says, 'the proposition seems to have complications. I hear it is against the law in Florida to push people off, even if they wish to be pushed.'

'Well,' Chesty says, 'Mr. Box thinks of this too. His idea is that the party who is to do this service for him will slip into his house over on the bay front some night and push him off while he is asleep, so he will never know what happens to him. You understand, he wishes this matter to be as unexpected and painless as possible. Then,' Chesty says, 'the party can leave that thing with which he does the pushing on the premises and it will look as if Mr. Box does the pushing in person.'

'What about a club?' The Macarone says. 'Or maybe a shiv? That thing makes a lot of racket.'

'Why,' Chesty says, 'how can you make a club or shiv look like anything but something illegal if you use them to push anybody? You need not be afraid of making a racket, because,' he says, 'no one lives within hearing distance of the joint, and Mr. Box will see that all his servants and everybody else are away from the place every night, once I give him the word the deal is on. He will place the dough at my disposal when he gets this word. Of course he does not wish to know what night it is to happen, but it must be some night soon after the transaction is agreed to.'

'Well,' The Macarone says, 'this is one of the most interesting and unusual propositions ever presented to me. Personally,' he says, 'I do not see why Mr. Box does not get somebody to put something in his tea. Anybody will be glad to do him such a favour.'

'He is afraid of suffering,' Chesty Charles says. 'He is one of the most nervous characters I ever encounter in my life. Look, Mac,' he says, 'this is a job that scarcely requires human intelligence. I have here a diagram that shows the layout of the joint.'

And with this, Chesty Charles outs with a sheet of paper and spreads it out on the table, and begins explaining it to The Macarone with his finger.

'Now,' he says, 'this shows every door and window on the ground floor. Here is a wing of the house. Here is Mr. Cleeburn T. Box's room on the ground floor overlooking the bay. Here is a French window that is never locked,' he says. 'Here is his bed against the wall, not two steps from the window. Why,' Chesty says, 'it is as simple as WPA.'

'Well,' The Macarone says, 'you are dead sure Mr. Box will not mind being pushed? Because, after all, I do not have any reason to push him on my own account, and I am doing my best at this time to lead a clean life and keep out of unpleasant situations.'

'He will love it,' Chesty says.

So The Macarone finally says he will give the matter his earnest consideration and will let Chesty Charles have his answer in a couple of days. Then we all have some more Scotches, and it is now past closing-time, and The Macarone and Willie take their departure, and I say to Chesty like this:

'Chesty,' I say, 'all this sounds to me like a very strange proposition, and I do not believe anybody in this world is dumb enough to accept same.'

'Well,' Chesty says, 'I always hear The Macarone is the dumbest character in the Middle West. Maybe he will wind up taking in the South too,' he says, and then Chesty laughs and we have another Scotch by ourselves before we leave.

Now, the next afternoon I am over on South Beach, taking a little dip in the ocean, and who do I run into engaged in the same pastime but The Macarone and Willie. There are also numerous other parties along the beach, splashing about in the water in their bathing-suits or stretched out on the sand, and The Macarone speaks of Chesty Charles's proposition like this:

'It sounds all right,' The Macarone says. 'In fact,' he says, 'it sounds so all right that the only thing that bothers me is I cannot figure out why Chesty does not take it over one hundred per cent. But,' he says, 'I can see Chesty is getting old, and maybe he loses his nerve. Well,' The Macarone says, 'that is the way it always is with old folks. They lose their nerve.'

Then The Macarone starts swimming towards a float pretty well out in the water, and what happens when he is about half-way to the float but he starts flapping around in the water no little, and it is plain to be seen that he is in some difficulty and seems about to drown. In fact, The Macarone issues loud cries for help, but, personally, I do not see where it is any of my put-in to help him, as he is just a chance acquaintance of mine and, furthermore, I cannot swim.

Well, it seems that Willie cannot swim either, and he is saying it is too bad that The Macarone has to go in such a fashion, and he is also saying he better go and get The Macarone's clothes before someone else thinks of it. But about this time a little Judy with about as much bathing-suit on as will make a boxing glove for a mosquito jumps off the float and swims to The Macarone and seizes him by one ear and holds his head above the water until a lifeguard with hair on his chest gets out there and takes The Macarone off her hands.

Well, the lifeguard tows The Macarone ashore and rolls him over a barrel and gets enough water out of him to float the *Queen Mary*, and by and by The Macarone is as good as new, and he starts looking around for the little Judy who holds him up in the water.

'She almost pulls my ear out by the roots,' The Macarone says: 'But,' he says, 'I will forgive this torture because she saves my life. Who is she, and where is she?'

Well, the lifeguard, who turns out to be a character by the name of Dorgan, says she is Miss Mary Peering and that she works in the evening in a barbecue stand over on Fifth Street, and what is more, she is a right nifty little swimmer, but, of course, The Macarone already knows this. But now nothing will do but we must go to the barbecue stand and find Miss Mary Peering, and there she is in a blue linen uniform and with a Southern accent, dealing hot dogs and hamburger sandwiches and one thing and another, to the customers.

She is a pretty little Judy who is maybe nineteen years of age, and when The Macarone steps forward and thanks her for saving his life, she laughs and says it is nothing whatever, and at first The Macarone figures that this crack is by no means complimentary, and is disposed to chide her for same, especially when he gets to thinking about his ear. But he can see that the little Judy has no idea of getting out of line with him, and he becomes very friendly towards her.

We sit there quite a while with The Macarone talking to her between customers, and finally he asks her if she has a sweet-pea anywhere in the background of her career, and at this she bursts into tears and almost drops an order of pork and beans.

'Yes,' she says, 'I am in love with a wonderful young character by the name of Lionel Box. He is a nephew of Mr. Cleeburn T. Box, and Mr. Cleeburn T. Box is greatly opposed to our friendship. Lionel wishes to marry me, but,' she says, 'Mr. Cleeburn T. Box is his guardian and says he will not hear of Lionel marrying beneath his station. Lionel will be very rich when he is of age, a year from now, and then he can do as he pleases, but just at present his Uncle Cleeburn keeps him from even seeing me. Oh,' she says, 'I am heartbroken.'

'Where is this Lionel now?' The Macarone says.

'That is just it,' Miss Mary Peering says. 'He is home, sick with the grip or some such, and his Uncle Cleeburn will not as much as let him answer the telephone. His Uncle Cleeburn acts awful crazy, if you ask me. But,' she says, 'just wait until Lionel is of age and we can be married. Then we will go so far away from his Uncle Cleeburn he can never catch up with us again.'

Well, at this news The Macarone seems to become very thoughtful, and at first I think it is because he is disappointed to find Miss Mary Peering has a sweet-pea in the background, but after a little more talk, he thanks her again for saving his life and pats her hand and tells her not to worry about nothing, not even about what she does to his ear.

Then we go to the Shark Fin Grill and find Chesty Charles sitting out in front with his chair tilted up against the wall, and The Macarone says to him like this:

'Chesty,' he says, 'have the dough on call for me from now on. I will take care of this matter for Mr. Cleeburn T. Box. I study it over carefully,' The Macarone says, 'and I can see how I will render Mr. Box a service and at the same time do a new friend of mine a favour.

'In the meantime,' The Macarone says, 'you keep Willie here amused. It is a one-handed job, and I do not care to use him on it in any manner, shape or form. He is a nice character, but,' The Macarone says, 'he sometimes makes wrong moves. He is too handy with that thing to suit me. By the way, Chesty,' he says, 'what does Mr. Cleeburn T. Box look like?'

'Well,' Chesty says, 'he will be the only one you find in the room indicated on the diagram, so his looks do not make any difference, but,' he says, 'he is smooth-shaved and has thick black hair.'

Now, several nights pass away, and every night I drop into the Shark Fin Grill to visit with Chesty Charles, but The Macarone does not show up but once, and this is to personally view the five thousand dollars that Charles now has in his safe, although Willie comes in now and then and sits around a while. But Willie is a most restless character, and he does not seem to be able to hold still more than a few minutes at a time, and he is always wandering around and about the city.

Finally, along towards four bells one morning, when Chesty Charles is getting ready to close the Shark Fin Grill, in walks The Macarone, and it is plain to be seen that he has something on his mind.

A couple of customers are still in the joint and The Macarone waits until they depart, and then he steps over to the bar, where Chesty Charles is working, and gazes at Chesty for quite a spell without saying as much as aye, yes, or no.

'Well?' Chesty says.

'Well, Chesty,' The Macarone says, 'I go to the home of your Mr. Cleeburn T. Box a little while ago. It is a nice place. A little more shrubbery than we like in Kansas City, but still a nice place. It must stand somebody maybe half a million. I follow your diagram, Chesty,' he says. 'I find the wing marked X and I make my way through plenty of cactus and Spanish bayonets, and I do not know what all else, and enter the house by way of an open French window.

'I find myself in a room in which there are no lights, but,' The Macarone says, 'as soon as my eyes become accustomed to the darkness, I can see that is all just as the diagram shows. There is a bed within a few steps of the window and there is a character asleep on the bed. He is snoring pretty good too. In fact,' The Macarone says, 'he is snoring about as good as anybody I ever hear, and I do not bar Willie, who is a wonderful snorer.'

'All right,' Chesty Charles says.

'Show me the dough again, Chesty,' The Macarone says.

So Chesty goes to his safe and opens it and outs with a nice package of the soft and places it on the back bar where The Macarone can see it, and the sight of the money seems to please The Macarone no little.

'All right,' Chesty says. 'Then what?'

'Well, Chesty,' The Macarone says, 'there I am with that thing in my hand, and there is this character on the bed asleep, and there is no sound except his snoring and the wind in some palm-trees outside. Chesty,' he says, 'are you ever in a strange house at night with the wind working on the palm-trees outside?'

'No,' Chesty says. 'I do not care for palm-trees.'

'It is a lonesome sound,' The Macarone says. 'Well,' he says, 'I step over to the bed, and I can see by the outline of the character on the bed that he is sleeping on his back, which is a good thing, as it saves me the trouble of turning him over and maybe waking him up. You see, Chesty,' he says, 'I give this matter some scientific study beforehand. I figure that the right idea in this case is to push this character in such a manner that there can be no doubt that he pushes himself, so it must be done from in front, and from close up.

'Well,' The Macarone says, 'I wait right over this character on the bed until my eyes make out the outline of his face in the dark, and I put that thing down close to his nose, and just as I am about to give it to him, the moon comes out from behind a cloud over the bay and spills plenty of light through the open French window and over the character on the bed.

'And,' The Macarone says, 'I observe that this character on the bed is holding some object clasped to his breast, and that he has a large smile on his face, as if he is dreaming very pleasant dreams, indeed; and when I gently remove the object from his fingers, thinking it may be something of value to me, and hold it up to the light, what is it but a framed stand photograph of a young friend of mine by the name of Miss Mary Peering.

'But,' The Macarone says, 'I hope and trust that no one will ever relate to Miss Mary Peering the story of me finding this character asleep with her picture, and snoring, because,' he says, 'snoring is without doubt a great knock to romance.'

'So?' Chesty Charles says.

'So,' The Macarone says, 'I come away as quietly as possible without disturbing the character on the bed, and here I am, Chesty, and there you are, and it comes to my mind that somebody tries to drop me in on a great piece of skullduggery.'

And all of a sudden, The Macarone outs with that thing and jams the nozzle of it into Chesty Charles's chest, and says:

'Hand over that dough, Chesty,' he says. 'A nice thing you are trying to get a respectable character like me into, because you know very well it cannot be your Mr. Cleeburn T. Box on the bed in that room with Miss Mary Peering's photograph clasped to his breast and smiling so. Chesty,' he says, 'I fear you almost make a criminal of me, and for two cents I will give you a pushing for your own self, right here and now.'

'Why, Mac,' Chesty says, 'you are a trifle hasty. If it is not Mr. Cleeburn T. Box in that bed, I cannot think who it can be, but,' he says, 'maybe some last-minute switch comes up in the occupant of the bed by accident. Maybe it is something Mr. Cleeburn T. Box will easily explain when I see him again. Why,' Chesty says, 'I cannot believe Mr. Cleeburn T. Box means any fraud in this matter. He seems to me to be a nice, honest character, and very sincere in his wish to be pushed.'

Then Chesty Charles goes on to state that if there is any fraud in this matter, he is also a victim of same, and he says he will surely speak harshly to Mr. Cleeburn T. Box about it the first time he gets a chance. In fact, Chesty Charles becomes quite indignant when he gets to thinking that maybe Mr. Cleeburn T. Box may be deceiving him and finally The Macarone says :

'Well, all right,' he says. 'Maybe you are not in on anything, at that, and, in fact, I do not see what it is all about, anyway; but,' he says, 'it is my opinion that your Mr. Cleeburn T. Box is without doubt nothing but a great scalawag somewhere. Anyway, hand over the dough, Chesty,' he says. 'I am going to collect on my good intentions.'

So Chesty Charles takes the package off the back bar and hands it over to The Macarone, and as The Macarone is disposing of it in his pants' pocket, Chesty says to him like this : 'But look, Mac,' he says, 'I am entitled to my twenty-five per cent. for finding the plant, just the same.'

Well, The Macarone seems to be thinking this over, and, personally, I figure there is much justice in what Chesty Charles says, and while The Macarone is thinking, there is a noise at the door of somebody coming in, and The Macarone hides that thing under his coat, though I notice he keeps his hand under there, too, until it turns out that the party coming in is nobody but Willie.

'Well,' Willie says, 'I have quite an interesting experience just now while I am taking a stroll away out on the Boulevard. It is right pretty out that way, to be sure,' he says. 'I meet a cop and get to talking to him about this and that, and while we are talking the cop says, "Good evening, Mr. Box," to a character who goes walking past.

'The cop says this character is Mr. Cleeburn T. Box,' Willie says. 'I say Mr. Box looks worried, and the cop says yes, his nephew is sick, and maybe he is worrying about him. But,' Willie says, 'the cop says, "If I am Mr. Box, I will not be worrying about such a thing, because if the nephew dies before he comes of age, Mr. Box is the sole heir to his brother's estate of maybe ten million dollars, and the nephew is not yet of age."

' "Well, cop," I say,' Willie says, ' "are you sure this is Mr. Cleeburn T. Box?" and the cop says yes, he knows him for over ten years, and that he meets up with him every night on the Boulevard for the past week, just the same as to-night, because it seems Mr. Cleeburn T. Box takes to strolling that way quite some lately.

'So,' Willie says, 'I figure to save everybody a lot of bother, and I follow Mr. Cleeburn T. Box away out the Boulevard after I leave the cop, and when I get to a spot that seems nice and quiet and with nobody around, I step close enough for powder marks to show good and give it to Mr. Cleeburn T. Box between the eyes. Then,' Willie says, 'I leave that thing in his right hand, and if they do not say it is a clear case of him pushing himself when they find him, I will eat my hat.'

'Willie,' The Macarone says, 'is your Mr. Cleeburn T. Box clean-shaved and does he have thick black hair?'

'Why, no,' Willie says. 'He has a big mouser on his upper lip and no hair whatsoever on his head. In fact,' he says, 'he is as bald as a biscuit, and maybe balder.'

Now, at this The Macarone turns to Chesty Charles, but by the time he is half turned, Chesty is out the back door of the Shark Fin Grill and is taking it on the Jesse Owens up the street, and The Macarone seems greatly surprised and somewhat disappointed, and says to me like this:

'Well,' he says, 'Willie and me cannot wait for Chesty to return, but,' he says, 'you can tell him for me that, under the circumstances, I am compelled to reject his request for twenty-five per cent. for finding the plant. And,' The Macarone says, 'if ever you hear of the nephew of the late Mr. Cleeburn T. Box beefing about a missing photograph of Miss Mary Peering, you can tell him that it is in good hands.'

All Horse Players Die Broke

It is during the last race meeting at Saratoga, and one evening I am standing out under the elms in front of the Grand Union Hotel thinking what a beautiful world it is, to be sure, for what do I do in the afternoon at the track but grab myself a piece of a 10–to–1 shot.

I am thinking what a beautiful moon it is, indeed, that is shining down over the park where Mr. Dick Canfield once deals them higher than a cat's back, and how pure and balmy the air is, and also what nice-looking Judys are wandering around and about, although it is only the night before that I am standing in the same spot wondering where I can borrow a Betsy with which to shoot myself smack-dab through the pimple.

In fact, I go around to see a character I know by the name of Solly something, who owns a Betsy, but it seems he has only one cartridge to his name for this Betsy and he is thinking some of either using the cartridge to shoot his own self smack-dab through the pimple, or of going out to the race course and shooting an old catfish by the name of Pair of Jacks that plays him false in the fifth race, and therefore Solly is not in a mood to lend his Betsy to anybody else.

So we try to figure out a way we can make one cartridge do for two pimples, and in the meantime Solly outs with a bottle of apple-jack, and after a couple of belts at this bottle we decide that the sensible thing to do is to take the Betsy out and peddle it for whatever we can, and maybe get a taw for the next day.

Well, it happens that we run into an Italian party from Passaic, N.J., by the name of Giuseppe Palladino, who is called Joe for short, and this Joe is in the money very good at the moment, and he is glad to lend us a pound note on the Betsy, because Joe is such a character as never knows when he may need an extra Betsy, and anyway it is the first time in his experience around the race tracks that anybody ever offers him collateral for a loan.

So there Solly and I are with a deuce apiece after we spend the odd dollar for breakfast the next day, and I run my deuce up to a total of twenty-two slugs on the 10–to–1 shot in the last heat of the day, and everything is certainly all right with me in every respect.

Well, while I am standing there under the elms, who comes

along but a raggedy old Dutchman by the name of Unser Fritz, who is maybe seventy-five years old, come next grass, and who is following the giddyaps since the battle of Gettysburg, as near as anybody can figure out. In fact, Unser Fritz is quite an institution around the race tracks, and is often written up by the newspaper scribes as a terrible example of what a horse player comes to, although personally I always say that what Unser Fritz comes to is not so tough when you figure that he does not do a tap of work in all these years.

In his day, Unser Fritz is a most successful handicapper, a handicapper being a character who can dope out from the form what horses ought to win the races, and as long as his figures turn out all right, a handicapper is spoken of most respectfully by one and all, although of course when he begins missing out for any length of time as handicappers are bound to do, he is no longer spoken of respectfully, or even as a handicapper. He is spoken of as a bum.

It is a strange thing how a handicapper can go along for years doing everything right, and then all of a sudden he finds himself doing everything wrong, and this is the way it is with Unser Fritz. For a long time his figures on the horse races are considered most remarkable indeed, and as he will bet till the cows come home on his own figures, he generally has plenty of money, and a fiancée by the name of Emerald Em.

She is called Emerald Em because she has a habit of wearing a raft of emeralds in rings, and pins, and bracelets, and one thing and another, which are purchased for her by Unser Fritz to express his love, an emerald being a green stone that is considered most expressive of love, if it is big enough. It seems that Emerald Em is very fond of emeralds, especially when they are surrounded by large, coarse diamonds.

I hear the old-timers around the race tracks say that when Emerald Em is young, she is a tall, good-looking Judy with yellow hair that is by no means a phony yellow, at that, and with a shape that does not require a bustle such as most Judys always wear in those days.

But then nobody ever hears an old-timer mention any Judy that he remembers from back down the years who is not good-looking, and in fact beautiful. To hear the old-timers tell it, every pancake they ever see when they are young is a double Myrna Loy, though the chances are, figuring in the law of averages, that some of them are bound to be rutabagas, the same as now. Anyway, for years this Emerald Em is known on every race track from coast to coast as Unser Fritz's fiancée, and is considered quite a remarkable scene, what with her emeralds, and not requiring any bustle, and everything else.

Then one day Unser Fritz's figures run plumb out on him, and so does his dough, and so does Emerald Em, and now Unser Fritz is an old pappy guy, and it is years since he is regarded as anything but a crumbo around the race tracks, and nobody remembers much of his story, or cares a cuss about it, for if there is anything that is a drug on the market around the tracks it is the story of a broker.

How he gets from place to place, and how he lives after he gets there, is a very great mystery to one and all, although I hear he often rides in the horsecars with the horses, when some owner or trainer happens to be feeling tender-hearted, or he hitchhikes in automobiles, and sometimes he even walks, for Unser Fritz is still fairly nimble, no matter how old he is.

He always has under his arm a bundle of newspapers that somebody throws away, and every night he sits down and handicaps the horses running the next day according to his own system, but he seldom picks any winners, and even if he does pick any winners, he seldom has anything to bet on them.

Sometimes he promotes a stranger, who does not know he is bad luck to a good hunting dog, to put down a few dibs on one of his picks, and once in a while the pick wins, and Unser Fritz gets a small stake, and sometimes an old-timer who feels sorry for him will slip him something. But whatever Unser Fritz gets hold of, he bets off right away on the next race that comes up, so naturally he never is holding anything very long.

Well, Unser Fritz stands under the elms with me a while, speaking of this and that, and especially of the races, and I am wondering to myself if I will become as dishevelled as Unser Fritz if I keep on following the races, when he gazes at the Grand Union Hotel, and says to me like this:

'It looks nice,' he says. 'It looks cheery-like, with the lights, and all this and that. It brings back memories to me. Emma always lives in this hotel whenever we make Saratoga for the races back in the days when I am in the money. She always has a suite of two or three rooms on this side of the hotel. Once she has four.

'I often stand here under these trees,' Unser Fritz says, 'watching her windows to see what time she puts out her lights, because, while I trust Emma implicitly, I know she has a restless nature, and sometimes she cannot resist returning to scenes of gaiety after I bid her good night, especially,' he says, 'with a party by the name of Pete Shovelin, who runs the restaurant where she once deals them off the arm.'

'You mean she is a biscuit shooter?' I say.

'A waitress,' Unser Fritz says. 'A good waitress. She comes of a family of farm folks in this very section, although I never know much about them,' he says. 'Shovelin's is a little hole-in-the-wall up the street here somewhere which long since disappears. I go there for my morning java in the old days.

'I will say one thing for Shovelin,' Unser Fritz says, 'he always has good java. Three days after I first clap eyes on Emma, she is wearing her first emerald, and is my fiancée. Then she moves into a suite in the Grand Union. I only wish you can know Emma in those days,' he says. 'She is beautiful. She is a fine character. She is always on the level, and I love her dearly.'

'What do you mean – always on the level?' I say. 'What about this Shovelin party you just mention?'

'Ah,' Unser Fritz says, 'I suppose I am dull company for a squab, what with having to stay in at night to work on my figures, and Emma likes to go around and about. She is a highly nervous type, and extremely restless, and she cannot bear to hold still very long at a time. But,' he says, 'in those days it is not considered proper for a young Judy to go around and about without a chaperon, so she goes with Shovelin for her chaperon. Emma never goes anywhere without a chaperon,' he says.

Well, it seems that early in their courtship, Unser Fritz learns that he can generally quiet her restlessness with emeralds, if they have diamonds on the side. It seems that these stones have a very soothing effect on her, and this is why he purchases them for her by the bucket.

'Yes,' Unser Fritz says, 'I always think of Emma whenever I am in New York City, and look down Broadway at night with the go lights on.'

But it seems from what Unser Fritz tells me that even with the emeralds her restless spells come on her very bad, and especially when he finds himself running short of ready, and is unable to purchase more emeralds for her at the moment, although Unser Fritz claims this is nothing unusual. In fact, he says anybody with any experience with nervous female characters knows that it becomes very monotonous for them to be around people who are short of ready.

'But,' he says, 'not all of them require soothing with emeralds. Some require pearls,' he says.

Well, it seems that Emma generally takes a trip without Unser Fritz to break the monotony of his running short of ready, but she never takes one of these trips without a chaperon, because she is very careful about her good name, and Unser Fritz's, too. It seems that in those days Judys have to be more careful about such matters than they do now.

He remembers that once when they are in San Francisco she takes a trip through the Yellowstone with Jockey Gus Kloobus as her chaperon, and is gone three weeks and returns much refreshed, especially as she gets back just as Unser Fritz makes a nice score and has a seidel of emeralds waiting for her. He remembers another time she goes to England with a trainer by the name of Blootz as her chaperon and comes home with an English accent that sounds right cute, to find Unser Fritz going like a house afire at Belmont.

'She takes a lot of other trips without me during the time we are engaged,' Unser Fritz says, 'but,' he says, 'I always know Emma will return to me as soon as she hears I am back in the money and can purchase more emeralds for her. In fact,' he says, 'this knowledge is all that keeps me struggling now.'

'Look, Fritz,' I say, 'what do you mean, keeps you going? Do you mean you think Emma may return to you again?'

'Why, sure,' Unser Fritz says. 'Why, certainly, if I get my rushes again. Why not?' he says. 'She knows there will be a pail of emeralds waiting for her. She knows I love her and always will,' he says.

Well, I ask him when he sees Emerald Em last, and he says it is 1908 in the old Waldorf-Astoria the night he blows a hundred and sixty thousand betting on a hide called Sir Martin to win the Futurity, and it is all the dough Unser Fritz has at the moment. In fact, he is cleaner than a jay bird, and he is feeling somewhat discouraged.

It seems he is waiting on his floor for the elevator, and when it comes down Emerald Em is one of the several passengers, and when the door opens, and Unser Fritz starts to get in, she raises her foot and plants it in his stomach, and gives him a big push back out the door and the elevator goes on down without him.

'But, of course,' Unser Fritz says, 'Emma never likes to ride in the same elevator with me, because I am not always tidy enough to suit her in those days, what with having so much work to do on my figures, and she claims it is a knock to her socially. Anyway,' he says, 'this is the last I see of Emma.'

'Why, Fritz,' I say, 'nineteen-eight is nearly thirty years back, and if she ever thinks of returning to you, she will return long before this.'

'No,' Unser Fritz says. 'You see, I never make a scratch since then. I am never since in the money, so there is no reason for Emma to return to me. But,' he says, 'wait until I get going good again and you will see.'

Well, I always figure Unser Fritz must be more or less of an old screwball for going on thinking there is still a chance for him around the tracks, and now I am sure of it, and I am about to bid him good evening, when he mentions that he can use about two dollars if I happen to have a deuce on me that is not working, and I will say one thing for Unser Fritz, he seldom comes right out and asks anybody for anything unless things are very desperate with him, indeed.

'I need it to pay something on account of my landlady,' he says. 'I room with old Mrs. Crob around the corner for over twenty years, and,' he says, 'she only charges me a finnif a week, so I try to keep from getting too far to the rear with her. I will return it to you the first score I make.'

Well, of course I know this means practically never, but I am feeling so good about my success at the track that I slip him a deucer, and it is half an hour later before I fully realize what I do, and go looking for Fritz to get anyway half of it back. But by this time he disappears, and I think no more of the matter until the next day out at the course when I hear Unser Fritz bets two dollars on a thing by the name of Speed Cart, and it bows down at 50 to 1, so I know Mrs. Crob is still waiting for hers.

Now there is Unser Fritz with one hundred slugs, and this is undoubtedly more money than he enjoys since Hickory Slim is a two-year-old. And from here on the story becomes very interesting, and in fact remarkable, because up to the moment Speed Cart hits the wire, Unser Fritz is still nothing but a crumbo, and you can say it again, while from now on he is somebody to point out and say can you imagine such a thing happening?

He bets a hundred on a centipede called Marchesa, and down pops Marchesa like a trained pig at 20 to 1. Then old Unser Fritz bets two hundred on a caterpillar by the name of Merry Soul, at 4 to 1, and Merry Soul just laughs his way home. Unser Fritz winds up the day betting two thousand more on something called Sharp Practice, and when Sharp Practice wins by so far it looks as if he is a shoo-in, Fritz finds himself with over twelve thousand slugs, and the way the bookmakers in the betting ring are sobbing is really most distressing to hear.

Well, in a week Unser Fritz is a hundred thousand dollars in front, because the way he sends it in is quite astonishing to behold, although the old-timers tell me it is just the way he sends it when he is younger. He is betting only on horses that he personally figures out, and what happens is that Unser Fritz's figures suddenly come to life again, and he cannot do anything wrong.

He wins so much dough that he even pays off a few old touches, including my two, and he goes so far as to lend Joe Palladino three dollars on the Betsy that Solly and I hock with Joe for the pound note, as it seems that by this time Joe himself is practically on his way to the poorhouse, and while Unser Fritz has no use whatsoever for a Betsy he cannot bear to see a character such as Joe go to the poorhouse.

But with all the dough Unser Fritz carries in his pockets, and plants in a safe-deposit box in the jug downtown, he looks just the same as ever, because he claims he cannot find time from working on his figures to buy new clothes and dust himself off, and if you tell anybody who does not know who he is that this old crutch is stone rich, the chances are they will call you a liar.

In fact, on a Monday around noon, the clerk in the branch office that a big Fifth Avenue jewellery firm keeps in the lobby of the States Hotel is all ready to yell for the constables when Unser Fritz leans up against the counter and asks to see some jewellery on display in a showcase, as Unser Fritz is by no means the clerk's idea of a customer for jewellery.

I am standing in the lobby of the hotel on the off chance that some fresh money may arrive in the city on the late trains that I may be able to connect up with before the races, when I notice Unser Fritz and observe the agitation of the clerk, and presently I see Unser Fritz waving a fistful of bank notes under the clerk's beak, and the clerk starts setting out the jewellery with surprising speed.

I go over to see what is coming off, and I can see that the jewellery Unser Fritz is looking at consists of a necklace of emeralds and diamonds, with a centrepiece the size of the home plate, and some eardrops, and bracelets, and clips of same, and as I approach the scene I hear Unser Fritz ask how much for the lot as if he is dickering for a basket of fish.

'One hundred and one thousand dollars, sir,' the clerk says. 'You see, sir, it is a set, and one of the finest things of the kind in the country. We just got it in from our New York store to show a party here, and,' he says, 'she is absolutely crazy about it, but she states she cannot give us a final decision until five o'clock this afternoon. Confidentially, sir,' the clerk says, 'I think the real trouble is financial, and doubt that we will hear from her again. In fact,' he says, 'I am so strongly of this opinion that I am prepared to sell the goods without waiting on her. It is really a bargain at the price,' he says.

'Dear me,' Unser Fritz says to me, 'this is most unfortunate as the sum mentioned is just one thousand dollars more than I possess in all this world. I have twenty thousand on my person, and eighty thousand over in the box in the jug, and not another dime. But,' he says, 'I will be back before five o'clock and take the lot. In fact,' he says, 'I will run in right after the third race and pick it up.'

Well, at this the clerk starts putting the jewellery back in the case, and anybody can see that he figures he is on a lob and that he is sorry he wastes so much time, but Unser Fritz says to me like this:

'Emma is returning to me,' he says.

'Emma who?' I say.

'Why,' Unser Fritz says, 'my Emma. The one I tell you about not long ago. She must hear I am in the money again, and she is returning just as I always say she will.'

'How do you know?' I say. 'Do you hear from her, or what?'

'No,' Unser Fritz says, 'I do not hear from her direct, but Mrs. Crob knows some female relative of Emma's that lives at Ballston Spa a few miles from here, and this relative is in Saratoga this morning to do some shopping, and she tells Mrs. Crob and Mrs. Crob tells me. Emma will be here to-night. I will have these emeralds waiting for her.'

Well, what I always say is that every guy knows his own business best, and if Unser Fritz wishes to toss his dough off on jewellery, it is none of my put-in, so all I remark is that I have no doubt Emma will be very much surprised indeed.

'No,' Unser Fritz says. 'She will be expecting them. She always expects emeralds when she returns to me. I love her,' he says. 'You have no idea how I love her. But let us hasten to the course,' he says. 'Cara Mia is a right good thing in the third, and I will make just one bet to-day to win the thousand I need to buy these emeralds.'

'But, Fritz,' I say, 'you will have nothing left for operating expenses after you invest in the emeralds.'

'I am not worrying about operating expenses now,' Unser Fritz says. 'The way my figures are standing up, I can run a spool of thread into a pair of pants in no time. But I can scarcely wait to see the expression on Emma's face when she sees her emeralds. I will have to make a fast trip into town after the third to get my dough out of the box in the jug and pick them up,' he says. 'Who knows but what this other party that is interested in the emeralds may make her mind up before five o'clock and pop in there and nail them?'

Well, after we get to the race track, all Unser Fritz does is stand around waiting for the third race. He has his figures on the first two races, and ordinarily he will be betting himself a gob on them, but he says he does not wish to take the slightest chance of cutting down his capital at this time, and winding up short of enough dough to buy the emeralds.

It turns out that both of the horses Unser Fritz's figures make on top in the first and second races bow down, and Unser Fritz will have his thousand if he only bets a couple of hundred on either of them, but Unser Fritz says he is not sorry he does not bet. He says the finishes in both races are very close, and prove that there is an element of risk in these races. And Unser Fritz says he cannot afford to tamper with the element of risk at this time.

He states that there is no element of risk whatever in the third race, and what he states is very true, as everybody realizes that this mare Cara Mia is a stick-out. In fact, she is such a stick-out that it scarcely figures to be a contest. There are three other horses in the race, but it is the opinion of one and all that if the owners of these horses have any sense they will leave them in the barn and save them a lot of unnecessary lather.

The opening price offered by the bookmakers on Cara Mia is 2 to 5, which means that if you wish to wager on Cara Mia to win you will have to put up five dollars to a bookmaker's two dollars, and everybody agrees that this is a reasonable thing to do in this case unless you wish to rob the poor bookmaker.

In fact, this is considered so reasonable that everybody starts running at the bookmakers all at once, and the bookmakers can see if this keeps up they may get knocked off their stools in the betting ring and maybe seriously injured, so they make Cara Mia 1 to 6, and out, as quickly as possible to halt the rush and give them a chance to breathe.

This 1 to 6 means that if you wish to wager on Cara Mia to win, you must wager six of your own dollars to one of the bookmaker's dollars, and means that the bookies are not offering any prices whatsoever on Cara Mia running second or third. You can get almost any price you can think of right quick against any of the other horses winning the race, and place and show prices, too, but asking the bookmakers to lay against Cara Mia running second or third will be something like asking them to bet that Mr. Roosevelt is not President of the United States.

Well, I am expecting Unser Fritz to step in and partake of the 2 to 5 on Cara Mia for all the dough he has on his person the moment it is offered, because he is very high indeed on this mare, and in fact I never see anybody any higher on any horse, and it is a price Unser Fritz will not back off from when he is high on anything.

Moreover, I am pleased to think he will make such a wager, because it will give him plenty over and above the price of the emeralds, and as long as he is bound to purchase the emeralds, I wish to see him have a little surplus, because when anybody has a surplus there is always a chance for me. It is when everybody runs out of surpluses that I am handicapped no little. But instead of stepping in and partaking, Unser Fritz keeps hesitating until the opening price gets away from him, and finally he says to me like this:

'Of course,' he says, 'my figures show Cara Mia cannot possibly lose this race, but,' he says, 'to guard against any possibility whatever of her losing, I will make an absolute cinch of it. I will bet her third.'

'Why, Fritz,' I say, 'I do not think there is anybody in this world outside of an insane asylum who will give you a price on the peek. Furthermore,' I say, 'I am greatly surprised at this sign of weakening on your part on your figures.'

'Well,' Unser Fritz says, 'I cannot afford to take a chance on not having the emeralds for Emma when she arrives. Let us go through the betting ring and see what we can see,' he says.

So we walk through the betting ring, and by this time it seems that many of the books are so loaded with wagers on Cara Mia to win that they will not accept any more under the circumstances, and I figure that Unser Fritz blows the biggest opportunity of his life in not grabbing the opening. The bookmakers who are loaded are now looking even sadder than somewhat, and this makes them a pitiful spectacle indeed.

Well, one of the saddest-looking is a character by the name of Slow McCool, but he is a character who will usually give you a gamble and he is still taking Cara Mia at 1 to 6, and Unser Fritz walks up to him and whispers in his ear, and what he whispers is he wishes to know if Slow McCool cares to lay him a price on Cara Mia third. But all that happens is that Slow McCool stops looking sad a minute and looks slightly perplexed, and then he shakes his head and goes on looking sad again.

Now Unser Fritz steps up to another sad-looking bookmaker by the name of Pete Phozzler and whispers in his ear, and Pete also shakes his head, and after we leave him I look back and see that Pete is standing up on his stool watching Unser Fritz and still shaking his head.

Well, Unser Fritz approaches maybe a dozen other sad-looking bookmakers, and whispers to them, and all he gets is the old head-shake, but none of them seem to become angry with Unser Fritz, and I always say that this proves that bookmakers are better than some people think, because, personally, I claim they have a right to get angry with Unser Fritz for insulting their intelligence, and trying to defraud them, too, by asking a price on Cara Mia third.

Finally we come to a character by the name of Willie the Worrier, who is called by this name because he is always worrying about something, and what he is generally worrying about is a short bank roll, or his ever-loving wife, and sometimes both, though mostly it is his wife. Personally, I always figure she is something to worry about, at that, though I do not consider details necessary.

She is a red-headed Judy about half as old as Willie the Worrier, and this alone is enough to start any guy worrying, and what is more she is easily vexed, especially by Willie. In fact, I remember Solly telling me that she is vexed with Willie no longer ago than about 11 a.m. this very day, and gives him a public reprimanding about something or other in the telegraph office downtown when Solly happens to be in there hoping maybe he will receive an answer from a mark in Pittsfield, Mass., that he sends a tip on a horse.

Solly says the last he hears Willie the Worrier's wife say is that she will leave him for good this time, but I just see her over on the clubhouse lawn wearing some right classy-looking garments, so I judge she does not leave him as yet, as the clubhouse lawn is not a place to be waiting for a train.

Well, when Unser Fritz sees that he is in front of Willie's stand, he starts to move on, and I nudge him and motion at Willie, and ask him if he does not notice that Willie is another bookmaker, and Unser Fritz says he notices him all right, but that he does not care to offer him any business because Willie insults him ten years ago. He says Willie calls him a dirty old Dutch bum, and while I am thinking what a wonderful memory Unser Fritz has to remember insults from bookmakers for ten years, Willie the Worrier, sitting on his stool looking out over the crowd, spots Unser Fritz and yells at him as follows:

'Hello, Dirty Dutch,' he says. 'How is the soap market? What are you looking for around here, Dirty Dutch? Santa Claus?'

Well, at this Unser Fritz pushes his way through the crowd around Willie the Worrier's stand, and gets close to Willie, and says:

'Yes,' he says, 'I am looking for Santa Claus. I am looking for a show price on number two horse, but,' he says, 'I do not expect to get it from the shoemakers who are booking nowadays.'

Now the chances are Willie the Worrier figures Unser Fritz is just trying to get sarcastic with him for the benefit of the crowd around his stand in asking for such a thing as a price on Cara Mia third, and in fact the idea of anybody asking a price third on a horse that some bookmakers will not accept any more wagers on first, or even second, is so humorous that many characters laugh right out loud.

'All right,' Willie the Worrier says. 'No one can ever say he comes to my store looking for a marker on anything and is turned down. I will quote you a show price, Dirty Dutch,' he says. 'You can have 1 to 100.'

This means that Willie the Worrier is asking Unser Fritz for one hundred dollars to the book's one dollar if Unser Fritz wishes to bet on Cara Mia dropping in there no worse than third, and of course Willie has no idea Unser Fritz or anybody else will ever take such a price, and the chances are if Willie is not sizzling a little at Unser Fritz, he will not offer such a price, because it sounds foolish.

Furthermore, the chances are if Unser Fritz offers Willie a comparatively small bet at this price, such as may enable him to chisel just a couple of hundred out of Willie's book, Willie will find some excuse to wiggle off, but Unser Fritz leans over and says in a low voice to Willie the Worrier:

'A hundred thousand.'

Willie nods his head and turns to a clerk alongside him, and his voice is as low as Unser Fritz's as he says to the clerk:

'A thousand to a hundred thousand, Cara Mia third.'

The clerk's eyes pop open and so does his mouth, but he does not say a word. He just writes something on a pad of paper in his hand, and Unser Fritz offers Willie the Worrier a package of thousand-dollar bills, and says:

'Here is twenty,' he says. 'The rest is in the jug.'

'All right, Dutch,' Willie says, 'I know you have it, although,' he says, 'this is the first crack you give me at it. You are on, Dutch,' he says. 'P.S.,' Willie says, 'the Dirty does not go any more.'

Well, you understand Unser Fritz is betting one hundred thousand dollars against a thousand dollars that Cara Mia will run in the money, and personally I consider this wager a very sound business proposition indeed, and so does everybody else, for all it amounts to is finding a thousand dollars in the street.

There is really nothing that can make Cara Mia run out of the money, the way I look at it, except what happens to her, and what happens is she steps in a hole fifty yards from the finish when she is on top by ten, and breezing, and down she goes all spread out, and of course the other three horses run on past her to the wire, and all this is quite a disaster to many members of the public, including Unser Fritz.

I am standing with him on the rise of the grandstand lawn watching the race, and it is plain to be seen that he is slightly surprised at what happens, and personally, I am practically dumbfounded because, to tell the truth, I take a nibble at the opening price of 2 to 5 on Cara Mia with a total of thirty slugs, which represents all my capital, and I am thinking what a great injustice it is for them to leave holes in the track for horses to step in, when Unser Fritz says like this:

'Well,' he says, 'it is horse racing.'

And this is all he ever says about the matter, and then he walks down to Willie the Worrier, and tells Willie if he will send a clerk with him, he will go to the jug and get the balance of the money that is now due Willie.

'Dutch,' Willie says, 'it will be a pleasure to accompany you to the jug in person.'

As Willie is getting down off his stool, somebody in the crowd who hears of the wager gazes at Unser Fritz, and remarks that he is really a game guy, and Willie says:

'Yes,' he says, 'he is a game guy at that. But,' he says, 'what about me?'

And he takes Unser Fritz by the arm, and they walk away together, and anybody can see that Unser Fritz picks up anyway twenty years or more, and a slight stringhalt, in the last few minutes.

Then it comes on night again in Saratoga, and I am standing out under the elms in front of the Grand Union, thinking that this world is by no means as beautiful as formerly, when I notice a big, fat old Judy with snow-white hair and spectacles standing near me, looking up and down the street. She will weigh a good two hundred pounds, and much of it is around her ankles, but she has a pleasant face, at that, and when she observes me looking at her, she comes over to me, and says:

'I am trying to fix the location of a restaurant where I work many years ago,' she says. 'It is a place called Shovelin's. The last thing my husband tells me is to see if the old building is still here, but,' she says, 'it is so long since I am in Saratoga I cannot get my bearings.'

'Ma'am,' I say, 'is your name Emma by any chance and do they ever call you Emerald Em?'

Well, at this the old Judy laughs, and says:

'Why, yes,' she says. 'That is what they call me when I am young and foolish. But how do you know?' she says. 'I do not remember ever seeing you before in my life.'

'Well,' I say, 'I know a party who once knows you. A party by the name of Unser Fritz.'

'Unser Fritz?' she says. 'Unser Fritz? Oh,' she says, 'I wonder if you mean a crazy Dutchman I run around with many years ago? My gracious,' she says, 'I just barely remember him. He is a great hand for giving me little presents such as emeralds. When I am young I think emeralds are right pretty, but,' she says, 'otherwise I cannot stand them.'

'Then you do not come here to see him?' I say.

'Are you crazy, too?' she says. 'I am on my way to Ballston Spa to see my grandchildren. I live in Macon, Georgia. If ever you are in Macon, Georgia, drop in at Shovelin's restaurant and get some real Southern fried chicken. I am Mrs. Joe Shovelin,' she says. 'By the way,' she says, 'I remember more about that crazy Dutchman. He is a horse player. I always figure he must die long ago and that the chances are he dies broke, too. I remember I hear people say all horse players die broke.'

'Yes,' I say, 'he dies all right, and he dies as you suggest, too,' for it is only an hour before that they find old Unser Fritz in a vacant lot over near the railroad station with the Betsy he gets off Joe Palladino in his hand and a bullet-hole smack-dab through his pimple.

. Nobody blames him much for taking this out, and in fact I am standing there thinking long after Emerald Em goes on about her business that it will be a good idea if I follow his example, only I cannot think where I can find another Betsy, when Solly comes along and stands there with me. I ask Solly if he knows anything new.

'No,' Solly says, 'I do not know anything new, except,' he says, 'I heard Willie the Worrier and his ever-loving make up again, and she is not going to leave him after all. I hear Willie takes home a squarer in the shape of a batch of emeralds and diamonds that she orders sent up here when Willie is not looking, and that they are fighting about all day. Well,' Solly says, 'maybe this is love.'